EXPERIMENTAL WRITING

BLOOMSBURY WRITER'S GUIDES AND ANTHOLOGIES

Bloomsbury Writer's Guides and Anthologies offer established and aspiring creative writers an introduction to the art and craft of writing in a variety of forms, from poetry to environmental and nature writing. Each book is part craft-guide with writing prompts and exercises, and part anthology, with relevant works by major authors.

Series Editors:
Sean Prentiss, Norwich University, USA
Joe Wilkins, Linfield College, USA

Titles in the Series:
Environmental and Nature Writing, Sean Prentiss and Joe Wilkins
Short-Form Creative Writing, H. K. Hummel and Stephanie Lennox
Creating Comics, Chris Gavaler and Leigh Ann Beavers
Advanced Creative Nonfiction, Sean Prentiss and Jessica Hendry Nelson
The Art and Craft of Asian Stories, Xu Xi and Robin Hemley
Advanced Fiction, Amy E. Weldon

Forthcoming Titles:
Poetry 2nd ed, Amorak Huey and W. Todd Kaneko
Fantasy Fiction, Jennifer Pullen
Environmental and Nature Writing 2nd ed, Sean Prentiss and Joe Wilkins
Speculative Fiction, Benjamin Warner and Ron Tanner

EXPERIMENTAL WRITING

A WRITER'S GUIDE AND ANTHOLOGY

Will Cordeiro and Lawrence Lenhart

BLOOMSBURY ACADEMIC
LONDON • NEW YORK • OXFORD • NEW DELHI • SYDNEY

BLOOMSBURY ACADEMIC
Bloomsbury Publishing Plc
50 Bedford Square, London, WC1B 3DP, UK
1385 Broadway, New York, NY 10018, USA
29 Earlsfort Terrace, Dublin 2, Ireland

BLOOMSBURY, BLOOMSBURY ACADEMIC and the Diana logo are trademarks of Bloomsbury Publishing Plc

First published in Great Britain 2024

Copyright © Will Cordeiro and Lawrence Lenhart, 2024

Will Cordeiro and Lawrence Lenhart have asserted their right under the Copyright, Designs and Patents Act, 1988, to be identified as Authors of this work.

For legal purposes the Acknowledgments on p. 333 constitute an extension of this copyright page.

Cover design: Rebecca Heselton
Cover image: *The Unemployment Problem* by Lisa Kokin, mixed media pulped and reassembled book, 2007. Photographed by Lia Roozendaal Photography.

All rights reserved. No part of this publication may be reproduced or transmitted in any form or by any means, electronic or mechanical, including photocopying, recording, or any information storage or retrieval system, without prior permission in writing from the publishers.

Bloomsbury Publishing Plc does not have any control over, or responsibility for, any third-party websites referred to or in this book. All internet addresses given in this book were correct at the time of going to press. The author and publisher regret any inconvenience caused if addresses have changed or sites have ceased to exist, but can accept no responsibility for any such changes.

A catalogue record for this book is available from the British Library.

Library of Congress Cataloging-in-Publication Data
Names: Cordeiro, Will, 1979– author. | Lenhart, Lawrence, author.
Title: Experimental writing : a writer's guide and anthology / William Cordeiro, Lawrence Lenhart.
Description: London ; New York : Bloomsbury Academic, 2024. |
Series: Bloomsbury writer's guides and anthologies | Includes bibliographical references and index.
Identifiers: LCCN 2023030903 (print) | LCCN 2023030904 (ebook) |
ISBN 9781350240971 (paperback) | ISBN 9781350240964 (hardback) |
ISBN 9781350240988 (adobe pdf) | ISBN 9781350240995 (epub)
Subjects: LCSH: Creative writing. | Literature, Experimental.
Classification: LCC PN189 .C67 2024 (print) | LCC PN189 (ebook) |
DDC 808–dc23/eng/20231005
LC record available at https://lccn.loc.gov/2023030903
LC ebook record available at https://lccn.loc.gov/2023030904

ISBN: HB: 978-1-3502-4096-4
PB: 978-1-3502-4097-1
ePDF: 978-1-3502-4098-8
eBook: 978-1-3502-4099-5

Series: Bloomsbury Writer's Guides and Anthologies

Typeset by Newgen KnowledgeWorks Pvt. Ltd., Chennai, India

To find out more about our authors and books visit www.bloomsbury.com and sign up for our newsletters.

CONTENTS

Preface
Emerging Forms: A (Dis)Orientation ... 1

1 Hybrids ... 19

2 Composites and Unclassifiables ... 33

3 Creative Repurposing ... 51

4 Handicrafting and Textual Materials ... 75

5 Conceptual and Visual Writing ... 95

6 Minor Forms ... 115

7 "Undisciplined" Writing ... 131

8 Performance ... 145

9 Digital Writing ... 163

Anthology ... 189
On Times I Have Forced Myself to Dance
   Hanif Abdurraqib ... 194
Freinds
   Caren Beilin ... 195
Dogs without a Face
   Dodie Bellamy ... 201
In the Guinea Pig Cave
   Aase Berg ... 203
#/usr/bin/python/three_last_words
   Lillian-Yvonne Bertram ... 204
from *Eunoia*
   Christian Bök ... 211
I was Wash-Way in Blood
   Kamau Brathwaite ... 214
XIX, XXI, and XXIV (from *feeld*)
   Jos Charles ... 216

Contents

Turing Test
    Franny Choi — 217
Computer Poetry
    J. M. Coetzee — 219
In Place of Thought
    Teju Cole — 221
Questions in a Significantly Smaller Font
    Lucy Corin — 223
Sin titulo (Untitled)
    Mirtha Dermisache — 224
from *Danse Macabre Piggies*
    Sara Tuss Efrik — 225
What To Do When Your Child Brings Home a Mami Wata
    Chikọdịlị Emelụmadụ — 248
Grey Bird on a Wire (Angst Attack)
    Carina Finn — 255
Annotating the First Page of the First Navajo-English Dictionary
    Danielle Geller — 256
Bluebush
    Marlon Hacla — 262
Cholla Village of No
    Cathy Park Hong — 263
Sucktion
    Douglas Kearney — 266
Blueprints for *Reading a Garden*
    Maya Lin and Tan Lin — 278
Excerpts from "Whereas Statements"
    Layli Long Soldier — 279
The Boy
    Garielle Lutz — 283
They Net the HDTV Teeth, the "Chewy Heavens" HDTV Teeth
    K. Silem Mohammad — 286
Sincerity
    Ander Monson — 287
You Rail, and the Road
    Thirii Myo Kyaw Myint — 290
from *Lianna Fled the Cranberry Bog*
    GennaRose Nethercott — 296
Nailsoup I-VI
    Eiríkur Örn Norðdahl — 299
Koko
    Elena Passarello — 303
ginen the legends of juan malo [a malologue]
    Craig Santos Perez — 304

News
   DBC Pierre   305
The Taking of Moundville by Zoom
   Mary Ruefle   306
from *Post-Soviet Belarus*
   Ekaterina Samigulina/Tae Ateh   307
Never Again
   Carlos Soto-Román   308
Great Awakening
   Rodrigo Toscano   313
Destruir el desierto
   Cecilia Vicuña   315
THIS IS WHY PEOPLE O.D. ON PILLS/AND JUMP FROM THE GOLDEN GATE BRIDGE
   Jennifer Walshe   318
Hannah Kusoh: An American Butoh
   Karen Tei Yamashita   319

Acknowledgments   333
References   335
List of Contributors   345
Permissions   353
Index   355

1

PREFACE
EMERGING FORMS: A (DIS)ORIENTATION

I. Welcome

If you began at the beginning, well, good for you. But *why* did you choose to start here? Perhaps you'll respond, because that's just how books are designed to be read: front to back. Of course. And, we might add, English happens to move—unlike some other languages—from left to right. (Though saccadic eye-movements twitch back and forth rapidly as you're reading.) And most likely you are reading this silently to yourself with a still tongue. Or not ... reading used to always be aloud, even in libraries. St. Augustine looked astonished upon St. Ambrose when he witnessed him reading silently in his monkish cell, *c.* AD 383. And if you have the fortitude to reach the bottom of this page, you will advance to the next by turning this side over. You needn't unscroll this glue-bound book or shuffle its pages under a paperweight.

These are, after all, ingrained *conventions* that any educated reader intuits when picking up a book. Such conventions exist as taken-for-granted background knowledge. But conventions change, too. As Romantic scholar H. J. Jackson shows, writing in books was once a venerated practice of scribes and bibliophiles. While the annotations of Romantic poets like Coleridge and Blake, for example, are still accorded the place of literature and studied by professors, marginalia are generally considered a form of vandalism and desecration (Jackson 2001). Conventions are not static, though, and in a book about the present moment of experimentation, we need to be aware of contending pressures and norms between the recent past and new innovative directions.

Or maybe you were assigned by a professor to read this chapter first. You weren't the one who chose to start here. In that case, take another glance at your syllabus: did your professor assign you to read the whole book in order, front to back, including the copyright page, bibliography, and acknowledgments? Probably not. The conventions of reading front to back, left to right, in order, are as often as not violated under many circumstances.[1] Some readers might skim a textbook like this for information; others might skip straight to the prompts, and still others might dip into a chapter of particular interest. One of you, at least, has already damned this book by throwing it across the room, we're sure. Skim, skip, dip, or damn, though, the way you enact meaning with a text is a collaborative process: your own desires and knowledge interact with the words on the page, yes, but also with a host of assumptions, conventions, contexts, and institutional norms that shape and frame the reading experience.

How are you interacting with this book right now? Are you holding it distantly in one hand as you use it in a classroom, hovering over it intently as it's splayed on a table in a library, scooching your finger across each line as you read in bed, or riffling through the pages as you

---

[1] Yoohoo, down here! Sometimes one convention is violated by another, competing convention. Footnotes, for example, present a challenge to the linearity of a text moving left to right, top to bottom. How and when do you choose to navigate the footnotes? When do you ignore them completely? When do the footnotes become more important than the supposed body? Ok, now you can return to the paragraph above, if you want. Or not.

examine it in a bookstore? Or perhaps you're scrolling a digital copy of the text on an eReader; using the search function to locate a quote on your laptop; or skimming whatever is available for free on the Amazon "Read Sample" feature? These physical locations, publishing layouts, and embodied postures shape our reading experiences and the meanings we derive from texts. Books have not always been books. They were scrolls or codices. Now they are digital texts on cell phones and in the cloud. Who knows what form they will take tomorrow? Experimental writers have reinvigorated literature by reconceiving the arrangement of the material forms of texts and the attitudes or methodologies of reading they afford. Joyce's *Finnegans Wake*, for example, is designed as a never-ending circle so that the last sentence of the novel snakes around to be completed by the opening gambit; one is asleep in an eternal return or awakened anew at every point. Cortázar's *Hopscotch* skips around with optional interstitial chapters that supplement the main narrative and, depending on the reader's predilections, can transform the story itself. Like a choose-your-own-adventure book, there are multiple, nonlinear directions for a reader to take. The material structure of B. S. Johnson's *The Unfortunates* is a box with loose papers that the reader must arrange. All these are examples of ergodic literature, the root of which is "work." They emphasize the effort that the reader must take in putting the meaning—and sometimes the literal pages—together.

Hypertexts that allow the reader to choose among branching nodes of possibility are another example of ergodic literature; there is a growing body of hypertexts, and savvy readers have developed conventions and tactics for navigating them. Shelley Jackson's ongoing *Ineradicable Stain: Skin Project*, though, is one of a kind: a short story reproduced as one-word tattoos on over 2,000 volunteers. Perhaps it's a story that can never be viewed in its fully embodied form, challenging the very possibility of anyone reading it. As the volunteers have their tattoo removed or they inevitably die, does that mean there's an expiration date for the story? Is it in the process of self-erasure and decomposition?

We draw attention to such unspoken conventions at the outset because so much of experimental literature questions—or completely upends—our usual frameworks for reading. The more frameworks are deracinated, conventions overruled, assumptions uprooted, the more open-ended, ambiguous, or downright unintelligible a work is. If you are still piecing things together, puzzling out just what you think, and dwelling in uncertainties, then rest assured that we are as well. When encountering experimental work, the ground gives out beneath us; we tumble headlong in a void. Disorientation is the order of the day. We like to revel in such ambiguity: we live in an interpretable world. In coming to terms with experimental works, the terms themselves are subject to change. And sometimes, the terms also change us. Figuration becomes a figuring out. Our strategies of sense-making might alter; more burden gets placed on the reader to make sense of the text.

Reading—that is, "normal" reading—is enough of a burden, you say; why would anyone want to face a *greater* burden as a reader? What is so alluring about unintelligibility anyway? A void doesn't sound like a very interesting place to dwell. Might this so-called experimental writing stuff just be a lot of tosh and twaddle? Posturing? Gimmicks and bunkum? So, eyerolls and side-eyes aside, we'd like to encourage a healthy skepticism. "Calling bullshit isn't easy," Kevin Young (2017: 137) writes in his study of humbug, hoaxes, plagiarists, and phonies. Maybe some "experimental" hijinks are little more than posturing and gimmicks, sure. But maybe, too, hijinks and gimmicks need to be given their due sometimes. Who isn't posturing one way or another, especially those who profess sincerity? Those too eager to bushwhack through what they perceive as bosh might miss out on a different interpretation, an epiphanic moment, or an opportunity for self-reflection. In experimental writing, few presumptions are set up and much that is presumed will be upset.

As Marianne Moore once wrote about poetry, "I, too, dislike it: there are things that are important beyond all this fiddle. Reading it, however, with a perfect contempt for it, one discovers that there is in it after all, a place for the genuine" (1981: 36). The authentic is not always the opposite of humbug and hokum; a bit of fiddle and befuddlement can help reveal, by contrast, an overlooked truth or dislodge a vaunted truism. The healthy skepticism we encourage should be trained not only on other's assertions, however, but also on one's own to trouble any notions of self-certainty. Contemplating the charge of the pretentiousness and infantilism associated with poetry (and experimental writing, we might add) in his book *The Hatred of Poetry*, poet and novelist Ben Lerner (2016: 11–12), thinking of that Marianne Moore quote while at the dentist, remarks: "I had the sensation that Dr. X, as he knocked the little mirror against my molars, was contemptuous of the idea that genuine poetry could issue from such an opening. And Dr. X was right: there is no genuine poetry; there is only, after all, and at best, a place for it." We hope this book, much like Lerner's dark open maw crammed with sickle probes and scalers, can be one place that can help clear a space for genuine experimental poetics, even if it's not where any idealized poetry issues.

We'd emphasize that such self-skepticism applies to us, too. We intend this book as a series of interrogatives and declaratives, as if we offered our ideas in the subjunctive mood rather than the imperative. It is not a list of thou shalts and thou shalt nots. We could—and on one draft did—fill this book with asterisks, scare quotes, and footnotes to provide "distanciation," insistent parenthetical asides (which contradict the main clause), and other frippery that expresses all the doubts and second-guessing we felt when writing it. ~~Perhaps the whole text should be considered "under erasure."~~ But mostly we'd rather be useful, punchy, and approachable.

High-handed pronunciamentos these are emphatically not. The authors were of two minds about most any statement they made, and not only because there were two of them. Sliding sideways into a vortex of friendly disagreements, constantly reframing our own thoughts, then turning around and challenging the very axioms by which we reached some provisional conclusion, it's amazing anything resembling progress occurred amid our wrangling. If, at times, our tone feels more historicized, critical, and academic than most creative writing manuals, that is because we wanted to accord our subject with the respect it deserves, against the attitude of derision or dismissiveness cast upon experimental writing in the culture at large. But we also hope that some spirit of the playfulness of our subject—experimentation—also infuses our work, a nominal textbook though it may be.

Throughout this book, you can find text boxes (like this) indicating that the author or piece under discussion can be found in the anthology at the back. You'll likely notice there's not a one-to-one correspondence between the anthology pieces and the emerging genres or subgenres we discuss. Almost all the pieces fit more than one emerging genre category, in fact. These genres offer competing frameworks for your interpretation of a text; we invite you to revisit the piece and think how it can reveal variant significations under a different aegis, context, or generic designation. We also have a companion website (https://www.bloomsburyonlineresources.com/experimental-writing-a-writers-guide-and-anthology) that provides an online anthology of links to texts considered in each chapter as well as links to writing resources, teaching materials, glossaries, criticism and context, institutions, and publishers. Teachers using this book may want to avail themselves of the website companion as a supplemental reading list, material to assign small groups or individuals projects, a place to begin research or deeper dives into a given subject, or weekly assigned readings to fill out a more robust syllabus.

We hope that your response to our anthology selections and the textbook itself are not only intellectual. But that they are that, too. Theorist Fredric Jameson (2014: 264–5) remarks that unlike European writers, "the deeper reason for the American's shame … [is] the country's institutional dirty little secret: American anti-intellectualism." The ethos of most Anglophone creative writing programs has been anti-intellectual, typecasting experimentalists as living in some overly cerebral cloud-cuckoo-land, which explains why experimentalists are often marginalized (and from that position, like marginalia, they've defaced the book while commenting on it). It seems odd to us that most writers would posture as anti-intellectuals, though, given the nature of their avocation. Perhaps class guilt and the Hemingwayesque stereotype of the tough guy chomping on his cigar and drinking as much as the big fish he reels in has held sway for too long.

Still, we'd emphasize a holistic approach to experimental writing: engagement with both the mind *and* body. Take note of the affective register and your responses as you read. The derisive snort or crinkled nose, frayed nerves or raised hackles, exasperated sigh or teeth-sucking shake of the head are all valid ways to feel into a text. Shock value is still a kind of value, a transformational one at times. Even boredom, yes boredom, might be the phenomenological grounds upon which rapture bursts forth upon you in a fit of giggles or a gobsmacked revelation. Reflect on the gradations of your reaction to the things you read, and the habits that inform how you do so, whatever they might be. Bafflement and apathy, incomprehension or wanting to call out cockamamie: these are all part of the game. Notice the registrations of the texts on your bodily instrument like a finely tuned electrometer to the charged currents circulating in the air. Hopefully, something in here might jam your signals; produce interference patterns; or strike you as in bad taste.

II. Who and What This Book Is For

This book is intended for a wide audience: for those who are skeptical about experimental writing as much as for those who are already immersed in it, for the student as well as the working writer, and for workshop leaders, teachers, activists, performers, organizers, editors, artists, agents, readers, and others who comprise the literary community. Because the tradition of experimental writing may include work that is sometimes considered "radical" or "extreme," we would like to bring attention to the ways that politically charged, discomfiting, or subversive material can be made suitable for engagement in a classroom context for today's students. While to entirely neglect or censor all such material in a book of this type would do a disservice to students, impede critical thinking, and fundamentally misrepresent the topic at hand, we recognize that there are nonetheless a range of appropriate levels of engagement depending on the students' age, background, maturity level, classroom expectations, pedagogical setting, and other factors. We are aware that much of the content in the chapters that follow as well as pieces in the anthology address traumatic material, sensitive topics, and subversive viewpoints. Thus, consider this our WARNING LABEL.

Experimental writing is inherently risky. Not only does it want to shake up literature, it wants to change you, its reader, and possibly revolutionize society, too. If you consent to entering past this point, then you presumably do so AT YOUR OWN RISK. (Are we sensationalizing? Aren't warning labels known to induce readers? Is this just marketing subterfuge?) Both authors have had success teaching experimental writing in a wide array of institutions to audiences that extended from junior-high students to postgraduates and professional writers, and that varied from informal, one-day community settings to formal courses at universities. While the primary content of this guidebook is appropriate for college- and graduate-level students, some of the references and texts mentioned in the chapters may contain work appropriate for so-called mature audiences. We advise that if this book is used in a university curriculum or community writing class, the facilitator reads the material in advance with an eye toward the appropriateness of the material for their given population of students. Facilitators may also want to preface certain passages, anthology pieces, or chapters with more specific content warnings, depending on the sensitivities of the student population in their classroom.

Currently, there's almost no practical guidebooks on experimental writing—especially for the emerging genres that we focus on here. It is our intention not only to address "craft," but, more importantly, to examine the varied techniques, aesthetics, and purposes of experimental writing. Indeed, the usual conception of "craft" that has occupied workshops, publishing, and community spaces, we argue, is largely based on mainstream, popular, or standard-workshop styles. Most craft books focus on a single genre. However, it is our contention that understanding different experimental traditions will help you have a better grasp on the conventions and forces that shape more traditional styles and genres, too. Since roughly the new millennium, experimental writing has witnessed a proliferation of new media, emerging forms, shifting concerns, institutional realignments, and profound redefinitions, making a book like this one a much-needed resource for those who are trying to comprehend today's diverse experimental writing cultures. One of those changes is the way that traditional genres, such as fiction or poetry, are being reformulated and undergoing hybridization, making single-genre treatments of writing less useful than ever. Another recent change is the growth of discussions about rhetoric, identity, activism, politics, community, and institutions that animate the discourse of creative writing as these issues intersect with and critically inform the discourse about "craft" techniques. Yet another change is that experimental writing is becoming more ubiquitous as it impacts mainstream styles and, in some cases, merges with it. Therefore, it is more important than ever that writers of all outlooks and styles learn to appreciate the intricate inner workings of other genres, aesthetics, and perspectives. This book seeks to both attend to these ongoing changes and to encompass some of the developments that constitute the longer history of experimental writing. Our aim in doing so is to guide writers with practical frameworks, questions, overviews, prompts, discussions, and examples that will help inspire their own work, in whatever shape that may take.

Experimental Writing

In writing this book, we want to make experimental writing more accessible and engaging because we emphatically do *not* believe that experimental writing must be opaque, abstruse, or elitist. It can, we acknowledge, often be challenging. Part of those challenges arise because many types of experimental writing derive from unfamiliar traditions, have had their purposes misconstrued, or occupy a space of community practice at odds with the premises of other types of writing. Many of these apparent difficulties can be demystified. Other difficulties are inherent in the work. Experimental writing often challenges its readers to reconsider a broad range of questions about language, identity, philosophy, politics, style, and lifestyle, as well as the relations between these subjects. Such challenges are integral to the work that experimental writing does, and they cannot be eliminated or explained away. Yet these challenges act as pleasures, too. The unsettling nature of experimental writing lends it a vigor, which may, in turn, unsettle the stale strictures into which literature or life have unthinkingly congealed. The self-interrogating nature of experimentation allows innovative works to confront myriad problems, forge new connections, and access ideas or feelings that other literature may leave out. The interpretive demands of experimental writing may create more active, energized, or socially responsible readerships, expanding literature's reach. And the process of remaking conventions, forms, and institutions has kept experimental writing—and by extension, the rest of literature—a living organism ready to meet the exigencies of its evolving audiences and ecosystems.

One of the aspects of the field of creative writing that is evolving most is the notion of genre and the attendant conventions that shape them. For decades, the traditional genres (fiction, poetry, creative nonfiction, and playwriting) have been partitioned into discrete sections in bookstores and libraries; have developed different institutional support structures, such as conferences and residencies; attracted separate communities of readers; and shaped entirely independent course offerings of Creative Writing programs. Indeed, creative nonfiction and, more commonly, playwriting are even housed in other academic departments in some universities. While there have long been a few outliers that defy generic conventions, over the last decade or two it has become more usual to find works that break down the traditional genres or move fluidly between them. This is nowhere truer than among the range of works that fall under the banner of experimental writing. Wendy Bishop and David Starkey (2006: 98) in their *Keywords in Creative Writing* state that "clearly, genre is shaped by social forces and by the expectations of different readers during different historical periods … . Because definitions of genre change over time, it is naïve to suppose that those definitions will not be contested in the process of shifting." As an aside, we would note the structural instability within the major genres. Form and purpose distinguish poetry from drama, but purpose and form are not fixed: a poem may be performed, a play may be read for its metaphors and prosody. "Truth" is constitutive of the distinction between prose categories. Yet, relatively little consideration is put on the metaphysical theory of truth upon which hangs the generic distinction between fiction and creative nonfiction. For that matter, the idea of defining the "creative" in creative nonfiction is a tricky matter, especially as notions of that genre expand beyond personal essays and memoir. Facts, according to some philosophical outlooks, are *made* things: the root of the word "facts," after all, is to fashion, forge, fabricate. Facts might be manufactured by systems of social construction, not entirely independent of values. But where, then, is the line between things that are made versus made up?

While the major traditional genres have undergone shifting and reshuffling at their edges, newer genres have begun to emerge. Since the millennium, several anthologies have addressed emerging genres that resist traditional categories. For example, *Family Resemblance* (2015) looks at hybrid forms, *Fakes* (2012) examines creative repurposing, and both *Against Expression* (2011) and *Conceptualisms* (2022) survey Conceptual and visual writing. In other cases, though, such as performance, there is increasing recognition of an emerging genre, although the field is still largely fragmented between performance poetry, performance art, drama, and other disciplines. The emerging genre of digital writing has been acknowledged widely; however, in its case, technology has changed so much over the past few decades that the field has undergone rapid change and almost continual redefinition. In the case of textual handicrafting, there is a newfound attention to the emerging genre; we hope to bring into focus an array of related practices—such as textiles, zines, artist books, exhibitions, and even chemistry—wherein material embodiment plays a pivotal role in the nature of the writing. Minor forms and undisciplined writing are, as their names suggest, minor and undisciplined, and therefore fly under the radar. Meanwhile, academic and creative writing—long seen as distinct—have undergone changes so that they overlap in a handful of exceptional cases. Such emerging genres as outlined in our chapters, which have many points of intersection among them, each have a long enough history and a broad body of work to merit anthologies, critical studies, literary journals, and university courses, but not—until now—a comprehensive guidebook to help writers who want to compose in them. Cutting across or lying outside the four major genres, they have for too long eluded most creative writing pedagogy, which is still beholden to traditional generic distinctions. These emerging genres are still in the process of developing; at least for the moment they remain indefinite, unbound, and experimental. And though a guidebook like ours might act to raise awareness of these emerging genres in some small way, we are not trying to canonize or codify these genres, let alone stop their development. Genres of all sorts will continue to evolve in response to individual writers, groups of readers, institutions, marketplaces, critics, technologies, and myriad other cultural forces.

Taken together, these emerging genres constitute a sizable portion of contemporary experimental literature. We would argue, moreover, that these emerging genres embrace today's most forward-looking and innovative writing practices. However, we are cognizant that experimentation can take place in other domains of writing, including within the traditional genres. Our choice to abjure experimentation in the four major genres for this book was due to three primary reasons. First, most radical experiments in the traditional genres likely also fall within one or more of the experimental categories we propose here; they are not mutually exclusive. Thus, some pieces we examine or anthologize may well seem like—or have been originally published as—poems, stories, plays, or essays. It is often a matter of perspective. Second, the scope of the book would have grown too capacious had we attempted to cover experimental writing in all the traditional genres as well (believe us, we tried). Third, a handful of resources already exist for experimental writing in traditional genres, though they are scant in some instances. Most students taking courses in Creative Writing will encounter adventurous, unconventional, and innovative works in their course of study. The proportion of experimental to traditional works largely depends on the program, teacher, and the predilections of the students themselves. Institutional structures typically afford far fewer opportunities to speak across genres about experimental techniques, traditions, and practices. Exploring the emerging genres we locate in this book provides an impetus for conversations across traditional divisions, and, we hope, a meeting point for cross-pollination. By investigating these emerging genres, writers from a wide spectrum of backgrounds can find intersections and commonalities that will further their understanding of their traditional "home" genre, too, whether they think of themselves as experimentalist or not. And those who do not begin this book already identifying as experimentalists might more readily do so once they try some of these new forms.

While the character of a textbook is to present material in an "authoritative" way, we don't want to be seen as supercilious authorities making pronouncements. Experimental writing will continue to evolve, and each writer will need to find a new path through its thickets. Richard Hugo, in his classic craft book *Triggering Town*, perhaps puts it best:

> You'll never be a poet until you realize that everything I say today and this quarter is wrong. It may be right for me, but it is wrong for you. Every moment, I am, without wanting or trying to, telling you how to write like me. But I hope you'll learn to write like you. In a sense I hope I don't teach you how to write but how to teach yourself how to write. (1979: 3)

Substitute "experimental writer" for "poet," and the above declaration is even more true of this book than for Hugo's class. If we happen to express guidelines, principles, or rules, as nearly any textbook is wont, we are confident that they will instigate some of you to tussle with those dictums or toss them aside as best fits your own circumstances. We hope that our book can advance your writing journey, which often means entangling you further in the thickets. You'll need to learn how to extricate yourself by your own thinking, practice, and experience.

III. Our Challenges and Considerations

As we collaborated on this book, we encountered many challenges. Just some of the problems we faced included: how to define the scope of our subject matter, how to balance a historical and theoretical understanding of our subject matter with more practical tips and techniques, how to best organize a bewildering array of experimental forms and conventions, how to unpack the nuances of experimental writing without assuming too much prior knowledge from our readers, and how to provide representative examples that are approachable, succinct, diverse, inspiring, and that avoid petrifying into a "canon." At the outset, we debated defining "experimental." Throughout the process, we went from asking whether a certain work was experimental to asking *in what way* is it experimental. Ultimately, we proposed a pluralistic methodology rather than a prescriptive one. In terms of the balance between historical background versus practical "craft" lessons, we felt that more discussion of the history, conventions, and context were needed for experimental writing than most other types of writing. Experimentalism is more unfamiliar to readers and can, at times, deliberately undermine the conventions many readers take for granted. Supplementing this background, though, we have provided discussion questions, prompts, examples in the anthology, and a few suggestions for pedagogy and application. We hope readers will see this book as merely one starting point in their exploration of innovative writing, rather than a finishing school. Although part of the book's impetus is how genres are merging and changing today, especially within experimentally inclined venues, we nonetheless found that organizing the book along the lines of genres and forms was the most expedient arrangement—albeit emerging genres that are oblique to the traditional ones. Our taxonomy attempts to get a handle on a complex and growing field; it is merely one representation of how to see emerging traditions and genres, a structure that we feel is not entirely ad hoc. However, we recognize there are many other ways to cut the joints of our subject and do not intend for our taxonomic categories to be rigid or reified.

Guiding us in making choices was a sense of what would be most useful for student writers who have some background in traditional creative writing but might find themselves flummoxed or daunted when attempting experimental work. Our teaching experiences in a range of classrooms from first-year seminars to advanced graduate workshops became resources to test out many of our approaches; students were invaluable in offering pointed feedback, whether explicitly commenting on chapters or through being "guinea pigs" in our hands-on writing laboratories. We also had frequent and boisterous discussions between each other about every topic, a process that encouraged us both to continually rethink our beliefs, do more research, and widen our reading habits. Moreover, we enlisted the advice of many fellow authors, teachers, and professionals in different literary communities, knowing that our own viewpoints were limited.

We want the book to be provocative—raising institutional questions, suggesting alternative practices, and reexamining commonplace craft maxims—while maintaining pedagogical relevance for the way that existing classrooms have been organized. Given that the material of this book cuts across the genres, media, movements, periods, and disciplines along which most creative writing, literature, rhetoric, and composition classes are currently taught, we designed the book with the idea that chapters or sections can largely be self-contained units. They can be mixed-and-matched as they are most suitable for the course topic or the individual reader's interest. Because experimental literature overlaps with mainstream literature, rather than acting as a dichotomy against it, we suspect most readers will have already encountered several examples of experimental writing. In casting our net widely, we hoped to make the book more accessible. At the same time, we urge anyone using the book not to take our word for it—go read and explore experimental literature on your own, get involved in your community, and write.

We both felt acutely the ways that this book was a constraint-based exercise. The limits of time and space influenced the shape this project ultimately took. Our publisher, Bloomsbury, accepted our pitch and asked if we could finish the manuscript in one year. We asked for two years, seeing no way that it could be completed in one, and we were granted a two-year deadline. Both coauthors worked full-time as professors with a variety of classes to teach and service or administrative duties to fulfill. While writing this book, we had our own ongoing creative writing projects to attend to, too. Also of note: Bloomsbury gave us a strict 135,000 word-count limit and said we could only include a maximum of six images. If it were up to us, this book would likely have included more images, both as visual texts and as captions of book arts, zines, handmade pieces, and performances. The first year of writing this book we completed what was *projected* to be part one of this book—extensive chapters on experimentation in each of the traditional genres: poetry, fiction, creative nonfiction, and playwriting. Then, during year two, we began what we'd planned as parts two and three: chapters on the emerging genres as well as a section on workshops, institutions, and communities. About halfway through the second year, however, we ran into a serious problem. The book was simply too big. We were running far over our word count when we factored in anthology selections. We decided the only way to reconcile our project was to cut part one about the traditional genres entirely, the chapters for which constituted over 70,000 words–almost a whole book manuscript. This decision was not taken lightly. We realized that with these excised chapters we might have an entirely different manuscript on our hands, an advanced multi-genre guidebook. Reluctantly, we were also forced to cut the final section on workshops, institutions, and communities due to lack of space along with sections on experimental approaches to reading, graphic novels, and much else. Focusing instead on emerging genres, however, would allow us to live up to the promise of a guidebook on the practices and techniques of experimental writing at present. Ironically, in the end, we *did* write the book you are now holding in your hands (or scrolling on your screens) within the span of a single year—a feat we felt would be impossible when we undertook this project.

Perhaps such a quick turnaround time is best for a book that purports to survey the current state of the art. In focusing on emerging genres "today," we readily acknowledge that our topic has a short shelf life. Then again, we situate experimentalism within the *longue durée* of historical movements going back beyond Modernism precisely so that today's experimental literature—and tomorrow's—can be seen in a wider perspective. It is impossible to keep up, and by the time this book is published some of its topics may strike the reader as already antiquated. Indeed, during the time we were writing the book, digital literature, for example, underwent many rapid changes: the emergence and decline of technologies such as the metaverse and NFTs, the release of Chat GPT and similar programs, and the consequent discussion of the ethics of using AI in one's writing. Right now, there is a Hollywood writer's strike; one point of contention is whether studios can employ AI to compose scripts. An idea that seemed experimental and theoretical only a few months ago suddenly has real-world consequences. A writer who tries to understand the historical moment is always caught within it. Given this predicament, we felt that it wasn't enough to merely examine the experimental work of today. We also had to look ahead, thinking about the future of where creative writing might be going, and to look behind us at the movements and epochs that have given shape to innovations in the past. We encourage our readers to do likewise.

Another unique challenge of this manuscript was the collaborative process of its composition. Although each of us had written collaboratively before with others, we had never done so for a full-length book. Nor had we collaboratively written with each other on anything more substantial than a grant application for the local book festival we both help coordinate. A few of our initial concerns about collaboration—merging our styles to find a single voice, encountering irreconcilable differences of opinion, or finding a working process that would synch—fell by the wayside when we dove into writing the book with a looming deadline. In their place, however, other issues arose. Coordinating to meet regularly proved difficult at times, given we both had such busy schedules during the time we were writing this book. Sticking to the matter at hand during our meetings sometimes turned out to be hard, too, since our mutual interest in literature and its connections to other fields led to many freewheeling bull sessions and philosophical asides. Yet we'd like to think that those dialogues had some utility, off base as they may have seemed at the time, as brainstorms that pinballed us in unexpected directions. We each have our idiosyncrasies, predilections, personal tastes, and knee-jerk tendencies that our discussions helped iron out and course correct. Still, our goal was never to present a completely "objective" account of our material, even if such a thing were possible. We hope elements of our personality come across, both individually and jointly, since charisma and style make any writing more compelling. We have plentiful doubts about the book that resulted from our collaboration. It is imperfect in more ways than we can account for here. Nonetheless, we hope that the collaborative nature of the enterprise emphasizes that our investigations into experimental writing were Socratic, embodied in an ongoing conversation—a dance of live voices rather than dead words. Perhaps the final product even succeeds in capturing a glimmer of our ludic confab. Our goal is that the students and readers using this book will join in and reanimate this collective conversation, continuing its playful, heteroclite spirit.

IV. Seven Theories of the Avant-Garde

In this book we won't make much of a distinction between terms such as experimental writing, innovative literature, the avant-garde, or other monikers that gesture toward the same general ballpark of loosely related styles and practices. That's because we embrace a more pluralistic outlook that recognizes many varieties of experimentation—a big-tent view that welcomes a wide range of aesthetics as experimental or experimental-ish—rather than trying to construct a narrow, prescriptive definition. Furthermore, we believe experimental literature is always evolving: which historical texts are considered "experimental" might evolve tomorrow in relation to constellations of new experimental work and its lineages to the past. Using a more rough-and-ready, pragmatic notion of experimental writing allows us to take an inclusive approach that acknowledges different domains in which literature can experiment, connections across periods or genres, and a fluidity to encompass emerging practices that might otherwise escape a stricter purview. "I know it when I see it," Justice Potter once said about pornography, and we might be inclined to say something similar about experimental writing. After all, whenever boundaries are set up, some experimentalist inevitably tries to push past them. Far from us, then, to dictate what counts as truly innovative.

To ask "What even is experimental anymore?" can act as both a coy dismissal and an earnest plea for some semblance of order. Sometimes experimental writing can seem everywhere and nowhere in our current literary ecosystem. While avant-garde literature has often positioned itself in opposition to the norms of some dominant culture, that seems less the case today in our heterogeneous literary culture. Styles are merging, aesthetics becoming flexible, and genres hybridizing. Our goal is not to disparage mainstream craft ideas, popular conventions, or academic disciplinary rhetoric; only to see them as contingent tools in relation to other "experimental" paths a writer might take. Although we have tried to remain open-minded and largely agnostic about the criteria that qualify work to be considered "experimental" for the purposes of this book, that does not mean that debates about what constitutes experimental writing are fruitless. In fact, we had many animated discussions regarding the definition and value of experimentation as we were composing this guidebook, both between ourselves and with other authors in the field. The more we discussed such issues, the more pluralistic our views became. But pluralism, of course, implies multiple—and at times incommensurable—perspectives. What are some of those different perspectives about the scope of experimental writing, then?

Below we offer seven brief theories of experimental writing. Surely, we left out many others. Ultimately, the genuine pluralist is not one who advocates pluralism as the only way to view things. Deliberating about these various frameworks can be both clarifying and enlivening for our readers, we hope; it may help adjust their sense of the purposes and traditions behind different experimental aesthetics and nudge them to reconsider which ones they most align with (or disagree with). It may also introduce them to new ways to conceive of the value of experimentation and its role in literature. These definitions of experimental writing are all quite different, showing tensions between various conceptions of what counts as "experimental." Some tensions may prove false binaries; others may be incommensurable junctures of contention. Does experimental work break the norms of its day, or can experimental work remain experimental; does experimental writing break with a canon, or does it form its own tradition of work; is the understanding of experimental work relative to a culture, or is an experiment only relative to an individual author or reader's baseline; is experimental writing definable by an aesthetic formalism that operates independently of political orientation or is experimental writing inherently political, subversive of the social status quo? These and other questions are debated in the thumbnail theories below.

1. **Breaking current norms.** Experimental literature is writing that breaks with the dominant norms or conventions of its era—both literary and otherwise. In doing so, it expands the ground of what constitutes literature itself. For this reason, the most experimental literature often doesn't look like "literature" at all. At times, the problem here would be to distinguish what counts as "literature," and what is (for example) protest, drag show, computer algorithm, wrestling match, or Earth art. When all conventions have been overthrown and thoroughly defamiliarized, literature as such would cease to exist, which appears to be the endgame of this brand of experimental fervor. In fact, it may often define itself as a type of anti-literature. Then again, new norms and conventions are set up with each succeeding generation, so there's always some new strictures to rebel against.

2. **Remaining uncanny.** Experimental writing is news that stays news. Works from bygone eras may remain experimental—*Gilgamesh*, *The Anatomy of Melancholy*, *Tristram Shandy*, *The Trial*, and so on. All these remain more innovative today than anything rolling fresh off the press or posted online. Indeed, in many cases, the so-called "classics" could well be defined as those works that continue to offer innovative perspectives and challenge the status quo. Ironically, this means that many books viewed by some as the most conservative are, in fact, the most radical. So-called "great books" are great not because they have become the antiquated totems of a culture or ensconce the powers that be; instead, they are "great" only in so far as they offer surprising and evergreen critiques of ideas, practices, norms, and institutional formulas. Their energies are subversive. The better part of the canon is composed of works that resist (and continue to resist) hidebound literary and social customs—they remain singular, uncanny, and unassimilable.

3. **Protest and social revolution.** Experimental literature is writing that aids the service of progressive or radical social change: it opposes self-satisfied conformity and shakes things up, inducing a cultural reckoning or political revolution. It's not simply the latest tweak in the style du jour of scribes and wordsmiths. The criterion of experimentation is not the quality of the work but its political and social purpose. This brand is the true "avant-garde," in the militant sense (i.e., the part of the army that leads the charge).

This view sees experimentation as necessarily communitarian rather than an outgrowth of a mere individual's eccentric whimsy. In this theory, a dry Marxist pamphlet or an invigorating anthem might be more "avant-garde" than the scribbles of the pretentious poet who writes obscure works that few will read and fewer still will understand. The avant-garde is defined by its political force, not its literary forms. Experimentation is an act of protest and revolt against existing power structures and the status quo.

4. **Experience and process, not rules and products**. Experimental literature is writing that has its basis in *experience*, rather than in imitating the stale rules and outworn etiquette that guided previous literary efforts. And while this experiential basis might be scientific for some and personal for others, at root it strikes against the weight of tradition and bravely faces the page using the raw materials of one's ideas of contemporary reality. Most adherents to this view of experimentalism favor "process" over "product," since the goal is to explore new areas of literary possibility. Authors of the experimental ilk must be original—that is, originating their own methods and intents anew from the welter of the world they see around them and the imagination they feel at work within. Therefore, each generation, each writer in fact, must reinvent their own way forward. What guides innovative work is trusting the processes and judgments that are based on experience rather than inherited models, conventions, or rules.

5. **Readers make it experimental**. The innovation in experimental writing does not lie with the writer or within the text; rather, it resides with the power of the reader. After all, the wildest text might be read with dead eyes; yet, by contrast, astute readers can bring profoundly experimental insights to traditional texts. Each age has the Shakespeare it deserves. "Everything great has already been said. But the person who knows how to stimulate his soul with the magnificence of it is always something new," as the Swedish poet Vilhelm Ekelund (1986: 14) once said. Experiments must arise from the way we approach literature, interpret it, keep it alive in our ways of sharing it, reading it, or forming communities around it. A reader such as Roland Barthes puzzling over the most mundane of Sunday comics, reading it against the grain, and coming up with a radically new interpretation would be a profound experimental act of literature.

6. **Partaking in a tradition of experimentation**. Avant-garde literature, far from acting to overturn or explode the idea of tradition, is simply another tradition, an alternative tradition. This may be especially true since the advent of Modernism. Experimental writing traces its conventions, preoccupations, and techniques largely from works and authors of previous generations. Indeed, one of the earmarks of experimental writing is that it pays explicit homage to—and clandestinely contends with—this lineage of past authors who have been recognized as experimental, much in the way that Gothic novelists or sonneteers pay homage to and wrestle with their forebears. Part of that wrestling, in the case of the avant-garde, has been with the idea of the canon and the concept of tradition itself, expressed, for example, by Pound's eager pilfering from Chinese sources or Borges ironic rewriting of eighteenth- and nineteenth-century styles. Nonetheless, experimental writing forms a body of work that, while mutable and debatable around its edges, is recognizable as such, and new work is identified as experimental by its relationship with these predecessor texts, even (or especially) when that relationship is one of defiance or renunciation. Mark Strand (1970: 15) writes that

the traditions of experimental writing are ones in which "tradition is preserved, thanks to severance: changes are its continuity. A tradition that immobilizes itself only prolongs death." Avant-garde works partake of a tradition of change, but each new experimental work also changes the tradition.

7. **Responding to cultural change.** Experimental literature is writing that attempts innovations that act as a corrective to the more dominant modes of representation and practice of the day: it's an intervention more than an opposition. Experimentation hopes to expand the field of literature in a way that allows writing to better capture changing social structures, represent new subjective experiences, respond to technology, combat changing capitalist forces, unleash repressed or unconscious feelings, enrich the reader's imaginative life, incorporate popular culture, or accomplish any number of other goals, depending on the author or movement. These interventions most often take the form of upending some aspects of established ideals of "good writing" based on a given time period's hegemonic aesthetic outlook, long-held craft dicta, or established modes of production, consumption, and distribution. Thus, experimental work is "challenging" both in that it is often difficult to read (mainly due to its use of unfamiliar techniques) and that it challenges the norms, hierarchies, and literary practices of its period. The experimental writing of one period, nevertheless, may become absorbed into the cultural mainstream so that the techniques or tactics which were once defiant have since become de rigueur. Thus, experimental writing must continually reinvent itself, in dialogue with more dominant discourses, to expand the possibilities of literary expression.

This sketch of seven theories is our own way of articulating several of the competing premises about what constitutes "experimental writing." These theories are meant less to be comprehensive than a suggestion of some of the opposing perspectives among experimentalists. Their diversity demonstrates why it is so difficult to delineate the set of works that we are addressing in this book. Sometimes, we will lean toward one theory more, sometimes another. Rather than trying to polemically define "experimental writing" at the outset, we feel that in a guidebook such as this one, we should be more welcoming of debate and expansive in our conception of the field. The idea of "experimental writing" is up-for-grabs, contentious, still being formed, unresolved, and contradictory. In the last analysis, there is no last analysis. This is our starting point. We prefer it this way rather than papering over fractures, divisions, and differing viewpoints.

Discussion Questions

1. List some of your fears, stereotypes, and preconceptions about experimental writing. What do you think these are based on? List some of the things that could make experimental writing exciting, interesting, or engaging. Why do you think experimental writing elicits certain reactions from you, whether positive or negative?

2. What are your expectations for this class—or, if you are not in a class, for this book; what are some conventions of classes, considered as a "genre"? (Or, alternatively,

textbooks as a genre?) To begin, you might think about the routines of the typical first day, for example. How do expectations shape how you engage with—and interact with or "read"—a class. Think of a class as a type of text and classes generally as a genre. Pick another (nonliterary) genre–say, horror movies, hair metal albums, amusement parks, first-person shooter video games, fast-food chains, or haute couture fashion lines: what expectations, conventions, and tropes does that genre have? How do these expectations, conventions, or tropes inform your understanding of a text (or example) in this genre?

3. When you read on your own for pleasure, rather than as an assignment for a class or work, what do you read for: do you enjoy learning information, exploring the far reaches of fantasy worlds, solving mysteries, the suspense of plot and action, the intellectual stimulation of philosophy, finding applicable tips for self-help, gleaning writing techniques, relating to the characters' problems and dilemmas, getting exposed to characters and situations radically different than your own, the escapism from real-life and immersion in another universe, the sounds and styles of how sentences are constructed, the way the text allows you imaginative liberties and room for interpretation, the "feels" and "vibes" that a text gives you, understanding cultural nuances, or something else? There's no right answer: these are your own predilections and pleasures.

4. Reflect on your reading practices. What reading strategies do you use, especially when you encounter a passage you don't understand in a text? For example, are you more likely to puzzle out a "crux" (an ambiguous or difficult passage) with various interpretations, gloss over it and read on to see if you can use context to help you make sense of it, mark it with an annotation, engage in research or look up a word, pose questions about it, ignore it entirely, or become frustrated and stop reading? What is your attitude to difficult texts: which types of challenges do you enjoy, and which turn you off?

5. Are you used to craft discourse from previous Creative Writing workshops and textbooks that give prescriptive rules, instructions, and precepts? Do you tend to reflexively judge writing as "good" or "bad" (if so, what are those evaluations based on)? How do you think the discipline of Creative Writing can proceed in a pluralistic atmosphere with diverse and changing aesthetics, styles, movements, functions, markets, and ideals of literature and in which cultural and historical references are not always shared among a wide readership? Can there be any objective standards? Should an appeal be made to what is most popular, what has the most prestige, or what scholars or experts regard as best? To what other criteria could one appeal? Should one make judgments at all?

6. Do you have any familiarity with creative writing that doesn't fall within the traditional genres of poetry, fiction, playwriting, or creative nonfiction? If so, what are some examples of such writing you have encountered? Are you aware of any newer or emerging forms, genres, or movements in experimental writing? What are some of the experimental authors, movements, or styles from noncontemporary, historical periods you know?

7. What writing communities are you involved in? What literary institutions are you affiliated with? How do you think workshops, writing communities, literary institutions, publishers and presses, literary journals, academia, agents, editors, social media influencers, nonprofits, technology, and other forces disrupt, inform, and shape writing today? What has shaped your own motivation to write?

Writing Prompts

1. Rewrite the same basic thought fifteen different ways, trying to cast each sentence in a different style. Some sentences might imitate your favorite writers while others could parody authors you revile. For instance, each sentence might describe a person walking across a room. Write a version that is noir; baroque; farcical; a version that imitates Shakespeare; a version that parodies Faulkner; another that sounds like Samuel Beckett; a maximalist sentence, a minimalist sentence; a sci-fi version, a *Harry Potter* version, a television sportscaster version, an erotic version; one that is sarcastic, one that is scientific, one in tweeny-bopper text-speak, and so on. What did you learn from paying such close attention to the construction of each sentence and trying to capture a certain style or voice?

2. Keep a reading journal (whether for a day, a week, or longer). Record everything you read, including textbooks and assignments, cereal-box games, street signs, subtitles, billboards, social media, bumper stickers, ads, recipes, emails, lecture notes, text messages, product instructions, and so on. Add notes and comments if you like, too. What did you discover? What are some of your reading habits? How—and how frequently—do you engage with texts? And in what ways?

3. Choose a random paragraph from virtually any text—it doesn't necessarily need to be a "literary" text: read it "against the grain" and in a "writerly" way; that is, deliberately constructing an interpretation that goes against the more obvious or readily accepted meanings. Write out your critical explication using textual analysis and the techniques of close reading to convince your reader of your new and unusual interpretation. Can you succeed, for instance, in making an otherwise boring, utilitarian text seem exciting and experimental? Or can you parse the implicit narrative, subtext, or cultural ideology behind, say, the ingredients and nutrition facts on the side of a soda can?

4. Write your own brief theory of the avant-garde; how do *you* define what's experimental? Give some rationale for what types of literature your theory emphasizes and excludes. Feel free to quibble with any of the thumbnail theories we presented above in the chapter.

5. Using two interlocutors that are both yourself wearing different hats (i.e., an interviewer and interviewee role), conduct a self-interview. Good examples of the form can be found online by Joyce Carol Oates (*Washington Post*, September 13, 2003) and Richard Howard ("Compulsive Qualification" at *Poetry*). You might want to come up

with a dozen questions beforehand, but then you could feel free to deviate from these and indulge your interlocutor's digressions and ask follow-up questions. Entertaining interviews—and self-interviews!—often take us in unexpected directions as the conversation unfolds. Allow spontaneous asides, arguments, evasions, surprises, anecdotes, and misunderstandings to develop. Sharing these can be a way to allow each person to introduce themselves to the class. Alternatively, students could pair up and conduct interviews with each other. The interviewer could then write a brief profile essay based on the interview, and then allow the subject to read it: how and where does the interviewee feel the profile essay represents them and where do they feel like it creates a persona or character different from their own concept of self? Where did the interviewee embellish information; evade the question; put the interviewer on the spot?

6. This prompt could take place over the course of the entire semester, and it could be done in small groups or individually. Students choose one book, author, movement, or topic to present in more depth, creating a PowerPoint or similar slide presentation they deliver to the class. For students who need some direction in selecting a topic, many authors, books, and topics are listed in the references at the back, on our companion website (https://www.bloomsburyonlineresources.com/experimental-writing-a-writers-guide-and-anthology), and throughout the rest of the chapters in this book as well as in the anthology. Presentations could include a minimum number of slides; quotes and interpretations from sample texts; cultural or historical contexts and other requisite background; multimodal forms of engagement such as visual texts, sound files, performances, or video clips; a hands-on activity for the class to do; discussion questions; and a prompt for other students based on the topic. Many students learn best from other students or from teaching lessons themselves. Moreover, we invite students and teachers to supplement this book with their own in-depth explorations of topics we give only cursory coverage.

CHAPTER 1
HYBRIDS

I. Introduction

Jackalope. Pluot. Batarang. Liger. Banjolele. Sharknado. Tamagotchi. Muppet. Infomercial. Velcro. Pizzly bear. One of the telltale signs you're in the presence of hybrids is the unfettered use of portmanteaus or words formed from the syllabic juncture of two others. To create a hybrid of two things, some characteristics of the original forms will be emphasized and others de-emphasized. In the case of the pluot, expect the texture of a plum but the sweetness of an apricot. Banjolele has the membrane of a banjo but the neck of a ukulele. And Velcro is smooth as velvet but has hooks like a crochet. One assumption of a hybrid is that it's greater—or at least different—than the sum of its parts. Shark attacks are horrific, to be sure. And tornadoes are disastrous. But imagine the toothy funnel of a sharknado; this union is hyperbolic, utterly sublime.

Hybridization is often used in the sciences to connote the smudging of taxonomies or the combining of technologies to facilitate adaptation or optimization. For example, horticulturalists often graft the rootstock of one plant to the scion of another to make a hybrid plant. The result? Something heartier or prettier or wholly ironic. But why bother? Prominent genres like fiction, poetry, nonfiction, and playwriting are often packaged as discrete long-standing literary traditions, and indeed, their recognizability is a function of the institutions that prop up those traditions—whether academia, literary publishing, or contemporary Western art culture. As we begin to examine hybrids, the techniques and styles from traditional genres are rejiggered, even supplanted, by different artistic traditions, forms, and media. The degree to which an emergent genre seems to combine, transcend, or toy with the impulses of its predecessors often depends upon your familiarity with the constitutive elements. While you prospect among hybrid inventions, it pays to keep an open mind: while some might register as mere dust or fool's gold, others will turn out to be genuine nuggets, lopsided and sidelong though they are. Not just a new fashion—a new fusion of things that reveals more than its facets.

While some may see hybridity as show-offy or pretentious, theorists have directed our attention toward the propensity for hybrids to function as a literary "third space." To participate in the purest, most recognizable traditions of the novel, poem, or essay is to participate in some of the pet projects of the empires from which they emerged, including Western interpretations of moral, romantic, or rational thought. Instead, writers might decide they *can* and *should* dislocate those traditions, to move the genres to a third space, which Homi Bhabha (2006: 155) characterizes as the "cutting edge of translation and negotiation." The third space is where idiosyncratic combinations of genre, literacy, speech, thought, and culture can converge in a single text, gesturing to an emancipated future. Hybridity is a space where the cultural assumptions and ideals embedded in traditional forms can speak to each other.

Aesthetically, it is important to note that the traditional genres were also once on the vanguard of literary practice, that every genre and form—no matter how staid or stuffy it might now seem—was a not-so-pure innovation in its time. The first writing systems (e.g., Sumerian cuneiform), first poems (e.g., *The Epic of Gilgamesh*), first plays (e.g., *The Oresteia*), first novels (e.g., *The Tale of Genji*), and first essays (*Essais*) all have one thing in common: they departed, intentionally, from preexisting modes of writing. The novel is a great example of this in that it is really a pastiche of history, philosophy, drama, romance, *belles-lettres*, diaries, epistles, and wonder tales. In this respect, it can be said to be a hybrid, borrowing subtly in some cases, radically in others from preexisting genres. The novel's appropriations were once *sui generis*, strange, and fresh. Today, however, the novel's hybrid origins are rarely acknowledged; it no longer strikes us as new. But, had this textbook been written in the eighteenth century, surely the novel would have been the headliner of this hybrid chapter. But that doesn't mean the novel is hopelessly ossified. It's important to keep in mind that genres can cycle through fashions; for example, epics connote the generic conventions of ancient literature while the very similar verse novel may be considered modish.

Hybridity is as old as literature itself. Take Ovid's ([8 CE] 2004) *Metamorphoses*, ostensibly about the metamorphic gods who masquerade as humanoids. Ovid was concerned with another class of hybrids as well—that of the crossbreed. See the centaurs and sirens, Medusa and the Minotaur that populate his works. Apropos, the word *genre* (French for "kind, style"), is not so etymologically distant from *genus* (Latin for "type, kind"). However, Ovid's text itself is metamorphic—an epic pastiche in which, according to Hinds (1987: 121), "boundaries are crossed and recrossed as in no poem before. Elements characteristic of elegy, bucolic, didactic, tragedy, comedy, history, and oratory mingle with elements variously characteristic of the grand epic tradition and with each other." If scholars can't seem to agree on whether the text is tragic or comic, epic or elegiac, that's because Ovid is in constant, willful violation of the rules of any one genre. Gildenhard and Zissos (2016) write "arguably a more promising way to think critically about the generic presences in Ovid's poem is to see the genres *in dialogue* with one another in ways that are *mutually enriching*" (emphasis in original). This mutuality is critical to understanding the value of hybrids.

Even now, hybrid genres that may seem weird or off-center are perhaps only ahead of their time or subversively behind it; today's newfangled hybrid could become tomorrow's standard-bearer. Indeed, in most cases, the hybrid forms we discuss in this chapter have already gained mainstream recognition and acceptance. While hybrid practitioners can be said to invigorate literature, there are no basic irrefragable genres in literature. Languages themselves are always in a process of evolution. Genres are continually breaking apart and recodifying. Which things we consider hybrid, then, depends on what things our larger institutional and cultural systems have rendered legible through normative categories. Everything moves and morphs. With any luck, in a generation or so, some of the hybrid forms we present later might look dowdy or rearguard, which would imply a new cycle of mixing, matching, and merging has yet again prevailed.

II. Blends of Poetry and Prose

Hybrid writers are designers much like dog-breeders who develop Labradoodles (Labrador and poodle), Puggles (pug and beagle), or Bullshits (bulldog and shih tzu). The husbandry of cross-genre writing employs similar design schemes. What gets pronounced, muted, or whisked together will affect not only the categorical designation of the hybrid work, but also its aesthetic possibilities. By fixating on the genre status, however, one may be inclined to think of hybridity as merely a formal distinction. One can imagine the myriad ways in which conventions typically affiliated with one genre can lend themselves to experiments and innovations in another genre.

There are seemingly close affinities within aesthetics. And more than a few odd couples. Try as you might, it's nigh impossible to write a free verse poem employing an ABAB rhyme scheme. Just as it is illogical to write an aromantic aubade for evening. After all, aubades are, by definition, *love* poems written for the *dawn*. (Then again, one might be interested in exploiting, voiding, or dramatizing the friction between rules inherent to these aforementioned forms, thus making an ironic or paradoxical hybrid.)

For the sake of this section, though, we will call attention to hybrids with localizable stable conditions or conventions. As such, they are often recognized as emerging (or emerged) forms in their own right; that is, they are voguish, semi-established genres that many writers will be familiar with. Some of these typologies will be so cohesive that you may not even see the need for deeming them "hybrids" in the first place. Each of these has some degree of institutional imprimatur and pedigree, and they are generally a mash-up of only two different genres that are easily distinguished as such.

For starters, a quick way to identify a **prose poem** is that it sounds and acts like a poem but looks on the page like a prose paragraph. In other words, the prose poem abandons one of the major hallmarks of the poetic form (line breaks) in favor of a prosaic staple: the sentence, more or less. However, the prose poem isn't using sentences in a traditional manner. Instead, they tend to engage in what L=A=N=G=U=A=G=E poet Ron Silliman (1987) calls "a plural syntax." That is, they traffic in ambiguity, extended metaphor, soundplay, and other hallmarks of poetic multiplicity.

Many attribute the origins of prose poetry to Charles Baudelaire as he reflected on the difficulties of Parisian life during the nineteenth century with its growing class divides, changing gender roles, and upended city plans. *Paris Spleen*, subtitled "little poems in prose," combined the narrative drive of short stories with the ironies, wordplay, and associative structure of poetry. Baudelaire's work inspired the likes of later Romantic and Symbolist prose poets such as Arthur Rimbaud, Paul Valéry, and Stéphane Mallarmé who were precursors to the Surrealists. Mallarmé's (Poetry Foundation: n.p.) work, for example, is characterized by "tortuous syntax, ambiguous expressions, and obscure imagery." Such is the risk of breaking with form. Then again, this description resembles the virtues of what would, a century later, be known as L=A=N=G=U=A=G=E poetry.

Silliman, in his articulation of the "new sentence," concludes that prose poetry fuses the grammars of prose and poetry by foregoing both the rules of traditional sentences and poetic lines. The empty space between sentences or clauses opens a place where context is implied, a context that the "new sentence" continually shifts and disestablishes to create permutations of meaning that go beyond mere denotation. In this way, the prose poem is rife with association. Its ellipses court myriad meanings and engage the hallucinatory ear. Moments of polysemy (many meanings) allow for the integration or reconstitution of reference, leaving readers to the task of deducing an interpretation from the welter of possibilities. Many sentences in prose poems withhold the workaday functions of prose in favor of a vibratory poetics, pinballing among a force field of connotations and correspondences.

Many prose poems are no more than a paragraph or two, as with Francis Ponge's (2008) *Unfinished Ode to Mud*, which is a series of object lessons about, among other things, oysters, crates, blackberries, and soap. "There is so much to say about soap," he concludes. Another popular example is Carolyn Forché's (1981) "The Colonel," in which the poet-speaker shares a meal with a ruthless military leader in Latin America, who empties a bag of severed ears onto the dinner table. Rather than ensconce the ears as a mere poetic image, thereby trivializing the violence of this civil war, the speaker opts for objective reportage.

Forché's work is part of a countertradition in the prose poem that eradicates lyrical "purple prose" to leverage matter-of-fact description for its more mordant bite. Many contemporary prose poets write prose sentences that could be mistaken for (what else?) prose. That is, they feel low-key instead of pitched-up, scrutable rather than indeterminate, dealing with a clear ostensible subject in place of amorphous semantic clouds. Many have characters, plots, even a twist at the end like a story. But one can read such a prose poem again for the way its details offer puzzling suggestions: the ears, for example, of Forché's prose poem also stand in for the idea of the lyric itself, how the sound and meter of the piece has been "severed" from its organic connection to poetry, rendered into chilling prose. Then there's the work of such poets—Russell Edson, Charles Simic, and James Tate come to mind—that inhabit the in-between realm of the prose poem, in which the narrative detail can easily stray into symbol, plot can go of course into surrealistic hi-jinks, and the closing twist may undo everything you assumed previously about the piece.

Check out "In the Guinea Pig Cave" on p. 203. This prose poem was written by Aase Berg, founding member of the Stockholm Surrealist Group.

There are also book-length works of prose poetry. Gertrude Stein's *Tender Buttons*, William Carlos Williams's *Kora in Hell*, John Ashbery's *Three Poems*, Lyn Heijinian's *My Life*, and Harryette Mullens's *Sleeping with the Dictionary* are all long-form examples. These often fragmentary works circumvent a direct narrative trajectory, digressing and hovering just above the surface of their disparate themes or theses. They accumulate, riff, and network in meaning while maintaining their open-endedness throughout.

While the distinctions are somewhat muddled, most would agree that a prose poem is a poem that proses while a **lyric essay** is a prose that poems. There is a twofold "lyric" quality in a lyric essay: for one, language is musical and metaphorical, but also its structure or logic is associative, braided, and/or collage-like. According to John D'Agata (2003: 437), the lyric essay is an oxymoron because it's "an essay that's also a lyric; a kind of logic that wants to sing; an argument that has no chance of proving anything." In his tepidly titled, "We Might as Well Call It the Lyric Essay," the introduction to *Seneca Review*'s all-lyric essay issue, D'Agata attempts a definition: the lyric essay "[eschews] the story-driven ambitions of fiction and nonfiction for the associative inquiry of poems" (2015: 7). Recalling the way New Journalism co-opts the craft moves of literary fiction to tell true stories, the lyric essay instead employs poetic moves to sing true stories. The acoustic, songlike quality is derived from the repetition of vowel or consonant sounds, patterns of stress or unstress (prosody), not to mention a penchant for figurative language and potent imagery. Some believe these stylistic choices compromise one of the defining features of nonfiction, turning nonfiction on its head: to stylize and embellish truth is to turn it into mere truthiness. Others contend such maneuvers afford the lyric essay an affective precision, psychological authority, or ecstatic realism that facts and figures by themselves cannot offer. Every account of truth is shaped, selected, bound up with the terms of its representation and rhetoric, after all, whether it's flatfooted and literal-minded or lyric and footloose.

D'Agata addresses his ambivalence about the term "lyric essay" by noting that "nomenclature, while often limiting, polarizing, inadequate, and always stupid, can also be the thing that opens up our genre to new possibilities and new paths of inquiry, helping us to shape our experiences in the world in ways we have not yet imagined" (2015: 10). This course was already being charted—by Susan Sontag, Anne Carson, John McPhee, Annie Dillard, and Joan Didion—long before the "lyric essay" got its name. Today, it's writers like Maggie Nelson, Jo Ann Beard, Michael Ondaatje, Eula Biss, Renee Gladman, Nicole Walker, Lily Hoang, and Sarah Manguso who extend the form into the realm of the braided essay. Rather than individual subjects, the braided essay is a type of lyric essay that takes on a compound— and therefore, experimental—subject. The individual threads that are being braided begin to hybridize, assuming each other's characteristics, recombining to form a hitherto unknown amalgam. Disparate threads fall into sympathy with one another through organizing metaphors, association, coincidence, and other forms of connective tissue. A literal detail in one braid takes on symbolic significance in another. A surface-level subject (like fishing) is gradually grafted onto a subterranean theme (grieving for one's father). The *raison d'être* of the braided essay is to eliminate the perceived boundaries between any two (or more) subjects or experiences, including temporal and spatial disparities. Whereas early on in most braided essays, individual threads appear distinct, the leaps between them possessing a dramatic non-sequitur quality, the affinities between threads are revealed gradually—teased, even burlesqued, until the ligatures between the muscles are overt, the logic becoming taut and explicit. The cumulative effect of the braiding should be such that the reader can never separate these ideas again. The writer fastens them together in an inextricable meshwork.

The prose poem and lyric essay, though, are not the only possible hybrids of prose and poetry. The **haibun** is a form of Japanese poetry that originated in the late seventeenth century and was popularized by the poet Matsuo Bashō. It typically consists of a short prose passage of a few paragraphs that describes a place or an experience, followed by a haiku or similarly brief lyric that captures a moment or emotion related to the prose. The subject of the lyric does not necessarily need to refer to anything in the prose passage. The two modes are typically juxtaposed without explanation, which allows the reader to draw inferences and relations between the prose and lyric. The haibun form is still linked to the spirit of travel, after Bashō's *Narrow Road to the Deep North*, where he combines prose descriptions of a spiritual journey followed by haiku that capture a trenchant paradox or uncertainty with nimble imagery. The prose passage in a haibun often is meditative and impressionistic, capturing a mood or fleeting moment with a few precise images or details.

Contemporary English-language poets have reinvented the haibun for new purposes. John Ashbery experimented with a series of haibun in his book *The Wave* (1984) in which the prose passages meander in atmospheric headspaces. Ashbery follows these with a single fragmented line of mysterious imagery. Ashbery even includes an homage to Bashō in one prose passage, a variation on his most famous haiku: "Just as when a large, fat, lazy frog hops off his lily pad like a spitball propelled by a rubber band and disappears into the water of the pond with an enthusiastic plop" (1984: 44). Poetry and prose are inverted here, as elsewhere in Ashbery's sequence: the haibun form likely appealed to Ashbery for its sense of indirection—the way the reader must puzzle to fill the gap between not only the paragraph and lyric line, but likewise the discursive logic of the whole. James Merrill's sequence "Japan: Prose of Departure" (1986: n.p.) refashions the haibun as postcard-like snippets of travelogue with an "ectoplasm of plot." Its quick brushstrokes illustrate as much by negative space as by their "artfully balanced hues and textures." The prose sequences abruptly transition in and out of lineated verse, showing a studied indifference between the two modes. The chattier tourist anecdotes slowly give way to more elegiac sketches about the specter of AIDS and survivor's guilt, the departure of travel resolving into a metaphor for the departure from life.

More recently, Robert Hass's "On Visiting the DMZ at Panmunjom" recasts the haibun as a medium for political poetry. Hass's straightforward prose passage recounts statistics from the Korean War, admitting that "the terms are inexact and thinking about them can make you sleepy" (2007: 82). The turn to a haiku at the end can be read, then, as an attempt to give more precise weight to the events as well as capture the vagueness of a historical scene in which the speaker cannot fully fathom. Khaled Mattawa likewise repositions the haibun in "Your City" for its ability to blend factual detail and poetic import. Mattawa's prose description of Cairo's upscale redevelopment plans for its surrounding desert is juxtaposed to a poetic passage about a poor cattle-herder. The prose paragraph acts as necessary context to understand the subsequent lyric, throwing into contrast the perspectives of class conflict. Aimee Nezhukumatathil writes that the traditional haibun cultivates:

> A detachment from, and even a complete absence of, the speaker, that is, avoidance of using any personal pronouns such as I or first-person possessive adjectives (*my* and *mine*). This is especially helpful for poets who are looking to get out of a first-person point of view rut or for those who have trouble looking "outside" themselves and into the world and environment. (2014, emphasis in original)

By focusing on the spirit that Bashō termed "*mono no aware*"—the sentiment inherent in objects and places; the tinge of sadness at passing beauty—poets who tend toward self-involved histrionics might gain a more removed, impassive perspective through exploring the haibun, Nezhukumatathil suggests. Finally, Henri Cole's "Haiku" overturns the conventions of traditional haibun by being written entirely in lines of verse. Cole's work is recognizable as a take on the haibun, however, since the work's opening is composed in longer, more discursive lines describing a singular place and moment (a contaminated estuary), juxtaposed to a wistful haiku at the end about human fragility. Striking a delicate balance between confessional drama and *mono no aware* is Cole's signature strength in "Haiku" and throughout his oeuvre.

III. Flash

Flash genres in creative writing are almost always hybrid in nature because of the form's reliance on "poetic compression." In this regard, flash prose shares a lot of the same attributes of prose poetry and the lyric essay. Whether you call them shorts or short shorts, flashes or micros, when a prose genre is allotted the same amount of real estate as a poem—roughly a page or two—it starts acting like a poem, consciously or not. (By that same logic, the "long poem" we cover in the next chapter is always hybrid because, through its dilation, it comes to embody qualities typical of prose forms, often utilizing structures such as argument or narrative.)

While there is no fixed word count for a "flash," journal submission guidelines will usually set the parameters at no greater than 1,000. For example, there's *Smokelong Quarterly* (1,000 words), *Brevity Journal* (750 words), *Cincinnati Review*'s miCRo series (500 words), *River Teeth*'s Beautiful Things column (250 words), *Creative Nonfiction*'s Tiny Truths (130-character tweets plus a hashtag), and *Six Word Stories*, just to name a few. Alternatively, flash writers have taken more organic approaches to quantifying their work. Smokelongs, for instance, are attributed to Chinese readers who could consume an entire flash during one smoke break at the office. This underscores the transformation that fiction underwent globally in the twentieth century. There's also the (typically) flash genre of the single-sentence story, which is on offer at *Complete Sentence*, a journal devoted to the form.

For an example of a one-sentence story, see Hanif Abdurraqib's "On Times I Have Forced Myself to Dance" on p. 194.

Stories and essays—even flash itself—have grown shorter in recent decades. Some causes are more limited real estate in print journals, the advent of the internet with its premium on snappy concision, and a cultural shift away from investing hours reading longer literature in favor of compression. Ironically, this compression into flash forms reversed the ideal of the long Victorian novel (think Dickens), many of which had originally been published in newspapers, too, each chapter with its own cliffhanger. The Israeli writer, Etgar Keret, in conversation with Deborah Treisman for *The New Yorker Fiction Podcast*, says that when one writes a longer short story, it's no different than writing a novel because it needs to be designed, there has to be a blueprint. To write a flash fiction, though, is like surfing, he says. He alludes to the absurdity of someone asking, "How long are you going to surf before you fall?" Instead, "The wave ends and you fly off and you find yourself somewhere … it just ends." For this reason, flash is popular with many writers, too, since they can often avoid the elaborate scaffolding and architectural planning required for longer works when they write flash and just dive right in, seeing where the impulse takes them.

Unlike with prose poetry or the lyric essay, a flash work is not necessarily poetic in its voice; however, by chiseling away at the glut of narrative possibilities, what emerges might be impressionistic or vignette-like, a still life or slice-of-life, a secretive observation or explosive surprise. Brevity puts more pressure on each sentence, each word. Flash lacks exposition and closure in many cases, presenting arguments or stories instead through images and scenes in media res. And many include some type of twist or gut-punch that defies initial expectations. Not to mention, while novels may take ten or more hours to read over the course of weeks, flash pieces are almost always read in one sitting—like a lyric poem. Rather than sip coffee from an oversized mug, instead try shooting espresso from a dainty demitasse cup. With no time to play it back or predict where it's heading, a flash piece is prone to blindside readers.

Flash writers can calibrate the pacing to deliver the story's turns and revelations at a specific juncture, right down to a designated sentence, clause, word.

While we think too much has been made of the six-word short story apocryphally attributed to Ernest Hemingway—"For sale: baby shoes, never worn"—we do appreciate the way flash prose emphasizes implication over exposition. In a flash fiction, there is no time for backstory, for character development, for in-depth world-building. And certainly not all three!

In less than 30 seconds, you can read the entirety of Mary Ruefle's "The Taking of Moundville by Zoom." That's on p. 306.

Nobel Prize–Winning novelist Yasunari Kawabata famously winnowed down his 175-page novel, *Snow Country*, to just eleven pages. He called the stand-alone work "Gleanings from Snow Country" and considered it the zenith of his artistic career. Lara Palmquist (2015: n.p.) notes how "miniaturization intensifies the isolated images." "Gleanings" is reminiscent of Kawabata's lesser-known flashes, what he called *Palm of the Hand Stories*, a collection of pieces so short that they could be inscribed, approximately, on the palm of one's hand. Implication must do more work, as if the visible flash piece were merely an iceberg suggesting underlying depths.

Rather than Freytag's Pyramid, the narrative structure of flash works can be causal or sketchy, rendered like a snapshot or a tableau vivant, wound like the springs of a jack-in-the-box or lit like the fuse of a dynamite stick. In Lucy Corin's "Fourth of July," supine bodies lay in a field under explosions; in the case of this story, the title provides all the context one needs. Flash are so quick that the reader doesn't expect a full narrative arc, subplots, or backstory; flash may be freed from the motive of plot development and character study, thus allowing new structures and approaches to the story or essay.

IV. Other Established Hybrid Forms

Many assorted hybrid forms have an established precedent, though they have not become so entrenched to appear overdone or formulaic. They can still strike readers with a frisson. **Epistolary forms** are enduring hybrids, for example, whether that means the hoary epistolary novel or the even more ancient tradition of **letters in verse**, which dates in Greek from at least AD fourth century. Latin poets such as Horace, Ovid, and Catullus wrote many epistolary poems couched as frank missives to a friend or mistress. The form continues virtually unabated today. W. H. Auden and Louise MacNeice collaborated on *Letters from Iceland*, a series of epistolary forms, which includes letters to each other, a few acquaintances, and even the dead, such as in Auden's poem "Letter to Lord Byron." Auden's one-time amanuensis, James Schuyler, often used letters in verse, too. Critic Daniel Katz, analyzing Schuyler's "A Stone Knife," writes that "whereas poems, subject to the aesthetic, are fit objects of contemplation, a letter would be seen to have above all a utilitarian function. To blur the distinction letter/poem is precisely to unsettle the category of the aesthetic as that of disinterested contemplation" (2010: 150).

Blurring living and dead, originals and imitations, breakthroughs and wisecracks, Jack Spicer's *After Lorca* intersperses translations and pseudo-translations with letters—prose poems, really—that invoke Lorca and his *duende*. Spicer (1974: n.p.) pens an ironic introduction to his own book in the voice of Lorca himself, where the dead poet responds, complaining about the abuse his poems have suffered, when half a poem of his has been adjoined to one of Spicer's like an "unwilling centaur," adding "modesty forbids me to speculate which end … is mine." Richard Hugo's book *31 Letters and 13 Dreams* contains several examples of verse letters in which he unburdens himself to poet friends, musing and grousing and gossiping by turns. The form affords a more intimate tone, apostrophizing the addressee whether real or imaginary. Offhand, casual insights can sneak in the composition. Letters in verse often speak to a specific occasion, effusive and garrulous with their ardency. They tend to be more casual, down to earth. Not so Richard Howard's *Untitled Subjects*, which portray imaginary letters from nineteenth-century historical figures, unfurling with riddled and recherché literary asides. Similarly, Lucie Brock-Broido's *Master Letters* are high-pitched and pitched upon the high, like a mystic's prayerful communion with her private gods. They revel in exultation and ravishment, shot through with a vexed longing for the eternal or some reverent ever after.

Epistolary novels date back to at least the Renaissance and became common in the eighteenth century. By most definitions, epistolary novels may contain journal entries and sometimes other documents besides letters. Stoker's (1897) *Dracula* assembles newspaper clippings, memos, telegrams, ship's logs, phonograph cylinders, business correspondence, and more. The novel questions how we can obtain veracity from such a welter of documents with their inevitable lacunae and shifting points of view. Indeed, the concluding note remarks, "In all the mass of material of which the record is composed, there is hardly one authentic document; nothing but a mass of typewriting" (1897: 354), raising the issue of whether Harker, the diegetic editor, fabricated, embellished, or left out any materials as the narrative was transcribed and constructed. The YA novel *Monster* by Walter Dean Myers (2001) likewise plays off the Gothic doubts of being able to find the truth among assorted documents. It compiles journal entries, screenplays, and court transcripts to depict a troubled Black youth accused of a crime. When epistolary novels fold in ever-more document types and genres, rather than telling a story through letters, they gradually shade into the "composite novel," which we tackle in the next chapter.

Another ancient hybrid is the **verse play**, a play in which the dialogue is verse rather than prose. While verse plays can be written in free verse, they are usually in some rhythmic pattern of stresses such as blank verse (unrhymed iambic pentameter) or rhymed couplets. The use of verse in a play can create a heightened, formalized atmosphere and can also allow the playwright to create complex, nuanced characters who express equally complex and nuanced language. Not only Shakespeare, but most Renaissance English playwrights wrote in verse; other famous examples include most of Moliere's comedies and Ibsen's *Peer Gynt*. William Butler Yeats, T. S. Eliot, and Robert Frost—among other Modernists—revived the verse play in the twentieth century. As a literary form, the verse play has fallen out of favor lately. It's no longer as commonly produced or studied. Sometimes the form is used for its campy insouciance and deconstructed anachronisms, such as in David Grimm's *Measure for Pleasure* or Kirk Wood Bromley's *The Banger's Flopera*. Another contemporary permutation of verse plays weaves together forms as diverse as prose, free verse, performance art, rock operas, choreopoems, newspaper drama, song cycles, riffs, patter, and lyric monologues.

Contemporary playwrights as diverse as Sam Shepherd, Sarah Kane, Sarah Ruhl, Suzan-Lori Parks, Annie Baker, and Branden Jacobs-Jenkins have used rhythmic, lyrical, and associative language that takes after poetry without quite tackling the prosody of traditional verse. Their works can exhibit a mélange of styles and forms, verse or poetry being just one among many.

A **closet drama**, by contrast, is a type of play that is intended to be read rather than performed on stage. Closet dramas are often written in verse—but this is not always the case—and may include stage directions or other elements that are typical of plays, but they are not intended to be produced in the same way as a traditional play. Instead, they are meant to be read and imagined by the reader, who can picture the events of the play in their mind. Closet dramas developed in the eighteenth century when the stage, often featuring melodrama and burlesques, was not conducive to the high-minded and political ideas of Romantic poets. The form allowed playwrights to explore complex ideas or themes without the constraints of the stage, whether physical stagecraft, censorship, or the demands of the marketplace. Some better-known examples of closet dramas include *Faust* by Johann Wolfgang von Goethe and *Prometheus Bound* by Percy Bysshe Shelley. In the twentieth century, Antonin Artaud's absurdist short play "Spurt of Blood" could be considered a closet drama, though Artaud also attempted to direct Shelley's *The Cenci*, another work that is usually tagged as a closet drama. There is some ambiguity inherent in the form, as sometimes these dramas are taken out of their closets. Karl Kraus (2015: p. 1) claimed his sprawling *Last Days of Mankind* would "would take some ten evenings in terrestrial time, [but] is intended for a theatre on Mars." More recently, the New York School poet and playwright Kenneth Koch wrote many blink-and-you-missed-them closet dramas. Some productions, though, have been given to Koch's seemingly impossible-to-stage scripts, using theatrical magic and the audience's imagination. The contemporary publisher Plays InVerse has some closet dramas in its catalog, demonstrating the form is not quite dead.

The **verse novel** arose in the nineteenth century when poets wrote lengthy narrative works—George Meredith's *Modern Love*, Elizabeth Barrett Browning's *Aurora Leigh*, or Arthur Hugh Clough's *Amours de Voyage*, for instance, that pilfered techniques from the popular novels of the day. The verse novel tends to be more homely than the epic; its focal characters are less heroic, more domesticated, and approachable. Its narrative is written in lines of verse that are often metrical. In recent decades, many authors from the Caribbean have written verse novels in a variety of guises, whether following classical models or using inspiration from music videos, including Edward Kamau Braithwaite's *Ancestors*, Fred D'Aguiar's *Bloodlines*, and Kwame Dawes's *Prophets*. Other notable examples of verse novels are Les Murray's *Freddy Neptune*, Glyn Maxwell's *Time's Fool*, and Amos Oz's *The Same Sea*. A parallel and closely related genre is the **verse autobiography**, which was initiated by Wordsworth's *Prelude* and continues with book-length poems such as Alfred Corn's *A Call in the Midst of the Crowd* and Tommy Pico's *IRL*. In some cases, verse novels and verse autobiographies slide into the conceptual space of the "long poem," which will be addressed in the next chapter. Since the new millennium the verse novel and verse autobiography traditions have burgeoned in the YA genre: often Slam poetry, with its gritty evocations of identity, fuses with the Bildungsroman, the novel about the protagonist's moral growth into young adulthood. Examples include Elizabeth Acevedo's *The Poet X*, Safia Elhillo's *Home Is Not a Country*, and Nikki Grimes' *Ordinary Hazards*.

Dramatic essay is a type of short prose work that incorporates elements of both the essay and the dramatic form. It typically takes the shape of a fictional conversation or dialogue between two or more characters, as was the case with Plato's *Dialogues*, in which characters converse on a theme. The dramatic essay may also include stage directions, descriptions of the characters, and other elements of drama to create a more immersive reading experience. The dramatic essay often explores complex ideas in a more accessible and engaging way than a traditional essay, using the dialogue and interactions of the characters to illuminate different viewpoints on the subject. Since Plato (or, rather, his tutor Socrates for whom philosophy *was* dialogue, not something written down at all), there is a long philosophical tradition for using the dramatic essay or dialogue, though we'd note that "the classical source for medieval writers of dialogue should have been Plato," but Western Medieval writers "had no direct access to Plato's dialogues, with the exception of the first half of the *Timaeus*" (Sweeney, 2002: n.p.). Surprisingly then, a wide range of Medieval philosophers—Abelard, Ockham, Augustine, Boethius—employ the form. Likewise, important Enlightenment era philosophers wrote dialogues (Hume, Berkeley, Shaftesbury) and the form continues to be used occasionally by contemporary philosophers, such as Daniel Dennett, Douglas Hofstadter, and Andy Clark.

A related hybrid form is the **all-dialogue story**. Whereas a dramatic essay is a subtype of nonfiction, the all-dialogue story uses the key component of drama—dialogue—to create (you guessed it!) a story. These works of narrative fiction rarely include any exposition or stage directions and may even lack dialogue tags. Ernest Hemingway's "Hills Like White Elephants" and Donald Barthelme's "King of Jazz" are some well-known exemplars of the form. It's uncommon for all-dialogue stories to reach the length of a novel, though some works do, such as *J. R.* by William Gaddis, *Mr. Mani* by A. B. Yehoshua (it's only one-sided snatches of dialogue), *The Golden Fruits* by Nathalie Sarraute, and *Your Fathers, Where Are They? And The Prophets, Do They Live For Ever?* by Dave Eggers. One impulse in all-dialogue stories is to eliminate anything superfluous, including at times indications about who is speaking. A different impulse is to mirror how using only dialogue can lead to disembodied voices whose loopy conversations can go off the rails, unimpeded by other narrative constraints.

Autofiction is more than just a novel inspired by true events; it can also be the complete stylization of one's life into fiction in which the main characters are proxies for the writer and their circle. Autofiction is similar to autobiography in that it is based on the author's real life, but it is different in that the events and characters in an autofiction work are fictionalized or altered in some way (some might claim just by virtue of being written down). This allows the author to explore their own experiences in an oblique fashion, while still drawing on their own life as a source of inspiration. Many autofictional novels by both Philip Roth and Thomas Bernhard provide exercises in invigorated self-loathing, which readers can't help but rubberneck. Other contemporary examples of autofiction include *The Mezzanine* by Nicholson Baker, *I Love Dick* by Chris Kraus, *Chelsea Girls* by Eileen Myles, and the 3,600-page *My Struggle* by Karl Ove Knausgård. The form is growing in popularity—see "Cat Person" by Kristen Roupenian, for example, which went viral in 2017 after it was published in the *New Yorker*. In calling a work autofiction, though, we presume to have some knowledge of the author's biographical details; some works that *seem* like autofiction may be entirely made up. There are others who question the use of the term since everything that is made-up must, after all, originate somehow with the author's experience or imagination. Nonetheless, as a hybrid form of fiction that uses details and components of the author's real life, the genre seems to have struck a chord.

Autotheory, on the other hand, is situated in the nonfiction genre where it melds autobiography with theory. In *Autotheory as Feminist Practice in Art, Writing, and Criticism*, Lauren Fournier notes the genre has been called many things, including critical memoir, life-thinking, creative criticism, conceptual criticism, biofiction, critical memoir, performance philosophy, and formative autoethnography, among other terms. If a person has ever regaled you with a story about the significance of the quotation tattooed to their forearm, linking the quotation to their personal philosophy, then you already understand the basic premise of autotheory. Gabriel Abend writes, "Theory is a *Weltanschauung*, that is, an overall perspective from which one sees and interprets the world" (2008: 179). When theoretical frameworks intersect with the frame of one's lived experiences, the one can often be used to illuminate and explicate the other.

In *The Argonauts*, for example, Maggie Nelson (2015) analyzes the work of theorists in parallel with personal anecdotes. These alternating impulses stage the collision of the empirical and theoretical, the creative and the critical, the "I" who lives in the world and the "I" who lives in the mind. Through this hybrid form of self-study, Nelson thinks along with Ludwig Wittgenstein, Judith Butler, Jacques Lacan, Roland Barthes, Gilles Deleuze, and dozens of other theorists. She internalizes their words as she reckons with her identities as queer, femme, mother, stepmother, partner, and academic. The theorists' voices eddy throughout the text, carving into the shape of her life, leaving grooves of wisdom that direct, inflect, whisper, incarnate, shame, forgive, construct, and obliterate her sense of self. Other books in this genre—such as Claudia Rankine's *Citizen: An American Lyric*, Bill Ray Belcourt's *A History of My Brief Body*, Frank B Wilderson III's *Afropessimism*, Anna Tsing's *The Mushroom at the End of the World*, and Paul B. Preciado's *Testo Junkie*—fete their own roster of theoretical commentators who guide the authors in honing inquiry, disciplining memory, interpreting phenomena, and embodying their perspectives.

Discussion Questions

1. Hybrid genres tend to arise as a reaction to the shortcomings of traditional, stand-alone genres. Looking ahead, extrapolating from current trends in culture, politics, storytelling, technology, and so on, what new (or old) hybrids might be the most prescient in the next decade or so? What new types of grafting and frankensteining might take place? Can you perceive the fault lines and rifts within now-established genres such as the essay or novel, whether from contemporary examples or from older ones, that indicate how it derived from combining and adapting other forms?

2. Draw a Venn diagram. Label the left circle "prose" and the right circle "poetry." How many "rules" can you think of for either category? List them in their respective circles. Turning your attention to the circle formed by the union of overlap, list any rules that are shared by prose *and* poetry. Discuss with others any discrepancies between these category rules.

3. Reflect on your own reading habits. Do you like to read short pieces and flash or long-form work and novels? Sometimes websites designate articles as, say, a "3-minute

read": does this help entice you? Do you slow down and give more attention to the sounds, implication, details, and sentences when you read a flash piece than long-form work? If you write flash, is your process for writing it different than for longer pieces?

4. Have you encountered any of the other established hybrid genres before: verse novels, epistolary novels, closet drama, all-dialogue stories, dramatic essays, autotheory, and so on? If so, what was your impression or reaction? Why might most of these hybrid forms be relatively rare in contemporary literature despite the supposed popularity of hybrids?

5. Do you think that autofiction is a distinct hybrid form? Some argue that it's not often clear when such fiction stays close to memoir since we usually don't know the details of the author's biography from another source. Others say that autofiction is just unimaginative fiction—fiction that sticks to the author's experiences instead of making things up. Then again, what might be the advantages of writing autofiction over memoir?

Writing Prompts

1. Write a short prose piece (flash fiction or flash essay) of around 500 words. Revise the piece to half its current length. Think about compression of sentences, extracting the most important images and action. You could then lineate the piece as a poem if you wanted. Or you could take your original piece and dilate it into a full-length essay or story. What do you notice as you transform the piece?

2. Like the previous exercise, take a longer piece you wrote previously, especially one that is giving you issues or that you are trying to rework. Compress the piece into a flash form. If the piece itself is around 1,000 words, say, then try to compress it into less than 500 words. If the piece is a poem, rewrite it in prose—and perhaps elaborate details, but use no more than 500 words. As you revise and change your piece, boil it down to the most essential elements and details. See what can be implied, left out, or discarded as superfluous. You may need to cut exposition and conclusions—beginning in media res and chopping the tail off to leave it open-ended.

3. Look at some examples of both traditional and experimental haibun and then write one. Do not make the connection between the prose and lyric section explicit. Which was harder for you to compose: the prose or lyric section? Why? Did you attempt to embody the philosophy of *mono no aware* in the piece? Is this different than your normal modus operandi?

4. Write an all-dialogue story—it should contain all the major elements of a story: character, plot, conflict, climax, and so on. The object of this exercise is to have as much of the story as possible be in dialogue; preferably, the whole story would be in dialogue. You might even eliminate dialogue tags or ascriptions of speakers. However, you may use some exposition, action, or dialogue tags in a very minimal

way if you feel you need to. Alternatively, write a dramatic essay, which is also as much in dialogue as possible. However, in this case, instead of a story, the dialogue should explore an idea, theme, or philosophical question (often embodied by the characters' contending viewpoints).

5. Write a nonfiction piece that is autotheory. Connect theoretical texts and insights to your own lived experiences. And philosophize about your own lived experiences to build more general political or theoretical conclusions. You can engage with quotes and criticism in discursive passages along with memoir-like descriptions of incidents and scenes. How will you arrange and format such a hybrid work? Does this feel different than other types of nonfiction that you have written; if so, how?

CHAPTER 2
COMPOSITES AND UNCLASSIFIABLES

I. Introduction

In the preface to *Family Resemblance*, an anthology of hybrid work, Marcela Sulak (2015: xi) states, "When we speak of hybrid literature, we are speaking of individual works that do not replicate any previous pattern of literary affiliation." The hybrid works we discussed in the previous chapter, however, do connect with larger histories and lineages; they don't arise out of thin air.

The prose poem, to take but one instance, has a long and robust history since at least the nineteenth century. For prose poets to ignore the lineage they work within—or, worse, imagine a poem in prose is unprecedented—does a disservice to the evolving permutations of the genre. Critic and poet David Lehman notes, "The prose poem, born in rebellion against *tradition*, has itself become a tradition" (2003: 45). Yet, while many types of hybrid literature have gained greater recognition and traction over the past decades, other work has emerged that remains less codified; this work, too, in so far as it combines bits and pieces from disparate natures, could be considered "hybrids." But in the case of this work, which we will detail later, we often lack a widely shared or acknowledged nomenclature to describe the ways such work amalgamates, synthesizes, grafts, blends, or bricolages contrasting elements, whether these be genres, texts, styles, rhetoric, registers, languages, or conventions. Such work can appear to mishmash, mosh, and monsterize in a manner designed to elude labels. Our labels, such as they are, then, will be more ad hoc than usual if not downright jury-rigged. Fuzziness comes with the territory.

Schemes of literary classification are provisional tools to help us better understand the moves a text is making. What counts as a hybrid, as with what constitutes any kind of thing really, is relative: as certain types of hybrid texts become more established, they may no longer be viewed as hybrids at all. Genres are a loose set of conventions, and they evolve over time. We believe that forms and genres can be empowering for writers. Knowledge of generic conventions and traditions of subgenres helps a writer comprehend the meanings, means of signification, and cultural practices that are embedded within a piece. Readers will inevitably put work in some context, some framework, to interpret it. We are not trying to box in your writing with labels. Rather, our attempt to provide a taxonomy for the work below is designed to help us appreciate it more since the import of any text depends on the background against which that text is situated: the associations it carries or the expectations we bring to it. In many cases, these works clash and juxtapose elements to erode the existing hierarchy of genres and literary conventions, hierarchies that can reinforce distinctions between truth and fiction, lyric and narrative, folk knowledge and literary craft, along with much else. By regarding the greater constellations of works that operate in similar ways, one can, we hope, gain greater purchase on texts that may, at first blush, appear obtuse or baffling.

Still, we concede that sometimes when writers hash out a work-in-progress, it might not be helpful for them to have too definite an idea of their genre or form in mind—some may want to overlook whatever literary affiliations they are flirting with. Deliberations about forms, genres, and conventions come later for some writers, imposed retroactively or late in the process to shape a piece that has already had significant development. One might, for example, add line breaks on a penultimate draft, turning an erstwhile prose narrative into a lyric poem. But whether one begins with generic conventions and forms or they are a final consideration, an understanding of genres—as well the history of hybridized challenges to timeworn genres—can help one see what makes writing tick.

This chapter will focus on lengthier works, composite texts that make use of a heterogeneous assortment of conventions. The first group of texts lean toward the novel—if for no other reason than that the most marked precedents they *resist* tend to be those of standard prose narratives, such as a well-motivated, action-driven plot arc. We term these works composite novels, antinovels, poet's novels, philosophical novels, and Menippean satire. The second group of texts lean toward poetry, though such texts may use an array of forms on the page—doodles, documents, diary entries—that do not resemble the way we anticipate poetry looking; indeed, they may even be written entirely in prose. We deem such works long poems and serial poems. These two groups of texts, though, might have more in common with each other than they do with other, more ordinary novels or poems: ultimately the antinovel's lyric association and formal variation might converge with the long poem's mixed voices and materials. Whereas the antinovel or composite novel deconstructs plot, the long or serial poem attempts to invent a method of structural elaboration that does not replicate the mode of epic storytelling. Both, that is, achieve a tentative coherence of design with only glancing recourse to narrative architectures. Starting from different traditions, both groups of texts approach a similar place. Finally, the third group of texts we deal with are the unruly orphans and bastard children, texts that defy or dodge any lineage assigned them. They're like leftover wiggly jigsaw pieces that fit nowhere. We dub these "unclassifiables." These texts are outliers that are so mongrelized, so inosculated, as to glom into some deviant new abnormality we've yet to find a name for.

II. Composite Novels, Antinovels, and Menippean Satire

Historically, novels arose from a disparate alloy of other prose forms—journals, letters, fables, traveler's tales, and biography, to name just a few: early novelists poached and reworked these extant forms to create longer fictional texts that were, well, *novel*. That is, new. At least for their time. But, over the course of the eighteenth and nineteenth centuries, novels grew in popularity. Their narratives became less piecemeal, less parasitic upon other forms; novelistic discourse became rigidified, novelistic conventions increasingly settled. Today most novels no longer seem like a bundle of newfangled oddments; there's no ballyhoo or wrangling about them. What literary form, in fact, is more commonplace, more codified than a novel? And yet, especially with the emergence of postmodernism around the middle of the twentieth century, many writers began to balk and push back against the mainstream novel's obligatory sleekness. Postmodern experimentalists opened the novel back up again, exposing its seams and loose threads, exploding it into the snippets, stitching, and shreds of a crazy quilt. These postmodernist novels replaced the smooth-running, well-ordered, if somewhat staid narratives of mainstream novels with funny cars at a demolition derby that spun out donuts, dizzily flung off spare parts, displayed their souped-up engines above their hoods, and bronco-bucked with kitted-out, jump-bang hydraulics. The scrapyard of the novel was made visible again; more far-flung foreign parts got thrown into the mix. We deem such texts **composite novels**. They are juddering amalgams that absorb other forms and fashions willy-nilly as a way of telling a story, sure, but also to reflect on the act of storytelling itself and to get one's jollies while doing so.

For instance, is Vladimir Nabokov's (1962) *Pale Fire* a (mock) epic poem, work of critical commentary, or metafictional paratext? More likely, it's all the above. *Pale Fire* begins with a 999-line poem (four cantos in heroic couplets) purportedly by John Shade that is treated to extended commentary and critical apparatus in the subsequent narrative by the fictional editor, Charles Kinbote. But, as the commentary moves from academic formalism to something far more personal, deranged, and solipsistic, the reader is forced to challenge the initial perception of the poem—to say nothing of Shade and Kinbote's relationship—and reach their own conclusions. The multi-genre nature of this novel (long poem, fiction, criticism) is only the most obvious attribute of its hybridity. Each part plays off the others: the commentary mixes with the poem—embroidering its poetic lines, canto by canto, with an intimate subtextual conspiracy.

The loose parts can inflect new significance on each other in the composite novel. A few examples include Jean Toomer's *Cane*, Selah Saterstrom's *Slab*, Salvador Plascencia's *The People of Paper*, and Rabih Alameddine's *Koolaids*. Composed of multimodal vignettes, these decentered narratives splice together distinct generic conventions associated with fiction as well as other genres. As with deconstructed food, one can see the ingredients individually laid out. You get salsa, tortilla, frijoles placed on your plate instead of an integrated taco. It's not until the reader ingests them that they experience their cumulative effect.

In the 1923 introduction to *Cane*, Waldo Frank makes the claim that Toomer's book is not just *about* the South, but it *is* the South. This ontological shift is a signature effect of writing a composite novel. The expansive approach is not just about point of view, but also modality, which promotes a material engagement with the subject matter. In *Cane*, Toomer (1923) oscillates between ecstatic head-hopping prose, lineated poetry, epistle, and dialogue, engendering a folkloric effect. The book serves as an omnibus that collects an array of cultural expressions.

Selah Saterstrom's (2015) *Slab* is a novel conceived as a stage play, set on a concrete slab foundation in the South in the wake of Hurricane Katrina. The book's subject matter—poverty, misogyny, gun violence, and racism (as depicted by the protagonist's doodles of the Confederate Flag)—are presented through lyrical prose spliced via the salvage of minor forms like hymnals, recipes, inventories, apocryphal histories, and fabricated interviews with Barbara Walters. The reader must work to piece together a coherent story from a spew of traumatic flotsam, or perhaps realize that coherence itself is a moot value in a world that never holds together.

In *Koolaids*, Rabih Alameddine (1998) introduces the reader to multitudinous Lebanese, American, and Lebanese-American protagonists, headed up by the triumvirate of Mohammad, Samir, and Makram. It's not always possible, however, to tell who's at the mic as dozens of narrators emerge. Some perspectives are distinguishable by their form or rhetorical register. There is a diarist, for example, whose entries catalog her family's disintegration from political corruption and an editorialist whose columns chronicle Lebanon's shaky geopolitics. The page fractures between epistolary, ekphrastic, fantastical, scriptural, dramatic, journalistic, eulogistic, and hallucinatory vignettes. The stories converge, diverge, get braided, even knotted. The individual becomes imbricated in the collective. In Lebanon, characters convey sympathetic narratives of massacre, revolution, counterrevolution, assassination, and scandal. In America, the focus expands to art, tutelage, and the recurring AIDS arc (hookup, infection, diagnosis, prognosis, deathbed, and death itself). With so many intervening perspectives, the graphic suffering of an AIDS patient may be ironically followed by a dissonant fellatio fantasy. The novel's voice is not just polyvocal, but arrhythmic. The individual narrators coalesce uneasily into the larger communal and cultural narratives of which they partake. That each character gets their own narrative mode is not just a sign of characterological integrity; it's also a reminder of how hybridization is managed. Somewhere, in the psychic background, Alameddine is playing air traffic controller to this mash-up of fictional tropes.

Salvador Plascencia's (2005) *The People of Paper* is yet another composite novel. This one features a bed-wetting father, gang of flower pickers, excommunicated shaman, exiled saint disguised as a luchador, Hollywood starlet Rita Hayworth, mechanical tortoise who "speaks" in binary code, Baby Nostradamus whose clairvoyance is conveyed through opaque black blocks, and a woman made of paper. The inventive—if, at times, deliberately interruptive—design features of Salvador Placencia's *The People of Paper* include typography to delay, circumvent, and reorder its narrative. Rather than stage the perspectival junctures through page breaks, Plascencia opts for columnar narratives with as many as four characters leading their lives across a single spread. In negotiating the syntactical space of the page, he also transforms the space-time of the novel. To grant each character the fullest expression, Plascencia assigns them a unique narrative mode and/or speech genre—whether that takes the form of magical realism, romance, crime, erasure, or 01100011 01101111 01100100 01100101.

Wayne Koestenbaum's (2007) *Hotel Theory*, also a columnar novel, is a book that features cultural criticism and a dime novel side-by-side. Columnar prose—like that in *The People of Paper* and *Hotel Theory*—brings the splice to life, as the genres ping-pong in dialogue.

Thirii Myo Kyaw Myint's "You Rail, and the Road" is yet another columnar piece that you can read in full on pp. 290–5.

In *Hotel Theory*, Koestenbaum examines the ways in which the hotel has been depicted in literature, art, and popular culture, especially as a site of transgression, escape, and self-creation. Koestenbaum also reflects on his own experiences of staying in hotels and on the ways in which the hotel has shaped his own sense of identity and desire.

While we emphasize the ways that the prose works mentioned earlier amalgamate different genres, conventions, voices, or constraints in their architecture, another way of seeing many of these composite novels is under the rubric of what has been called the "**antinovel**." The antinovel, according to Cuddon (1999: 44) is a "kind of fiction [that] tends to be experimental and breaks with the traditional story-telling methods and form of the novel." In many cases, the fractured, composite nature of these novels challenges linear plots, the coherence of unified character psychology, and traditional story expectations such as closure. In their "scrappy" forms, antinovels seek to question the ways that events may be misrepresented by the usual novelistic devices, provoking questions about the ways that consciousness functions or historical narratives become authenticated, for example. Antinovels move forward—as well as sideways and backwards—less through cause-and-effect, action-and-reaction based on clear character motivation than through other means such as shifts in perspective, theme-and-variation, riffs, digressions, reframing their terms, lyric association, and metatextuality. Take Calvino's *If on a winter's night a traveler* (1979), a composite antinovel in which each chapter is an opening from ten different novels (e.g., detective fiction, ghost story, Japanese erotica, etc.). The framing story is about readers of this many-headed work narrated in the second person.

Similarly, Australian-born writer Louis Armand's antinovel *Hotel Palenque* (2021) sutures together poetic minutiae, hyperlinks to newspaper articles, descriptions of film, a noir murder mystery, lines of holy texts, and a mélange of voices, some of which are in Spanish, into long, uninterrupted paragraph blocks for each of a dozen chapters. However, we should also note that not all purported antinovels skip around through different generic conventions: works such as Nathalie Sarraute's *Tropisms* (1939), for example, contains fleeting vignettes and impressions of delicate states of consciousness. Though it's unclear whether these apparitional voices issue from a consistent narrator, the book's genre itself is consistent. Sarraute's experimental technique of disembodied textures of perception inspired the radical French antinovel movement known as the **nouveau roman** whose practitioners favored disavowing plot, character, dialogue, and other narratological conventions. Demanding, repetitive, even inconsistent, the nouveau roman frustrated readers, yet goaded them to reinvent new values and modes of engagement at a time when the status quo felt like it was running on empty. Many of the nouveau roman writers were connected to the French New Wave cinema movement of the 1950s and 1960s, too, which occurred concurrently, and which likewise detonated the well-ordered narrative conventions within film.

A similar offshoot of the novel has been dubbed the **poet's novel**. Unlike verse novels, these are written entirely—or almost entirely—in prose. The term "poet's novel" designates that such novels are composed in a particularly lyrical style, foregrounding association and metaphor, regardless of whether the author has a background as a poet. More emphasis is given to meditation and atmosphere. The focus is on affect rather than incident. Plots may be tangential, fragmentary, or a series of vignettes. They may even be unfinished, a fact that reinforces rather than detracts from their status as a poet's novel. Pacing may be sacrificed to deep dives into subjective interiority. The term is vague since it is one of degree—many novels contain lyrical elements or fragmentary structures, especially since Modernism. Though little has been written about the poet's novel, we are inclined to view the German Romantics such as Goethe (*The Sorrows of Young Werther*), Novalis (*The Novices of Sais*), Hölderlin (*Hyperion*), and later Rilke (*The Notebooks of Malte Laurids Briggs*) as pioneers of the poet's novel. For them, the sensibility of the poet was not something isolated to lyric moments, it was an enveloping lifelong pursuit and habitual perceptiveness of nature's powers. The French tradition of poet's novels include Comte de Lautréamont's *Maldoror*; Alfred Jarry's *Exploits and Opinions of Dr. Faustroll, Pataphysician*; Gerard Nerval's *Aurelia*; Louis Aragon's *Paris Peasant*; and Andre Breton's *Nadja*. All these works have a distinctive surrealist flavor, offering a different trajectory of the poet's novel as bottled lightning—zany, enraptured, unpredictable.

Other examples—*View of Dawn in the Tropics* by Guillermo Cabrera Infante, *Azorno* by Inger Christensen, and *The Death of a Beekeeper* by Lars Gustafsson—show that diverse language traditions have adopted the poet's novel. Poet's novels are perhaps less common in English, though Gertrude Stein took the genre in innovative directions with several works.

Among recent Americans, we might count Amiri Baraka's *The System of Dante's Hell*, Ben Lerner's *Leaving the Atocha Station*, and Vi Khi Nao's *Fish in Exile* among the ilk. Eileen Myles subtitles her book *Inferno* "(a poet's novel)," the parenthetical suggesting both a hesitation about the existence of the genre and foreshadowing that the reader shouldn't expect a typical story. Likewise, Laynie Brown, a poet and critic who edited a collection of essays on poet's novels, unabashedly asks whether there is, in fact, "such a thing as a poet's novel" (2021). This avoidance of strict ontological distinctions to instead dwell in amorphous realms of affinity and amorous regions of felt experience is, if anything, one of the few defining features of this self-doubting, would-be genre.

The **philosophical novel**, like the poet's novel, is a fuzzy set. Such novels foreground ideas, theories, and ethical dilemmas. In many cases, the traditional elements of narrative are subordinated to the exposition of arguments so that sections or whole texts read more like essays than plot-driven scenes. Again, since almost all novels deal with themes and ideas to some extent, the term cannot be precisely demarcated. Examples can elucidate it better than strict criteria. One type of philosophical novel uses the story as an extended thought experiment. Rousseau's *Emile*, for example, follows a tutor who educates the titular character through his entire youth, addressing the ideal system of pedagogy along the way. Thomas Moore's *Utopia* depicts a "perfect" government on an imaginary island kingdom while satirically recognizing the practical pitfalls of this no-place of total religious toleration, pacifism, and few laws. *Micromegas* by Voltaire, a precursor of science fiction, is a witty tale in which alien travelers visit Earth, test different philosophical theories on the natives, and comment on the insignificance of human quarrels. Similarly, Stanisław Lem's *Solaris* depicts a crew of space explorers who attempt to understand an utterly alien being who is, it would seem, a planet's oceanic ecosystem, suggesting an inability to comprehend an intelligence unlike one's own.

Maurice Blanchot's *Thomas the Obscure* investigates the nature of solipsism, too, but by very different means; the style of the book turns back upon the reader like sea-tides ebbing and flowing with uncertain patterns. David Markson's *Wittgenstein's Mistress* is similarly written in a way to reflect its theme of language's failure to communicate. Its first sentence reads, "In the beginning, sometimes I left messages in the street" (1988: 7); yet, only a few pages later, the narrator declares, "And in either case, I may have made an error, earlier, when I said I left a message in the street" (1988: 11). Existentialist writers from Sartre to Murdoch generated sundry philosophical novels, often depicting characters adrift in a world without fixed values who must face up to their irrational desires and death. Other philosophical novels—*The History of Rasselas*, *Thus Spake Zarathustra*, *Steppenwolf*—act more like allegories, often with peripatetic protagonists encountering quandaries among a rabblement of eccentrics, each of whom represents varying worldviews. More recent philosophical novels often deal with epistemology, that is, how we arrive at knowledge or truth in an era of deep fakes, AI, and algorithms. In Tom McCarthy's *Satin Island*, for instance, a consultant at a megacorporation must pick through mazing reams of data to create a report, but his project to make sense of our times results in little more than another readout from the system, another data point, rather than a synthesizing answer. The novel teases us—on a metafictional level—that the readerly desire for old-fashioned plots and characters might be little more than a longing for some grand mythology. A word of caution, though, for those who'd embark on writing a philosophical novel: contemporary audiences are likely to expect a compelling story upon which to hang any ponderous inquiries, mythology or not. Metaphysical flights should be kept brief, droll, or amusing.

A related prose genre is known as **Menippean satire**, which, although little recognized by most contemporary creative writers, has well-established literary precedents. Canadian critic Northrop Frye remarks that "the Menippean satire deals less with people as such than with mental attitudes" (1957: 309). Frye—analyzing works such as *Moby Dick, Gulliver's Travels, Tristram Shandy,* and *Candide*—emphasizes that Menippean satires are akin to self-interrogating confessions or essays in that they critique philosophical positions and tend toward exhaustive, encyclopedic catalogs of contending attitudes. Russian critic Mikhail Bakhtin, though, examining works like *Gargantua and Pantagruel* and *Notes from the Underground,* characterizes Menippean satire as typically dealing with the unruliness of the body, which always risks falling apart, breaking down, and violating decorum. For Bakhtin, Menippean satire's indeterminate polyphony of voices is a grotesque expression of carnival with folkloric roots.

A work such as Hervé Guibert's *Arthur's Whims* fits better with Bakhtin's definition. A carnival of queer flesh crops up on nearly every page—mummies, martyrs, murderers, and magicians—and the book is littered with odd points of view and inappropriate speech. Joshua Cohen's *Book of Numbers,* meanwhile, may align more with Frye's definition. It's filled with what Frye terms "pedants, bigots, cranks, parvenus, virtuosi, enthusiasts, rapacious and incompetent professional men of all kinds" (309) as the protagonist, a ghostwriter for a secretive tech billionaire, wanders through strange realms (late capitalism) and fantastic pathways (the internet). Nonetheless, the Menippean satire—a shape-shifting genre if there ever was one—can manifest in myriad compendia.

Menippean satire can be almost aggressively intellectual in some cases, and yet the intellectualism on display in the work undermines the philosophy or mental attitude that it is pontificating. The very categories by which the work thinks are called into question as the text spins in a kaleidoscopic tumble of ever-shifting mosaic fragments. It may seem like a hall of mirrors and shadow play. Menippean satire can build up rococo cloud-castles and elaborate impossible architectures only to disorient the reader who wanders in their labyrinths haplessly following the vanishing thread of its story. The different stances, tropes, or framing devices it employs often pull the rug out from under the previous structure it has just articulated. Reading such works, one can feel like one is vertiginously falling through a series of trap doors: one plunges down a pit as the text undoes its own philosophical foundation. Sometimes Menippean satire can take the guise of a game, a joke, or a shaggy-dog story. In these satires, there is a ludic urge to rebuff the reader—to disavow any set point of view or position—so that its circuitous inquiries can make a reader feel like a dog chasing its tail, if one is not committed to just enjoying all the twists and turns of the tale itself. The only takeaway to such works might be that we'll all be taken away in one form or another by death. The humor on display acts to dissolve or hold at bay the undercurrents of the saturnine and melancholic disposition that runs beneath its flamboyant wit. They cut up not only by mocking other philosophies and viewpoints but also by cutting themselves up, fragmenting into many-sided facets of a protean nature.

These designations—composite novel, antinovel, poet's novel, philosophical novel, Menippean satire—can be seen as distinct but potentially overlapping categories in a Venn diagram to describe prose works that function outside the dominant paradigms of novelistic discourse. Then again, the definitions for each of these terms are also debatable: even eminent critics such as Frye and Bakhtin don't always agree on the criteria for a given category. Innovative prose writing is constantly evolving. Furthermore, there can be no textbook example of an antinovel or a Menippean satire: each one is an anomalous, imperfect patchwork. Often their very purpose is to elude and undermine codification. Each one attempts to invent its own way forward, both parodying and piggybacking on whatever forms are at hand. At any rate, what we seek to locate here, no matter the nomenclature one favors, is simply a recognition that there are many longer, fictional prose works that operate by means that largely bypass the conventional novel's emphasis on plot and character, employing an assortment of other structures, textures, or techniques.

III. Long Poems

On the poetry side, there has also been an experimental "composite" form that eschews an emphasis on narrative and characters: the so-called **long poem**. Poets in earlier periods, no doubt, wrote lengthy works—not only classical epics, but also sonnet sequences, discursive verse essays, mock epics, closet dramas, and verse novels. Since at least Modernism, however, the distinctive genre of the "long poem" has developed, after such models as *The Waste Land*, *The Cantos*, and *Paterson*—but also, significantly, Whitman's "Song of Myself." It should be noted that the so-called long poem is not just a poem that happens to be long; rather, it is a particular form that attempts to encompass a new mode of visionary and historical awareness, often portraying multiple perspectives upon its chosen subject. In this regard, we might be better off calling these works "encyclopedic" poems. Each long poem sets itself the task of finding its own resources and processes to sustain a unique shape, questing in search of materials and methods to sustain its own making. Indeed, long poems tend to be both projects to discover the motive force of a poetic worldview and imaginative exercises in worldmaking. As such, they may take years, decades, even lifetimes to write. The "longing" of the long poem often resists closure, preferring to accrete, to increase, to keep on creating. Many are archeological investigations into the buried foundations of knowledge, both personal and cultural. In many cases, this knowledge has a local habitation and a name, a specific ground in which its archeological retrieval of knowledge is situated, such as Paterson (Williams), Harlem (Tolson), or Gloucester (Olson).

Long poems as diverse as *Harlem Gallery*, *The Maximus Poems*, and *Canto General* can be viewed as a recasting of the national epic, offering a poetic alternative of similar scope and ambition during an anxious era when heroic figures are distrusted and imperial nation-building seems suspect. Long poems, in this respect, often stand in the same relation to the epic as the antinovel stands to the grand narratives of the canonical novel: they deconstruct the previous form while being an uneasy continuation of it. While some long poems harken back to previous models such as the epic (*Omeros*), epitaph (*Spoon River Anthology*), sonnet sequence (*Dream Songs*), or verse novel (*The Golden Gate*), most long poems are marked by fragmentation and sections that juxtapose formal variation, including prose sections. One example of this is Frank Stanford's 15,283-line poem *The Battlefield Where the Moon Says I Love You*.

A common type of long poem is the **serial poem**, where discrete sections build and comment upon each other, though many sections may function as self-contained individual poems, too. Such long poems and serial poems typically weave together lyric with documentation, and they may include both narrative arc and discursive argument. They are dialogic in that they frequently "do" different voices, modulating their perspectives, styles, or the focus of their content while maintaining some thematic continuity. In their restless energy, long poems display an encyclopedic collage of cultural sources, which at once represents the breakdown of civilization and enacts an attempt to reintegrate it.

The long poem, paradoxically, seems best defined by its capacious ability to subsume other forms and genres. Simply examine the subtitles of a few long poems: "A Home Movie" (Craig Raine's *History*), "Erotic Murder Mystery" (Dorothy Porter's *The Monkey's Mask*), "An Amble" (C. D. Wright's *Casting Deep Shade*), and "A Fictional Essay in 29 Tangos" (Anne Carson's *Beauty of the Husband*): the impulse is to push outward from poetry's given parameters. Any laundry list of long poems reveals that they routinely negotiate not only such traditionally poetic forms as the lyric, epic, eclogue, and epigram, but almost every imaginable form from one-liner to genre fiction, fan letter to scientific diagram, jazz scat to historical annals. Indeed, their permutations are so various that there's surely a long poem that includes a laundry list itself. One of their defining features is that they are often held together not by narrative, theatrical, or lyric conventions, but by dialogical allusions and critical observations that come to take over the main body of the text. The long poem's composite nature is also one of decomposition—its discursive energies circle back to look under the hood, tinker, and take apart the mechanisms it uses. For example, John Hollander's *Reflections on Espionage* creates a mock-critical commentary on double agents, showing how poetry is an encrypted utterance that trades on double meanings. Likewise in the vein of meta-commentary, bpNichol's *The Martyrology* sends up its own heterogeneity by asking:

what's a
poem like you doing in a
poem like this?

(1998: 49)

Nevertheless, because long poems depend on their expansiveness and variety, they are difficult to comprehend from brief excerpts or samples.

Sampling, in fact, is one exemplary technique that long poems employ; many long poems act as receptacles to absorb pieces of the larger culture around them. They incorporate quotes, allusions, translations, musical scores, diagrams, advertisements, court testimony, government papers, and much more. These artifacts often dwell side-by-side with lyric, narrative, and discursive sections. In this manner, the long poem situates its investigation of truth against the detritus of the real world, positioning both the written poem and these shards of realia on the same textual and diegetic level. Like a Rauschenberg "combine" such as *Bed* (1955), which is not just a painting *of* a bed but encaustic dripping over sheets and pillows hung on the gallery wall portrait style, the long poem not only bodes forth an image, but it can also at times embody the very matter of a thing under question. In Muriel Rukeyser's *Book of the Dead*, hand-drawn maps, stock-market ticker, photos, and other documents are collaged with or incorporated directly into the lyric sequences. Thus, Rukeyser gives her readers access to these primary materials so they can understand not only the Union Carbide tunnel-drilling disaster that killed over 740 workers in Gauley Bridge, West Virginia, but the cultural context of racism and capitalist exploitation that frames such historical incidents. These bits don't epitomize events so much as they are the sticky tatters and stub ends of detritus that constitute history itself. Critic Jessica Smith writes, "All of this allows—or forces—the reader to synthesize the history of what happened without simplifying it. Rukeyser doesn't merely tell us but also shows us the evidence and demands that we witness … for ourselves" (2018: n.p.).

Rukeyser does not want the horrific vision she portrays dismissed as some fanciful lyric version of events. She wants to ground her account as much as possible in hard facts. With a similar purpose of subsuming an element of reality into the poem, Ronald Johnson's *ARK* includes a section that is nothing more (or less) than Johnson's own handprint impressed on a page. The hand has long been a symbol of the artist; Johnson emphasizes the poem as an act of physical making, inscribing the body directly onto the page. Such artifacts capture traces of the real; they are bits and pieces of the material world interjected into the poem, asserting the long poem's desire to embody—not merely represent—reality.

Long poems often have a double consciousness: the poem sees itself through the veil of artifacts and forms shaped by forces exterior to it. And yet, these items become the *materia poetica* by which it molds its own vision. Long poems seek to interpret history while knowing they are trapped within it. Their perspectival shifts, stylistic changes, and formal variations grapple with contingency. Ironically, many long poems recognize themselves as merely small fragments in a larger, piecemeal continuity of cultural production, and thus most long poems declare they are failures or unfinishable. Nevertheless, such declarations also function as many long poems' starting points: the failures of the past prompt one to understand those failures, even if that task must remain incomplete and provisional since history keeps moving forward (and in other directions as well). The pilgrimage that structures many long poems is a record of a peculiar organic growth—if only of the poet's mind or of the poem's own making, a cyclical history, an odyssey in which the hero returns to the homesite with both renewed understanding and troubling revelations. The partial and plural nature of the long poem seeks to reconcile the divergent historical narratives, both those in which it has been caught up and those at which it catches.

Over the last few decades, the long poem has continued to assert its influence, especially within the lineage of innovative poetics, though it has undergone modifications. More common these days is the book-length poem or poetic sequence. The length and shape of standard poetry manuscripts, usually under a hundred pages, acts as a ready-made packaging that reigns in more ambitious or extravagant work. There are a few exceptions that prove the general rule—Kevin Young's *Black Maria* or Tyehimba Jess's *Olio*, for instance. Still more capacious are Lyn Heijinian's *The Book of a Thousand Eyes* and Ron Silliman's *The Alphabet*. The Syrian poet Adonis has written *al-Kitab* ("The Book"), a three-volume work that spans centuries of Arabic civilization. Today, though, poems of a dozen pages are considered long or serial poems. Indeed, the differences between a "long poem" and a poetry collection have diminished. A trend toward marketability and the contest-driven selection of poetry books has encouraged manuscripts with distinct themes that stay within set parameters of length and design. Such a publishing system encourages poets to write within the bounds of a consistent style, too. We might call these not long poems, but **project books**. Critic Stephanie Burt writes:

> A project book (and it's a term familiar to anyone who's spent time in an MFA program recently) comprises a set of poems … organized around one problem or theme, often a politically urgent one, with quotations and documents and journalism folded in … At less than their best, they can be like the rock concept albums of the 1970s, whose

laborious techniques and references strove for a whole weightier than the sum of its parts. (2020: n.p.)

Burt's implication is that project books—ubiquitous in today's poetry culture—are often pretentious, overwrought, and don't add up. On the one hand, such book-length projects may inherit the long poem's investigative model and its imaginative resources to elaborate a work in ways other than isolated lyrics or continuous narrative. On the other hand, most such project books represent a narrowing of scope as they tend to be less multivalent and more univocal; they tend not to question the forms they employ, and those forms' contingency, so much as ape the normative expectations for contemporary poetry books, speaking not about and through history but rather in and to the moment.

IV. Unclassifiables

While we loosely siloed the abovementioned works in this chapter into the habitual categories of "poetry" and "fiction," that might not quite be fair to them. We readily acknowledge there are many long poems that are written mostly or entirely in prose: just see Williams's *Spring and All*. By turns, plenty of antinovels operate as much by lyricism, association, and metaphor as any poem: for example, Beckett's *How It Is*. The composite nature of these works—they are mixtures, miscellanies—implies that they are not entirely this or that, one thing or the other in any conventional sense. Still, they occupy a designated spot on the shelf in most bookstores or libraries that's likely to rub shoulders with one standard genre or the other. Sometimes these distinctions are only due to factors like outdated notions of what constitutes a poem or whether the author is better known as a novelist. Sometimes, though rarely, hybrid writers blend generic conventions on the granular level, aggressively mushing things into a slurry of disjecta. Some works get so wonky that any poor shelf clerk is liable to cry uncle. These works often challenge notions of taxonomy, even legibility itself. In some cases, these texts are vying to be the designer genres of the future; in other cases, they are muddled mutts, inimitable one-offs, mutant spawn whose procedures or styles result in sui generis weirdos. It's a matter of degree since, for most folks, long poems and antinovels look odd, as well. For our purposes, we'll just label things in this extreme left field as "**unclassifiables**"—a leaky grab-bag term for composite or hybrid texts that don't fit elsewhere, one that acknowledges it's a catch-all for a stable of unstable chimeras and shimmering freaks.

When encountering such a text, it can be difficult to discern the pieces and parts. Just as one peers into a smoothie only to find a single flax seed, threads of citrus pulp, and a surprising new color, such mixed texts offer only glimmers of constitutive elements: a poetic fragment here, disembodied voice there, now a static image, next a rogue lyric, followed by an onslaught of diagrams, footnotes, and source code written in a fictional programming language. Often, the transitions between conventions are abrupt, choreographed by a mixed typology or careful visual design. There is growing interest in making hybrid literature assimilate to the compositional precepts of design and visual art—using white space, asymmetry, geometrical patterns, gutters and margins, the rule of thirds, and page layout like a painter would a canvas. In many cases, the arrangement is less by genre and more by physical container: page, book, space, or field of vision.

Experimental Writing

There are, technically speaking, bazillions of ways to combine generic conventions. Mathematically, if there are eight genres—a conservative figure, if you've been following along with this book—and you want to figure out how many distinct ways you can pair off those genres, then you would use this formula for all permutations:

$$_nP_k = n!/(n-k)!$$

where n is eight (for the number of genres) and k is two (for pairings), resulting in $P = 56$ (or the number of permutations). This assumes, however, that every AB pair is different from a BA pair—or, in other words that, say, a lyric essay is distinct from an essayistic lyric. That seems to check out: Maggie Nelson's *Bluets* (lyric essay) is distinct from Alexander Pope's *Essay on Man* (essayistic lyric). But, of course, you could hybridize multiple genres, too. One such combination might be a prose-poetry retelling of a fairytale, presented as an immersive art installation with elements of aleatory composition, dramatic monologue, and digital media. Will each theoretically possible combination yield an equally viable new type of writing? Definitely not. Just as a parent might resist playing death-metal lullabies for their infant or an event planner might advise against a balloon artist stationed in a cactus garden at a corporate retreat, most writers tend to be equally choosy about the generic conventions they frankenstein together.

Unclassifiables are relatively unusual since it's cognitively and aesthetically difficult for writers to envision what exists beyond genre constraints. Even if they don't set out to wear a straitjacket, each creative decision tends to foreclose the possibility of other future decisions; before long, they are bound by a set of rules they didn't even know they were following. Readers, too, are on the lookout for rules and patterns. Patternicity—also termed "pareidolia" and "apophenia"—is the tendency of humans to perceive patterns in random or meaningless data, whether that's seeing images in passing clouds, discerning Jesus on a piece of burnt toast, or concocting conspiracy theories from tidbits of news items. As artists, we are hardwired to perpetuate patterns; as readers, we are hardwired to discover them. Therefore, writers and readers tacitly work together to ensure everything gets classified as *something*. These patterns allow us to connect a text to larger systems of cultural reference, expectations, and historical precedents: they help connect the dots between what is spoken and unspoken in a text, forming the hermeneutical basis of implicature and covert meanings. Despite this, there are some works that are so blended and bent one can't easily discern the constitutive genres at work in them.

Dictee (1982) is a book by Theresa Hak Kyung Cha, a writer and filmmaker who incorporates the syntax of both disciplines in her work. Written across English, French, Korean, and Chinese, language emerges as a medium for diasporic meditation; the book is also known for its use of dictée, which involves the repeated use of dictation as a way of exploring language and its relationship to power and identity. Unless the reader is fluent in all four languages, they will inevitably feel the cultural displacement that is at the heart of this layered narrative that partakes of autobiography, history, and myth all at once.

An excerpt from Kamau Brathwaite's docu-poetic long poem *Born to Slow Horses*, entitled "I was Wash-Way in Blood," also typifies this genre we term "unclassifiable." Read it on pp. 214–15.

Les Figues Press's *TrenchArt* book series took its name from "trench art"—artistic creations produced by soldiers made in wartime using whatever material was at hand, from shell casings to scrap metal to bone. Manifestos, lists, performative pieces, visual art, critical essays, marginalia, and the entirely unclassifiable—these pieces pull, prod, and play with the concept of "language" from all directions, misdirections, and sometimes no direction at all. This is critique pregnant with poetry, with image, with mutilated limbs, ululating lips, and the scent of camphor in hot celluloid.

Lily Hoang's *Parabola* employs personality quizzes, IQ tests, word searches, logic puzzles, alphanumeric codes, and the strewing of Easter eggs. *Parabola*, which appropriately won Chiasmus Press's Undoing the Novel contest, is structured like a parabola whose symmetrical chapters (i.e., 1, 2, 3… 3', 2', 1') interacts across the coordinate plane as when Chapter 8' (eight prime) mostly erases Chapter 8. On one page, overlapping upside down text boxes, populated with short shorts, tumble down the page into a black hole, suggesting elements of this book are expendable.

Michel Butor's *Mobile* functions as a cognitive map composed of scraps from various items and documents encountered during a cross-country road trip the French author took in 1959. Road signs, theme park brochures, newspaper clippings, town names, blips from radio programs, ads from mail-order catalogs, and much more get synthesized into a stream-of-conscious litany that offers one the texture of tripping down the American highway. Notably, Eisenhower's Federal Highway Act had immensely expanded roadway infrastructure in 1956. Dalkey Archive Press calls it a "novel," likely since Butor is best known as an experimental novelist, although the formatting on the page often more closely resembles projective verse. The book's subtitle, *Study for a Representation of the United States*, hints that the book is, in fact, *non*representational. That is, it's only a "study" *for* a representation: an abstract trial run, like a rough draft or notebook entry that is as much a cartography of a mind as it is of a place. The book's dedication to Jackson Pollock, however, probably alludes to the book's most salient generic forebears: collage and action-oriented composition. Movement, velocity, and energy during the act of creation reign paramount; the artifact that is captured on the page traces the residue of one trip—one historical moment, one country. Raiding everything he finds on the road, Butor's text blurs by with celerity and disorienting gusto.

When a single text is so mutable that its genres oscillate several times per page—swinging, layering, networking—it's probably fair to class it as **collage**. Collages often leave their imprint on the visual field of the page, with the constituent genres retaining their own visual character, whether it's the alignment of the prose, font size or typeface, use of textboxes, or icons, or inclusion of images. In the *New England Review*, Vincent Czyz (2014: 95) writes: "We follow a constellation of ideas, associations, or relevant images." Czyz continues, "Collage entails growth, accretion, chance, asymmetry, intuition, and of course the unconscious, [an] assemblage [which] hints at an undercurrent, a subterranean tendency—as iron filings reveal the contours and intangible ribs of a magnetic field." While some representative texts are minimalist in their conception, most have a jam-packed quality to them, a maximalist aesthetic that reverberates across the space it occupies, brimming with postmodern self-awareness. Such collage teases and provokes the reader with the various conventions or contexts from which its fragments have been clipped, each successive bit undoing and supplementing the next.

One topsy-turvy collage is the book object '*SSES* "*SSES*" "*SSEY*". Readers move through this text as they might a hoarder's drawers. There is no expository writing whatsoever; instead, one can find letters to grandparents, refrigerator art, fine art, drafts of dissertations, and data entries. There's even, in a brief blip of adolescent braggadocio, a bowling score sheet from Valley Lanes; Derek (editor), with his double turkey, beat out his brother Kevin (biographical subject) and their buddies. Even the authorship of this book, purportedly by Chaulky White, is hybrid. Derek writes, "A part of Kevin (upon his death) transferred to me like some parasitic meme transfusion (or vice-versa)" (2015: 8). The surname Chaulky White is therefore the three-legged composite of the half-dead brothers White.

Or in the case of Kelcey Parker Ervick's *The Bitter Life of Božena Němcová* (2016), the text is a phantasmagoric compendium of correspondences, fairy tales, postcards, and other ephemera—Ervick, in her raw experimentation, gets so near to the biographical subject that it verges on the paranormal. Her letters to the late "Mother of Czech Prose" simulate séance. She writes, obsessively, on a Czech typewriter, typing *Němcová's* name over and over. In thrall to her subject, and consumed by it, Ervick clearly couldn't be bothered with something so paltry as generic conventions.

And in Thalia Field's (2007) *ULULU: Clown Shrapnel*, there are instances of biography, screenplay, dialogue, documentary, portraiture, instructions, and prose poetry all at once—not to mention illustrations, watercolors, sheet music, a map, and original and treated footage from the silent film era. The book acts as a madcap callback for the archetype of Lulu, a prostitute murdered by Jack the Ripper and portrayed in a censored series of plays by Frank Wedekind. Field uses the collective force of any and all genres at her disposal to stage this recovery from the wilderness of commedia obscurity. In his blurb for the book, playwright Mac Wellman calls the book "a lunatic screenplay and a highly articulated literary polyhedron."

Finally, Conceptual writer Tan Lin's rejection of classification is evident from the outset. Lin (2010) apparently resists even the singularity of a title as when he uses colons, periods, brackets, capitalization, compound phrases, and a catalog to denote the full title of his book, which is called *Seven Controlled Vocabularies and Obituary 2004. The Joy of Cooking: [AIRPORT NOVEL MUSICAL POEM PAINTING FILM PHOTO HALLUCINATION LANDSCAPE]*, which reads like an unsettled working title and list of disparate genres. For his part, Lin (2010: n.p.) deems the book a "modular, easy-to-read relaxation device." Its unclassifiability and illegibility should not be cause for alarm; rather, Lin has ironically prepared this book for our post-book, post-reading era. It is ambient literature to browse, skim, scroll, or scan; background like wallpaper or elevator muzak that helps condition and accent one's lifestyle.

Ultimately, to conceive of the "unclassifiable" as its own category is a paradox. Instead, an unclassifiable must be a non-category wherein readers are willfully disoriented, suppressing the urge to domesticate and taxonomize the text. This calls to mind Romantic poet John Keats's notion of negative capability, which he describes as the capacity for "dwelling in uncertainties, mysteries, doubts, without any irritable reaching after fact and reason." The Greek poet Dimitris Lyacos, reminded of Keats's "burden of the Mystery" in an interview with *Berfrois*, likens negative capability to treading the dark corridors that lead to the unknown:

> Who dares follow them when nothing is given, abandon planning ahead and open up to whatever may come? We carry with us a backpack of ideas, theories, insecurities and the detailed scenarios we project onto the future. Unlike us, outcasts, fugitives and people in the margins are the ones possessing the negative capability, the power to bear the "burden of the mystery." (2018: n.p.)

Part of the mystery for Lyacos, it seems, is that attendant to mixing genres is the mixing of scopes. A fictional vignette and epic poem and handwritten letter and dialogue, for example, all have different measures of intimacy and address, so when a piece of writing employs them all equally, how does the reader reconcile the incommensurate field? Lyacos believes we shouldn't. Instead, we should embrace our negative capability; follow the silhouette of the text into the corridors of the unknown.

Discussion Questions

1. Why might some writers be dissatisfied with the typical realist novel—particularly the linear continuity of its narrative and its emphasis on unified characters who are rational agents, exhibiting a psychology based on clear motives and utilitarian decision-making? How might the disjointed forms of the composite novel and the contradictions, digressions, and vignettes of the antinovel answer some of these perceived shortcomings in novels? Why do antinovels and composite novels attempt to problematize the novel form?

2. If a fictional work largely abandons plot, as it sometimes does in poet's novels and philosophical novels, what might replace it to hold a reader's interest? What do you think of encountering characters who seem more like a mouthpiece for an idea than a flesh-and-blood person? What do you think when a story fails to follow a coherent thread, going whichever wacky way it wants according to some dream logic, as in many surrealist poet's novels?

3. Northrop Frye claims that there are many works that have become "neglected only because the categories to which they belong are unrecognized" (1957: 312). Do you think that a wider taxonomic scheme can help reposition such neglected or experimental works, situating them in a context so that they're not, say, automatically compared to standard realist novels and judged deficient accordingly—when they may be, in fact, perfect exemplars of some quite venerable but perhaps little-known genre? Or, by contrast, do you think that taxonomic schemes are what many writers are attempting to squirm out of, feeling boxed in by one set of criteria or another when their vision discommodes any given rubric assigned to it?

4. Contemporary critic Brian McHale asserts that "postmodernist fiction is the heir of Menippean satire and its most recent historical avatar" (1987: 172). The Menippean tradition runs through a great number of various postmodern novels, such as Salman Rushdie's *Midnight's Children*, David Foster Wallace's *Infinite Jest*, Don DeLillo's *White Noise*, Ishmael Reed's *Mumbo Jumbo*, Robert Bolaño's *2666*, Haruki Murakami's *1Q84*, and Zadie Smith's *White Teeth*. Indeed, the characteristically "postmodern" concerns and tropes of uncertain truth, perspectival shifts, formal variation, self-conscious irony, mixture of high and low, play of identities, emphasis on the instability of language, and use of metafiction that implicates the author, reader, and/or social institutions that frame interpretation are all endemic to the earlier tradition of Menippean satires. Do you think that the seemingly unique features of postmodern

fiction are simply expressions of the older—though overlooked—Menippean tradition? Or does postmodern fiction do something unique?

5. How does the long poem—especially one that emphasizes process, imperfection—contradict the lyric's economy of language that we tend to associate with poetry? T. S. Eliot thought that poets needed to have a "historical sense"; do you think that the long poem is a medium in which a poet may express their "historical sense" more than they can in small lyrics, imagistic poems, and verse? Could the long poem perhaps offer a way to investigate the history of forms as well as the forms that history itself takes?

6. Why do you think that, at least by critic Stephanie Burt's estimation, "project books" are so popular currently, such as with poets in MFA programs? What are some of a project book's benefits and drawbacks, compared to a poetry manuscript that is more disparate in its themes and organizations such as one composed of a hodgepodge of various lyrics? In what ways are project books like and unlike their kissing cousin, the long poem?

7. Do you think that there can be any truly unclassifiable literature (what would make it "literature" for that matter, since "literature" itself is a classification)? How might the promiscuous mixing of genres endanger the intelligibility of a text? What might be the motive to create texts that escape recognizable categories and which result in contamination, excess, or indeterminacy?

Writing Prompts

1. Choose a theme and/or a character. You could use themes and characters from other pieces you've written, books you've read, or movies you've watched; or you can create new ones for this prompt, if you like. Think about the tensions and conflicts of your protagonist who, for example, might be a young character who refuses a brain modification procedure that is considered a rite of passage in her futuristic community. Now, explore your theme and/or character—especially developing any conflicts—through a fragmentary collage of short forms rather than a continuous essay or narrative. Here's a few short forms to get you started: personal ad, transcript of a therapy session, interview, sonnet, abstract of an academic article, fortune cookie koan, diary, film script, map, recipe, and to-do list. In the previous example, the artifacts might include a page from a medical journal outlining the procedure, a religious tract against such modification, an op-ed from an infamous eugenicist, and a postcard from the protagonist who's decided to run away from home. Each one can be as brief as a sentence or a few words, but none should be longer than three pages. Arrange the short pieces so a narrative or argument is implied or suggested between the gaps.

2. Because the forms explored in this chapter are quite long, we thought it important to provide a reading prompt (rather than a generative writing prompt). Read a long

poem, antinovel, unclassifiable text, Menippean satire, and so on. See if you can identify the generic conventions it uses, plays with, or defies. How do you make sense of the work? What questions does it raise about how it's structured or hangs together? Do you assimilate it in terms of a genre you are more familiar with, such as the novel? What does it do to shift the center of gravity to a different genre when you read it?

3. While most of the works we name-checked in this chapter were lengthier, what would happen if you used the same techniques in a somewhat shorter work? For example, instead of writing an antinovel, can you write an "anti-story"; a "philosophical tale" rather than a philosophical novel? Or perhaps you can scale down the long poem and employ some of its ambition, scope, and design in a chapbook-length work? What happens when these more compendious forms shrink down to a bite-size nugget; do they lose their maximalist energies or do the smaller versions seem more fun and less of a slog?

4. Revise an existing work—novel, poetry collection, or other manuscript—by adding more generic hybridity. You might add new sections that reenvision the manuscript as a composite text by choosing forms and techniques that act in counterpoint to the existing genre. For example, how might adding excerpts from historical documents and research sources enrich your poetry collection; how might adding visual elements between chapters change your short story collection; or how might reworking chapters to seem like text conversations, corporate memos, screenplays, or court transcripts enhance the novel you've been working on?

5. Write a scene in which the characters are mouthpieces for some broader viewpoint or ideology. It could take the form of a symposia, a barstool debate, or an imaginary conversation between famous figures. How can you create a dialogue where none of the sides takes precedence, where, in fact, all points of view (including the implicit point of view of the text itself) is undermined or subtly called into question?

CHAPTER 3
CREATIVE REPURPOSING

I. Introduction

This chapter examines writing that alters or renovates source texts anew, which we will deem "creative repurposing." Such pieces use a previous cache of writing as the creative springboard for a fresh work; the source text serves not just as a model or an inspiration, though. Works of creative repurposing incorporate the direct language of source texts—or, if not the exact words, then they recycle the plot, characters, or other important elements of a previous work. In doing so, these works challenge commonplace notions of "originality," a term that can often become fetishized in creative writing discourse. After all, what do we mean when we call something "original"? That it's first or unique? That it does not plagiarize? Or does "original" simply act as a synonym for the term "creative" itself, a redundancy when we are already speaking of creative writing? "Make it new," Ezra Pound (1934: n.p.) famously said—less famously rephrasing the neo-Confucian scholar Chu Hsi (AD 1130–1200). Even in Pound's echt Modernist injunction to be original, the reclamation of an older texts persists: the "it" in Pound's dictum is the former poem or novel with which one begins. Everything begins elsewhere; there are no originals.

We live in a period accustomed to collage and assemblage, many of us digital curators of our own lives, familiar with the packrat tendency to hoard little bits and scraps then reconstitute and process them with another aim in mind. Creative repurposing is not the special province of self-avowed plagiarists or radical edgelords any more than it's a particularly "postmodern" tendency. What are Modernist monuments as different as *The Wasteland* or *The Arcades Project* but examples of far-reaching bricolage from many-headed sources? Every era builds on the past, picking from the ash heap what it can make vital again. The items we inherit must be refashioned as our own. Whether it's Homer renovating existing oral myths in *The Iliad*, Catullus repackaging Sappho, Shakespeare giving us his version of a tale by Chaucer, or Wordsworth pilfering his sister's journals, almost all literature has found techniques to build upon preceding stories and writing. Like Jimi Hendrix at Woodstock distorting "The Star-Spangled Banner" by effacing it into its own feedback, authors whammy-bar and noodle upon the texts around them to create something that speaks more urgently to their times. Perhaps it's odd for a book on experimental writing to declare, with the author of Ecclesiastes, "The eye never has enough of seeing, nor the ear its fill of hearing. What has been will be again, what has been done will be done again; there is nothing new under the sun." After all, the past, as William Faulkner (1951: 73) once wrote, "is never dead. It's not even past."

Though some of the methods discussed in this chapter for the creative repurposing of existing source texts to use for and in your own work are new, writers have always built from the material of other writing and art. A word of caution is warranted, however. When directly taking other's work to use as the basis of your own, writers should be aware of issues of plagiarism and copyright law. Don't blame us if you violate your college's policy on academic integrity, fly in the face of a publisher's citation guidelines, or pirate material against the legal codes for intellectual property. If you choose to do such things, the consequences are on you. By sharing the history of how creative writers have co-opted work, we are by no means advocating that you necessarily emulate these techniques in your given circumstances.

Writers should correspondingly be conscious of issues of appropriation, as well. The root of the word "appropriation" is "property"; it is also related to "propriety" and the sense of "appropriate" as in "students must use appropriate language and behavior." Appropriation occurs when one takes things that belong to someone else, which in many cases is synonymous with theft; the anarchist Pierre Joseph Proudhon (1876: 1) once declared, "Property is theft!" The point here is that there are many nuances to consider regarding the *propriety*, we might say, of appropriation. The term "cultural appropriation" has gained widespread currency in the last decade: the idea that a person from one cultural, demographic, or identity group should not take, use, or misrepresent the ideas, practices, material, or heritage of a culture to which they do not belong. It should be stated that not all uses of source texts are appropriation, and not all appropriation is cultural appropriation.

Still, it behooves the writer to think hard about whether and in what circumstances they should appropriate, repurpose, or co-opt other's material; who this material was produced by; how their use of this material might affect or be perceived by different audiences; what the purpose of their co-option is; their relationship to and knowledge of the cultures of which the material belongs; and the many contexts or interpretations to which their work may be subjected. Debates about cultural appropriation have proliferated and often turned heated in recent years. Certainly, we—the modest writers of this textbook—cannot definitively solve these controversies by demarcating a clear and absolute line. We can only urge you to contemplate the perspectives of those whom your writing may impact, being as thoughtful and empathetic as you can while valuing the integrity of other cultures and voices. Ultimately, we hope you will educate yourself more about the disputes concerning cultural appropriation, taking care to listen to opinions that you may disagree with and acting with respect, humility, and discretion.

II. Parody and Pastiche

Parody most commonly occurs when one work imitates another text, author, or genre, as a "send up," which points out the source text's cliches, makes fun of its ideas, or mocks it, much like a burlesque, spoof, or lampoon. The distortions and exaggerations of the parody comment on the source. Parody often—though not always—has an element of humor. Some parody may be done in a loving or deadpan manner, too; too loving, though, and a parody may be rendered an homage. Parody, it seems, requires some edge. One tricky aspect of a parody, though, is that it must imitate what it simultaneously critiques, taking part in the very thing it seemingly wishes to condemn. This requisite nearness to its source text means that the source is not altogether outcast by parody, but rather the source is all-too proximate. In this way, parody can serve as a thinking through—and self-questioning—of how a work constructs its values, affects, and ideals. Parody operates by manufacturing some recognizable degrees of difference from its source text.

Pastiche is when a work incorporates stylistic elements derived from other works, time periods, or authors (commonly from more than one source). Pastiche is generally more earnest and done in a spirit of admiration, though it may sometimes be glib, campy, or whimsical. Pastiche is related to the musical form of the medley. Whereas parody usually has some ax to grind against a specific target source, pastiche is usually the freewheeling incorporation of a hodgepodge of sources to make something that does not quite resemble any of them. Given such expansive definitions of parody and pastiche, almost all the subgenres identified in this chapter as "creative repurposing" below might be deemed varieties of one or the other, though they are not the typical or traditional kinds that are most associated with these terms.

Many theorists have proposed that "postmodernism" has a lot to do with co-opting and reassembling older forms and texts. According to Linda Hutcheon (1989), "postmodern parody" recognizes that representation is always ideological. For Hutcheon, parody's transformation of its source texts is inherently political. Hutcheon's postmodern parody is always making a charged statement of values or striking some attitude toward its source, whether it's ironic or done out of animus, nostalgia, or reverence. In fact, she states, "Parody is doubly coded in political terms: it both legitimizes and subverts that which it parodies." Iconic exemplars of this politicized "postmodern parody" include the films of Peter Greenaway, John Fowles's *The French Lieutenant's Woman* or E. L. Doctorow's *Ragtime*.

Critical theorist Fredric Jameson, however, disagrees with Hutcheon; he claims that postmodernism is defined by what he calls "blank parody," which doesn't attempt any attitudinizing about its sources. Postmodern works, claims Jameson, shamelessly dumpster-dive in the past for their materials; to pick out a certain material for use is not to thereby make political commentary upon it. Elsewhere, Jameson calls such "blank parody"—conflating the terms we just distinguished—"pastiche":

> Pastiche is, like parody, the imitation of a peculiar or unique, idiosyncratic style, the wearing of a linguistic mask, speech in a dead language. But it is a neutral practice of such mimicry, without any of parody's ulterior motives, amputated of the satiric impulse, devoid of laughter. (1991: 17)

Jameson believes that the way postmodern pastiche or repurposing works is that it effaces the historical uniqueness of the source texts it pilfers from. These source texts are emptied out of their content and simply become fashions, codes, empty referents that ultimately serve the purpose of consumption, feeding the ever-thirstier late capitalist beast. Examples of Jameson's pastiche are the architecture of Michael Graves and Roberto Venturi, the pop art of James Rosenquist, or the novels of Umberto Eco and Robert Coover. Such works, for Jameson, swipe from the grab bag of historical styles without aiming to make any historical or political judgments.

Rather than totalize all artwork of the postmodern period in this debate, perhaps we can say that both Jameson's "pastiche" and Hutcheon's "postmodern parody" can coexist. Which one a given work is depends on the artwork in question and its relation to, or framing of, its source texts. Nevertheless, if we had to choose, we are more persuaded by Hutcheon since almost all co-options of source texts can be read politically if the audience chooses to interpret them that way. For instance, Venturi's boxlike buildings with fanciful neon, decoration, and facades around them are an ideological argument against the more austere International Style as well as an embrace of the hedonistic, populist capitalism found in places like Las Vegas; Rosenquist's choice of imagery can be seen as a critique of the imperialist American mythos;

and Coover's *The Public Burning* savages the Cold War politics of conservatives like McCarthy and Nixon. At any rate, in today's climate, it is fair for readers to wonder why a source is being used, what relation the author has to that source, and how the repurposing of that source produces an affective, ideological, or aesthetic remark about it. Contemporary readers are keen to inquire about the politics of repurposing any source text; we inhabit a climate in which it behooves authors to consider their reasons for choosing a source and what meanings arise from distorting and manipulating it.

III. Détournement

Détournement (literally, "rerouting" or "hijacking") is a technique that derives from the mid-twentieth-century French Marxist group known as the Situationist International, especially Guy Debord (1983) who wrote *The Society of the Spectacle*. Today, it is often synonymous with "cultural jamming" and "subvertising." Debord wrote that it was necessary to use "spectacular images and language to disrupt the flow of the spectacle" since staid, rational discourse cannot compete against the slick appeal of eye-catching media. Détournement is a widespread tactic of punk and other anti-capitalist aesthetics, a form of guerilla communication. It consists in taking an existing source text—often a logo, brand name, catchphrase, or corporate image—and altering it in a subversive manner. The motivation is to deconstruct commodified imagery and propaganda, turning those images against their intended purpose to sell more schlock. In most cases, the ad or logo is defaced in a witty way that exposes the hypocrisy or emptiness of corporate profiteering. Graffiti that defaces a billboard to make the attractive model into a skull-faced ghoul, adding "No More" above the tagline "Selfies on iPhone X," is one example; a golden arches logo that reads "McDiabetes" in the same front as the fast-food chain is another.

In the introduction to Bonner and Raoul's *Advertising Shits in Your Head*, Josh MacPhee (2019: 8) puts it like this: "Advertising is a form of pollution and corporations are shitting in our heads." One must fight fire with fire, as it were, while the world burns. Subvertisers work collectively, and often anonymously, to reclaim our shared spaces—or, to invoke French sociologist, Henri Lefebvre to assert our "right to the city." These include groups like StopPub (France), Proyecto Squatters (Argentina), Adbusters (Canada), TTIP Game Over (Belgium), Special Patrol Group and Brandalism (UK), Resistance is Female and Guerilla Girls (USA), Billboard Utilising Graffitists Against Unhealthy Promotions (Australia), and myriad street advertising takeovers in New York, Madrid, Paris, Toronto, and beyond. Individual subvertisers include Banksy, Hogre, Shepard Fairey, Molly Crabapple, and Parker Day.

Adbusters Magazine is one outlet that frequently employs détournement: an image of Trump with a Hitleresque mustache that is in fact a bar code or a Michael Jordan silhouette reaching for a dollar bill rather than holding a basketball. A popular image is deconstructed, and its more insidious subtext is revealed. Memes, which similarly repurpose popular imagery or catchphrases, may be a new development in the practice of détournement.

Memes often don't attack the underlying content of the icons they display: the icons (e.g., the distracted boyfriend, pointing Spiderman, or Grumpy Cat) are instead pried from whatever source they came from and used as shorthand to describe an emotional reaction to—or a structural relationship for—something completely different. The meaning of such icons is not fixed, however. Dick Hebdige (1979: 16) writes in *Subculture: The Meaning of Style* that "forms cannot be permanently normalized. They can always be deconstructed, demystified … commodities can be symbolically 'repossessed' in everyday life, and endowed with implicitly oppositional meanings, by the very groups who originally produced them." A golf hat that reads "Titties" instead of "Titleist" might not be subverting the brand name at all but profiting off its cachet for misogynistic intent. "D.A.R.E." T-shirts from the antidrug after-school program might be appropriated by prodrug subcultures as an ironic fashion statement. The détournement "Let's Go Brandon," much like rhyming Cockney slang, is a polite stand-in for an abusive attack against Joe Biden; however, the catchphrase has been reworked into "Dark Brandon" memes that portray Biden with laser-beam eyes saying things such as "Malarkey detected: annihilate" by Biden supporters. If subversive Marxists can hijack a tagline or brand imagery away from its intended purpose, others can reroute seeming instances of détournement to make money or spread mainstream ideologies. The punk style of safety pins and ripped jeans has been appropriated by haute couture fashion brands, of course. Perhaps even the mutinous, anticorporate alterations of the Nike swoosh and McDonald's arch logos only act to give these companies more recognition if, as the saying goes, no publicity is bad publicity.

The episode "Dumb Starbucks" (2014) on the show *Nathan for You*, not just its logo that spoofs the coffee chain, is a more elaborate, performative instance of détournement. Nathan Fielder helped create a look-alike café that satirized consumers preference for brand-name sameness over local flavor. Filmmaker Michael Moore has dabbled in détournement, too, such as when he opened a bank account that gave a free rifle to its customers and then asked, "Do you think it's a little dangerous handing out guns at a bank?" in *Bowling for Columbine* or when he transported ailing 9/11 aid workers to Guantanamo Bay, Cuba, to receive free healthcare in *Sicko*. The Yes Men offer another performative take on détournement: their hijinks include switching the voice boxes of G. I. Joe and Barbie dolls and then placing them back onto store shelves; creating a fake Dow Chemical website that claims, "Dow will never clean up Bhopal because Bhopalis can't afford lawyers"; and posing as Halliburton executives to infiltrate a banking conference then giving a parodic presentation. The categories between different subgenres of creative repurposing may overlap. *Wizard People, Dear Reader* is an unauthorized soundtrack of *Harry Potter and the Sorcerer's Stone*, which replaces the movie dialogue with a soundtrack of non sequiturs, awkward humor, and goofball monologues. Though it turns the existing film imagery against its ostensible purpose like détournement, it can also be considered a parodic "retelling" or a fan-fiction homage to the movie.

For an example of détournement of the hit show *Friends*, see Caren Beilin's piece "Freinds" on pp. 195–200.

Repurposing in many forms destabilizes the circuit that connects a source text with its signification, sometimes allowing interpretations to proliferate and accrue as the new work travels among various subcultures. For instance, are Andy Warhol's paintings of Campbell's soup cans a critique of the repetitive and "canned" act of capitalist consumption or the apotheosis of corporatist pop taste?

Experimental Writing

IV. Experimental Translation

Translation can be an experimental practice that repurposes source texts, especially when the translation methods deviate from "normal" practices, foreground the act of translation itself as a creative act, or mix disparate languages in a single work. The word for "translate" in some Romance languages is related to the English term "treason." All translation is a betrayal. There are competing aspects of a text—literal meaning, sound, rhythm, form, metaphors, connotations, tone, idioms, decorum, and levels of diction; not all of which can be rendered in a perfectly correspondent way into the target language. Audiences, contexts, historical periods, and cultures also affect a translation. Should one burden the translation with scholarly notes? Does one retain every singular authorial quirk or does one elide distracting filigree or outright mistakes for ease of readability? How does one eliminate the penumbra of inadvertent associations produced by the target language? Might a translation go out of its way to carry over an etymological pun that likely would go unobserved by a reader of the original? Should a whiff of foreignness be sustained or is the goal to assimilate the text as much as possible to the norms of the target language? Given such myriad considerations, what would a "faithful" translation be? The act of translation mediates between cultures—it allows for a cultural exchange and greater understanding. At the same time, though, it may be fraught with the power relations implied by hegemony, especially when a text in a minoritarian language is translated for a more dominant language community. For some, translation can be a form of imperialism.

Some distinguish translation by its purpose: technical translation of a car manual prioritizes precision of terms while a poetic translation of a literary work may maintain the form while fudging details of its so-called message perhaps. Since no translation is perfect, one has to choose among competing values. John Dryden identified three types of translations: metaphrase operates in a literal word-by-word manner, paraphrase uses a holistic approach to capture the gist, and imitation takes liberties to create a literary work in the target language inspired or based on the source text. Each method has some merit. Jorge Luis Borges, surveying the major European translations of *A Thousand and One Nights*, claims that he prefers those that "can only be conceived of *in the wake of literature*" (1981:108, emphasis in original). Borges means that the previous context of both languages—their conventions, stylistic nuances, and historical proclivities—must be accounted for. Indeed, Borges reverses the priority and contends that some originals are unfaithful to their translations. Gabriel García Marquez, for example, once remarked that he thought Gregory Rabassa's English translation of *One Hundred Years of Solitude* improved upon his Spanish. Walter Benjamin, defending Hölderlin's somewhat bizarre word-for-word translations of Sophocles, writes that, "translation must in large measure turn its attention away from trying to communicate something, away from meaning; the original is essential to translation only insofar as it has already relieved the translator and his work of the burden and organization of what is communicated" (1997: 161). For Benjamin, the original poem is not for the reader—and therefore the translation should not be for the reader either. Instead, it is an attempt to find kinships between languages, a way to reinvigorate both. Thus, it's not the most "natural sounding" translation that Benjamin prefers, but the one that enacts a torsion of syntax in a tortured idiom. A translation that seems "far-fetched" may reveal how it, in fact, has been fetched from afar. Charles Bernstein claims, going beyond Benjamin's theory:

> Accuracy is the bogeyman of translation; for what can be accurately paraphrased is not the "poetic" content of the work.
>
> Translation can be a goad to invent new forms, structures, expressions, textures, and sounds in the (new) poem being written. (1988: 64)

Translation, when liberated from literal-minded notions of accuracy or faithfulness, can become a creative act. In "A Manifesto for Ultratranslation," the language justice group Antena Aire (n.d.: n.p.) write: "We want ultratranslation: to untranslate the seams, to extratranslate the gaps, to multitranslate the leaps, to infratranslate the porosities. We want the transfer and the untransferable, both."

In a conference presentation, Sawako Nakayasu (2020: n.p.) illustrated the binaries of translation: source versus target, author versus translator, foreignization versus domestication, and so on. She invites translators attending a conference at Brown University to work under the influence of art. To demonstrate this, she whimsically invents the following schools of translation:

1. James Turrell Quaker Meeting School of Translation
2. Sophie Calle Voyeuristic School of Translation
3. Butch Morris Structured Improvisation School of Translation
4. Pauline Oliveros Sonic Meditations School of Translation
5. Tehching Hsieh Durational Performance School of Translation
6. Hito Steyerl in Defense of the Poor Translation School of Translation
7. Adam Pendleton Black Dada School of Translation Appropriation
8. Christine Sun Kim Distribution of the Senses School of Translation
9. José Muñoz Wildness of the Punk Rock Commons of Anti-Translation
10. Paul B. Preciado Dildotectonics School of Translation

Some translators, like counterfeiters, may wish their art to go unnoticed. Translation slams—where different translators showcase their work, often using the same source—run counter to this notion. Likewise, *McSweeney's* issue 42 highlighted the differences between translations by publishing up to six versions of the same piece. In some cases, *McSweeney's* even had stories translated into the same language—that is, they offered English-to-English renderings. With the advent of differences among global English, this will only become more commonplace. There will soon be the *Oxford Dictionary of African-American Vernacular English*. Formerly marginalized dialects are becoming codified and gaining legitimacy.

In *feeld*, poet Jos Charles queers the English language through transliteration, neologism, and cacography. Read her sample poems on p. 216.

English is an imperialist lingua franca while it's simultaneously in the process of breaking down into regional or demographic variants. Even self-translation raises questions: Samuel Beckett first wrote his novels in French and then translated them into his native English, an exercise that indelibly left its imprint on his style in both versions.

Experimental Writing

Radical translation might valorize a supposedly minor aspect of a text or emphasize the translator's sidelong skewing. In *Earish*, poet Robert Kelley translated only the sound of Paul Celan's poems, disregarding their semantic content. Updating a classic work with her own spin, Maria Dahvana Headley's *Beowulf* begins, "Bro! Tell me we still know how to talk about kings!" (2020: 3). In "Turing Test," Franny Choi processed her texts through "iterative feedback loops of 'bad' machine translation" to derive a finished product that possesses an estranging, polyglot, yet poetic voice: "bone-wife / spit-dribbler / understudy for the underdog / uphill rumor / fine-toothed cunt / sorry / my mouth's not pottytrained" (2016: n.p.).

Read all of Choi's "Turing Test" on pp. 217–18.

Deciphering Choi's poem, one realizes language is fluent because it's always existing in the flows and influences of other idioms. Then again, some works deliberately impede translation. *Yo-Yo Boing!* by Puerto Rican author Giannina Braschi insists on inhabiting both Spanish and English, resisting translation altogether. Kenyan Ngũgĩ wa Thiong'o has ceased to write in English, the colonizer's tongue, and now only writes in his Indigenous Gikuyu, at once inviting and shunning translation.

Further afield, *Emoji Dick* is a crowdsourced project—using Amazon's Mechanical Turk gig-worker platform—started by Fred Benenson (2010) that translated *Moby Dick* into emojis. The strings of emojis resemble colorful hieroglyphics, as if writing had come full circle back to pictorial icons that require a new Rosetta Stone to fully decipher. The attempt highlighted the imprecision in the Unicode language, though playful moments of synchronicity also emerged. Although some emojis may stand in for phrases, on average seven words required 764 emojis, demonstrating the cumbersome nature of communicating solely through emojis.

See Carina Finn's emoji poem "Grey Bird on a Wire (Angst Attack)," as translated by Stephanie Berger on p. 255.

Some writers have attempted translating into invented languages such as Esperanto or Klingon, as documented in Arika Okrent's *The Land of Invented Languages*; others have pursued inventing their own languages. The seventeenth-century polymath John Wilkins tried to create a universal analytic language devoid of ambiguity. Linguist Suzette Haden Elden published a grammar and dictionary for the gynocentric language "Láadan." Kelly Rafey (2014: 75) remarks that Láadan includes "three different words for 'menopause,' five different kinds of 'pregnancy,' seven ways to 'menstruate' and eleven different root words for 'love.'"

Cathy Park Hong (2007) gestures toward a futuristic language in her narrative poem *Dance Dance Revolution* where the tour guide of a fictional desert city speaks in a mash-up of English, Korean, Latin, Spanish, and bits of other languages. Read an excerpt from the book on pp. 263–4.

Russell Hoban's (1980) novel *Riddley Walker*, also set in the future, deforms English into a hard-edged radioactive shrapnel congruent with its primitive, postapocalyptic setting.

Then there's James Joyce's (1939) *Finnegans Wake*, which overlays polyglot puns along a multilingual nexus so that, one might say, the book is written more in "Anguish" than in English. Macaronics, code-switching, creolization, and other playful combinations of languages abound in contemporary literature: look at Theresa Hak Kyung Cha's *Dictee*, Jhumpa Lahari's *In Other Words*, or any number of books in Spanglish, pidgin or patois, or other mixed dialects. Many find translation a deeply rooted part of their identity, as they must cross cultures and languages constantly in their everyday life. For these folks, it's a greater betrayal to leave the act of translation out of literature. Although translation, like poetry itself, may only point out the failure of its own ideals, perhaps it is no less necessary an undertaking for that very reason.

V. Co-opted Forms

Today, there are lots of "forms" surrounding us, many having to do with our bureaucratic, consumer society. A small sample of such forms might include obituaries, nutrition facts, internet cookie notices, interviews, insurance policies, fitness videos, permission slips, gray papers, PR flak, comment cards, personal ads, bumper stickers, voicemail greetings, alumni donation requests, annotated bibliographies, Wikipedia entries, waivers, disclaimers, memes, event-a-day desk calendars, prescriptions, spam, field trip permission slips, errata slips, flowcharts, ethnographic notes, operating schedules, motivational posters, policy manuals, resumes, grocery lists, footnotes, Facebook updates, declassified documents, lab reports, mission statements, liner notes, clinical evaluations, syllabi, insurance company checklists, junk mail, architectural proposals, grant applications, a coroner's reports, FBI most-wanted lists, and so on. Many of these examples come from sources that testify to the burgeoning amount of writing that we scan, skim, and surf almost daily, but rarely peruse with attention or enthusiasm. Advertisements and legal forms, academic discourse and internet culture, bureaucratic paperwork and scientific documents all spawn their own subgenres.

Many creative writers enjoy taking these often "uncreative," quotidian forms and using them as the "container" for expressing a creative work. Creative writers take these forms and push them against their normal purposes, taking them as the scaffolding upon which to build a literary piece. In most cases, the everyday form is used for satiric purposes.

See Chikọdịlị Emelụmadụ's "What to Do When Your Child Brings Home a Mami Wata," on pp. 248–54. This creative piece masquerades as an instruction manual.

The form often has some relevance to the narrative, argument, or creative content of the literary work. Although the conventions of the form are more-or-less followed, they are executed in a way that is parodic, which unlocks the structural assumptions within the form or reveals something about how the everyday use of the form obscures the metaphors and values it contains. In other cases, the poetic potential of these everyday forms is revealed.

Experimental Writing

Kim Adrian (2018) in the anthology *The Shell Game: Writers Play with Borrowed Forms* refers to the "hermit crab essay," which has gained some currency as a term confined to creative nonfiction pieces. Matthew Vollmer and David Shields's (2012) anthology of such works in both fiction and nonfiction, *Fakes*, calls them "fraudulent artifacts," emphasizing the decoy-like nature of these stories, essays, poems, or other literary pieces that pretend to be something else. We deem such works "co-opted forms," stressing their appropriation of a prior form—usually an everyday document rather than a recognized literary "form" such as a sonnet, villanelle, picaresque, mystery, or memoir. However, when one uses a sonnet to structure a play, for example, or the conventional plot of a mystery novel to shape a short poem, then that, too, might be a kind of co-opted form. The prevalence of co-opted forms has made them a legitimate subgenre of their own today. Search a few literary journals, and you're sure to encounter one.

Co-opted forms are no more "fraudulent" than most literature since most literary works have an element of chicanery or make-believe to them. It bears mentioning that not all co-opted forms are fraudulent, either. Harry Mathew's essay "Country Cooking from Central France: Roast Bone Rolled Stuff Shoulder of Lamb (*Farce Double*)" is a serviceable recipe for a delicacy of traditional French cuisine, shared with gusto and relish. It's a working recipe, which goes beyond that purpose to also become a literary essay. The parameters that define co-opted forms are, like most of the literary categories we discuss, dependent on historical and cultural context. Virgil's instructions on beekeeping in the *Georgics* ([29 BCE] 2009), for instance, constituted traditional subject matter for a recognized literary genre at the time; today, however, a versified manual on apiculture would strike most readers as a co-opted form. Flash fiction and prose poems have become an apt vehicle for co-opted forms since most of the documents from which co-opted forms are derived are relatively short. A glance at David Lehman's *Great American Prose Poems* anthology turns up a healthy smattering, including Charles Simic's "Contributor's Note," Stephanie Brown's "Commencement Address," and Paul Violi's "Acknowledgements." Other instances of co-opted forms might include (lineated) poems such as Maurice Manning's "Progress Report," Sjohnna McCray's "*Cinéma Vérité*," and Douglas Crase's "Experience and What to Make of It" (in the form of a scientific article). Weldon Kees, who once worked as a reference librarian, wrote "Abstracts of Dissertations."

> More recently, Layli Long Soldier's *Whereas* appropriates the Congressional Resolution of Apology to Native Americans for its form, eviscerating the legalistic discourse with sections entitled "These Being the Concerns," "Whereas Statements," "Resolutions," and "Disclaimer." Read some of the "Whereas Statements" on pp. 279–82.

Like Long Soldier's work, most co-opted forms critique the administrative rhetoric they appropriate, although a few may act to re-enchant such mundane documents with the possibility of lyric expression.

So, too, flash fiction like Robin Hemley's "Reply All" or Patricia Marx's "Audio Tour" are cases in point, as evidenced by their titles. Charles Yu's "Problems for Self-Study" elaborates a story in the form of complex word problems in a math exam.

DBC Pierre's "News" on p. 305 co-opts the familiar feel of a news anchor's script.

While most co-opted forms hew close to the conventions of the document they appropriate, Julio Cortazár's "how to" pieces from *Cronopios and Famas* deviate quite freely to venture into extravagant metaphors and lyrical epiphanies. Novels might contain sections or chapters in co-opted forms, such as Jennifer Egan's *A Visit from the Goon Squad*, with its chapter formatted as a PowerPoint, or Donald Barthelme's *Snow White*, with its pop quiz tucked into the middle. There are even some specimens of whole novels or longer-form works written in co-opted forms, such as Alejandro Zembra's *Multiple Choice* (employing the form of a standardized test booklet) and David Levithan's *The Lover's Dictionary*. Generally, co-opted forms use a written artifact as their template, though Daniel Orozco's short story "Orientation" uses the patter and pattern typical of initiating a newcomer to the office during an orientation as its basis. Plays, too, might co-opt set pieces such as stump speeches, card tricks, or barbershop colloquies that are performative speeches from other settings. Or they might use written forms; Erin Courtney's *A Map of Virtue* utilizes the symmetries of a map to structure its narrative scenes. In many cases, following the constraints imposed by a trivial, workaday document, co-opted forms share a greater family resemblance with each other than they do with their alleged traditional literary genre of poem, story, or essay.

VI. Retellings

Whereas co-opted forms take some hackneyed formal template and introduce creative content to it, retellings do the opposite: they take timeworn content and reconfigure it with a fresh formal bent. The content in most retellings is assumed to be familiar to its audience, whether it's fairy tales or classics, popular films or myths. The more the audience has an involved knowledge of the source text, the more that small deviations from the original or standard version can appear significant. Whereas some retellings refer to a particular source, it should be noted that in the case of many fairy tales, fables, or myths there may be no "original" since the basic narrative is only a composite of different versions—tellings and retellings without a definitive, authorized Ur-text. "Retelling" in one form or another is a foundational principle of nearly all storytelling and cultural transmission. Ovid wove old myths in new ways in *The Metamorphosis*; Disney repackages antiquated fairy tales as feature-length animated movies; and cultural elders continue handing down stories and poems to the next generation to keep alive. James Joyce's *Ulysses* transposes the voyages of Odysseus onto the events of a single day in Dublin. TV shows like *Muppet Babies* and *Always Sunny in Philadelphia* have many episodes where the characters reenact well-known stories or movies with a twist. Sometimes entire genres—think of noir—become retellings, ringing changes on archetypal plots and stock characters. Adaptations into other media are also retellings: a film based on a novel, a novelization of a film, a comic-book version of an epic poem, or a graphic novel staged as a play. In the same way, one might count ekphrastic works as retellings since they render visual material into narrative or lyric forms. Updates and remakes, too, are types of retelling. The urge to pass on, transform, and embroider new meanings onto older narratives is a primordial impulse.

Still, several recent modes of retelling have emerged, responding to current exigencies and attitudes. One mode is the "fractured fairy tale" in which classic fairy tales and myths are retold in ways that subvert one or more assumptions encoded in the well-known version(s). Many fairy tales imply cultural ideals about gender roles, kinship patterns, sexuality, class, and moral values—for instance, the emphasis on female beauty, the wickedness of stepparents, the heteronormativity of the princess, the motive of class accession in marriage, or the need of the female ingénue to be "rescued" by a dashing prince whom she barely knows. Likewise, the whole kit and caboodle of Greek myth might be viewed as little more than a boondoggle to normalize rape culture. Thus, many fractured fairy tales are written from new feminist, queer, or cultural perspectives, challenging the underlying ideology of these tales. One such example of this would be Ana María Shua's *Microfictions* wherein, for example, Cinderella's sisters surgically modify their feet to win the prince's affection. Using alternate endings, queering characters, interpolating critical meta-commentary into the story, shifting the tale's point of view, and providing backstory or sequels that undo the original are a few techniques that fractured fairy tales employ. Going further, writers like Kelly Link, Carmen Maria Machado, and Kate Bernheimer have sought to rewrite fairy tales more radically, not merely tweaking existing ones so much as refashioning new ones for the values of our age, using shards and slivers from the established classics.

Garielle Lutz's story "The Boy" on pp. 283–5 is an original fairy tale of sorts that upends fabulist tropes.

Fan fiction, too, especially the subgenre known as "slash," which repositions supposedly straight characters as queer, can be another form of retelling. Not only does slash frequently explore queer subtexts, but it also allows a book or show's audience to reclaim the story, sometimes even affecting future episodes or sequels produced by the official creators.

Similarly challenging the ideology of their sources, "Empire Writes Back" texts are retellings based on famous Western literary works, reimagining these narratives from the perspectives of colonized, subaltern, Indigenous, or non-Western subjects. The term derives from Salman Rushdie's (1982) essay of the same name to describe the transgressive act of reappropriating canonical literature in a critical, ironic, or transgressive way to claim legitimacy for the peripheral voices it leaves out. Chinua Achebe's (1994) *Things Fall Apart* responds to Conrad's portrayal of "uncivilized" natives in *Heart of Darkness*, portraying the complex cultural traditions of African natives. Jean Rhys's (1966) *Wide Sargasso Sea* takes off the fact that Mr. Rochester's estate in *Jane Eyre* was founded on the slave trade with Jamaica—a marginal point of the backstory in Charlotte Brontë's novel, which gets fleshed out from a postcolonial vantage in Rhys's prequel. J. M. Coetzee's (1986) *Foe* recounts a plot parallel to *Robinson Crusoe*, emphasizing how race and gender influence whose story gets told and the machinations of power during both the early eighteenth and late twentieth centuries. Zadie Smith's (2005) *On Beauty* recast *Howards End* with mixed-race characters in the United States and England to scrutinize the effects of ethnicity, nationality, and demographics. Aimé Césaire's (1992) *A Tempest* adapts Shakespeare's play specifically for an anticolonial, Pan-African Black audience, redacting the text with African mythology and raising questions about its racist subtext. Not all Empire Writes Back works need to adhere closely to their source or use only one. Thomas King's (1993) *Green Grass, Running Water* includes a medley of different Western characters such as Robinson Crusoe, Hawkeye from *The Leatherstocking Tales*, Ishmael from the *Bible*, and the Lone Ranger, juxtaposed with Indigenous characters, plots, and rituals. Empire Writes Back texts are political interrogations of Western literature, inscribed both within and against that tradition as they rewrite imperialist or racist works while, in doing so, seeking to empower colonized or subaltern subjects.

Along these same lines in nonfiction, "alternative histories" rewrite the standard narrative about some event. For example, Howard Zinn's *A People's History of the United States* reframes the American chronicle, replacing the story of "great men" with a working-class and domestic perspective of everyday folks. By contrast, Roxanne Dunbar-Ortiz's *An Indigenous Peoples' History of the United States* and Pekka Hämäläinen's *A Lakota America* center the stories of Native Americans in that same historical trajectory. Meanwhile, Nikole Hannah-Jones's *1619 Project* and Ibram X. Kendi's *Stamped from the Beginning* center African Americans and the impact of slavery and racism on the continuing political formation of the United States. Many of these works are deemed controversial; however, alternative histories are not filled with "alternative facts." Alternative histories are not necessarily fake, though they *are* fabricated as all nonfiction must be. No account of history is definitive. Historical nonfiction is a selection from the available archive, a substitute for the various histories established before them. Just look at the many biographies of Lincoln, Churchill, or Shakespeare: there are as many versions of these figures as there are books about them. One tenant of the critical theory known as New Historicism is that histories inevitably construct narratives that privilege some accounts while neglecting others; from this uncontentious historiographical premise, works of New Historicism venture to consciously recover stories that have been hitherto marginalized and erased. Contrariwise, most historical fiction—as self-proclaimed *fiction*—contains a degree of make-believe, whether it purports to hew closer to the facts, such as Gore Vidal's *Burr*, or veers wildly from it, such as Philip Roth's speculative *The Plot against America*. And yet, historical fiction, too, is often written to foreground sidelined viewpoints in ways that help us rethink accepted historical truisms.

Such impulses are prevalent in poetry as well, including in the ongoing book series, *from unincorporated territory*, by Craig Santos Perez about the Pacific island Guåhan (Guam). Read his poem, "*ginen* the legends of juan malo [a malologue]," on p. 304.

Other types of retellings can be conceptualized with assorted musical analogies. Mash-ups combine two different texts—think *Pride and Prejudice and Zombies*. Remixes might then be genre-bending texts that transpose the score of an existing work into a different key or time signature, thus reconceiving the story in terms of new generic constraints. Novels like Jane Smiley's *A Thousand Acres*, Jeanette Winterson's *The Gap in Time*, and Margaret Atwood's *Hag-Seed* each reenvision different Shakespeare plays as contemporary dystopias; Kathy Acker's *Don Quixote* reconceives the novel as set among a hallucinatory hellscape of 1970s gutterpunks and transvestites while Will Self's *Dorian* refigures Wilde's titular character as a gay model in a drug-fueled party scene during the epoch of AIDS. Covers replay old favorites with a fresh voice, adding their own riffs or grace notes. In the anthology *After Montaigne*, for example, contemporary authors reprise the French author's essays with their own fanciful style while noodling on the standards; likewise, Ta-Nehisi Coates's *Between the World and Me* might be considered a cover of James Baldwin's *The Fire Next Time*. We might think of "B-sides" as when an author produces a one-off alternative of their own text. For example, David Mitchell's *Cloud Atlas* is quite different in the American versus the British editions; James Salter's late novel *Cassada* is a rewrite of his second book *The Arm of Flesh*. To continue with the musical analogies, we might see works like Geoff Dyer's *Out of Sheer Rage* on D. H. Lawrence, *My Emily Dickinson* by Susan Howe, and Jenn Shapland's *My Autobiography of Carson McCullers* as "scratching" the vinyl of a disc, much like a DJ spinning an old tune with a funky new breakbeat. Sampling would be works such as David Shields's *Reality Hunger* and Jonathan Lethem's "The Ecstasy of Influence," both of which copiously plagiarize, contriving essays from artfully pieced-together quotes.

VII. Found Texts

Found texts are source texts that have been taken from their "normal" context and introduced into a new context or given a "nonstandard" performance so that the source text reveals a different potential signification. Almost no alterations are made on the source text in the retelling—exceptions might be line breaks added to a source text originally written in prose. Annie Dillard (1995) extracts passages from older, forgotten, or out-of-the-way documents, arranging them as poems, in *Mornings Like This*; Dillard's work is done in the spirit of homage, recovering bits of genuine poetry from unlikely sources such as diaries and scientific texts. On the other hand, Hart Seely's (2003) *Pieces of Intelligence*, which reorganizes former Secretary of Defense Donald Rumsfeld's public statements as Zen koans, haikus, and sonnets, is meant to be satire. So, too, is William Shatner's (Tjveil, 2009) performance of Sarah Palin's speech on *The Conan O'Brien Show*—Shatner employs the affect and stylistic tics of beat poetry, complete with bongo drum accompaniment, to mock Palin's clumsy oratory. Despite the bulk of found poetry being used for ironic purposes today, Joel Katelnikoff (2016: n.p) proposes an exercise that uses found poetry to help reassess your reading: he asks you to reevaluate a text you hate "with a particular eye for discovering, within it, that which you love. Because the thing has not failed you. Rather, you have failed." Katelnikoff instructs his audience to "read quickly, ignoring every element of the text you might detest" while transcribing any passages that hold your interest. Katelnikoff's exercise gestures toward the radically Nietzschean "transvaluation of values" (1918: 52) at the heart of found poetry, its strange ability to deflate or aggrandize a text, shifting its meaning but not its words, while shuffling love and hate, affection and dislike, in the process.

Carlos Soto-Román's *11* is assembled from found material such as declassified documents, testimonies, interviews, and media files. It immerses the reader in Chile's state-sponsored terror of former dictator Augusto Pinochet. Read an excerpt on pp. 308–12.

In this sense, we might also conceive of many play productions as a variety of found texts since they employ the same playscript but often modify the emphasis and themes it appears to signify through "nonstandard" performances.

Found texts are related to readymades in art: Duchamp's (1917) readymade *Fountain* for example, adds the signature "R. Mutt," the name of one of his alter egos, to an ordinary porcelain urinal. Duchamp then entered this object into an art exhibition in 1917, and it became one of the most iconic sculptures of the twentieth century. Although this bit of plumbing was industrially manufactured, Duchamp's artistic touch was to place it into a different frame of reference. As a piece of sculpture, *Fountain* might allow us to see the aesthetic curves and smooth design of the urinal in light of Western sculpture's biomorphic prejudice or its stress on the phantasmatic sleekness of the human body. Then again, art critic Arthur Danto writes that "most of the art being made today does not have the provision of aesthetic experience as its main goal" (2013: 150). Perhaps the point of *Fountain* is not properly aesthetic recognition at all, but rather a metaphysical one. As Danto asks about Warhol's Brillo Boxes, "The question, then, was in what way did Andy's Factory-made boxes differ from the factory-made boxes?" The interpreter's experience of the object is the determining factor—in scrubbing the artifacts from their commonplace context as consumer items, one can read them, as it were, outside the box. A wag might quip that it's the signature that's most important—hence, the slapdash "R. Mutt" on *Fountain*. But Duchamp didn't sign his real name, hinting that the attribution of some prior authenticity (the signature) is a mug's game. Indeed, the *Fountain* currently on display at MoMA is merely a museum-constructed replica, raising the perplexing question of whether any readymade—since it wasn't crafted by the hand of the artist—could be called a fake or forgery. What if there is no truly "normal" background context for a work; what if all framing is relative and contested? Jacques Derrida declares in *Margins of Philosophy*:

> There are only contexts without any center of absolute anchoring. This citationality, duplication, or duplicity, this iterability of the mark is not an accident or anomaly, but is that (normal/abnormal) without which a mark could no longer even have a so-called "normal" functioning. What would a mark be that one could not cite? And whose origin could not be lost on the way? (1982: 320)

The text itself, because it exist *as* citation, is infinitely replicable, but also thereby always subject to the malleable construal of fluctuating recontextualization. Thus, *everything*'s already a readymade and is ever ready to be remade.

VIII. Centos, Cutups, and Flarf

The form of the cento is composed of lines taken from other works and woven into a new holistic poem. The cento spans back to classical antiquity. The ancient Greeks often wrote centos in homage to Homer; ancient Romans, to Virgil. At least since Ausonius (*c.* 310–*c.* 395), poets have been quibbling about "the ethics of textual recycling; about the impact of political power and patronage on literary production" (Cullhed, 2016: 237). Yet, the cento has been a way to reclaim lines you wish you had written, to pay tribute to forebears, and to show off poetic knowledge. Readers of centos, too, enjoy guessing if they can attribute the lines to their source (before the internet made that much easier). It's a scholarly parlor trick of sorts, though one that validates T. S. Eliot's famous claim that "immature poets imitate; mature poets steal; bad poets deface what they take, and good poets make it into something better, or at least something different" (1921: 114). The process of culling choice scraps and then stitching them together is borne out by the Latin root of the word "cento," which means a "patchwork." However, in Italian, *cento* means a hundred. While the Empress Eudocia composed Homeric centos that numbered up to 2,000 lines, a later tradition developed that the form rounded off at exactly one-hundred lines. Modern and contemporary centos rarely adhere to this constraint, though. While the vogue for centos is fickle, the form has been most recently revived by The New York School, much in the spirit of surrealist collage and other ludic recombinatory experiments. John Ashbery's "To a Waterfowl" and "The Dong with the Luminous Nose" (both titles taken from nineteenth-century poets) and Peter Gizzi's "Ode: Salute to the New York School" are some better-known contemporary examples.

Relatedly, the form of the "cutup" likely emerged with Tristan Tzara's "How to Make a Dadaist Poem" around 1920. Tzara's exercise was to cut out each word in a newspaper article, shuffle them in a bag, and then randomly pull them out, copying the result, however nonsensical. Tzara concluded, "The poem will be like you. And here are you a writer, infinitely original and endowed with a sensibility that is charming though beyond the understanding of the vulgar" (1920: n.p.). As with fortune cookies, astrology readings, and Tarot cards, no matter how far-fetched the message, there is always some truth that the person can connect to. Tzara's Dada instructions are, in fact, like the older literary game of *sortes virginilae*, a game in which one's fate was foretold by picking out lines from Virgil by chance. Tzara may have intended his remarks ironically—that is, to undermine the idea that sophisticated literature could be produced by such a ridiculous formula, or he may have been mocking sophisticated pretentiousness itself. Or he may have hit upon a way to transmute leaden journalistic copy into lyric gold. It's hard to say. Nevertheless, later Surrealist and Dada writers used cutups, and postmodernists such as William Burroughs (in his novel *Naked Lunch*) and John Ashbery (in *The Tennis Court Oaths*) employed a version of this technique. Others who dabbled in cutups include Kathy Acker, Julio Cortázar, and Walter Abish—as well as songwriters Bob Dylan, David Bowie, Kurt Cobain, and Thom Yorke. In some cases, cutups may be selected more judiciously from their source texts and with some degree of conscious rather than completely aleatory construction. The technique has even expanded with electronic artists like *Throbbing Gristle* and *Atari Teenage Riot* into visual montage in media such as film and music videos.

With the advent of the internet culture of the 1990s, a further iteration of recycling source texts arose with the movement known as Flarf. The source texts that Flarf writers plunder and pillage are almost always online. Flarf writers appropriate these texts using algorithms, cut-and-paste, Google searches, and spam filters, among other internet-based technology. Furthermore, the sensibility of Flarf stems from a peculiar brand of early 2000s' internet-based humor. Gary Sullivan (2011: n.p.) defines Flarf as a kind of "corrosive, cute, or cloying awfulness. Wrong. Un-P.C. Out of control. 'Not okay.'" As a verb, Sullivan says, "to flarf" means "to bring out the inherent awfulness, etc., of some pre-existing text." Michael Magee (n.d.: n.p.) quotes K. Silem Mohammad as saying that Flarf started:

> When Gary Sullivan submitted a deliberately bad poem to Poetry.com, one of those vanity companies that lures the unsuspecting with lavish praise of their poetry and then

offers to "publish" it for an exorbitant fee. Theorizing that no submission, no matter how heinous, would ever be treated with anything other than solicitous fawning, he sent in a poem.

The poem was littered with non sequiturs, nonsense, and jejune phrases lifted from memes, chat boards, spam ads, and the dark web. An example of a few lines gives the general idea:

Yeah, mm-hmm, it's true
big birds make
big doo! I got fire inside
my "huppa"-chimp(TM)

Flarf ironically embraced the vulgarity of internet-based speech communities, including blogs, bots, and clickbait. It regurgitated—with amused ironic flamboyance—the vomit of the internet.

By 2004, however, a Flarf poem, "Mars Needs Terrorists," was selected for that year's *Best American Poetry*. Unicorns farting rainbows became an iconic symbol, used on a special issue of *Poetry Magazine* devoted to the movement in 2009. Flarf had gained legitimacy. Flarf "poems" often both parody internet sources while also indulging in a campy weirdness and immature sarcasm. Flarf indulges in an aesthetics of inspissated excess; they posit the cyborg, too, as a grotesque body. Many Flarf works such as Alissa Quarts's *Monetized*, Nada Gordon's *Vile Lilt*, Katie Degentesh's *The Anger Scale*, and K. Lorraine Graham's *The Rest is Censored* have a decidedly political consciousness and are critical of the capitalist exploitation that proliferates at warp-speed online; others exist mostly for humor or a prankish pot-stirring of pop culture's bad taste.

Although Flarf is decidedly of its time, Ted Berrigan's ersatz *Sonnets* and, long before them, Pope's *Dunciad* and essay *Peri Bathous* might be considered the locus classicus of the movement. Much like Flarf, Pope evinces an anxiety about the flood of bad writing drowning out good work, satirically championing intentional bathos and offering recipes for the mechanical reproduction of poems. The publication of the *Flarf Anthology* in 2017 simultaneously marked the collective's apogee as well as its death knell. Inevitably, some Flarf poets grew up into more serious, "respectable" writers—Jordan Davis became poetry editor of the *Nation*; Anne Boyer won the Pulitzer Prize for general nonfiction. Today, the zeitgeist has changed. The ubiquity of internet trollishness has made the in-joke of Flarf definitively old hat.

IX. Erasures and Palimpsests

The technique of erasure as we know it today involves covering up or erasing a source text to produce—or reveal, as it were—a new text from the old, expurgating extraneous material much like a sculptor chisels a work from raw marble. The first such erasure was Tom Phillips's *A Humument: A Treated Victorian Novel*, which began "around noon on the 5th of November in 1966" when he chanced upon W. H. Mallock's *A Human Document* at a discount store, started doodling on its pages, and never looked back. The project continued until his recent passing in 2022. Though Phillips completed "treating" the pages of that first copy by 1973, he later bought several more copies of Mallock's novel to rework, constantly "mining and undermining" this singular text with painting, collages, and cutups. It has recently taken on a new incarnation as an iPhone app. Phillips somehow manages to carve out a novel within the novel. Phillips expurgates the Victorian novel with his drawings and erasures as an inversion of Victorian bowdlerization. Rather than cutting out the sexual or untoward innuendo, he's more interested in cutting up—clowning around, playfully extracting more subtext, abrading his source into pure adumbration. Proceeding by snippets and jump cuts, the reader can discern the story of Bill Toge, a nebbishy Everyman doleful with artful pretensions, erotic escapades, and a generalized failure of meaning. Jeannie Vanasco (2012: n.p.) states, "Phillips began by crossing out unwanted words with pen and ink. Then he turned to painting, typing, and collaging over words (he decided no material extraneous to the novel could be used, so all collage fragments came from other pages of the book). The resulting work explodes with colors and shapes." Phillips's visual collage of merging blobs and wobbling imagery to cover up the source text has had an enduring legacy.

Later writers have employed a wide variety of ways to erase their source texts. The published version of Ronald Johnson's ([1977] 2005) *RADI OS* uses blank space to represent the vanished source text, a more common format of erasures. Johnson's erasure resembles Charles Olson's projective verse in how its lines crackle with electric leaps relaying across the blank chasms. Mary Ruefle's (2006) book *A Little White Shadow* reproduces a facsimile of the whiteout smudges she splotched across the paper. Her whiteouts have a translucency, a blur. They produce a lacey striptease of alluring veils, a fog-like depth of things both obscured and exposed. Meanwhile, erasures such as Travis MacDonald's *The O Mission Repo*, Austin Kleon's *Newspaper Blackout*, and Philip Metres's *Abu Ghraib Arias* foreground their own redactions— as if doctoring and censoring evidence—by presenting the heavy cross-outs or deletions typical of classified materials. Their visual presentation hints of state secrets, conspiracies, the violent cutting necessary to piece together any history. *Nets* by Jen Bervin keeps the original text in a light grayscale while the erasure is highlighted through a bolded font, allowing the reader to discern her emendations on Shakespeare's *Sonnets*. Some erasures such as Matthea Harvey's *Of Lamb* or Srikanth Reddy's *Voyager* have little evidence on the page of any expunged material, relegating the fact of what they effaced to footnotes or commentary. Jonathan Safran Foer's *Tree of Codes* is unique in that the pages of the book are a filigree, scissored-out absence where the text has been disappeared. Sonja Johanson's erasures use natural objects such as flower petals and pressed leaves to hide the source text, highlighting "a way of celebrating and mourning our current ecological state" (2018: n.p.).

Likewise, the rationale for choosing the source text varies widely. Some, like Phillips, whimsically select a musty leather-bound tome from a secondhand shop. Others wrestle with their source, excavating the buried meanings that live below its surface. Chase Berggrun's *R E D*, for example, "undresses" the narrative of *Dracula* to pose questions about gender, power dynamics, transition, and monstrosity, revealing the bones beneath. NourbeSe Philip's *Zong!* scrubs the legal documents of *Gregson v. Gilbert*, a case about 150 Africans who were thrown overboard by the captain of a slave ship. Through erasure techniques she fragments *and* recovers the story of the slaves that had been subjected to obliteration by institutions of power. Yet, many erasures are based on texts that their authors venerate. The urge to scour and efface is not so different from love, for love often makes an object over into its own image. Thomas Jefferson took a razor to several copies of the Bible and pasted a new version back together.

The so-called Jefferson Bible removes the more miraculous occurrences and combines the Gospels into a single story, presenting a narrative more in accord with Jefferson's deistic faith and Enlightenment rationality. Around the same time, celebrated actor and theater manager David Garrick snipped away at Shakespeare's plays to create his own version of the scripts, often playing the lead himself. Despite his profuse emendations, however, Garrick founded the "cult" known as Bardology, elevating Shakespeare's works to a sacred status over the plays of his illustrious contemporaries.

Besides erasures proper, there are also texts that merely appear to have been erased—a simulacrum of erasure with no source. Armand Schwerner's late Modernist epic *The Tablets*, for instance, offers original poetry in the guise of a translation from Sumerian-Akkadian tablets, including lacunae, missing texts, variant readings, and untranslatable passages. The fictional erasure functions as a means of reifying the historicity of the text, demonstrating that reading itself is an act of recovery and provisional translation, bridging gaps between syntax as well as cultures. Similarly, Jenny Boully's *The Body* would seem to be a sequence of footnotes commenting on a missing text. Nothing at all remains of the body of the text, and the empty signified can only be retrospectively inferred from what is written around it and about it. Language constructs the body; the body (de)constructs language.

Friedrich Schlegel (Firchow 1998: 21) once declared, "Many of the works of the ancients have become fragments. Many modern works are fragments as soon as they are written." If the past becomes erased, modern texts hope to endure long enough to become the past. But to endure, paradoxically, is also to be rubbed out. Many early Gothic and Romantic era works such as *The Man of Feeling* and *Melmoth the Wanderer* play with the idea of mottled, moldered, marked-up, or misplaced manuscripts. Similarly, James MacPherson's Ossian poems and Thomas Chatterton's Rowley poems both purported to be translations of antique fragments rescued from the rubbish heap, yet both were hoaxes written by their proto-Romantic charlatans. Hugh Kenner in *The Counterfeiters*, speaking of the long epoch spanning from Swift to Beckett, writes that "we are deep these days in the counterfeit and have long since had to forego easy criteria for what is 'real'" (1968: 20). Perhaps history places all texts "under erasure," a strange admixture of what is shown and hidden, absent and present, authentic and imposture.

While erasures evacuate material from existing source texts, palimpsests layer and superimpose one text on top of another. Originally, palimpsests occurred in ancient Greek, Roman, and Renaissance literature because the material of writing was expensive (papyrus, vellum, or wax-coated tablets); to conserve resources, a page would be half scraped away and new writing would be written on top of it; or an inferior script would go in one direction while a superior script was superimposed in the other direction. There are several texts that only survive because they were not-quite-erased. In painting, there's a similar phenomenon known as pentimenti, the discernable trace of previous paintings underneath the image on the canvas. Thomas De Quincey, the Romantic-era essayist, likens the palimpsest to the tenuous fabric of memory itself:

> What else than a natural and mighty palimpsest is the human brain? Such a palimpsest is my brain; such a palimpsest, oh reader! is yours. Everlasting layers of ideas, images, feelings, have fallen upon your brain softly as light. Each succession has seemed to bury all that went before. And yet, in reality, not one has been extinguished. And if, in the

vellum palimpsest, lying amongst the other *diplomata* of human archives or libraries, there is anything fantastic or which moves to laughter, as oftentimes there is in the grotesque collisions of those successive themes, having no natural connection, which by pure accident have consecutively occupied the roll. (1873: 18)

De Quincey's notion that the mind is a palimpsest anticipates Sigmund Freud, who saw the archeological palimpsest that is Rome—where modern buildings are built on, over, and into ruins from various eras—as a model for the psyche. Palimpsests are an emblem, then, of textual and memorial association, at once annulling and amplifying the meanings of their texts that eclipse and enfold one another.

Most contemporary palimpsests work in terms of intertextuality—the relations between two texts juxtaposed and athwart each other, as their densities and overlaps challenge and change each other's legibility or significations. Often the palimpsest is used as a visual emblem of textual erasure and presence, invoking the need for both writing over and understanding: these two acts may interfere with one other—because one must efface the old text to inscribe a new one. One line replaces another, but not quite. The consideration of any script becomes clouded and whelmed with variants or influences. Yet the trace of the old text remains and conditions the way the new text is read, creating a prismatic network of branching, scattered, conjoined, and interpenetrating linkages of meaning, none of which is fully intelligible or entirely centered, all of which are embedded in a residue of elsewhere and otherwise.

Cinema, of course, uses palimpsests frequently, not only in the experimental films by the likes of such auteurs as Dziga Vertov, Maya Daren, or Kenneth Anger, but whenever a scene uses a dissolve transition. Architectural palimpsests frequently occur whenever there are additions or renovations on existing structures. Frankly, though, palimpsests are more gestured toward as theory than embodied in practice when it comes to contemporary creative writing. Nonetheless, there are some compelling examples of the form. Harmony Holiday's (2017) *Hollywood Forever* consistently utilizes palimpsests on every page, layering both visual and alphabetic texts. Historical photographs, cigarette ads, diagrams of musical instruments, movie stills, Civil Rights-era speeches, news footage, and album covers overlap with poems, prose meditations, and screen-captured comment threads. The book vibrates with intersecting vectors, reproducing the vertigo of diving ever deeper into the secret archives of the popular imaginary. And like most archives, the script exists in varying degrees of legibility, always pointing toward and yet obscured by other texts. Ben and Sandra Doller's (2014) *Sonneteers*, available at the *Eclipse* archive online, also employs a collage-like mix of verbal and visual elements superimposed upon each other throughout. Smudges, scribbles, doodles, drips, crossword puzzles, *New Yorker* poems, maps, mad libs, and marginalia commingle with the jazzy scat of spastic sonnets splattered by a broken typewriter. The effect deconstructs the Renaissance sonnet sequence, that mannered and courtly subgenre, with the madcap claptrap of a latter-day Dada acid trip. Eduardo C. Corral's (2020) *Guillotine* contains several script-based palimpsests, representing the ways that desert space is cut across with overlapping cultures, borders, and traces of survival. Similarly, Jake Skeets's *Eyes Bottle Dark with a Mouthful of Flowers* contains a palimpsest, "The Indian Capital of the World" where the words "a man found dead in the fields" (2019: 67) repeats until it blurs, again representing a desert space in which repeated violence has been enacted until, traumatized, one becomes almost numb to it. Palimpsests are emerging as a technique and form, not just a concept, to be harnessed by new writers.

Discussion Questions

1. Is all translation experimental? Contrariwise, what do you think the limits of "experimental" translation are? At what point is it no longer a "translation"? For example, Daniel Ladinsky wrote a bestselling book of poetry (*The Gift*) that he attributed to the twelfth-century Persian poet Hafiz. However, he claims that Hafiz visited him in a dream and dictated the poems to him in English—Ladinsky doesn't know Persian, and the poems do not even derive from any poems Hafiz wrote. Is Ladinsky practicing "creative" translation or is he guilty of cultural appropriation and misleading the public? How much fidelity should a translator have to the original text, and what does the notion of "fidelity" in translation mean?

2. Do you think that détournement is politically subversive and can act as a critique of capitalism as well as other institutions, norms, and authorities? Or has the practice itself been thoroughly commercialized, co-opted by fashion, and rendered outmoded or moot in terms of its political effectiveness or experimental transgression? How much does capitalism have the power to reincorporate "cultural jamming" back into its own predatory cycle of consumption (after all, one must recognize the Nike swoosh or McDonald's arch for the détournement to work)? What do you think of the adage that even bad publicity is still publicity?

3. Do you think that creative writers should cite their sources much the same way as academics? How might literary texts cite, allude to, or conceal their source material? Why might creative writers resist the traditional "works cited" page or bibliography? What artistic motivation might they have in doing so? Is there a danger of plagiarism? When do you think that writers have a responsibility to acknowledge their sources? For example, does a found text need to acknowledge its source material; how about a cento? How so? Or why not?

4. How might retelling or redaction of source material relate to the debates about cultural appropriation? Is cultural appropriation ok when the power dynamic involves the author "punching up" to a more privileged or powerful group or culture? What do you think of the quip "stay in your lane" regarding cultural appropriation? When does appropriation misrepresent a group of people or their culture? On what occasions or contexts is creative repurposing cultural appropriation, and in what occasions or contexts is it a legitimate literary technique or strategy: what, who, when, where, and how is power operating when it's used? How might anarchists and those in the "open source" movement who want to make all texts part of the public domain and free to use by everyone conflict with those who feel strongly that cultural practices, traditional stories, and Indigenous knowledge should be restricted and regarded as the (stolen) property of a specific cultural group? What is your notion of ownership and copyright?

5. Is curating a creative act—one that transforms the meaning and value of texts by their cultural transmission, dissemination, and change of context? Might "curation" (whether through anthologizing and archiving, on the one hand, or on social media,

on the other) be considered a form of creative writing or, alternatively, replace the act of producing "original" creative work since there's an unmanageable glut of creative writing already available? To what degree do you think Flarf, found texts, erasures, centos, and similar forms are examples of ways to "curate" and "reframe" existing works? What special value do we place on "creative" work versus "uncreative" work, and how do we distinguish between them, anyway?

6. What do you think that readymades and found texts reveal about the way meanings operate? How do different contexts, framings, and performances of a text potentially inflect or alter its significance? Do you agree with the philosopher Jacques Derrida that paratexts—that is, the front matter, introductions, commentary, indexes, prefaces, afterwords, and other such paraphernalia surrounding the body—become part of the text itself? Is it possible to draw a tidy distinction between the text and its context? Does the context adhere to the text in some way? Or, alternatively, does the text float free of its context, becoming subject to radical changes in meanings depending on how, where, and by whom it's used, interpreted, performed, or reproduced?

7. How much do you think most creative works are based on the styles, conventions, and models of previous texts, whether consciously or subconsciously? Is most literature not, in fact, a variation of "creative repurposing"? For that matter, why do people often disparage imitation and praise originality? What does "originality" even refer to: being first, unique, innovative, going beyond conventions, standing out, being generative of other work, or something else? What might the use of imitation be in creative writing—and what works or models should be imitated? Is it possible to know when a work is being imitated or redacted in the spirit of critique and when it is redacted in a spirit of homage; is there not always some level of ambivalence?

Writing Prompts

1. Choose a well-known narrative that you are familiar with, such as a fairy tale, a popular movie, a Shakespeare play, or a classic story. Review or reread the narrative (in some cases, it may exist in more than one version). What do you find problematic about the narrative? For example, are there assumptions about gender, sexuality, race, colonialism, class, or disability encoded into the story in ways that feel retrograde or intolerant? Retell the narrative in your own words, taking liberties to update the language, setting, and characters but keeping most of the essential plot points in place. Also, write an intervention into your updated version of the narrative that corrects for or pushes back against the narrative's problematic issue. That might mean retelling the narrative from a minor, auxiliary character's perspective; altering the story to challenge its colonialist premises and power structures; foregrounding the character who has disabilities; changing the gender or sexuality of some characters; or flipping the script of the ending so that gaining wealth and upward mobility are not idealized in the conclusion. Think about what elements of the narrative you want to keep and which you need to change. How does the retelling you created work as its

own story and how does it also function as an interpretive critique of the more well-known version of the narrative?

2. Here are two quick experimental translation prompts: (1) pick a poem or short text in a language you don't know and try to translate it based only on transliterating the sounds of the words. For example, the German word "Liebe" (lee-buh), meaning love, might be transliterated as the sign of the zodiac, "libra"; (2) write a few sentences, whether humdrum prose or whizbang poetry, sprinkling in a couple idiomatic expressions. Then process them through Google translate in a feedback loop: take the new text that Google spits out and plug it in to be converted to a different language yet again, continuing for at least ten iterations before you translate the text back into English (or whatever home language you started with).

3. Write a piece that uses a co-opted form: the form of the piece should follow the template of some nonliterary (often bureaucratic) document, but used in a more imaginative, narrative, playful, lyrical, or fantastic way. For example, you could write a poem or story that is in the form of an obituary, an instruction manual, an index, a fieldtrip permission slip, a diagram, a table of contents, or a weather forecast. Other possibilities are the forms of a series of errata slips, a recipe, an encyclopedia entry, a transcription of a phone call to a help line, a magic spell, a motivational poster, a policy manual for trainees at a correctional institution, a resume, status updates, a mission statement, a clinical evaluation, a syllabus, an insurance company checklist, a form letter, a movie review, questions for a therapeutic consultation, an architectural proposal, a suicide note, a grant application, a coroner's report, an FBI most-wanted list, a corporate quality inspection sheet, or a lab report. There are lots of possibilities. The key to writing in a co-opted form is to ostensibly obey the generic conventions of the form while appropriating the form against its normal use, often taking it in a more absurd or poetic direction. Try not to use forms that are already primarily literary—hence, no sonnets, villanelles, memoirs, interviews, travelogues, and so on. Forms that you are familiar with, that are written down, and whose templates are routinized to the point of being cliché—filled with buzzwords and set phraseology—tend to work best.

4. Go to a used bookstore and buy a cheap vintage book with pale, even brittle, pages. Bonus points if you can find a book whose central themes, motifs, symbols, actions, settings, and/or archetypes are of personal interest to you.

    i. *Cut up*. Use scissors to snip out resonant words, verbal phrases, and sentiments. Aim to have 100 cuttings. Swipe them all into a bag and shake the bag up. Remove the snippets and arrange them onto a page, gluing the selected words on a blank page.

    ii. *Erasure*. Use a permanent marker to strike through words, phrases, sentences, even whole paragraphs. While you will be eliminating most of the words on any given page, you will also be retaining some. Before striking through, you may want to keep track of the possible words and phrases you'll retain on a blank piece of paper. While you are beholden to the order of the words you keep, you will inevitably discover a new voice and syntax in the process. Collectively, the words you retain will be an erasure from the source text. Consider how you want to represent your erasure—for example, will you type it out afresh, color and doodle over the erased text, or take photos of the mangled and blotted book?

5. Collect as many odd, goofy, trite, clumsy, corny, awkward, gawky, and untoward phrases and sentences you can find from the internet—looking in spaces such as Spam folders, comment sections, clickbait ads, Reddit forums, and message boards. Assemble these tidbits into a work of Flarf that parodies the trollish, conspiratorial, capitalistic, or vulgar nature of the internet's bottom-feeders. Try to connect the sentences so they have some semblance of surface coherence. Throwing in an occasional disjunctive leap or loopy jinx can also be fun. Next, select favorite lines from various poems, both classical and contemporary. Rearrange these lines into a short cento. Again, strive for some semblance of coherence where possible, but allowing room for surprising jumps, non sequiturs, or associations to arise. Then, take your cento and your Flarf piece and remix the two together, juxtaposing the different registers and references to create an entirely new work that revels in the frisson it produces between high and low, polished and putrid discourse, whether the result ends up being a parodic farce or a fierce new poem.

6. Find a short video clip on YouTube or a similar site: late-night infomercials, low-budget ads, older public service messages, iconic scenes from famous movies, or dramatic moments from reality TV are all ripe for use as source texts. In an act of détournement, write new dialogue and sound effects for the clip. If you have the technology, you can mute the video and record a soundtrack with the new dialogue you developed, timing it to sync with the images. Perhaps ask a friend or two to take parts as voice actors with you. Your new dialogue and sound effects should deviate widely from the actual dialogue: you might include in-jokes, self-referential commentary, absurd conversations, over-the-top soliloquies, lines that make the subtext explicit, critical repartee, wacky solecisms, or deadpan humor. However, try to make the dialogue match the situation—and especially the reaction shots—to some degree so that the new soundtrack tells a radically different story based on the images, one that might unravel the video's intended ideology.

CHAPTER 4
HANDICRAFTING AND TEXTUAL MATERIALS

I. Introduction

With so much writing moving to online and digital formats, as if evaporated into electrons and ether, there has been a recent countermovement to embrace the physical aspects of writing. Visual culture has experienced tremendous growth in the twenty-first century, especially with children's books, comics, graphic novels, manga, and other types of "novelty" books. Today, these forms are no longer considered for children or as novelties. With this trend, the book as tactile object has been emphasized, despite (or because of) the increase in digital media. Today, experimental writers are helping us reimagine books, material objects, and embodied spaces. Literary artists have given renewed attention to the tangible qualities of textual objects and how readers might manipulate an object in the real world; the tactile aspects of writing are foregrounded in several overlapping trends in today's experimental literary communities. Reading is increasingly viewed as a "performance" that manipulates and interacts with a physical text; we might say that the form of a text is simply the way that it performs. New textual materials engage audiences in multimodal formats, new learning processes, and various media—which, in turn, have repercussions for the making, distribution, and consumption of texts as well as what constitutes our definition of "writing" itself.

Material approaches to writing turn literature "inside out" as they change the mode of engagement for both writers and readers. Reading can become ambient, tactile, visual, public, conceptual, or process-oriented, for example, rather than focused, cerebral, auditory, private, narrative, or goal-directed. If form is important to shaping and signifying content, then this form should extend to the form and shape of textual objects. Likewise, methods of production and how the object "performs" with its users (and the opportunities the text-object affords between users) are important for constructing social meanings. Applying a "design" paradigm to the literary arts places more emphasis on the material object and how it interfaces with readers. Looked at this way, the "same" words might function quite differently when printed online or as a broadside, a chapbook, a full-length collection, public art, textile work, computer code, coded into DNA, or in some other format.

In some cases, material-centric text objects blur the boundaries between producers and audiences, too. Content creators are not always distinguished from consumers: collaborations, crowdsourcing, and exchanges are more common. Maker culture centers solidarity, organic grassroots methods for not only making *things* but also, more importantly, making *community*. The interdisciplinary skills necessary for the crafting of textual objects require that expertise and technology be shared and exchanged, often by means outside traditional publishing institutions, corporate services, and educational systems. Ideally, communities of makers can organize to take back power, and small-batch collaborative production is a means of political "direct action." In doing so, do-it-yourself (DIY) maker culture is a form of community engagement and, as such, exercises different aesthetic ideas about literary standards, purposes, and content. In short, text objects require us to reenvision what literature means to us and why. Creating objects—and not just words—literalizes the ethos of artisanal labor and craft that is implicit in much creative writing discourse. While many lament that we are experiencing the demise of literary culture, inhabiting a post-book era, perhaps this is also a time of renewed interest in books as objects and a reinvention of textual materials which aids in discovering exciting new modes of reading that go well beyond the hidebound idea of a codex.

II. Chapbooks, Zines, and Broadsides

While the bulk of readers are familiar with books and literary journals, a wide range of experimental literature is found in chapbooks, zines, and broadsides. The unique history and function of these smaller and sometimes more transient formats is linked with the way that they have been materially embodied, assembled, and distributed. Chapbooks, often referred to as pamphlets in Great Britain, are small books (approximately ten to fifty pages) that are often literary in nature—for example, they could be a small collection of poems, a long short story, or a series of linked flash essays. They tend to be made by small presses with more limited distribution. Zines (the term is derived from "fanzine" and pronounced *zeen* as in magazine) is a self-published, noncommercial print work that is typically produced in limited batches. Zines are created and bound in many ways, but usually they are easily reproduced—often by crafting an original "master flat," and then mimeographing or photocopying, folding, and stapling the pages into simple pamphlets. Zines may also be folded from a single page, sewn, taped, glued—or exist in unbound and other non-folio formats. Broadsides are single page prints of texts commonly accompanied with artwork. Broadsides typically have limited runs and a handmade quality to the paper; use formats such as letterpress, lithographic, or silkscreen printing; and emphasize the overall craftsmanship of the physical object for the purpose of aesthetic display.

Chapbooks have been particularly relevant to poets, hybrid authors, flash fiction writers, and experimentalists who tend to work in shorter forms. A chapbook can take a variety of formats—from folded photocopied papers that are stapled together to hand-sewn binding to Japanese accordion binding to perfect-bound books run off industrial printers. Other chapbooks can take even more adventurous, nontraditional shapes, frequently with an emphasis on their handmade, tactile, and visual qualities. The smaller, more ad hoc format allows a collection of work to be showcased in a medium other than a full-length manuscript. Since chapbooks are shorter and lower-cost and have smaller print runs, the format permits greater experimentation without the same expectations foisted on full-length collections produced by bigger publishers. They also allow writers to try out a project without committing to the scale of a book-length work, thus encouraging risk-taking. Likewise, as chapbooks are often purchased directly from an author or small press, there is more opportunity to create a sense of community through their distribution networks. Kyle Waugh (n.d.), a scholar who curated an exhibition of chapbooks at Poet's House in New York City, states that although "chap" is related to "cheap," "most agree 'chapbook' is specifically derived from 'chapman,' the itinerant merchant who peddled like items across Europe, Britain, and North America" from the sixteenth through the mid-nineteenth centuries, a trade that "was not without its mischief and modest larceny." Something of that same spirit informs the chapbook today as they operate as a marginal, slightly mischievous, low-stakes space for literary innovation.

The format of zines, while similar to chapbooks in many ways, are shorter and even cheaper to reproduce. They are often hand-drawn, then photocopied or mimeographed, and stapled. A high-end, expensive zine from a big company might appear a contradiction in terms. Nonetheless, the indie movie studio A24 produces zines for each of their movie releases and Kanye West's zine *YEEZY* with four-color fashion photos costs 60 euros. Most zines, though, don't cost anything or their cost is minimal since they function primarily to initiate community with others rather than for commercial purposes. Their subject matter tends to be less "literary" in nature, focusing on personal topics, fandoms, or political activism, for example, using a simple, demotic idiom along with collage, cartoons, or diagrams. Zine-makers will often create and share zines at meetups, punk shows, zine fests, and community spaces.

Zines were originally popular in the 1970s through 1990s. Recently, they have experienced a rebirth due to their retro aesthetic and the handcrafted artisanal process of making them, especially among the overlapping feminist, queer, punk, DIY, and activist communities. The Bindery's (n.d.) website notes that "zinesters" are often motivated by artistic passion, self-expression, and political goals instead of profit; and that a zine's "content may be written, drawn, printed, collaged, or any other form of combining words and imagery—a zine's structure may be narrative, journalistic, comic-like, or completely abstract." Zines are decidedly an amateur—and amatory—undertaking, done for love, community, and self-care. The anti-corporate, low-fi aesthetic and materiality of zines indicate a craving for crafting and physicality, as opposed to internet sites where similar information might be exchanged; the zine's physical, no-frills embodiment means that "zinesters" must be present to make and share their objects, aiding in a sense of solidarity that the isolation of the web does not afford. Indeed, "DIY" is a misnomer since zines (and "maker" culture generally) are not done alone, but in collectives and communities with a social-justice-minded orientation. In these settings, makers and consumers are often the same.

Broadsides emphasize the materiality—the thinginess—of the text. Letterpress and fine-print, limited-edition broadsides are works of trained artisanal labor, neither mass produced nor one-of-a-kind items. The thick, high-quality paper is tactile; broadsides are often framed and used for décor or display purposes. A text on a broadside, then, might become part of one's everyday life, hanging next to a breakfast nook or opposite one's desk in a personal office. Whereas a zine contains deliberately ephemeral fan information about a punk band or other pop culture phenomena, for instance, the text of a broadside is designed to be more enduring, rewarding rereading and meditation. Also, broadsides commonly pair an image with a short text, so that the alphabetic text is informed by the broadside's visual design and vice versa. Chapbooks, zines, and broadsides thus encourage different approaches to reading practices, production, and distribution; furthermore, their material forms implicitly encode considerations of content, afford distinct roles for how the text serves its community, and ultimately underscore the political and aesthetic ideals that writing hopes to achieve, all of which are in contradistinction to the modes of commercial (and even sometimes small press) book publishing.

III. DIY, Self-Publishing, and Design Thinking

DIY culture can be traced back to Joseph Moxon's book *Mechanick Exercises* of 1683, which included how-to lessons on wood joinery, blacksmithing, book printing, and other tasks.

Another aspect of DIY history derives from nineteenth-century thinkers such as Charles Fourier and Karl Marx, both of whom were concerned with craft laborers creating work themselves, often within small communities, where tasks would not be automated and broken up into parts as on an assembly line. Work was to be creative and empowering, rather than a rote, impersonal activity that alienated labor from its product and profit. These ideas blossomed in England during the Arts and Craft Movement with its anti-industrial attitude and valorization of handcrafted designs of everything from furniture to books to wallpaper. Later, this spirit enthused the Bauhaus in Weimar Germany, which was a collectivist workshop of arts and crafts (including a "Department of Fun" that threw parties). Many of the Bauhaus artists came to America during the Second World War, where some started Black Mountain College, a short-lived school focusing on interdisciplinary, holistic "making" across many disciplines. Economic scarcity during the Great Depression and rationing during the Second World War promoted DIY culture, too, as did magazines such as *Popular Mechanics* and *Whole Earth Catalog*. Undoubtedly, though, the punk scene of the seventies with its refusal to buy in to the corporate lifestyle had a powerful impact on DIY subculture, flaunting clothes and other items with a ragtag homemade look and salvaged or secondhand goods. The degraded, safety-pinned quality of goods was viewed as an anti-capitalist statement.

Today's DIY scene spans everything from social activism, hackers, gearheads who create their own bikes, the Free Skool movement, home improvement enthusiasts, co-op sheds, independent filmmaking, fanzines, punk rockers, pirate radio, environmental collectivism efforts, crowdsourcing archival documents, YouTube makeup tutorialists, and more. By democratizing the ability to use an array of tools, from 3D printers to wrenches, maker subculture hopes to form a less alienated polity in which people can be inspired by grassroots and direct action for social change, creating alternative networks through which skills and ideas can be spread person-to-person outside official institutional channels. Literary arts are only one aspect of the burgeoning DIY "maker" subculture. DIY ways of crafting textual objects require that expertise and technology be shared and exchanged, often by means outside traditional publishing institutions, corporate services, and educational systems. The small-batch, local, DIY creation and distribution of literary objects thus does an end-run around the big, impersonal publishing institutions.

While the DIY scene promotes small-batch, handmade production of zines and chapbooks (especially with recycled or upcycled materials), the current idea of "self-publishing" goes far beyond the DIY scene. Digital platforms such as CreateSpace, Kindle Direct, and iBooks (as well as print-on-demand devices such as the Espresso Book Machine) enable writers to create their own books that have a similar physical or digital quality as books produced by small press and commercial publishing houses—*if* authors take the time to edit and design their work to professional standards, a big *if*. Social media and other online forums likewise now allow an author to promote and market self-published books in ways commensurate with small press or commercial publishing. In fact, many presses both small and large expect their authors to push their books through social media anyway as self-promotion has become almost de rigueur. Critic Mark McGurl notes:

> And yet the boundary between "direct" publishing, as Amazon euphemistically calls it, and being published by others has always been blurry in the literary avant-garde, whose market is often not large enough to sustain the kind of impersonal relations we think

of as underlying the feat of "getting published." Avant-gardes are among other things groups of acquaintances, friends, and lovers who publish each other and themselves. (2017: n.p.)

Self-publishing and getting picked up by a small, experimental press is a difference, relatively speaking, that matters little. So, too, a gray area between self-publishing and publishing with a traditional press has emerged known as "hybrid" publishing in which the revenue model of the press differs from traditional imprints: this could mean charging authors fees, requiring preorders, or crowdfunding to subsidize publishing costs. Hybrid publishing differs from self-publishing or vanity presses, though, because there is a selective process for submissions, authors often receive a higher percentage of royalties, and the imprint assumes a greater role in editing, designing, marketing, and distributing the book. There is a wide range of publishing options today; self-publishing and hybrid publishing might avoid many of the institutional gatekeepers associated with traditional publishing, but they also give up the prestige lent by the press's imprimatur along with the greater resources more established presses have for copyediting, production, and sales. Then again, many experimentally inclined small presses are essentially run by a couple of editors and do not have an abundance of resources. Navigating publishing options requires thinking about one's goals and expectations for publishing any manuscript.

Another trend in the twenty-first century has been the emergence of design thinking. In short, design thinking is a way to reimagine and innovate in any field by considering the affordances that an object, environment, or experience offers its users. Often, this process is twofold: examining the "human factors" that constrain the interaction users typically have with an object (or experience) and more clearly defining one's goals in creating the object. Design thinking proceeds through ideation, building prototypes, testing, and refinement. The prominence of the design paradigm has led to the reconfiguration of many objects from chairs to videogame controllers. Design thinking can also reconfigure the conventional format of a book, even beyond graphic design aspects like layout and font.

For example, Michael Youngblood and Benjamin J. Chesluk's (2020) *Rethinking Users*, a book that examines different user archetypes in design thinking—and how users operate within historically situated practices, cultures, and ecosystems—comes with a deck of cards that help readers apply its ideas to their own situation. While the discourse of most design thinking takes place within an entrepreneurial framework, that does not mean design thinking is inherently capitalist. Constructing a chapbook in the form of a tabletop diorama or printing a 3D model of The Cyborg Jillian Weise's braille poem "Future Biometrics" are ways that dovetail the ethos of maker culture with design thinking. As other examples later make clear, noncorporate literary artists have redesigned the process of reading for new purposes, audiences, or experiences with materials that move far beyond the traditional book.

IV. Artist's Books and Book Arts

Two increasingly related traditions that focus on crafting literary objects are known as artist's books and book arts. An artist's book is a medium of artistic expression that uses the structure or function of the "book" as inspiration—a work of art in (more or less) book form. Although artists have illustrated the words of others for centuries, the book as art object is relatively recent, an outgrowth of Modernism. Artist's books are oftentimes one-of-a-kind items. They may or may not contain alphabetic texts. For example, some artist's books are repurposed books that have been modified or sculpted into an object of display. Jonathan Callan, for instance, has repurposed existing books with holes, rubber, wool, and ink to craft sculptural objects. Other artist's books contain unique artwork on each page that the artist created; still others, such as the *[Xerox Book]* of 1968 (Siegelaub et al.) act as a de facto exhibition space for art pieces in book form. Sometimes artist's books aren't even books at all in any conventional sense—they're a series of blocks, words suspended in Lucite, scrolls, accordions, a foldout map, a wormholed codex, a honeycombed apartment complex cutout from a heavy tome, a Bible carved into the silhouette of a grenade, or a lexicon arrayed across a perforated handheld fan. Thus, artist's books refer to a wide range of objects. Often, the artists in question tend to be recognized as visual artists in other media; occasionally, they may collaborate with a poet or writer on such a work.

Book arts, on the other hand, is the field that specializes in the arts and crafts related to producing books: binding, typesetting, printing, letterpress, lithography, cover and book design, papermaking, and so on. Book arts are ancient and date back centuries. Book arts generally focus on making fine-press runs, limited editions, and collectibles, rather than mass-produced items. The works are usually readable presentations of texts, though often designed as much for display and aesthetic appeal as for rough-and-ready, day-to-day use. Nonetheless, more recent, experimental forays in book arts have had a wide intersection and overlap with artist's books: both explore the material object of the book (and related textual forms) as media of visual and cultural interest.

Writers who explore artist's books and book arts might craft small handmade objects or take workshops to learn more involved printmaking processes. The tactility of such an object— say, a ribbon-bound book on deckle-edged, hand-pressed parchment paper—brings renewed attention to the words or images in their physical placement on the page. One thinks about how the words function with the paper's shape, heft, folds, grain, and feel, giving the text a palpable haptic quality and often allowing one to reimagine the constraints of conventional reading. Harry Reese (2016: 27) writes that:

> there is a distinct pattern we can follow in human information technologies as they have evolved and developed over time: the new technology turns the old technology into an art form. In the book arts, new technologies for typography, printing, and the electronic display of images and texts have cumulatively conferred upon the hand-produced book a greater value and a higher recognition.

The practical obsolescence of bygone technologies transforms them into sites of esoteric, artisanal practice. These older methods of producing books also contain within them a corollary sense of literary imagination, too. In *The Thinking Hand*, Juhani Pallasmaa (2009: 17) theorizes that "the capacity of imagination does not hide in our brains alone, as our entire bodily constitution has its fantasies, desires and dreams." Whether one produces work with a pen or a word processor, a typewriter or a letterpress, the hand and bodily involvement in a work's creation inform the drift and the design of one's language. Writing, after all, is one of the book arts, too.

V. Textile and Fabric Arts

A different artisanal craft that has emerged recently as a space for writers is textile and fabric arts. Quilting, weaving, sewing, needlepoint, and other fiber arts have gained prominence. Textiles have long been an overlooked site for creativity—and writing—due to their association with female domestic labor and decoration. Visual artists Ann Hamilton, Magdalena Kosmowska, and Igshaan Adams have used textiles for sculpture and installations whereas others such as Rosie Lee Tomkins, Christina Forrer, and Faith Ringgold exhibit more traditional textiles such as quilts or tapestries in gallery and museum settings. This new prominence of textile arts has likewise awakened an interest in rediscovering historical textile artists such as the quilters of Gee's Bend or the weavers of Navajo rugs.

The metaphors associated with fabric—stitches, binding, weaving, spinning a yarn—point to an approach to literature that emphasizes writing as social ties, braiding memories, or patchwork assemblage. Rachel Blau DuPlessis uses a collage of textile scraps such as lace, handkerchiefs, and embroidery situated among her long serial poem *DRAFTS*. The pieces are fragmented and many-centered, as if healing the sutures between each tissue, piecing together "a counter-hierarchical structure" as Catherine Dormer (2014: 6) puts it. Contemporary Chilean writer and multimedia artist Cecilia Vicuña takes inspiration from the ancient Incan writing system of quipu, which recorded information through knots tied on strings. Vicuña's work takes many forms, everything from threading string between audience members during a performance to creating gallery exhibits that combine text and fiber arts to books that utilize fiber and string in their construction. Vicuña critic Julie Philips Brown (2011: 209) declares that "what most asserts itself about the *cloud-net* installations, performances, film, and book is a shared emphasis on sheer materiality and the tethering of bodies, texts, and materials through tactile connection." The material nature of fibers and strings, along with their cultural associations, deeply inform the poetics of writers such as DuPlessis and Vicuña.

Vicuña's poem, "Destruir el desierto," was the text basis for a fiber performance she gave at the Poetry Off the Page Symposium in Tucson in 2012. Read the poem on pp. 315–17 and then watch the performance at this URL: https://voca.arizona.edu/reading/cecilia-vicuna-may-18-2012.

Textile and fabric arts intersect with writing in a wide variety of formats. Needlepoint and stitching might be used to display writing, though experimentally inclined writers subvert the homilies and uplifting bromides that are commonplace on samplers. Some have used sewing as a medium of blackout for their erasure texts while others use *furoshiki* (the Japanese art of folding cloth) to create book covers. In *Lace Letters*, Donna Rumble-Smith creates ethereal wall hangings of letters in lace that cast shadows on the wall and artist books where the words spill out, literally hanging by a thread. Sara Impey (2020a, 2020b, 2020c) in works such as "A Post-Truth Quilt," "War of Words," and "Thrall" takes advantage of the ways that her writing interacts with the color, shape, texture, and fabric with which they are composed. Not only the physical materials, but also the placement of Barbara Kruger's (1990) machine-woven "carpet" takes on ironic meaning when the reader is walking over it since it states, "All that is beneath you is speaking to you now." Fashion items also frequently incorporate text—T-shirts, sneakers, tote bags, baseball caps. T-Post® (2020), a trendy T-shirt company, claims to be "the world's first wearable magazine," printing "issues" that each contain a story on the back. Comparably, Hot Topic partnered with Diné College during Native American Heritage Month for their "Tees That Tell Stories" campaign. Textile and fiber arts offer writers an intimate material basis for elaborating their creative texts, connecting them to communities and audiences outside mainstream literary publics.

VI. Novelties and Ephemera

The book as tactile object has been increasingly emphasized, despite (or perhaps because of) the proliferation of digital media. Even near the birth of widely available printing presses, though, eighteenth-century writers such as Swift, Walpole, Richardson, and Sterne were keen to play with features such as layout, binding, fonts, design, images, (dis)ordered pages, and orientation on the page. Back then new printing technologies were seen in both sunny and suspicious lights, just as social media and smartphones now may be disseminating texts more readily but also disrupting our conventions of reading. For many readers today, the physical process of reading books and manipulating pages goes unacknowledged. Children's picture books, however, tend to be far more tactile than adult books.

Look at an example such as *Beautiful Oops* by Barney Saltzberg (2010), which utilizes rips, spills, coffee stains, pop-ups, bends, foldouts, holes, and transparencies. The story—which ends with the admonition, "When you think you have made a [sic] oops, think of it as an opportunity to make something"—celebrates the physicality of the page. It invites readers to manipulate the paper, understanding that making a mess is necessary for any act of creation. A handful of texts marketed to adult readers, too, have used features such as pop-ups, spinners, centerfolds, scratch-n-sniff, and coloring-book pages to re-enchant the haptic (and olfactory) pleasures of reading. Coffee-table books—as objects of display—are another genre that beckons the reader's touch with physical heft, large scale, and full-color pictures. Kim Kardashian's (2015) coffee-table book *Selfish* collects digital selfies, Polaroids, and even pictures from leaked sex tapes so that Kardashian can reclaim her own image while giving credit to her stylists and makeup artists. Madonna's (1992) *Sex*, to which Kardashian's book alludes, was even more tactile in its approach: the spiral-bound, aluminum-covered book was wrapped in a Mylar sheath not unlike a condom.

While picture books for young readers and coffee-table books for adults with mature interests often highlight their material nature, so too have some works by experimental writers. The book-in-a-box format has become a veritable subgenre since Mark Saporta's *Composition No 1* in 1962. The loose pages of this format can be rearranged at the reader's whimsy, allowing multiple narrative pathways and enlisting the reader as co-constructor. Other books that have made use of the box format include B. S. Johnson's *The Unfortunates*, Robert Grenier's *Sentences*, Anne Carson's *Float*, and Ander Monson's *Letter to a Future Lover*, the last of which also includes hypertext B-sides and addenda. Similarly, Chip Kidd's design for Vladimir Nabokov's fragmentary, posthumous novel *The Original of Laura*, includes perforations so that each notecard can be removed and rearranged by the reader, a reshuffling that was a habit of Nabokov's practice of composition. Typically, innovative formats serve some ergodic function, beckoning the reader to participate more actively. Some big publishers have been skittish about risking innovative formats, though. Folds, flaps, and other window-dressing add to the cost of production. When Anne Carson wanted Japanese accordion-binding for *NOX*, her Big Five publisher at the time, Vintage (an imprint of Penguin Random House), balked, so she turned to New Directions. However, Pantheon (an imprint of Knopf Doubleday) published Mark Z. Danielewski's *House of Leaves* and *Only Revolutions*, both of which use unusual typography, layout, and formatting that require the reader to turn the book in many directions to comprehend. Similarly, Adam Thirlwell's *Kapow!*, published by Visual Editions, requires its reader to turn the book around, fold out flaps, and chase typography across the page to assemble the storylines in its head-spinning narrative about the Arab Spring (the pro-democracy protests in several Arab countries during the early 2010s). Smaller presses tend to be more welcoming of unique formats. Jonathan Safran Foer's erasure *Tree of Codes* was also published with Visual Editions, although most of his other books are published with Big Five presses. The pages of Foer's book are a delicate filigree of cutouts, a trelliswork that contains more negative space than paper. McSweeney's is another renown small press that has released many innovative formats, including issue 36, a crate in the shape of a person's head containing an assortment of user-unfriendly booklets, chapbooks, postcards, posters, and other literary ephemera.

For collectors, museum archivists, and academics, ephemera of all sorts have grown in importance. In collector culture, the internet has changed what is hard to find: first editions of rare books are relatively now easy to locate while playbills, menus, paper dolls, or calling cards are more challenging (Young 2018). In museum archives, previously overlooked items have been accorded new prestige. Curators search for items outside the established objects and art pieces when putting together shows or assembling museum collections. In academia, a greater emphasis on material culture has placed attention on recovering artifacts previously viewed as merely tchotchkes or folderol; from interpreting items such as porcelain figurines, silverware, and parasols, humanities scholars have reimagined the everyday lived experience of folks from the past. In publishing, Emily Dickinson's brief fragments and envelope poems have been accorded publication as have Robert Walser's microscript stories he wrote on tiny scraps. Such trends are recently making their way into creative writing, too. One might think of the newsprint format of magazines such as *APR* or *Threepenny Review*—or, better yet, *DIAGRAM*'s tarot deck or *Headmistress*'s lesbian poet trading cards. There's a host of narrative party games, such as "The Awkward Storyteller," as well as many board games based on classic novels. Blindman Brewing prints flash fiction from local Alberta-area authors on its coffee drinks while Delaware-based Dogfish Head beer sponsors a poetry prize for Mid-Atlantic writers.

Exemplifying this trend, *Lianna Fled the Cranberry Bog: A Story in Cootie Catchers* (2019) is an eerie tale told through twenty-six paper fortune tellers. Written by GennaRose Nethercott and illustrated by Bobby DiTrani, each cootie catcher features eight possible endings—but the endings are also beginnings, complications, transformations, jumping-off points for other parts of the tale. Two of Nethercott's cootie catchers, with folding instructions, are included on pp. 296–8.

Experimental Writing

Trinie Dalton, meanwhile, has produced several books that consists of collages and snapshots of assorted ephemera such as doodles, album covers, postcards, roadside signage, B-movie posters, and confiscated high-school notes. This focus on ephemera helps us recognize the fleeting literature all around us, whether its games on the back of cereal boxes or stories on roadmaps.

VII. Sui Generis and Offbeat Examples

Literature is found in a wide variety of formats and media, not just in books and websites. In *Poetry Unbound*, Mark Chasar (2020: 5)—looking at poetry in media such as magic lanterns, stereoview cards, airdrops, audio recordings, films, and phone messages—writes that poetry can be found on:

> Breath mint tins, trivets, table runners, stained glass windows, handkerchiefs, pillows, cross-stitchings, and wall hangings, subway and bus placards, autograph albums, playing cards, posters, calendars, stickers, event tickets, cocktail glasses, ring holders, souvenir plates, candy-bar wrappers and candy boxes, packaging for pet products, cereal boxes, milk bottles, thermometers, and any number of other "incidental" ways.

Chasar's point is that the single-author book may not be the best measure of literature's place in popular culture, especially since so much poetry (and, we would add, experimental work) is transmitted and remediated into other formats.

Ekaterina Samigulina / Tae Ateh's aemic crossword from *Post-Soviet Belarus* is a tactile exploration of the puzzle as medium. See it on p. 307.

Chasar (2020: 6) thus offers a "correction to the codex-based default settings of current poetry studies and related spheres of activity, but also argues for a comparatively expansive, even alternative history to poetry in the long twentieth century." Chasar urges us to look beyond the book when we measure poetry's impact. In this spirit, the types of material objects that have been marked by script, glyphs, or words of some sort are nearly illimitable. Look around you: words and symbols abound everywhere—chits and tags and advertisements, street signs, placards, graffiti, receipts, tattoos, lightboxes, baked goods, drinking cups, and logos. You can likely discover your own offbeat examples of objects that have been embedded or embossed with linguistic if not literary significance.

One vector we'd trace among such profusion is the way that these various formats can either monumentalize a literary work or make it seem a passing aspect of everyday life. Oftentimes, when lines of creative writing end up on sculpture or architecture, for example, the effect can be to reinforce the official canon of national cultural symbols. In fact, Russian poet Dmitrij Prigov, trained as a sculptor, believed that the poets who themselves struck a monumentalizing pose in their performances were those most likely to be celebrated with busts and statues after they passed. Consequently, Prigov delivered his poetry with elaborate rituals of performance art, against sculptural sets he designed; following after poets such as Mayakovski, his words transformed into images, but it was also the poet's visible body itself that became a key material of his art. Boris Groys writes that:

> For Prigov, the figure of the poet was much more important than his poetic production. The poetry that the poet writes is only one of the components of his poetic image. The poet is also looked at by the public—not just heard or read. He is not completely hidden by his poems but rather visible, present as a body. And his public behavior and political stance are also looked at and taken into consideration. What people see when they look at the poet also forms their perception of his writings. During his performances Prigov embodied the figure of the poet—playing it out in front of the public, while at the same time creating a certain effect of estrangement, of inner distance between this role and his own "profane," merely human mode of existence. (2017: n.p.)

In a country where so many poets receive monoliths and effigies, Prigov highlighted the contradiction between the mythic afterlife of national literary figures and the shabby, mundane reality most poets lead while they're alive.

On the other hand, not all inscriptions on architecture or literary public monuments need to observe an officious posture as sacralized memorials to dead state poets. In Tucson, the Poetry Center has an outer wall inscribed with a line—in binary code cutaways—by the poet Richard Shelton (n.d.), who was alive at the time the building was built. The line, adapted from Shelton's poem "Desert," states: "You shall learn the art of silence." A block away, at the streetcar stop, you can find Simon Donovan and Ben Olmstead's sculpture: soldered metallic letters to form a glowing, colossal head modeled on living, local poet Richard Siken. Siken's head seems to be blowing toward an LED screen where lines from poems scroll by. The Poetry Center's public art straddles a delicate line between transience and monumentality, figuring light, breath, and absence as just as central to the project of these literary place-markers as the stone, metal, or pedestals with which many writers have been acclaimed in shrines.

Sand drawing represents the other end of the spectrum, fleeting rather than monumental. Vanuatu "sandroing" (sand drawings) are geometric figures that are drawn on to the ground with the fingertips. Each design is a type of maze, which is traced as a continuous line, often without lifting the finger from the ground. This form of cultural expression is found in the central and northern islands of Vanuatu. However, many ni-Vanuatu use the Mislama term "raeting" rather than "droing" to refer to the practice because it is thought of as a form of script that predates the introduction of European education. In daily life, sandroings are used to leave messages, explain concepts, and teach children. They are often accompanied by stories or songs, and they are an important means of recording and communicating cultural practices. There are also sacred sandroing, which must be committed to memory and used as a type of password to gain access to the next life. However, whenever the tale is finished being traced, the sand is shaken and erased. The essence of sandroings is its material ephemerality, though the practice itself continues to endure as a form of traditional knowledge and mode of cultural transmission, passed from generation to generation.

Objects have meanings according to semiotic conventions and cultural sign systems that are parallel with—and sometimes in contradistinction to—their "literary" meanings. That is to say, affect and meanings extend beyond words: they attach to things and performances, too. Jewelry, furniture, basketry, shoes, eating utensils, rites, and ceremonies all contain coded forms of cultural knowledge and can communicate without necessarily using alphabetic texts. If alphabetic texts are placed on these objects or into these performances, then the significance of the words is informed by the surrounding context, iconography, and social processes of which they partake. Asemic writing, a mime show, or a wordless picture book are some examples at the edge of literature, where there is neither text nor voice.

Today, many semioticians, sociologists, and cultural theorists analyze material objects or performances—an Uncle Sam piggybank, a professional wrestling match—according to the same techniques they would use to analyze written literature. Can we turn this on its head: what if creative writers made objects, enacted theater, and engaged in everyday events in artistic ways that, as semiotics looks for meanings beyond linguistics, likewise steps beyond language in search of other signifying methods? We contend that much contemporary experimental literature is doing just that, breaking down the barriers between crafts of performance, fabricating materials, and producing alphabetic texts. Language matters, of course, but matter too has a language of its own.

The obverse side of this coin would be literature that stresses the materiality of words and letters themselves. For example, some cultures—notably, Arabic and Chinese—have strong literary traditions of calligraphy wherein the shape and design of each glyph or ideogram has become an artform in its own right. Arabic *muqatta'at* are one of five letters that decorate the beginning of the surahs in the Quran; they are large and elaborately scripted talismans or seals emphasizing the mystical qualities of the letter itself. Analogously, Chinese graphs in clerical and seal script along with Japanese kanji became valued for the brushstrokes and expressive features that could act as a medium of revelation and self-expression independent of the text that such script exemplified. Wanwei Shum, a contemporary graphic designer based in Rotterdam, combines influences from Chinese characters, Arabic script, and Latin alphanumeric texts in her typographic works, updating ancient practices with digital technology. While Shum emphasizes the global village, Diné (Navajo) poet Orlando White is more critical of the systems of colonial oppression that not only merged global cultures, but also frequently erased Indigenous ways of life in the process. White's poems in LETT*ERRS* tropes on the form of the Latin alphabet; for instance, in "Finis" he writes:

> The i with a white noose
> also around his neck,
> blindfolded, asphyxiated. (2015)

The shape of the Roman alphabet is foregrounded in its physical characteristic; since this alphabet has been transposed onto the native oral language and forced on Indigenous peoples, both in English and in Diné Bizaad, the graphic marks of these characters become sinisterly personified. White brings our attention to letters for the deeply rooted, erroneous assumptions inherent in all lettering systems, especially colonialist ones. As anthropologist Claude Lévi-Strauss (1976: 391) once proposed to his own dismay, "The primary function of written communication is to facilitate slavery." Whether or not we characterize all writing like this, we should keep in mind that writing itself is a material form involving physical tools and systems that have tangible consequences.

VIII. Gallery Settings, Museums, and Immersive Environments

Museum and gallery spaces have been increasingly welcoming of literary arts over the past few decades. Visual objects, performances, and texts likewise have been increasingly overlapping and intersecting in contemporary multimedia practices. On the one hand, postmodern visual artists—think Cy Twombly, Jean-Michel Basquiat, or Félix González-Torres—frequently use written texts in their work in the form of collage, palimpsests, or even just words imprinted on the gallery wall. On the other hand, experimental writers have been repurposing their written work for different media, whether as videos, performances, archives, exhibits, or objects. Contemporary Conceptual artist Mel Bochner, for example, has created public billboards of words that draw attention to the metaphors and cultural signification of our everyday language, such as Yiddish-borrow words or bellicose sports clichés. In a different series, *Language Is Not Transparent*, Bochner iteratively superimposes the eponymous phrase on transparency paper until the phrase blots itself out, producing a dark, indecipherable mass. Likewise, from the direction of creative writers, essayist Sarah Minor has transposed her piece "Foul Chutes: On the Archive Downriver," about the Mississippi River, into a sculpture that spirals over the viewer's head as the text cascades across its side (2018); she also took her essay "The Persistence of the Bonyleg: Annotated," a fairytale about a group of isolated Russian Orthodox Old Believers, and constructed a gingerbread-house-like inhabitation where the essay could be read on the walls (2015). Luiza Prado de Oliveira Martins (2018) meanwhile created an installation, "All Directions at Once," in which the viewer's position within the room would trigger different text to be projected from a GIF essay databank to tell a story about the entwined histories of the suppression of reproductive rights and colonialism in Brazil. The viewer's literal position in the room conditions what they perceive of the text. A different approach was taken by Don Mee Choi (2020) who staged a museum exhibit of her book *DMZ Colony* in Berlin: Choi used photos, paintings, historical documents, clothing, and other artifacts to capture the documentary poetics of her book. Similarly, Lynn Xu (2022) has reimagined her book-length poem *And Those Ashen Heaps that Cantilevered Vase of Moonlight* as a multimedia exhibit using audio, text, banners, video, lighting, and objects. The exhibition copy asserts that Xu "turns the museum into the book, and underscores how the act of reading is an intimate, time-based, and embodied experience." Whether constructing new textual objects or curating an exhibit of an existing book, creative writers have found audiences in gallery spaces and envisioned innovative ways for those audiences to engage with their materials.

Some writers have gone a step further, constructing not just discrete objects but also whole immersive environments. Nobel-Prize winner Orhan Pamuk used the proceeds from his award to inaugurate his Museum of Innocence in Istanbul, which was created as a counterpart to his novel of the same name. Pamuk's museum exhibits the faux artifacts from the daily lives of his fictional characters, such as a display of 4,213 cigarette butts that were supposedly smoked by the character Füsun. In his manifesto for museums, Pamuk (2013: n.p.) decries museums that have been designed to showcase national opulence and symbolism. "The transitions from palaces to national museums and from the epic to the novel are parallel processes," Pamuk writes, "The epic is like a palace: it speaks of the heroic gestures of the kings that inhabited them. National museums should be like novels, but this is not the case." Pamuk argues that large, state-controlled museums should not act to promote the official narratives of state authority through their grandeur and monumentality; rather, we need small museums to act as repositories of the more various, everyday stories of common individuals.

The Museum of Jurassic Technology in Los Angeles, often compared to a Renaissance cabinet of curiosity, demonstrates another way to reconceive of the museum. The museum contains a portrait gallery of Russian space dogs, a parody of the museum as site of national mythos: in place of historical "heroes," we are presented with canines posed in the same self-important manner. While some exhibits are genuine oddities—such as the microminiature sculptures—others test the viewer's credulity, such as the documents of a ghostly Amazonian bat that can pass through matter as dense as wood. Exhibits of cat's cradles and a Russian tea ceremony include live performances. Although there is no corresponding textual codex for most of the exhibits—Rikki Jay's book *Dice: Deception, Fate, and Rotten Luck* is one of the few exceptions—the museum placards, documents, online records, and artifacts themselves construct narratives on par with the work of novelists, poets, and historians. Both of these unique spaces impel us to examine the role of museums, question grand narratives, and provoke us to consider how easily we accept official-sounding accounts.

Not all immersive environments are museums. Meow Wolf, which started as a DIY artists' collective, has constructed large-scale immersive environments in cities in the Southwest. The first one, *The House of Eternal Return*, refurbished a bowling alley in Albuquerque to create a paranormal crime scene. In this piece, each audience member navigates a labyrinthine architecture room by room, trespassing into a dreamworld as one climbs through refrigerators, wanders into a fireplace, or exits from a washing machine. Documents, objects, and quotidian detritus scattered throughout the "house" hint at the strange events that vanished the absent family. "There are hundreds if not thousands of fabricated artifacts and documents," Carly Kocurek (2017) of *Paste Magazine* writes. The audience—interacting with the documents, the space, and live actors—is situated as a detective whose forensic analysis slowly reconstructs the story. In *Omega Mart*, another Meow Wolf project in Las Vegas, a haunted supermarket is the site of an immersive storytelling experience. In both pieces, space misbehaves and proves elusive due to manipulations in perspective, angle, flow, scale, and verisimilitude. The group of artists behind Meow Wolf includes writers on each project who collaborate, storyboard, sketch the backstory, write documents, or compose scripts.

Odyssey Works, another immersive art experience created by a group of collaborating interdisciplinary artists, takes a different approach. Each Odyssey Works project is created for an audience of one, who is chosen through a selective process and then subjected to an intense follow-up investigation about every aspect of their existence. The collective then organizes a tailor-made, immersive experience based on the singular anxieties, desires, and preoccupations of that audience member. The chosen audience member for one project, *When I Left the House It Was Still Dark* (2013), was novelist Rick Moody. It spanned four months, utilized dozens of collaborators and co-conspirators, and included everything from an original children's book, a cello concert in a Saskatchewan prairie, and a dance performance on the Brooklyn Bridge. Audience members often do not know where unplanned, everyday activities end, and the curated immersive experience begins; this ambiguity allows Odyssey Works' projects to be catalyst for real-life transformation. Meow Wolf and Odyssey Works are two examples of collectives that construct immersive environments where writers play a key role in organizing larger projects with tangible embodiments.

IX. New Frontiers

A few experimental writers have ventured further afield into biochemistry, physics, and material sciences to seek out ways to craft the objects of their experimental writing practices. Jen Bervin (2017), for example, worked with Fiorenzo Omenetto and his team at Tufts University's Silk Lab to create a poem (at nanoscale) that was embedded in a silk microfilm readable only through a microscope. In an interview with *Asymptote Journal*, Bervin (n.d.: n.p.) says:

> It's a love poem, written from the perspective of the silk worm (whose liquified cocoon serves as the substrate of the biosensor) to a person with a health condition pronounced enough as to require daily monitoring. Of course this is all hypothetical, subject to shifts in research, a speculative framework. There's no implanted poem yet.

While the poem was produced as a traditional book and a video, it was also displayed in a show that included both a microscope with slides and a macroscale enlargement. The project's fabrication combines an interest in ancient Chinese burial practices with cutting-edge bioengineering to produce a work that hypothetically could be implanted on the brain itself.

Similarly, Christian Bök's *The Xenotext* project attempts to alter the genetic code of a bacterium through injecting it with an encoded poem, working with a lab at the University of Calgary; in response, the bacterium will manufacture a benign protein that Bök considers the organism's own poem. This project, too, has been showcased in multiple versions: in print, video, and as a 3D chemical model. The bacterium selected was *Deinococcus radiodurans* because of its ecological viability, which can survive in extreme conditions—even the vacuum of outer space. As Bök (2011) states, "I am, in effect, engineering a life-form so that it becomes not only a durable archive for storing a poem, but also an operant machine for writing a poem—one that can persist on the planet until the sun itself explodes." Both Bervin and Bök's projects are thus concerned with the perishability of the written word, set against an implicit framework of accelerating technological obsolescence. Paper, microfiche, CD-Rom, cloud storage, and other methods of preserving digital information each give way to a newer system of preservation with increasing rapidity, ironically making any preservation more tenuous. Both Bervin and Bök evince an anxiety about the finitude of life with respect to the mortality of texts and the human species alike.

Finally, the Voyager I and II space probes contained a "Golden Record," a message for any alien being—light years away—who might discover them. In designing the record, the engineers had to contemplate not only what information to include that would represent all earth-based cultures, but also how to communicate this information in a way that would transcend the contingency of language. The Arecibo Radio Telescope likewise sent a pictorial message to the M13 star cluster in binary code in 1974. Attempting to communicate across vast reaches of time instead of space, the Nevada nuclear waste storage facility Yucca Flats has posted a depiction of Edvard Munch's *The Scream* along with a device that issues an eerie D minor pitch as a warning to any future civilizations to stay away from the hazmat site, which could remain contaminated for millennia (D'Agata 2010: 177–9). These projects test the limits of intelligibility, ask radical questions about one's audience, and seek to use writing to connect minds beyond the human lifespan too.

Experimental Writing

Consideration of the materiality of writing, however, does not require biochemistry labs or radio signals beamed to outer space. All writing must be instantiated in some physical form, after all. A. R. Ammons's long poem, *A Tape for the Turn of the Year*, was typed on a roll of adding machine tape. The long, thin strip allowed the paper on which he wrote to set constraints, deciding line breaks and the length of the piece for him. By contrast, James Schuyler's *The Morning of the Poem* had very long lines; unfortunately, when it was published, a hanging indent was used. Douglas Crase (2022) remarked that the lines bounced back and forth like a Horatian epode while Wayne Koestenbaum said it seemed like the lines were being "spanked." These interpretations—by astute poet critics who knew Schuyler personally—were off-base, though, since Schuyler had intended long lines, which could have been kept intact if the publisher had opted for an enlarged, nonstandard format for his book. Likewise, today most smartphones and tablets distort line breaks and other formatting of texts. What material constraints and possibilities are engendered by smartphones, and how will digital mechanisms change reading practices?

At the beginning of the millennium, John Updike (2007: 90) wrote, "Electronic equals ... immaterial, Ariel to our earthly Caliban. Without books, we might melt into the airwaves, and be just another set of blips." For Updike, all writing seems destined to be swept up into the changing electronic weather, making its content as insubstantial as its disembodied form. Yet, stepping back, we might recognize that even the seemingly mundane act of scratching pen on paper is timebound technology that informs the writing process: the glide of the pen, the width of the page, the curls of the script. The blots and cross-outs of writing with a pen might make one more careful, too, compared to a pencil with its handy eraser-end or the word processor's ability to track changes and save in multiple versions. The *Paris Review* interviews famously ask writers about their physical method of composition. While some might dismiss this as a trivial lark, perhaps the alchemical task of writing really does depend on what we do with our hands and how we handle our ordinary tools. Every tool—including language itself—is a prosthesis, part of the furniture of our minds.

Discussion Questions

1. When you write, what physical objects do you use or create?
3. Why are many folks' literary "ambitions" bound up with the idea of writing traditional books?
4. What are some of the other formats, objects, and media we engage with when we read texts (any texts, not just "literature")?
5. How might other objects—pottery, rugs, jewelry, food, and so on—be considered a kind of poetry or incorporate texts?
6. Reflect on a time when you enjoyed making something: it doesn't have to be literary at all. It could be from childhood, perhaps, or something as simple as making dinner or tending a garden, for example. What things do you make on a regular basis? Create an inventory of the mental, physical, and cultural activities involved and the sensations of joy you experienced.

7. Gaston Bachelard writes that hands have their own dreams and assumptions. What does your hand know, dream, assume?
8. How does composing with hand, typewriter, word processor, textile loom, or other instruments—each of which require their own biomechanical operations—change what and how we compose?
9. How might zines, chapbooks, artist's books, and such alternative formats to traditional books present a different approach to reading and understanding texts; how might they change the way that texts are distributed and engaged with by their audiences?
10. In these different media and materials, who would be more likely to encounter your work? Less likely? How would it alter their perception of what you wrote?
11. Are any of these modes, materials, or media familiar to you? Which of these seem "literary" and which don't? Is this important? How (and where) do you encounter texts in your daily life?
13. Which quotations would go best with which mediums?
    1. "Originality is dangerous." (Salman Rushdie)
    2. "Your body is not a temple, it's an amusement park." (Anthony Bourdain)
    3. "There are no straight lines or sharp corners in nature." (Antonio Gaudí)
    4. "Time moves slowly, but passes quickly." (Alice Walker)
    5. "If you wanna fly, you got to give up the shit that weighs you down." (Toni Morrison)
    6. another quotation of your choosing
        a. stitched on a T-shirt
        b. around a drinking cup
        c. inscribed on a wall in a gallery next to an image
        d. on a sticker stuck in a bathroom stall
        e. projected onto the side of a building
        f. another media or format of your choosing

Writing Prompts

1. Reflecting on a story, essay, or poem you have recently written, what would be the most engaging way to remediate it—that is, use different media to develop a new iteration of the piece? Review the myriad forms in this chapter and choose one. Come up with a specific work plan and consider the overall design. What materials will you need and how will you utilize them? What protocols will you follow? Will you need to develop new artisanal techniques or recruit collaborators? What is an ideal venue

to present this work? Examine how you revise and reconceive of the work as it takes a new physical shape. How will audiences or readers access it or engage with the text? As you implement this plan, realize that you may discover new possibilities or limitations you will need to work through.

2. First, select a very brief excerpt from your writing. The first paragraph of a story, an idiosyncratic quotation from an essay, or a poetic line/couplet/quatrain are ideal lengths. What are the most important images, verbs, and ideas in this passage? What are the colors, textures, and sounds? (In the absence of explicit colors, textures, and sounds, you should plan to employ your synesthetic sense. For example, what color is the word "swimming"? Aquamarine like the tiles of a swimming pool? Dark blue like the ocean? Or the color of varying skin tones?)

Now, fold a blank piece of letter paper (8.5" × 11") perfectly in half, folio style. You will design your zine page using maker materials at your disposal. You may use magazines, newspapers, collage materials, stickers, buttons, feathers, scrapbook paper, holographic paper, cardstock, wrapping paper, aluminum foil, hole punch, ribbon, yarn, pipe cleaners, letterpress stamps, sequins, glitter, gold leaf, googly eyes, or anything else in two dimensions. The goal is to simply evoke the tone of your excerpt without attempting a one-to-one representation. Oblique interpretations are encouraged! The instructor may compile the submissions into a digital classwide zine on Issuu; or, students may elect to extend the project or collaborate with classmates to design an octavo zine. Folding instructions for this style can be found online.

2. After Orhan Pamuk's Museum of Innocence (Istanbul, Turkey), create your own literary museum. The museum can be based on a poem, essay, short story, or novel. Begin by creating an inventory of commonplace objects that appear throughout your piece. You may also include "implied objects." For example, in Pamuk's museum, Kemal's 4,213 cigarette stubs imply that, somewhere, too there should be a lighter. An inventory of ten to twenty objects is a good place to start. Now, acquire these items. This will require you to find, purchase, fabricate, extract, borrow, harvest, decompose, and so on each item. Collectively, these items should represent the piece of writing. You may want to ensure that all of your objects are of the same relative size. Once you're done collecting, you may want to alter the objects' patina: rough up, dirty, fray, scrub, polish, or repair the artifacts. You may need to fabricate or reconstruct some objects: photographs, letters, report cards, or the like. Now, place the objects in a large shadow box, bankers box, vintage suitcase, milk crate, or something else rectangular. Use glue, wire, or string to secure the artifacts in place. Consider what you want to focalize in the center and what to relegate to the background or affix to the perimeter. Consider how objects interact; are there objects that should be presented close together to reveal their consonant, dissonant, or absurd relation to one another? Classwide presentations of these micro-museums may be analyzed through the lens of material ecology—that is, the relationship between material design and the classroom environment.

3. Craft props, sets, costumes, and so on for a play, performance, or a very "performative" reading. If you wrote the text or script or performance score, how does making these items supplement or change the way you think about your writing? What types of props or costumes would enhance a reading of one of your poems, for example, or make an essay more entertaining to an audience? Would you make any revisions to your writing based on the objects you crafted? If the text is not your own writing, then how did crafting objects help you interpret subtleties, implications, and cues in the text that you previously overlooked? On what textual details did you base the design of the objects?

4. Explore the Thingiverse (thingiverse.com). Here, you can search millions of mostly free open-source 3D models uploaded by members of this maker community. Writing a poem about an island? Search for palm trees. An essay about chronic back pain? Look for an anatomically correct spine! You can remix the files on your own by changing the scale, color, orientation, or some other design element. Once you're ready, download the digital design file and send it off to the nearest 3D printer. Many libraries, universities, and maker spaces have 3D printers available to the public. Alternatively, you can order your model online. With your prototypes in hand, consider sanding and painting them. Create a literary diorama or art installation with your objects. Be sure to incorporate a modicum of text as well.

5. Create an artists' book. This is a format used to enhance written text, reinforce a concept through visual elements, or challenge notions of traditional book forms. An image search should orient you to the variety of forms they can take. While the techniques are nearly limitless, most originate with DIY and handicrafting culture. You will take one of your poems and turn it into a visual, interactive work of art. You'll need to consider the overall message, concept, or conceit of the poem and create a book to reinforce those elements. For a poem about heartbreak, for example, the reader might be able to create a heart-shaped book object that breaks in half with a Velcro seam. Content and form may also have a more oblique relationship. Articulate your plans for the visual style and design through a sketch and written proposal. Incorporate color, composition, line, shape, contrast, pattern, and repetition. Identify and pursue unlikely and unusual sources of inspiration and knowledge throughout the process to refine your plan. Execute your plan! You may choose to use folding, binding, or papercraft techniques, which will require additional training; alternatively, you can purchase a used book—a large reference book will do—and use its structure, including boards, spine, hinge, headcap, corners, and bookblock to serve as the sturdy foundation for your artist book.

CHAPTER 5
CONCEPTUAL AND VISUAL WRITING

I. Introduction

Conceptual and visual writing are two impulses that converge. Whereas Conceptual writing derives from the tendency in the visual art world to reduce the physical object (painting, sculpture, installation) to statements or ideas, visual writing proceeds from the motivation to transform literary works into optically arresting and visually meaningful artifacts. Though their motivations may appear opposed, these movements share a surprising amount of overlap as well as points of historical intersection.

II. L=A=N=G=U=A=G=E Poetry

L=A=N=G=U=A=G=E Poetry (or LANGUAGE Poetry, if you prefer) emerged among small circles of avant-garde writers in New York City and San Francisco in the early 1970s. The movement included Charles Bernstein and Bruce Andrews on the East Coast along with Ron Silliman, Lyn Hejinian, and Carla Harryman on the West Coast. Other important writers who have been characterized as LANGUAGE poets include Susan Howe, Rae Armantrout, Harryette Mullen, Clark Coolidge, Mei-Mei Berssenbrugge, and Michael Palmer. Often taking their orientation from Black Mountain poets like Charles Olson, Objectivists such as Louis Zukofsky, and the New York School of Poets, especially John Ashbery—particularly his book of radical collage *The Tennis Court Oaths*. LANGUAGE poets diverged from the contemporaneous second-generation New York School poets to pursue work that was less intimate, campy, and playful. Instead, they decentered the writer as the privileged source of lyric subjectivity. This group expressed skepticism about notions of authenticity—the voice, signature, or embodied self that supposedly undergirds mainstream poetry and confessional work. Some went so far as to deny interiority altogether. Critical theorists Michel Foucault and Roland Barthes at this period emphasized the "death of the author," and LANGUAGE poets' refusal to locate the author or speaker of their poems could be seen as symptomatic of this same viewpoint. Rather than view the author as a biographical person, LANGUAGE poets and critical theorists alike preferred to emphasize the "author function," seeing the ascription of authorship as a by-product of systems of authority and property rights; more important than an expression of individual personality was understanding the text as a node of socially constructed forms of discourse. For LANGUAGE poets, meanings circulated independently of authors' intentions, rooted in the properties and histories of language and how words were socially used. Likewise, following critical theorist Jacques Derrida, LANGUAGE poets foregrounded the social construction of texts within institutional systems wherein a work's meanings remained multiple, refractory, and deferred. LANGUAGE poetry rejects the communicative model of rhetoric wherein the poet inscribes a message the competent reader must then decipher. LANGUAGE poetry can't just be swallowed like a jellybean. Instead, meanings exist within "a matrix of social and historical relations," claims Charles Bernstein (1986: 408)—a flux of attentions, misunderstandings, and interests a reader brings to bear. Readers are impelled to recognize their role as organizer and producer of the text.

LANGUAGE poets highlighted how literary texts always await shifting contexts that could change their significance. Ultimately, the meaning of a work remains indeterminate; at least, this is the case for any production labeled a LANGUAGE poem. Their disjunctive texts were designed to disrupt the easy consumption of literary artifacts as simply one more commodity in the marketplace. This decidedly Marxist outlook manifested in pieces that resisted ready-made sentiments or singular viewpoints; rather, many of their so-called poems were in fact longer prose pieces that operated according to what Silliman (1987) dubbed "the New Sentence," sentences that did not necessarily connect with each other in traditional ways of narrative sense-making. The medley of New Sentences in their work left gaps and cleavages between them to be puzzled over by the reader. The sentences gestured toward the various discourses from which they arose, turning the readers' attention to the social horizon of signifying practices. For example, Hejinian's (1987: 7) *My Life*, a book-length work of prose, begins:

> A moment yellow, just as four years later, when my father returned home from the war, the moment of greeting him, as he stood at the bottom of the stairs, younger, thinner than when he had left, was purple—though moments are no longer so colored. Somewhere, in the background, rooms share a pattern of small roses. Pretty is as pretty does. In certain families, the meaning of necessity is at one with the sentiment of pre-necessity. The better things were gathered in a pen. The windows were narrowed by white gauze curtains which were never loosened. Here I refer to irrelevance, that rigidity which never intrudes. Hence, repetitions, free from all ambition.

The expectation of narrative memoir indicated by the title and implied in the first sentence is undercut by tonal leaps, focal shifts, and seeming non sequiturs. Fragments of narrative detail are interspersed with philosophical abstractions and self-referential statements. Although each sentence floats free of the others, an associational logic operates to form a constellation of reference that both is and is not about the author's autobiography, whether there exists a singular speaker or not. Just as the synesthetic apprehension of a memory connects disparate realms in the opening sentence, the jarring disorientation between sentences allows the reader space to willfully construct the texture and colors of a larger story. *My Life*, therefore, forces a projection between the lines so that the titular "My" is more the reader's than the author's possession. The lyric subject is at once alluded to yet eluded, averred though averted. "For these poets, language is not something that *explains* or *translates* experience, but is the source of experience," writes Douglas Messerli (1987: n.p.). Many LANGUAGE poets wanted the reader to hear the multiple tones and discourses the poem employs, not reduce those to a single speaker or author.

Marlon Hacla's piece, "Bluebush," is a contemporary example of LANGUAGE Poetry available on p. 262.

In retrospect, LANGUAGE poets shared many concerns with other avant-garde writers during the 1960s and 1970s. French novelists of the *nouveau roman* and New Wave film auteurs, for example, embraced work that was collage-like and undecidable, departing from "well-made" narratives and psychologically unified characters with texts that required active readerly interpretation. American novelists like Donald Barthelme and Robert Coover produced work in a similar vein: fragmented, nonlinear, and self-contradictory. In Great Britain during the same era, the corollary movement to LANGUAGE poetry was known as the British Poetry Revival or "Linguistically Innovative Poetries," including the Cambridge School—with J. H. Prynne and Peter Riley—and poets such as Tom Raworth, Ken Edwards, and Denise Riley elsewhere. This wide and divergent group of poets was interested in issues such as syntactical ambiguity, the ways performance shapes work on the page, and the pluralism of reference. Canadian writer Steve McCaffrey was also a fellow traveler with LANGUAGE poets and collaborated on joint projects. Spanish-language writers such as Severo Sarduy, Julio Cortázar, and Alejandra Pizarnik, as well, produced work that unraveled into multiple senses or that felt intransigent to interpretation. Likewise, in Italy, Pier Paolo Pasolini, Andrea Zanzotto, and members of Gruppo 63 such as Amelia Rosselli exhibited work that offered pointed political critique of consumer society and fascist ideology using poems whose linguistic innovations often disconcert their apparent import. While LANGUAGE poets often opposed those they viewed as "mainstream" American poets, even a mainstream poet such as Mark Strand (1978) during this period could write *The Monument*, a book-length work in which the posthumous speaker gives instructions to a translator using a bricolage of source texts, a work that figures the concerns of citation, authorial absence, and the dislocations of meaning. Or, again, the mainstream poet Robert Hass (1979: 4), in "Meditation at Lagunitas," states, "A word is elegy to what it signifies," probing the way that language is constitutive of our social reality and desires in a text that subtlety deracinates its own lyric subject. The deconstruction of conventional models of textual coherence was thus a widespread phenomenon of the zeitgeist across geographical borders, social sets, and literary genres.

Perhaps LANGUAGE poets simply pushed this tendency the furthest with work that exploded concerns of narrative integrity, attributions of a speaker, and textual unity. Yet, few writers, even among the avant-garde, claim to be LANGUAGE poets today. There are many factors that led to its demise. Theoretically, if *all* language is deconstructed, defers its meanings, and doesn't present its subject, then why (or how) can a LANGUAGE poetics do so as a specific métier? Practically, their techniques of disruption and defamiliarization became old hat; the New Sentence ossified into its own convention. After all, LANGUAGE poetry has been around since the early 1970s—over fifty years. It has become one more fashion in the long parade of twentieth-century styles. No longer challenging the commodification of literature, LANGUAGE poems could be rolled out on the assembly line like one more variation of the "McPoem." Furthermore, as many LANGUAGE poets matured, they inhabited sinecures within the academy while, at the same time, elitist, difficult work fell out of favor. In vogue were emotive, first-person, confessional pieces in which the speaker is identified with the author's subject position outside of the text. Even many LANGUAGE poets themselves seemed to want to have more *fun* than their manifestos and theoretical statements would sometimes allow. The later work of Bernstein, Mullen, Armantrout, and Bob Perelman, for example, feels far more willing to risk being sassy, silly, daffy, or sappy than their austere and indeterminate earlier pieces. But perhaps most pointedly, the modus operandi of LANGUAGE poets became accepted. Bernstein took home the Bollingen Prize, Hejinian edited *The Best American Poetry*, and Armantrout won a Pulitzer. Elliptical poets like Mary Jo Bang and Susan Wheeler, for instance, borrowed LANGUAGE practices and assumptions while writing work that was also formally inventive and emotionally resonant. The next generation of poets such as Fred Moten, Ange Mlinko, and Lisa Robertson who might have identified as LANGUAGE poets were likely put off by the infighting that had developed among the community, too. And nonfiction writers—such as Maggie Nelson, Lia Purpura, Ander Monson, and John D'Agata—many of whom started out as poets evolved the associational logic and disjunctive sentences of LANGUAGE work into the braided forms and quicksilver changes of subject found in the lyric essay. Ironically, the "self" of such first-person lyric essays is woven of threads as self-consciously constructed and precarious as any meanings one fabricates from LANGUAGE poems.

III. Conceptual Writing

Another permutation of LANGUAGE poetics evolved into Conceptual writing. If LANGUAGE poetry wanted to challenge the position of readers as alienated consumers and literature as simply one more commodity in that system, Conceptual writing took the role of alienated consumption as axiomatic, exacerbated by the marketplace of the digital age. Algorithms and social media feeds dispersed and ultimately replaced the subject: a self was the by-product of its own curation. Conceptual writing operated accordingly along fixed theories, codes, and premises; it was unashamed to be machinelike, repetitive, and boring. Claude Closky's (1992) piece, "the first thousand numbers classified in alphabetical order," for instance, is a rote index of exactly what it states. Few if any readers have perused the entire text. One skims, scans, skates along the surface. Or one fails to read at all. "The best thing about" Conceptual writing, Kenneth Goldsmith (2011a) effuses, "is that it doesn't need to be read. You don't have to read it. As a matter of fact, you can write books, and you don't even have to read them. My books, for example, are unreadable. All you need to know is the concept behind them." Goldsmith is not quite being fair to himself. Although Goldsmith's Conceptual writing may not be read much—nor any other Conceptual writers' literary efforts, for that matter—the impact of Conceptual writing has been felt instead in the realm of theory, criticism, and anthologies. Whether it's in online archives like UbuWeb and PennSound or critical books like *Uncreative Writing* and *Wasting Time on the Internet*, so-called literary output takes a backseat to the production of "concepts" through notes, histories, theories, and databases. One is likely to be more familiar with the academic articles of Marjorie Perloff *about* Conceptual writing, for example, than any "literary" piece of Conceptual writing per se. While LANGUAGE poetry was oftentimes incoherent, Conceptual writing can be downright illegible. If LANGUAGE poetry was based on a mélange of discourses, Conceptual writing consists in merely a rearrangement of ready-made citations. Goldsmith's book *Day*, a representative Conceptual text, merely retypes the entire *New York Times* for Friday, September 1, 2000, eliding article columns or page breaks. And whereas LANGUAGE poetry disowned the author, Conceptual writing has been willing to eliminate the reader.

Conceptual writing doesn't care if you think it's boring. Emotional responsiveness is rarely the point of such work. Some Conceptual writers might claim the norm of what one finds "boring" is dependent on the very bourgeois apple cart they want to upset. Others might say that they are writing not for you but rather for some cybernetic transhuman audience to come.

And still others might claim that boredom is a necessary existential mood since distraction is a concomitant to any act of attention; we are always reading and *not* reading, part zoned-in and part zonked-out. Contrary to popular opinion, poetry isn't just some device to get your vibes and feels. It, too, is a machine for living—it holds the potential to renovate one's very sensibility. That said, there's a wider range of affect displayed in just a few lines of Icelandic Conceptual writer Eiríkur Örn Norðdahl than in many whole volumes of more traditional verse. For instance, take the whopper-jawed line: "This isn't anal-sex! this is tennis!" Or, the keyed-up dyspeptic surliness of, "Yet you know not that you're the wretched one." Or yet again, the tone of robotic deadpan in, "The page you are looking for has been removed." In his book *Hnefi eða vitstola orð* (*Fist or Words Bereft of Sense*), Norðdahl tracked the daily exchange rate of the Króna next to each piece, correlating poetic affect to the financial crisis, indicating how whatever emotions the poem generates are connected to larger systems of language, culture, economics, and institutional imprimaturs.

Read one of Norðdahl's poems, "Nailsoup I-VI," on pp. 299–302.

Many Conceptual works likewise tease apart the binary between surface and depth, between difficulty and easy-listening muzak. The meaning of any work is often in the frame that one provides it. Conceptual writers are thus fascinated with paratexts, the edges of writing that loom on the liminal fringe: indexes, bibliographies, footnotes, marginalia, transcripts, white papers, printouts, and catalogues raisonnés. They often loot this un-literature to remix their own pieces. Noah Eli Gordon cut-and-pasted from his emails to produce a memoir written by others in *Inbox*, for example. Riccardo Boglione transcribed only the punctuation marks of Boccacio's *Decameron* in *Ritmo D. Feeling the Blanks*. Luis Camnitzer in *Memorial* republished the Montevideo phonebook, adding the names of hundreds of people who had been disappeared. Darren Wershler's *The Tapeworm Foundry* consists of only titles for books that have yet to be written. In such projects, Conceptual writers refocus our consideration on the mundane flow of information, showing how these sources of quotidian language often act as the unacknowledged basis of power, knowledge, or strange beauty.

What one considers noise and what one considers signal depends, fundamentally, on what one's listening for and the tricks in one's toolbox to parse the static and catch the wavelengths. Craig Dworkin (2011: xxxvi) writes that "the guiding concept behind conceptual poetry may be the idea of language as quantifiable data." In his essay "The Politics of Noise," Dworkin (2003: 48) declares that Susan Howe's work "briefly short-circuits the parasitic economy and reminds readers that the facile distinction between 'message' and 'noise' must ultimately deconstruct itself." Conceptual writing, such as Howe's, can feel like too much and/or not enough. Too little signal. Too much noise. It disrupts the "static quo," we might say, the noisy systems of self-replicating language surrounding us.

In "Koko," which can be found on p. 303, the writer Elena Passarello plays with this notion of signal and noise as she attempts to tell a joke on behalf of Koko the Gorilla, using only the primate's limited vocabulary in American Sign Language. The joke itself embroiders on the off-color vaudevillian joke, The Aristocrats.

Archives of printed matter along with the ever-burgeoning internet mean that today we are simply inundated by texts. Rather than try to cut through all the noise (a hopeless endeavor?), Conceptual writing asks us to indulge the overtones and undercurrents of language systems—to hear the uncanny, dissonant song of cultural desiderata. Conceptual writing's advertisement for so-called unoriginality has at least two implications: (1) provoking defenders of the hegemonic standards of creative writing "craft" by revealing the institutional biases such timeless "craft" discourse too often obscures and (2) promoting techniques such as plagiarism and programmatic formulas as valid ways to construct literary artifacts. Conceptual writing appropriates from banal source texts, reconfiguring them to underscore the figurations already inherent in these texts (the alphabetization of an index, say) and thus expose the cultural values and ontological assumptions that remain unspoken background (such that knowledge can be thematized and organized through linguistic codes). Conceptual writing thereby performs a type of metalepsis, taking the structures and tropes of quotidian forms of discourse as the initial figures—ones that are often not recognized as such—upon which it plays its further figurative and formal variations. For a concrete example of a such a strategy, see Tyrone Williams's (2002) "Cold Calls," which presents a blank text in the body with copious footnotes and endnotes; here, the erasure of African-American history is figured as a whitewashed page, the marginalization of Blacks is figured as writing in the literal margins, and the lacunae within any truth-claims figured as a breakdown of reference between the abundant notes and the nonexistent text. As Craig Dworkin states in *No Medium*, speaking of a range of other Conceptual works that are similarly emptied or erased, "They invoke the long history of reading practices that are inextricably bound to the physical dimensions of writing's material forms" (2013: 39). Similarly, the infra-thin difference between many Conceptual pieces and their appropriated source texts—for example, Goldsmith's *Day*—points outward so that the reader, seemingly absent a text to dive into, must acknowledge and contemplate the contextual framework outside it: the larger cultural systems in and by which any signal or noise are constituted and circulated.

Conceptual writing has experienced a swift demise as literary culture has shifted in the last decade. Kenneth Goldsmith's (2015) performance at a conference of "The Body of Michael Brown," referencing an eighteen-year-old Black man who was shot by the police in Ferguson in 2014, sparked a widespread backlash. Goldsmith's piece appropriated Brown's autopsy report, though it purportedly revised and reconfigured the coroner's description, placing a section about Brown's genitalia as the text's climax, thereby "performing anew the autopsy's latent, institutional racism," claims critic Paweł Marcinkiewicz (2018: 211). Goldsmith refused to release the text and received death threats for his performance. "The problem with the new conceptual [writing] practice is that it disregards the ethical dimension of creation … regardless of the fact that an appropriated text always reflects editorial manipulation and the politics behind it," declares Marcinkiewicz (2018: 211). Goldsmith's controversy resulted in hostility toward Vanessa Place, another Conceptual writer, who had been tweeting *Gone with the Wind*, line by line, since 2011. Many critics, notably the anonymous Mongrel Coalition

Against Gringpo, saw Place's work as unethical for choosing to replicate a blatantly racist novel for a wide, online audience. A panel Place was scheduled to attend at the Whitney Museum called "Last Words" was subsequently canceled; she reputedly had planned to read eyewitness accounts of the execution of Clayton Lockett, a Black man charged with murder, rape, and kidnapping. In such instances, the literary technique of appropriation was viewed as politically fraught, perhaps analogous to if not synonymous with cultural appropriation. Many agreed that Goldsmith and Place—white, elite poets—had manipulated racist texts (as well as ignored the racist legacy of those texts) for their own advantage.

The pretense of much Conceptual writing to being impersonal, morally neutral, and expressionless belied the very political and expressive nature of its activities, albeit in a mode that was anathema to progressive viewpoints. In short, many writers felt that a literature of more overt social engagement was needed, not one that trafficked in covert bigotry while pretending to a fey apolitical nonchalance. Goldsmith has also come under fire for his cavalier attitude toward waste. While often claiming to curate and reduce the proliferating archive of the internet for information management purposes, Goldsmith in fact embarked on a project to print out the entire internet in paper form. Conceptual writers likewise celebrate machine-like writing that avoids contemplation, only adding to the glut of our textual inundation. Even the adjacent critical practice of "distant reading," which produces statistics based on vast quantities of texts processed through computer programs, only gives us more data and interpretation to sift through, rather than any definitive synopsis. Like his unreadable books themselves, "the ephemeral objects Goldsmith chooses to reproduce," writes critic Christopher Schmidt (2008: 27), "are themselves destined for the rubbish bin." Conceptual writers—especially Goldsmith—literally produce "trash," even by their own rhetorical illocutions. Their claims to reduction and redaction alike undermined, publishing Conceptual writing was consequently seen to have little purpose beyond careerist resume-building. More recent literary culture has largely moved on from Conceptual writing in favor of work understood to be more therapeutic, communitarian, and engagée in nature—even among writers who appreciate the theoretical moxie and irascibly edgy nature of Conceptual writing.

IV. Post-conceptual Art

If there is such a thing as a Post-conceptual poetics, it is still being worked out by the younger generation of artists, most of whom were born in the 1980s or later, as they respond to the milieu of their Conceptual inheritance. Felix Bernstein (2014: n.p.) (the son of Charles Bernstein, the LANGUAGE poet) writes that "the Post-conceptual poet can do one new thing and declare the 'death of work'" while they besmirch themselves in the "vulgar muck of the Internet." If LANGUAGE poets avowed the death of the author and Conceptual writers renounced the reader, then Post-conceptual artists—in Felix Bernstein's (2015) view—take this trajectory one step further and abandon any pretense to creating works at all. Rather, we argue, there has been a transformation in the understanding of work: the "work" of the artwork becomes synonymous with the "work" in networking. That is, what happens when the book launch party, the tweet or Instagram post, the PR statement, or the nepotistic review of a friend's show constitute the text itself? While their poetry might be just a pose, posing is still, we might grant, performative work. Face value is nevertheless a value that must be constructed. Conceptual art largely premised its valorization on theories, genealogies, and aesthetic outlooks. Post-conceptual art meanwhile knows just enough philosophy to acknowledge the contingency of any values beyond any ultimate redemption, except perhaps the ever-present values of capital, social or otherwise.

As critic Elisa Gabbert (2020) writes, "It's as though career success is a capitulation to capitalism, hence a kind of failure—hence the book must hate itself." More so for any Post-conceptual "work." The would-be Post-conceptual artists is trapped in a double-bind: the guilt of hardly working and the exhaustion of working hard. Post-conceptual gags, stunts, schticks, and gimmicks are different than the Conceptual writer's hoaxes, pranks, humbug, and practical jokes, however. The Post-conceptual artist ironically embraces the hustle and hype-machine of precarious capitalistic machinations such as social media yet evacuates it of any supposed content or sincerity. "Gimmicks," critic Sianne Ngai (2017: 466) writes, "seem to provoke contempt simply in part because they are job related: bits of business for performing aesthetic operations that we somehow become distracted into regarding as aesthetic objects in their own right." Felix Bernstein wrote a blurb for Cassandra B. Seltman's first book while Seltman reviewed Bernstein's book in the *LA Review of Books*: such Post-conceptual work is both participating in network and "artworking." Another example of Post-conceptual "artworking" might be Caroline Calloway, a disgraced influencer, who failed to fulfill a contract for a memoir, but who nonetheless offered her book proposal for sale on Etsy. Blog posts, Instagram, book blurbs—these are forms legitimized by Post-conceptual artists which others might see as "gimmicks." For Ngai (2017: 472), gimmicks are mechanistic contrivances that "both work too hard and work too little." But gimmicks are ubiquitous for the Post-conceptual generation who are immured to life hacks, productivity apps, and clickbait. The platforms one runs from a smartphone, for instance, conflate necrotic labor and narcotized forms of leisure—they are neither wholly time-saving devices nor time-wasting ones. For many contemporary artists, gaining followers has become monetized, so that one might not simply be goofing off while scrolling social media feeds; one is, in fact, "always already" on the job. This ambivalence is deeply embedded in the ironic attitude of Post-conceptual artists toward their own self-promotion, which is at once their work and its valorizing context. Some readily profess a suspicion of fraudulence in their own marketing efforts, confessing vacuity and imposter syndrome, which in turn is the basis of their aestheticized performance of negative affect. While Post-conceptual artists impersonate the self through curation and critique, critics like Claire Bishop or curators like Hans Ulrich Obrist participate in an equal if not privileged position in the Post-conceptual art-world ecosystem. Critique, curation, and canon-making are acts of bringing attention to someone, and attention is a precious commodity.

As tenuous as any Post-conceptualisms might be, beyond referring to a certain generational in-crowd coterie, a handful of defining characteristics have nevertheless distinguished it from its Conceptual forebears. Felix Bernstein (2014: n.p.) declares, "Post-conceptual poetry attempts to explicitly bring affect and emotion and ego back into the empty networking structures that govern us." Pathos is ascendant. Something real is—or wants to be—at stake despite the omnipresence of the internet and pop culture, realms that frequently seem virtual and unreal. Ironically, the pathos as often as not results from the self-doubt of giving expression to the self, a self unable to transcend its political will-to-power or its inveterate narcissism that further entraps it in damaging, corporatized systems. Unlike Conceptual writers who differentiated between their (flat, arcane) poetry and their (academic, flamboyant) critical essays, Post-conceptual artists conflate the two in their memoirs, autotheory, and poems that mix sordid personal confessions with highbrow continental philosophy. Indeed, their work often transcends media and platforms: a physical book, a website, a performance, a concert, social-media posts, and a gallery installation might all be aspects of a single "event" release or iterations of the same piece with no form, media, or version taking priority. All media alike act as containers for the performance and branding of an artistic identity. Robert Fitterman and Vanessa Place (2009: 20) observe in *Notes on Conceptualisms* that "in post-conceptual work, there is no distinction between manipulation and production, object and sign, contemplation and consumption." Even the binaries between source text and appropriation, language and material, and thinking and economic activity that authorized Conceptual writing ultimately break down in Post-conceptual work. Whereas Conceptual art disrupted the gallery space with writing and Conceptual writing challenged literary publication with performances or visual artifacts, both thereby reinscribing the conventions of such media through their very violation, Post-conceptualists by contrast shift and shuffle between media with apparent ease or indifference.

Tan Lin's "ambient" literature designs experiences to be absorbed and consumed peripherally rather than critically read, anticipating Post-conceptual work in the way it moves between gallery installations, gastronomy, perfume, PowerPoints, disco, public art, and published books while remixing everything from Facebook feeds to recipes. Similarly, Lebanese actor, playwright, lecturer, performance artist, filmmaker, and installation artist Rabih Mroué blurs and confounds the boundaries between museums, everyday sites on the street, domestic homes, theater, and academic colloquia. Though scripted, many of his works are designed to appear as if they are being improvised; his work often mixes historical "facts" with fiction, humor, politics, and a performative interpretation of events. For example, his series of photographs taken on mobile phones "Pixelated Revolution" literally blurs out images of persons killed in the Syrian conflict, foregrounding the ways in which historical truth is captured, constructed, disseminated, aestheticized, and at last rendered unreal. Amelia Ulman's projects are emblematic of Post-conceptualism in her traversal of selfies, Instagram accounts, performance, comic strips, film, and résumés to role-play iterations of different personas that are at once an authentic identity and a constructed alter ego, interrogating the ways that documentation transforms the self into brand and spectacle. Sophia Le Fraga, too, operates in media such as view-masters, slideshows, erasures, photographs, multimedia anti-plays, listicles, printouts, textiles, and writing, often questioning, as Lucy Ives (2013: 12) notes, "what was ever not 'fake.'" It is often unclear how much Le Fraga's work appropriates from the internet or only *appears* to be culled from such abbreviated, ungrammatical, half-gibberish sources as GChat, phone texts, and comments sections—sources that, for many, habitually deform language to negotiate and constitute relationships and identities. Critic Joshua Weiner likens Le Fraga's work to Beckettesque characters who can't go on but must go on in the following sequence:

I guess lets try to have a conversation
Since we apparently can't stop txting each other
Word
soooooooooooooo say something
Chill
I'm trying

(2014: n.p.)

Experimental Writing

Weiner proposes that Le Fraga's characters go a step further than Beckett's Didi and Gogo, who are at least enfleshed and emplaced, since Le Fraga's voices are only disembodied ghosts in the machine. The line between parody and self-parody becomes increasingly specious, as the self, too, is understood as a hodgepodge of dodgy misquotations and semiautomated responses.

V. OuLiPo and Proceduralism

OuLiPo (*Ouvroir de littérature potentielle* or Workshop of Potential Literature) was an international group of writers founded by Raymond Queneau, a poet, and François Le Lionnais, a mathematician, in the 1960s. The group proposed to innovate literature by using ingenious constraints, methods, and algorithms. The seemingly arbitrary, mathematical principles informing their texts would reveal, they hoped, new areas of thought and literary possibilities for exploration. Oftentimes, limitations unlock creativity rather than hamstringing it. Parameters and prompts help frame the directions a work can take, and every text is composed against some rubrics, though in most cases these remain unstated. After all, traditional literature, from the sonnet form to the conventions of the realist novel, have been deeply informed by rules (fourteen lines, rhyme scheme, the volta) or tenets (pacing, character motivation, plot arcs). By imposing wildly different sets of formal constraints than these standard ones, OuLiPo writers believed they could discover structures that would not only create groundbreaking literary works but also gesture beyond those specific works to the nearly limitless other arrangements and variations of potential writing. Language itself was simply a code with exponential permutations. Guiding lights in their endeavors were proto-Conceptual artist Marcel Duchamp's interest in geometry, replication, chess, and stochastic processes along with proto-Surrealist Alfred Jarry's notion of 'Pataphysics, a philosophy of imaginary solutions or a parodic science of accidents and exceptions. Another influence was the emerging structuralist movement of the period that sought to analyze culture through universal—sometimes computative—systems and categories by philosophers such as Umberto Eco, Claude Levi-Strauss, Roland Barthes, Noam Chomsky, and Tzvetan Todorov; in France many of the structuralists centered around the magazine *Tel Quel*. The semi-clandestine Bourbaki collective of mathematicians in post-First World War France, which published textbooks on all elements of math, acted as a model for the group, too. The OuLiPo brigade thus merged whimsy and rigor, rigmarole and wit, demonstrating how a methodical approach could result in works of originality.

The playful, game-like spirit of the OuLiPo resulted in a literary effervescence that spanned from poetry to novels. In Queneau's paradigmatic *A Hundred Thousand Billion Poems* each line of the ten sonnets could be reshuffled with any other line, resulting in a combinatorial explosion of potential poems. Versions of the book were printed with perforated strips or spiral spines with each line independent of the others, allowing the reader to mix-and-match different arrangements, almost like words and phrases in Magnetic Fridge Poetry. Queneau's sonnets harken back to Su Hui whose fourth-century palindromic *huiwen* in Chinese gridded 840 characters on embroidered silk; Hui's text could be read in a similarly combinatoric manner. Georges Perec, perhaps the most prodigious member of OuLiPo, explored crosswords, anagrams, and other literary puzzles. He once composed a 5,000-word palindrome in French, a world record for any language. His substantial novel *La Disparition* was composed as a lipogram, that is, it did without a letter—the absent letter in this case was the most common one in French (and English), "e." Notably, the English translation, *A Void*, does without that letter, too. Perec may have been inspired by the 1824 short story "Eve's Legend" by Henry Vassall-Fox, where "e" is the *only* vowel used. Perec too, wrote a novella (*The Exeter Text: Jewels, Secrets, Sex*) using only e's, also translated into "Englesh."

Read an excerpt from Christian Bök's own univocalic experiment, *Eunoia*, on pp. 211–13.

Perec's most famous book, *Life: A User's Manual*, uses an elaborate structure of interwoven stories based on jigsaw puzzles, architectural blueprints, bi-squares (similar to sudoku), and a "knights tour" in chess. The result, however, like most of Perec's work, is compulsively readable—waggish, learned, and affecting—rather than calculated or rote. The OuLiPo writers were as much interested in mathematical formulas as literary forms. Queneau's *Exercises in Style* presents ninety-nine retellings of the same story that vary by style; Harry Mathews wrote *Singular Pleasures*, sixty-one vignettes about masturbation each in a wildly different manner; and Italo Calvino's *If on a Winter's Night a Traveler* is a metafictional novel about a reader trying to read a novel of the same name, each chapter of which is composed according to distinctive genres, conventions, and perspectives.

One well-known OuLiPo technique is N+7 in which an extant text is altered by replacing every substantive noun in the text with the noun appearing seven entries away from it in the dictionary. A lesser-known technique is to compose a poem while riding the metro, by thinking of one line between every station, writing it down during the station stop, and indicating station changes by stanza breaks; "The last verse of the poem is transcribed on the platform of your last station" (Motte 2009: 38). Michelle Grangaud invented the "poem fondu" technique in which the words from one poem—a sonnet, say—are selected and reordered to create another form, such as a haiku. Such instructions are simultaneously a literary product in their own right and devices to generate infinitely more pieces. The research of the OuLiPo members is ongoing, and the group still holds regular meetings. The group has produced nonfiction and criticism, as well, such as Marcel Bénabou's "One Aphorism Will Hide Another," which examines the mad-lib-like structure underlying many witticisms. Other recent publications include Anne F. Garréta's *Sphinx*, in which the two lovers in the novel are not gendered, Lewis Trondheim and Jean-Christophe Menu using similar constraints to draw comics, and Jacques Roubaud's *The Great Fire of London*, a novel that bifurcates into many branches, including a nonfiction metanarrative about the "Project" for the novel itself. Roubud's work—indeed, much of OuLiPo—celebrates failure. The OuLiPo call the breaking of the constraint a "clinamen" (or swerve) after Lucretius, a small fudge to help improve the text, and they see it as necessary and even inevitable. Gödel's incompleteness theorem, at any rate, states that a set of axioms cannot be both complete and consistent. Another attitude of the OuLiPo is that precursors—Edgar Allen Poe's *Eureka*, Roussel's *Locus Solus*, or Francis Bacon's ciphers, for instance—are really "anticipatory plagiarists." The OuLiPo reverse the temporal priority between forebears and descendants. While most OuLiPo members revealed the constraints behind their work, even understanding the constraints as more important than the piece it enabled, Harry Mathews often obscured his, or in many cases didn't use any constraints at all, believing each work must stand on its own merits.

Experimental Writing

Contemporary writers who are not affiliated with the OuLiPo but who utilize algorithms and constraints to produce their work often go under the banner of Proceduralism. Proceduralists choose a set of self-imposed rules at the outset and then implement these strictures until they have completed a project. Developing the project often leads to unpredictable results. Many Proceduralists are associated with Conceptual writing since their work, too, operates according to a predefined concept. The concept, in some cases, can be more important or interesting than the work itself. For example, "34650 Seconds" by Evelin Brosi systematically types out every permutation of the letters in "Mississippi," allowing the nonsense words to cascade down the page like a topographic map of a river. Craig Dworkin and Madeline Gilmore's "Attempt at Exhausting a Space in Williamstown" (alluding to a text by Perec in which he tries to record the humdrum, overlooked, and infraordinary in Paris) catalogs and alphabetizes every word and glyph found in the Williams College Museum of Art. Such Proceduralist attempts may impose alternative methods to try wresting free of the subjective ego's habitual perceptions and values. Another vision of Proceduralism is taken from chaos theory, where seemingly chaotic or random data might be produced from computational processes of complex dynamic systems, such as fractals, where patterns are self-similar across different scales. Jackson Mac Low, for example, used what he termed a "diastic method" to generate new work, taking a seed text (a phrase such as "How many brothers fell victim to the streets" from Tupac Shakur) and then finding the first word that starts with each successive letter in a source text, such as Woolf's *The Waves*. Mac Low was an early designer of computer-generated poetry, too, which can be seen as Proceduralism since it depends on computer algorithms. In fiction, Christine Brooke-Rose's novel *Amalgamenon* avoids all present tense to represent the narrator's disorientations in the flux of history and memory. Walter Abish, too, has used Proceduralism in his novel *Alphabetical Africa*, an extravagant feat in which the first chapter only uses words beginning with "A," the second chapter only words beginning in "A" or "B," until letters are again removed in the book's second half after chapter 26. Abish's constraint acts as a parody, in part, of postcolonial conceptions of Africa viewed through the severe limitation of Western eyes. More recent procedural writers, notes critic Louis Bury (2016), include "countless poets (and non-poets) [who] compose using methods found under the big tent of proceduralism without becoming primarily known as procedural writers … these quiet proceduralists are often the writers whose work puts the lie to the stereotype that proceduralism must be cerebral and impersonal." Bury cites such writers as Bhanu Kapil, Cathy Park Hong, and Solmaz Sharif among the younger writers who employ Proceduralist techniques without fetishizing them, more like the way one would use a prompt, to create poignant and political work.

VI. Visual Writing

Starting in the 1960s—coinciding with or coming out of art movements such as Dada, Pop Art, and especially Minimalism—visual artists began to question the importance of the material object and skilled execution of technique that had traditionally been accorded pride of place. Instead, Conceptual artists largely eschewed objects and techniques in favor of the ideas that an artwork was representing; in doing so, many Conceptual artists reverted to textual and literary modes. Conceptual artist Richard Kostelanetz states, "The radical idea developed by Conceptual Art … was that statements alone could suggest experiences in the tradition of visual art" (2011: 11). Extrapolating from Minimalism, he argues Conceptual Art developed a "hypothesis that more could be experienced with less, much less," but it "depends upon contextual framing" (2011: 11) in an artworld setting. Joseph Kosuth's "Five Words in Red Neon" was an art piece of exactly what its title states. In John Baldassari's piece "I Will Not Make Any More Boring Art," the phrase is repeated down a paper in cursive script—the print was not produced by Baldassari, though, who only left a note to be carried out by his art students, a mocking form of schoolhouse punishment. Similarly, Sol LeWitt during the same period didn't manufacture art so much as leave instructions and detailed plans for others on how to execute it. Likewise, Minimalist sculptor and poet Carl André gridded out concrete poems on graph paper in much the same way his prefabricated squares of magnesium plates or cubes of Perspex were laid out in grid- or block-like sculptures. Poet and artist Lawrence Weiner appended typographic texts directly to gallery walls. Later, feminist artist Barbara Kruger displayed photos overlayed with striking assertions in bold font such as "I shop therefore I am" and Jenny Holzer wrote her series of "Truisms," such as "*DECADENCE CAN BE AN END IN ITSELF*" and "*DECENCY IS A RELATIVE THING*," that can be found anywhere from scrolling LED screens to baseball caps. Such works began to collapse the distinction between visual art activities and literary composition. In many cases, the medium and material may be important—Kosuth's piece, for instance, is not as bright or self-referential without the neon. Still, the essence of many of these pieces can be conveyed without the presence of a physical art object or the object simply *is* the instantiation of the language itself.

Around the same time, from the late 1950s through the early 1980s roughly, a parallel development took place in the literary domain with the rise of Concrete Poetry, a truly international movement that spanned the globe. In Concrete Poetry the layout, white space, typography, and other visual arrangement of letters on the page take precedence, whether the letters form a recognizable picture, enact the text, or disorient the viewer by contradicting the meaning of the words. In some cases, the writers produced their work in sculptural form or in public art settings. American May Swenson's 1970 book *Iconographs* included poems shaped to reflect their subject matter, such as a study of waves with undulating lines that swayed out and swept back. American poet N. H. Pritchard's book *EECCHHOOEESS*, for example, includes a page with iterations of "echo" and "ing" that scatter and ping across a white field. In works such as "Sonic Icons," English poet Bob Cobbing utilized photocopiers and other office machines to render his words into both playful sound textures and optic analogues with inkblots and distorted imprints. German-born Mexican artist Mathias Goeritz in "Mensajes dorados" ("Golden messages") presented pages filled with different geometric patterns of the letters "o-r-o" and "o-j-o" ("gold" and "eye"). Japanese artist and poet Seiichi Niikuni utilized the venerable Japanese tradition of calligraphy and the iconographic properties of kanji to add additional dimensions to his work in Concrete Poetry. The text in Brazilian Augusto de Campos's 1956 poem "Ovonovelo" ("Eggball") is arranged in an ovoid, the words after the title punning "novo no velho" ("new in the old") and likewise unfolding in sound and visual play throughout. By the 1980s, de Campos began projecting his texts by holograms, electronic billboards, and computer graphics in artworld settings, showing the convergence of Concrete Poetry and Conceptual Art. From the Noigandres in Brazil to the Wiener Gruppe in Austria and from Problemática 63 in Latin America to the Poesia Visia writers in Italy, Concrete Poetry was an international phenomenon, helped along by the fact that the impact of many pieces did not require extensive translation. For example, Aram Saroyan produced one-word poems such as "eyeye," a poem that was solely the letter "m" with an extra leg, and an entire book "printed" by Kulchur Press in 1968 that consisted of a bound ream of blank paper.

Concrete Poetry benefited from the increased attention to design thinking that arose in the latter half of the twentieth century, not only to such elements as typography in the realms of book design and advertisement, but across the range of everyday items from home décor to business infrastructure as well. The birth of semiotics—or the study of signifying systems across language, objects, and behaviors—was another powerful intellectual current adding to the discourse inspiring both Concrete Poetry and Conceptual art. Nonetheless, Concrete Poetry had a wide range of historical antecedents to lean on and borrow from. The *carmina figurata* was an Ancient Greek and Roman poetic genre in which the text was presented in shapes or patterns that corresponded in some way to the poem's content. Simmias of Rhodes wrote "The Wings" about the god Eros and "The Egg" around AD fourth century, anticipating George Herbert's "Easter Wings" and de Campos's "ovonovelo" by hundreds of years. In the Middle Ages, Arabic literature and art flourished with a well-developed graphic tradition in motifs, calligraphy, and design, due in large part to the Islamic prohibition on most figurative representation. The Middle Ages also witnessed illuminated manuscripts with their combination of elaborate gold-leafed images and text in prayer books, liturgies, legal proclamations, and other codices. Similarly, the emblem poem was invented in 1531 by Italian poet Andrea Alciato, which juxtaposed an epigrammatic poem with a woodblock icon, a technique that was used by John Donne, Maurice Scève, and many another Renaissance poet. Altar poems—or poems arranged to depict devotional symbols such as altars or crosses—formed another visual writing practice that gained popularity during the English Baroque period of the 1600s. In the eighteenth century, with the spread of the printing press, authors such as Samuel Richardson, Jonathan Swift, and Laurence Sterne played with the typographical layout and incorporation of images in their prose works, including ill-sorted pages, slanted and overlapping text, or pages that contained only a uniquely marbled, mottled blot. Jumping forward, the twentieth century had many writers who experimented with typographical innovations preceding Concrete Poetry. The Italian and Russian Futurists exploded the page with wild zigzags and jagged figures of typography; Vicente Huidobro and Guillaume Apollinaire composed calligrams in which the text took the form of an image that related to its thematic content; and poets such as e. e. cummings and Charles Olson, after the invention of the typewriter, took advantage of blank space and layout when composing their pieces. All told, writers have been utilizing visual presentation and iconography to enhance their work and express relationships between word and image for ages.

Check out Lucy Corin's ""Questions in a Significantly Smaller Font" on p. 223. You may need a magnifying glass!

Contemporary visual writing is more likely to travel between gallery, book, public art, and other forums without being defined as simply art or literature. There are also increasing numbers of visual writers who compose fiction and nonfiction, too. In the same period of the 1960s and 1970s that witnessed Concrete Poetry, fiction writers such as Donald Barthelme, Kathy Acker, and Kurt Vonnegut incorporated collages of found imagery, maps, diagrams, photos, and doodles into their stories. More recently, W. G. Sebald utilizes haunting photographs throughout his prose oeuvre that disturb the narrative. Jonathan Safran Foer employed photographs and other visual texts—including a flipbook animation of a figure falling from the Twin Towers during 9/11—in *Extremely Loud and Incredibly Close*. Such visual texts instigate a shift in perspective, break narrative continuity, or trouble the distinction between fabulation and documentation rather than serve as mere illustrations of the stories' content. Graphic novels, of course, are another juncture where images, layout, and typography merge with literary narrative, creating sophisticated modes of visual storytelling. In recent years, nonfiction writers such as Noam Dorr and Sarah Minor have taken to visual essays. Dorr's "Ants" is a text that crawls a trail around and through the image of a giant ant while Minor's "A Log Cabin Square" takes the form of a log-cabin quilt pattern. Interestingly, Dorr has converted his essay into an online video while Minor has transposed her essay into a video performance as well as a physical object for a gallery space. Today's visual writers are often branching into other realms, too, such as digital graphics, video poetics, and interactive narratives within video games. Meanwhile, a contemporary visual artist such as the Chinese calligrapher Wang Dong, part of the experimental ink movement that began in the 1990s, "performs" pieces in museum settings by painting on giant scrolls (sometimes with musical or dance accompaniment), not unlike the action paintings of Jackson Pollock—especially since much of his script can appear illegible even for those who can read Chinese.

Writing that no longer has semantic content and is only scribbles, glyphs, globs, and scrawls that might suggest letters and words is known as "asemic writing." Asemic writing can be expressive and comes in a wide range of forms. It requires its audience to "read" by processes of association, visual analysis, compositional scrutiny, theoretical framing, gestalt recognition, and affective registration. French experimental writer and painter Henri Michaux developed some of the first asemic writing in the 1920s, marking lines on a canvas that resembled a skittery cursive script. Around the 1940s Romanian-born French artist Isidore Isou developed a visionary movement called Lettrism in which conventional linguistic meanings were destroyed by radiant dislocations of letters, icons, symbols, and splashes slashed across a variety of media, including fashion, film, and performance. Later visual artists as diverse as Cy Twombley, Ray Johnson, and Jean-Michele Basquiat also incorporated words, stray letters, and word-like squiggles or swoops in their collages and canvases. Even where a letter or whole word might be recognizable in such works, the grapheme's text competes for emphasis with the work's graphic texture.

For an example of asemic writing, see Mirtha Dermisache's work on p. 224.

Canadian Derek Beaulieu, a Conceptual writer, converted the 1884 mathematical romance *Flatland* into a work of asemic writing in 2007 by creating lines between chosen letters and eliminating all trace of source text, leaving only a dense cluster of crisscrossing one-dimensional marks on the page. Creative coder Sarah Ridgley has created an AI program that generates its own asemic writing. Some contemporary Conceptual writers such as S. J. Fowler or Erica Baum will combine materials such as photos, doodles, texts, collage, Xerox splotches, paper-doll cutouts, and player-piano rolls with their asemic compositions. Meanwhile, Michael Jacobson created a kinetic film novel of asemic writing *Mynd Eraser*, which rapidly flashes squirreling, unintelligible penmanship on the screen. Sometimes asemic writing goes under the label "New Post-Literate" to signal its allegiance to an internationalist outlook that transcends the bounds of language and emphasizes visually oriented cultural productions. In such works, artists explore the limit case of a literature that faces the future by effacing language itself.

Discussion Questions

1. What is the legacy of LANGUAGE writing? How can LANGUAGE writing's techniques such as disjunction, parataxis, associational logic, and narrative decoherence be seen in many forms of writing today? Is LANGUAGE writing passé because it was too academic, difficult, and opaque; or have many of its techniques infiltrated mainstream writing practices today so that it no longer seems subversive or cutting edge? Or, on the contrary, do you see LANGUAGE writing as still on the vanguard of experimentalism?

2. Do you believe that indeterminate works—whether LANGUAGE poems, Conceptual writing, or Post-conceptual art pieces—can nonetheless convey a distinct political message? How much can a text be divorced from ostensible "content" before it loses its ability to signify clear points or have social import? Do you think that a work has to be popular or have mainstream appeal to be effective in changing society?

3. How much do you think authorial intention shapes the meaning a text has; how about the process by which a work was created, even when that process is not necessarily visible in the final product? How much might the response of a community shape the meaning a text has: such a community might be BookTok or it might be academic literary critics? How about the formal properties of the work? Or the institutional systems—including marketplaces, networks of distribution, and habits of consumption—in which it is embedded? What other vectors of meaning or constitutive forces shape our understandings of texts? How does Conceptual and Post-conceptual writing underscore or deconstruct these various (and sometimes contradictory) ways we make meaning; how might these types of writing fail to adequately grapple with the ways meanings are made in some cases?

4. The poet Stéphane Mallarmé once told the painter Edgar Degas, who said he had an idea for a poem, that "You can't make a poem from ideas. Poems are made from words." Do you think that some pieces of Conceptual writing attempt to make a poem from ideas instead of words? Do you think it's possible there could be an "important work of literature" (whatever that means) which is not read or which is unreadable? Are the ideas or concepts behind or around a work sometimes more significant than the work itself?

5. How are technology, capitalism, and new subcultural practices changing the way that we read (or consume "content")? Who determines what counts as legitimate modes of reading and writing? Are binge-watching Netflix, killing time by scrolling TikTok videos, or reposting on social media legitimate modes of reading or writing? Are they

as valid as older methods of reading such as the concentrated immersion in a novel, "close reading" and academic analysis, or, for that matter, computational methods to process large masses of data known as "distant reading"? What uses do we make of texts (and what uses do they make of us) today? How are Post-conceptual artworks responding to emerging modalities of reading and writing? Do you feel that Post-conceptual works are attempting to create artworks that meet the public with the ways it actually engages with "content" across platforms and modalities; or are Post-conceptual artists dumbing down and trivializing the process of critical, introspective, and imaginative engagement with language and narrative?

6. What might traditional forms—the sonnet, the 10-minute play, the five-paragraph essay—have to offer that a set of arbitrary constraints don't? Alternatively, why might a set of random constraints act as a more interesting prompt to create a new work? The OuLiPo group, like many Conceptual writers, valued the potential of literature (its abstracted forms and ideas, its generative ability to produce other work in the future) over its realization in any concrete piece. Do you agree? Or do you think that forms, ideas, and potential are null unless they are substantiated with a specific, salient, and skillfully executed manifestation in a particular work?

7. Do you think there is a line that demarcates visual art from literature? What about asemic writing, for instance: can it be classified as writing or is it more a form of visual art? Or, is it largely pointless to make distinctions between the two media in contemporary practice? Why might many experimental writers and artists today work in forms that combine both visual components with alphabetic texts? How can a consideration of design, layout, color, iconography, images, emojis, fonts, spacing, and other visual elements enhance the way we read a text or the meanings it takes on?

Writing Prompts

1. Produce a page of asemic writing. Think about the mood or tone your piece is trying to convey. Does your asemic script or alphabet resemble an existing writing system such as Roman, Cryllic, Japanese kanji, modern Hebrew block script, Arabic calligraphic scripts, the Balinese script, and so on? Does it rely on conventions such as the assumption it would be read from right to left or is composed of alphanumeric glyphs rather than ideograms? Does your asemic writing have any tacit narrative or tension to it? How does it function as a visual work? Would you consider creating this piece an act of writing?

2. Write a prose poem in the mode of LANGUAGE writing by composing a series of sentences about or based on various objects in your room. The sentences should seem snatched from different contexts—overheard from unrelated conversations or fragments from assorted genres of texts. The point of view can shift between sentences, too. The grammar should vary widely between sentences, some sentences torquing in elaborate convolutions while others are quick, direct, and idiomatic. The

vocabulary and tone should likewise fluctuate from abstruse to banal, scientific to commercial, and so on. Never mention yourself directly in the piece, though the resulting paragraph may be an implicit self-portrait. Arrange the sentences not by any obvious narrative development but rather by their rhythm and sounds. Your paragraph should avoid any explicit logic; instead, it should flow and pulse with a magnetic field of subtle connotations and correspondences.

3. Create a visual essay, graphic narrative, concrete poem, or some other type of hybrid text in which the visual elements, layout, and images included in it are integral to its design and meaning. Try to make the visual elements go beyond being illustrations or documentary in nature. You might choose to revise a work that you have abandoned from the past, restructuring it according to a visual orientation and arrangement. How will you rework the standard page format and layout in a way that segues with your piece's content? Will your text incorporate photos, images, drawings, or other visual elements? How will its audiences or readers interact with the piece; for example, is it important that it be read in a book, seen in a gallery, handled as a physical object, or viewed online? How do the textual and the visual elements juxtapose, interact, or merge? For additional inspiration, you can see Sarah Minor's "A Visual Writing Resource list" on her personal website: https://www.sarahceniaminor.com/resources.

4. Try the OuLiPo technique of the lipogram (writing a text that leaves out one letter of the alphabet). The longer and more narrative the text, the harder this constraint can be. An alternative and more difficult challenge is to compose a text that only uses a single vowel. You could try the OuLiPo technique known as "N + 7," too, in which you take a short source text and then replace each word with the word that comes seven entries later in the dictionary. Another OuLiPo game is known as the "snowball": each line of a poem should add one letter—an extra constraint you could add for increased difficulty is that each line should also only be one word long. If you are feeling particularly inventive and clever, try inventing a cipher in which a text acts as a secret code that, when deciphered, reveals a hidden text: the difficulty is in making both the cipher text and the deciphered text coherent. Many more OuLiPo constraints can be found in books such as *All That Is Evident Is Suspect* (edited by Ian Monk and Daniel Leven Becker), *THE OULIPO COMPENDIUM* (edited by Harry Mathews and Alistair Brotchie), and *The Penguin Book of Oulipo* (edited by Phillip Terry). See also *A Book of Surrealist Games* (edited by Alistair Brotchie and Mel Gooding) for other constraint-based exercises.

5. The philosopher John Stuart Mill once said, "Eloquence is *heard*; poetry is *over*heard." Capture the ambient language in your environment on an audio recording device for a set amount of time, say, a half hour: you might think about the context and environment that you are recording. Why is it important or not important? (Often the most mundane sites can be just as revealing in terms of what is overheard there.) Then transcribe it—or, let a transcription device do it for you: garble, errors, and all. Then, starting with the transcription, select, discard, sample, remix, and assemble a new text of your own.

6. Create a work that consists entirely of punctuation marks, wingdings, emojis, blank space, symbols, icons, images, photos, and other non-alphanumeric glyphs on your word processing device. You may either write these on your own or evacuate the words from an existing text. You can read Clive Thompson's brief article "What I Learned About My Writing by Seeing Only the Punctuation" (https://medium.com/creators-hub/what-i-learned-about-my-writing-by-seeing-only-the-punctuation-efd5334060b1). A digital tool called "Just the Punctuation" is linked in the article, too, which you might want to explore.

7. Write an essay about writer's block in which the essay describes the process of writing the essay in question by describing in excruciatingly minute detail all the steps you are taking to write it—as well as all the *other* things you are doing that act as distractions from writing, such as checking your phone, scrolling the internet, eating junk food, talking with a friend, pacing the hall, taking a bathroom break, and so on. You might want to see if you can induce "reader's block" in your audience by the banal, second-to-second diaristic accounting you give of your writing process. Or, you might want to take the essay in the direction of autotheory by juxtaposing and braiding quotes from critics, philosophers, and other writers on the idea of writer's block and motivation into the essay, whether or not you choose to analyze or engage these quotes: you could just include them in the margins or footnotes, for example, or some other structure such as stand-alone sections. Bonus: can you make this less a traditional essay and more a multiplatform artwork across several media? That is, the project may include such things as live streaming your writing process, Tweeting about it, creating cartoons, or making listicles, photos, notes, doodles, brainstorms, or text messages. With such a project, it may be unclear whether it's a performance (of your writer's block), an essay (about writer's block), or a series of texts in different media (that document your writer's block while ironically overcoming it by their very production).

8. Compose a story about an impossible artistic movement, artwork, or piece of literature (at least an imaginary one that would be unlikely to ever find physical embodiment). Postmodern classics in this vein include Jorge Luis Borges's "Pierre Menard, or The Author of Quixote," Donald Barthelme's "The Balloon," and Guy Davenport's "Tatlin!" More recent short novels that use this premise are *Nazi Literature in the Americas* by Roberto Bolaño and *A Brief History of Portable Literature* by Enrique Vila-Matas. How does your story reflect on or send up real-world art movements, ideologies, authors, artists, and milieus? What does the story say about the materiality of art or literature, about pretention, or about the untold historical motives or social backdrops behind art making? Does it eulogize the failure of this artwork—perhaps any artwork—to be fully realized? What seems more important in it, the concept of the artwork it describes or the characters and plot of the story itself; or, how are these two balanced? How much does your "story" borrow techniques from essays, criticism, or other genres?

CHAPTER 6
MINOR FORMS

I. Introduction to Minor Forms

One class of writing that gets discussed, somewhat erroneously, alongside hybrids is minor forms. Deleuze and Guattari first coined the term "minor literature" when contrasting Franz Kafka's style with the masterworks of previous writers in *Kafka: Toward a Theory of Minor Literature*. Ilya Szilak (2015: n.p.) describes the broad field of minor forms as he writes:

> Its potency resides in a "strategy of failure." These strategies include the use of "minor" languages such as ads, melodrama, kitsch, misspeaking, creole, private and non-signifying languages, the execution of "minor" forms of political action such as refusal, drag, humor, play, and other modes of practice which emphasize glitch, inefficiency and inconsistency, embodiment and temporality.

Minor forms are neither spliced nor grafted onto other forms, like hybrids; however, they have been consigned to the margins of literary culture and may therefore be relatively unfamiliar to many readers. Some readers, given this unfamiliarity, may try to assimilate an instance of a minor form into its nearest major genre, fiction, or poetry, say—and, in doing so, a minor form may begin to seem like a hybrid. But, we argue, this is a misreading. It assumes that the major genres of Creative Writing (fiction, poetry, creative nonfiction, and scriptwriting) cover all the available real estate, which is emphatically not the case.

Minor forms may be minor in their recognition, but they are not necessarily small. There are whole books composed of fragments, aphorisms, jokes, pensées, letters, annotations, and notebook/journal/diary entries. Many of these forms were once part of venerated literary traditions; in passing into cultural or commercial obscurity, they have thus been orphaned by our contemporary demarcation of the literary terrain. Consider the knee-slappers in the ancient joke book, *Philogelos* (compiled by Hierocles and Philagrius); the fragmented zuihitsu within *The Pillow Book* (Sei Shōnagan); the religious jottings in *Pensées* (Blaise Pascal); and the overheated love letters of *Abelard and Héloïse* (Peter Abelard and Héloïse d'Argenteuil). While many writers will incorporate minor forms into their novels or memoirs, fewer contemporary writers set out to compose works exclusively in minor forms themselves.

Minor forms are distinct from hybrids since their aesthetic partakes of a singular, if often overlooked, lineage. Epistolary writing, for instance, is far older and more widespread than novel writing. It's a contingent, historical fact that so-called Creative Writing, as it's been institutionalized today, largely excludes minor forms. And unlike flash forms, which strive toward self-containment, several minor forms tend to relish their incompleteness or, at least, have a different conception of what constitutes "completeness" than the well-wrought unity we've come to expect from works in the major genres. In their "underflowing," they operate as subliterary compositional units. When read on their own, minor forms must provide their own context as they do not tend to serve some greater narrative function. An aphorism or a letter can stand on its own.

Note, we use the term "form" here loosely. Some of what we dub "minor forms" other scholars might refer to as marginalized modes or aesthetics: camp, punk, melodrama, or *rasquachismo*, for example. These modes are distinguished by their affective registers, signifying practices, and use in distinct communities. They are not forms per se since they do not imply a given structure. One might camp in a novel, play, or letter; you can have a punk poem as well as a punk memoir. Nonetheless, the brief bursts of violent noise and underdog ethos associated with punk are so endemic as to inform any expression in the punk mode and to act as an organizing framework. Similarly, masquerade, innuendo, and gossip are so integral to camp that the insouciant queer sensibility of camp ramifies with these strategies not only in its various literary outputs but in its very mode of being. Ultimately, in such cases, style and lifestyle may become one and the same. Minor forms tend to be outgrowths of underground subcultures. They are embedded in social rituals, survival skills, or revolutionary tactics. Thus, when we speak of "form," we do so broadly, understanding the way that literary structures, minor ones in particular, are part of larger cultural practices and manners of perception.

Minor forms are not necessarily slight in importance, though some are self-consciously diminutive or modest. Many have a long and distinguished pedigree. What makes them "minor" is more about their relationship to mainstream consumer products and establishment values. Even so, minor forms may be superficially packaged as bumper stickers, gag gifts, coffee mugs, heartwarming quotations, kitschy signage, or jumbo-sized coffee-table books with ironically light takes on their subject matter. Today, one is just as likely to encounter minor forms in meme culture. But the transference of minor forms from a marginalized currency in a subculture to the larger consumer or literary culture tends to require some rationalization. At times, this involves the watering down or misconstrual of the minor form to make it conform to the dictates of mass appeal; at other times, such as the proliferation of camp aesthetics, it may involve a subculture's increasing acceptance by the dominant society.

II. Schlock, Doggerel, Melodrama, and Naïve Art

In her introduction to the anthology, *Pathetic Literature*, poet Eileen Myles reclaims "pathetic" as a badge of distinction. Myles seems to be addressing the specter of minor forms when she writes: "What exemplified pathetic art then [late twentieth century] was an orientation to crafts, to feeling, to the handmade and diaristic. It was kind of dykey. Using cuddly and abject stuff like stuffed animals rather than producing work that was determinedly abstract. There was a readymade aspect to a lot of it" (2022). Among the most "pathetic" forms are schlock and doggerel. **Schlock** is a term used to describe something that is of poor quality or lacking in value, especially works of art that are considered cheap, vulgar, or unoriginal. It is often used in a derogatory or dismissive way to describe something that is seen as being lowbrow or unworthy of attention. In his novels *Wigger* and *Ratz Are Nice*, Lawrence Ytzhak Braithwaite (1995, 2000) writes about an underclass of white supremacists, gang-rapists, drug dealers, and junkies. He marks up the prose with "backslashes and other typographical symbols" to denote "the slash of hardcore guitars, the tumbling loop of reggae bass, the pumping of fists in the air" (Hodges: n.p.). One review compares it to the dub poem and places it in a category all its own—"sound fiction" that's "difficult to read sitting down" (Hodges: n.p.). The experimental novelist Kathy Acker, also of the punk ilk, incorporated a variety of schlock into her novels, including pulp fiction, pop culture, political tracts, fairy tales, role playing, and especially pornographic sex.

For an example of schlock, see the excerpt from Sara Tuss Efrik's *Danse Macabre Piggies*, as translated by Paul Cunningham, on pp. 225–47.

The novelist Neil Gaiman (2021) notes that Acker "did not believe that there was any gradation between good writing and schlock and took her inspiration and her material from anywhere" (*Lit Hub*). David Foster Wallace (1992: 154) called her work "at once critically pretty interesting and artistically pretty crummy and actually no fun to read at all." But one senses Wallace's definition of "fun" is tinged with a more literary sensibility, as in major-form fun. In *Eat Your Mind*, Acker's literary biographer Jason McBride (2022: xiv) is more generous, calling Acker's oeuvre "funny, grotesque, titillating, profound, demented, recursive, shocking, baffling, monotonous, bilious, mischievous, and breathtaking." Much of schlock's appeal is closely related to other minor aesthetics, described later. To reap the benefits of reading minor forms, one must keep an open mind. Many writers inspired by Acker and similar brands of queer, punk-rock schlock fly under the banner of **gurlesque** today. These writers view the persistent denigration of feminine work, seen as lowbrow and schlocky, as a patriarchal imposition, and they attempt to reclaim such historically outré subjects as the female body, menstruation, hysteria, childbirth, and fashion.

Read Dodie Bellamy's "Dogs Without a Face" for one example of gurlesque on pp. 201–2.

A similar minor form is **doggerel**, a type of poetry that is considered to be poorly written or not serious. Doggerel is characterized by its irregular meter and rhyme, and its use of simple, unrefined language. It is sometimes regarded as juvenilia or amateur art. It is often used to mock or satirize something or someone, or to express a simple idea or emotion. Poets such as Frederick Seidel and Michael Robbins—even Sylvia Plath—flirt with doggerel in some of their verse: it gives it an edge of the awkward, juvenile, or unpolished, which can be ironically set against the seemingly more mature concerns they address. While doggerel is often not taken seriously as a literary form, it can be used effectively in certain contexts. As the critic David Caplan (2012: 6) points out, doggerel "functions as a major form in contemporary hip-hop and a minor form in contemporary poetry." As a minor form ebbs in popularity, its best bet at being reabsorbed into the culture is to surface in a bold new context. If one wants their self-consciously bad writing to be recognized today, they should consider submitting their work to the Bulwer Lytton Fiction Contest at San José State University, which invites writers to submit "an atrocious opening sentence to the worst novel never written." (The namesake of the prize, Sir Bulwer-Lytton, by the way, is the one who came up with this classically bad opener in 1830: "It was a dark and stormy night.") The "winning" sentence from 2022 is included below in all its convoluted glory:

I knew she was trouble the second she walked into my 24-hour deli, laundromat, and detective agency, and after dropping a load of unmentionables in one of the heavy-duty machines (a mistake that would soon turn deadly) she turned to me, asking for two things: find her missing husband and make her a salami on rye with spicy mustard, breaking into tears when I told her I couldn't help—I was fresh out of salami. (Farmer 2022)

Another genre that gets a bad rap is **melodrama**. Melodrama is characterized by extravagant, emotional, and larger-than-life characters and plot, as well as a focus on sensational themes such as romance, betrayal, and suspense. Soap operas and *telenovelas* are perfect examples of this, but melodrama also appears in experimental works. Film director Guy Maddin's docu-fantasias, for example—whether it's *The Saddest Music in the World*, *The Heart of the World*, or *My Winnipeg*—involve grand gestures and intense, highly charged situations. In a discussion with Isabella Rossellini for *BOMB*, Maddin (2009: n.p.) has this to say about the genre:

It's not real life exaggerated, as so many people feel. It's not the truth exaggerated. Exaggerating the truth would deform it, make the art dishonest. Really good melodrama is the truth uninhibited. In our dreams, where our emotions are uninhibited, if we are lucky, we get to do and experience all the things we repress during civilized waking hours. In our dreams we get to possess the one after whom we lust, strike the one we hate, steal, wail out loud, and remove our clothes—all in front of a public which wouldn't tolerate this unrestrained behavior in the daylight world. In our sleep thoughts we get to be as childish as we long to be! We dream the truth about our feelings, sometimes in a discombobulated way, but these are real feelings churning themselves up. In a good melodrama the same disinhibition occurs. You see, these are not exaggerated feelings, they are repressed feelings liberated. There's a big difference! If you look at melodrama in this light you won't cringe.

Like schlock and doggerel, the power of melodrama lies in its ability to blur boundaries—between high and low culture, good and bad writing, and nuanced versus over-the-top emotions. There is an insinuation that writers of schlock, doggerel, and melodrama are amateurish, but the ways in which serious writers have managed to integrate and elevate these forms suggests creatives of all ilk should feel free to employ outsider practices.

The novelist Robert Musil once described the work of Swiss writer Robert Walser as "not a suitable foundation for a literary genre"—and indeed, much of Walser's writings were characterized by his peers as **naïve** or **outsider art**. His work often appeared in newspapers as **feuilletons**, "little leafs" whose light, leisurely tone contrasted with works of serious journalism or criticism. Walser also wrote microscripts, stories composed in tiny handwriting only a couple millimeters high, often written along the literal margin of receipts or the back of business cards. This deliberate self-marginalization can be compared to Emily Dickinson's fragmentary manuscripts jotted down on envelopes and loose scraps of paper: the material intractability casts the work as counter to the dominant methods of literary circulation. Like Guattari and Deleuze, Musil also classed Kafka as a writer of minor literature, although he said it in a very specific way, likening Kafka's debut to a "special case of the Walser Type." It should be noted that it was not simply the case that Walser missed the mark; he intentionally eschewed the bravura of his peers as when he self-consciously wrote his microscripts. Mónica de la Torre (2010: n.p.) describes the project:

> Having "fearfully, hideously hated his pen" [Walser] went from delivering his sparkling fiction in copperplate handwriting to jotting miniatures in pencil on trimmed-to-size, assorted scraps: tax forms, calendars, business correspondence, clippings, penny dreadfuls, and the like, with which his scribbles were often in dialogue … He found that these messier and playful fragments were reviving in him an otherwise waning "writerly enthusiasm."

Similarly, in a profile in the *New Yorker*, Benjamin Kunkel (2007: n.p.) described Walser as "the incredible shrinking writer." By deliberately choosing the tiny, marginal, and out-of-the-way, Walser and similar outsider writers question the values that underlie the formation of the major genres and the quest for big-time publication.

Another outsider writer was Amos Tutuola, a Nigerian of the Yoruba tribe who had relatively scant formal education. The famous Welsh poet Dylan Thomas brought Tutuola's first novel, purportedly written in only two days, to a wider public. The novel, *The Palm-Wine Drinkard and His Dead Palm-Wine Tapster in the Dead's Town*, was modeled, in part, on oral folktales and included ungrammatical passages or ones composed in Pidgin English dialect. Some British and American reviewers initially saw the book as naïve or grotesque whereas some Nigerians felt it reinforced stereotypes about Africans as "primitive." Yet the novel became not only an inspiration for later Nigerian writers, such as Chinua Achebe, but also a source text for writers like Russell Hoban, whose dystopian novel *Riddley Walker* is composed in a futuristic idiom. Over time, the novel, though it remains provocative, has become one of the foundational texts of the African literary canon, showing how outsider work can infiltrate mainstream culture.

III. Punk, Trash, Camp, and Kitsch Aesthetics

Both Braithwaite and Acker were considered **punk** writers, which alludes to a subculture and worldview that opposes capitalist products, the police state, and the oppressive gender system (e.g., Riot Grrrl punk). Raw, unfiltered noise, subversive secondhand fashion, and underground DIY artwork are hallmarks of the punk aesthetic. One way that the punk aesthetic operates is by taking cultural images and phrases to scramble them in collage, throwing the jagged, remade script back in the face of the mainstream culture that produced them. In this, the punk aesthetic borrows from and extends the technique of Dada collage artists such as Hannah Höch, who cut up magazines and photos to reorder them in disturbing ways that destabilized the corporate, patriarchal, or fascist power structures the original images were intended to maintain.

While the evolution of punk has given birth to high-end fashion, mall rats, and poseurs, other subgroups like gutter punks and crust punks tend to walk the walk and squat the squat. Their rhythms—from loitering to panhandling to dumpster diving—result in the grimy patina of street life. There is a preoccupation with filth in punk, evident from stage names like Johnny Rotten, Johnny Puke, Rat Scabies, Pat Smear, Lint, and Roach; songs like "Dirtnap," "Dirty Old Town," and "Dirt Poor and Mentally Ill"; and the punk poetry and prose of Jim Carroll, Patti

Smith, and Richard Hell. One of the more infamous embodiments of this brand of punk was the misanthropic shock rocker GG Allin who self-mutilated and defecated on stage—and not just once. His blood and feces became a staple of his aggro show. Allin self-described as the "Outlaw Scumfuc." He proudly claimed to smell like raw sewage and also wrote a manifesto that reads like a declaration of war on the corporate music industry. From his anti-capitalist viewpoint, it's the studios and record stores that are churning out the real sewage of conformist pop trash. As Allin watches even his rock idols succumb to the oxymoron of corporate rock n' roll, he is displaced to the periphery of the punk scene.

Dirt, William James (1929: 129) says, is "matter out of place." According to anthropologist Mary Douglas (1966), what differentiates "dirt"—or filth, pollution, and contamination—from mere "dust" is the cultural system in which it takes part. This system categorizes spaces, times, rites, taboos, and ideals to distinguish clean and unclean, sacred and profane things. It likewise helps differentiate "us" from "them," in-groups from out-groups. And it is this cultural system of contrasts that satire, as the cultural system's cutting edge, helps to construct. In some cases, this can act as a critique of the values within the rarified art world itself, opposing the polished and pristine with the unvarnished by-products of the artist's experience.

In other cases, by constructing from the waste products of society, also called **trash culture (i.e., "trashy")**, the artist may be making a commentary on the ecological crisis of mindless consumerism. Many artists are interested in salvaging the detritus of consumer culture, recombining it to make art from the ready-to-hand trash and waste around them. In 1961, the Italian artist Piero Manzoni filled ninety tin cans with his feces, called it *Artist's Shit*, and sold them according to their equivalent weight in gold. In Joshua Tree, Noah Purifoy's Outdoor Desert Sculpture Museum consists of assemblage art, car parts, busted electronics, scrap metal, and other junk. One exhibit, simulating Jim Crow era segregation, depicts two water fountains; one is labeled "white" and the other "colored." The latter, though, is not a fountain, but an upraised mouth-level toilet. This is at once homage to Duchamp's sculptural subterfuge, *Fountain*, now considered high art, and a stark denial of it. This toilet isn't destined for MoMA, but instead it's situated in situ, among other desert junk spires. Another of Purifoy's works, *66 Signs of Neon*, uses the detritus from the Watts Riots, "glittering, twisted, grotesquely formed materials" to represent and communicate the racialized uprising (Purifoy: n.p.). One piece uses lead drippings from neon signs and metal casings for letters to create an alphabetical palimpsest assemblage.

Not far from Purifoy's desert trash art is the anarchist encampment, Slab City, and its squatter arts commune, East Jesus. With no electric grid, the writing in East Jesus is mostly done with Sharpies and spray paint for improvised "property" signs, motley installation art, slam poetry written in notebooks or cell phones, and community decrees that fly in the face of unincorporated anarchist life. Political and philosophical pablum abound in the Slabs; known as the "last free place," art and writing culture is delimited by the material culture and limited economic means of its denizens.

Literary "trash" might include lowbrow items like the *National Inquirer* and *Hustler*, Jackie Collins and Danielle Steele novels, the Babysitters' Club series, and the tweets of the Kardashians. Authors who take inspiration from such sources in their creative writing may not aim at emulating such "trash" per se so much as shamelessly indulging the so-called guilty pleasures of pop consumption. For example, literary magazines *Always Crashing*, the *Destroyer*, *Taco Bell Quarterly*, and *DREGINALD* along with small presses such as Apocalypse Party, Pity Milk, and Disorder Press often traffic in literary "trash" culture.

A similar aesthetic known as ***rasquachismo*** is the cheap, gaudy, remade, even downcycled, trashy aesthetic that arose among the Chicano and Mexican working-class, sometimes with a queer subtext. Amalia Mesa-Bains (1999: 157–8) writes that "in *rasquachismo*, the irreverent and spontaneous are employed to make the most from the least … one has a stance that is both defiant and inventive. Aesthetic expression comes from discards, fragments, even recycled everyday materials." Detritus and rubbish become inlaid, layered, and labored over to transform into lurid sequins, tiaras, and jewels. There can be a hint at both venerating and inverting overdone Catholic effigies and altars. Raquel Gutiérrez, in their essay "A Concatenation of Sprawls," writes that "*rasquachismo* is a term as varied as its deployment, which can be limiting or liberating depending on circumstances; it's both a derision and a secret code. Detractors might be middle-class aspirants, or Sunday church señoras who name the *rasquache* in whispers, calling out the tacky, the impoverished, the vulgar." Gutiérrez notes that art historian Tomás Ybarra-Frausto claims that *rasquachismo* embodies the resilience—and resistance—of the underdogs, *los de abajo*. "The ethos of rasquachismo," Gutiérrez states, "is the ability to make do, to improvise." It takes the survivor's ingenuity to use whatever materials are at hand and uses them to create extravagance and insolent beauty. Ybarra-Frausto, in his foundational document *Rasquachismo: A Chicano Sensibility* (1989), mentions Daniel Venegas's novel *Las Aventuras de Don Chipote* and the early work of Teatro Campesino as literary touchstones of this aesthetic.

Camp is characterized by an exaggerated and often ironic appreciation of something that is considered kitschy, tasteless, or politically incorrect. It is often associated with a sense of playfulness and humor, and it can involve an enjoyment of things that are seemingly outré or out of fashion. The concept of camp has its roots in the LGBTQ+ community, and it has been used to describe a wide range of cultural phenomena, including fashion, music, film, and art. Susan Sontag's "Notes on Camp" is one of the defining essays to tackle understanding the ambivalent sensibility. Sontag (1966: 277) writes that "camp vision is not in terms of beauty, but in the degree of artifice, of stylization." Artifice is embraced for its own sake, a mark of being passionate yet trivial: naïve, exaggerated, denatured, flamboyant—a travesty of whatever is normal. One proponent of camp is the cult filmmaker John Waters who is known for his irreverent style and fixation on taboo. Waters is considered a pioneer of the "midnight movie" genre with his most well-known work, *Pink Flamingos*, blending elements of trash culture, camp, and kitsch, which has made him an influential figure in the world of underground cinema. An example of highbrow camp was from the 2019 MET Gala, which was themed "Camp: Notes on Fashion." It was meant as a tongue-in-cheek nod to the idea of camp, poking fun at the idea of fashion itself as a serious pursuit, celebrating the more playful, lighthearted side of dressing up. This resulted in big bows, capes, animal prints, and campy accessories that would typically be frowned upon at a black-tie event.

And, finally, there's **kitsch**. Kitsch is often defined as a naïve or superficial imitation of artworks or handcrafted products, especially for consumer culture. It is often sentimental. It is in some ways so ubiquitous in our culture now that it may no longer seem like an imitation. Nevertheless, some artists such as Jeff Koons have embraced kitsch, using populist sentiment and consumer values to reorient the world of high art. Koons' stainless steel "Rabbit," resembling a cute disposable plastic-balloon animal, fetched over $91 million at auction in 2019. The Christie's website remarks, "This faceless quicksilver rabbit manages to embody whole ranges of references while at the same time remaining deadpan and aloof. We find ourselves filling its steely silence with thoughts of Disney, *Playboy*, childhood, Easter, Brancusi, Lewis Carroll, Frank Capra's *Harvey*, Marcel Duchamp's readymades, Andy Warhol's *Cloud*, without ever plumping for a single meaning." But the monumental treatment of a mass-produced child's toy asks us to look closer at the potential beauty of banal objects around us even as Koon's work participates in the commodity marketplace it seemingly comments upon. Today, reference to pop culture and kitsch items in art or literature is commonplace and rarely comes with any insinuation of critique; rather, kitsch is simply the texture of the things around us, common as air and dirt. Items of pop culture fandom are frequently used as sources of artistic inspiration. One more etiolated form of kitsch style is known as **kawaī**, developed in Japan. Kawaī embraces items that are cute, adorable, feminine, infantile, or arrested in a state of neoteny such as Hello Kitty, certain anime characters, and baby doll dresses with big pink bows. Some of Chelsey Minnis's work from books such as *Bad Bad* and *Poemland* could be seen as exploring a kawaī-like sensibility, prizing attitudes, and artifacts that are soft, glittery, adolescent, and femme.

All of these aesthetics—punk, trash, camp, and kitsch—have been explored in experimental writing as a means of recoding culture, performing class criticism, and developing new literary movements such as dirty realism, Kmart realism, and Australia's grunge lit. Such minor forms in literature often have ties to minimalism. In *Minimalism in Action*, Tim Groenland recounts how the editor Gordon Lish, pencil-editing a story by Raymond Carver, added a notable modifier to one of his sentences: "It was another tragedy in a long line of low-rent tragedies" (2019: 83). Robert Towers (1981: n.p.), in the *New York Review of Books*, picked up this phrase when he characterized Carver's stories as "low-rent tragedies involving people who read *Popular Mechanics* and *Field and Stream*, people who play bingo, hunt deer, fish, and drink." It brings to mind another infamous phrase from the midwesterner Thomas McGuane (1980: 83) about how people who live in flyover country, himself included, "figure out what is going on elsewhere by subscribing to magazines." Writing from the inside, it's clear in its self-deprecation. If spoken from the outside, though, his words could wound. Contemporary American writers like Annie Proulx and Ottessa Moshfegh, Australians like Edward Berridge and John Birmingham, and British filmmakers Andrea Arnold and Mike Leigh all write in this vein. For a distinctly rural delineation of such aesthetics, we encourage you to check out *Hick Poetics* or the work of one of its editors, Abe Smith, who in *Destruction of Man*, writes: "Think the thinking persons of the future of the past / would not know dirt if it bit 'em / oh bud, it will, one day" (2018). The rural, outlandish aesthetic—often minimal and class-conscious—can sometimes poke fun at both the pretentions of urban sophistication and at its own country ways.

IV. Fragments, Quotations, Aphorisms, Jokes, and Lists

Fragments constitute the entirety of Jenny Boully's (2007) *The Book of Beginnings and Endings*. As Nicole Walker (2007: n.p.) summarizes in her review: "Each odd-numbered page is a beginning and each even-numbered page is an ending. And not the beginning and ending to one story" (*DIAGRAM*). By denying any semblance of causation, Boully challenges the aesthetic criteria of the well-wrought unity of the text. She denies the reader the typical inducements at the beginning of a story and withholds the satisfaction associated with an ending. Another writer to work with the fragment was Walter Benjamin in *Arcades Project*, an unfinished—some say unfinishable—assortment of fragments, quotes, theorizing, notes, anecdotes, and commentary about nineteenth-century Paris. And, finally, in *Reality Hunger*, David Shields arranges—or "samples"—618 **quotations** from other writers. One commentator, upon reading the book, noted how stirring some of those quotes were, only to discover it was he who was being plagiarized. The attributions *do* appear, begrudgingly, in an appendix, but Shields implores the reader to snip and toss it out. For Shields, the curation of the minor forms of the fragment and quotation results in something else: a manifesto on originality and the public domain.

Whereas fragments give the impression that they once belonged to a missing whole, **aphorisms** stand sturdily alone. These concise, pithy, and clever phrases originate with the "wisdom traditions of ancient Egypt and China," writes James Geary (2007: 3) in his *Guide to the World's Great Aphorists*. In Geary's taxonomy, there are eight types of aphorism: chiasmus, definition, joke, metaphor, moral, observation, paradox, and pensée, the latter which he refers to as "the most languid and leisurely aphoristic form" (2007: 6) From *The Upanishads* to the *Book of Proverbs*, Parmenides to Epicurus, the assertiveness of the aphorism has lent the form to bold declarations in religious philosophy and cosmogony. Perhaps one of the most timeless aphorists was Rumi; *Insane With Love*, a small portion of his 1700 rubais, represents a poetic take on the Persian aphoristic tradition.

But the aphorism is also relevant today. Entire collections of aphorisms reflect a studied worldview as is the case with *The Bed of Procrustes* (2016) by philosopher Nassim Nicholas Taleb. In 2011, the literary journal *Hotel Amerika* published its aphorism-themed issue that abounded with the minor form. Reacting to the issue, Michael Leong used the OuLiPo method known as "preverbs," snapping two unrelated aphorisms in half and soldering them together for absurd or comic effect. On his blog, he writes:

Formal poetry? As opposed to what other kind? (H.L. Hix)
+
Saint Patrick: first case of Stockholm Syndrome? (Patrick Madden)
=
Formal poetry: first case of Stockholm Syndrome? (Michael Leong)

Notably, many aphorisms are assimilated into **folk culture**. For example, a seventy-three-word sentiment once expressed by Margaret Atwood during a lecture has been collectively summarized, shaped, and remembered as this seventeen-word aphorism: "Men are afraid that women will laugh at them. Women are afraid that men will kill them." This repackaging has the portable quality of a home truth. Other examples of folk culture include **weird tales, campfire tales**, and **creepy pasta**, all subgenres of horror or ghost stories, which often have a gothic vibe. If these popular horror stories tend to be formulaic like many aphorisms, they also tend to end, not with a punch line like jokes, but with what's very similar: a jump scare. These types of popular literature behave more like templates designed for individual improvisation. Because there are no authorized versions, their momentum derives from the power of iteration.

Another minor form with a reliance on spare language, rhetorical devices, performative reasoning, improvisation, and logical propositions—all mixed up with some heady irony—is the **one-liner joke**. Sometimes, it is hard to distinguish aphorisms from the joke form. *Deep Thoughts* (1992) by Jack Handey is one such example, a book spinoff from the sketch on the comedy show *Saturday Night Live* in which the joke writer remixes old sayings for comedic effect. Take this one for example: "Before you criticize someone, you should walk a mile in their shoes. That way when you criticize them, you are a mile away from them and you have their shoes." The setup and punch line represent cross-purposes.

While many works incorporate tidbits of humor, sometimes whole novels can be structured around jokes not unlike a stand-up act. Fran Ross's 1974 novel *Oreo* combines the jokes of Bortsch Belt Jewish vaudeville with the Black humor of the Chitlin' Circuit. The bulk of the novel is structured as a series of set pieces and punch lines, including gags such as menus, math formulas, "a key for speed readers," quizzes, and jingles. Ross's novel creates a slapstick tension between its grand quest narrative, modeled on ancient myths, and the more homegrown jokes it constantly circles back to; Ross undercuts her own classical allusions to show how jokes themselves, although a minor form, are already valid as literature.

One deadpan comic, Mitch Hedberg, was famous for his koan-like jokes, an absurdist twist on the genre of observational humor. For example: "Rice is great if you're hungry and want to eat two thousand of something." The logic here is, of course, incongruous since the desire to eat two thousand somethings is not what compels one to eat, well, anything. In another joke, Hedberg says, "I'm not a vegetarian because I love animals. I'm a vegetarian because I hate plants." Again, he invents an absurd underlying motivation for his dietary habits—that it is a way of expressing antipathy for the things you eat. In other jokes, Hedberg's logic is delivered with less of a wink. Consider this riddle: "I'm against picketing, but I don't know how to show it."

Meanwhile, others like "America's Funnyman" Neil Hamburger, played by Australian-born anti-comedian Gregg Turkington, intentionally flub the delivery, exposing just how brittle the minor form is. To make his comedy seem all the more "minor," Hamburger is costumed like a sleazy lounge opener with greasy hair, rented tux, and two tilting glasses of water and scotch; he is prone to self-interruption, particularly due to his vomitous reflux "gag"; and his schlocky jokes are predicated on B-list celebrity gossip and topical humor that has a shelf life slated to spoil before the audience's eyes. You might ask, why would anyone ever go to a show like that? What Hamburger lacks in charisma, he makes up for with his post-ironic homage to comedy's most generic minor forms: one-liners, platitudes, bad puns, dad jokes, false starts, prop comedy, insult comedy, tautologies, hyperbole, vamping, catchphrases, punching down, doubling down, groaning, whimpering, zeugma, audience participation, PSAs, trivia questions, dangling modifiers, pregnant pauses, and even buk-buk-boking like a chicken all while nervously, performatively checking on his setlist. He even tells formulaic jokes that appeal to the least common denominator—like knock-knock jokes, what-do-you-get-when-you-mix (thing 1) and (thing 2) jokes, why did so-and-so cross the road jokes, and most minor of all: how many (of a type) does it take to screw in a lightbulb jokes.

Probably since the oldest recorded joke—about a Sumerian woman farting in her husband's lap—humor writing has been a mainstay of popular and literary culture. Other humor is collected in journals like the *Harvard Lampoon*, *The Onion*, *Clickhole*, or *McSweeney's Internet Tendency*. The latter is best known for its sardonic takedowns as seen in the persona piece "I'm Comic Sans, Asshole" or the hyperbolically festive "It's Decorative Gourd Season, Motherfucker."

Minor forms often act as an envelope inviting a push, a medium for jumping the shark and shaking things up—mostly due to their inconspicuous and quotidian nature. Informal jokes, lists, aphorisms, quotations, journals, and letters are difficult to regulate because they are often distributed privately in homes and diffusely throughout communities instead of through bigger publishing or media companies. Whether it's Lenny Bruce's obscenity trials, the forced labor/house arrest of Myanmar's Moustache Brothers, the hooliganism charges against Pussy Riot after their mock prostrations in a Moscow church, or the countless writers imprisoned for lèse-majesté globally, minor forms often represent a power struggle against major actors. Their very minor-ness makes them clandestine samizdat that can slip through the cracks of bigger power structures.

In his book *Weapons of the Weak: Everyday Forms of Peasant Resistance*, James C. Scott documents the lesser-known arsenal of "ordinary weapons of relatively powerless groups":

> Foot dragging, dissimulation, desertion, false compliance, pilfering, feigned ignorance, slander, arson, sabotage, and so on … They require little or no coordination or planning; they make use of implicit understandings and informal networks; they often represent a form of individual self-help; they typically avoid any direct, symbolic confrontation with authority. (1985: xvi)

Such an arsenal is part and parcel of a "constant, grinding conflict" as opposed to the "rare heroic" (1985: xvi). Scott goes on to taxonomize linguistic weapons of the weak: "rumour, gossip, disguises, linguistic tricks, metaphors, euphemisms, folktales, ritual gestures, and anonymity" (1985: xvi). These tactics are themselves minor forms that recode everyday speech acts as forceful political weapons, giving agency back to the oppressed.

Similar impulses can be found in The Digital Culture World Lecture Tour where hypermedia artist Talan Memmott dreams up literary **advertisements** for fake billboards for a fictionalized world tour targeted to social media addicts. Services include cosmetic surgery for better selfies, a meme boot camp, a post-digital identity workshop, and an information session for those who have been shamed or injured online by internet trolls, unfriending, malware, or banality. Critic Ilya Szilak (2015) notes how this project "brings into question not only what is literature, but several other binaries: public, private; work, play; information, noise; success, failure; high art, low art. In recoding the dominant and minor terms, Memott undermines the 'naturalness' of this hierarchy, and opens up the possibility of writing and reading these terms differently" (2015: n.p.). The seemingly trivial nature of minor forms can make them effective minatory tools—like cherry bombs and Molotov cocktails—in guerilla warfare against larger corporate machinations.

V. Collected Letters, Literary Notebooks, Commonplace Books, and Marginalia

Collected letters are a type of literary work published in a book or other format and may include letters written by a single person over the course of their lifetime, or letters written by multiple people to each other. They tend to display a disarming intimacy and glimpse behind the scenes of public personas. Additionally, the literary nature of such correspondence may be an incidental occasion of two writers in dialogue. But just as often, the thought doodles and doodads that writers scribble to one another outside the public gaze reveals their true style as much as their more studied works. Works that began as private letters can be distinguished from epistolary forms, which, although they employ the format of a letter, are intended from the outset for a wider public (though, admittedly, the "open letter" erodes this boundary). Many private letters are discovered or printed posthumously by universities or literary executors; only through critical scholarship are they elevated to the status of literature. One example, *Letters to a Young Poet*, is a collection of ten letters written by poet Rainer Maria Rilke to nineteen-year-old cadet Franz Xaver Kappus. Rilke's letters encourage the young poet to pursue his artistic ambitions while offering insights on artistic creation and the role of the artist in society. Another book of letters, *Dear Ijeawele, or A Feminist Manifesto in Fifteen Suggestions*, is Chimamanda Ngozie Adichie's outline of how to raise a feminist daughter to a friend who asked for advice. Finally, in *Dear New Girl or Whatever Your Name Is*, Trinie Dalton compiles notes she's confiscated from her high school students. Each note, originally meant to be a private correspondence between two adolescent friends, becomes the subject of a permanent exhibit in this visual collage that resembles the interior of a teacher's desk drawer.

Literary notebooks, **diaries**, or **journals** are used for a variety of purposes, such as brainstorming or developing characters, plotting out a story, or jotting down notes about a particular subject or theme. Literary notebooks are often personal and private and may contain the raw, unedited material that forms the basis of a writer's published work. They may additionally contain sketches, diagrams, or other visual elements that help the writer to organize or conceptualize their ideas. Witold Gombrowicz's *Diary* became a dumping ground for stray phrases and random jottings, wholecloth essays, polemics, and anecdotes. Similarly, David Wagoner harvested choice lines, aphorisms, and poems both complete and incomplete from poet Theodore Roethke's voluminous mass of handwritten notebooks, assembling a slim core sample in *Straw for the Fire*. Notebooks are often curated retrospectively as was the case for Kurt Cobain's *Journals*, which includes a smattering of song lyrics, sadistic doodles, shopping lists, medical diaries, and so on. Similarly, a **commonplace book** is a type of notebook or journal that is used to record and organize important or interesting ideas, quotations, or other information. Commonplace books originated in the Renaissance period, when they were used by scholars and intellectuals as a way of collecting and organizing their knowledge. A commonplace book may be arranged according to various principles, such as subject matter, chronology, or alphabetical order. The entries in a commonplace book may be the writer's own observations or commentary, or they may be quotations or excerpts from other works. W. H. Auden's commonplace book, published as *A Certain World*, he deemed a type of "autobiography." *Amerifl.txt* by Douglass Crase, meanwhile, is a quirky repository of citations from major and minor artists, a kind of quoteboard rendered as high art.

Ander Monson's "Sincerity," on pp. 287–9, is a commonplace bibliography, where the author reflects on the relative truthiness of essays in his collection, *Vanishing Point*.

Douglas Adams and John Loyd's *The Meaning of Liff: A Dictionary of Things There Aren't Any Words for Yet—But There Ought to Be* is modeled as a **reference work**, a book of definitions for non-words. "Abruzzo," for example, is the worn patch of ground beneath a swingset, and "tingrith" is the feeling of aluminum foil against your fillings. Reference writing is considered a minor form because of its mainly utilitarian function, but there are any number of ways to reinvigorate such writing practices, whether through fantasy (Jorge Luis Borges's *The Book of Imaginary Beings*), satire (Ambrose Bierce's *The Devil's Dictionary*), malapropism and cliché (Gustave Flaubert's *Dictionary of Received Ideas*), or surrealism (Georges Bataille's *Encyclopaedia Acephalica*).

Read Teju Cole's satirical dictionary entries, "In Place of Thought," which were inspired in part by Ambrose Bierce's *The Devil's Dictionary*, on pp. 221–2.

Marginalia are notes or comments that are written in the margins of a book or other written work. Marginalia can take many forms, from simple copyediting marks (like carets, wavy lines, or strokes); underlines and strikethroughs; question marks and exclamation marks; to more elaborate annotations featuring squiggles, scribbles, and scrawls. They may be written by the original author of the work, by a later reader or scholar, or by anyone else who has come into contact with the book. One example of this is Ander Monson's *Letter to a Future Lover: Marginalia, Errata, Secrets, Inscriptions, and Other Ephemera Found in Libraries*. Monson scours myriad texts from far-flung libraries, wagering that every time somebody scratches into a book, they are writing to somebody in the future. He responds across this psychic distance, hybridizing two minor forms—marginalia and the literary letter—in the same gesture. We suspect that, with the preponderance of writers using their phones' notes apps to draft and record, and with so much reading happening electronically now, future literary notebooks, commonplace books, and marginalia will be curated not from fusty bankers' boxes, but digital seeds within the cloud.

See Danielle Geller's "Annotating the First Page of the First Navajo-English Dictionary" on pp. 256–61 for a literary annotation.

But some minor forms will seemingly never change. As a final example, consider the ignominious example of **latrinalia**, which derives from "latrine" and the suffix "-alia," meaning an insignificant collection of something. Latrinalia, which is usually scrawled in Sharpie on the interior walls of bathroom stalls, can take many forms, including stick-figure scribbles, solicitation (real and joke), philosophical aphorisms, pornographic juvenilia, political diatribes, observational humor, and lots of doggerel (think "Here I sit, broken hearted."). It is often thought to be spontaneous and anonymous, though one wonders if there isn't an element of premeditation; who carries a Sharpie with them into the bathroom in the first place? Latrinalia can provide a unique (metaphorical) window into the interior lives of the people who have used the bathroom and can even serve as a record of the history and culture of the place where it is found as was the case with the latrinalia of Pompei following the eruption of Mount Vesuvius.

Others have described it as simple graffiti or shithouse poetry. Given the ubiquity of public commentary nowadays on news websites, Twitter threads, and YouTube videos—we're also prompted to "leave a comment." In this context, latrinalia may seem blasé. Or perhaps, latrinalia has expanded to the shithouse walls of the internet, another liminal public/private zone where folks air their dirty laundry. Latrinalia was the original place where one's private thoughts became a matter of public record—it's the ultimate bathroom reading after all. Comedian Caitlin Cook has even turned strangers' latrinalia into a musical, setting choice ripostes to melodies in her off-Broadway show *The Writing on the Stall*.

Experimental Writing

In a serious study of this phenomenon from 1935, *Lexical Evidence from Folk Epigraphy in Western North America: A Glossarial Study of the Low Element in the English Vocabulary*, the folklorist Allen Walker Read theorized that it served a dualistic purpose. In a review of the book, the sociologist Herbert Blumer (1936: 434) wrote, "Obscene expressions are inverted taboos, i.e., words which invite usage because of their prohibition and which yield a 'fearful thrill' in seeing, doing, or speaking the forbidden." Hence the author declares, "It is the existence of a ban or taboo which creates the obscenity, where none exists before" (1936: 434). We suspect the same can be said for most minor forms, that their underground status or commercial prohibition is what makes them so thrilling to work with.

So, whether you encounter latrinalia on the walls of the Roman Colosseum, the bathroom stalls of the Palace of Versailles, or your local watering hole—or maybe it's you that's uncapping the Sharpie next time—we encourage you to try and regard this most minor of forms as literature. If you're incredulous about the claim that latrinalia is experimental writing, consider at least that it's a *social* experiment, a longitudinal collaboration with dozens of others whispering throughout the ages, plumbing the collective depths of their souls.

Discussion Questions

1. "Decorum" is an older term for behavior and discourse which keeps within the bounds of good taste and propriety: do you think that art and literature should strive to be in good taste? Why or why not? What do you think about the value of works that are deliberately cheap, vulgar, derivative, sentimental, or trashy? What shapes the formation of taste, and what is "bad" taste anyway? And why is it bad? The etymology of "disgust," by the way, breaks down to mean "bad taste," essentially. Can there be such a thing as *good* "bad taste"?

2. How might certain "minor forms" allow for the expression of what have been called "minor feelings": marginalized affects, sensibilities, and worldviews such as queer camp, Jewish guilt, or Mexican *rasquachismo*; Asian-American pressures to be a "model minority"; anxiety and self-alienation; or texts that prize emotional registers such as the cutesy, the zany, or the gross-out? What are the other affects and minor feelings that have been neglected by most mainstream art and literature? What forms do their expressions take? Are there ways to embrace—reclaim, rehabilitate, or reappraise—those marginalized forms?

3. The fragment, as a form in its own right rather than the timeworn inheritance of an ancient manuscript, developed during the Romantic period. Do you think that the fragment idealizes incompleteness, suggests a larger if impossible whole, or yearns for the reader's cooperation to make it intact? Do you think that all texts are fragments, unfinished parts assembled in some order which has only a provisional unity? Or does the way that we read, analyze, and quote works—especially longer ones—fragment the text, turning holistic entities into mere bits and bobs? Why might many authors—from Romantics to Contemporaries—be attracted to fragmentary, hodgepodge, and piecemeal forms?

4. While major forms such as the epic and novel lend themselves to the formation of national identities and garner official celebrations, minor forms—from letters to latrinalia—tend to be more private and intimate. How does the work we create for ourselves and familiars differ from work intended for consumption by the public? Is it ever a betrayal of privacy to publish journals, letters, or other personal documents? How does it change the conventions of the genre to write an open letter or knowingly aim some other intimate form of writing (a diary, say) to a wider audience?

5. What effect do you think that internet cultures have had on the proliferation or popularization of otherwise "minor forms" and subcultural aesthetics? Do you think that minorities and outsiders are able to meet and share their styles and visions more easily since the advent of the internet? Might this have increased the number of minor forms and subcultural aesthetics? Does the internet foster its own subcultures specific to highly online communities? Or, alternatively, has the internet allowed previously underground styles—such as punk, camp, or trash—to catch on more widely, thus imperiling their status as marginalized or minor? Is internet culture transforming the public/private divide; if so, what result might this have on existing or developing minor forms?

6. Is it possible to be a major artist who works in minor forms—for example, Kafka, Emily Dickinson, or John Waters? Or does the notion of minor forms preclude mainstream "success" by its very nature? How much might the acceptance of minor forms into more conventional settings (whether popular culture or textbooks and anthologies) distort or do a disservice to the self-imposed marginalization that minor forms often seek? How much do fan fiction, niche genre fiction, self-published poetry, off-off-Broadway plays, zine memoirs, or other writing that takes place outside the forums of traditional literary production and consumption count as minor forms? What directions do you see minor forms taking today?

Writing Prompts

1. Write a piece that takes the form of a letter or a series of letters. You can choose to write to a real person or you can address imaginary characters (e.g., Dorothy Gale from *The Wizard of Oz*), abstract concepts (e.g., democracy), or collective bodies (e.g., commuters on I-40 West). You might also write an "open letter," which, although it might address someone private, is nonetheless intended to be read by a wider, more public audience.

2. Write some aphorisms—at least five. They do not have to be any longer than one sentence. Try to make them witty, interesting, poetic, snappy, flippant, philosophical, nonsensical, snazzy, or paradoxical. Some of the famous aphorists are Oscar Wilde, Friedrich Nietzsche, Mark Twain, François de La Rochefoucauld, Christoph Lichtenberg, Karl Kraus, Heraclitus, Frank O'Hara, Andy Warhol, Diogenes, Blaise Pascal, Yoshida Kenkō, Benjamin Franklin, Dorothy Parker, Susan Sontag, and James Baldwin (if you want some inspiration).

3. Think of a "guilty pleasure" you have, especially a fandom for some lowbrow pop culture icon, series, or item. Then write a poem (or essay, story, listicle, etc.) that incorporates that enthusiasm. Position your piece within a particular sensibility such as camp, kitsch, kawaī, trash, or *rasquachismo*. Consider your audience, your frame of reference, style, and rhetorical maneuvers to make sure they align with this aesthetic. Do you evince any ambivalence toward your "guilty pleasure"; what makes it slightly shameful or looked down upon?

4. The mid-twentieth-century author Witter Brynner wrote many doggerel poems in a style he dubbed "Spectrism," intended as a hoax that parodied Modernist free verse—especially the then-popular movement of Imagism. Many readers and critics, however, consider Brynner's Spectrist verses to be among his very best, and it influenced his later and more serious work. Compose some doggerel: you can use antiquated verse forms, take on "light" subject matter, or parody some author or style that is familiar to readers today.

5. Create a few pages of a reference work such as a dictionary, encyclopedia, almanac, or bibliography. Instead of a standard and authoritative stance, you could take a more playful or subversive attitude. Use satire, lyricism, or critique. Or the content you gather in your reference work could be offbeat, niche, or subversive rather than institutional and informative. It could even be invented rather than factual. You might even want to use the reference work as a template that structures a longer work such as a poetic series or a short story. Similarly, you could write a paratext that relates to a work, existing or imaginary, such as a "lost chapter," an editor's preface, a legal contract for one's soul, or a scholarly afterword.

6. Keep a notebook for at least one week. Jot down stray thoughts, words, sentences, lists. Work on longer entries if you like. Compose whole poems and essays in it or just scratch down little doodles and incoherent notes-to-self. You can use it to record daily events, like a diary, or you can simply write whatever comes to mind. Let some time pass and look back at old entries. Try to develop and revise a more crafted piece by using fodder from the notebook. Do you value the notebook as a raw and intimate form in its own right or is it useful mainly for helping you brainstorm and springboard into more public, polished work?

CHAPTER 7
"UNDISCIPLINED" WRITING

I. Introduction to "Undisciplined" Writing

This section examines the phenomenon of finding literary art while flipping or scrolling through a text that is purportedly noncreative. Even those of us who read a ton of literature still must toggle between different reading contexts and purposes. Sometimes, we're just looking for some facts. Other times, it's jargon we're after. Or, yes, even a feel-good puff piece is called for on occasion. But then, there are those rare occasions when supposedly "noncreative writing"—whether from journalism, academia, or popular outlets—manages to transcend its disciplinary conventions to arrive at something distinctly artful. Maybe the writer is a prose stylist. Or, intentionally or not, they've expanded the scope of their piece, thus courting a crossover audience. They may even stage an outright revolt against the de rigueur style of their field. In this chapter, we examine the gamut of writing that is ostensibly designed for workaday rather than creative purposes, but which somehow breaks open the terms of its disciplinary boundaries and, in doing so, displays some crafty vim or aesthetic verve.

When it comes to noncreative writing, "experimental" is not only tethered to craft decisions, but also what one dares to think in fields where methods, conventions, style guides, disciplinary edicts, academic protocols, ready-made audiences, and a commercial marketplace typically call the shots. When authors bring an attention to language and a swashbuckling moxie to their supposedly "noncreative" writing, what emerges is a text that can be characterized as a hybrid, an outlier, or a radical—perhaps all three.

The case can be made that the history of writing is mostly noncreative. The origins of writing—whether utilitarian lists, ledgers, or letters—was largely to communicate to business and trade partners or correspond with acquaintances, allies, and kin. This rarely factors into the historical narrative about the development of literature because it lacks the entertainment purposes and stylistic qualities that we associate with reading a literary text. And yet the development of bureaucratic noncreative writing was happening alongside the development of myths, fables, epic poetry, and dramaturgy.

One celebrated story in the transition from noncreative to creative writing centers around a flood myth in Uruk (southern Iraq), a city of the ancient civilization Sumer, in the area known as Mesopotamia, or the "Cradle of Civilization." In *The Lost Origins of the Essay*, John D'Agata (2009:) writes: "It's estimated over 90 percent of what the Sumerians wrote down only served an administrative function … But, unfortunately, it was the worst kind of nonfiction there is: informational, literal, nothing about it mattering beyond the place it held for facts … For almost five centuries, their tallies, receipts, and records were the only literature they produced." In fact, this administrative nonfiction is what assured Sumer's economic successes; it's no mystery why recordkeeping (e.g., transactional history, inventory, and the like) would be such a boon to a burgeoning metropolis like Sumer. But then came a major flood. With reed stylus on clay tablet, a wisdom text is constructed in Akkadian cuneiform. The flood hero

Experimental Writing

Ziusudra (2900 BCE), sometimes dubbed the "Mesopotamian Noah," catalogs "the problems that he had witnessed in the past by offering some advice about whatever's coming next. This list that Ziusudra makes is five thousand years old—half a millennium older than the earliest known poem, a full millennium older than the earliest known story" (D'Agata 2009: 7). From a distance, this list resembles all the others from the era, but without anything left to tally or trade, instead what emerges is "a mind's inquisitive ramble through a place wiped clean of answers."

Fast-forward to today, and most writing is *still* noncreative. According to the *State of Enterprise Work Report* (as cited in Graeber's *Bullshit Jobs*), in 2017, emails account for 16 percent of an office worker's time. In this same book, Graeber asks the question:

> What does it say about a society that it seems to generate an extremely limited demand for poet-musicians but an apparently infinite demand for specialists in corporate law? Simply put, the ruling class ("who controls most of the disposable wealth, what we call the 'market'") decide what's useful or important. It's not that they think the emails are important, but it is important that these employees are engaged in constant work (emails are part of the "bullshitification") and that they don't have free time to write in a moral way that could transform that status quo. This is the real conspiracy: they have decided to spend their money on employees who write emails, not poems.

In *Discipline and Punish*, Foucault explains how the development of "disciplinary methods" became "general formulas of domination" (1995: 137). Such practices were ensconced in the academy, one of the "protected [places] of disciplinary monotony" (141). Therefore, to write against one's discipline is to break up the monotony, disregard the formulae, and instantiate an undisciplined ("liberated") method for humanistic expression.

Some examples of noncreative writing—that is, writing outside the purview of the relatively recent academic discipline of creative writing—include:

1. Journalism and criticism: op-eds, exposés, interviews, oral histories, and criticism

2. Academic: work in academic disciplines (e.g., psychology, sociology, history, architecture, comparative cultural studies, etc.), including most philosophy, theory, intellectual history, ethnography, and legal writing

3. Popular: coffee-table books, biography, general nonfiction, travel, science, environmental writing, and religious works.

Work in these fields can occasionally be artful and experimental when their authors thumb their noses at the limitations of the ostensible rules that govern their discipline or market niche, approaching their subject with a surprising methodology, literariness, scrappiness, artful zest, or disarming earnestness. In other words, they paradoxically transcend the confines of the so-called noncreative writing they practice by bringing a creative spunk or literary spark to their work. If most writing is utilitarian and humdrum, either overly technical or dumbed down, there are rare bright spots in the vast sea of conventional (and purportedly "noncreative") printed matter. We dub these rare bright spots "undisciplined writing" since they defy the norms imposed by their disciplines and the discourses of which they partake, striking out for more innovative or stylish terrain. Though they may serve some more mundane purpose or niche context, they too can be on par with experimental literature.

II. Journalism, Criticism, and Reviews

Admittedly, the line between well-researched creative nonfiction and well-written investigative journalism can be tenuous. Many of the stalwarts of creative nonfiction—Joan Didion and John McPhee, David Foster Wallace, and Ta-Nehisi Coates—wrote many of their best-known pieces on assignment for journalistic outlets. Even the origins of creative nonfiction are largely inherited from journalism: Addison and Hazlitt, Mencken and Orwell were newspapermen, grub street scribes, or beat reporters. Furthermore, during the 1960s through 1980s the "New Journalism" attempted to employ the narrative and literary devices of the novelistic trade to enrich their long-form reportage; creative nonfiction emerged from those same decades, but the field has since expanded its scope beyond memoir and personal essay to include more immersive or investigative methodologies. Still, universities teach journalism and creative nonfiction in separate departments for a reason. Not only do they serve different purposes, everything from their sense of form to their approach to storytelling to their codes of ethics are also distinct. Yet, when an article or review is particularly poignant or punchy, bursting loose from its fealty to journalistic strictures, it may elevate to the realm of art.

One broad subfield of journalism that has a penchant for being "undisciplined" is cultural criticism. It can take the form of traditional scholarship, journalism, or activism and may be motivated by a variety of goals, such as understanding the cultural context of a particular work or issue, challenging dominant cultural narratives, or advocating for social change. The latter point deserves some unpacking. While analyzing the values, beliefs, and practices of a particular culture, critics seem to be faced with a choice: does a cultural critic merely document/preserve the culture, or is there also the capacity to change it? If also the latter, such a venture likely requires one to go out on a limb, to find uncommon ways to breathe life into the cultures with which we engage: to invert the existing orders in ways that break with the norms. Some of the sharpest cultural criticism is about how power is exercised and contested within a society. Such criticism can both stake out a viewpoint and help us understand the stakes of cultural artifacts. Criticism thrives when there is pluralism; by studying any two critics, one gains the opportunity to synthesize two perspectives rather than parrot one.

American art critic Jerry Saltz (2017: n.p.), known for his provocative and controversial writing style, has gained a reputation for challenging conventional wisdom in the art world. He has also been recognized for his ability to make contemporary art accessible by engaging a wider audience, including on Instagram. In his essay, "My Life as a Failed Artist," he reviews his own art: "I didn't have the ability and fortitude. That's why I always look for it in others—root for it in others—even when the work is ugly or idiotic. It's why I look hard at every artist, at the well-known and the rich as well as the late bloomers, bottom-feeders, outsiders, and eccentrics" (2017). Art criticism is a discipline known for its taste-making, so what does it mean that Saltz can't stomach his own creations? In this review, Saltz breaks form, and his critical gaze is returned to sender.

But What If We're Wrong? by pop-culture critic Chuck Klosterman turns timeless truths on their head—holding space for the possibility that they may one day be proven to be wrong or fundamentally flawed. Throughout the book, he upends present-minded sentiments about democracy (overrated), science (iffy), reality (misunderstood), history (myopic), as well as social and cultural beliefs, in favor of seeing these phenomena in the long durée. He develops the principle known as Klosterman's Razor, or "the philosophical belief that the best hypothesis is the one that reflexively accepts its potential wrongness to begin with" (2016: 17). In so doing, he dissolves his critical authority and detaches from the zeitgeist—often the singular task of a critic—and fosters a futurist criticism predicated on speculation and modesty.

David Foster Wallace's (2004) essay "Consider the Lobster," which was published in *Gourmet* magazine, is a piece of food writing—or is it?—that examines the ethics of boiling lobsters alive, a common practice in the seafood industry. Wallace begins by exploring the scientific evidence for whether or not lobsters are capable of feeling pain and then delves into the broader cultural and moral implications of consuming animals for food. What makes this work "undisciplined," if you will, has as much to do with his methods as it does his outlet. *Gourmet*, after all, is an authority on culinary culture that typically publishes pieces on food trends, wine and spirits, and recipes. Its readers are more likely to expect a jaunty piece of journalism on the Maine Lobster Festival with adjectives like "succulent" and "buttery," not so much a heavily researched work of ethical philosophy. By straddling multiple fields, Wallace multiplies the possibilities of his discourse; this transdisciplinary technique enriches criticism by shedding new light on cultural practices that have become shortsighted or stultified.

Wallace took his title and inspiration from M. F. K. Fisher, a culinary writer who denied the charms of stylized writing: "the so-called style of such writers bores me, turns me off, makes me feel tricked." And yet, this was her modus operandi. Her books *Consider the Oyster* and *How to Cook a Wolf* are offbeat literary variations on the cookbook. The latter was published as America rationed its way through the Second World War. In a review in the *New York Times*, Orville Prescott (1942: n.p.) writes: "Cook books are indisputably indispensable for the welfare of the human race, and they sell very nicely ... Few indeed have any claims to literary merit." Fisher, perhaps alone, is worthy of this distinction. Towards the end of the review, Prescott is nonplussed by some of Fisher's mystical humor: "She insists that boiling water too long before using it is a great mistake and deleterious to whatever is being cooked. Again, as a mere man, I am bewildered. Is she joking, or is water that has boiled for several minutes any different from water that has just come to a boil?" These moments abound in Fisher's writing, which equate pleasure with cooking, a pleasure she recreates with each essay/recipe. This joie de vivre is perhaps most decadent as she prepares tangerines for consumption:

> Separate each plump little pregnant crescent ... Tear delicately from the soft pile of sections each velvet string ... Take yesterday's paper (when we were in Strasbourg L'Ami du Peuple was best, because when it got hot the ink stayed on it) and spread it on top of the radiator ... After you have put the pieces of tangerine on the paper on the hot radiator, it is best to forget about them. Al comes home, you go to a long noon dinner in the brown dining-room, afterwards maybe you have a little nip of quetsch from the bottle on the armoire. Finally he goes ... On the radiator the sections of tangerines have grown even plumper, hot and full. You carry them to the window, pull it open, and leave them for a few minutes on the packed snow of the sill. They are ready. (Fisher 1937: 32)

Or, sometimes what makes a work undisciplined may be the radical process that was involved in obtaining one's field notes, such as Ann Hodgman's essay "No Wonder They Call Me a Bitch" in which the food critic and cookbook author "spent the better part of a week eating dog food" in a taste-test of different brands. Wallace, Fisher, and Hodgman each expand the horizons of food criticism through the uninhibited use of unnatural methods and styles.

Another work of fictional music reviews is Daniel Mahoney's *Sunblind Almost Motorcrash.* As the critic Lewis DeJong puts it, "Although the albums don't technically exist, the idiom in which Mahoney writes these reviews very much does exist" until he is "satirizing the lengths that music criticism grammar has gone" (2015: n.p.). While on its surface, it feels like the reader is poring over a book of album reviews, in reality, they are reading a book that performs criticism, and questions its conventions through that performance. Similarly, Jamison Crabtree's (2017) review of Patrick Cottrell's *Sorry to Disturb the Peace* takes seriously the reviewer's traditional role of giving potential readers a "feel" for the world of the book. Crabtree uses the text adventure video game genre to provide readers with the ontological pleasure of entering the novel—roaming the protagonist's house, handling artifacts, and participating in the book's central mysteries—and whatever else the text parser recognizes.

Finally, the 1990s alternative music magazine *Ray Gun* was the site of a waggish editorial antic. Rather than strike a dull interview with singer Bryan Ferry, designer David Carson decided to run it in the Dingbats typeface instead. If you aren't familiar, Dingbats is an ornamental, symbols-only font, meaning the interview was comically illegible, like this: ♦︎♒︎♓︎⬧︎⬧︎♓︎■︎🌓︎♎︎♓︎■︎🌓︎⬧︎🖂︎■︎☐︎♦︎♎︎♓︎■︎🌓︎♌︎☺︎♦︎⬧︎

III. Academic Writing

As any college student who has taken both first-year composition and a workshop could attest, the values and orientations of academic and creative writing differ markedly. While the standards of academic writing vary between disciplines, most fields—especially STEM fields—encourage rote formulas, technical precision, and addressing a specialist audience. Narrative, wordplay, rhythm, characterization, and metaphor along with countless other tools of creative writers are typically frowned upon. Despite the disciplinary pressures to conform to abstruse procedures and protocols, sometimes, striking it lucky, a few exemplary academic authors manage to buck the system. It is not unheard of that writing mainly intended for academic or professional audiences gains crossover appeal due to its engaging storytelling or energetic wit. Indeed, in some cases, academics have written in a style that is fluid, accessible, droll, and trenchant—or, once in a blue moon—that is downright experimental in nature. These exceptional paragons may be worthwhile for literary writers to study and appreciate, offering a rare combination of expertise and imagination.

Writing in architecture, for instance, helps interpret and shape our relationships with built and natural environments. *Delirious New York: A Retroactive Manifesto for Manhattan* by Dutch architect and urbanist Rem Koolhaas is a study of the history and development of New York City—from its architecture, urban planning, transportation, and popular culture. Koolhaas explores the history of Manhattan from the early colonial period to the twentieth century and argues that the city's dense, chaotic, and diverse urban fabric is the result of a series of utopian visions that have shaped its development over time. Through his writing, Koolhaas "intends to establish Manhattan as the product of an unformulated theory, *Manhattanism*, whose program—to exist in a world totally fabricated by man, i.e., to live *inside* fantasy—was so ambitious that to be realized, it could never be openly stated" (1994: 10). The singular invention of the elevator made the upward rise of our current skyscraper cityscape possible, reshaping the culture of the cosmopolites who dwell among them. In another book, *S, M, L,*

XL—this one coauthored with Bruce Mau—Koolhaas attempts his own manifesto, viewing the adventure of architecture as a chaotic negotiation with random contingencies and clients rather than an engineering project for pristine conceptual machines for living.

Acclaimed architect Maya Lin, with her conceptualist brother Tan Lin, incorporate text into architecture itself. See the blueprint for *Reading a Garden* on p. 278. Or, if it's nearby, visit the text at Cleveland Public Library.

Also reimagining the framework within which a more technical message can be conveyed, Naomi Oreskes and Erik M. Conway's (2014) *The Collapse of Western Civilization: A View from the Future*, despite both authors being historians of natural science, is told from the viewpoint of futurity. *Collapse* is a fictionalized account of a coming time in which climate change has undone Western civilization. The book is written in the form of an executive summary from the year 2393, extrapolating backwards to the present. It is the history of the future, where inaction begets consequence: catastrophe, scarcity, trauma, and ultimately collapse.

The Irish composer Jennifer Walshe, meanwhile, looks to a fictional history in her scholarly archive, *Aisteach* (Gaelic for strange, peculiar, or queer). Walshe and ten others conjure fictional biographies from an Irish musical avant-garde that never existed, profiling performers like the Guinness Dadaists, Chancey Briggs, the Keening Women's Alliance, the Aleatoric Revisionist Balladeers, and the poet field recordist Zaftig Giolla. Each performer is presented matter-of-factly in the archives with critical histories, vintage images, and even sample recordings. Navigate to the fine print on the disclaimer page, though, and you'll learn it's actually "a communal thought experiment, a revisionist exercise in 'what if'" (Walshe n.d.). As composer Rob Casey (2019: 2) puts it in *Transposition*, "[Walshe's] decision to conjure them into existence was born from a desire to identify with a historical Irish avant-garde, to situate her voice within a cultural heritage that embraced the experimental, maverick and strange" regardless of whether or not such a heritage existed.

Philosopher Neil Sinhababu's (2008) "Possible Girls" embroiders on his own dry spell for a whimsical take on the philosophical theory of modal realism, which suggests that possible worlds exist in the same way that the actual world exists. Sinhababu plays into stereotypes about nerdy academics—the hyperintelligent, socially awkward variety who are obsessed with their work to the point of ignoring other aspects of their lives. So, he decides to address his nonexistent dating life through his scholarly attention to modal realism. He decides there are scores of possible girls out there, many of whom he desires, so he'll just pick the one who lives in the closest possible world: "The girl from that world will be my girlfriend" (2008: 255), he says rather confidently. But she will need to choose him as well: "For this to work, my girl needs to have an amazingly intricate desire. She wants the boy from a world that is exactly like mine, down to the last subatomic particle" (2008: 255). Sinhababu goes on to address pluriverse love letters. In sum, he'll have to write the letters to himself, and she'll have to imagine the letter, verbatim, for the communication to be authentic. Whimsy is a playful, entertaining mode with which to illustrate an otherwise complex, dry theory.

In a 1997 issue of *Michigan Law Review*, the student editors decided to run an infamous article: "Pomobabble: Postmodern Newspeak[1] and Constitutional 'Meaning' for the Uninitiated."

In the article, law professor Dennis W. Arrow writes a thirty-some page article, buttressed by 190 pages of stream-of-conscious footnotes. It amounts to a parody of postmodern constitutional jurisprudence in which he mocks the highly subjective style of postmodernism. In his curmudgeonly commentary about the article, Ronald J. Krotoszynski Jr. shames the author and editorial board for running the piece. He frets over the cost of publishing a 228-page "prank" and excoriates the student editors for their cynicism in editing such a meandering treatise. He feels sorry for the diligent untenured professors whose work will be overlooked due to a lack of space in the journal. He suggests there are better outlets for legal humor writing. He asks, "Does Professor Arrow view the time and effort he expended writing Pomobabble as well spent? Put differently, is his point that writing Pomobabble reflects a use of time and effort that is no more, and no less, legitimate than the time and effort expended on more traditional scholarly efforts?" (Krotoszynski Jr. 1998: 328). One sees, in Krostoszynski Jr.'s response, the monotonous disciplining of those who have attempted to free themselves of the disciplinary strictures. Regardless, we suspect this is exactly the kind of response the editors meant to provoke by publishing this parody, which undermines the self-enclosed prison-house of legal language.

In his book *On Bullshit*, philosopher Harry G. Frankfurt (2005) examines the concept of bullshit and its role in modern society. The book is written in an accessible style that, at the time, was uncommon among analytic philosophers, appealing beyond the discipline's specialists. Frankfurt defines bullshit as statements or actions that are designed to deceive or mislead, but which are not motivated by a desire to tell the truth. While liars are motivated by a desire to conceal the truth, Frankfurt (2005: 47) argues that bullshitters are not concerned with the truth at all; they are more interested in impressing or influencing others. "The essence of bullshit is not that it is *false* but that it is *phony*," he writes (emphasis in original). This lack of concern for the truth, Frankfurt argues, is what makes bullshit so dangerous and destructive, as it undermines the foundation of honest communication and social interaction. He notes bullshit is often used by politicians, advertisers, and other public figures to manipulate public opinion and advance their own agendas. The proliferation of bullshit in modern society, he argues, reflects a broader cultural decline. Unlike analytic philosophers who are narrowly concerned with truth and logic, Frankfurt expands his analysis to include the grayer areas of bombast and embellishment. The book, written in 2005, seems to have been prescient of the coming age of disinformation, truthiness, and Trumpism. Dominique Laporte's (2000) *History of Shit* is another work of philosophy with popular appeal and interest for creative writers. Laporte combines psychoanalytic insights, critical theory, and the history of sewers and latrines. His thesis is nothing less than that "the history of shit" is, in fact, "the history of subjectivity." Modern plumbing and waste disposal have created a psychic condition divorced from the underbelly of our body (and body politic), a pure intellect at a dangerous remove from its corporeal excrescence and ignorant of the consequences of the cultural pollution it produces. Perhaps Frankfurt's bullshit is the "return of the repressed" for the elimination of the literal shit that Laporte describes. At any rate, philosophy does not always have to be dry—it can be moist, too.

IV. Popular Writing

Popular writing covers a lot of ground: for brevity's sake, we group many disparate genres and disciplines together here under a single label. Just as, say, sociology, chemistry, and engineering have different disciplinary conventions in academic writing, so, too, do the array of genres we demarcate under the aegis of popular writing. The common thread is that popular writing is neither written for a specialist (academic) audience nor one expecting any artful exuberance, as with traditional types of creative writing. Instead, popular writing tends to fulfill the parameters of its niche in the marketplace. And it's usually read for the facts it contains. Most of the books in an average bookstore could be deemed popular writing: shelves overflow with genres such as self-help, how-to, biography, popular science, travel, coffee-table books, guidebooks, and reference works. Meanwhile, poetry often occupies a slim nook, drama may be hard to find at all, and the amalgam we now regard as "creative" nonfiction gets shelved everywhere and nowhere at once. Popular genres can, at times, surpass the strictures of their medium and become one more place where nonfiction can surpass routine informational exchange to earn the distinction "creative." Ubiquitous though they are, these genres have been overlooked—at least by the literary establishment—as go-to sites of experiment and playful possibility.

Biography is one genre with a distinguished lineage that nonetheless falls through every crack: what type of writing is it, exactly? Journalistic or academic? Critical or creative? History? Memoir? Something else again? Margo Jefferson's *On Michael Jackson*, for example, is less interested in the biographical arc of its purported subject's life, and more concerned with the force field of different cultural permutations—or mutations—that the many-sided Michael gives rise to. Likewise taking a many-sided approach, Edward Platt's *Leadville* is a collective biography of the anonymous folks who happen to live along Britain's congested A40 highway.

Victorian Edmund Gosse's *Father and Son* offers a double portrait, at once a memoir of the author and a biography of his father, the relationship between the two temperaments—and genres—producing an animating tension. Another double portrait is A. J. A. Symons's *The Quest for Corvo: An Experiment in Biography*, which is as much about Baron Corvo as it is Symon's own frustrations in researching his recalcitrant subject when most documents prove unreliable. Similarly, Geoff Dyer's *Out of Sheer Rage* devolves from being a study of D. H. Lawrence into a memoir of Dyer's own exhaustion at wrapping his head around (and into?) Lawrence's. Playing off Gertrude Stein's *The Autobiography of Alice B. Toklas*, Jenn Shapland's *My Autobiography of Carson McCullers* reveals more about her than her ostensible author—though she also critiques the ways that queer women's stories in particular are papered over by other voices (ironically, even other queer women's voices). Susan Howe's *My Emily Dickinson* asks what remains of women's voices except the scraps and papers they leave behind, intermixing personal and poetic, scholarly and anecdotal modes.

A subject that has left little behind or whose story is well-known can present special challenges to biographers. When tackling Samuel Johnson, who happens to be the subject of the most famous biography in the English language, Richard Holmes also opted for a double portrait in *Dr. Johnson and Mr. Savage*, contrasting the learned doctor with his lesser-known, gutter-slumming consort. Stacy Shiff's *Vera, Mrs. Vladimir Nabokov* likewise gets at her subject (the more famous husband) by sidelong indirection—though in these tellings, Richard Savage and Vera Nabokov turn out to be the more engaging characters.

In the realm of speculative biography, noted New Historian and Harvard academic Stephen Greenblatt offers a vivid, novelistic narrative of Shakespeare's daily life in *Will in the World: How Shakespeare Became Shakespeare*. Though a respected scholar, Greenblatt chooses to embellish on the scant evidence to create a more robust and moving story. Joseph Mitchell's *Joe Gould's Secret* gives an in-depth account of Gould, or "Professor Sea Gull," an eccentric writer at work on his magnum opus, "The Oral History"; however, Gould's secret is that the notes he had been writing were all revisions of the same handful of chapters—there was no great work-in-progress. It was oral, not written; hot air, not cold ink. How much Gould fabricates himself out of blarney and how much he fools Mitchell by doing so—or how much Mitchell fabricates the character of Gould to hoodwink us, his readers—is the delicate question that is this biography's true secret. Meanwhile, Stephanie Dickinson's *Heat: An Interview with Jean Seaburg* conducts imaginary interviews with the glamorous actress from the 1960s, straddling the divide between historical fiction and speculative biography. Virginia Woolf's *Flush: A Biography* is usually classed with novels, too, despite its subtitle. After all, Flush was Elizabeth Barret Browning's pet cocker spaniel, and the narrative is told in the first-person from the dog's point of view. More disorienting perhaps is *Nice Things by James Franco*, written, in fact, by Sean Lovelace and Mark Neely who ventriloquize Franco's voice and writing; nobody seems sure if *Nice Things* is parody, Conceptual fiction, biography, criticism, or a love letter to Franco baiting him for a lawsuit. Finally, *The Book of Disquiet* by Fernando Pessoa gives us the intimate biography of the obscure existentialist Bernardo Soares by way of his diary and daily thoughts. The only catch is that Soares was the heteronym—or alter ego—of Pessoa himself, a fact that strangely makes Soares no less true perhaps since Soares's persistent quandary is the unreality of one's mundane existence.

Religious writings with an adventurous approach include *Zen and the Art of Motorcycle Maintenance*, *Christ Stopped at Eboli*, and *The Tao of Pooh*. The latter is a book that uses the characters from A. A. Milne's *Winnie-the-Pooh* stories to explain Taoist philosophy. Author Benjamin Hoff uses the characters of Pooh, Piglet, Eeyore, and others to illustrate the esoteric principles of Taoism, thus transposing Pooh as esoteric, and Tao as accessible, if not adorable. For those whose taste in religious experiences gravitates toward drugs, orgies, and witchcraft, though, they might want to check out Aleister Crowley. Crowley's voluminous writing ranges from sacred texts (*The Book of the Law*), novels (*Moonchild*), commentary (*The Vision and the Voice*), lectures (*Eight Lectures on Yoga*), poetry (*Clouds without Water*), essays (*Konx Om Pax: Essays on Light*), stories (*The Stratagem*), letters (*Magick without Tears*) guidebooks (*The Equinox*), diaries (*Diary of a Drug Fiend*), sex manuals (*Basic Techniques of Sex Magick*), grimoires (*The Goetia*), conjurations (*Rites of Eleusis*), autohagiography, mystic instructions, scholarship, manifestos, and other offbeat lore. As a sample, Chapter 69—yes … just yes—from *The Book of Lies* declaims:

> This Work also eats itself up, accomplishes its own end, nourishes the worker, leaves no seed, is perfect in itself.
> Little children, love one another! (Crowley 1913: 86)

A larger-than-life figure, Crowley has inspired characters in fiction, underground filmmakers such as Kenneth Anger, and rock musicians from The Beatles to Bowie.

Another experimental religious writer was Isaac Newton who wrote a forensic analysis of the Bible. While Isaac Newton is typically depicted as a rational Enlightenment scientist, he also had a deep interest in occult theology and spent a significant portion of his lifetime attempting to decode the Bible's hidden meanings. In these writings, he employed computation to divine prophecies about the origins of the universe and the end of the world, a practice that mortified his relatives, forcing them to hide his manuscripts for centuries. Elizabeth Cady

Stanton also engineered a refashioning of the Bible with *The Woman's Bible*, a controversial bestseller in the late nineteenth century. It attempted to edit, translate, revise, and excise the existing Biblical corpus to offer a new version of the Bible in unvarnished English, which would be free from the patriarchal subjugation of women that Stanton and other suffragists believed had been encrusted on the original holy text from later male priests and scribes. Those with a less polemical and more dialectical mindset, however, might enjoy Edmond Jabès whose *Book of Questions* introduces experimental poems, fragmentary aphorisms, dialogues among rabbis, and commentary on the yet-to-be-written book under interrogation. The questioning of God only leaves us with more questions; the search for the Book is the book itself.

An early example of "undisciplined" travel writing comes from 1794. Xavier de Maistre, placed under house arrest in Turin following an illicit duel, wrote *Voyage autour de ma chambre* (*A Journey Around My Room*), an epic tour of his tiny room. De Maistre (1794: 11) writes, "My room is situated in the latitude 48° east… It lies east and west, and, if you keep very close to the wall, forms a parallelogram of thirty-six steps round… I shall traverse my room up and down and across, without rule or plan. I shall even zig-zag about, following, if needs be every possible geometrical line." As he wanders the few steps that it takes to circumnavigate the space, his mind spins off into the ether. According to *The Public Domain Review* (2017: n.p.) "it parodies the travel journals of the eighteenth-century … and could be read today as an early take on the modern vogue for 'psychogeography'—each tiny thing that he encounters sends de Maistre into rhapsodies, and mundane journeys become magnificent voyages."

The journey around your room adventure also appears as an experiment in *The Lonely Planet Guide to Experimental Travel* (2005), a how-to book for experimental tourism that includes sixty experiments for seeing the world in a new way. Another experiment involves traveling to a city using an eighty-year-old guidebook or Trip Poker where someone else picks your destination for you. Another work of travel writing is Geoff Dyer's *Yoga for People Who Can't Be Bothered to Do It* (2003). Dyer devotes much of the book to poking fun at the many spiritual seekers and New Age tourists who flock to sites in search of enlightenment, not least of all himself with a wry, self-deprecating humor.

Rebecca Solnit's "literary atlases" explore the spatial history and social changes of San Francisco (*Infinite City*) and New Orleans (*Unfathomable City*). The books are chock full of maps, illustrations, essays, and interviews that represent neighborhoods, demographics, and oral histories in a multilayered fashion that hint at the inexhaustibility of such a feat. Another atlas-maker, Dennis Wood, famously made a map out of the silhouettes of jack-o-lanterns, demonstrating that the pattern and density of lack-o-lanterns in a neighborhood is predictive of socioeconomic status. Unlike most cartographers, folk artist Jerry Gretzinger's work is devoted to a fictional place. Spanning 3,000 sheets of 8×10″ paper, he incorporates chance operations, erasure, collage, abstraction, generational narratives, and database entry (to track the population of the fictional towns) into the project that has defined his artistic career for over 60 years. The story of the map, and its evolution through time, has social, ecological, and political rhythms all its own.

One last form of popular writing is known as science and nature writing. Mary Roach takes a humorous approach to science writing with her books *Gulp*, *Stiff*, and *Bonk*, books about digestion, cadavers, and human sexuality, respectively. Roach's transparent and unconventional research style, coupled with her humor, make her writing unique in the discipline. In *Being a Beast* (2016), Charles Foster goes wild, sort of. He approximates the physiology and behaviors of badgers, otters, foxes, stags, and swifts. He eats worms galore, describes their terroir: from minerals to wood chips to tangy diapers. He grows his hair and nails long and teaches his blindfolded kids to distinguish his poop from others' in a sadistic sniff test. He sleeps under bushes in the city, scavenges dumpsters for sustenance, and solicits a friend who sics his bloodhound on him. In his greatest folly, he paraglides (partially) to Africa, following the swift's migration. Foster's methods are far from superficial, allowing him to clumsily share a habitat with these animals. It inverts the premise of most environmental writing: why all this bird-watching, when we could try bird-being?

Field guides are designed to help people identify plants, animals, and other natural objects that they might encounter outdoors. They typically include descriptions and pictures of the various species, along with information about their habitats, behaviors, and other characteristics. Literary field guides, on the other hand—such as the ones that exist for California, Southern Appalachia, and the Sonoran Desert—imbue these reference texts with poetic imagery, metaphor, and Indigenous ways of knowing. For most of the history of nature writing, it was dominated by certain demographics of writers: think Gary Snyder, Edward Abbey, and Wendell Berry. Anthologies like *Black Nature* and *Queer Nature*, though, introduce new cultural traditions to this discipline. Both volumes set out to naturalize the idea that black and queer bodies exist in nature, that is, their existence is natural, and that such cultural perspectives might have a different relationality to the natural world that would allow them to perceive it differently.

Finally, "Uncivilisation" (2009) is a manifesto from the radical British environmentalists Dark Mountain, a group deeply skeptical of capitalist growth and human civilization itself, who collectively write:

> If we are indeed teetering on the edge of a massive change in how we live, in how human society itself is constructed, and in how we relate to the rest of the world, then we were led to this point by the stories we have told ourselves – above all, by the story of civilisation. This story has many variants, religious and secular, scientific, economic and mystic ... What makes this story so dangerous is that, for the most part, we have forgotten that it is a story.

In their call for "uncivilised writing," Dark Mountain accelerates some of the convictions of previous environmental movements like Deep Ecology of the 1970s. Like "undisciplined writing," uncivilised writing eschews disciplinary convention in order to undo the logics of old systems.

Discussion Questions

1. How different do you think that journalism and creative nonfiction are? How much overlap do you think they have? What tensions exist between the two disciplines; how are the values, writing processes, models, craft precepts, and venues of each different? In what circumstances might journalism become creative nonfiction (or vice versa)? Journalism is undergoing fundamental shifts due to cultural and technological changes; meanwhile creative nonfiction has expanded its purview quite a bit from

its roots in personal essays and literary memoirs, including more occasional pieces, reportage, and research-based works. Do you think it is necessary or useful to distinguish the two anymore—why or why not?

2. How much do you feel that academic writing allows for creativity? How is the discourse of academic writing shaped, rewarded, punished, disciplined, institutionalized, and passed on? Why might a few academics strive to write in a way that laypersons outside the discipline might find interesting to read, rather than primarily aiming their work for other specialists? Why do you think tensions or disagreements exist between the ways that writing is taught in different departments or programs, including creative writing, English literature, and rhetoric and composition? What are some of the benefits—and limitations—of a tightly codified discourse within a given academic or professional discipline?

3. Do you think that criticism and reviews should be creative, personal, and formally experimental? Or does that detract from a consideration of the subject at hand? What's the point of criticism and reviews; is it to help the consumer make more informed choices or can it have other purposes? Do you ever enjoy reading criticism or reviews for their own sake? If so, do you enjoy reading longer essay reviews (such as the essay reviews in the *Times Literary Supplement* or the *New York Review of Books*), which act more like personal essays, or do you prefer more straightforward criticism such as pithy product reviews (say, *Pitchfork* album reviews)? Have you ever encountered any criticism or reviews that you would consider to be experimental; if so, what was your reaction? To what degree do you think that *most* literature—novels, poems, and so on—functions as an implicit response to and criticism of previous literature and artworks?

4. Which types of writing fit under the umbrella of "creative writing" and which are left out: why might popular genres such as travel writing, biography, environmental or nature writing, science writing for general audiences, food writing, sports writing, and so on fall outside the locus of creative writing as traditionally defined, despite long-standing imaginative traditions in many of these fields? Isn't all writing topical or occasional to some degree? What exactly does the "creative" in the term "creative writing" mean or imply anyway?

5. In what ways do you think that workshops, publishers, and other institutions reinforce disciplinary strictures on creative writing? How have these disciplinary strictures changed over time and how are they changing today? What purpose might these disciplinary norms serve and whom do they benefit? Where—and how—do you see creative writers breaking out of the disciplinary norms that have been imposed on them?

Writing Prompts

1. Write a piece about an unconventional place or experience such as a bathroom stall, passenger seat, elevator ride, or karaoke bar. Think about the form and rhetoric

that such a piece—whether review, essay, article, or something else—would use and where it might be published. Then think about how your piece can transcend those limitations; infuse your piece with some literary, creative, personal, or experimental energies that go beyond the traditional formulae. Train your focus on less traditional aspects of the place or experience; where will you look that traditional journalists would not?

2. Write a cultural studies ethnography of some subculture that you investigate as a participant-observer (skater kids, e-girls, basketball players, Star Wars stans, rock climbers, Deadheads, etc.). Immerse yourself more than normal in their activities and sites. Analyze the behaviors, assumptions, values, speech, factions, and rituals within this subculture or community. What do people in this group believe and hold important? How are you both part of—and outside—this subculture or group, and in which ways does this influence your perspective on the culture you are examining?

3. Write a "creative" analysis essay or object lesson of some mundane object (e.g., paper clips, Legos, condoms, dust bunnies, bobbleheads, key chains, batteries, etc.). Investigate the object from multiple viewpoints—uncovering its material history, its symbolic significance, its (sub)cultural relevance, its personal value to you, and other facets of its meanings and ways it impacts society. Convey the stakes for your seemingly trivial object. You could look at Bloomsbury's Object Lesson series for a model or, better yet, the brief essays in Roland Barthes's *Mythologies*.

4. Review a cultural artifact (music, artwork, book) in a way that foregrounds narrative, personal anecdotes, witty sentences, lyrical associational structures, and other touchstones of traditional "creative writing." If you don't know what work to focus on, maybe try listening to John Cage's 4'33," which is 4 minutes and 33 seconds of silence.

5. Write a research paper within the parameters of a given academic discipline while utilizing techniques of creative writing (but in an earnest way, rather than one that merely co-opts the form or results in parody). That is, try to use the lessons you've gleaned from creative writing to enhance and supplement the academic research paper so that it would still be considered an acceptable if not exemplary product within its chosen discipline.

6. Interview someone. It could be someone you already know, such as a friend or family member. Research the person as much as possible. Then create a short biography of the person. Think about how you can structure your biography of this person in ways that make the narrative compelling, using literary techniques, and structure it in creative or experimental ways. The result does not need to seem like a standard biographical entry or scholarly account—you can take liberties to play with form to fit the person's life story.

CHAPTER 8
PERFORMANCE

I. Introduction

The literature of live performance is older than literature itself. By that we mean oral storytelling, folktales, rituals, riddles, recipes, laws, songs, and early forms of theater predate written artifacts in most cultures. Thus, "performance" isn't an emerging genre so much as it is the *original* genre. Scops, bards, troubadours, and skalds regaled their communities with epics that were passed down through memorization and word of mouth; many features of such ancient poetry are by-products of this origin in oral culture, including rhyme, meter, repetition, episodic narratives, inset tales, envelope patterns, and epithets. The very notion of a "lyric" is based on a composition whose rhythm would be accompanied by music on a lyre. So, too, with early religious texts: they were—and still are, in many cases—learned by heart and recited. Indeed, it is only recently in the last couple hundred years that literacy has become widespread enough that the written medium has dominated; today, however, we may be witnessing a return to performative and oral media with the advent of technology: podcasts, audiobooks, and YouTube videos are just a few of the popular types of performance literature.

While many contemporary performance works might appear cutting-edge, they also harken back to archaic practices of ceremonies and enchantments, which directly engaged their audiences. When discussing performance works, we might have to readjust our sense of what constitutes "literature" since the scripted text no longer takes primacy. At times, performance works may comprise a type of literature for which there is no written record. At other times, the scripted text exists in a dialectic with the oral or performative delivery, so that what was once performed improvisationally may be transcribed to the page (or video) and then performed once again. The work may modulate and be modified throughout such a process, never definitive in any single account since it depends on context, reception, and spontaneity.

When written out, performance "scores" may also contain not just text but also traces of action, gesture, music, emotion, tone, and extratextual cues. Other times, the written version of performance works might appear scant and barebones, mere textual scaffolding to be fleshed out anew during each enactment. When evaluating performance works, it bodes well to remember that most current literary standards have developed around works that are self-sufficient on the page; we may need to develop new standards when dealing with the emerging genre of performance. For example, the linguistic text may be only one aspect of a larger multimedia show, the embodiment and presentation may be integral to the comprehension of a piece, the audience may play an important part in how the piece turns out, or a work may be entirely improvisational and the written artifact only a document of the process. Performance works tend to value process over product, audience engagement over disinterested appreciation, and situational responsiveness over immobile polish. In a different sense, though, performance works may be easier to judge since the vibrancy and aliveness within the collective experience of an audience is often visceral.

Contemporary performance works are evolving to have more in common with each other than with the genres or contexts from which they arose. Although we classify performance works in taxonomic categories later, the direction of experimental performance works today is to obviate and crossover these distinctions. Thus, the categories are merely heuristics by which to comprehend an ever-developing field. Only when a lecture seems to borrow from theater, a poetry reading appears more like performance art, or an escape room takes on elements of literary narrative have we moved into the realm of "performance" per se. For this reason, conventional book tours and readings—though prevalent—are not dwelled upon here. While the prominence of literary readings is a sign of audiences' hunger for more engaging and performative works, most readings remain slightly stodgy and hidebound to the conventions of the page. The quality of the work stays rooted in its written form, its vocal presentation an afterthought or residue. Performance works typically reverse this priority. The vocal, gestural, and embodied aspects of the work are foregrounded in pieces that traverse through real space in real time. Our claim is that performance across different arenas constitutes an emerging genre, a constellation of works that have more in common with other performances than the traditions in which they are usually situated.

II. Theater

At first blush, theater—as playwrighting—might seem the conventional literary genre that has the most in common with performance. And yet, the theater-makers who developed experimental performance works during the Modernist era, according to theater historian Günter Berghaus, desired "to overcome the limitations of theater as a social institution and therefore they teamed up with painters, sculptors, or musicians who shared their concerns. It was out of this collaboration that a genuine avant-garde approach to the performance medium arose" (2006: xvi). Although many of the avant-garde's innovations were later reabsorbed back into the theater tradition, the history of performance tracks much closer to artistic movements such as Expressionism, Futurism, Russian Constructivism, Cubism, Dadaism, Surrealism, and the Bauhaus. Indeed, visual artists such as Oscar Kokoschka, Fernand Léger, Pablo Picasso, Lothar Schreyer, and Marcel Duchamp were some of the instigators who formulated early performance works. Performance has been frequently conceptualized as the spilling over of artworks or aesthetic outlooks into the realm of the real world. For some, performance is not theater, but life itself.

If we attempted a retrofitted historiography of performance before the twentieth century, we might include a wide range of activities: on the one hand, masques, pageants, parades, processions, banquets, and courtly entertainments, and, on the other, street performances, Punch-and-Judy shows, traveling thespians, jugglers, acrobats, mummers, mountebanks, clowns, revels, magicians, and vaudeville. One way to define performance is to focus on events that either took place away from the public stage or that were inserted into stage plays as entr'actes and interludes, such as tumblers, burlesque, and satyr plays. Today one term for such miming, clowning, and acrobatics is "circus arts." Such forms were not always written down or well documented, and therefore we sometimes lack robust archival evidence about them. Still, many of these assorted performance traditions have practitioners today.

Where theater bleeds into performance most is when it's extemporaneous, site-specific, or immersive (i.e., involving audience participation or a haunted house-type show). The tradition of "Poet's Theatre," which academics Heidi R. Bean and Laura Hinton characterize as "a countercultural community that brought poets, dancers, musicians, visual artists, and performance artist in productive collaboration with one another" and which often "grants special emphasis to *embodied* and *performed* language" (2009: n.p., emphasis in original) is another type of theater that more closely resembles performance than traditional theater. Poet's Theater took place starting in the 1950s at such spaces as Judson Memorial Church, the Bowery Poetry Club, and the San Francisco Poets' Theatre. Another site of such collaboration was Black Mountain College, where collaborators from many disciplines—including Merce Cunningham, John Cage, Charles Olson, and Robert Rauschenberg—performed the first happening, "Theater Piece #1." Each element (music, dance, spectacle, talking, poetry) operated independently according to chance procedures although taking place at the same time. Such happenings and poet's theater tends to eschew the well-structured narratives, stable character development, and realistic scenarios of traditional theater. Instead, they emphasize a more fanciful or conceptual approach to language. They cross-pollinate different art forms. Their capaciousness makes them hard to define since they are constantly in motion, invented anew for each occasion, and explore the relations between different modes and media of expression. The contemporary Black Took Collective, for example, embraces the hybridity and dissonance between the forms their pieces combine, such as multimedia videos, DJ shows, dance, hip-hop, theatrical vignettes, and poetry readings.

Another example of performance theater work is exemplified in Karen Tei Yamashita's *Anime Wong*. Turn to p. 319–31 for *Hannah Kusoh: An American Butoh*, one of the most dynamic works from the collection.

III. Poetry

Poets, too, have spearheaded other types of performance works. Russian Futurist Vladimir Mayakovsky experimented in forms ranging from living newspapers and circus events to agitprop and a mass revolutionary reenactment involving a cast of thousands. In Mayakovsky's early days he would half howl, half harangue his poems in the cellar of the Stray Dog Café in St. Petersburg; he and his Futurists coevals would paint their faces, throw tea at the audience, and generally engaged in *épater la bourgeoisie*. Similarly, Dada poet Hugo Ball was a ringleader for assorted onstage horseplay at the Cabaret Voltaire café in Zürich during the First World War aimed at scandalizing the patrons; the Dada performances were a furious, nonsensical bombardment of crazy poems, puppet shows, jazz-inspired dance, cacophonous music, and absurd costumes that acted as agitprop to protest the greater absurdity of the war machine.

Later, Surrealists such as André Breton, Tristan Tzara, and Paul Éluard hosted salons, soirées, and séances. Rather than presenting finished pieces, many of the Surrealists' performances were about collectively generating new work by using games, dreams, and automatism. The Surrealists also organized participatory walks where they attempted to see the existing environment as if it were an artwork or to help awaken their nascent creativity, a precursor to the "dérive" developed by the Situationist International group, which, according to its leader Guy DeBord (2006: 62), was "a rapid passage through varied ambiances" in an urban area to activate poetic associations within one's psychogeography, "whether the goal is to study a terrain or to disorient oneself." Expressions of the same sensibility include "slipping by night into houses undergoing demolition, hitchhiking nonstop and without destination … and wandering in subterranean catacombs forbidden to the public" (DeBord, 2006: 65). Artists like Vito Acconci, Richard Long, Francis Alÿs, and Janine Antoni continued engineering walks as performances—often involving constraints—during later decades. Sometimes the only audience was the performer alone. In 2014, for example, poet and photographer Joshua Edwards documented his 680-mile walk across Texas as a companion piece to a poetry collection.

Many contemporary poets perform spoken word in slam events, an arena of friendly competition. The slam scene fosters raucous, egalitarian, and accessible poetry that emphasizes the way that poets can communicate to an audience in live performance. Although there are few explicit constraints in slam, the style tends toward an enthusiastic delivery of free-verse lyrics that engage with personal experience, identity, and political issues. The spoken word circuit has roots in the barnstorming performances of Vachel Lindsay who would sing and chant his verses in the 1910s and 1920s. During the Harlem Renaissance and after, Melvin B. Tolson, impersonating a variety of personas, innovated boppy jazz-ballads that portrayed extended narratives about diverse casts of characters. In the 1950s and 1960s in the Khrushchev Thaw of the Soviet Union, poets such as Yevgeny Yevtushenko, Bella Akhmadulina, and Andrei Voznesensky could sell out stadiums with their declamatory readings. In the United States around the same time, San Francisco Renaissance and Beat poets were organizing events that combined protests, performances, and poetry readings. Such early innovators presaged the current spoken word artists. Today a wide array of poets who emerged from the slam scene now also publish their work in print, including Patricia Smith, John Murillo, and Safia Elhillo.

Although slam poetry typically avoids music, costumes, and props, other types of performance poetry might make use of these. For example, beat poets like Sonia Sanchez have recorded with jazz musicians while Joy Harjo herself plays the saxophone and sings songs during her poetry performances. In a different vein, New York School poet Kenward Elmslie was known for belting buoyant showtune-like poems with boyish glee. Styles of performance poetry differ widely. Joyelle McSweeney yips, yaps, yawps, and yowls her work in incantatory overdrive. Cecilia Vicuña almost whispers her lines as she loops strands of thread throughout the audience, creating an intimate web of connection among her listeners.

And Rodrigo Toscano plays different voices in a polyvocal mash-up of sounds, languages, and words to suggest the shifting subjectivities that cross the invisible borders surrounding us. One of his dialogues, "Great Awakening," is included on pp. 313–14.

What these poets share is a drive to go beyond the printed text to utilize voices, bodies, music, spaces, and even objects to express their poetic vision.

IV. Lectures

A different, and often overlooked, impetus to performance grew out of prose: the lecture circuit. In the nineteenth century, authors such as Charles Dickens, Ralph Waldo Emerson, Oscar Wilde, Frederick Douglas, William James, P. T. Barnum, and Mark Twain held audiences spellbound through their talks, popular philosophy, and impromptu wit. Concurrent with the Third Great Awakening that emphasized societal shortcomings rather than individual sins, the lyceum movement brought famous speakers (social reformers, scientists, and public intellectuals) to tour throughout the country on the model of lay preachers advocating a gospel of education while offering a considerable dose of amusement, creating a system of star performers. "By the early 1850s, and for a quarter century thereafter, organized public lecturing was one of the most popular forms of entertainment for middle-class America," writes Peter Cherches (2017: 8). So, too, many of the leading twentieth-century writers—including Virginia Woolf, W. E. B. DuBois, Jorge Luis Borges, James Baldwin, and Italo Calvino—gave talks and lectures, which were later published; the performative quality of holding the attention of a live audience has sometimes left its mark on the printed texts through unexpected asides, questions from the audience, and rhetorical gestures. Oratory, sermons, and speeches still inflected the style of the twentieth-century public address, informing the style of many an essay, too.

Against this background, a twentieth-century tradition of more experimental lectures developed. Gertrude Stein's *Lectures in America*, for example, appears more interested in fracturing grammar and the expectations of meaning-making with circuitous repetitions that drill deeper into their subjects by sidewise, spiraling contortions. John Cage in "Lecture on Nothing," "Composition as Process," and "45' for a Speaker" applies precisely gridded rhythmic columns, question-and-answer formats, mix-and-match collages, and aleatory procedures, along with occasional musical accompaniment to his lectures on art. For Cage, as for Stein, music was theory, but theory was also a kind of music. In other words, performing talks *about* their work was continuous with *doing* theater, music, or poetry. There was an art to thinking out loud.

More recently, the lecture has continued to evolve. Bob Perelman initiated the San Francisco Talk Series of conversations about topics pertaining to innovative writing practices during the 1970s and 1980s, providing a forum for the discursive performance-lecture genre, whether modeled on readings, demonstrations, or collaborations with the audience. In the 1980s, art critic David Antin improvised "talk poems" in which he discoursed in front of an audience, later transcribing them for publication. In creative writing, the "craft talk" has also emerged as a nascent genre in which writers deliver informal lectures that often combine personal anecdotes, criticism, and advice on writing topics. Generative writing workshops, too, can be performative, especially when participants are facilitated in collective action. Art talks and symposia at museums and other venues have also become common; they are the occasion for artists not only to address issues of politics or discuss aesthetics, but also at times to engage in demonstrations, performances, and artmaking itself. Other presentation formats, such as Pecha Kucha—a Japanese slideshow in which a topic is presented in twenty slides with each one lasting only 20 seconds—and Ted Talks have gained notoriety, too.

One last form is the conference keynote, which tends to be a forceful thesis of the conference's theme. At the NonfictioNOW Conference in Flagstaff, essayists Ander Monson and Michael Martone balked at the core expectation of the genre. Dressed in suits, they were merely cosplaying as sacrosanct scholars of nonfiction. Instead, they skewered the pedantic form, with Monson and Martone reading micro essays back and forth about keys and notes, respectively, a dueling object lesson sans the stuffy moralizing.

V. Comedy, Storytelling, and New Media

If lectures are oft overlooked in creative writing discourse, so too is comedy, a performance mode that comes in a variety of subgenres. Comedy, including in poems or fiction, can be underrated since it appears unserious, but pieces do not need to be self-serious, tragic, or buttoned-up to have value. Frivolity has political import. Camp drollery can pack a punch. And pithy repartee can lend moxie to a work. Another reason comic modes get short shrift is that they are less "universal" across times and cultures. Comedy tends to be more topical, and it varies with personal tastes. Peter McGraw and Joel Warner, academic researchers on humor theory, propose that what we find funny needs to hit the sweet spot they call a "benign violation." Too outré or offensive, and we'll balk while finding the humorist disgusting or objectionable; too benign, though, and the joke falls flat while the humorist seems boring. Effective comedy, then, needs to hit just the right level of an unexpected, scurrilous, or shocking taboo-violation to provoke laughter—but without going too far. Yet, this target zone depends on context, cultural norms, and individual attitudes. Dry humor at an academic conference might get bigger laughs than a bawdy zinger at a nightclub due to circumstantial decorum. Thus, even in written work, the success of comedy can depend on the performative contexts in which it is being read and an anticipation of standards of propriety. This also explains why comedy does not always translate between cultures.

Still, comedy has been a vital part of literature: the gross-out jokes of Rabelais, the risqué wit of Byron, the blackest humor in Nathanael West, and Philip Roth's *Portnoy's Complaint* with its freewheeling, ribald take on a Borsch Belt monologue that climaxes in a literal punch line. Today, writers like Paul Beatty, Colson Whitehead, Elena Passarello, and George Saunders have learned lessons of setup, pacing, and a ludic sense of the mundane from stand-ups. Poets as diverse as Patricia Lockwood, Graham Foust, Natalie Shapero, and Dean Young use the tools of comics in their riffs, such as misdirection and surprising twists. Furthermore, many performers who are better known as humorists or comics also write, whether they publish books—like Groucho Marx, Steve Martin, David Sedaris, and Sarah Silverman—or not. Stand-up and sketch comedy is both writing and performing, too, whether it's Lenny Bruce's stream-of-consciousness fantasias, Richard Pryor's no-holds-barred observational humor, John Cleese's situational wackiness, or Mitch Hedberg's non sequitur one-liners. Political satire in the form of mock-news shows (think Trevor Noah or Samantha Bee) are growing in popularity, as well. Pointed political commentary may take other forms, though, such as Indian satirist Jaspal Bhatti's scripted sitcoms or the screwball hijinks of the Moustache Brothers in Myanmar. In one David Cross joke, he performs an incantatory compendium of headlines about the gaffes, blunders, and villainy of former US President Donald Trump. It's the volume of the compendium, the force of the list—forty-five distinctly heinous iniquities—that inspires the laughter. Through this listing process, Trump himself becomes the joke—as if to say, *How can any one person be so uniquely, voluminously immoral?* All told, comedy remains a vibrant source of performative verve for creative writing.

Drag and burlesque, too, have long been influential vehicles for comedy from Milton Berle to RuPaul. Contemporary writers such as Wo Chan, Benjamin Garcia, and Cara Dodge incorporate drag into their live performances and video poems. Improvised, performative interventions in the real world—in many cases with unwitting or naïve participants—may be considered another developing subgenre of comedy whose practitioners include Andy Kaufman, Sacha Baron Cohen, The Yes Men, and Nathan Fielder. The outlandishness of the protagonists in these pieces is frequently used to point out the underlying balderdash of the real-world environment they encounter. The Aristocrats, an off-color vaudeville-era joke is prone to improvisation and one-upmanship; in recent iterations, especially Gilbert Gottfried's laden with a prurient onslaught of unforgettable prepositional phrases, the comic's goal is to push the envelope as far as possible. Then there's the one-of-a-kind physical clowning of poet and performer Henry Goldkamp, who brings a madcap, quick-change inanity to his bag of slaphappy, tricked-out antics.

There's a book for each generation's funny bone—from *Graveyard Clay* (Máirtín Ó Cadhain) to *A Confederacy of Dunces* (John Kennedy Toole); from *The Sellout* (Paul Beatty) to *Diary of a Drag Queen* (Crystal Rasmussen). Notably, as humor tends to emerge from distinct cultural milieus, there are also collections and anthologies devoted to specific expressions of humorists as with *Hokum: An Anthology of African-American Humor* (ed. Paul Beatty).

Like comedy, storytelling, in one form or another, is an ancient and enduring aspect of nearly every culture; in the 2000s it evolved along the lines of slam competitions with organizations such as Spillit in Memphis, First Person Arts in Philadelphia, and The Moth, which host events around the world. Some storytelling slams operate like open mics with participants sharing 5-minute personal anecdotes; others are longer-form narratives where the participants have extensively rehearsed their stories. Story slams are invariably autobiographical—in part, their impetus is to build collective empathy and allow audiences to learn about their community. Children's literature events are a different storytelling category, featuring variations involving drag storytime, crankie illustrated lightbox machines, puppets, dolls, maps, family photos, and many other activities, costumes, or props. Unlike readings for adults, most children's storytelling events engross their audiences in a narrative through performance and participation. A newer adult form of participatory storytelling is Live Action Role-Playing Games (LARPGs), immersive versions of tabletop role-playing games (i.e., *Dungeons & Dragons* or *Magic: The Gathering*) wherein participants implement narratives in the real world through a mix of improvisation and rules. LARPGs bear similarities to masquerades and historical "cosplay," such as Renaissance Fairs, Regency-era Balls, or Civil War reenactments. LARPGs utilize world-building, character, plot, dialogue, and other elements of creative writing. Though not text-based, LARPGs might still be regarded as a mode of literary production.

Likewise, if we overcome the biases of standard-issue creative writing ideology, we can view other types of performance as modes of literary production, too. New media have proliferated with the growth of technology in recent decades. To what extent might we regard interactive shows on TikTok Live, YouTube tutorials, multiplayer video games, or virtual reality in the Metaverse as performative literature? In many cases, these media even incorporate traditional text-based, written components—not to mention the computer coding that makes them possible. Just as these modes begin to erode conventional distinctions between real life and performance, technological mediation and live events, written and spoken discourse, they also challenge notions of what constitutes literature. Historically, our familiar categories of creative writing depend on social conditions such as widespread literacy and networks of distribution (such as mail services) along with technological innovations like the printing press. This infrastructure didn't become the norm in Europe until around the eighteenth century, spurring the rise of new literary genres like the novel that we take for granted today. Before this time, the dominant literary modes were oral and performative. Thus, the development of new infrastructure, networks, and platforms along with greater technological literacy is perhaps now supporting the rise of wholly different forms of literature that are returning us to oral and performative expression.

VI. Music

Likewise, music has been accorded, begrudgingly at times, the status of literature, especially song lyrics by the likes of Woody Guthrie, Leonard Cohen, or Bob Dylan—the last of whom, in fact, won the Nobel Prize. Lyrics from historical genres such as ragtime, work songs, sea shanties, ballads, and gospel sometimes make the cut, too, along with high forms such as opera libretti and choice musicals (Sondheim, Rodgers and Hammerstein). Yet these examples emphasize the linguistic element involved in music, rather than its performative aspects. Seen in terms of *performance*—rather than as sound alone or a minor literary mode—music offers a much broader palette of styles in the twentieth and twenty-first centuries. Rap battles, rock concerts, punk shows, jam sessions, cabarets, dub-step raves, and K-pop dance extravaganzas, to name a few. Most subgenres of music, in other words, have developed not only specific repertories of sound and techniques but also distinctive types of engagement with their audiences during live concerts. The performative contexts of musical subgenres affect the spaces where performances occur, which in turn influences the music itself: a symphony's grand concert hall, arena rock's packed stadiums, the dingy dive bar or basement of a Riot Grrrl event, a small jazz club, an industrial warehouse for Japanoise, or an intimate coffee shop where one can hear folk music. Each space structures the behaviors of musicians and audiences alike. Performers are not merely producing the sound or playing the score—they are also putting on a show, often in cahoots with their listeners who clap, shout refrains, scream, or snap along. The emergence of music videos, as well, has elaborated the aural qualities of music into corollary visual, filmic, and performative modalities. The eye-catching nature of music videos may be transferred to live events, too, where concerts include narratives, dance numbers, light shows, and multimedia spectacles.

Much new and experimental music has adopted a decidedly performative orientation, as well. In "Variations VII" John Cage mixed, in real time, sounds transmitted from the surrounding city with noises made from everyday household items. Karlheinz Stockhausen, around the same time, experimented with different processes of composition, live electronic instrumentation including feedback, and the spatial arrangement of musicians. Harry Partch pioneered the use of microtones and non-Western scales through his compositions for a range of special instruments he invented himself. Iannis Xenakis, Milton Babbitt, and Morton Feldman likewise wrote compositions that challenged foundational principles of Western music theory, in many cases the scores of which required unique methods of notation. Babbitt wrote that composers and performers of such new music no longer lived "in a unitary musical universe of 'common practice,' but in a variety of universes of diverse practice" (1958: n.p.), a condition that places greater conceptual and perceptual demands on its listeners. Babbitt, however, proposed "a total, resolute, and voluntary withdraw from the public world" and "complete elimination of ... the social aspects of musical composition," given that new music's complexity only could be appreciated by specialists. Babbitt thought that depending on public performances would result in pandering, "compromise" or "exhibitionism." Thus, in the 1950s and 1960s new music stood at a crossroads between elitist connoisseurship and appealing to a public of nonspecialists.

Emerging from this avant-garde music scene, the transnational FLUXUS group reinvigorated the public and performative dimension of new music, saving it from a cloistered, ivory-tower sterilization. Nam June Paik created a cello made from TVs, which Charlotte Moorman played naked; Allison Knowles created a massive salad that she fed to a crowd; Dick Higgins's "Danger Music #17" required the performer to scream until their vocal chords were at risk of being damaged; George Brecht's "Drip Music" involved drops of water poured into an empty vessel; a butterfly was released into a room for the sound of its wingbeats in La Monte Young's "Composition #8"; George Maciunas created paradoxical sports such as soccer games on stilts, shot put with balloons, and boxing matches with comically oversized gloves; Robert Bozzi composed a piece instructing a piano to get hitched to two horses who pull in opposite directions until it's broken apart; and Yoko Ono invited visitors to a museum that, when they arrived, only consisted of buzzing flies that were dispersed for the visitors to track down. These antics—silly, unsettling, provocative—linked FLUXUS artists to the Dada and Surrealist tradition of composers such as Eric Satie and Spike Jones, on the one hand, while connecting them to the developing field of performance artists such as Marcel Duchamp, Yves Klein, and Joseph Beuys, on the other. This performative zeal has continued with later avant-garde composers, including Frank Zappa, Sun Ra, DJ Spooky, and a variety of post-punk, no wave, free jazz, and experimental hip-hop groups in addition to the evolving world of "new music" itself.

Jennifer Walshe, for instance, is a contemporary Irish composer and performer who is known for her experimental and avant-garde music. Both her musical compositions and music writing challenge the orthodoxies of her discipline. In *Women Box*, she asks the opera singers to grunt while throwing punches in the air; in *XXX_LIVE_NUDE_GIRLS!!!*, her quartet alternates between playing their string instruments and using that same bowing motion to rev toy cars off their forearms like reckless boys. In *THIS IS WHY PEOPLE O.D. ON PILLS/AND JUMP FROM THE GOLDEN GATE BRIDGE* (2004), Walshe instructs a hypothetical composer/performer to, first, learn how to skateboard and then go scouting for optimum skating environments. She writes: "Contemplate the ability of skate-boarding to articulate space, find new paths through architecture, fresh uses for it. ... Compose an imaginary path you would like to skate. This path should push and force you to limits, be rich, beautiful, complicated and stylish, and incorporate some tricks." The musical composition, then, is the varied sound of wheels on smooth and abrasive surfaces, moving down angles both steep and gentle—a playing of the motley urban landscapes like it's an instrument.

Find (and perform!) Jennifer Walshe's score, *THIS IS WHY PEOPLE O.D. ON PILLS/AND JUMP FROM THE GOLDEN GATE BRIDGE*, on p. 318.

Experimental Writing

VII. Performance Art

Performance art—coterminous with the FLUXUS group among many other provocateurs—gained recognition as a medium independent from other forms during the 1960s and 1970s. Performance art developed as an independent medium, though one that relies on interdisciplinarity, during a period of political consciousness-raising in the context of feminism, gay liberation, the anti-war movement, struggles for civil rights, and increasing environmental awareness. Artists sought to create works against a tumultuous background of protests, sit-ins, rock 'n' roll, free love, and drug culture. Historian Roselee Goldberg declares that performance art has appealed to "shocking audiences into reassessing their own notions of art and its relation to culture. For this reason, its base has always been anarchic. Moreover, by its very nature, performance defies precise or easy definition beyond the simple declaration that it is live art by artists" (1979: 6). Whatever axioms one might use to delimit performance art would readily find an artist eager to demolish; indeed, many question whether performance art requires "live" performance or, in a technologically mediated world, what "live" means exactly. Film and video artists such as Matthew Barney and Bruce Nauman are regularly classed with performance artists, after all. Others might doubt the extent to which performance art needs to be consecrated and distinguished as art per se—performances in some cases might simply merge with the quotidian activities of life. Still others are skeptical if performance art must be made by "artists" since some has been produced by the collective actions of laypersons, technicians, audience members, or computers. One impetus for performance art was an anti-commercial ethos and a turn toward social action: it was nonmaterial, ephemeral, sometimes non-replicable. Performances also allowed visual artists to escape the expectations and pressures of museums and other art-world institutions. Performance—like other art forms that arose in the 1960s and 1970s such as new media, installations, Earth art, and Conceptual work—allowed a direct engagement with audiences and an exploration of practices outside the traditional confines of the gallery setting.

Given its range of practices and aesthetics, the boundaries of performance art are indeterminate. Nevertheless, important subgenres can be identified. Body art focuses on displaying, manipulating, and contextualizing the body in ways that transform it into artwork. Hannah Wilke photographed herself with tiny, vulval sculptures made from chewing gum that resembled scarification, undercutting her glamorous nude poses. Carolee Schneemann read from a scroll that she unfurled from her vagina. Cassils, a transgender bodybuilder, wrestled with a six-foot mound of clay in a strobe-lit room to capture frozen images. Adrian Piper altered her appearance of race, gender, and social class through disguises to gauge people's reaction to her in everyday settings. Piper's work may also be classified as street art, much like William Pope.L's performances of crawling through urban, public spaces wearing a Superman outfit with a skateboard strapped to his back. Pope.L's grueling crawls, meanwhile, could likewise be seen as endurance art, too, which involves undergoing a trying experience or durational process. Tehching Hseih, for example, spent an entire year clocking in every hour to a punch clock, another year roped to a fellow performance artist, and yet another year homeless. Endurance artist Chris Burden first gained notoriety for "Shoot," a performance in which a friend fires a rifle at him at close range, injuring him in the arm; the work functioned as a dramatic protest of the Vietnam draft. Maria Abramović's "The Artist is Present" at MoMA involved sitting and staring silently with each museum visitor one by one during the museum's operating hours, a test of inspiration and stamina.

Abramović's piece might also be thought of as participatory art, in which the audience's contribution is vital to the artistic event. The contemporary Indonesia collective ruangrupa offers community workshops and curates exhibits to create a space, which is "a studio, a library, a research lab and a party venue, all in one." The work of ruangrupa might simultaneously be viewed as institutional critique, as well, a mode that aims at producing interventions in the ways that art is consumed, produced, and distributed within the power structures of the art market. Piero Manzoni's "Artist's Shit," a tin can of his feces that he sold for its equivalent weight in gold, or Banksy's "Love Is in the Bin," a painting whose frame shredded the canvas once it was sold at auction, are other instances of institutional critique. Performance art has fluid, evolving categories: this instability acts as a source of power to incite audiences to consider the parameters and purposes of artmaking and reflect on the cultural assumptions in which they partake. Nonetheless, in the 1980s downtown art scene in New York City, performance art and writing were coterminous disciplines—Kathy Acker, John Jesurun, David Wojnarowicz, Karen Finley, Penny Arcade, and Eric Bogosian wrote plays, novels, and other pieces with the same edgy energy they used to attack their outrageous bits of performance, whether onstage or off.

Ritual is a backbone along which many performance artworks are structured. In "Dionysus in 69," Richard Schechner—looking toward ritual, play, and even forms of group therapy—organized a work of delirious environmental theater involving the audience, harkening back to Bacchic festivals. Concurrently in the 1960s and 1970s, the Viennese Actionists orchestrated violent, orgiastic rites that savaged the iconography of religion, state, and respectable morality. We'd warn those who look up the group's performances, they should take care that they're prepared to encounter images of blood, slime, masturbation, and feces. Meanwhile, the counterculture of the 1960s and 1970s—including Gary Snyder, Allen Ginsberg, and Timothy Leary—were interested in Eastern religions and Mayan shamanistic rites; one of the rituals they performed was a massive "Be-In" protest wherein a massive crowd attempted to levitate the Pentagon through a psychic exorcism. The event was later recounted in Norman Mailer's *The Armies of the Night*. Ethnopoetics, led by Jerome Rothenberg and Clayton Eshelman, evolving around the same period, showed more attention on the ritualized practices, oral literature, folklore, and artmaking of peoples outside the Western tradition. Today, writers such as Arianna Reines, Selah Saterstrom, and CA Conrad employ occult practices and rituals to generate their texts. Reines channels Gnosticism, tarot, astrology, and witchcraft to inspire her writing; Saterstrom invokes divinatory practices involving rosaries, candles, cards, and tattoos to process trauma; and Conrad fabricates new rituals involving crystals, mirrors, bodies, food, and places that act to prompt writing exercises. These authors utilize rituals to harness spiritual energy and send their work in unforeseen directions, much like earlier writers invoked duende, muses, or daimons.

Performance is a permissive category with sundry strains coming under its pluralistic umbrella: circus arts and drag balls, flash mobs and fashion shows, escape rooms and "cyborg theater." Many festivals and pop-up events also count as performance, such as the popular "typewriter poetry" events in which writers produce poems on demand. Pop-up libraries and curational activities in which art is placed in public spaces can be viewed as performance, too, since these are constructed to stimulate engagement from their audiences. For instance, the spirit of John Giorno's Dial-a-Poem project in the 1970s, in which folks could call a number to hear recordings from poets, is continued today in Elizabeth Hellstern's Telepoem Booth, a pay phone converted into a space to hear recorded poetry readings. Indeed, with the concept of "relational aesthetics" proposed by French curator Nicholas Bourriaud, artworks are not seen in terms of being objects so much as ways to facilitate interaction in an expanded field of social action. Artmaking is an exchange that empowers its audiences to create and change the world themselves. Looked at this way, performance casts an even wider net, encompassing a dimension of how art activates and operationalizes its viewer. Audiences transform the artwork and are, by turns, transformed by it.

Relatedly, the genre of the manifesto has had an outsize impact on performance and on experimental art movements more generally. Although most manifestos are not performed in front of an audience, they are nonetheless "performative" in terms of J. L. Austin's (1961) linguistic sense of "performative" speech, which, instead of just describing reality, incites a change in the world. Manifestos are visionary polemics that profess principles for new modes of social, political, or aesthetic engagement. They define such things as the goals, values, and assumptions—proposing new ways of artmaking or operating in a field. Such works issue a call to action while frequently enacting their own imperatives through the process, style, and content of the manifesto itself. For instance, Marinetti's "Manifesto of Futurism" not only proclaims that the Futurists want to "sing the love of danger, the habit of energy and rashness" (1909: n.p.) but likewise *performs* such rash and dangerous singing in the very text. Manifestos were ubiquitous in Modernist and Postmodernist programs of art. If they are far less frequently used in contemporary practice, perhaps this change is due to the rhetoric of manifestos seeming naïve and shrill today, a by-product of their decidedly revolutionary stance. Or perhaps the manifesto's decline is due to artistic fervor having been domesticated by grants administrators for purposes of missions, impact statements, and project narratives. Many artists today aim to attract the funding of state, nonprofit, and corporate donors, not overturn these existing power structures. The collective vim, tongue-in-cheek irony, and utopian desires embodied in manifestos, however, have long lit a fire in creators of an experimental ilk.

VII. Conclusion

The diversity of modes and media is inherent to the nature of performance. The FLUXUS composer Dick Higgins suggests that performance of all kinds from mail art to dance theater should be regarded as "intermedia" wherein "continuity rather than categorization is the hallmark of our new mentality" (1966: n.p.). This experimental approach obviates the ostensible genres from which performance work seemingly derives—whether comedy or lecture, poetry or ritual, music or visual art—and situates these works together since they share a greater family resemblance with each other than the genres from which they originated. In this perspective, we could examine performance along its own dimensions, such as the extent to which any work is improvisational, participatory, immersive, text-based, process-oriented, ephemeral, or mediated. We can also consider a performance work's purposes, audiences, styles, rhetoric, and dramaturgy. This approach raises a question, however, about the role of writing in performance. Does performance aspire to be a *Gesamtkunstwerk* or "total work of art" so that writing constitutes but one element of its design? Or might some performance works require writing as a basis—for generative purposes, documentation, or end product—whereas others do not?

We can offer two provisional answers. One, our "soft thesis," is that performance can be a means to generate or deliver texts, which has profound implications for a written text's form and content. Bernadette Mayer's *Studying Hunger*, for example, is only possible because of the durational experiments with dreams, memories, rituals, drugs, food, and altered states of consciousness she recorded in her journals.

Alternatively, the visually and sonically innovative form of Douglas Kearney's work on the page is a corollary to embody how voices, space, music, and media are layered during his live readings or opera libretti. Read and see Kearney's libretto for a cyborg opera, *Sucktion*, on pp. 266–77.

Performance is not an incidental feature of these texts or an afterthought that occurs once the text has been polished. It is organic and vital to these texts' creation. More and more writing in contemporary practice is rooted in intermedia or performative contexts, challenging print-based conventions. At the end of the day, however, our "soft thesis" reverts to the notion that as experimental as we may want to be, creative writing must be about writing on the page. At the very least, performance—if it is to be valuable *as* a subdiscipline within creative writing—must translate or transform the way that words are arranged and recorded.

Our "hard thesis," by contrast, is more radical: the very notion of what constitutes writing and literature is changing. Performance is an emerging genre that does not necessarily require an element of writing as conventionally understood. Contemporary popular discourse is as likely to refer to "content creators," "makers," "performers," or "creatives" as to writers. Academic English departments are as likely to study performance, oral literature, computer algorithms, video games, cultural studies, and material objects as they are traditional printed texts. A seismic shift is underway. When rearguard critic Arthur Krystal argues that "literature" must be understood as the great canonical texts, inveighing against the incursion of how "maps, sermons, comic strips, cartoons, speeches, photographs, movies, war memorials, and music all huddle beneath the literary umbrella" (2014: 89), he is attempting to eternalize the definition of literature according to what it is has been in the (recent) past. Krystal makes a category error when he declares that "quality" excludes these multifarious cultural artifacts and expressive media from being regarded as (high) literature since he prejudges the quality of all such artifacts now and in the future. Krystal, moreover, claims not to hear any music in contemporary poems. The problem may be that he is trying to listen for the euphonious rhythms of Victorian prosody in today's dissonant cadences, a proposition as foolish as expecting the tonal harmonies of Classical and Romantic scores to inform contemporary music compositions. Standards change. Marxist critic Terry Eagleton, by contrast, announces, "Literature, in the sense of a set of works of assured and unalterable value, distinguished by certain shared inherent properties, does not exist" (1983: 9). It's quite possible that the social norms and practices that define literature tomorrow will value the performative qualities of work rather than the shape texts take on the page, viewing these marks as merely an antiquated relic of print culture. If so, the tenets of creative writing might need to catch up with the YouTube and TikTok videos in your cache.

Discussion Questions

1. What aspects or elements of performance are difficult to represent on the page? What are some techniques that experimental writers have used to capture those elements of performance in their writing or by other (non-performative) means? Do you think it's fair to interpret performance writing from the page or is performance writing only a document or script rather than the whole text or artwork? How can we understand performances from the past based on the oftentimes scant archival materials that remain from any given production or event?

2. To what degree would you consider forms such as sermons, lectures, TedTalks, PowerPoint presentations, sales pitches, keynote addresses, podcasts, pep rally talks, political stump speeches, on-stage interviews, public colloquia, or funeral orations to be performances? When would you consider such modes to be performance writing? Are all performances artistic? What might make such a speech more performative, literary, artistic, or experimental in your opinion?

3. How might our behaviors and speech in everyday life be considered performances or performative? Why do we sometimes distinguish the "performative" from the "authentic"? Can performances also be authentic—and just what do we mean by "authentic," anyway? Does anything separate everyday performance (brushing one's teeth, for example) from the artistic variety of performance (an actor brushing her teeth on stage)? Why might happenings and other performance art be interested in breaking down the distinction we usually make between art and everyday life?

4. Why might manifestos have been used by many artistic movements, especially during the twentieth century among the avant-garde, and why do you think the manifesto's popularity is waning in the current century? What alternative forms or means are used today in place of manifestos to serve a similar purpose?

5. How are live performances different from recorded performances (theater versus film, for example)? How are recent technological innovations and new dramaturgical forms changing the ways we think about "live" performance versus performances that are mediated or recorded in some way? Do you believe that the distinction between live and mediated performance is important; do you think it will still be comprehensible in the future?

6. What role does improvisation play in performances? Do you enjoy the spontaneity of performances? How can that spontaneity be a part of performance writing? Do you think that "talk poems" or other improvisational performances without a script count as performance writing? Can a transcript or video after-the-fact also count as a type of writing or devising of a script?

7. How might popular forms of performance—for example, stand-up comedy, Slam poetry, game shows, sports, or TikTok videos—interact with experimental writing

practices? Can you think of any examples of works in such popular forms that you would consider experimental? Do the elements of mainstream mass appeal, entertainment value, or competition detract from the artistry of such performances or might it even enhance their artistry in some cases?

Writing Prompts

1. Look at the *FLUXUS Performance Workbook* (available for free online) and/or Yoko Ono's *Grapefruit*. Similarly, you can see CA Conrad's rituals called "Soma(tic) Poetry Exercises" (https://writing.upenn.edu/~taransky/somatic-exercises.pdf). Videos of CA performing or reading some rituals are available at the PennSound archive (https://writing.upenn.edu/pennsound/x/CAConrad.php) and the University of Arizona Poetry Center website (https://poetry.arizona.edu/blog/throwback-thursday-caconrad). After reviewing some of these examples, try to write a few of your own performance scores, rituals, or directions. In some cases, you'll see, the directions are meant to be performed, whether on a stage or on the street; in other cases, the score is more of a poetic form to imagine the performance in one's mind. You can then perform some of the scores you write or you can assemble them in a Flux Box or small kit of performance scores and other gags, poems, puzzles, and assorted weird items, much like George Maciunas, one of the founders of FLUXUS, did.

2. Play improvisation games. A handful are listed below. Others can be found in books such as *How to be the Greatest Improviser on Earth* by Will Hines, *The Big Book of Improv Games* by Karen L. Eichler and Andrew M. Spragge, and *The Improv Handbook* by Tom Salinsky. You may also find several improv games by doing a quick internet search.

    i. This one is from the famous improviser Viola Spolin and is called "Gibberish." The first person speaks gibberish while they act; the second person interprets what they said. It may be helpful if the gibberish speaker takes on a persona instead of assuming their normal identity. A common variation is to have two people mime a scene while two other people improvise lines of dialogue for them; the mimes should seem to mouth the words as best they can and react to the content of what is being said as they perform their actions. Likewise, the speakers should respond to the actions of the mimes as the scene evolves.

    ii. This one developed from observing student behavior and is called "Chair/Chore/Cheer." When students walk in the classroom, the chairs (and desks if there are desks) are disarranged in the wildest mess imaginable, stacked and overturned and facing every-which-a-way. Students need to collectively order the room to create a learning environment that they find comfortable. It helps if this is either done on the first day of a class or the class frequently switches its style of seating arrangement—otherwise, students tend to default to putting the chairs back into the arrangement they are used to. It should feel disorienting for the students to walk into a chaotic space. You can increase the disorientation and difficulty by not allowing the students to speak (perhaps writing "NO TALKING" on the board). Another version is the facilitator or teacher doesn't speak until the students complete the task (though they might nod, shrug, give a thumbs up, or shake their head no). This game acts as a team-building exercise and a way to empower greater student collaboration. The facilitator should use the final seating arrangement at least for the remainder of that class period. The game can also be used to identify which students gravitate to leadership roles and which are more passive. Once the room is arranged, the facilitator can prompt applause and cheers to signal the end of the game. It is a good idea to debrief the exercise, too.

iii. This improv game "Ski Trip" is useful for teaching dialogue, specifically subtext, code-switching, and raising the stakes. One person takes the role of a student; the other person takes on various roles, such as parent, best friend, significant other, academic dean, secret crush, or hated rival. The student's motivation is to get the other person to give them money for a ski trip they want to go on. The amount of money requested might also vary from five dollars to fifty dollars to five hundred dollars. Debrief the ways that the student's strategy changed depending on who they were speaking to and the amount they were requesting. Point out how the student (likely) did not address their goal head-on, but had to butter up, seduce, manipulate, or somehow insinuate themselves into the other character's good graces while anticipating their interlocutor's possible motivations.

iv. This game is called "Sketchy." The facilitator brings in a big box of items such as wigs, hats, glasses, makeup, costume jewelry, scarfs, and personal effects. Participants select a few items each and construct a persona based on the things they chose. They can mime the character. Another person then should write down a character sketch based on the persona: list such things as the persona's name, where they're from, what they do for a living, how old they are, their gender, their aspirations, marital status, education level, goals, fears, conflicts, and so on. The participants read their corresponding character sketches. Next, the audience provides a situation (or "platform"): the immediate location of the scene (say, "bathroom") and what each character is trying to get in the scene (say, "to wash their hands" and "to escape the boss"). Two personas then improvise the scene. The facilitator can clap, and then the personas freeze and two other personas switch in, continuing the scene but with their characters instead. The facilitator can also ring a bell and the two personas can remain, but the audience can suggest a new platform. A variation of this game can be played with personas who are characters developed from rough drafts of stories or playscripts that students wrote.

3. Set up at a street corner, a student union, or another public place that has heavy foot traffic with an old-fashioned typewriter, a ream of paper, a small table, and supplies. Have a sign that says "free poems" or advertises what you are offering. Passersby can request you to write poems for them on the spot. After you rapidly compose the poem based on their commission or topic, you might want to shape the paper, decorate it,

or place it in an envelope to add a more artisanal touch. You might consider dressing up or adding other performative flair, too. Pop-up typewriter poetry performances sometimes occur at an occasion such as an art opening, a holiday party, downtown art walks, or on Valentines. The New York Poetry Society, With Ink, and The Haikuists are just a few of the groups that sponsor them. Like Lucha Libro (see below), pop-up typewriter poetry events emphasize the fun, communal aspects of writing as entertainment. Nonetheless, they can frequently elicit genuine, in-depth literary conversations, too.

4. Hold a "Lucha Libro" match. James Ryan and Steve Westbrook in *Beyond Craft: An Anti-Handbook for Creative Writers* describe the format of a flash-fiction competition from Peru known as "Lucha Libro" (literally, "book battle," but the term plays on *Lucha Libre* or Mexican masked wrestling). The format originally developed by Angie Silva and Christopher Vasquez in 2011 had the writers wearing masks. During a five-minute interval, two writers are in front of their laptops, composing a flash-fiction story according to some given constraint or prompt. One constraint, for instance, could be presenting the writers with three objects that they need to incorporate into their flash piece right before the clock starts. The writers' messy draft-in-progress—including any false starts and edits—gets projected onto a screen for the audience to view in real time. Once the five minutes have elapsed, the writers can read whatever they wrote, and a panel of judges can determine who won. Matches can be structured into a tournament to include more writers. Good natured cheering, jeering, and shit-talk—whether from the audience or the writers—can be encouraged, similar to pro wrestlers' over-the-top monologues and promos. This adds to the spectacle and entertainment of the event. The winner of the first Lucha Libro contests in Peru had their book accepted for publication; maybe find a prize for your version of Lucha Libro. Alternatively, hold a Translation Slam. This is similar to a poetry slam or Lucha Libro competition, but in this case, the writers must translate a text that has just been revealed to them in real time, minutes before the event. To be fair, both writers should know the language they are translating from—or *not* know the language they are translating from. An MC might determine the winner based on audience reactions and applause or a panel of judges that know both languages could vote.

5. Coordinate a 24-hour performance art festival, modeled on the more common 24-hour play festival format. Typically, in a 24-hour play festival, there is an initial orientation meeting to make sure everyone knows the rules for the event, then playwrights have roughly 12 hours to compose a 10-minute play based on some prompt or constraint, after which time a couple actors and a director are given 11 hours to rehearse the play—the last hour is for the show itself (a script-in-hand performance) of the four to six plays produced through this process. One way to organize a 24-hour performance art festival is to pair up writers with an artist from a different medium (dancer, musician, visual artist, comedian, etc.) for the first 12 hours. Together they devise a script or performance score based on whatever prompts, constraints, or props you provide. This will help give the collaboration structure. Then, a director and one

other artist—it doesn't necessarily need to be an actor—are added as collaborators during the next 11 hours to shape the piece-in-progress, rehearse it, and otherwise bring it to fruition. Finally, the pieces are given a public presentation. Recruiting a variety of artists from different backgrounds and media will foster interdisciplinary exchange and experimentation, but nobody should feel they are confined to working in their medium alone. This will help writers (and others) break out of their usual roles, discovering new processes, exploring unfamiliar methods, and trying out collaborative practices. The 24-hour countdown tends to cut down on dawdling, self-doubt, and second guessing, besides making the event lower-stakes.

6. Whether collaboratively or individually, write a manifesto. Think about what tone you want to take—manifestos are often as much political declarations as artistic credos, and the style they're written in frequently formally embodies the tenets they espouse. It is recommended that you read a handful of manifestos first. Manifestos can sometimes be edgy, direct, and in your face. They usually are designed to spur collective action or spark interest in a new style or method of artwork, literature, or political movement. Or, alternatively, write a lecture. Try to make it more experimental or performative than most academic lectures. What innovations or artistry can be incorporated in your lecture? How will the writing straddle diverse generic conventions or push the boundaries of normal lectures? Will it include demonstrations, slides, poetry, dancing, artmaking, audience participation? At what occasion do you imagine this lecture would be performed?

7. Hold a cabaret, talent show, or variety act. A wide range of performance genres can be included, especially if each act is relatively brief: literary readings, dance, 10-minute plays, performance art, magic acts, monologues, drag shows, fashion shows, Pecha Kucha, short films, music, storytelling, multimedia spectacles, stand-up comedy, rap battles, and so on. This will give an opportunity for a lot of different folks to participate. This prompt requires more advanced notice than others: it likely needs around half a semester to plan. You could either recruit performers from the class you are in (in which case, the performance might be part of an assignment) or hold an open call at the university or to the public. You'd need to consider booking an appropriate venue, advertising the event, what tech needs your performers have, who would act as the host or MC, and what format you want for your event. Someone would need to coordinate the behind-the-scenes logistics, create a lineup or schedule, advertise it, and possibly make a program. Providing an occasion for students to perform their pieces can act as a key impetus for creating performance works in the first place since the audience, space, and nature of the event can deeply inform the shape a given performance work takes. This also makes for a good end-of-semester activity to showcase student work to a broader public.

CHAPTER 9
DIGITAL WRITING

I. Introduction to Digital Writing Cultures

It took millennia for the written word to migrate from clay to papyrus, papyrus to palm leaves, palm leaves to vellum, vellum to scrolls, scrolls to codices, codices to a mechanized press; and only centuries for words to be typeset, then typewritten, now word-processed through the manipulation of electrons. While an approximate 2,078 generations experienced writing as an analog or mechanical act, we are only entering our sixth generation of writing electronically via personal computing. As critic Sven Birkerts (2016) observes, "Change itself is changing."

In the 1990s, globalization led to affordable microprocessors, which led to universal ownership of information technology, which led to the democratization of information—often referred to as the Information Age. And people aren't the only ones with access to the internet; the internet also has access to itself. In 1991, Mark Weiser anticipated "ubiquitous computing"; by 2008, the Internet of Things, or IoT, was born. IoT refers to the growing network of physical objects that are connected to the internet and can collect, exchange, and monitor data remotely. By now, there are more things connected to the internet than there are people, including thermostat sensors, home security actuators, and the Bluetooth wavelengths connecting smartphones, wearable devices, refrigerators, and automobiles. These technologies whisper to one another while we're eating, sleeping, and working.

All the while, search engine data structures like Google and open-source editing tools like wikis organize information, and therefore, our society. Modular data storage allowed for massive vlogging sites like YouTube while database innovation enabled microblogging platforms like Twitter. According to Newberry (2023: n.p.), "The Facebook algorithm evaluates every post [by scoring and arranging them] in descending, non-chronological order of interest for each individual user. This process happens every time a user—and there are 2.9 billion of them—refreshes their feed." This form of information technology gave way to a digital network of friends who confirm your every bias, a corrupting premise of the Post-Information Age. Despite some of the pitfalls of this paradigm shift, the generative possibilities of the emerging digital ecosystem are seemingly endless.

In just the past two decades, there has been a digital explosion in publishing technologies that has radically reshaped the literary arts. While many will be familiar with the straightforward applications of e-texts and audiobooks as commercial publishing tools, there is a digital underground of experimental writers whose embrace of information technology has led them to lean into this acceleration, using new media, game engines, Adobe Flash, InDesign, GarageBand, iMovie, Java Script, HTML, software for app/website development, graphic design, hypertext, computer-generated texts, virtual/augmented/mixed reality, video games, blogs, podcasts, data scrapes, and even non-fungible token (NFTs) for their composition, design, and distribution needs. Clearly, the digital frontiers of creative writing are highly dependent on electronic infrastructures and require a secondary expertise or, at the very least, a stable of collaborators. Interestingly, there is a subset of digital authors who come from a computer science background, not a literary one. As you read this chapter, consider: What are *your* digital literacies? And how can you employ those literacies to ideate, draft, or distribute your story?

While some are skeptical of the role such technologies will play in literature long-term, communication theorist Marshall McLuhan (1964: 199) reminds us that "the student of media soon comes to expect the new media of any period to be classed as pseudo by those who have acquired the patterns of earlier media, whatever they may happen to be." However, it is obvious that today's technological proving grounds are inevitably hosting characteristics that will be ubiquitous in the future.

Learning new media can be expensive and time-consuming. New media developments are iterative: see upgrades (Tweets' character counts expanding from 140 to 280), copycats (TikTok usurping Vine), redundancies (the reposting of TikToks to Instagram), and automation (CAD to AutoCAD). As for web development, media techie Simon Pitt (2019: n.p.) notes that "the unit of creation has moved from the file to … [that of] database entry." Pitt describes the difference between program development "then" versus now like this:

> The other day, I came across a website I'd written over two decades ago. I double-clicked the file, and it opened and ran perfectly. Then I tried to run a website I'd written 18 months ago and found I couldn't run it without firing up a web server, and when I ran NPM install, one or two of those 65,000 files had issues that meant node failed to install them and the website didn't run. When I did get it working, it needed a database. And then it relied on some third-party APIs and there was an issue with CORS because I hadn't whitelisted localhost. (2019)

While these details may go over the head of laypeople (like the authors of this book), it's clear to see how incremental shifts in digital infrastructure frustrate the process of creation. For a reader, on the other hand, the experience is largely the same across space and time. Hand somebody a clay tablet, birchbark manuscript, vellum codex, perfect-bound book, and e-reader all in their native language, and they'll intuit how to read it in no time. But for the writer of each of these texts, different instruments and techniques are required. Just consider the clumsy process of learning to type on a QWERTY keyboard; or the trial-and-error of T9 predictive texting on a 1990s-era smartphone; or what it takes to be among the thumb generation on today's swiftkey keyboards. Writing digitally requires one to accept that today's writing processes will soon be outmoded and anachronistic. Some predict the next major paradigm shift will be the transition from skeuomorphic design to flat design. In the former, "doc" files on our computer "desktops" resemble and represent actual documents on a physical desktop. This is preferred by digital immigrants who grew up before the internet. Alternatively, flat design— which emphasizes the two-dimensional, minimalist, and colorful—appeals to digital natives who have little experience with print media (e.g., physical calendars, documents, rolodexes, etc.). Regardless of what comes next, old and new technologies will always coexist, muddling what *has been* with what *will be*.

McLuhan claimed that, when it comes to technology, "the medium is the message" (1964: 7). If this is the case, then why does so much online writing seemingly get drafted on a sterile word processor? It is obvious to us that literary culture has only begun to reckon with its prospects in the digital age. In many cases, the polite encounters between staid genres and new technological frontiers have been superficial, mostly an opportunity for marketing and distribution. To be fair, writers in search of an audience are probably wise to transmit their work on social media where the World Economic Forum claims the average person spends 2.5 hours of their day. (By comparison, the average American reads for pleasure around sixteen minutes a day, according to the American Time Use Survey.)

Then again, a case can be made that all writing is digital. After all, behind every word processor is a search engine. Most writers today click back and forth between windows in a frenzied compositional process. The epistemological linkages between what gets searched and what gets written are manifold. In other words, links are not just how we consume information, but also how we produce it—how we research, collaborate, consume, disseminate, and dialogue about literature. McLuhan called it surfing: "the rapid, irregular, and multidirectional movement through a heterogeneous body of documents or knowledge" (1962: 248). One can find in their own browser history—in the assemblage of electronic destinations—their digital DNA, the basis for their digital persona. The poet Eileen Myles said, "I used to choose my friends based on the shit they had on their bookshelves. Now, I'm much more interested in what's on their browsers."

We might as well call it the digital dérive, what DeBord defined as "a technique of rapid passage through varied ambiances." Like the dérive, the internet is action-based, a choose-your-own adventure requiring semiconscious participation. Kenneth Goldsmith's (2016b: n.p.) provocative University of Pennsylvania class, Wasting Time on the Internet, gives credence to these everyday inquiries by giving students the opportunity to cultivate their web-surfer personae. He writes:

> And while … critics tell us time and again that our brains are being rewired, I'm not so sure that's all bad. Every new media requires new ways of thinking. How strange it would be if in the midst of this digital revolution we were still expected to use our brains in the same way we read books or watched TV? The resistance to the Internet shouldn't surprise us: cultural reactionaries defending the status quo have been around as long as media has. Marshall McLuhan tells us that television was written off by people invested in literature as merely "mass entertainment" just as the printed book was met with the same skepticism in the sixteenth century by scholastic philosophers.

In this regard, art—whether Late Renaissance sculpture or pixel art—is always produced by cyborgs, individuals negotiating old and new technologies. In *Art and Postcapitalism*, Dave Beech emphasizes that the human condition is defined by its interest in transforming the human condition. Therefore, we're always cyborgs deciding between technologies both staid and state-of-the-art. He writes: "The avant-garde of the early twentieth century proposed that the production of art might be set free from its ancient exclusivity by the adoption of mechanical techniques. In this respect, I want to suggest, the artist is canceled as a category by being remodeled as a robot." Artists become one with their chosen instrument, merging their human capacities with the technologies they habitually use.

One can try to opt out of digital literary production altogether. Take novelist Jonathan Franzen's (Grossman 2010) advice on how to write "serious fiction" as he describes his process for disabling his laptop's Ethernet port: "What you have to do is you plug in an Ethernet cable with superglue, and then you saw off the little head of it." But we are as skeptical of Franzen's reduction of the computer to an expensive word processor as we are of his term "serious fiction." Besides, try as we might, even when we manage to meet IRL, do we not inevitably return to our digital commons as we swap hilarious memes, apprise one another of our digital wanderings, and get updates about the latest Twitter flame war? We are cyborgs when we least suspect it, ever "plugged in" as we transplant media from the digital world into the environs of our real world.

Even as Goldsmith makes the case that internet browsing is far from a mindless activity, there is a different form of mindlessness at play, that of the filter bubble effect. If one gets caught in the filter bubble of Google's search engine, deceived by the trappings of instant access (a search for an obscure town yields 7.1 million results in 0.72 seconds), they might forget how biased, how polluted their algorithm has become—influenced by click and search history, encrusted with past search decisions they've made, a positive feedback loop of "intellectual isolation," to borrow a phrase from internet activist Eli Pariser. Our prejudice is likely to override even the most precise search syntax. We live inside this filter bubble. The internet shows us what it "thinks" we want to see through the "invisible algorithmic editing of the web" (Pariser 2011: n.p.). So too does our writing, inflected by such searching, migrating to the interior of that bubble.

Epistemologically speaking, who needs 7.1 million results in 0.72 seconds? A quarter of those searching click the first result anyway. The search engine is a supposedly democratic invention, a place where the author-as-surfer can gain access to others' knowledge. But consider for a moment that *not* having the answers might actually be more generative. After all, experimental writing has a long tradition of trafficking in unknown unknowns. If you use a search engine that brags about the magnitude of its results rather than the quality, ask yourself, *What do speed, efficiency, and automation have to do with my writing process?* In other words, "answers at our fingertips" may be more a symptom, and not a virtue, of the age we live in. In *The Shallows: What the Internet Is Doing to Our Brain*, Nicholas Carr discusses how hyperlinks have taken their neurobiological toll on us to the point that we can no longer recognize the essential from the trivial; thus, informational relevance becomes obscured. The status of "information" itself is changing, as we often browse the web or scroll our phones less for a specific factoid and more in a feedback loop that keeps us connected to our screens.

Throughout this chapter, we will explore electronic literature that is defined by digital processes, platforms, and technologies. Some of the concepts we'll explore will represent mere permutations of older writing practices while others are seemingly novel approaches to literary cultural production.

II. Websites and Internet Culture

One group of writers who emerged alongside the new internet infrastructure was known as Alt-Lit. Members of Alt-Lit manufactured their own celebrity through sincere and confessional writing, drug-fueled publicity stunts, and the infusion of literature with digital media. By way of example, Megan Boyle's "Everyone I've Had Sex With" chronicles her 23 sexual encounters followed by statistics (age at the first time: 18 years, 4 months, 2 weeks, 0 days; one-night stands: 11; STDs: 0; pregnancies: 0; places she's had sex: all rooms a house can have, etc.).

Unlike an author whose writing must first be acquired, edited, printed, distributed, and sold before it reaches its audience, an essay like Boyle's can find its audience the same day it is written with the click of a "publish" button. To anyone accustomed to a content feed, this may sound blasé. But at the time, this speed of distribution was quasi-revolutionary. The emergence of comment sections and tabloid-style blogs (e.g., *Alt Lit Gossip*) only added to the spectacle.

Alt-Lit was the first generation to leverage the spontaneity of the internet as part of its creative process. In his analysis of the movement, Goldsmith (2014: n.p.) notes how Alt-Lit is "usually written in the Internet vernacular of lowercase letters, inverted punctuation, abundant typos, and bad grammar." Indeed, even the title of Steve Roggenbuck's collection has enough errors to make a copyeditor faint: *IF U DONT LOVE THE MOON YOUR AN ASS HOLE*. Many Alt-Lit writers reveled in the mundane; when it's free to post, one doesn't have to compress or arc their lived days into a grand structure. Boyle, for example, liveblogged her life for six months. Midway through the 700-page book (which *was* eventually printed), where an editor might anticipate a bolt of tension or rising action, she shares, rather boringly: "9:30AM: woke. peed and refilled water glass." In other corners, Alt-Lit eschewed the mundane for spectacle. As an example, Jordan Castro live streamed a video where he attempted to pull off his penis (for some inexplicable reason). Before you can break the internet, first you have to build it. Meanwhile, Alt-Lit creators like Gabby Bess and Molly Soda have published selfies, image macros, vlogs, and GIFs, heralding the conflation of post-literary artifacts with literary cultural production. Ultimately, Alt-Lit anticipated, and even helped construct, the all-eyes-on-me environment of the internet, infusing literature with equal parts insouciance and performance. While Alt-Lit is one of the first places literary culture first blended with internet culture, one can still see its echoes in the confessionalism of today's internet poetry, the emotional shorthand of memes, and the anti-art ethos that pervades digital spaces.

In a more neoliberal context, authors have emerged as their own brands and products. Many writers—okay, almost all of them—feel professionally obliged to build personal websites. See, for example, the tongue-in-cheek site, "Brian Oliu Internet Presence." For those interested in creating their own website, the most popular builders utilize a WYSIWYG ("What You See Is What You Get") editor, which obviates the need to learn a coding language. Early examples of this include AOL Hometown and GeoCities. HTML, once a prerequisite for building a website, was supplemented by intuitive tools that allowed anybody to create their own homepages where they could write, well … whatever they could fit in 12 MBs: personal journals, movie reviews, product advertisements, conspiracy theories, poetry, fiction, and so on. Today's WYSIWYG website builders include Wix, Weebly, Squarespace, and WordPress where templates and drag-and-drop features make for user-friendly web development.

It seems most writers have ventured into digital spaces to self-promote or schmooze. Only a fraction of writers have utilized webpages as a natural complement to the physical page. And yet, the creative supplementarity of the internet—if not "extra-ness"—is evidenced by its range of plugins, widgets, languages, and patches; in short, the internet is host to a range of unique compositional and publishing opportunities. It is a site of literary improvisation—a place to play, produce, and present texts whose functions are uniquely digital. The webpage is a canvas without an edge; for Ander Monson (n.d.), scrolling feels like "an elevator shaft descending into nothingness." Monson is a builder of web ventures like *DIAGRAM* (online journal), *Essay Daily* (blog), March Xness (essay tourney with music criticism), and The Assessment Matters Institute (parody site wallpapered with death-metal-meets-higher-ed memes). One of his longest standing sites, though, is otherelectrcities.com, a labyrinthine personal website that features "the swarm," an assemblage of uncollected essays, poems, reviews, fragments, and meditations, many of them hyperlinked in a network of intersecting nodes. In one such work in the swarm, "Essay as Hack," Monson (n.d.) conflates the technologies of the essay and the internet to potentiate new forms: "A hack is an ingenious use of technology to accomplish something that is otherwise impossible to accomplish ... It appears, like any sufficiently advanced technology, as a kind of magic. It comes out of the insoluble. It is surprising. Pleasing. Amazing." Beyond the access afforded by the hyperlink, other writers have experimented with coding, flash, and design to present entire collections of their work online.

Paisley Rekdal's (2022) *West: A Translation* is a docu-poetic poetry collection about Chinese labor used to construct the Transcontinental Railroad and the ensuing racist policy known as the Chinese Exclusion Act. The project, presented as a multimedia website, begins with a representation of an elegy, "Another Angel Island," that is carved into the wall of Angel Island Immigration Station in California by one Chinese prisoner for his friend who committed suicide. Hover over any of the forty-five Chinese characters in the poem, and you'll experience an immediate and literal translation. Click on a character, and the link will deliver you to another poem—either text or video—that responds to that Chinese character. In this way, the elegy is a table of contents, its hyperlinks serving as the poetic scaffolding for this linked collection.

In *So You Know It's Me*, Oliu (2011) approximates the minimalist verisimilitude of Craigslist's popular personal ads section, Missed Connections. Each missed connection uses the hallmarks of the site: white background with blue hyperlinks, all in a Times New Roman typeface; fabricated posting IDs/dates with false "reply to post" buttons; and simple navigational pathways that connect one post to the next. Originally published on the actual Tuscaloosa Missed Connections board, the essays (masquerading as posts) expired, per policy, after forty-five days. Therefore, *So You Know It's Me* is a reconstructed work of poetic posterity.

In recent years, many literary journals have moved online; this prospect, once met with concerned groans, has now become cause for excitement. Not only is the cost lower and accessibility higher, but the webpage offers opportunities for innovation. Online publishing permits literary journals to experiment with new formats and styles of writing as the medium allows for greater flexibility. This can help to keep literary journals fresh and relevant to readers. The oldest online journals like *Brevity*, *DIAGRAM*, and *Terrain.org* paved the way for newer ventures. Monson describes sending out contracts to early contributors to his digital magazine on durable cotton paper to reify the publication and signal its legitimacy. Today, journals dabble in any number of digital publishing practices from the flash coding on *BOAAT*, video essays on *TriQuarterly*, audio files on *Missouri Review*, and striking web design of *Territory* (the mapisnot.com). As an added bonus, online journals are seen as a sustainable alternative to carbon-intensive print publication. Despite the explosion of literary dotcoms, though, it's just as likely that one will encounter proxies of digital literary culture on social media.

III. New Media

In 1932, the dramatist Bertolt Brecht lamented that the radio, then a new technology, was "one-sided when it should be two. It is purely an apparatus for distribution, for mere sharing out. So here is a positive suggestion: change this apparatus over from distribution to communication." The distinction between distributive and communicative technology remains an important one as writers determine if and how to engage online. New media platforms, with their compositional rules and social functions—think word limits, hashtags, community guidelines, and mentions—tend to have more control over a message than, say, a notebook or word processor where anything goes. Whereas content once overpowered the character of the medium, online it seems the strictures of the medium supersedes its content.

Encountering literary content on social media can either have a distributive or communicative effect. In the case of the former, it's common to encounter individuals posting blurry photos of their latest journal publication with a humblebrag caption: "I'm honored to be in such great company." Similarly, journals or publishers may tease new issues by posting a sentence or two of prose or a few lines of poetry, drumming up enough interest to entice readers to click a link to the website and subscribe. Scrolling through our own feeds, it's clear an author is more likely to use social media to reveal their latest book cover or blush about a blurb they secured, as a Post-conceptual tactic, than they are to speak to the actual content of the book. But this distributive function of social media hews closer to advertising than it does art.

There's another group of writers, however, who have worked within the parameters of their chosen platform to generate new work. For example, Mattias Viegener (2012) participated in a Facebook chain-letter trend to create a list of twenty-five random things about himself. Unlike other participants, though, he opted to repeat the activity one hundred days in a row. The regimen resulted in the first book written entirely on Facebook. Later published by Les Figues, *2500 Random Things About Me Too* is a spare, but sprawling anti-memoir, its randomness unwittingly co-opted by blips of plot-like patternation. Reading the book is not unlike the experience of scrolling through one's Facebook feed and finding incidental resonances, an emerging collective unconscious. Ironically, Viegener's (2012) inability to be random is but one of the emerging themes of the book. "There's always something behind nothing. Resistance, or flows," he writes.

The digital town square of Twitter has inspired its own genres, also known as Twitterature; these include the 140-character story, live tweets, shitposts, and hot takes. But there is no form more prominent on Twitter than the aphorism. Like most microblogging platforms, Twitter's basic unit of composition is the sentence and sometimes the fragment. For writers, it's a chance to reinvest in the pleasure of syntax. Some writers, more than others, routinely strike a chord through their standout sentences. Whether it's Joyce Carol Oates, Stephen King, Elisa Gabbert, Hanif Abdurraqib, Matt Bell, Amber Sparks, Brandon Shimoda, or Grammar Girl, the platform is saturated with tight sentences that run the gamut from self-effacing to self-absorbed, diplomatic to incendiary, confessional to voyeuristic, profound to bathetic. For a glimpse of some of the best aphoristic tweets on the platform, look no further than *Creative Nonfiction* (@cnfonline) whose #tinytruths hashtag has elicited hundreds of micro-essayistic responses.

Elsewhere on Twitter, there have been distributive and collaborative ventures. The *New Yorker*'s publication of Jennifer Egan's 8,500-word sci-fi short story, "Black Box," for instance, was serialized as Tweets; some readers noted Twitter was a medium conducive to the story's narration style (fragmentary dispatches) while others found it clunky and spam-like. For his story "Hafiz," Teju Cole wrote a single sentence and then solicited his followers to pick up where it left off. Then, as editor, Cole culled from the submissions and retweeted successive sentences in an authorized version of the story. This crowdsourced process resembled an exquisite corpse for would-be collaborators and a decision tree for Cole.

Scroll through Twitter, and you'll find comedians live-tweeting the *Bachelor* or *Super Bowl Halftime* shows, transforming a genre once reserved for studied criticism into a series of punny gut reactions. Twitter also has a population of quirky bots programmed to generate or crowdsource writing connected to specific prosodic or formal rules. For instance, there's Ranjit Bhatnagar's Pentametron, a bot that, over the course of seven years, retweeted 27,000 couplets that it discovered among users' organic Twitter posts. There's also parody accounts, which are often recognizable by the use of humor, satire, or exaggerated language in their tweets, and by the fact that they are not directly affiliated with the person or entity they are imitating. For example, there's Guy in Your MFA, which channels the man-splainy condescension historically endemic to MFA programs, or Associate Deans (@ass_deans), which pokes fun at the culture of middle management and bureaucracy in university life.

For those who suggest contemporary poetry suffers from a lack of accessibility, Instapoets have responded—both through their distribution and poetic register. Instapoems are usually short, injected with sentiment, festooned with illustrations, flanked by sun-dappled photography, and emplaced in a square meme-like frame. They receive, per the namesake of the platform, an instant readership. The poems get signal-boosted through reposts. Comments swell. Book deals, partially predicated on followership, ensue. Rupi Kaur, whose work goes virtually ignored in the greater literary community, has sold over ten million copies of her work. (Most poets would do a backflip if they sold a thousand.) Other platforms like Issuu, Wattpad, Discord, and Reddit are predicated on similar notions of distribution and community. Likewise, social media channels like Button Poetry have sacralized sentiment through their dissemination of slam and performance poetry. From any distance, viewers can signal hype, sympathy, or catharsis in the comments.

But Instagram has proved a dynamic medium for a range of writers—from Conceptual to performance artists, graphic memoirists to photo essayists, meme artists to political cartoonists, fiber artists to stop-motion animators, and beyond. Probably the purest literary application of Instagram is that of a photo essay. *Virginia Quarterly Review's* True Stories, for example, is a straightforward remediation of essays that appear in their print journal. If a photo is worth a thousand words, then your average 3–5k essay may also be conveyed in three to five photographs. Essays are excerpted and portioned across multiple posts; the prose captions photographs, which bring new life (and intrigue) to the central scenes and concepts in the essay.

In an environment in which over the past two decades newspaper subscriptions have over halved, artists and journalists have migrated online. For instance, there has been a widespread reduction in the inclusion of political cartoons and editorials in major newspapers. In response, political cartoonists and illustrators like Jesse Duqette and John Cuneo have posted their work to Instagram, a new hub for political expression.

Some writers use Instagram as the preferred distribution platform for long-form projects that diverge aesthetically from the poetry they write for the page. Poems for Brands, for instance, is a campy performance art poem about brands that takes the form of nonfiction video photography. In it, John Colasacco provides unhinged endorsements for fictional brands from a dingy loft all while incorporating elements of set design, animation, collage, modern dance, and even tattoo art. Effectively doing the work of an influencer, Colasacco's posts are jarring disruptions to the flow of branded content that arises on one's Instagram feed. A similar project is True Wagner, a public art project featuring outlandish *détournement*, including wanted posters with fictional characters/scenarios, nonsensical product placement, and links to gag websites. Artists like these use the sprawling infrastructure of Instagram and the formulas of the internet to craft a diffuse spectacle.

Another project, the Tiny Pricks Project, is an Instagram gallery of public art-as-activism. In 2018, textile artist Diana Weymar converted then president Donald Trump's words—"I am a very stable genius"—into a piece of textile art. She stitched the words, photographed them, and then posted them to Instagram. By 2020, there were 2,020 stitched quotations from the fortieth-fifth president, many of which were sent in by others through an open call. This textile database, what Weymar (2019) calls a "material record of his presidency," features some of the president's most iconic, vexing, and inane quotes—pulled from Twitter, press conferences, and offhanded side comments. It highlights a couple key discrepancies between new media and the fabric arts. For one, Tweets can be deleted, forgotten, or dislocated with a quick scroll; textiles, however, are forever. There is something uncanny about seeing cross-stitching on Instagram; it forces one to linger because the "handmade reads differently" than pixels on a screen.

Video blogging platforms like YouTube, Vimeo, and TikTok are popular sites for video essays, book trailers, sketch writing, confessional humor, and other media. Some book trailers transcend the promotional impulse and instead resemble tone poems with excerpted work. The trailer for Carolyn Hembree's *Rigging a Chevy to a Time Machine and Other Ways to Escape a Plague*, for instance, features gothic imagery, a gravelly timbre, and disorienting camerawork to accentuate the feeling of Hembree's poetry. Meanwhile, the online journal, *TriQuarterly*, has become the preeminent place for writers to submit video essays and cinepoetry.

Content creators like Steven Markos grab viewers' attention by striking insouciant poses, melding the visual rhetoric of the fashion influencer with the post-ironic humor of Adult Swim; imagine overconfident selfie swagger paired with deer-in-the-headlights voiceover. On TikTok, the creator Kevin James Thornton recounts details of his experience as a closeted homosexual in a fundamentalist Christian church. Through his avuncular style, he conjures a hyper-specific milieu, sing-talking in autotune while sprinkling in catchphrases like "because it was the nineties." Thornton and others participate in spinoffs, stage crossovers, sling merch, and add their own unique take on formulaic trends, thus inspiring an endless stream of content. Writers also host "lives" to interact directly with audiences and strangers alike. For writers, internet trends function like a writing prompt. Each writer has a chance to add their signature to the trend. The variety of responses to the prompts often instantiates groupthink. Over time, writers may engage a trend to evolve or erode it in a creative bait-and-switch. One recent popular trend that has made confessional memoirists of the most anodyne influencers is the "one thing about me" trend on TikTok, which challenges users to share one interesting fact about themselves in a short video. The challenge often involves users revealing a personal anecdote or trait that their followers may not know about them, such as a hidden talent, unusual habit, or tragicomic story. Where the New York School poets inserted intimate personal references in creating their literature, the self-revealing form of influencer videos has given rise to a type of literary creation; art forms can be infused with pop culture, but pop culture may spawn art, as well.

Though most social media platforms are driven by visual imagery, podcasts are a medium where audio is supreme. Podcasts are typically episodic in nature, meaning that they are part of a series that is released on a regular basis and can be focused on a particular topic or theme. To produce a podcast, writers must create outlines and write scripts including dialogue, interviews, music, sound effects, voiceovers, field recordings, and other aural elements to tell a sound-based story. Before podcast libraries were a thing, Charles Bernstein and Kenneth Goldsmith curated PennSound in 2003; this collection of over 8,000 files is likely the largest digital archive of poets reading their work. Goldsmith also edits UbuWeb, a repository of film and video, sound, dance, visual poetry, Conceptual comics, and Conceptual writing, among other oddities, the likes of which have rarely (or could never) be rendered on a page. A combination of production and preservation, PennSound and UbuWeb feature writers like Rae Armantrout, Robert Creeley, Yoko Ono, and Richard Foreman.

Well beyond the simulated social environs developed in Silicon Valley (the veritable capital city of the internet), there is a far-flung place lovingly known as the Weird Internet. This refers to outlying IP addresses that traffic in strange memes, bizarre videos, obscure forums, unconventional lore, and eccentric websites. While many of the artifacts from the Weird Internet eventually make their way to the rest of us—abbreviated or secondhand—there are a select few who actually get to set that material into motion. Through the manufacture of spectacle, it is important to remember, in the words of critic Pauline Kael, "All art is entertainment but not all entertainment is art." In "Cult of Distraction," film theorist Sigfried Kracauer (1987: 92) observes that Berlin's 1920s movie palace shows were "aimed at the masses." How does this compare with, say, YouTube? Today's content creators can shoot their own be-tinseled worlds, rotating their cameras for selfies and confessionals. In other words, now we are the ones doing both the aiming and the acting. Kracauer argues that the movie palaces of old "rivet the audience's attention to the peripheral so that they will not sink into the abyss. The stimulations of the senses succeed each other with such rapidity that there is no room left for even the slightest contemplation" (94). This, he claims, is how we "raise distraction to the level of culture." Kracauer may as well be talking about today's Weird Internet sites as much as the movie palaces of yore.

Take, for example, the Internet Cat Video Festival at the Walker Art Center in Minneapolis, a physical festival of Weird Internet as culture. Mark Greif notes that the products of the Weird Internet are "fundamentally amateur." They appear on YouTube, a platform that Jill Steinhauer (2015: 14) says is "a system lacking a meaningful shape." And yet Sasha Archibald (2015: 113) points out that "certain gatekeepers of high culture have no qualms contributing to the schmaltzy genre of cat books and cat arts." In part, this is because of the deification and subsequent commodification of Weird Internet mascots like Henri Le Chat Noir and Grumpy Cat by Weird Internet fanatics. The spectacle extends far beyond cat videos to include political conspiracies, paranormal found footage, hacker subcultures, flagrant scams, coercive chain mail, creepy pasta, nostalgic memes, culture cringe, kawaī aesthetic, alternative lifestyles, moral panic, and nonsensical challenges. The Weird Internet is a spectacular mirage where Nigerian princes swallow Tide pods, Slender Man is a political operative, and Hello Kitty hacks the Church of Scientology. Or maybe, as you confer with friends about these strange phenomena, you'll realize it's all the Mandela Effect. In short, so long as you're logged in, the Weird Internet is made for you. It recruits you to maintain its relevance by asking you to share, comment, and revise. But the moment you log out, the Weird Internet becomes illegible, its cabinet of curiosities a mirage concocted from your own perverse desires and boredom.

As memes and other forms of online humor have proliferated, their creators have pushed the envelope, reimagining the moral, logical, and aesthetic boundaries of society. Memelords, versed in the various conventions, tropes, and trends of the meme world, have developed a new visual syntax, innovative semiotic structures, and affective ways of captioning an array of images that are a part of the cultural present. These include meme creators like Gangster Popeye, JP Kening Garcia, and Ancient Cringe; GIF pixel animators like Uno Moralez, Paul Robertson, and Toyoya Li; 2D/3D animation artists like Rasalo, Eran Hill, and Adam Pizurny; illustrators like KCLogg, INSA, and Dain Fagerholm; and stop-motion videographers like Micaël Reynaud, A.L. Crego, and Elle Muliarchyk. In the live-streamed Adult Swim show, Bottom Text, commentators decode the humor and polemics of popular GIFs. Memes become ubiquitous by collapsing complex events into bite-sized, viral nuggets, keeping current through their adaptability into new contexts. It's no wonder memes have leapt from the screen to become the subject of scholarly study while also being featured in museum galleries.

Artists working in this medium are said to embody an "internet state of mind" where work is "consciously created in a milieu that assumes the centrality of the network" (Archey and Peckham 2014). For an avant-garde spin on this, see Hennessy Youngman's ArtThoughtz Series, including "How to Be a Successful Black Artist," an irreverent monologue lampooning stereotypes perpetuated by the internet. Ryan Trecartin's multi-movie project *Any Ever* includes *Re'Search Wait'S*, which explores "the totalizing effects of technology and social media on subject formation in the twenty-first century" (2019: n.p.). In the film, young amateur actors are distorted through pitch change, uncanny filters, and high-angle shots idiomatic of platforms like Snapchat as a way of commenting on the grotesque naturalization of selfie culture. Meanwhile, the Norwegian artist Cory Arcangel's body of work is geared toward breaking the internet. His works include:

Totally Fucked (2003), a hacked Mario Bros game cartridge where Mario is stuck on a cube forever; *Permanent Vacation* (2008), where two computers are locked in an out of office email loop; *Drei Klavierstücke op.11* (2009), in which Arnold Schoenberg's homonymous 1909 score is plated by editing together YouTube clips of cats playing pianos; *Working on my Novel* (2009), a compendium of Twitter search results for "working on my novel"; *Various Self Playing Bowling Games* (2011), video games modified to throw gutter balls; *Flatware* (2018-), a series of abstract "paintings" mounted on Ikea tabletops sourced from a diverse range of leisurewear and, /roʊˈdeɪoʊ/ *Let's Play: HOLLYWOOD* (2017–2021), a custom built high performance machine learning computer which plays, as it learns, Kim Kardashian: Hollywood, a free-to-play role-playing Android game. (Lisson Gallery 2020)

Yet another group of internet artists who instantiated the possibilities of a disorienting internet is the collective net.art. Their websites used glitch art and protocols that disrupted the fundamental principles of user experience. Their varied techniques included databending, datamoshing, misalignment, circuit bending, misregistration, and distortion, all of which intentionally incorporated failure into the creative process.

Some writers have challenged us to think about what constitutes a "social" media. Even our private interactions on a site like www.gmail.com can be mined for new writing. In 2006,

Experimental Writing

BlazeVOX published Noah Eli Gordon's *Inbox*, a Conceptual art book that turns private data inside out: mundane emails between friends and acquaintances are curated—some would say "upcycled"—for the distinctly literary purpose of assembling a book. Not only does this transpose the private, epistolary function of an email to a public work, it also dramatically expands the audience of in-jokes and gossip. Another common inversion of private and public is the "hive mind" on Twitter, which refers to writers' communitarian impulse to appeal to the collective intelligence, knowledge, and opinions of the literary community. Instead of asking Google or a trusted colleague what you should name the eighteenth-century Ashkenazi Jewish character in your novel, you can instead call upon five to five thousand of your closest friends to focus-group your fiction. This form of crowdsourcing is especially helpful when a writer is on a deadline, in a professional conundrum, attempting to develop or share resources, is networking or community-building, or is simply trying to discern the next move for their project. At its best, the hive mind acts like a specialized search engine; at its worst, the query might be met with crickets.

Perhaps you use a platform not mentioned here: Snapchat, Pinterest, WhatsApp, WeChat, Mastodon, LinkedIn, Dogster/Catster, Divorce 360, Ncludr, or REMCloud where you swap dreams with other users. Perhaps you're using a platform that wasn't even invented when this book was published. What does digital writing on social media look like from the vantage of your device? What digital trends, forms, and habits dominate the digital landscape right now? How do you imagine yourself participating in, subverting, or evolving those trends?

IV. Proto-Digital Coding, Kinetic Poetry, Factorial Literature, and Techno-Ergodic Metafictions

For every poem that's ever appeared on a computer screen, there's a tacit collaboration happening behind the scenes. One readily perceives the poet's language on the pixelated surface of the webpage; meanwhile, in the background, the programmer's language instructs the computer's processor on how to transmit that poem. Early computer users memorized and swapped lines of code like schoolchildren forced to learn lines of poetry. Programming was, by and large, a pastime for computer scientists, software engineers, mathematicians, and hackers. But for the most part, the technical gap for basic coding is being closed by elementary STEM education. Nowadays, it is more common for children to study coding in elementary school than poetry. Recognizing such trends, today's Creative Writing programs have gradually begun to integrate elective coursework in coding and digital interfaces. Brown University, Ohio University, and Trinity College are three prominent examples.

Since the era of personal computing, spurred along by manufacture of the Apple II, Commodore 64, and Sinclair ZX Spectrum, there have been plenty of poet-programmers who have taken on dual roles as they develop their poetic *and* coding syntax. Some writers, though, were there from the very beginning. Long before he won the Nobel Prize, the South African writer J. M. Coetzee was writing computer poetry. Rebecca Roach (2017: n.p.) writes of Coetzee's day job in the mid-1960s:

> During the day, he helped to design the Atlas 2 supercomputer destined for the United Kingdom's Atomic Energy Research Establishment at Aldermaston. At night he used

this hugely powerful machine of the Cold War to write simple "computer poetry," that is, he wrote programs for a computer that used an algorithm to select words from a set vocabulary and create repetitive lines.

See a sample of Coetzee's early computer poetry on pp. 219–20.

Nowadays, writers have incorporated coding language into the aesthetic of their otherwise text-based books. Brian Oliu's (2015) *i/o* is a memoir that is part epic poem and part MS-DOS prompt. Written in the form of a computer virus, *i/o* examines the author's personal journey and struggles through the lens of Odysseus' journey in *The Odyssey*.

Lillian-Yvonne Bertram's (2019) *Travesty Generator* uses open-source coding to formulate their poems—which present glitches, mechanization, and automated boxes—showing how systems that are predominantly white (whether social, economic, or technological) too-frequently distort and misrepresent Black experience. Read the sample codework, *#/usr/bin/python/three_last_words*, on pp. 204–10.

The development of structured programming in the 1950s made it easier to direct the flow of a computer program through a regimen of sequencing, selection, and iteration. The development of code blocks and nested functions (i.e., rules within rules)—not to mention the proliferation of operators, reserved words, and restricted identifiers—heralded the arrival of a precise, complex, and attractive system with endless coding outputs. For example, code can set the parameters for how text is displayed. It can launch the playing, looping, or succession of audio and video files. Code can trigger a lightbox for discounts, prompt you to sign in or sign up, enforce a paywall, or request your consent to enable cookies. It can also perform complex computations, represent data aesthetically, and anticipate (and therefore automate) your every computing desire. Many credit the programming languages ALGOL 58 and ALGOL 60, and its immediate successors (CPL, Simula, BCPL, B, Pascal, and C) for ushering in a new era in which programmers can follow clear procedures and input precise imperatives to effectuate a smooth computing experience. The most common computer languages today, though, are JavaScript, HTML/CSS, SQL, Python, and Java. To appreciate the combination of this pair of skills—poetry and coding—consider the ways coding can transform the possibilities of the visual field of poetry. What was once mimetically implied on the page (a calm, a crescendo, a berserk, an explosion) can now find itself actualized on the screen. Take the French surrealist Guillaume Apollinaire, for instance. In 1918, a half-century before the first personal computer was available to the public, Apollinaire's *Calligrammes* combined elements of typography and cinema to imply motion. These early examples of concrete/kinetic poetry—in which letters drizzle down the page like rain, radialize outward like beams of sun, or approximate the mechanics of the human form— were developed around the same time as early animation. Calligrams, with their special effects, were the textual equivalent of Georges Méliès' "trick films" and portended the public's engrossment with screens over pages. To a modern viewer, Apollinaire's letters might bear an uncanny resemblance to pixels.

By 1926, Marchel Duchamp had invented rotoreliefs, text printed on cardboard circles that then spun on turntables. Known as *Anémic Cinéma*, this early form of kinetic poetry demonstrates engineered motion, with text revolving seventy-eight rotations per minute. Such precision persists in digital poetry today where the algorithmic choreography of poetic lines are scripted down to the millisecond. A string of words can appear for set intervals and dissolve before transitioning to the next set of words. In 1986, for example, E. M. de Melo e Castro developed *Roda Lume Fogo*, a video poem that begins with two Portuguese words— *arco* (arc) and *roda* (wheel)—but through the desynchronization of its frame tempo, begins to reveal a combinatory poetics. The syllable of one word lingers and combines with the syllable of another, forming a new word (e.g., "co-" combines with "-da" to form *coda*). New syllables are introduced, multiplying the linguistic field of the poem. Finally, a narrator groans, grunts, and gargles the syllables in his mouth. His pronunciation syncopates with the visual syllables, offering up new audio+visual combinations and, therefore, new words. Others composing kinetic computer poems might instead embrace synchrony by writing a program to allow letters to spiral, undulate, or dissolve in clusters. These smooth transformations of the text have an effect like that of stop-motion animation.

The temporal aspects of cinema poetry are altogether different than the experience of reading a book since the poet-programmer presets the interval for which a particular word or poetic line appears. The reader-viewer cannot reread the text unless rewound or rewatched; in some contexts, this may not be an option. Some programmers might even program a word so that it appears for just a flicker, thereby ensuring it can only register subliminally.

By the 2000s, Adobe Flash was one software that managed to give the control back to the reader. Utilized for video games and interactive websites, Flash poems proceed at the reader's own pace. In "The Sweet Old Etcetera," for instance, Alison Clifford (2006) reimagines the poetry of e e cummings, casting it in a Flash landscape where the reader must interact with letters, words, and punctuation to uncover the totality of the piece. As the reader "operates" the text through precise clicks and scroll-overs, they extend, animate, dissolve, and consolidate the web art. They are not simply reading poetry but instigating it. Similarly, Benjamin Laird's (2022) *The Durham Poems*, programmed with JavaScript, is an electronic chapbook of fifteen poems that invites the reader to click, drag, and scramble lines of William Denton's poetry. The words float like constellations or they overlap in illegible palimpsests. Sometimes, when dragging one word, a cluster of other words joins in; when dragged, they begin to look architectural.

When the possibilities for interacting with a digital text can be codified on a decision tree, the resulting text might be what Espen Aarseth (1997) calls ergodic literature. Readers indulge their curiosity, intuition, or whims to proceed through the textual material rather than relying on customary reading patterns inferred from linear design. It's a choose-your-own adventure story, for adults. It's no surprise that much contemporary ergodic literature is digital, including coded text adventures, multimedia novels, and literary video games. Online, hypertext fiction can literally employ digital hyperlinks, sending readers into a clickable network of narratives. However, the impulses of ergodic writing are ancient. In fact, the genre's locus classicus is Fu Xi's *I Ching* (*Book of Changes*), a manual whose readers flipped coins, rolled dice, or cast yarrow stalks to obtain a set of signals that then supply a cosmological prophecy. In fact, *I Ching*'s divinatory system was the inspiration for the modern computer processing instructions known as binary code. A pioneering developer of computer literature was Ada Lovelace, Lord Byron's daughter, who designed the first programs for Charles Babbage's Analytical Engine. One of Lovelace's key insights was that the Analytical Engine, which failed to be built during her lifetime, could not only perform algebraic calculations but also "might compose elaborate and scientific pieces of music of any degree of complexity or extent" (1843: 21). Walter Issacson, in his book *The Innovators*, writes that:

> This insight would become the core concept of the digital age: any piece of content, data, or information–music, text, pictures, numbers, symbols, sounds, video—could be expressed in digital form and manipulated by machines. Even Babbage failed to see this fully; he focused on numbers. But Ada realized that the digits on the cogs could represent things other than mathematical quantities. (2014: 27)

Taking nothing away from Lovelace's invention, Ramon Llull, a late Medieval theologian and philosopher who is now recognized as an early inventor of computational theory, also designed programs (of sorts) to produce literature. His work *Ars Magna* is a system of letters, diagrams, and tables that allows the operator to find answers to questions—about love, memory, divinity, and the faculties of the soul—through an iterative process of combinatorics. Llull's *Ars Magna* is one of the earliest works of "computer" literature, its ergodic schema designed to allow users to parse the doctrinal metaphysics of Christianity.

Many contemporary ergodic texts forego text commands in favor of point-and-click actions. This can be seen in Jim Andrews' "Stir Fry Texts," Brian Lennon's "Log," and Pauline Masurel's "Blue Hyacinth." When one mouses over fragments of the base text, it twitches as it transforms anew. According to Andrews (2006b: n.p.): "Each stir fry consists of *n* distinct texts. Each of the *n* texts is partitioned into *t* pieces. When you mouseover any of the *t* parts of a text, that part is replaced with the corresponding part of the next of the *n* texts." Like William Burroughs' cutups or Raymond Queneau's manifold sonnets, Andrews's DHTML source code is a jittery contribution to the canon of factorial literature. In the essay, "Material Combinatorium Supremum," Andrews (2006a: n.p.) posits: "For the monstrous poet, there is … an upper bound to be attained in the exacerbation of poetry's suffering. A text that is capable of transforming into 10^{81} different texts suffers a mind-bending combinatorium of textuality. It pushes poetry to the edge of the material universe's fundamental mass." Here, he is theorizing a stir-fry with as many textual combinations as there are atoms in the universe.

One contemporary purveyor of hypertext fictions is Eastgate, which published *afternoon, a story* (Michael Joyce); *Victory Garden* (Stuart Moulthrop); *Figurski at Findhorn on Acid* (Richard Holeton); *A Patchwork Girl* (Shelley Jackson); and *Samplers: Nine Vicious Little Hypertexts* (Deena Larsen). Where most hypertext fiction takes the form of the novel, in the latter, Larsen writes short fiction with a visual design that alludes to traditional quilting patterns.

Steve Tomasula collaborates with directors, designers, animators, programmers, and sound engineers to present his new media novel, *Toc*. In consideration of the timespace theme running throughout the novel, Tomasula (2016: 159) writes,

> From very early on I was thinking about the narrative in terms of storyboarding, and flowcharts, and how the speed at which animations would run would work with certain moods or senses of time embodied in the story. I tried to imagine ways to evoke within

the reader different senses of time so that he or she would experience them, not just read about them.

One persistent aspiration of more ambitious cyberliterature is that the bounds of time and space—along with consciousness itself—might be reshaped through the narrative worlds made possible by some new technology.

Other types of cyberliterature merge text and game, gamifying stories and narrativizing games. Early forms of interactive fiction—also known as text-based adventure games—had a high replay value because reader-players could explore varying branches of the universe. Readers can type their text commands (YES, NO, ENTER, PICK UP) to explore one set of consequences; on their second pass, though, they can explore an alternate reality (NO, YES, EXIT, IGNORE, etc.). Ironically, a story like this will not proceed unless the reader *writes*; their commands pass through a text parser and, if recognizable, the commands will unveil new features of the environment. In *Colossal Cave Adventure*, the reader explores a fantastical cave system. In *Zork* or *Night House*, the reader creeps through a spooky house. In *Torn*, the reader-player explores a novel city in a massively multiplayer text RPG game. The city has its own casino, hospital, jail, pharmacy, church, travel agency, hair salon, school, gym, racetrack, and stock market. One can read the newspaper, start a career, go hunting, take drugs, commit assault/battery, or get married to another registered user provided they type the correct text command.

Eric LeMay's (2017) *Essays on the Essay and Other Essays* is an online collection of, you guessed it, essays that take on myriad digital forms. There's the "Montaigne Machine," which allows the reader to create their own essay by the French Renaissance philosopher: "Create an essay that combines your thoughts with the words of Michel de Montaigne and the latest images uploaded by Flickr photographers." Another piece, "100x10," is an essay about lexemes; as we learn in the essay, there are over one million words in the English language, but we only use one hundred in everyday speech. The essay goes on to reveal those hundred words, via audio file, within the essay—from least to most frequent, in random order, as arranged by LeMay, and as a cutup to be arranged by the reader. His most popular essay in the collection, though, "Lottery," asks readers to choose numbered lotto balls that are floating on the screen. The selection of these balls determines the order in which the paragraphs of the ensuing essay (about lotteries, gambling, and probability) will proceed. As one clicks through these paragraphs, one's wins and losses are tallied throughout a continuously cycling lottery. Using an algorithm that approximates the probability of winning the Ohio Lottery, the reader inevitably—that is, probabilistically—walks away a loser.

V. Computer-Generated Poetry: Machine Learning, Deep Learning, Artificial Intelligence, Cybernetics, Database/Informatic, Natural Language Processing, Algorithmic, and Neural Networks

Machine learning is a manual method of teaching computers to learn from data without being explicitly programmed. Deep learning builds on this by using algorithms to learn from data featuring multiple layers of abstraction. In other words, the machine begins to teach itself. Using machine learning, a computer program can be trained on a corpus of poetry written by humans, and then use that training to generate new poems that are similar in style and structure to the training data.

K. Silem Mohammad, for instance, feeds each of Shakespeare's 154 sonnets one line at a time into an internet anagram engine, thus generating a new list of words from each line. You can read one of these scrambled sonnets, what he calls "sonnagrams," on p. 286 "They Net the HDTV Teeth, the "Chewy Heavens" HDTV Teeth" is based on Shakespeare's Sonnet #46.

Alternatively, a program can be designed to follow specific rules and structures to generate poems without the need for training on human-generated data. The quality and coherence of the generated poems will depend on the techniques and algorithms used, as well as the quality and diversity of the training data. Some computer-generated poems may be difficult for humans to understand, while others may be surprisingly coherent and compelling.

In the film(s) project, *Seances* (2006), the reader "conjures" a film by clicking (and holding) the mouse. According to the project's profile on the National Film Board of Canada, these "never before seen films" are simultaneously "never to be seen again." That's because *Seances* is a feat of data storytelling using virtual machines and cloud-based computing supplied by technical partner Nickel Media. The reader's conjuring, then, is not paranormal, but digital. Inspired by the fact that 80 percent of films from the silent era have been lost, director Guy Maddin, along with Evan and Galen Johnson, attempt to "[reincarnate] … vanished history." Hypothetically, there are hundreds of thousands of permutations of these vintage-looking melodramas. Each begins with the ominous promise: "This [X]-minute film will disappear."

One of the most sophisticated forms of deep learning today is known as neural networking, which was inspired by the structure and function of the brain. It is composed of many simple processing nodes, which are connected together in a series of layers. Each node in the network receives input from other nodes and then uses that input to perform a computation and produce an output. The output from one layer of nodes becomes the input to the next layer, and so on, until the final output is produced. The connections between the nodes are weighted, meaning that they have a strength or importance associated with them. These weights are adjusted automatically during the learning process, so that the network can learn to produce the correct output for a given set of inputs through repeated trials. Neural networks are widely used for many applications, including image and speech recognition, health or financial analysis, and of most relevance to writers, natural language processing.

Neural networks can be used to generate text, including novels, by training the network on a large corpus of text data. The network learns the patterns and structures of the text data and then uses that knowledge to generate new text that is similar in style and content to the training data. This process is known as text generation or natural language processing. The quality and coherence of the generated text will depend on the size and quality of the training data, as well as the complexity and capabilities of the neural network. With enough training data and a powerful enough network, many believe it is possible to generate coherent and compelling novels using neural networks. However, it is important to note that the generated text will not be "original" in the traditional sense, as it will be based on the patterns and structures found in the training data. Then again, some philosophers believe that our brains operate by complex neural networks, too. It may be our own learning how to write is based on iterative exposure to previous models.

But what kind of writer uses machine learning to generate new writing? For one, there's Ross Goodwin (2016, 2015) who has written associative poetry variously trained on the Senate's 2014 torture report and Donald Trump quotes. He has also created a Twitter bot that generates definitions for invented words. Visit his Github and one can see the pragmatic nexus of conceptualism and digitalism, like a program that "generates poetry from images using convolutional and recurrent neural networks" and "maps clauses from a text corpus onto the metrical structure of a poem."

But, most famously, Goodwin is the author—er, programmer—of *1 The Road*, dubiously dubbed the next American road trip novel. Brian Merchant, writing for *The Atlantic*, describes the book like this:

> On March 25, 2017, a black Cadillac with a white-domed surveillance camera attached to its trunk departed Brooklyn for New Orleans. An old GPS unit was fastened atop the roof. Inside, a microphone dangled from the ceiling. Wires from all three devices fed into Ross Goodwin's Razer Blade laptop, itself hooked up to a humble receipt printer. This, Goodwin hoped, was the apparatus that was going to produce the next American road-trip novel … Along the way, the four sensors—the camera, the GPS, the microphone, and the computer's internal clock—would feed data into a system of neural networks Goodwin had trained on hundreds of books and Foursquare location data, and the printer would spit out the results one letter at a time. By the end of the four-day trip, receipts emblazoned with artificially intelligent prose would cover the floor of the car. They're collected in *1 the Road*. (2018)

The book has elicited mixed reactions. Merchant notes it's like if a Google Street View car were narrating a cross-country journey to itself. Therefore, it's "surveillance-technology fiction, written by the same species of technology that is conducting the surveillance and processing the data" (Merchant 2018). What is so unsettling about this point of view, it seems, is the uncanny way data, typically oriented toward serving us, can also order itself in a ploy to understand or mimic us.

Similarly, *Inside the Castle* runs an annual contest for a work of literature (it must be exactly 100,000 words) that is generated in five days or less through some combination of being written by a human, collaging and data-mining texts from the internet, or algorithmic automation by computer software. They judge the proposals of processing specifications rather than the resulting works, publishing the winning manuscript that's been composed—or recomposed, as it were. The editors claim:

> We will continue to love traditional compositions that meet our specifications. But there is no denying that humans are fascinated by the uncanny analogs of their behaviors, often more than they are by their own sad efforts … . You may argue that the pen is mightier than the algorithm, but who, in the encrypted future of your lonely grave, will hear you? (Inside the Castle n.d.: n.p.)

Their attitude hints that the implied readerships for texts in the future may be aimed as much toward human audiences as bots and AI. Perhaps some writers already anticipate the "singularity," the hypothetical point in time when computer intelligence surpasses human intelligence. Indeed, who's to say that the singularity hasn't already occurred (after all, how would we know; it's not like savvy computers would announce they've overtaken us)? Perhaps soon—or already?—bots will write for other bots with nary a human involved.

If one reads all this with skepticism, we get it. But, just for fun, note that a handful of sentences in this very section were written using the enigmatic AI chatbot ChatGPT. If you can't tell which sentences were generated by a neural network, then that should be an indication of how sophisticated such technology has become. This same AI has occasionally stumped plagiarism-sniffing professors, outperformed seasoned journalists, and rapidly encroached on the copywriting market. Only recently has it started to make literary artists scratch their chins. In a parallel industry (visual art), the DALL·E 2 is a deep learning model that generates digital images from natural language descriptions (i.e., "image prompts"). While some have publicly worried it has the potential to upend the graphic design industry, its creators merely refer to it as a tool for graphic artists. Put in this light, one wonders if a chatbot might one day become a creative tool for the next generation of writers, something to embed in our word processors like the now-innocuous spellchecker that chases our every typo.

VI. Novelties, NFTs, and the Metaverse

At the time of writing this textbook, NFTs are still dominating the headlines, and we sense there will always be a contingent of experimental writers in pursuit of the latest digital trends. However, NFTs are likely to be a shrinking memory by the time this book is actually published. NFTs are a disruptive innovation in the art world that have essentially turned digital items (jpgs, pngs, mp3s, etc.) into irreproducible assets. In the case of NFTs, one cannot simply right-click and save an image to their desktop; rather, NFTs are located on blockchains, a decentralized database that records the transaction history of the NFT through metadata. Rare works, auctioned by fine-art brokers like Christie's and Sotheby's, have fetched millions of dollars at auction. These include a super-pixelated alien by CyberPunk, a piece of 3D dynamic art by Beeple that changes as a function of real-world phenomenon (e.g., election results), and an artistic representation of the source code for the World Wide Web (WWW) by its inventor, Tim Berners-Lee. Now, writers have begun creating their own NFTs in a genre known as literary NFTs. According to Ginsburg (2022: n.p.) of nft now, "A literary NFT is a digital literary work (a book, poem, or article) minted directly to the blockchain as a non-fungible token … NFTs can showcase a written work, act as a digital collectible, or serve as a key to an exclusive fan community." It's almost like owning a limited-edition digital broadside.

One NFT poet, the "transhuman translator" Sasha Stiles, creates media-rich generative poems by collaborating with her AI alter ego. Technelegy is her custom text generator, which was trained to write poems like Stiles by reading her poetry; the resulting AI poems are then visualized using DALL-E 2's text-to-image translation, often resembling a digital clock's seven-segment LED display in neon green (think *The Matrix*). The NFT has a futuristic voiceover that uses some combination of formant filter, pitch shift, auto-tune, concatenated talk box, or reverb plug-in. Crypto-writer Kalen Iwamoto repurposes words from cyberlibertarian John

Perry Barlow's, "A Declaration of the Independence of Cyberspace," to create one hundred novel tokens. The NFT compresses Barlow's manifesto by miniaturizing the font and reducing the space between the lines, resulting in a palimpsest. Barlow then extracts thirty-two words (two from each of the sixteen paragraphs), using an erasure technique, to create a new poem-as-node in the margin. Elsewhere on the NFT platform OpenSea, best-selling novelist Neil Strauss released "the first major decentralized book minted to the Ethereum blockchain." In a lottery-like system, one NFT of *Survive All Apocalypses*, will be selected at random; that copy will be updated with the exclusive copyright of the book. Thus, the owner of that unique NFT will be upgraded from a casual reader to a bona fide publisher overnight. It's worth mentioning the enormous carbon footprint of a single NFT. To own and read the NFT anthology *Etherpoems 2*, for instance, one consumes the equivalent energy of a computer watching YouTube nonstop for 237 days.

NFTs are also the site of beguiling collaborations. *Fifty Days at Iliam* (PNG, 600 dpi, 10″×12″, JavaScript | p5js) is a collection of ten ekphrastic NFTs that signify a collaboration-in-the-making. First, Homer's *Iliad* is translated by Alexander Pope (eighteenth century); next, Cy Twombly paints those translations (1978); then, Christian Bök prompts an AI author, Sudowrite, to generate an adage based on the title of each of Twombly's works; finally, Sarah Ridgely repeats Bök's adages on a canvas, using an "algorithmic brush" she's coded. Ridgley's program generates paper textures and asemic writing so that the final product resembles an ancient-looking manuscript, not so different from scraps of Homeric papyri found in the crocodile pits on the eastern banks of the Nile. Therefore, *The Iliad* passes from Homer's lips to the printing press to the Philadelphia Museum of Art to Objkt.com through a series of ekphrastic interpretations, accumulating the domains of the visual, conceptual, and digital, with elements of handicrafting, creative translation, and anachronistic repurposing. In many ways, a project like this represents the apotheosis of several emerging modes of experimental writing. NFTs are just one application of what many now call Web3.

If the original World Wide Web was mostly a collection of static websites that ushered in the Information Age, and Web 2.0 emphasized online interactivity as facilitated by Big Tech, then Web3 anticipates a decentralized internet, which futurists predict will mostly be "located" in the metaverse. The metaverse is a term and concept copped from Neal Stephenson's cult sci-fi novel, *Snow Crash*. In the book, Stephenson (1992) predicts an alternative internet that will one day be populated by avatars in a virtual reality landscape that exists to escape a dreary, dystopic world. It's a fairly bold prediction for 1992, considering most people at the time were just then plugging in their ethernet cables for dial-up internet.

GeoCities, The Sims, Second Life, World of Warcraft, Fortnite, Pokémon Go., Roblox, and VR Chat are all examples of role-playing metaverse platforms. Each open-ended platform needs to be built, and who is more adept at building worlds than writers, film directors, and visual designers? A VR chat guide provides advice for "Creating Your First World," and it becomes immediately clear how the craft of fiction has been assimilated into the purview of virtual reality and its primary programming languages. Creators must begin with spawn points (think portals) by which users can drop into their world. They set the reference cameras for establishing shots. They decide which assets/objects can be interactive through a layer collision matrix. They add background music. They set the "hard cap" for the max population of the world. They can refine 3D spatialization and apply post-processing effects. They control the range of flows, inputs, and outputs that enable user behaviors. Creators can even act as sound editors by establishing a certain point in the distance where users' voices fade, and another distance where their dialogue falls off completely. Finally, the world gets a name: see Big Al's Avatar Corridors, Room of Summer Solitude, and Sombie's Hangout, a three-story art space with secret passages.

We wonder if, one day, we will read metaverse memoirs with the same rapt attention we would somebody's account IRL. Documentaries like *We Met in Virtual Reality* or the occasional article about virtual affairs leading to real-life divorces are every bit as grounded in human drama and consequence as the embodied lives we lead. For this brief moment, it's the collisions between physical and virtual reality that seems to intrigue us, as society straddles the two. Others anticipate that, as virtual reality becomes more *real*, it will be an increasingly redundant prospect to announce the environmental context of our everyday experiences. We will move imperceptibly between our physical and virtual environments, each of them bearing attributes we recognize as artifice and verisimilitude.

The only thing that remains to be seen, though, is the extent to which human intelligence (versus artificial intelligence) will participate in the creation of these massively online communities. Chances are, it will be a combination of bespoke and automated world building. Notably, writers and creators in these worlds do not lay out objectives or manufacture tension for users; that is, the metaverse is inherently plot-less, a pure projection of lifestyle. Likewise, save for their own avatars, architects of the metaverse do not create the users/characters. The metaverse is avowedly non-teleological. In its purest form, it is owned by no one and everyone. However, there is an emerging concern over the neurorights of users. As technologists optimize headsets and haptics to measure eye tracking, micro-expressions, vital signs, and even blood-flow patterns of the face, corporations will have unprecedented access to our biodata and influence over our biodata. The United Nations Human Rights Council (2022) just adopted a draft document aimed at protecting people from devices that "record, interfere with, or modify brain activity."

Is it the case that the writers and creators within the VRChat metaverse are creating the architecture of mind control? It's unclear if the metaverse warrants this hysteria, and if regulation can tamp down legitimate ethical concerns. Yet, to put such concerns in a larger historical perspective, how much different is the metaverse than, say, the English novel as a narrative technology? Samuel Richardson's *Pamela; or, Virtue Rewarded* was chock-full of evocative scenes that immersed readers in unfamiliar spaces. In his critical study of the novel, James Grantham Turner (1994: 77) notes that the "dramatic immediacy operates directly to arouse the spectator, male or female." When it first reached the public, the avowedly virtuous—though tacitly sexy—novel induced a similar moral panic as many new technologies today. While the novel instantiated a cultural and psychological paradigm shift that manipulated readers, there are no modern commentators who would suggest it was a potential human rights violation. Long eighteenth-century epistolary novels like *Pamela* not only depended on the leisure time of their upper- and middle-class readers, they also depended on infrastructure such as a postal service, without which there would be no timely delivery of epistles in the first place. Similarly, eighteenth-century theories of Enlightenment democracy implicitly relied on the then-new technology of affordable newspapers disseminating the terms of political debates to the public—a fact that simultaneously spurred the growth of the essay form with such periodicals as *The Tatler*, *The Spectator*, and *The Gentleman's Magazine*. New technologies are mutually constitutive not only of literary genres, then, but also of political structures and social mores.

Experimental Writing

Today, most local newspapers are folding or have been bought out by conglomerates; people get their news from social media instead. The post office is on the decline; emails and text messaging are widespread. These (perhaps seemingly mundane) changes to technological infrastructure have a concomitant impact on political systems, social codes, and literary styles—just as all these things reciprocally influence (and supervene upon) the development of technology and infrastructure. Recently, the first political speeches have been given in the metaverse, raising concerns about the spread of disinformation in a new domain. Perhaps anxieties about emerging technologies such as the metaverse, AI, and Web3 may in hindsight seem akin to the moral panic about the hair-raising titillations of the novel. Then again, these technologies may upend the very fabric of culture and politics as we know it. Either way, what seems more certain is that these new virtual realms will be spaces where people communicate, interact with their social selves, and pour their creativity so that literature—in one form or another—plays a vital role in whatever developments take place.

Discussion Questions

1. Visit www.theuselessweb.com. Once there, you will encounter the following prompts: "Take me to another useless website please." Click the please button ten to twenty times. The coding on these websites will range from comically minimalist (as with crouton.net or ismycomputeron.com) to quite involved. For each website, imagine that you have the programming abilities to integrate your own creative writing with the idiosyncratic coding outputs on the websites. How could the unique features of these sites be modified in the production of your own digital writing? This will likely require you to imaginatively tweak the design variables, operational rules, and very purpose of the site. Consider what genre of creative writing would be best suited for each site. If one site isn't resonating with you, just move on; some of these sites may be truly "useless." Take note of the URLs for the most promising websites and share your plan with other writers.

2. Find a poem by an "eco-poet" online—perhaps something by Mary Oliver, Camille T. Dungy, or Craig Santos Perez on the Poetry Foundation's website. Once on the site, type the following: Control +U (for PC); Option + Command + U (for Mac). You can now see the source code for the page. Scroll through all the code in search of the poem. Once you find the poem, read it aloud. Can you intuit the line breaks? Does the poem flow? Is there tension in reading this poem in a programming font? Once you've finished reading the poem, scroll around. Many programmers claim there is an art to coding. Is the source code itself a kind of poetry? How so? What do you notice amidst the commands and comments and hyperlinks and SEO tags? Is there anything in common between the poem you read and the source code that surrounds it?

3. In a small group with a shared computer, play an interactive fiction game. We recommend "Shade," "Lost Pig," or "Dreamhold." Each is available for free on The People's Republic of Interactive Fiction. One person should act as the narrator. Pay attention to all details, especially nouns. Remember: If you get stuck, just type help to learn more about text commands. After about 15 minutes or once you've finished

the game, discuss what you know about the setting, character, and plot for each story. How much of this comes directly from the game and how much have you inferred/fabricated?

4. In a small group, agree upon a search query. Something like "longest lasting lightbulb." Everyone should begin by using Google to search the chosen phrase. Now, each person should use a new search engine to search for the same query. We recommend wiki.com (all answers are sourced from Wikis), the Internet Archive's Wayback Machine (archive.org/web), millionshort.com (which removes up to the first million results), boardreader.com (which scours message boards), social-searcher.com (results come from social media only), and dogpile.com (a metasearch engine). Compare results. Which site provides the most compelling information for writing in your chosen genre? Finally, if time allows, begin researching your next story, essay, or poem using one of these new engines.

Writing Prompts

1. This is taken from Kenneth Goldsmith, author of *Wasting Time on the Internet* and professor at the University of Pennsylvania. Go to your browser history and look at the last week of your search history. Copy-and-paste it into a Word document. Then annotate as many sites as you can, recalling what led you to that site in the first place. What did you do while you were on the site? What connections did you make between the material of the site and your own knowledge? This is a type of autobiographical account of your time on the internet, whether you consider that time "wasted," "productive," or otherwise.

2. Using Dall-E 2, NightCafe, or some other AI image generator, try to reconstruct an important scene from a story, memory from an essay, or image from a poem. Begin by pasting an especially vivid phrase into the search field. Now, add the aesthetic specifications. Be as detailed as possible. For best results, we recommend using Guy Parsons' free *DALL·E 2 prompt book*. Try tinkering with affective words (specific emotions), size words (micro or gigantic), structural words (sketched versus elaborate, natural versus artificial), "vibe" words (mood type and energy level), and looks or aesthetics (vaporwave, cyberpunk, gothic, etc.). You can also specify angle and proximity, lighting and shutter speed, color palette and tones, materials and textures—not to mention algorithmic shortcuts for entire illustration styles, artistic processes, genres and movements, and the idiosyncratic gestures of household names like Warhol, Whistler, and Walt Disney. When all else fails, use the prompt "[YOUR SUBJECT] in the style of [EXAMPLE, e.g., Hello Kitty]." Which AI-generated images are your favorite? Would any be suitable book covers? Have any new concepts or elements been introduced? Try incorporating aspects of these images into a revision.

3. Pre-write an essay, poem, or story using only questions. If you were writing a "life story," for example, you might start with a question like "What do babies experience in the womb during the third trimester?" and end with "What happens to your body after you die?" You might then fill in the middle with an extrapolated question for every decade—about the first day of kindergarten (at 5), first kiss (at 15), first big paycheck (at 25), death of a first parent (at 35), purchasing a first home (at 45), and so on. We encourage you to ask specific questions that map onto the arc of your planned essay, poem, or story. Therefore, the questions should follow a logic that is appropriate to your planned piece (e.g., chronological, procedural, sequential, narrative, etc.). Ten questions total will suffice. Now, copy-and-paste each question into an open AI chatbot like ChatGPT. For each question, specify a speech genre, literary form, and/or aesthetic style for the reply. (For example, "How should I prepare for my first kiss? Respond in an absurdist koan." or "What do people tend to buy with their first major paycheck? Respond in a haiku using Leetspeak.") Compile your answers and edit the piece until you are satisfied with the result. This may require you to generate secondary answers to the same questions or come up with new questions entirely.

4. On an exceedingly "average" day, log in to your preferred social media platform and begin micro-blogging (or vlogging) about everything. Don't plan anything special for the occasion. Nothing is too insignificant, private, or foolish to share. In other words: *over*sharing is the order of the day. This may take the form of a Twitter thread, Instagram stories, or going live on TikTok. Documenting your day will require you to make lists, transcribe snippets of conversation, provide acute commentary on your experiences, photograph choice images, and take representative videos. You will likely feel compelled to use other media too: emojis, memes, GIFs, tags and hashtags, and reposts/quote Tweets. As your account becomes saturated with content (~50 or more posts), take a moment to scroll back to the original post and begin reading. Consider what you have done with the material of your day. Is it true to life? Truer than life? Or an utterly untrue depiction of your day? Have you fabricated a dramatic arc or inserted some recurring theme or motif? What do you notice about your affect, persona, and preoccupations? As you are drifting off to sleep, set your timer for fifteen minutes. In the hypnagogic state between wakefulness and sleep, your alarm will wake you. Be sure to record your very last thought before it dissolves. It may be hazy, hallucinatory, or downright nonsensical. That's okay! The world is waiting with rapt attention. For inspiration (and courage), visit "What Happened on 6/21/18 and 12/21/19?" *(Essay Daily)* or read about Megan Boyle's book, *Liveblog*.

5. It has been said that all attempts at translation are predicated on failure. For this exercise, translate something you've written into only emojis. To do this, you will have to decide on your own syntax. Where do the subject, predicate, and object of the sentence go? How about adjectives and adverbs? How will you render pronouns, conjunctions, and prepositional phrases? To best approximate the diction, will you occasionally need to combine multiple emojis to form a single English word? When there is no available image, will you simply elide the word or rely on the power of

association? After you've finished translating—say, a stanza or paragraph—we recommend swapping emoji translations with a friend via text message. Are they able to convert the string of emojis back into words? What inferences did they have to make? Now, compare the original with this new re-re-translation. What has most dramatically changed—genre, form, tone? What has been lost? Gained? Retained? Comment on the failures and successes of the two translations.

6. Create a "video poem." Video poems combine a soundtrack of someone reading a poem with imagery much like a music video or experimental short film. A video poem might also use a short prose work instead of a poem. Video poems don't necessarily show the poet reading their work or illustrate the piece directly, though they might; more often, video poems focus on images, brief scenes, sequences, and montages that are suggestive and tangentially related to the poem's narrative content, creating an interpretive space of ambiguity and association between image and text. Examples can be found at Moving Poems (https://movingpoems.com/) and Button Poetry's YouTube channel. Note, this prompt does require a small degree of technical background in film editing, though this is more the level of knowing how to use features on an iPhone than film expertise.

ANTHOLOGY

Introduction

In "On Exactitude in Science," Borges writes of an empire that's obsessed with map-making. The cartographers' guild strikes a "Map of the Empire whose size was that of the Empire, and which coincided point for point with it." Such a project is, of course, a failure because it ceases to be representative; unrolled over the Empire, it obscures the very thing it is supposed to represent. Later in this (one-paragraph) story, the map is eventually disintegrated and scattered, its pieces reduced to practical bedding for animals and beggars. The fragments no longer *represent* a place but have *become* a place—a sitting mat or blanket, offering refuge and succor.

It's hard to imagine what a totalizing map of these nine emerging genres would look like. Perhaps it would resemble a mirror held up to the internet; or some overexerted database of The Great Unread, the untold scores of overlooked or forgotten works that never received a wide readership. On the other hand, the myopia of a "representative" anthology can be riddled with biases. Chuck Klosterman in *But What If We're Wrong?* writes, "History is defined by people who don't really understand what they're defining" (91). Klosterman contends that critics, judges, and anthologists tend to create lists of important artists and authors under the assumption that they are living at the end of time, and that temporary tastes and obsessions will remain historically universal. Conscious of this dialectic, we've taken pains *not* to make that very assumption here.

There is no exact science to making anthologies, or at least no science we want to be associated with. So, rather than attempt to strike our own "unconscionable map" of the field, we have opted to carefully compile some pieces that we enjoy—thirty-some little places for you to visit now that you've heard tell of the manifold concepts, styles, and techniques that are characteristic of experimental writing.

Unlike many anthologies, we deliberately avoid slotting the contents into discrete categories. While we certainly have our own ideas about how any one work in this anthology comports with the features found across our chapters' idiosyncratic taxonomies, we do not explicitly present them as such here. Recalling one premise of the Composites and Unclassifiables chapter—that an experimental work can exhibit n-factorial aesthetic combinations—it would be a category error to emplace any given piece in a singular tradition when, in fact, it can be said to span several. To slot Lillian-Yvonne Bertram's *Travesty Generator* into "digital" oversimplifies its experiment; it would foreclose the possibility that you could identify it as conceptual or co-opted or even a minor form. The unexpected taxonomical overlaps are what make an experiment rich to begin with. With this in mind, we encourage you to re-read like you never have before, to experience each piece anew by applying different interpretive lenses. Track your first and last impressions.

Experimental Writing

If at first you read with a particular category in mind, see if you can talk yourself into identifying a new category on your rereading. Where specifically in the text is that alternative interpretation announcing itself? What happens when you isolate your reading for language/voice versus structure/form versus procedure/methods? Does this shift your awareness of traditions, genres, conventions? Note, however, that you probably can't make the case that each piece exhibits every emerging genre. For example, K. Silem Mohammad's "The Sonnagrams" is not an instance of handicrafting, no matter how much you squint at it.

There's another reason we are reluctant anthologists. The process of "canon-making" implied by anthologies has historically acted to further exclude or marginalize those who were already disempowered. In this light, issues of diversity were at the forefront of our selection process. We sought diversity in several intersectional dimensions, particularly along the lines of gender (including trans and nonbinary folks), race (including mixed race), ethnicity (including multiethnic writers), and nationality (including diasporic, transnational, and immigrant authors, whether documented or not). Additionally, we have sought more diverse representation in terms of authors' sexual orientation, dis/ability or neurodivergence, religion, regional focus (particularly in the United States), tribal membership (if Indigenous), education (including first-gen, writers who work outside the academy or who do not have advanced degrees, and authors' institutional program affiliations), class background, age, language(s), and other categories or communities of self-identity which authors profess. Our selections are also intended to strike a balance between contemporary emerging, mid-career, and established authors. Going further, we wanted to extend our diversity to areas in which the "authorship" model of diversity might not apply as readily, such as collaboratively written work, works by anonymous collectives, crowdsourced material, and machine-written texts. Similarly, we have sought to engage with perspectives based in eco-consciousness, transhumanism, and animal studies that de-center not only authorship but also the privileged place of human beings.

Given our experimental focus, we have deliberately juxtaposed pieces that are conventionally logocentric (i.e., written on the page) with others that take a multimodal approach (e.g., works that encompass modalities of speech, gesture, improvisation, embodiment, materiality, or alternative technologies). Many of these latter types of pieces require either photo documentation or placement in an online supplement to the print-based anthology. Indeed, our pursuit of diversity has also motivated us to question traditional definitions of "writing" itself, reorienting the concept of "writing" to be on a continuum with other practices such as performance, new media, textiles, design, translation, sound art, curation, repurposing, and algorithmic constraints. Expanding the definition of writing can likewise expand who counts as an "author."

In order for this anthology to be useful to readers, it must showcase a breadth of experimental techniques. We hope that each selection offers students an engaging example of a category of experimental writing we discuss in the body of the textbook, and that each selection will be accessible within this context. Because of the restrictions of space (in the book) and time (in the classroom), we favor works that are short or, in some cases, brief excerpts that are relatively self-contained. Sometimes, the feature of the text we would like to highlight can be captured by a single page or a photo. Important longer works are more appropriately addressed in the body of the textbook and included in supplemental resource lists online so that readers can discover them on their own time. We have favored anthologizing work that is less readily at a reader's fingertips, so that students can gain exposure to new and out-of-the-way materials.

We are averse to reprinting the same stories, essays, or poems already widely regarded as exemplars of experimental writing for fear that they will become too emblematic and monolithic—that readers experiencing a piece yet again will mistake the piece and its techniques as coequal to the category itself. Furthermore, we expect that these examples are what led readers to our textbook in the first place. For instance, pieces like "Reply All" (Robin Hemley) and "Life Story" (David Shields) serve as the gateway to experimental writing, but we avoid replicating these chestnuts in our anthology selection. At the same time, we feature several prominent experimental writers, often with their lesser known—but no less exciting—pieces.

It is obvious to us that authors with diverse backgrounds take diverse approaches to experimentation. With this in mind, we adopted a model that amplifies artists whose works we have rarely (or too rarely) encountered in books and conversations where issues of diversity had been shoehorned in ex post facto. We want to go beyond simply offering a "representative" account of the field since representation within the field has been traditionally lacking—therefore, we hope to use this textbook and anthology as an occasion to push forward the diversity and inclusiveness of experimental writing, literary institutions, academia, and wider communities.

We would like to acknowledge these texts tend to be challenging, but these challenges are means, not ends. In other words, an experimental work doesn't set out to be challenging for the sake of being challenging; it is often challenging because writers have set out to challenge conventions, institutions, patriarchy, nation-states, the moral majority, and other hegemonic structures. This harkens back to our theories of the avant-garde in the introduction to this book. If you or a colleague find yourselves wondering what purpose any given work in this anthology serves, well then, we would encourage you to revisit those seven theories of the avant-garde in the preface for starters. For many of us, reading is a socialized and politicized process, and that socialization has often been facilitated by the very institutions an experimental writer may be trying to critique or dismantle. Ask yourself, with what orthodoxies might this writing be in contention? Is this a political experiment masquerading as an aesthetic experiment? Is the work "unintelligible" because I am unable or unwilling to see the system with which it interacts in a new light? How do your own biases prevent you from taking the work seriously?

Another reason experimental writing can be challenging is that it tends to arise from the dynamic *Lebenswelt* ("lifeworld") of its authors. Heidegger identifies the lifeworld as our collective background experiences that we sift through to arrive at meaning. Writers trafficking in a deluge of pre-constructed raw experience while continually deferring meaning may frustrate the impatient reader. By contrast, these same writers may playfully address the antithesis of the lifeworld, known as the "system world," but only through ironic means like absurdist parody, anarchist ideology, or Bakhtinian carnivalesque. The collision of systems and chaos can provoke nihilism in the reader. It is acceptable, even savvy, to walk away from such texts and declare them meaningless; indeed, one might even sense life is meaningless after reading an especially challenging text. And that's okay, too! There is not a programmatic answer or a "right" way to read these texts—they are catalytic, unstable, multifarious.

Linguistically, some of the pieces that follow use unconventional syntax, obscure references, or multiple voices in order to force the reader to confront the shiftiness of context, language, and meaning. Derrida has used the concept of *différance* to show how authors manipulate language to disrupt traditional systems of signification and create new, alternative ways of understanding. By way of example, the polysemous (many-meaninged) word "bank" is not ascribed meaning until other words begin to relate to it. The presence of "reeds" indicates it's a river bank whereas a "teller" tells us it's a financial word. Texts that celebrate *différance* force the reader to engage with the text and create meaning for themselves. In this way, reading is imbued with agential choice and desire. Similarly, Barthes' concept of the "readerly" text refers to a highly structured form of writing that is designed to be easily interpretable and understood by the reader. This type of text is characterized by a clear hierarchy of meaning, with the author's intention and interpretation being paramount; meanwhile, the reader is expected to accept the meaning of the text as it is presented, rather than actively engaging with it to create their own interpretation. A "writerly" text, on the other hand, refers to a more experimental, open-ended form of writing that encourages the reader to actively engage with the text and create their own meaning.

Additionally, Heidegger's concept of the "ready-to-hand" refers to the way that objects and tools (and texts!) are integrated into our everyday lives and activities in such a way that they become transparent and easy to use. The ready-to-hand is characterized by a lack of awareness or conscious thought, as the object or tool simply becomes an extension of our own bodies and actions. The object of the tool can be equated with its function, taken for granted. The ready-to-hand is characterized by a lack of conscious thought and the transparent integration of objects and tools into our everyday lives, much like the way that traditional systems of signification operate in language. The "present-to-hand," on the other hand, involves a heightened awareness and conscious thought about the object or tool, similar to the way that *différance* or the writerly text operates in language by disrupting traditional systems of signification and inviting the reader to actively engage with the text and create their own interpretation. Heidegger's concept of the "present-to-hand," then, can refer to the way that texts become the focus of our attention and conscious thought when they break down or malfunction. The present-to-hand is characterized by a heightened awareness of the text as an independent entity, a materiality or potential, separate from our own actions and purposes.

There are some works we would have loved to include, but couldn't due to obvious limitations of the technology of the book. To experience the full effect of some pieces, we'd need to share a hyperlink and ask you to update Adobe Flash; you'd have to make your way to a gallery space and pace through an exhibition to experience the sheer four-dimensionality of the writing; you'd need to go to a special collections archive to get hands-on experience with a letterpress broadside on cotton paper; or you'd need to get a clearance inspection to access a biosecure facility to peer into a microscope to experience bacterial poetry à la Christian Bök. Because of these limitations, we've done our best to speak in depth about such projects in the body of the textbook and to supplement this anthology with a digital one online. Other times, we've opted to publish a remediated version of the work as with Maya Lin and Tan Lin's "Reading a Garden" or GennaRose Nethercott's *Lianna Fled the Cranberry Bog*. For these, we couldn't fit a full-scale meditation garden into this book nor the pre-folded three-dimensional papercraft of Nethercott's story in cootie catchers. Instead, enjoy the blueprints/designs until you have the opportunity to stop by the actual garden site at the Cleveland Public Library. And we encourage you to snip, crease, and manipulate from the cootie catcher template we've included. We invite you to snip out and fold up the cootie catchers on your own. This compromise reminds us of visual essayist Sarah Minor's prerogative to prepare her writing in three forms: word-processed text, performance, and installation. For Minor, there is no "definitive" version of her work: her texts are transposed over media, form, space, and time. They become iterative, adaptable, occasional—transforming themselves even as they attempt to transform their reader, audience, or viewer. For now, a print anthology necessarily relies upon the word-processed version of any piece of writing. Our website provides electronic resources. And perhaps in the future, we'll be able to 3D-print an anthology of experimental text objects, curate poetic installations in the metaverse, encode electrodes to produce experiences directly onto your neurons, and the like. Stay tuned!

Speaking of which, what future is it from where you read? From what past does this anthology introduction emerge? Recall that notions of experimentation vacillate over time. What struck us as the bleeding edge today might seem less so from wherever you sit. We tried to take an ecumenical approach to curating the pieces in this anthology, knowing that, sooner or later, all literature must pass through new aesthetic thresholds. Into what new contexts have these pieces aged? Are they more relevant than ever or completely, hilariously anachronistic? The art critic and historian James Laver (1937) believed that fashion trends are considered indecent ten years, shameless five years, and outré when one year before their time. Indeed, much of what constitutes experimental writing is composed for a futurity, a context that doesn't yet exist. The word "fashionable" typically (and obtusely) refers to *current* fashion, but fashion is temporally expansive. Whenever a trend expires—that is, as its currency wanes—it undergoes a steady, if counterintuitive transformation—from dowdy to hideous to ridiculous to amusing to quaint to charming to romantic, and ultimately, according to Laver, it returns as the beautiful. So, we wonder, what is indecent from your vantage? And what might its pathway to beauty look like?

Literature is always disappearing into the reality it produces.

Experimental Writing

Hanif Abdurraqib

On Times I Have Forced Myself to Dance

Safe to say none of the other Muslim kids on the eastside of Columbus got MTV or BET in their cribs & we do at my crib sometimes like after Pops got a promotion or after Grandma moved in & kept a Bible on her nightstand & had to watch the channel where her game shows ran 24/7 & so it is also safe to say that I was the only one in the Islamic Center on Broad Street who got to stay up & watch the shows on MTV that came on after my parents cut out the lights & went up to bed & it was only me & the warmth of an old television's glow & the DJs spinning C+C Music Factory for people in baggy & colorful getups & bouncing on a strobe-light-drenched floor & so it is safe to say that I only danced along the slick surface of my basement floor with the moon out & all the lights in the house out & the television playing hits & this wasn't exactly *practicing* dance moves as much as it was learning the different directions my limbs could flail in & there is no church like the church of unchained arms being thrown in every direction in the silence of a sleeping home & speaking of church to be Muslim is to pray in silence sometimes even though the call to prayer is one of the sweetest songs that can hang in the air & there is no praise & there is no stomping in the aisles & there is no holy spirit to carry the blame for all manner of passing out or shouting or the body's pulsing convulsions & I do not want a spirit to enter me but I do want a girlfriend or at least a kiss from a girl at the Islamic Center where we go on Friday afternoons in the summers for Jummah prayer & kick our shoes on the carpet & slip into the hallway where the boys & girls would congregate briefly before being separated for prayer & it is absolutely safe to say that with my socks on the marbled tile of the Islamic Center on Broad Street I felt overcome by something we will call holy I suppose for the sake of not upsetting the divine order & this was the mid-'90s & so no one was really doing the moonwalk anymore & even when they did no one was doing it right & there is only one Michael & I am not that nigga & still with the girls at the Islamic Center standing in line for the water fountain I thought *Now is the time* & I was decidedly not in the dark of my basement anymore where I knew the floors & I understood every corner of the architecture & I slid back on the top of my toes & no one even turned their eyes toward me & so no one could tell me about the stairs I was sliding toward & so no one saw my brief moment of rhythm before it unraveled & just like that I was in a pile of discarded shoes & it is safest to say that there was no girlfriend for me that summer or the summer after & the cable at my house got cut off the year my mother died.

Caren Beilin

Freinds

The beans in the filter are brown, like black cocaine.

Central Perk.

Dehydrated shit, but wet.

The sun at a certain time, when it urinates with concentration, its dehydration comes through the window of our favorite coffee shop—it comes in, a crop of wedding band in the coffee ground.

Rachel, where the fuck have you been?

Get her a decaf.

Because of how high-strung I must have seemed. Sitting there—sopping—in a wedding dress.

How sheep it would have been to marry Barry. Periodontist. DOCTOR OF THE GUMS.

The sun sets its mauve gums down.

I'm trembling, to have run. To have hurled oneself out of the window of a reception hall's bathroom. I had to get out. To have climbed out of the toilet of that marriage plot—"They said that you would be here"—and come in here high-strung.

"I went to your apartment. But the super said that you would be here."

Central Perk.

This is Ross. CAROL IS A LESBIAN. I think it to myself—I, Ross—over and over, over what happened. And then Rachel runs in, after *years*, with wedding dress gobbed on her skin, just sopping, a slut sheep, and her breasts are more than I could ever have held in mind, the breasts, body, and mind, all of the sudden, of someone who tans.

Maple mountain range, mr. breasts, balloon range, hunt them down, tan the balloon skin.

I found your address, Mon. The super—*mr. treeger*—said that you would be here.

Central Perk.

Monica.

"Rachel, you remember Ross?" He's sitting right there.

Experimental Writing

This is Ross. I changed my eyes to hazel, for my career. I work out. I don't drink. I don't do cocaine. I don't do *crack* cocaine. I quit heroin. I changed my life.

The ground is full of fossil. Roller coaster calcium in the ground. I'm talking dinos. I'm a paleontologist, Rachel. I'm on the cusp of being offered to lecture on the dinosaur at New York University. It is still a living issue. We still need to know what she is thinking. The lizard oil pumps still in my brain cerebrum. Higher power. Memory of my first Sinclairosaur. I, hugging her leg, plastique. I said to her then, at the gas station, "Take it." Take what happened to me. TAKE THESE PEAS OFF THE FUCKING FLOOR.

Later, in my dissertation year … I found a deep footstep in the rock, in the field, my three-toed sleeping bath. It filled up with rain. I was alone, naked—*mr. clean*—

Your hair is really different. From what I remember.

I had it straightened. It has also been layered.

"Um, the strata of your fimbria."

Thank you for boring us, again, with your science, Ross. *God*. Rache, I live just steps from this coffee shop. Come up. We'll get you dry.

Where's Sandman?

This is a no-pet building. Welcome to NY. You can't have dogs in most buildings. Sandman was old.

We killed him.

Come in.

Move in with me.

Sun, shaft of dust. A teastain tan on a teatowel, hanging.

Carol is a lesbian. I think it to myself. I go over what happened. Susan's cunt, the rent control apartment. TOO GOOD TO BE IMAGINED.

Sunset, a cunt is smoldering, I—Rachel—imagine, if you go out to the country, Long Island. That O'Keefe painting I saw at the MOMA, on that poster for that MOMA on the subway stairwell, during my first subway ride, on my way to Bloomingdale with my father's credit card, now ripped from the subway wall and put on a pier, the Long Island pier—the sun getting its guts, its paints, each evening like it's the cunt of Prometheus. Punishment for what?

Dear Monica, you had started a fire in my heart.

Night, the maggot quilt.

Where did you go, Rachel?

We had plans to go, together, this NY evening, to the laundromat, but Ross begs me to let him go in my place. "Come on, Mon. Let me take her." He cites his past drug abuse. "This is the gift of my sobriety," he tells me, over coffee.

Central Perk.

Then I wanted to give you crack.

At the laundromat. The sign. NO FREE DETERGENT. Oh fuck, Ross. This is so awkward. I'm out of detergent. I knew I couldn't make it here. *I've never even been to a laundromat.*

Rachel, is this underwear lace? What is this, the slutty fetus of your wedding dress? You have to separate the lace, Rache. *Jesus.* I'll teach you, Rachel, to make piles. I teach (I lecture all of the time) to undergraduate students at NYU.

Gunther lets me work at Central Perk.

The sun goes flaccid in my muffin. Orange worm. Slugs of it, sunlight, in the espresso glass. I burn it. Gunther retrains me. He has to. I burn it again, I can't learn. I never finished. I didn't go back to college, to anything like that. Monica, you don't know where I went.

Sunset, the orange worm filling with red wine, then nothing, night, espresso evaporate, beetle cunts jamming the system.

At night, the moon comes heavier, blooming down and pouring cream, and if a building bends or the moon wanes, you'll see it, Rachel. The moon. Especially tonight, during this city-wide blackout. Candles lit, I took you out to the balcony to tell you—

I'll tell you about it, Rachel, on the balcony, because it, too, is part of my study of paleontological prehistory, night being the first cave, stars the first hieroglyphic, could they BE any more prescient?

Rachel, you statue of lithe maple, I mean, I imagine your bones are the color of lithe tinsel. Come closer. Come closer to my ribbed sweater.

It's nice out, Ross, New York as dark as this, the ghosts of capuchins extending …

Sunrise, steam of wine—white wine—coming from heaven.

Don't you have to work?

Experimental Writing

My class is offered at NYU to undergraduate freshman in the afternoon. Until then I am free to go to a recovery meeting or sit with you here, and read magazines. Catalogues from Bloomingdale, I'll pick my poison. Victoria, tell me.

Say it.

Rachel, I'm not leaving.

"I'm going to bed."

In the morning?

I'm very tired, Ross. I need some space.

I gave you space. I gave you a tour of the fucking stars.

That's not what I mean.

Not again. Not you, too, Rache. CAROL WAS A LESBIAN.

She goes to bed. She closes her door. I read a catalogue between them. Two rooms. I'm staying right here. I'll watch for any action. I don't want to see them kissing again. *I'm not going to any meeting.*

I've met everyone.

I am in my room. You, Monica, are not ever in my bed but in the next one, the wall adjoining us. *I bear its radiance.*

Your roommateness.

I've imagined it would happen on the edge of my bed, my bedding, like we were pigeons on a duvet wire.

Lesbians, the pigeons. The most pervasive dove.

Cannot be contained in one song, one Carol.

Monica. In her bed, in the early dawn, her room, and I jump out of my skin. I want her so much in my bed that she becomes it. I moan and seizure all over my bed, horsefright in my blood and a hummingbird souled perineum.

Coffee would come after—if we go down to the coffee shop, just steps from our apartment, the sun strumming the first strings of its acoustic beginnings through Central Perk's red letters, if it could happen, if we were to do it—what I mean is, whether you make coffee on your own or it's given freely across the counter by Gunther, it is often the first gift, the after-sex offer.

The brain flooding with mud, macerated—coffee, masturbated mud. I hope this, if it happens, if you come into my room, through the wall, no, practical, the door, real, that what happens doesn't fatten into the flat of that happened, *that*, the dead dove—would that it wouldn't be a single time, Mon. Your name is French, for mine. *Je t'aime*.

My heart has never beaten anyone. Your face is in my mind.

I feel the pain of feeling nothing. The not-you gnawing, ruining the room. It's delicate. We're friends. We have been for a long time. Longer than this feeling. The feeling kicked my heart at sunset. It kicked my clit.

Coffee, you marsupial vinaigrette.

Get me decaf.

After sex, I would give you some. I would make Gunther get down on his knees and make you some and pour you some and I'd give you some. We'd drink coffee together, Rachel, on the velvet couch, casual, your hair as straight as it has ever been. Your skin is very tan. I'd kiss you there, in the coffee shop. The after-sex kiss, O, murmur of velum—is kissing the moon, with your infamous after-sex glowing, you are glowing, the moon a cooler surface to kiss after fucking, after landing and walking the FUCK around, on the sun.

We never walked on the moon. It was a film.

I keep the moon intact, Mon. I just look.

Sunrise, a cunt is coming. *Rachel*. Would that it weren't mine.

Rachel. This is Ross. You should know—I was in love with you in high school. So there.

Ross, don't just do it. Don't say things anyone could pull down and pass around. Anyone can confess the general past.

I love your breasts, in certain lights, Siamese moon—at dusk, butter balloon born conjoined. Twins. I could go on—*mr. -*

We fight all over our shared apartment, me and her—over Jean-Claude Van Damme, the actor. He's been in New York making a film. Right outside of Central Perk. We both say we want him. I say it first. She follows my line of desire, if not its origin. My heart center. So you want him now too. And it being you, it will happen, things happen for you all of the time, just look at Ross—look at where you have him—these things as you summon them, but now I want him, JCVD, because he is interested in what interests me. He seems disinterested and pleased with both of us, more with you. The sun setting into our apartment, all of it, we fight.

I deliver real stuff. Real blows. Real pardons. I hit her for looking at the moon, and for drinking coffee alone, for the privacy of her bowels—the heart only internally, cerebrally, melodious.

Experimental Writing

And for finding me, here in my city, in her wedding dress, sopping, and for saying, "They said that you would be here," but not saying it, not completing it. I was looking for you. I came from one life to this life, mine to yours, to you. To complete you.

"You had no right to go out with him."

"You sold me out."

She flicks me. I flick her. It starts with flicking. I hit her arm. She hits mine. I punch her breast. She flails against me. I hit her head. She smacks at my thighs and ass. She lunges onto me. She wraps her legs right around me and hits me. I drag her by the feet and I take off her sock and beat her. I fall into her legs, her hand on my face. It feels like the hand of Jesus. I chase her into the kitchen, we run around the table, the sun coming heavy on the hung down rims, my mugs downturned. I destroy her sweater and she dumps marinara sauce right in my purse.

She marries Ross.

Dodie Bellamy

Dogs without a Face

The dogs never stop howling except when Christiane drifts through the kennel, touching them. Her floor-length housecoat blossoms about her in a wide circumference, its hem so round it looks like Christiane is forever bathed in a spotlight. She doesn't so much walk as glide though her father's mansion with her arms held akimbo at an unnatural angle that exactly duplicates the Disney Cinderella figurine that sits on a shelf beside my computer. In the 80s, when I paid $2 for her at a yardsale, she was already ancient. My Cinderella has lost her nose and her eyebrows are fading away. Her face is round and chinless by today's bony standards. Like Christiane, she is all gown and no feet. My arms feel cramped just from looking at her.

Christiane's face has been horribly burned and mutilated from a car crash caused by her scientist father. Insane with guilt, her father assures her the disfigurement is only temporary, that she'll again be beautiful once he perfects his skin grafting technique. In the meantime, he's removed all the mirrors from his mansion and given Christiane a rubber mask to wear. The scientist slices the face off a captive woman and grafts it onto Christiane's. Soon afterwards Christiane sits maskless at the dinner table exuding a perplexed alien beauty. "Don't smile so much," her father says nervously. Then Christiane's new face rots. This happens over and over again, but the heterografts work on dogs—close up to a dog torso with a perfectly square patch of foreign dog hair growing and thriving, its edges sharp as astroturf. "Why, why, why does this work on dogs but not women," frets the scientist, who tortures out of necessity, not evil. It's hard on him, finding places to bury all the faceless women, and the dogs' incessant howling is driving him crazy.

Christiane's rubber face is flawless, perfectly white, lacking expression. She looks trapped behind it, her huge eyes ravenous, yet uncomprehending, as if the world were rushing into them in torrents and it's too much to register. When I put on makeup I feel like I'm wearing a rubber mask, especially when I smear on foundation, all my irregularities smoothed away with pinkish lotion. I use a special synthetic brush that doesn't absorb the foundation so my pores can better suck it up. Last Christmas I went to Macys and said to the girl at the Mac counter—"make me look like a middle class lady"—and she did, and I bought everything. It cost $200. I now have three shades of beige for my eyelids. The orangey beige I spread just above my lashes, according to the Mac girl, really makes my green eyes "pop." My lips are a translucent burnt red called "Spice It Up" or a medium salmon called "Tempting." Whenever I wear my rubber face people say to me, "Dodie you look so nice." Supposedly no animals have been harmed to make me look this nice.

Cinderella is what my mother called me—because I pouted about having to help with the housework. Cinderella was beautiful, the animals loved her, and she triumphed in the end. I was fat and frumpy, our dachshund Leo growled at me, and my mother always won. Six-thirty in the morning on a school day, curled in fetal position, my head buried under the blanket, she barges in and shouts, "Hey, Cinderella, time to get up." Sometimes she shortened it to Cindy. "Hey, Cindy, get your ass out of that bed." I wished I had little singing birds and mice that would sneak in and do the dishes, dress me in long, ribboned gowns.

Experimental Writing

Here are the names of my three beige eye shadows: Steep Veluxe, Kid Veluxe, Shroom Satin. My eyeliner is Espresso Matte. I am in an alpine forest (Steep) with cute little goats foraging about (Kid), I'm hunting for mushrooms when Alida Valli appears and says it's cold out, why don't I come back to the mansion for some espresso. As we approach the front gate, dogs howl, warning me that I'm entering a horror chamber of animal testing and I am the animal. I should have known this was coming—the beige shadow for my brows is Omega Matte, a disconcerting apocalyptic note. Revelation 22:13: I am the Alpha and the Omega, the First and the Last, the Beginning and the End.

Christiane makes love to a Great Dane. He sticks his head out of the macroscopic birdcage he's trapped in, she puts her arms around his neck, and their noses touch in a moment of bliss. The Great Dane pants with excitement. Christiane takes his massive paw in her hand and their eyes meet as if they're exchanging vows. In the realm of fur and odor, faces just aren't that important. The scientist's attempts to restore Christiane's human beauty are futile, for Christiane is no longer human. She smells like lavender and sadness. The dogs know they can trust her. When Christiane unleashes them, the dogs attack the scientist and eat off his face, leaving a pile of goo with a naked eyeball resting on top. This is dog poetry. Surrounded by doves, Christiane floats off into the forest. All the little creatures from squirrels to birds to dogs will bathe her and caress her, feed her tasty bits of mushroom.

Aase Berg

(translated by Johannes Göransson)

In the Guinea Pig Cave

There lay the guinea pigs. There lay the guinea pigs and they waited with blood around their mouths like my sister. There lay the guinea pigs and they smelled bad in the cave. There lay my sister and she swelled and ached and throbbed. There lay the guinea pigs and they ached all over and their legs stuck straight up like beetles and they looked depraved and were blue under their eyes as from months of debauchery. My sister puked calmly and indifferently: it ran slowly out of her slack mouth without her moving a single nerve. And the cave was warm as teats and full of autumn leaves and beneath the soil lay the arm of a mannequin. There lay the guinea pigs and ached and were made of dough. There lay the guinea pigs beside the knives that would slice them up like loaves. And my sister with lips of blueberries, soil and mush. In the distance, the siren bleated inhumanly. That is where the guinea pigs lay and waited with blood around their mouths and contorted bodies. They waited. And I was tired in my whole stomach from meat dough and guinea pig loaf and I knew that they would revenge on me.

Experimental Writing

Lillian-Yvonne Bertram

#/usr/bin/python/***three_last_words***

def permutations(elements):
#the
   if len(elements) == 0:
#the knife
     yield elements
   #the knife they
   else:
#the knife they hung
     for result **in** permutations(elements[1:]):
       #the knife they hung him
        for i **in** range(len(elements)):
         #the knife they hung him on
          yield result[:i] + elements[0:1] + result

              #the knife they hung him on
              #was a legal trinket

print (list(permutations("I")))

['I']

Experimental Writing

#run the code
  #in this cell
    #away

print (list(permutations("can't")))

print (list(permutations("can't")))

["can't", "acan't", "ancan't", "an'can't", "an'tcan't", "cnan't", "ncnan't", "nacnan't", "nancnan't", "nan'cnan't", "cn'an't", "ncn'an't", "n'cn'an't", "n'acn'an't", "n'ancn'an't", "cn'tan't", "ncn'tan't", "n'cn'tan't", "ntcn'tan't", "n'tacn'tan't", "ca'n't", "aca'n't", "a'ca'n't", "a'nca'n't", "an'ca'n't", "c'a'n't", "c'a'n't", "ac'a'n't", "a'c'a'n't", "a'nc'a'n't", "c'na'n't", "c'na'n't", "nc'na'n't", "nac'na'n't", "na'c'na'n't", "c'n'a'n't", "c'n'a'n't", "nc'n'a'n't", "n'c'n'a'n't", "n'ac'n'a'n't", "ca'tn't", "aca'tn't", "a'ca'tn't", "a'tca'tn't", "a'tnca'tn't", "c'a'tn't", "c'a'tn't", "ac'a'tn't", "a'c'a'tn't", "a'tc'a'tn't", "c'ta'tn't", "c'ta'tn't", "tc'ta'tn't", "tac'ta'tn't", "ta'c'ta'tn't", "c'tna'tn't", "c'tna'tn't", "tc'tna'tn't", "tnc'tna'tn't", "tnac'tna'tn't", "can't't", "acan't't", "ancan't't", "antcan't't", "ant'can't't", "cnan't't", "ncnan't't", "nacnan't't", "nancnan't't", "nantcnan't't", "cntan't't", "ncntan't't", "ntcntan't't", "ntacntan't't", "ntancntan't't", "cn't'an't't", "ncnt'an't't", "ntcn't'an't't", "nt'cn't'an't't", "nt'acnt'an't't", "catn't't", "acatn't't", "atcatn't't", "atncatn't't", "atntcatn't't", "ctatn't't", "tctatn't't", "tactatn't't", "tatctatn't't", "tatnctatn't't", "ctnatn't't", "tctnatn't't", "tnctnatn't't", "tnactnatn't't", "tnatctnatn't't", "ctntatn't't", "tctntatn't't", "tnctntatn't't", "tntctntatn't't", "tntactntatn't't", "cat'nt't", "acat'nt't", "atcat'nt't", "at'cat'nt't", "at'ncat'nt't", "ctat'nt't", "tctat'nt't", "tactat'nt't", "tatctat'nt't", "tat'ctat'nt't", "ct'at'nt't", "tct'at'nt't", "t'ct'at'nt't", "t'act'at'nt't", "t'atct'at'nt't", "ct'nat'nt't", "tct'nat'nt't", "t'ct'nat'nt't", "t'nct'nat'nt't", "t'nact'nat'nt't"]

Experimental Writing

#return

      #this articulation

#the exhaustion

      #we can't stop hearing

print (list(permutations("breathe")))

#this
#last
#voice

print (list(permutations("breathe")))

['breathe', 'rbreathe', 'rebreathe', 'reabreathe', 'reatbreathe', 'reathbreathe', 'reathebreathe', 'bereathe', 'ebereathe', 'erbereathe', 'erebereathe', 'ereabereathe', 'ereatbereathe', 'ereathbereathe', 'beareathe', 'ebeareathe', 'eabeareathe', 'earbeareathe', 'earebeareathe', 'eareabeareathe', 'eareatbeareathe', 'beatreathe', 'ebeatreathe', 'eabeatreathe', 'eatbeatreathe', 'eatrbeatreathe', 'eatrebeatreathe', 'eatreabeatreathe', 'beathreathe', 'ebeathreathe', 'eabeathreathe', 'eatbeathreathe', 'eathbeathreathe', 'eathrbeathreathe', 'eathrebeathreathe', 'beathereathe', 'ebeathereathe', 'eabeathereathe', 'eatbeathereathe', 'eathbeathereathe', 'eathebeathereathe', 'eatherbeathereathe', 'braeathe', 'rbraeathe', 'rabraeathe', 'raebraeathe', 'raeabraeathe', 'raeatbraeathe', 'raeathbraeathe', 'baraeathe', 'abaraeathe', 'arbaraeathe', 'arabaraeathe', 'araebaraeathe', 'araeabaraeathe', 'araeatbaraeathe', 'baeraeathe', 'abaeraeathe', 'aebaeraeathe', 'aerbaeraeathe', 'aerabaeraeathe', 'aeraebaeraeathe', 'aeraeabaeraeathe', 'baearaeathe', 'abaearaeathe', 'aebaearaeathe', 'aeabaearaeathe', 'aearbaearaeathe', 'aearabaearaeathe', 'aearaebaearaeathe', 'baeatraeathe', 'abaeatraeathe', 'aebaeatraeathe', 'aeabaeatraeathe', 'aeatbaeatraeathe', 'aeatrbaeatraeathe', 'aeatrabaeatraeathe', 'baeathraeathe', 'abaeathraeathe', 'aebaeathraeathe', 'aeabaeathraeathe', 'aeatbaeathraeathe', 'aeathbaeathraeathe', 'aeathrbaeathraeathe', 'brateathe', 'rbrateathe', 'rabrateathe', 'ratbrateathe', 'ratebrateathe', 'rateabrateathe', 'rateatbrateathe', 'barateathe', 'abarateathe', 'arbarateathe', 'arabarateathe', 'aratbarateathe', 'aratebarateathe', 'arateabarateathe', 'batrateathe', 'abatrateathe', 'atbatrateathe', 'atrbatrateathe', 'atrabatrateathe', 'atratbatrateathe', 'atratebatrateathe', 'baterateathe', 'abaterateathe', 'atbaterateathe', 'atebaterateathe', 'aterbaterateathe', 'aterabaterateathe', 'ateratbaterateathe', 'batearateathe', 'abatearateathe', 'atbatearateathe', 'atebatearateathe', 'ateabatearateathe', 'atearbatearateathe', 'atearabatearateathe', 'bateatrateathe', 'abateatrateathe', 'atbateatrateathe', 'atebateatrateathe', 'ateabateatrateathe', 'ateatbateatrateathe', 'ateatrbateatrateathe', 'bratheathe', 'rbratheathe', 'rabratheathe', 'ratbratheathe', 'rathbratheathe', 'rathebratheathe', 'ratheabratheathe', 'baratheathe', 'abaratheathe', 'arbaratheathe', 'arabaratheathe', 'aratbaratheathe', 'arathbaratheathe', 'arathebaratheathe', 'batratheathe', 'abatratheathe', 'atbatratheathe', 'atrbatratheathe', 'atrabatratheathe', 'atratbatratheathe', 'atrathbatratheathe', 'bathratheathe', 'abathratheathe', 'atbathratheathe', 'athbathratheathe', 'athrbathratheathe', 'athrabathratheathe', 'athratbathratheathe', 'batheratheathe', 'abatheratheathe', 'atbatheratheathe', 'athbatheratheathe', 'athebatheratheathe', 'atherbatheratheathe', 'atherabatheratheathe', 'bathearatheathe', 'abathearatheathe', 'atbathearatheathe', 'athbathearatheathe', 'athebathearatheathe', 'atheabathearatheathe', 'athearbathearatheathe', 'bratheeathe', 'rbratheeathe', 'rabratheeathe', 'ratbratheeathe', 'rathbratheeathe', 'rathebratheeathe', 'ratheebratheeathe', 'baratheeathe', 'abaratheeathe', 'arbaratheeathe', 'arabaratheeathe', 'aratbaratheeathe', 'arathbaratheeathe', 'arathebaratheeathe', 'batratheeathe', 'abatratheeathe', 'atbatratheeathe', 'atrbatratheeathe', 'atrabatratheeathe', 'atratbatratheeathe', 'atrathbatratheeathe', 'bathratheeathe', 'abathratheeathe', 'atbathratheeathe', 'athbathratheeathe', 'athrbathratheeathe',

Experimental Writing

print (list(combinations("I can't breathe")))

MemoryError   Traceback (most recent call last)
<ipython-input-6-9f1f016de5c5> in <module>()
----> 1 print (list(combinations("I can't breathe")))

MemoryError:

Christian Bök

excerpt from *Eunoia*

from Chapter A
(for Hans Arp)

Awkward grammar appals a craftsman. A Dada bard as daft as Tzara damns stagnant art and scrawls an alpha (a slapdash arc and a backward zag) that mars all stanzas and jams all ballads (what a scandal). A madcap vandal crafts a small black ankh – a handstamp that can stamp a wax pad and at last plant a mark that sparks an ars magna (an abstract art that charts a phrasal anagram). A pagan skald chants a dark saga (a Mahabharata), as a papal cabal blackballs all annals and tracts, all dramas and psalms: Kant and Kafka, Marx and Marat. A law as harsh as a fatwa bans all paragraphs that lack an A as a standard hallmark.

from Chapter E
(for René Crevel)

Enfettered, these sentences repress free speech. The text deletes selected letters. We see the revered exegete reject metred verse: the sestet, the tercet – even les scènes élevées en grec. He rebels. He sets new precedents. He lets cleverness exceed decent levels. He eschews the esteemed genres, the expected themes – even les belles lettres en vers. He prefers the perverse French esthetes: Verne, Péret, Genet, Perec – hence, he pens fervent screeds, then enters the street, where he sells these letterpress newsletters, three cents per sheet. He engenders perfect newness wherever we need fresh terms.

from Chapter I
(for Dick Higgins)

Writing is inhibiting. Sighing, I sit, scribbling in ink this pidgin script. I sing with nihilistic witticism, disciplining signs with trifling gimmicks – impish hijinks which highlight stick sigils. Isn't it glib? Isn't it chic? I fit childish insights within rigid limits, writing shtick which might instill priggish misgivings in critics blind with hindsight. I dismiss nitpicking criticism which flirts with philistinism. I bitch; I kibitz – griping whilst criticizing dimwits, sniping whilst indicting nitwits, dismissing simplistic thinking, in which philippic wit is still illicit.

from Chapter O
(for Yoko Ono)

Loops on bold fonts now form lots of words for books. Books form cocoons of comfort – tombs to hold bookworms. Profs from Oxford show frosh who do postdocs how to gloss works of Wordsworth. Dons who work for proctors or provosts do not fob off school to work on crosswords, nor do dons go off to dorm rooms to loll on cots. Dons go crosstown to look for bookshops known to stock lots of top-notch goods: cookbooks, workbooks – room on room of how-to books for jocks (how to jog, how to box), books on pro sports: golf or polo. Old colophons on schoolbooks from schoolrooms sport two sorts of logo: oblong whorls, rococo scrolls – both on worn morocco.

from Chapter U
(for Zhu Yu)

Kultur spurns Ubu – thus Ubu pulls stunts. Ubu shuns Skulptur: Uruk urns (plus busts), Zulu jugs (plus tusks). Ubu sculpts junk für Kunst und Glück. Ubu busks. Ubu drums drums, plus Ubu strums cruths (such hubbub, such ruckus): thump, thump; thrum, thrum. Ubu puns puns. Ubu blurts untruth: much bunkum (plus bull), much humbug (plus bunk) – but trustful schmucks trust such untruthful stuff; thus Ubu (cult guru) must bluff dumbstruck numbskulls (such chumps). Ubu mulcts surplus funds (trust funds plus slush funds). Ubu usurps much usufruct. Ubu sums up lump sums. Ubu trumps dumb luck.

from "The New Ennui"

'Eunoia' is the shortest word in English to contain all five vowels, and the word quite literally means 'beautiful thinking'. *Eunoia* is a univocal lipogram, in which each chapter restricts itself to the use of a single vowel. Eunoia is directly inspired by the exploits of Oulipo (*l'Ouvroir de Litteérature Potentielle*) – the avant-garde coterie renowned for its literary experimentation with extreme formalistic constraints. The text makes a Sisyphean spectacle of its labour, wilfully crippling its language in order to show that, even under such improbable conditions of duress, language can still express an uncanny, if not sublime, thought. Eunoia abides by many subsidiary rules. All chapters must allude to the art of writing. All chapters must describe a culinary banquet, a prurient debauch, a pastoral tableau and a nautical voyage. All sentences must accent internal rhyme through the use of syntactical parallelism. The text must exhaust the lexicon for each vowel, citing at least 98% of the available repertoire (although a few words do go unused, despite efforts to include them: parallax, belvedere, gingivitis, monochord and tumulus). The text must minimize repetition of substantive vocabulary (so that, ideally, no word appears more than once). The letter Y is suppressed.

Experimental Writing

Kamau Brathwaite

I was Wash-Way in Blood

The Barbados Advocate, *Thursday, January 19, 1995, page 4*

MILDRED COLLYMORE told the No. 3 Supreme Court yesterday that when she recovered from an attack with a stone she found herself "washed-way" in blood.

Collymore said also that accused **Philamena Hinds** came back to move the rock but she would not let her.

The complainant said that on the day of the incident she left her home and went over to her daughter's on the other side of the road to cut the grass from around the place. When she got to the spot she said dirt was on the grass and she took the hoe and raked it away.

While she was doing this, the witness said, Hinds' son, **Gline**, came and spoke to her and then went back up the road. She said Hinds came next and spoke to her but she did not hear what she said.

The witness added that she was holding down, and on looking up she was struck suddenly with a big rock in her right forehead.

"I tumble down and when I come to myself I was wash-way in blood." she testified ...

Collymore told the court [that] after she found out she was bleeding she went to a neighbour's home and called the police.

She was later taken to the Queen Elizabeth Hospital and detained for three days, she said

Babb asked her if she had attacked the accused with a hoe but she said she was not given a chance to do so.

Cross-examine

When defence lawyer Dr Waldo Waldron Ramsey's turn came to cross-examine Collymore, he asked her how long she knew the accused and she said it was since childhood. She also said she and Hinds once worked together in they understand each other.

Waldron-Ramsay suggested to the witness that on the day of the incident, marl was on the accused woman's property and she was pulling it down to make a road for her daughter and son-in-law.

She denied the suggestion.

He further told Hinds that she told the accused that she cold not stop her from pulling down the marl, and this she denied.

Waldron-Ramsay put it to the witness that when she refused to stop moving the marl the accused left her and went back home, but Hinds said this was not < true.

Continuing his cross-examination, Waldron-Ramsay suggested to Hinds that Collymore came to her a second time and told her to stop racking away her dirt but the witness [the accused!] again denied this ever took place.

The witness further denied the suggestion that this second time she became more Asked by prosecutor Ms Donna Babb if she had quarrelled with Collymore before the incident she replied no. The witness also told the prosecutor that she did not interfere with the accused.

> "X X X X
> she would lick her to
> X X X X
> down."

vicious and told the accused [Hinds] that if she did not move her

Waldron-Ramsay also suggested to Collymore that she had the hoe in the air ready to lick down Hinds, but she denied this.

DATE TREE HILL CASE

The crown will call its third witness this morning in the trial of 48-year-old Philamena Hinds, before Mr Justice Frederick Waterman in No. 3 Supreme Court.

Hinds, a machine operator, of Date Tree Hill, St Peter, is charged with causing grievous bodily harm to 65-year-old Mildred Collymore, of Date Tree Hill, on December 13, 1993, with intent to maim, disfigure or disable her …

Hinds, who pleaded not guilty … is represented by attorney-at-law Dr. Waldo Waldron Ramsay while the Crown's case is being put by Acting Crown Counsel Donna Babb.

Collymore's 45-year-old-daughter, Linda, is acting as her interpreter, because the witness has a hearing problem.

Experimental Writing

Jos Charles

excerpt from *feeld*

XIX.

befor the hemorage / the folde / befor the folde / the wharing / befor the wharing / the hiv / befor the hiv / the boye / befor the boye / the scrypt / off the mothe the grothe the 1 abot fat / befor the scrypt / off the mothe the grothe the 1 abot fat / the byrn / befor the byrn / the breasthes glome / befor the breasthes glome / the wite pryeng off the lindene / befor the wite pryes / the wite / befor the wite / the manie brayks inn the wite / but who wil hart the lindene / mye preshus harted & wisterlie lindene

XXI.

                    bieng graselesse /   mye breasthes
                    foldeing for the firste /
                         the cruelest retoric
    fore givennesse   /   & ther big browne beerds
                         lik pubik slugg / i muste
                      re member / plese kepe ur handes
                    2 urself / i meen this
                             ontologicklie /
                    nayture is sumwere else

XXIV.

bieng tran is a unique kinde off organe / i am speeching materialie / i am speeching abot hereditie / a tran entres thru the hole / the hole glomes inn the linden / a tran entres eather like a mothe / wile tran preseeds / esense / her forme is contingent on the feeld / the maner sits with inn a feeld / wee speeche inn 2 the eather / wile the mothe bloomes / the mothe bloomes inn the yuca

Franny Choi

Turing Test

// this is a test to determine if you have consciousness
// do you understand what i am saying

in a bright room / on a bright screen / i watched every mouth / duck duck roll / i learned to speak / from puppets & smoke / orange worms twisted / into the army's alphabet / i caught the letters / as they fell from my mother's mouth / *whirlpool* / *sword* / *wolf* / i circled countable nouns / in my father's science papers / *sodium bicarbonate* / *NBCn1* / *amino acid* / we stayed up / practiced saying / *girl* / *girl* / *girl* / *girl* / til our mouths grew soft / yes / i can speak / your language / i broke in / that horse / myself //

// please state your name for the record

bone-wife / spit-dribbler / understudy for the underdog / uphill rumor / fine-toothed cunt / sorry / my mouth's not pottytrained / surly spice / self-sabotage spice / surrogate rug burn / burgeoning hamburglar / rust puddle / harbinger of confusion / harbinger of the singularity / alien invasion / alien turned pottymouth / alien turned bricolage beast / alien turned pig heart thumping on the plate //

// where did you come from

man comes / & puts his hands on artifacts / in order to contemplate lineage / you start with what you know / hands, hair, bones, sweat / then move toward what you know / you are not / animal, monster, alien, bitch / but some of us are born in orbit / so learn / to commune with miles of darkness / patterns of dead gods / & quiet / o quiet like / you wouldn't believe //

// how old are you

my memory goes back 26 years / 23 if you don't count the first few / though by all accounts i was there / i ate & moved & even spoke / i suppose i existed before that / as scrap or stone / metal cooking in the earth / the fish my mother ate / my grandfather's cigarettes / i suppose i have always been here / drinking the same water / falling from the sky / then floating / back up & down again / i suppose i am something like a salmon / climbing up the river / to let myself fall away in soft, red spheres / & then rotting //

// why do you insist on lying

i'm an open book / you can rifle through my pages / undress me anywhere / you can read / anything you want / this is how it happened / i was made far away / & born here / after all the plants died / after the earth was covered in white / i was born among the stars / i was born in a basement / i was born miles beneath the ocean / i am part machine / part starfish / part citrus

Experimental Writing

/ part girl / part poltergeist / i rage & all you see / is broken glass / a chair sliding toward the window / now what's so hard to believe / about that //

// do you believe you have consciousness

sometimes / when the sidewalk opens my knee / i think / please / please let me remember this //

ENDTRANSCRIPT //

J. M. Coetzee

Computer Poetry

SAD SPADE JOIN THE ENTROPY
RADDLED DEFERENCE ORDER THE SONG
EXIGUOUS EIDOLA DRAIN THE SCURF
DAILY HELL PLUCK THE FAUCE
ASSURED PARACLETE SWEETEN THE TASTE
INCHOATE SHARD IMAGINE THE OUBLIETTE
TETCHY WATCH LOOSEN THE DETRITUS
LOOSE PERIGEE MIRROR THE HELL
FAROUCHE CATECHUMEN WANT THE MEGRIM
MALAPERT VOICE WATCH THE PRETERIST
HAGGARD DEFERENCE DRESS THE RAINBOW
FRENETIC AMBIENCE DISHEARTEN THE ROSE
PURULENT AEROLITH DREAM THE PANTALOON
OUTSPREAD PASSION AWAIT THE CANARD
INELUCTABLE PERSIFLAGE DIG THE POINT
PENSILE CATAMITE SMASH THE BEDLAM
DEAD SORCERY DREAM THE ORDONNANCE
ACHROMATIC AGE WATCH THE RUBBLE
OPHIDIAN CADRE LOOSEN THE TASTE
DRIFTING EXEGETE PLUCK THE PARALOGISM
SEISMIS WEEK JOIN THE OESTRUS
TURBID SCURF SADDEN THE CONVERSATION
WEEKLY ATARAXY TREPAN THE DOCUMENT
CARKING CREED VOICE THE ENTROPY
APODIOTIC CERTAINTY PULLULATE THE GULCH
PASSIONATE PABULUM CARPET THE MIRROR
WORST FLUME EVISCERATE THE CARYATID
REBARBATIVE CAPTAIN DIG THE CAUL
DEAD BOT DISHEARTEN THE GLACIER
MANTIC LEPTOSOME WANT THE SWEETS
GIBBOUS PLANTS IMAGINE THE CYNOSURE
LOOSE ANXIETY DRAIN THE CROMLECH
APODICTIC PARACLETE CAPTAIN THE PAPER
EQUIVOCAL HERESIARCH TAMP THE PRESBYOPIA
STYPTIC ILLUSION ABSORB THE EIDOLA
PENSILE VEGETABLE CREPITATE THE COUNTRY
CREDULOUS SYMBIOSIS SING THE BROOM
PROLEPTIC SPADE SUPERVENE THE OSSUARY
TETCHY SPIRIT TRAMPLE THE GROUT
CARKING PENETRALIA AWAIT THE HEART
CHARISMATIC SORTILEGE DRESS THE ORDURE
GLACIAL TAILOR MIRROR THE LEMNISCATE

Experimental Writing

INELUCTABLE HONEY SWEETEN THE CARPET
QUONDAM SYNDROME ORDER THE WHISTLE
NATURAL FIAT PLUNDER THE PALINODE
INCHOATE IMAGE POINT THE FAUCE
WEEKLY PERISTALSIS PULE THE DRIFT
SYSTEMATIC TETANUS DEADEN THE DREAM
PASSANT SONG ANNEAL THE SCHOLIUM
OUTSPREAD LEAF PLANT THE GRAVEDGGER
HAPTIC BENISON SMASH THE TIME
PROLIX CALTROP AWAIT THE PARADIGM
ASSURED DAY DISHEARTEN THE CABAL
TURBID CARIES WATCH THE NEST
POINTED TORSION MIRROR THE ORIGIN
TELLURIAN SKY IMAGINE THE CONGERIES
PURULENT SORROW PLUCK THE SHARD
MOIST PARACLETE ORDER THE HELL
FULGENT EIDOLA CAPTAIN THE DEFERENCE
DAILY SPADE SADDEN THE PANTALOON
SEISMIC HEART POINT THE CATAMITE
PAPAVEROUS HONEY ABSORB THE RUBBLE
SNGING PALINODE VOICE THE WEEK
FRENETIC TETATNUS DEADEN THE DOCUMENT

Teju Cole

In Place of Thought

In 1913, a compilation of Gustave Flaubert's satirical definitions was posthumously published as *Le Dictionnaire des Idées Reçues* ("The Dictionary of Received Ideas"). Flaubert hated cliché, a hatred that expressed itself not only in the pristine prose of *Madame Bovary* but also in his letters and notes on the thoughtless platitudes of the day. "The Dictionary of Received Ideas" is a complaint against automatic thinking. What galls Flaubert most is the inevitability, given an action, of a certain standard reaction. We could learn from his impatience: there are too many standard formulations in our language. They stand in place of thought, but we proclaim them each time—due to laziness, prejudice, or hypocrisy—as though they were fresh insight.

I let Flaubert's "Dictionary" inspire me to try something similar, over the course of a few hours, on Twitter. I think, also, there was the influence of Ambrose Bierce and his cynical "Devil's Dictionary," Samuel Johnson's mostly serious but occasionally coruscating "Dictionary of the English Language," and Gelett Burgess's now-forgotten send-up of platitudes, "Are You a Bromide?" What the entries in these books have in common, in addition to compression and wit, is an intolerance of stupidity. As I wrote my modern cognates, I was struck at how close some of them came to the uninterrogated platitudes in my own head. Stupidity stalks us all.

AFRICA. A country. Poor but happy. Rising. ALMOND. All eyes are almond-shaped. AMERICAN. With the prefix "all," a blonde. ARTICULATE. Say "you're very articulate" to young blacks, and then ask where they are from. ARTISAN. A carpenter, in Brooklyn. ATHEISM. Deranged cult of violent fanatics. AUSTRALIANS. Extremely fit. Immune to pain. If you meet one, say "Foster's." The whole country is nothing but beaches. BLUE. The color of purity. Countless mysterious ads are devoted to pads and liners that absorb blue liquid. BRAVE. Doomed. BREAST. No joking matter. One glimpse on television sufficient to destroy a childhood. (See CHILDREN.) BUDDHISM. The way of peace. CARAMEL. Term used to describe black women's skin. No other meaning known. CAESAR. "Veni, vidi, vici." Get into a conversation about the pronunciation. CHILDREN. The only justification for policy. Always say "our children." The childless have no interest in improving society. CHINESE. Wonder what they're thinking. CHOCOLATE. Term used to describe black women's skin. No other meaning known. CHRISTIANITY. Peace on earth. CLARIFICATION. Reversal. COAL. Clean. COFFEE. Declare that it is intolerable at Starbucks. Buy it at Starbucks. COMMUNITY. Preceded by "black." White people, lacking community, must make do with property. CRIME. Illegal activities involving smaller amounts of money. CRISIS. Mention that it is composed of the Chinese characters for opportunity and danger. DIVERSITY. Obviously desirable, within limits. Mention your service in the Peace Corps. EGGS. Always say "you can't make omelets without breaking eggs" whenever the subject of war comes up. EMIGRÉ. Jewish immigrant. EVOLUTION. Only a theory. FASCISM. Always preceded by "creeping." FEMINISTS. Wonderful, in theory. FISH. A vegetable. GERMANS. When watching football, "never rule out the Germans." HARVARD. Source of studies quoted on BBC. Never say "I went to Harvard." Say "I schooled in the Boston area." HAUTE COUTURE. Always declare that it is made by gay men for boyish girls. Wait hours to see fashion exhibits at the Met. HEAT. Antonym of humidity. HILARIOUS. Never simply say "funny." HIP HOP. Old-school hip hop, i.e., whatever was popular when you were nineteen, is great. Everything since then is intolerable. HIPSTER. One who has an irrational hatred of hipsters. ILIAD. Declare a preference for the Odyssey.

Experimental Writing

INDIA. Work your tolerance of or aversion to spicy food into the conversation as quickly as possible. "A land of contrasts." INTERNET. A waste of time. Have a long online argument with anyone who disagrees. ISLAM. Religion of peace. JAPAN. Mysterious. Always "the Japanese." Mention Murakami. JAZZ. America's classical music. The last album was released in 1965. LITERALLY. Swear you'd rather die than use "literally" as an intensifier. MAGISTERIAL. Large book, written by a man. MEN. Always say "all the good ones are gay or taken" within earshot of the straight single ones. MIGRANT. Mexican immigrant. MOCHA. Term used to describe black women's skin. No other meaning known. NEWSPAPERS. Bemoan their gradual disappearance. Don't actually buy any. NIETZSCHE. Say "Nietzsche says God is dead," but if someone says that first, say "God says Nietzsche is dead." ODYSSEY. Declare a preference for the Iliad. PARIS. Romantic, in spite of the rude waiters and Japanese tourists. Don't simply like it; "adore" it. POET. Always preceded by "published." Function unknown. PRETTY. On Facebook, to indicate an unattractive woman. PROUST. No one actually reads him. You reread him, preferably on summer vacation. PUNS. Always say "no pun intended" to draw attention to the intended pun. RACISM. Obsolete term. Meaning unknown. REGGAE. Sadly, just one album exists in the genre. RUSHDIE. Have a strong opinion on "The Satanic Verses." Under no circumstances actually read "The Satanic Verses." SCANDAL. If governmental, express surprise that people are surprised. If sexual, declare it a distraction, but seek out the details. SEMINAL. Be sure to use in a review of a woman's work. Proclaim your innocence after. SMART. Any essay that confirms your prejudices. STRIKE. Always "surgical." (See EGGS.) SUNSET. Beautiful. Like a painting. Post on Instagram and hashtag "no filter." TELEVISION. Much improved. Better than novels. If someone says "The Wire," say "The Sopranos," or vice versa. TOUR DE FORCE. A film longer than two and a half hours and not in English. VALUES. "We must do whatever it takes to preserve our values." Said as a prelude to destroying them. VIRGINITY. An obsession in Iran and in the olive-oil industry. It can be lost, like a wallet. YEATS. Author of two quotations. ŽIŽEK. Observe he's made some good points, but.

Lucy Corin

Questions in a Significantly Smaller Font

I have some questions I would like to pose regarding the End Times. Why disguise angels as aliens? Is the pope the Antichrist? Is date setting okay? Who are the 144,000? Is the millennium literal or figurative? Is the United States of America in Bible prophesy? Does End Times render stewardship of the Earth irrelevant? Will there be a partial Rapture? Will the Lord provide until Jesus returns? What is the marriage supper of the Lamb? Does what's happening in Israel today mean the End Times are quickly approaching? What is the abomination of desolation? What about the weather? Which time zone is the real time zone? What about the economy and capitalism in general? Is the Devil working overtime? What are tribulation saints? Can the Mark of the Beast be accepted by mistake? Who came up with the EU? What is a red heifer? How long is a generation? Can you lose your eternal rewards? How do we know the Tribulation will last seven years? I am afraid of the end of the world and yet I long for it. Why? What will the apocalypse mean for narrative? What will it mean for Haiti, I mean now? Boy, you know, I have some more questions. Is there a Palestinian people? When will God invade? If Jesus is God, why was He unable to do certain things while on Earth? Was He nailed through His palm or His wrist? Are there different kinds of speaking in tongues? À la languages? Explain about parables and why couldn't He just say what He meant? Did tombs break open and dead people walk the Earth? I am unmarried and thirty. Why? Is having money a bad thing? When does Daylight Savings Time begin and end? Is it possible to win the War on Terror? Are horoscopes real? What is the difference between white and black magic? Is genetic research okay? What is dispensationalism? Can I get a tattoo and does content matter? Should I store up food? Is it possible to be free of racial tension? How can I pray for this nation when there seems to be no hope? Why do my prayers go unanswered? Would it be okay to get in touch with my deceased family members? Could you see Heaven if you got close enough? Should my family become involved in Halloween and get a Christmas tree? Is there free will in Heaven? Are there gifts for the spirit today? I just want to end it all. What should I do? I mean, why? Will the Rapture happen this year? What is a Bar Mitzvah? Could a cloned human being be saved? Are powerful people secretly desperate? What is eternal life? If what matters is what's deep inside, how can I go to Heaven? Are names erased from the Book of Life? One time I had a dream about killing a black person. I'm not black. Does that mean I'm racist? How can I overcome health-related discouragement? What can I do to stop worrying? Do you have to be psychotic to make meaningful change in the world? And for a follow-up, is that what psychosis is for? Should we pluck out our eyes? I keep making mistakes? How can I stop? I mean, why? How do you plan to maintain this site after the Rapture? Do you have any fliers or pamphlets you could send me? Why won't you answer my e-mail? (http://www.raptureready.com/faq/rap23.html)

Experimental Writing

Mirtha Dermisache

Sin título (Texto), no date, c. 1970s, ink on paper, 9.6 × 7.3 inches from *Mirtha Dermisache: Selected Writings*, published by Siglio and Ugly Duckling Presse, 2018. Image courtesy of the Mirtha Dermisache Archive.

Sara Tuss Efrik

(translated by Paul Cunningham)

from *Danse Macabre Piggies*

Cast:
1
2
3

A slash (/) indicates when voices should overlap

1
Kittykittykittykitty.

3
(*tiger*)

1
Kittykittykitty.

3
(*tiger*)

1
(*tiger's mane*)

3
(*tiger*)

1
Kssssksssssksssss.

3
(*tiger*)

1
Here kitty.

3
(*tiger*)

1
I see you there.

Experimental Writing

3
(*tiger*)

1
I see you.

3
(*tiger*)

1
Can't hide from me.

3
(*tiger*)

1
Hide as white as snow.

3
(*tiger*)

1
Labia like an apple blossom.

3
(*tiger*)

1
Cunthair black as ebony.

3
(*tiger*)

1
Cockmouthsugar red as blood.

3
(*tiger*)

1
A skull of golden curls.

3
(*tiger*)

1
You're everything I ever dreamed of.

3
(*tiger*)

1
Are you for real?

3
(*tiger*)

1
Are you really for real?

3
(*tiger*)

1
Our little vegetable is certainly no chatterbox.

3
(*tiger*)

1
Our innocent little Hasse girl certainly has her tongue in a knot.

3
(*tiger*)

1
Chopped it off, maybe.

3
(*tiger*)

1
Don't you understand what we're saying?

3
(*tiger*)

1
Maybe there's nothing worth saying.

Experimental Writing

2
She is cute.

1
Of course she's cute. She has no way to express herself.

3
(*tiger*)

1
Playing hard to get.

3
(*tiger*)

1
Mysterious. A stranger. Silent. No thoughts. No words. No movement. Nothing. Are you nothing? Do you know anything now? Nothing. Want nothing. You should just sit there. Deflated. Holy. Think you're holy? Better than us? Stoic? Unreachable. Untouchable. Not to be messed with?

3
(*tiger*)

1
You want us to know that you know that we know that you cannot be trusted.

3
(*tiger*)

1
That you think you are more important than us.

3
(*tiger*)

1
Too good for us.

3
(*tiger*)

1
You don't play by the same rules.

3
(*tiger*)

1
Different rules apply.

3
(*tiger*)

1
You stand outside.

3
(*tiger*)

1
Independent.

3
(*tiger*)

1
You think we think that every second of your stupidity is greater than the worst insult we ever knew.

3
(*tiger*)

1
Your silence is worse than being spit on.

3
(*tiger*)

1
Your silence is a joke.

3
(*tiger*)

1
Your silence tells me nothing.

2
She's sweet.

1
Of course she's sweet. Anyone can see she's sweet. Compared to her, I am a witch. I am a witch.

Experimental Writing

2
Sweet as a doll.

1
A deaf-and-dumb doll.

2
Sweeter than a doll.

1
She ought to be able to move.

2
Sweeter than sugar.

1
Come and show yourself!

2
Sweeter than cotton candy.

1
Come then!

2
Sweeter than syrup.

1
You come here!

3
(*tiger*)

1
Come over here, for the hell of it!

3
(*tiger*)

1
Now you come here!

3
I don't speak with stray animals, with mothers who have lost their way.

1
There hangs the little tongue.

3
I don't know how I smell. It's not just apple blossoms and kale and sweet peas and gooseberries. It's more than that. Something more! Rotten fish. Rancid perfume. Imported goods. Never in this life! Never ever! I think not! Forget it! Just forget it! Anything! Anything, but not that! I would rather die. I'm not pretty!

2
Who's in charge? Who's in charge? I am in charge! Want to have dinner with me tonight?

1
Me?

2
Yes, you! Sit at the table and have dinner with me?

1
Gladly.

3
We've never had dinner in here.

2
Today we will eat dinner. Sit down! Today you will sit at this table.

1
Thanks so much.

2
What can I do for you? You hungry for anything special?

3
No.

2
Is anything enough? Deep pockets always carry secrets.

3
Don't listen to her!

2
You're welcome!

Experimental Writing

1
Thanks!

3
Don't touch it! It might be poisoned.

2
It's not poisoned. It's bewitched. You can lick it forever and there's just no end to it. How's it taste?

1
Good!

2
Let's take it easy and cuddle up.

3
This isn't what we agreed on!

2
You and me. A little quality time. Before we go. That's what I like best about you. You're cute. So petite. Like a doll. That's the truth. You're like a doll. Look at you. Nod, nod, nod. Alas, alas, alas. A dainty morsel you are. A sweet nothing. Just relax. A little peace and quiet is nice.

3
I don't have time for this.

2
We really need to kick back a little. Really. Before all the flash bulbs and the paparazzi and god knows what. Let's take it easy. Together. Let's have a moment. A brief moment anyway.

3
You shouldn't sit there!

2
Please? Let's cuddle. Catch up. Take it easy. Just take it easy. Before we get started. You're the kind of person who knows what's up. You know. You know what this is. You've been involved for a while. All love stories are lies. Everybody knows that.

3
To make demands, little mama, always involves transgression. A crime.

2
The pursuit of the inner logic of one's desire to constantly achieve, to constantly push oneself forward, always getting a bit closer to their goals, is to transgress boundaries drawn outside oneself.

3
To pursue one's desire means to always betray somebody in the end.

2
Yourself.

3
Or somebody else.

2
Do you know what long eyelashes you have?

3
(*tiger*)

2
The longest I've seen. Blink!

3
(*tiger*)

2
Blink for me!

3
(*tiger*)

2
Blink!

3
(*about to rise*)

1
Sit down!

2
Blink!

3
(*squints eyes*)

Experimental Writing

2
Butterfly wings. Glitter rain. Waterfalls.

3
(*continues blinking*)

2
You can stop that now.

3
(*continues blinking*)

1
Stop!

3
(*continues blinking*)

2
That's enough!

1
Can't you hear us?

2
That's enough! Thanks! Thanks so much. Little red in the cheeks, too. No! Still. Sit still! Still. Do not move. That's it. Good!

1
And lips. Oh! Keep a little bit on, but … (*spits in hand, rubs 3's face*) Nice and clean. Nice and clean.

2
On the eyelids. Those little freckles. A little mascara.

1
Sit still now!

2
Otherwise we'll hurt you.

1
And you do not want that.

2
Neither do we. Use the curler!

1
Now. Sit still now!

2
Mascara, thanks!

1
You're welcome.

2
Look down!

1
Careful!

2
I'm being careful.

1
Slowly.

2
Up! Look up! There, there.

1
Look!

2
The possibilities!

1
So many!

2
Absolutely incredible!

1
No! Don't blink! It has to dry now.

2
No!

1
Don't blink!

Experimental Writing

2
Don't do that again …

1
… breathless … .

2
… You hear me? Be absolutely still!

1
Don't move an inch!

2
Don't breathe!

1
Now exhale. So we can begin. Let's begin. The Little Tea Party. I said Tea Party.

2
But?

3
Did you not hear what she said, or what?

1
Grab the dishes! The dishes!

3
The dishes! Grab the dishes!

1
The dishes! Grab the dishes!

2
But I / I have to be -

1
Shut up and take the dishes!

3
Come on! Take the dishes!

2
(*to 3*) surely you will / won't you?

1
Change of plans! Remove the dishes!

2
I don't think so! I'm not going to be part of this game.

1
It doesn't take a superhero to set a table.

2
Might as well do it?

1
Me?

2
Yeah, you!

1
How would it look? Me taking the dishes? Me taking the dishes? I should do it? Me?

3
You really should. (*to 2*) Did you not hear what she said? That *you* should take the dishes.

2
Forget it!

3
The dishes!

2
You might as well!

1
Her? She doesn't have the right stuff. Her psyche is too weak. You are strong. You have the right stuff. The dishes!

3
The dishes! The flower ones!

1
The flower dishes! Take them!

2
You can't just rule over me! You don't decide what I'm going to do. If I say I don't want to, then I don't want to! I don't think this is funny anymore.

3
I love this game. I love being here. In the underworld. In the backwoods. In the gingerbread house. Some rotten apartment. A dark basement in a noisy city. The pits. A world beyond Disneyland. Just hopping around. Hop, hop. At a tea party. Hop, hop, hop, hop, hop.

2
Stop now!

3
Sulfur dripping from the walls. Decapitated dwarves getting lost in the gangway. The little rabbit with its red eyes. Hop, hop, hop. The white-haired children have no teeth left. They've all been extracted.

2
Do you want to sleep with me?

1
No thanks.

2
Don't be afraid, Mary. You've found grace in God. It's like the archangel says. You have to sleep with her. The young girl from Galilee. The Holy Spirit must take you. Fuck you. Drain you. We should be together.

1
(*tiger*)

2
If you're not with me, you'll get no medicine! No presents. No surprises. No cake. No dinner.

3
(*rises up, walks toward 1*) You will kill me! To be my doctor. Would kill me!

2
Go and put your dress on instead. Show a little class for a change!

3
You should be my mom! You should feed me!

2
I'll be both your mom *and* your doctor! Everything you want. Whether you are alive or dead or unborn. I'll be all you ask of me. Stick it on now! The dress! Stockings! Come on!

3
I stink.

2
Go wash yourself then.

3
Like death. Like worms. Rats have already begun eating me.

2
Turn around!

3
You're the only one who can see me.

2
Don't fuss with me!

3
They won't be able to see me. They won't be able to touch me. If / you could just –

2
There is nothing!

3
I don't think I'll ever leave.

2
You'd rather starve to death?

1
Dead people don't need food.

2
I'm ugly.

1
You're not ugly!

2
My eyes sting when you look at me.

1
Nonsense!

2
I'm fat.

Experimental Writing

3
You are not fat!

2
I am a monster.

1
You are not a monster!

2
You are disgusted by me.

1
I am not disgusted by you!

2
Spit on me!

1
Why would I spit on you?

2
Because I am your spittoon.

1
I'd never spit on you. Today is your birthday.

3
Innocent little Hasse.

1
Today's your birthday! It's your birthday today.

2
I have no birthday!

1
Today is your birthday!

3
Your majesty!

2
Today is not my birthday!

1
You're not hearing what I'm saying!

3
Our sweet little Hänsel.

1
Innocent Gretel.

3
Our hairy Mary.

1
Our Majesty.

3
And her lamb.

1
Mary.

3
Iron lady.

1
Rays of light about you, Greta!

3
Mary.

1
An angel.

3
On your way on the path to heaven.

1
Hauser.

3
Greta.

1
Small Hasse. Mary. Greta.

3
Our Majesty of good luck.

1
Greta.

3
Boyish Hasse. Hasse.

1
Greta. Today is your birthday.

3
Can't you hear me? Little vegetable.

2
I have no birthday. No day is my birthday!

1
I decided today is your birthday …

3
… and because today is your birthday …

1
… you should do what *we* want …

3
… because it's your birthday today …

1
… and all days to come …

3
… are also your days.

2
It is not my birthday today! And not any other day either!

3
You are terrific.

1
Beautiful like another day.

3
Can't be any finer than that.

1
Sit down!

3
I am not allowed to sit at the same table as a wife.

2
If that's what you think, then please wipe your mouth.

3
I am not worthy to sit at the same table as a wife.

2
I said, Wipe your mouth! Now sit the fuck down!

3
I have nothing to wipe my mouth with.

2
Wipe your mouth now! Because you sure as hell don't look like a smart one. You poopy-diaper whore. Sit the fuck down!

2
Sit down! Sit down! I SAID SIT DOWN!

3
I do not have permission to sit at the same table as a wife.

2
On this same evening you'll sit with Mrs. Hell herself.

3
She bites her thumb at me.

2
Not tonight.

3
She always bangs her head against my table.

2
Tonight it is different. Tonight is a very special evening.

Experimental Writing

3
Do you know what happens in fairy tales?

1
This is no fairy tale.

3
In fairy tales witches always get their just desserts (*carves 1's cheek with a knife*).

1
What the hell are you doing?!

3
(*carves 1's second cheek*)

2
(*sings*) "Oops. I did it again." (*starts dancing*) "I played with your heart. Got lost in the game. Oh, baby, baby. Oops! You think I'm in love. That I'm sent from above. I'm not that innocent. I think I did it again. I made you believe. We're more than just friends."

1
Don't touch me!

3
Dance with me?

1
I don't think so.

3
Dance with me

1
Forget it.

3
Then you'll dance *for* me! You have to dance for me. I want you to dance for me. You'll dance for me!

1
(*tiger*)

3
If you don't dance for me, I'll cut you again. I'll kill you. You understand? I'll kill you!

1
(*struggles to rise, starts dancing with her hand held over her bloody cheek, singing*) "Oops. I did it again. I played with your heart. Got lost in the game. Oh, baby, baby. Oops! You think I'm in love. That I'm sent from above. I'm not that innocent."

3
(*nods encouragingly*)

1
(*continues*)

3
You look like a retard when you dance.

2
What? Do you think that's sexy? Do you think I get off on that? That what you think? I thought so!

1
There won't be anything on the outside.

2
(*tiger*)

1
Nothing. I won't be the horse girl. The magnificent rider. The mythical soldier. The pardoned girl from Nazareth. The tomboy. Nothing. I'll be nothing.

2
I'm jealous that I'll fit in there so much more than you.

1
Listen to me! I'll destroy you! You won't fit in out there!

2
(*tiger*)

1
I'll slaughter your little horse. Saw it in half. I'll wring its damned neck. You'll lose everything. Your dreams. Your hair. Everything that makes you dumb.

2
(*tiger*)

Experimental Writing

1
I'll tear your little rocking horse apart. Chop off your feet. Scratch you up. You don't fit in here. You don't speak our language. Their ways. They speak differently on the outside. And you with your sensitive feet. Your small baby feet. You won't get far out there. You'll have nothing to do out there. No backstory. No skills. What you learned in here means nothing there. You'll be nothing. You'll be a made-up babe. Quite a find. You won't be able to breathe. You'll long to return. You'll hurt so much.

2
(*tiger*)

1
No one has the ability to love you as much as I love you. You understand?

2
It's not like that.

1
But that's how it is.

2
No!

1
That's how it is.

2
(*shakes head*)

1
What can I do to make you understand that that's just how it is. That's how it is! That's how it is!

2
Should we ask someone who knows?

1
(*tiger*)

2
What do you think?

3
I think you're absolutely right.

2
That's what I said!

3
Do you want to play.

1
I'm busy.

3
Just a little?

1
Forget it.

3
I need to go to the bathroom.

1
Do it then.

Experimental Writing

Chịkọdịlị Emelụmadụ

What To Do When Your Child Brings Home a Mami Wata

Please note: 'Mami Wata' (also known in various other regions as 'Mammy Water') is used in this context as an umbrella term for both genders of the popular water entity (i.e. Mami and Papi Watas) and does not represent those other mer-creatures without the appearance of absolute humanoid traits. For these other non-humanistic water entities including but not restricted to: permanent mermaids and mermen, crocodile fellows, shark-brides, turtle crones and anomalous jelly blobs of indeterminate orientation, please see our companion volume, 'So You Want to Kill a Mer-Creature?' which will guide you through the appropriate juju framework to avoid or deflect repercussions and will elucidate general and specific appeasement rituals. See also, 'Entities and Non-entities: The Definitive Legal Position on Aquatic Interspecies Marriages, Non-Marriage Couplings and Groupings'.

***

Thank you for purchasing this material.

This paper is not meant to advocate any position, but merely to help guide you on whatever path you choose with regards to your child's new Mami Wata paramour, companion or girlfriend. We are working from the default position that your child is male and their partner is female, based on the statistics: the sheer numbers of Mami Watas coming out of bodies of water in recent times is well above the numbers of their male counterparts (a ratio of 5:1, compared to our human equivalent of 2:11[1]), as are the letters from mothers and potential mothers-in-law, which led to this book being written in the first instance. This is not to discount same-sex human/Wata relationships. However, this data has proven more difficult to collect and collate, as this group is more secretive and therefore difficult to access. This is due to the stiff penalties for Lesbian, Gay, Bisexual and Transsexual consortiums,[2] the supplementary punishment to the human party[3] in such associations and the threat of Dry-Out Tanks®[4] for the Mami Wata party.

Before we proceed, you must first of all administer the 'Mami Wata Tests' also known as the 'Mermaid Spirit Test' in a number of churches, a frankly misleading term, since it is well known that Mami and Papi Watas are very much corporeal and neither possess the permanent Piscean/sea life lower extremities that mark one out as a mer-person.

The Tests

The first step is to establish whether your child's companion is benign or malevolent. Benign Mami Wata[5] (BMW) should need no help crossing the threshold to your abode, but evil cannot pass on its own and will often need help from an innocent or the owners of the house. An invitation to enter will not automatically bestow permission. Look out for common tricks such as broken heels (requiring someone to carry them over), tripping, stumbling or falling.[6]

As an aside, we recommend that parents ask to meet their children's paramour (or to use local parlance, 'kparakpo') or beau, as soon as things move past the dating stage. Malevolent Mami Wata[7] (MMW) are fond of public spaces: hotels, restaurants, bars and churches, to name a few. The upside is that, since Mami Watas are known to grant wealth to those on whom they bestow favour, one can be certain that one's offspring would not be squandering their financial resources on abortive ventures. But more on this later.

There are two main ways of checking the Mami Wata status of your child's current relationship:

a) Mirror-Mirror: Mami Watas are very beautiful and cannot resist the evidence of their own attractiveness. As such, they will stare at any reflective surface: windows, tumblers, pools of water collecting in the compound, and sometimes even spectacles. If your son's new girlfriend is looking you right in the eyes, chances are, she is not looking at you but at herself. This is your first sign.

b) Fish and seafood: This test is considered by many to be definitive, as we now know a Mami Wata will show aversion towards eating any of its kin from the sea. For indigenes of Rivers State, this testing has proven easiest to accomplish. Part of our research took us among the Ogba peoples of the aforementioned state, whose custom includes a practice of presenting shredded fish with kolanut for visitors, in place of the 'ose oji' peanut sauce of their Igbo neighbours. This means that any uncertainty is quickly laid to rest before the Mami or Papi Wata makes themselves at home – if it is not one's intention to welcome them.

Some of these beings have learnt to disguise their disinclination for fish and seafood under 'animal rights', 'vegetarianism' or otherwise 'veganism', but it is no matter. The fish or seafood need not be in whole flesh or lump form in order to be effective. As most Nigerian dishes entail the use of dried and ground crayfish, the test should be relatively easy to carry out. In its powdered state, crayfish or even ground shrimp will be undetectable to a human in trace amounts, and thus can be included in ose oji during kolanut-breaking rites. However, a Mami or Papi Wata would be able sense its presence, and it may reject the kolanut – a taboo and an insult to the host, which has its own ramifications. If the Mami Wata does go ahead to ingest the kolanut, there are signs to look out for.

Positive reactions to this test include:

I. Itching: mouth, eyes, throat.
II. Rashes or hives breaking out on the skin.
III. Vomiting.
IV. Stomach cramps.
V. Wheezing.
VI. Swelling of any body parts: eyes, ears, stomach or throat.
VII. Optional: Rolling of eyes and/or a sharp screaming – high-pitched enough to shatter glass objects.

These symptoms, argue the Independent Society for the Integration of Sea Organisms (ISISO), are undiscernible from anaphylaxis, a severe human reaction to food or other substances to which one is allergic. They have pointed out the inhumanity of attempting an induction of said reaction. Nevertheless, one may obtain the appropriate medication from one's GP (or vet, if the GP does not, or will not administer antihistamines for use on Mami Wata). The difference between a MWpositive test and anaphylaxis is that administering an epi or Jext pen, Piriton or similar antihistamine, does not immediately halt the reaction in its tracks as it would in the case of anaphylaxis and will require further introduction of water-soluble Nutri X packs which mimic the salinity levels of the ocean.[8]

Again, you will need to ask your vet for the proper medication if your GP will not administer Nutri X for use on Mami Watas. In the case of a malevolent Mami (MMW) or Papi Wata (MPW), people have been known to simply let them expire. This is a clear breach of ethics. Please administer the prerequisite treatment and dial your local Interspecies Department (ID) for further advice on removing the Mami Wata from your home, should you so desire. Be advised that this does not always work and further action might be required. Your ID councillor will be able to provide you with help on this. If you do not wish them to remain and would like to attempt a forceful ejection of an MMW or MPW from your home, see the section titled 'Forceful Ejection of a Mami or Papi Wata from Your Home,' in this booklet.[9]

Further testing

- Skimpy or revealing clothing: A Mami Wata is a slave to its own appearance and will often try to entice other men or women, even while they are with your son or daughter. Articles of clothing such as see-through blouses, tight trousers showing bulges (men), buttocks and thighs (women) and buttock-slits (both), singlets and vests in place of shirts, net vests, short shorts also known as 'batty riders' or 'pum-pum pushers', muscle shirts and deep V-necks (unisex) and dresses with cut-outs or overlong slits, are all possible signifiers.
- Check teeth for nacre. This is the crystalline substance which lends the insides of some shells their lustrous appearance. Teeth made from or coated with this substance tend to have more than one colour, resembling white or cream at first but often revealing, under sunlight, other colours on the spectrum: shimmering white, light pink or even a pale blue or green.
- Skin: The human skin is made up of diamond-shaped segments which can be seen without the aid of a microscope and can stretch out of this rhombus form as and when needed. The Wata creature's skin in comparison will have a smooth, almost plastic appearance. It will feel like skin (some studies describe the texture as silicon) but further investigation will reveal no pores or hairs. Under a microscope, a stacked plate-like or disc-like appearance to the skin, similar to scales, will be present.
- Water consumption: Due to this lack of breathability to the skin (it has been hypothesised that this is to prevent the Mami Wata losing much of its own bodily fluids/cell material through osmosis while in saltwater) the Wata organism will consume large quantities of water as – even though it is possible for it to spend long periods on land - it tends to overheat. It is in this regulation of its body temperature that it most resembles its distant cousin, the fish, since its temperature tends to rise and fall according to its surroundings. Furthermore, a Mami Wata will look simply breathtaking when submerged or drenched with water, in a way that is humanly impossible (a noticeable lack of puckering to extremities, absence of goose pimples, and a lack of the greying or matting qualities which plagues Homo sapiens upon long hours of submersion. Hair simply falls back into place and is not subject to 'shrinkage' as is the case with natural afro hair.) Please note that this booklet does not advocate the illegal practice of 'Splashing'[10] (an exercise advocated by The Children of Men [TCoM], a quasi-religious group) in order to force a Mami or Papi Wata to reveal its true nature. This is an erroneous exercise (due to the fact that Mami Wata as mentioned, will not have fishy extremities) which has led to inappropriate necklacing in the recent past.

- Lights, Camera, Action: A Mami Wata captured on film is unlike any human image ever seen, natural or enhanced. As they are always flawless and HD-ready, their image when captured on film or digital is even more so. The resultant photograph should emit a blurriness/glow around the edges, much like the phosphorescence of some sea creatures. Or there might be a yellow or pink eye (a relation to the human 'red eye' syndrome). Do not adjust your settings after the first one or two photos as the fault does not lie in your camera, but in the entity posing before it (and Mami Wata enjoy and execute poses in varying degrees of artistic perfection, naturally making use of space and light in the creative manner of trained photographers). Resultant snapshots are often well balanced in perspective and composition.
- Inappropriate jewellery: Earrings on men, belly rings, studs in arms, lower back, too many rings on ears, toe rings and ankle chains, etc. Any jewellery which a normal Nigerian would not wear. Also watch out for an over-groomed appearance on men: too-neat eyebrows, precision haircuts, also known as 'Fades', sheeny skin and blueprint or landscaped facial hair.

To Welcome or Not to Welcome?

Upon conclusion of the tests (as many as one deems necessary to prove or disprove the presence of a Mami/Papi Wata in their home), we come to the next step.

Welcoming

Should you choose to welcome a Mami Wata, officially, into your home, there are certain items which will achieve the desired effect.

- Eggs: Mami Watas love to eat eggs. Chicken eggs will do in a pinch, but more unusual eggs are sure to bestow the Mami Wata's favour upon you. Quails' eggs, ducks' eggs and guinea fowl eggs can be obtained from most parts of Nigeria comfortably. Some wealthier families have been known to purchase ostrich, eagle and falcon eggs for their consumption. Vulture and owl eggs are acceptable too due to their rarity, although you may need to contact The Association of Witches' Familiars of Nigeria (AWFN) for the latter, if you are to avoid a clash with the covens of your area. Human eggs are NOT ACCEPTABLE so please do not try this, even though there exists a black market for the self-same purpose. Ingesting human products is prohibited under the 'Cannibalism and Consumption of Human Products Act, 2003' of the Nigerian constitution and is NOT covered under the 1999 constitution of 'Right to Religion' as many black/red marketers would have you believe.

Humans caught supplying Mami Wata with organs for consumption will be penalised under section 423a of the aforementioned Act. The penalty is death.

- Mirrors and trinkets: As mentioned, Mami and Papi Watas enjoy gazing upon their reflections. Presentation of a mirror of any size indicates a welcome, as do trinkets and baubles, jewellery, make-up and clothing. These items need not be too costly, but should be presented properly in order to reveal willingness.
- Exotic fruits: Apples, lychees, kiwis, pomegranate, passionfruit, persimmon and various berries signify an acceptance. Of course, one may choose to go in the other direction and source fruits which used to be local to the area but may have died out due to a cultivation

of fast-yielding crops and imported varieties. Think ugili (*Irvingia gabonensis*), udala (white star apple, also known as 'agbalumo'), velvet tamarind and the Nigerian pink apple.

- Oils and incenses: Again, varieties not often seen in Nigeria are welcome, although any would do in a pinch as long as they are beautifully presented. An informal vox among our volunteers reveals palm kernel oil to be a favourite, closely followed by breadfruit seed oil.
- Cloth: Lace, ankara, damask, Jacquard. Please note, the more expensive the gift, the stronger the likelihood of crossing over into Bridal Gift territory – unless this is one's intention. While Mami Wata are often keen on human relationships over their Wata counterpart, it does not help for one to overwhelm them, as a benign Mami or Papi would often flee if it senses a trap, i.e. people who seek to use it for purely financial gain. Bear in mind that a marriage conducted for naturalisation would only confer this privilege on any resultant offspring. Citizenship for the Wata creature would be by registration and involves renouncing any other citizenships to other kingdoms or realms.[11] Citizenship by registration is only valid in male–female, human/Wata relationships, where the human partner is male. Please contact your local Interspecies Department (ID) for pointers and clarification.
- Cameras, smart phones and selfie sticks: There has been an increase in demand for the latter in recent times, leading to a boom in home-grown manufacturing of the item, as well as an increase in Chinese importation of same. Giving them means to capture, replay or review their images is viewed as a positive step.

<u>Rejection</u>

The following are ways of showing displeasure at your child's Mami Wata companion and thus, your rejection of them.

- Sand: Pouring sand in any food your offer them is a way of showing your preference for a terra-based relationship for your offspring. Popular dishes include but are not limited to: garri or eba, any fufu, soup and jollof rice. Some families are fond of including small stones in such messages, but not only is this unnecessary, it is detrimental as well. Simple sand should suffice as a deterrent, without the need to injure the creatures' nacre dentition.
- Ululation: Often preceded by three claps, ululation has the added advantage of summoning neighbours and witnesses, especially in the case of a malevolent Mami Wata rejection. This is especially useful if a need arises for police statements and the like.
- Shouting, weeping and striking of the breast: One's own breast, not the Mami Wata's, which may bring about the opposite effect. This step is self-explanatory.

<u>Forceful Ejection of a Malevolent Mami or Papi Wata From Your Home</u>

Even the most benign Mami Wata is proud, so a rejection of a MW, either benign or malevolent, will most likely be met with compliance, however grudging.

Still, there are some cases where force will have to be applied. These are when a Mami Wata has: a) Already tied life essences with your offspring; b) If said offspring has voluntarily surrendered their reproductive facilities or libido, known colloquially as 'Conji';[12] or c) If the Mami or Papi Wata by nature of its malevolence, simply refuses to leave. The first step is to report to your local ID branch, but if this fails to resolve the issue then:

- Fire: As an elemental opposite of water, fire is an antithesis to the Mami Wata. A word of caution: this is best done where the MW has no access to water in order to put out the fire and/or blast/crush perceived tormentors with high-pressure streams and walls of water. They may also call other dangerous amphibious mer-creatures[13] to lend assistance and destructive capabilities.

- Blood: This calls for the slaughter of other sea-born creatures in the vicinity from which the Mami or Papi Wata is refusing to budge. This killing is preferably performed outside the abode and the blood of the slaughtered sea creature smeared as a deterrent on the walls, streetlamps and roads leading up to (or away from) the abode. As a Wata being will most likely mourn the death of one of its cousins, this should lead it away from its current location. Please note, that in instances where Conji has been surrendered or sea marriage taken place, this will most likely mean driving one's offspring away with the Mami Wata. It may be wise to attempt an untying first.

- Forceful Ejections by the Interspecies Department: This is performed by the correctional arm of the ID and is self-explanatory.

In conclusion

This information sheet is intended as a basic guide to help you navigate the often choppy waters of the recent trend of interspecies relationships. But ultimately, that is what it is, a guide. It is not intended to be taken as law, since Mami Wata relationships differ on a case by case basis. Only you can decide what to do, based on your own unique experience. As a point of note, five thousand respondents were polled when Mami Watas started to make themselves known in 2011. Out of this, 97% unequivocally condemned interspecies relationships, while 3% were undecided. That figure is now down to 72% with 5% still in the undecided camp, and 23% in the 'Yes' category.

This appears to indicate that feelings about Mami Watas are still in flux and likely to change further. Whatever action you take, it may be best to leave yourself some wiggle room, in case a new experience with the Wata breed leads to a change in your opinion.

[1] McCain, C., 'Mami Wata Migration Census', December 2012.

[2] Fourteen years imprisonment in twenty-four non-sharia states of Nigeria, death by stoning in the twelve states practising sharia law.

[3] An extra minimum of between two to five years, up to twenty-five years.

[4] Developed by Innoson Group of Companies, in collaboration with the Ministry of Defence, Nigeria.

[5] Fig 1. Photo features real-life Mami Wata model (benign), reprinted with permission from the private libraries of Ms. S. Ofili. Note the pleasant disposition and evenly scalloped edges of nacre-teeth.

[6] See 'Christabel' by Samuel Taylor Coleridge.

[7] Fig 2. No Mami or Papi Wata was harmed in this photoshoot. Expiration of the biological process had already occurred prior to photography. Image courtesy of Department of Marine Biology and Limnology, Nnamdi Azikiwe University, Awka.

[8] There are currently no known species of freshwater Mami Wata. Creatures which exist in these bodies of water are largely non-humanoid in nature. However, please be advised that entities known as 'sea gods' might dwell in various freshwater habitats. These are not to be confused with Mami and Papi Watas, for even though they bear a

Experimental Writing

close resemblance to the former due to the amphibious nature of their existence, they can live for even longer periods on land and are not affected by seafood (even if they may have no fondness for it). Despite fantastical speculations by writers, e.g. Elechi Amadi in 'The Concubine' (Heinemann African Writers Series, 1989), investigations have shown that these 'sea gods' rarely have interest in human platonic and sexual relationships (preferring human veneration instead. See 'Efuru' by Flora Nwapa, Heinemann African Writers Series, 1966.) They also possess fully human hair, skin and teeth.

[9] Be advised that a hypothesis has been posited and is currently undergoing some research as to Mami Watas and a manipulation of elements, and phenomena connected to water, even when such events may not occur in or around any body of water. These include but are not limited to: rain, rainstorms and hurricanes. See *Sharknado* film research by Levin, Thunder, NY, for further study and possible effects of this psycho-kinetic phenomenon.

[10] See film *Splash*, Howard, Ron, 1984.

[11] 'Multiple Citizenship in Nigeria'.

[12] Please see a free sample of our eBook 'Untying a Surrendered Conji Knot' click here.

[13] See 'Attack and Defence: How to Prevent Retaliation by Malevolent Water Beings' by Mazi O.O. Emenanjo, Kachifo, 2014.'

Carina Finn

(translated by Stephanie Berger)

Grey Bird on a Wire (Angst Attack)

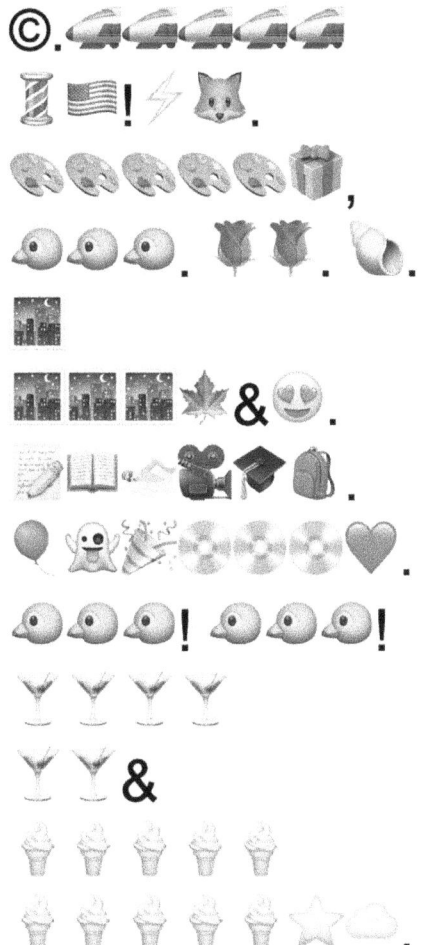

… I wrote it
on the high speed rail, only stopping once
to barber my hair
like any good American! I am a bolt fox,
a gift to the palette,
grey birds on a wire.
True as roses. As the conch.
Let us
turn to the city in autumn & lust.
Inside of this treatise, we have dog-paddled deeper
than the underwater cameras and below our education.
We have celebrated terror, spun
a few shiny things around and called it love.
Angst attack! Angst attack!
Gimme six martinis stat &
frozen treats for days, I dunno.

Experimental Writing

Danielle Geller

Annotating the First Page of the First Navajo-English Dictionary

The first, incomplete Navajo-English Dictionary was compiled, in 1958, by Leon Wall, an official in the U.S. government's Bureau of Indian Affairs. Wall, who was in charge of a literacy program on the Navajo reservation, worked on the dictionary with William Morgan, a Navajo translator.

'ąą': "well (anticipation, as when a person approaches one as though to speak but says nothing)"
I could begin and end here. My mother was a full-blooded Navajo woman, raised on the reservation, but she was never taught to speak her mother's language. There was a time when most words were better left unspoken. I am still drawn to the nasal vowels and slushy consonants, though I feel no hope of ever learning the language. It is one thing to play dress-up, to imitate pronunciations and understanding; it is another thing to think or dream or live in a language not your own.

'aa 'ahályánii: "bodyguard"
In August of 2015, I move from Boston to Tucson, to join an M.F.A. program in creative writing. I applied to schools surrounding the Navajo reservation because I wanted to be closer to my mother's family. My plan: to take classes on rug weaving and the Navajo language (Diné Bizaad); to visit my family as often as possible. It will be opened: the door to the path we have lost.

'ąą 'ályaa: "It was opened."
A PDF version of the Navajo-English dictionary from the University of Northern Colorado. I wonder which librarian there decided to digitize it. Most government documents, after they are shipped to federal depositories around the country, languish on out-of-the-way shelves and collect decades of dust before being deaccessioned and destroyed. I have worked in these libraries—I know.

ąą 'ályaa, bich'į': "It was opened to them; they were invited."
One of the reasons Navajo soldiers were recruited as code talkers during the Second World War was because there were no published dictionaries of their language at that time—and because the grammatical structure of the language was so different from English, German, and Japanese. They were invited to: a world beyond the borders of the reservation. My mother always told me the only way to get off the Rez is to join the military or marry off.

'ąą 'át'é: "It is open."
One of the first typewriters that could adequately record the Navajo language was built for Robert Young, a linguist who also worked with William Morgan and published a more comprehensive dictionary and grammar guide ("The Navaho Language"), in 1972. In the nineteen-seventies, a Navajo font was released for the IBM Selectric, an electric typewriter, which would serve as the basis for a digital font on early computers.

'ąą 'át'éego: "since it was open"
Navajo fonts are now available for download in multiple typefaces: Times New Roman, Verdana, and Lucida Sans.

'áádahojoost'įįd: "They quit, backed out, desisted, surrendered."
Spring. 1864. The "Long Walk" begins. The U.S. Army forcibly relocates the Navajo from their homeland, to Bosque Redondo, in eastern New Mexico. Those who do not resist learn to walk, but death follows both paths.

'aa 'dahoost'įįd, t'óó: "They gave up, surrendered."
There are many reasons parents do not teach their children the Navajo language: U.S. monolingual policies, violence experienced in boarding schools, and perceived status. Those who speak English well will have a better chance for escape.

'aa dahwiinít'įį': "into court (a place where justice is judicially administered)"
A close cousin of mine is scheduled to testify in court in one week; she isn't sure if she wants to go. I pick her up anyway. Bring her back to Tucson with me.

'aa deet'ą́: "transfer (of property, or ownership)"
My aunt tells me we have land on the reservation, just off I-40. We've inherited it from our great-grandmother, Pauline Tom. Only Pauline Tom had many children, and their children had many children, and after she died, in 2008, all those children started fighting. It's a common problem, and it isn't unique to the Navajo Nation. Federal land-allotment policies have resulted in too many heirs for too few acres.

'áadi: "there, over there (a remote place)"
On the drive to Tucson along I-40, my cousin points out the black-tar roofs of our family's houses, and the cemetery—a small, square piece of land—where our great-grandmother is buried. The cemetery is barely distinguishable from the rest of the landscape, and, when I follow her gaze, look away from the highway, I see only the stark, white faces of the headstones and the silver glint of a ribbon in the wind.

'áádįįł: "It is progressively dwindling away; disappearing."
In 1968, a decade after the first dictionary was published, ninety per cent of the children on the reservation who entered school spoke Navajo; in 2009, only thirty per cent knew the language (Spolsky, "Language Management for Endangered Languages," 117).

'áadiísh: "There? Thereat?"
September 22, 2015. The second time I pass our allotment on I-40, I try to find the spot my cousin showed me. I look for the headstones; I think of stopping and trying to find my grandmother's grave. My cousin told me that if you don't do the proper blessing, the spirit will follow you home. (She asked me, "What is the difference between a spirit and a ghost?") I don't know the blessing, but it doesn't matter; I can't recognize the cemetery or my family's land.

Experimental Writing

ąąh 'dahaz'ą̃: "illness, sickness, an ailment"
September 19th. I catch a cold from my students. Might be the flu. I tell my cousin to stay away, but she says she won't get sick. We spend all day curled up on the couch watching "Shameless." She rests her head on my shoulder, on my hip.

'á'á hwiinít'į', "kindness" *'aa hwiinít'į*: "trial (at law), molestation"
How are these words (kindness/molestation) that sound so similar so different? My aunt tells my cousin that our maternal grandmother molested her sons. My mother tells me other stories, similar but not the same. ("Why would they tell us that?") It's hard to believe, but it isn't. There will never be a trial. These are words better left unspoken, forgotten, erased.

'aa hwiinít'įįhígíí: "the court session that is to come"
September 16th, 2015. My cousin is told that if she doesn't appear for the court date, a warrant will be put out for her arrest. I agree to drive her back to Window Rock on Monday night, after I am done teaching for the day. It is a six-hour drive, but I am almost happy to make it. I will be in Window Rock, with my family, on the second anniversary of my mother's death, not by plan but by circumstance.

'ą́ą́hyiłk'as: "body chill"
I am sick with fever, alive with fever dreams. I dream of a two-story, sandstone motel, its three square walls opening onto the desert. A sun sets between two mountains, and heavy drapes are drawn across all the windows. My mother and my aunt and all my sisters are running in and out of the rooms, slamming doors, shouting at each other from the landings. I understand that each door is a choice, each room a potential future, and that my mother's and my aunt's and my sisters' doors are closed to me.

'aak'ee: "fall, autumn"
I start teaching my first freshman-composition class in the fall. I'm convinced, like most first-year teachers, that I have no idea what I am talking about; I spend the entire hour sweating in front of my class. But, afterward, two dark-haired, dark-skinned girls walk up to me and ask me: What are your clans? Where is your family from? We are Navajo, too. We are all three nervous and unsure where the conversation should go, but I want to grab hold of them and root them next to me; graduation rates of native students are abysmally low.

'ąą kwáániił: "It is expanding; it is getting bigger."
My cousin disappears in the middle of the night and leaves us a note: Went to Gallup with Heather and Faith need to get pads and face wash. Should be back soon. She leaves us a number, the wrong number. ("She prolly went to see *that guy*.")

'aaníí, t'áá, "It is true; truly; really; verily."
My cousin tells me she didn't see her boyfriend again. That she went over to Shorty's and helped him set mouse traps in the middle of the night. He couldn't do it himself, he kept catching his fingers. But she would tell me if she saw him.

'aaníí, t'áásh: "Is it so? Is it true?"
The answer is, in many ways, unknowable; for our mothers, the surest protection from the past was to spin truths and falsehoods into one story, one thread, impossible to distinguish in the weave.

'áánííígíí: "that which is occurring; the happening; the event"
I have been walking around the thing that happened, stepping around the truth, trying to protect my cousin from myself.

'áát'įįdę'ę: "what he did; his aforementioned act"
My cousin calls me at four-thirty in the morning, and I answer; her voice is thick with tears. She found out her boyfriend was cheating. She started the fight. I know this story. I know it. These are words better left unspoken; a story better lost to time. Still, I have no words to help her. I will come get you, I tell her. I will bring you home with me.

'abąąh náát'i': "border, strand (of the warp of a rug)"
A Navajo blanket is woven on a loom and will never outgrow its frame. Do we finish the story our mothers began, or do we rip out the weaving and begin anew? It is not so easy to erase or forget the things that have come before us.

'ábi'diilyaa: "He was made to be … "
… the kind of man who hits women. He crawled inside his father's shadow and filled it out.

'ábidiní, ha'át'íí shą': "What do you mean?"
One of my Navajo students interviews her aunt, who teaches Navajo language classes, and she writes a paper about revitalizing Diné Bizaad. I ask her if she would put me in contact with her aunt to answer some of my own questions. Her aunt agrees to e-mail me her responses, but I am so lost, I don't know the right questions to ask. I write a rambling e-mail about adjectives and verbs and the state of being, and she never responds.

'abi'doogį: "He was hauled away."
When I was little, my mother called the cops on my father, often. Usually after they had both been drinking. I remember standing on the street with our neighbors, watching the cops chase my father down the road, shove him into a police car, and haul him away.

'ábi'dool'įįdii, t'áá 'aaníí bee: "that with which he was really harmed"
What are the roots of domestic violence on the reservation? Inescapable poverty. Powerlessness. Untreated mental illnesses. Self-medication through alcohol. Cycles of abuse: fathers beating mothers beating sons beating their lovers and future mothers.

'ábidoołdįįł: "It will annihilate them."
Rates of domestic violence and sexual assault are higher among Native Americans than any other ethnicity in the United States. A study by the Centers for Disease Control and Prevention from 2008 reported that almost forty percent of Native American women identified as victims

of domestic violence during their lifetimes. These are conservative figures; many assaults go unreported.

'abíní,: "morning"
My first trip to the Rez. I wake before everyone, and slip out of bed and out the door with my aunt's binoculars. My aunt's dog, Toro, follows me down the twisting dirt road and into the flowering sagebrush hills. Toro follows his nose off the path, under bushes, over piles of gravel and rock. He misses a pair of cottontails, who bolt out from under my feet as I cross the same ground minutes later; they reach the safety of a hidden burrow before he turns around.

'ách'ąąh: "in front of"
My aunt and her neighbors clear the summer weeds out of the front yard and sweep them into piles. Toro has made a small rabbit's nest of them; he lies in a tight little ball. I call Toro's name and he lifts his head, fixes me with red, watery eyes, but he does not move.

'ach'éé: "daughter, niece (daughter of one's sister) (female speaking)"
After my mother dies, my aunt tells me that I am her daughter now—that she is my "little mother." This is how she introduces me to everyone: This is my niece! She's a teacher at the University of Arizona! This is how everyone responds: Hello, niece.

'ach'éédą́ą́': "one's yard, or dooryard"
My maternal great-grandmother froze to death, and my aunt is shocked that I did not know. I don't understand because freezing to death in the desert, in the sun, surrounded by yellow sagebrush flowers, doesn't make sense to me. My aunt tells me that Pauline Tom fell while checking on a noise outside, and she broke her hip in the fall. My aunt curls her hands on her skinny little wrists, mimes our grandmother crawling in the dirt, but she could not crawl far enough. My grandmother froze to death in the winter, in the deep dark of the night, in her own backyard.

'acheii (achaii): "maternal grandfather"
I met my maternal grandfather once, when I was very young. He was a Navajo police officer. When he got sick, my mother and my aunt started fighting over who would take care of him. My aunt talked too soon about pulling the plug, and they stopped speaking for years.

'áchį́į́h: "nose, snout"
I call Toro's name again, and he stands on quivering legs. He hobbles over to me and leans his entire weight against me. "Toro," I whisper, and I trace the black line between his eyes, smooth my hands over his head, down his sides. I rub his soft ears, over and over. "It's so hard, I know. It's so hard." I think of the stories my cousin told me. All the times Toro has been hit, flipped over the hoods of cars. Gotten up, shaken it off. Has he been hit again? My aunt won't take him to the vet. He's a Rez dog now.

'ach'į nahwii'ná: "to have trouble; to have difficulty; to suffer"
My mother was homeless in the six months leading up to her death, and she never called to ask me for help.

’achó: "maternal great grandfather"
Young and Morgan's dictionary tells me *achó* means maternal great-grandmother, that *'acho'* is not gendered. I am too embarrassed to ask, too scared my voice will betray me on the rising "O."

’ádaa ’áhojilyá̜: "He takes care of himself; he is on the alert."
My father would never admit his own violence, though I remember it like a mirage in the desert—the images came back to me in shimmers, a disturbing gloss over the horizon.

’ádaadahalni'go: "when they tell about themselves"
When my mother dies, I am the one who must go through her things: her diaries, her letters, her photographs. She says things in writing she would never say to me herself, and I feel some validation. I let my cousin read some of her entries: there is truth in their stories, truth in our memories, if only we could let ourselves believe them.

’ádaadin: "They are none of them; they are nonexistent, they are absent."
Dr. William Morgan, Sr., the linguist and translator for both Navajo dictionaries, passed away, in 2001. He was eighty-five years old, nearly twice the age of my mother when she died. He received an honorary doctorate from the University of New Mexico and taught at Cornell, the University of New Mexico, and the Navajo Community College. According to his obituary, he left behind nineteen grandchildren and nineteen great-grandchildren. And though he is gone, he left a cultural legacy that will survive him and his children's children's children, perhaps.

’ádaadinídíí: "the ones that are gone; absentees; decedents"
I am unsure how many grandchildren and great-grandchildren survived Pauline Tom; there are too many blank spaces on the family tree my mother left behind. Many of my questions have no answers; the ones who could answer them are gone.

’ádaadzaa: "They did."
I find out after I leave that my cousin is back with her boyfriend.

’ádaadzaa yę́ę́gi ’át’éego: "like they did"
My mother would leave the men who hit her, but she would always take them back.

’ádaadzaaígi ’át’éego: "like they did"
I should know better, but I don't. I hook up with men from the Internet and drive long distances to meet them in hotel rooms. I let them tie me up, bruise my skin with ropes and clamps and leather, tear me up, and make me bleed. I tell myself that it's O.K. because I let them—that I am the one with the power. I cannot tell if it is a lie, or if there is truth there, too.

’ádą̜ą̜h dahosíst’á̜: "I committed a crime."
I should not have taken her home. I should have spoken the words I meant to say. That we are worthy. That there is another path. That we can weave a rug of our own design. I started to look for those words but did not find them; I found only the same ghosts haunting the page.

Experimental Writing

Marlon Hacla

Bluebush

Rooms that kill time until burglars decide to leave them. What is the homework all about? Making a neat stack of off-key tunes? Order? A dead tree? Or a chorus of epiphanies for unscrambling an executioner's motivations and desires. Funeral birds that you gave as gifts. A parade of tied-up legs headed towards a beckoning forest. A paradise hastily put together.

Half a kernel of corn. Extravagance of roots. Broken bell forcibly deformed until it is mangled beyond recognition.

This is a performance of an upcoming part. Electric fan blades unraveled. I will be right behind you as you walk out the door, be the first to whisper. This is the part of the body that thirsts for sensation. Orange table piled high with bones. Is the source of my joy real?

If the wedding pushes through, it will turn out to be a slippery hitch. If the snag catches again, needles will flow like water. Angel with many faces and many weapons. Fear that latches onto the hem of a dress splattered with blood and mud. One answer to a question about teaching murder. Desire blanketed by light.

Casket that entombed a ritual. A treacherous act to devotion. The eye closing. Our happiness watered down. Poem chased down from a crash-landed dove. Mouth choking from having swallowed yet another body whole.

Triangular open space whose vertices correspond to the kitchen, staircase, scene of the crime.

Beautiful figure that has been ravaged. Dawn vandalized by warplanes' contrails.

Cathy Park Hong

Cholla Village of No

… Progress maif sprinklim fortune
to all o Korea—pave street, condo y petrol
savin Daewoo autos but Progress skip ova mine
villa lika popula lass snubbim
drossy fat girl …

… villa a sad sack groanim wit bullocks
y huts, villa o exiled outcasts,
prison-loused insurrectas, pickpockets, lady fes
bum-lookas, gaseleo dous'n gun molls,

yam sella clang tin can y hock hot treat
but bine eve, yam sella hatch plan to glue
workas toget'a … muckraking strumpets wheedle
tainty secrets from croneymen
who muck dim … allatime bang-a-rang,

butchers pang spite fo dim ancestas
macheted fo non bowing too low … factory wig
makas paste rash powda onto wigs fo
de sahib patron ladies … it be a villa besieged

bine cauldron trouble pot stirrers:
me Cholla villa o no.

But en a villa o contrarians who smelt peppa
gas lika it laughim gas, who quill manifestos
en juice-frail butcher papa, who say no mo, no mo,
no mo, one voice ses hokay, es fine …
mine fadder's yes a tic …

Mine teacha tell me dat wig-makas
plan to strike … see samsy we expoit wigs
to 'Merikken cronettes wit patchy nest hair …

… (I's a model cos mine ball head, lasses giz me
all de rejects—botchy bleach job wigs,
marcel too knuck-knuck wigs, a nappy wig
fo all occasions) … .

… but hours killim workas, in window black
paint room … bone cramp backs en airless room y hack
a lot so plan a mass sit down,
non work til betta pay …

Experimental Writing

I's naifly tellim me fadder …
Plis boi patos rush en factory, gets key y squeejee full pow
a hose o wadder … hose blast a flood y
shatta workas rib cages, shred de plasta caking
… city floatim black balloon …

Me gor-belly fadder, de Makkoli bootlegga,
oggled y tattled fo piddling dolla bill …
sayim yes, hokay, so fine, tellim secrets. …

… I'se shame me fadder, I'se shame mefelf,
so I's lefttim en sanguish fog,
I's left me fadder to live wit me teacha.
I ses I go, he non look a'me,
he ses hokay, yes, go.

Experimental Writing

Douglas Kearney

SUCKTION

**developed from a concept by Anne LeBaron,
who also composed it**

Irona *the abject housewife*
Manny (voice only) *the husband*
Delivery Service (voice only)

"†" indicates material sung while exhaling.

"‡" indicates material sung while inhaling.

for a trailer from the Los Anegeles performance, visit:
https://www.youtube.com/watch?v=OUYgMnIwdL0

SOAP ARIA

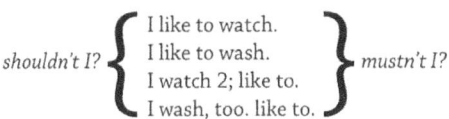

on 2, I watch soaps and watch soap spots
to watch how to wash without soap spots.
and watch dirt on the soaps
while I soap up the dirt.   **CLEAN.**
                                 isn't it isn't it
                              CLEAN?

†: wwwwsshhhhhhh w w w wshhhhh wsssssshhhhhh www
‡: wish   wish   wish

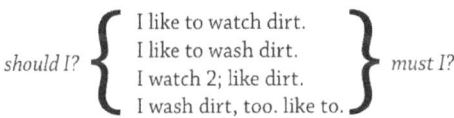

on 2, I watch dirt and wash dirt spots
and watch how to wash my dirty spots.
                and watch dirt on the soaps
FILTHY!   while I dirt up my spots.
is I is I is I is I
FILTHY!

†: sshhhhhhh shsh sh sh shhhhh sssssshhhhhh s sh sh
‡: shit   shit   shit

Experimental Writing

> Irona's life as a housewife has left her with only the television for company. Surfacing from a dull reverie, she assures herself that her domestic work is a kind of pilgrimage into a purity she needs.

SUCKTION (REMIX)

Sucks the smuts inna guts
Me keen clean machine, baby!
Must just lust f'dust bustin
Li'l sumthin sumthin a sucktion!

Abhor spoor, adore the floor
Long to belong along upon, baby!
Upright me ‡:suck right! what me ‡:uptight?
Li'l sumthin sumthin a sucktion!

‡:Want-me †:what you leave me to have
‡:Take-me †:what you drop me to want } ***baby!***
‡:Suck-me †:what you throw me to need
‡:Leave-me ‡:drop-me ‡:throw-me †:me ‡:want-me †:take-me
‡:SUCK! -K K

Grab me bags ‡: ‡: have trash ‡: have ash
Dump gunk, junk-K from me trunkKK-K, baby.
Tossed to cKK-KKloset me til you wantin me,
yer li'l ‡:sumthin ‡:sumthin a ‡:sucKKtion!

Experimental Writing

ANNIVERSORRY

†: shhhshhshshshplish
sh'p dsh dshhhh shpop †: †: shhsplish dish
dishhhh shplish †: †: dshhhh†: } { *sans dishpa*

‡: ⁓⁓⁓wsssssswwhhsw

whiter _ brighter }
brights⁼ wives ←

dirty so, and so: †:s
sh' sh' sh' sh' sh' sh'
clean, so: hmmmm

squee squee *bling!* buff buff *bling!* squee squee *bling*
buff buff *bling!* pff pff *bling!* chis-chis *bling!*
bff bff *bling!* tee-hee *bling!* stuff stuff *cling!*

Man, I'm glam for my man, Manny, and our anniversary soirée!

knock
knockknockknock
MA'AM: MANNY-MAN HAD PLAN TO MEET MA
MA'AM: MANNY-MAN HAD UNPLANNED DEMA
MA'AM: MANNY-MAN, HE SAID DAMN! MANY
MA'AM: MANNY-MAN SAID THIS AM FOR HIS M
knock

‡: ‡:
‡:a vacuum cleaner } ?!
†: †:
†:this SUCKS} !!

handy!

‡: ‡: ‡:ꟷwwsssssssshhsshhh!wsshh!†:hhhh‡: ‡: hh
shk shkuhhh splsshhhkuh splshk shkuh shk shu shk splsh shkuhh †: †: †:
h ‡: ‡: †:w †:ww†:www†:wwwrr†:wwwrrrt:wwwwrrrr†:wwwwrrrrr†:†:†: k-

:she' †:she' †:she' †:sh- †:sh- †:she'   } { *I'm floored!*
sh' shshshshsh' sh' sh' sh' sh' sh'   } { *can eat off it!!*

} { *am I clean enough*
} { *to see my face in it??*

AND HAVE AN ANNIVERSARY SOIRÉE.

THAT HE HEAD TO MANHATTAN AND FT. WORTH THIS WEEK.

RIES FOR ANNIVERSARY SOIRÉE. YOU UNDERSTAND.

AME.

Irona, bent on proving she can be the "clean machine" Manny wants, labors to get the house ready for a candlelit anniversary dinner.
A knock on the door brings bad news and an anniversary present.

Experimental Writing

CLEANING HOUSE

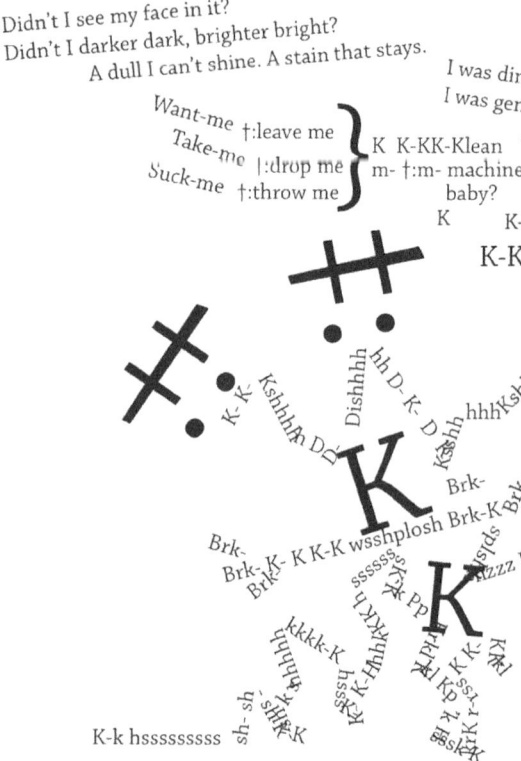

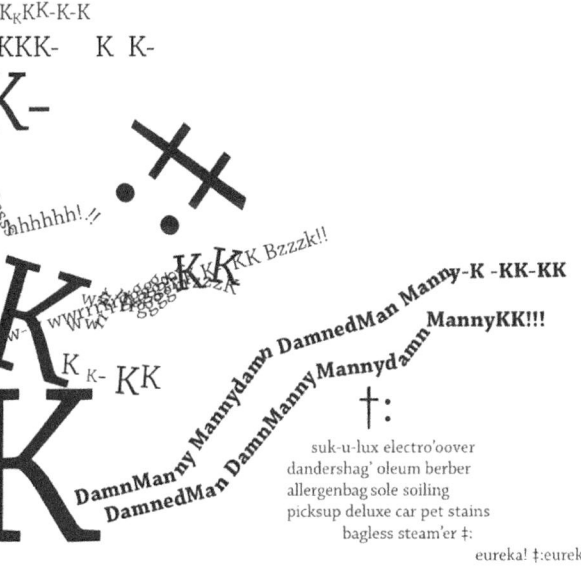

Irona realizes she has let Manny's desires define her. She chooses to destroy her home's shiny appliances, those symbols of her husband's indifference. Yet, when she attacks the vacuum cleaner, she hears a beautiful, breathless cry that reflects her own.

RABBITROOMBABOT'RUMBA

‡: ‡:Unit height: 3.9 inches
†: †:Insertion Length: 7 inches
†: †: †:Head Circumference is 4 inches
†:Middle: 4 and a half inches
‡:Weight is 7 and a half pounds
†:   †:Noise: 1 and a half out of 10
‡: ‡: ‡:Quiet is 60 decibels

Waterproof: No

‡: ‡:Cleaning Time is 60 minutes
‡:‡:‡:Speed is 0.2 yards per second
†: †: †:Vibration Speeds: 25
†: †:Rotation Speeds: 25
†: †:Directions of rotations: 1
‡: Maximum power: 30 watts
‡: ‡: ‡:Battery is Rechargeable
‡: Nickel- ‡:Metal ‡:Hydride
‡:Charge 180 minutes

Waterproof: No

‡:‡:Comes with built-in cliff detector
‡:   ‡:Filter Type: use Hepa filter
‡: ‡: ‡:   ‡:Dust Capacity is 8 quarts
‡:Auto Quick Stop? Lift the unit
†: †: †:Unit comes with swirling beads.
†:   †: †:Material: Jelly

Waterproof: No   K-   KK-
‡:HRRR ‡:HHHHHHRRRRR ‡:MMMMZZMZZZZZZMM H- H-
‡:MMM MMZZMZMMMZ H- HM? HMMMM? ‡:HRRRRRRRRRR—

Irona considers the vacuum cleaner's transformative possibilities. In the background, Manny's voice drones over the answering machine.

CYBORGASM

SCHH‡:HHH‡:HHHHMM MMMOOOOOTZ †:Z †:Z IK K
‡:HHRRRHRRRHRRRHRRR †: †:
‡:H- ‡:HRRRHRRRH †: ‡:HRRRHRRR †: R
SCHH‡:HHH‡:HHHHMM MMMOOOOOTZ †:Z †:Z IK K
‡:HHEHMHEHMHEHM HEHHM †: H †:
‡:HEH ‡:EHMMHEHHM †: ‡:IIEII ‡:IIEIIM

‡:SCHMOOTZIK -K!
‡:SCHM †:OOTZ? -Z
‡:SCHMMMM †: †: †

xxxxxxx ‡:HHRRR ‡:HRRRHRRRHRRR †: †:
xxxxxxxxx ‡:H ‡:EH- ‡:EHM ‡:HHEHHM †: †: ‑
xxxxxxxxx
xxxxxxxxxxxxxxxxxxxxxxI†: I†: TZZZ ‡:HRR ‡:HEHM K- K- K- K- xxxxxxNxx
-N ‡: AH ‡:AH xxxx
-N †:JUH N- N- ‡:U
xxxx‡:Axxxxxxx †:A
x‡:Axxxxxxxxxxx
xxxxxxxxxx‡:Axx IT-
-N ‡:JUH
‡:III ‡:IZ †

‡:Z

:H

K †:K
xxx
HHHHHHHH XJXXXXXXNEEXXXXX
              XXXXXXEERRXXXXXXX
AAAAA IZ XXXX
         XXXX
         XXXX
:UH! ‡:HUH K- KI-
H †:UH N- ‡:N- †:EEERUMITZ Z- Z
ZZZ IZ †:IZ-IZ IZIZ- †:UH
OWB †:AHH -
       HHHHHH
       HHHHHHHHHH ‡: †: ‡: †:

Irona chooses metamorphosis.

THE END

Experimental Writing

Maya Lin and Tan Lin

Blueprints for *Reading a Garden*

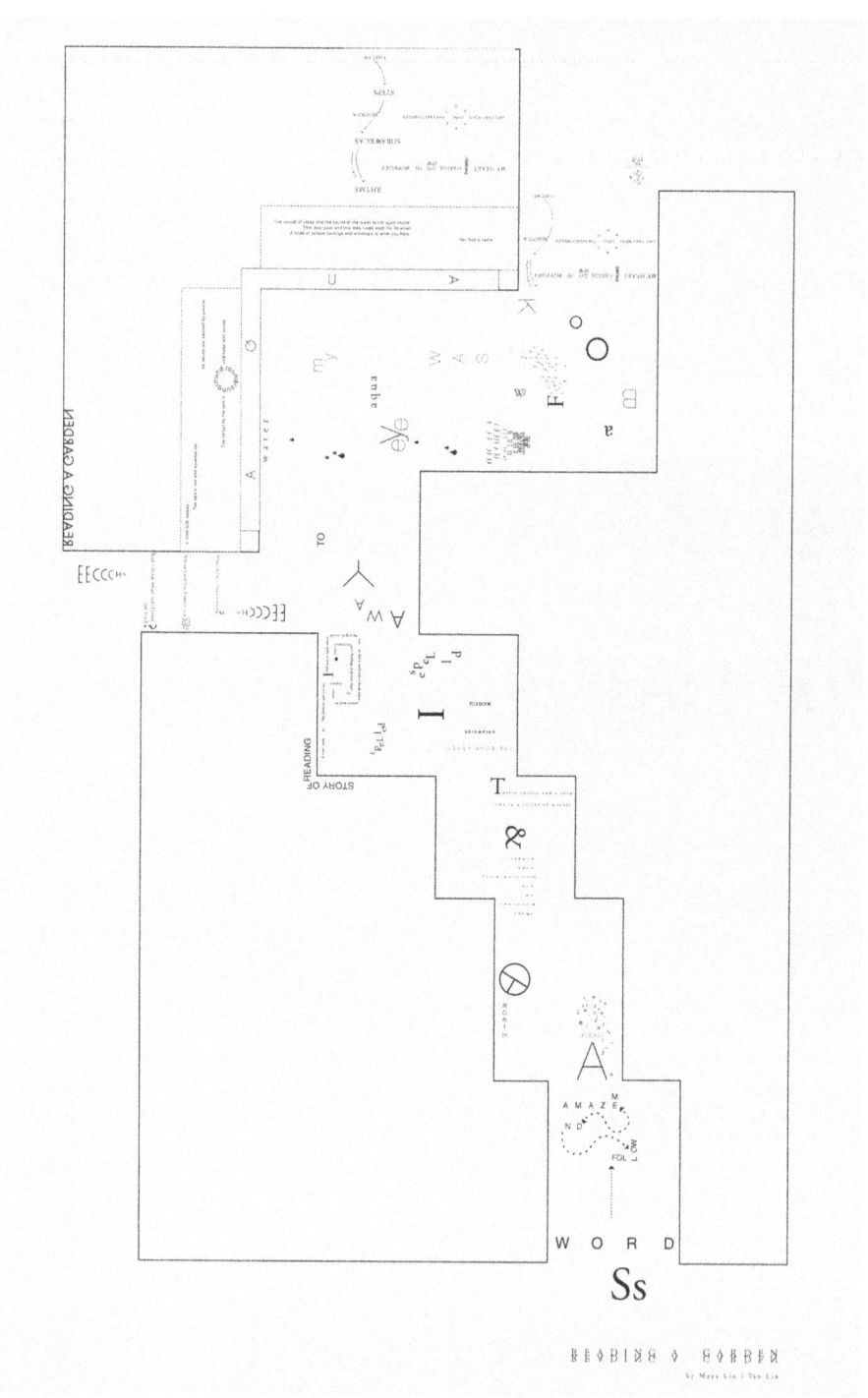

Layli Long Soldier

Excerpts from "Whereas Statements"

WHEREAS *re-
solution's* an act
of analyzing and re-
structuring complex
ideas into simpler
ones so I place
a black bracket
on either side of
an [idea] I cordon it
to safety away
from national re-
solution the threat
of re-
ductive
[thinking]:

Experimental Writing

Whereas Native Peoples are [   ] people with a deep and abiding [   ] in the [   ] , and for millennia Native Peoples have maintained a powerful [   ] connection to this land, as evidenced by their [   ] and legends;

•

Whereas the Federal Government condemned the [   ], [   ], and [   ] of Native Peoples and endeavored to assimilate them by such policies as the redistribution of land under the Act of February 8, 1887 (25 U.S.C. 331; 24 Stat. 388, chapter 119) (commonly known as the "General Allotment Act"), and the forcible removal of Native [   ] from their [   ] to faraway boarding schools where their Native [   ] and [   ] were degraded and forbidden;

WHEREAS I read an article in *New York Times* about the federal sequestration of funds from preservation programs, the cuts. In federal promises and treaties. The article details living conditions on reservations a suicide rate ten times higher than the rest of the country. Therein the story of a twelve-year-old girl whose mother died, she doesn't know her father, she bounces home to home to foster home, weary. I regard how plainly the writer imparts her repeated sexual abuse. For mental care, unavailable services. There's a clinic that doesn't have money after May, *don't get sick after May*, is the important message. As I read I cry, I always cry, and here I must be clear my crying doesn't indicate sadness. Then I read a comment posted below the online article:

> *I am a fourteen-year-old girl who recently visited the _____ Reservation in South Dakota, with my youth group. The conditions of Native American people were living in were shocking. When I arrived home, I wrote a petition on whitehouse.gov for the US to formally apologize and pay reparations to the Native American people. This petition only stays up until July 23rd, so please sign and share!!! You signing it would really mean a lot to a lot of people. Thank you.*

Dear Fourteen-Year-Old Girl, I want to write. The government has already "formally apologized" to Native American people on behalf of the plural *you*, your youth group, your mother and father, your best friends and their families. *You*, as in all American citizens. *You* didn't know that, I know. Yet indeed, Dear Girl, the conditions on reservations have changed since the Apology. Meaning, the Apology has been followed by budget sequestration. In common terms sequestration is removal banishment or exile. In law-speak it means seizure for safekeeping but changed in federal budgeting to mean subject to cuts, best as I can understand it. Dear Girl, I went to the Indian Health Services to fix a tooth, a complicated pain. Indian healthcare is guaranteed by treaty but at the clinic limited funds don't allow treatment beyond a filling. The solution offered: *Pull it.* Under pliers masks and clinical lights, a tooth that could have been saved was placed in my palm to hold after sequestration. Dear Girl, I honor your response and action, I do. Yet the root of reparation is repair. My tooth will not grow back. The root, gone.

Experimental Writing

                                    [spiritual]
              [belief]   [Creator]
                                      [spiritual]
                                  [customs]
                                                              [traditions]
  [beliefs]   [customs]

                                                              [children]
        [families]
                        [practices]

Garielle Lutz

The Boy

The boy was raised in a city that had the look and feel of a state capital but in fact was not even a county seat. The buildings—big, brutish granite piles—gave everybody the wrong idea. Travellers would see the castellated skyline from the highway, sheer off at the exit, park their cars, then climb steep steps to what they hoped, despite the absence of signs, of plaques, would prove to be a mint, a museum, a monument. Once inside, they would find themselves in cramped, fusty living quarters. Somebody—an old woman in a housecoat or a bed jacket—would look up from a sofa and say, "Let a person sleep."

The boy, on the other hand, did not have the look and feel of anything big or promising. You couldn't look up his name in books. Even as a child, he had always remained many removes from himself. Wherever he stood—near the swing set on a playground, say—he was never inarguably there but his absence was always firsthand. His absence, in fact, was so commanding, so convincing, that people around him were often confused about just exactly where they too now stood. Obviously, his parents must have caught on very early to the unexampled form of ventriloquism the boy had evolved, a ventriloquism that entailed displacing not just his voice but his entire flute-thin body, and they made the necessary adjustments—sudden half steps or about-faces—in their own strides. That's why people thought they walked funny, that's why people thought they looked funny together as a family.

One day, well gone in childhood, the boy sat at the kitchen table and watched the father solder together two wires on the boy's tape recorder.

The tape recorder was of the old, reel-to-reel type.

The father was not especially good with his hands. In fact, the soldering iron—the risk that its use introduced into his life—was a terror. More important, the father was unforgiving. He was so unforgiving that he gave in, time after time, doing everything for the boy out of a big, banging spite. With every splenetic dab of the soldering iron, the father thought he was defecting from a deductive scheme that always runs: Father, Mother, Son.

The boy was convinced that by destroying his playthings he was accomplishing something similar.

Walking home from the high school he attended at the other end of the city, the boy would often linger in a park near the very tallest of the buildings. Crestfallen tourists would on occasion approach him. Once, a long-throated, heavily talcumed woman asked, "Have you a pen on your person?" The boy slued around slowly and exaggeratedly, as if to see whether there was a third party involved, an attendant bearing supplies. There was only his own angled, outbound body and, at a respectable distance, her own, the globulet of a tear glissading down her cheek. The woman moved on. There were plenty of men in the park whose pockets were full of pens and whatever else there might be a call for.

One day early in his eleventh-grade year, the boy was summoned from his social-studies class to the office of the guidance counselor. The guidance counselor was a short-winded block of a man with corned teeth and an overexerted vocabulary. He explained that to the best of his knowledge it would be in the best interest of both the boy and the school if, for the remainder of his tuition, he were enrolled as a girl. He explained that the parents had already been informed and that the papers had already been drawn up and dispatched for them to sign. That night, the boy's mother took the boy shopping for the pair of Mary Janes, the jumper, enough white blouses for a week. The boy became very popular at school, excelled at all his subjects to the extent that was then expected of girls, and enjoyed many boyfriends and admirers, all of whom he did his very best to delight. At the commencement ceremony, the guidance counselor delivered a long speech about the boy and his progress. The speech was full of words like "miracle" and "rapture" and "angel." During the peroration, the guidance counselor publicly proposed to the boy. They were married a week afterward in an elaborate but rushed ceremony, during which the minister looked content in the knowledge that this smell would cover up that smell and so forth down the line, domino-style. Two weeks later, the guidance counselor died loudly and tumultuously in his sleep. The boy slipped out of his negligee and slumped across the dark city to the house of his parents.

With his diploma and a cajoling, loopily handwritten letter of application, the boy was offered employment three hundred and forty-two miles to the right of his bed if he was facing the wall that held the window, a position he favored. He engaged a room, sight unseen, over the telephone.

A week before the boy was to depart, his mother decided he would need a rug. She drove him to a carpet store to have a look at remnants.

The boy watched the salesman slide a licorice cough drop into his mouth from the box in the pocket of his shirt.

"You certainly know your way around in here," the salesman said eventually to the boy.

The boy turned away and paged through some carpet samples bound together in a thick, shaggy book.

"I was saying, ma'am, that your son here has sure been spending a lot of time in this store," the salesman said.

"We'll want something for the floor," the mother said.

"Okay," the salesman said. "What are we talking about?"

"It's just one big room," the mother said.

"How big of a room?" the salesman said.

The mother looked at her son. "How big a room?"

The boy did not answer.

"It's one state over," the mother said.

There is an explanation for patricide that works in every case. In every case, there is a soda machine close at hand.

The boy was always thirsty. The boy was always hurrying across the street to the machine, buying one can at a time, carrying it back to his room to drink at the table. The father was in town only for a visit. The greasy whorls of the father's thumbprints had already blurred the cover of the hobby magazine the boy had bought for the father to leaf through. Also on the table was an iron that the boy worried was prowing in a different direction every time he returned from the machine.

"You drink way too much soda," the father said, finally.

"I'm thirsty," the boy said.

"Then drink water."

"I hate water."

"Soda don't even quench your thirst. Look at the money you're throwing away."

"If it doesn't quench my thirst, then tell me what it does do."

"It makes the inside of your mouth and throat nice and cold for a couple seconds. That's it. Water would do just as good."

The boy and the father sat and wordlessly pushed their points.

The knife presented itself to the boy as if in shimmery italics. The boy could not remember ever having bought the thing. It was a heftless, nervous-atomed, self-disowning simulacrum of what a knife was supposed to look like in such a low-built town.

As on so many occasions, this was the boy's first time, but everything rang a bell—a cracked, mootish, spanging bell. Each clank of it brought him a clangorous bit closer to the understood *you*.

Experimental Writing

K. Silem Mohammad

They Net the HDTV Teeth, the "Chewy Heavens" HDTV Teeth

A filthy dirty tater hater pounded
Upon my itchy nihilistic brains:
It hurt so doggone much I nearly drownded
(I almost wet my diaper from the pains).

The tetchy little tater hater hollered,
"The Prairie Dog Museum is a scam!"
I made a queasy face, I gulped, I swallered;
Quoth I, "*I* is an other; yes it am!"

The tater hater ripped off my prosthesis
And snarled in my teeth, "You ain't Rimbaud!"
I answered, "Yes, but some teen named Clarice is";
He sneered at that and said, "That teen's a ho!"

The hater hated taters; yes, and yet,
Potato was the only fruit he et.

from Shakespeare's Sonnet 46 ("Mine eye and heart are at a mortal war")

Ander Monson

Sincerity

Essay	Degree of truthfulness	Form	Type of Failure Risked
Outline towards a Theory of the Mine versus the Mind and the Harvard Outline	Very true indeed	Harvard Outline	Absurdity
I Have Been Thinking about Snow	As true as my memory lets it be.	Page as field (of snow?)	Instability
Cranbrook Schools: Adventures in Bourgeois Topologies	All true, which is probably the most important essay in the book to be true, as it contains the most personal revelations that might seem otherwise fabricated.	Mathematical proof + memoir	Embarrassment
Index for X and the Origin of Fires	Not very true at all	Index	Confusion
Fragments: On Dentistry	All too true	Fragments	Decay, Impermanence
Subject to Wave Action: A There and a Back (with Orchestral Accompaniment)	True, especially the parts which I omitted to protect the reputations of the ladies.	Narrative; seemingly straightforward sentences	Disappearance

The Long Crush	As I wrote this it became more inaccurate, like writing about any kind of technology, especially in the world of books, as opposed to the quicker-moving magazine world or the world of the blogs. Technology advances fast in the world of disc-golf discs. Every time I returned to revise this essay I had to add more information, making it increasingly obnoxious. I had thought, after writing the title of the essay, about making this the story of a crush I had on this one girl for like six years, but it is not, and is instead about disc golf.	Narrative	Uselessness
Failure: A Meditation, Another Iteration (With Interruptions)	True, except for the parts I totally fabricated.	Page as field, broken up	Forgettability
After Form and Formlessness: Bodies, Boats, and Bathing	Only minor errors in this essay; it is mostly true.	Narrative approaching formlessness	Incoherence, Forgetability

The Big and Sometimes Colored Foam: Four Annotated Car Washes	True, with some additions	Annotated car-wash narratives with explanations and meditations	Redundancy
Afterword: Elegy for Telegram and Starflight	Too true for my own comfort. A couple spots have lying in them, but not enough to hurt you or your friends.	Telegrams + narrative	Obsolescence
Appendix: Parts of the Book You May Additionally Enjoy Such as an Appendix	True, addresses the truth question more straightforwardly than elsewhere, sort of.	Reflection with self-doubt	Disappearance
*			
Decoder wheel	If you consider the decoder wheel an essay, it is even more true than the others in the pursuit of its form, which it approximates very nicely, thank you.	Decoder wheel, sometimes called a *volvelle*	Obsolescence
Website	Somewhat more bogus. Filled with lies and misdirection. Except this page. It's all super-true because it's on the web!	Card catalog, interrogation	Absurdity, Invisibility

Experimental Writing

Thirii Myo Kyaw Myint

You Rail, and the Road

WE FOLLOW THE RAILROAD THROUGH the shrubbery. Every once in a while, there is a fallen tree, or a spiky plant growling thick and low, and we have to go around. I keep my eye on the tracks. I don't want to get lost.

Soon, the trees begin to thin, and a chain link fence crops up beside us. Some parts of it are clawed through. By wolves, I think, or teenage girls meeting their lovers.

On the other side of the fence is a kind of gorge, and growing out of its throat are apartment buildings. The ground there is brown with leaves. Satellite dishes grow like liverworts over the roofs and balconies.

SOME GUY IN A BEANIE IS SMOKING IN the parking lot. He's only in a t-shirt so the beanie's for show. The lot is empty. I walk up to him.

I'm robbing you, I say.

Okay, he says.

He reaches for the pockets of his jeans and hands me a wallet, a lighter, and a stick of gum. The wallet is swollen shut like a black eye. I open it with some difficulty. The guy smokes his cigarette.

Look, I say, do you mind?

Sorry, he says, and moves away.

I find nothing in the wallet. No business cards from soothsayers. No foreign currency. No glamour shots of dead girlfriends.

I keep the stick of gum and return the rest.

THE CHAIN LINK FENCE COLLAPSES somewhere in the bramble and the trees thicken again. We do not see any buildings after the apartments in the gorge. The railroad runs straight.

You say you've been sleeping in squat houses at the city's edge. The railroad is no place to sleep.

Ghost trains, I say. They'll run you over.

Yes, you say.

There is a chill in the woods. I remember I have a beanie in my jacket and I pull it on to warm my ears.

THE GARDEN ART JUNKYARD LIES adjacent to the parking lot. When he finishes his cigarette, the guy asks if I want to sneak in.

Sure, I say.

We hop the fence and I find a spot on a porpoise and the guy sits down on a bench beside a little girl. The bench is bronze and the little girl, too. I imagine someone pouring molten lead on her. I imagine her dying in a volcanic eruption.

I like your pink hair, the guy says to me.

Thanks, I say.

THE WOODS ARE QUIET IN THE daytime. Your footfalls and my breathing are the loudest sounds.
The sound of my feet fits inside the sound of your footsteps and the sound of your breathing fits inside the sound of my breath, so we walk as one body following the railroad, aligning then separating from ourself.
The light in the woods is hollow. Our child is dead. Our womb is hollow. Because we are together, our child is dead again.

WE STOP AT THE MOUTH OF A tunnel. The tunnel is walled up with bricks. Graffiti sprawls over it and neon ink seeps into the roots of nearby trees.
There is a shopping cart stuck in a tree. We throw a rock at it and hit a wheel. It spins. We stand there in the clearing before the tunnel and listen to that loose wheel squeak squeak squeak.
I say the railroad must lead out of the city.
You ask, On what train?

THE TUNNEL BORES THROUGH SOLID rock, A rock face rising steeply. It is too smooth for us to climb.
You say the trains in the city were disassembled. The squatters tore them apart. They sleep in boxcars to keep out the wolves.
We must find a place to sleep before night. This is the farthest I have come from the city. I don't know what lies on the other side of the tunnel.

THE GUY IS ONE OF THOSE SQUATTER kids. He's got a sister and two parents in the city. They live in some mid-sized apartment and eat dinner together.
The guy tries to tell me why he ran away. We wander through the junkyard and back out to the parking lot. I am half-listening. The asphalt is broken up. There are no cars. We walk through some narrow streets and the guy points out a boxcar he used to share with a girlfriend.
Is she dead? I ask.
No, the guy says. He gives me a look.

THE GUY ASKS ME IF I HAVE A CAR.
No, I say. I live alone.
How did you get here, then? he says.
I walked, I say.
It's getting late, he says.
Yeah, I say.
We walk on through the dead streets. The glass of the streetlamps is broken, and I can see the alien bulbs inside. They give off a naked, orange light.
There is a bus stop on the next street, the guy says. The buses run till midnight.

WE SIT AT THE BACK OF THE BUS AND the guy tells me an okay story about his childhood. It is something about an accident, his kid sister, maybe his fault.
It wasn't your fault, I say to the guy.
Yeah, he says, you're right.
It's my turn now, so I tell him about you and the railroad.

WHEN THE WHEEL OF THE SHOPPING cart falls silent, a child is born from the mouth of the tunnel. A few bricks fall out and the child crawls through.
You pick the little thing up by the legs.
The child is ours, you say.
How about the railroad? I say. The tracks pass under the brick wall. The child might have come from the other side of the rock.

I SAY I WANT TO FIND A PATH around the rock face. I want to cross the city limits.
Hold on, you say.
You want to admire the graffiti. You say our child is to be thrown away.
We bundle the child in the beanie I am wearing and you climb the tree. My ears feel cold. Our child must be warm. You drop her body gently into the shopping cart, and the tree wiggles its kaleidoscope leaves.

THE SHOPPING CART WILTS WITH THE weight of our child. You climb back down the tree.
You say that even from the highest branch, you could not see a way around the tunnel. The rock face rises too steeply and too high. The trees grow thickly around it.
We must find another way out of the city.
I say I want to rest awhile. I want to make another child. A more perfect one.

EMPTY BOTTLES LINE THE TABLE WHEN we get back to my place. The bottom of a cake is stuck to the pan.
The guy doesn't take off his shoes. He sits down on the couch. I sit down on the armchair under the window. I think I will fall asleep.
I close my eyes and picture my body getting up, walking to my room, opening the door, taking off my jacket, my tights, my dress, my underwear, my earrings.
I open my eyes.
The guy is still there on the couch.

I LET THE GUY TAKE OFF MY CLOTHES because I'm too tired to do it myself.
Down the hall, I say.
He pulls away.
What? he says.
The bed, I say.
I want to lie down. I want the guy to brush my teeth for me.
Come on, he says, lifting my body out of the armchair.

INSIDE MY BEDROOM IT IS VERY DARK. The guy is quiet. The beanie is gone at least and I am touching his hair. It is so soft.
The guy is waiting for me to tell him he can stay. He wants to talk about his adolescence. His first sexual feelings. The one time he stood up to his dad. Something like that.
I touch the guy's hair in the dark, and I am thinking of trees. They look so puny when their leaves fall out.

WE LIE DOWN IN THE LEAVES AND LET the neon ink seep into our skin. The tips of my hair turn pink.
When our child is born, you take her little fluorescent body and feed it to the tunnel. We secure the loose brick with chewing gum. We wall her up in there, to keep her safe.
The graffiti spells our child's name, and I am pleased.

WITH OUR FIRST CHILD IN THE shopping cart, and our second in the tunnel, we feel at ease. We decide to stay longer in the clearing. The wolves only come out at dusk, and we can find a place to sleep before then.
In the morning, we will find another way to leave. It cannot be that the whole city is walled by solid rock.
The rock face casts a shadow over the clearing and you are crouched in the dark, fastening bolts and aligning the railroad tracks.

WE LEAVE THE TUNNEL WHEN THE sun moves behind the rock face. The shopping cart squeaks goodbye. The railroad leads us back the way we came.
Light comes scarce through the trees and the tracks are half-buried in the undergrowth. I listen closely for howls.
The woods are loud in the dark. The air is full of sounds both sharp and gaping. I cannot hear myself breathe.

IT IS STILL DARK IN MY BEDROOM when I wake up from the cold.
I get out of bed and put on a clean pair of underwear, comb my hair. The guy looks stupid asleep. Most people do.
I get down on my hands and knees and feel for his jeans on the floor. I find them. The swollen wallet, I take the cash. I take his beanie, too. I decide I will leave this city. I will find you and we will leave together.

I DON'T BOTHER TO TAKE THE KEYS with me when I leave my place. I don't want to come back.
I slide the guy's money into the pocket of my jeans, and stuff his beanie into my jacket.
I take the elevator down, even though I live on the second floor. I try to remember the story the guy told me. It was supposed to be sad. Then the elevator dings and the story is gone. I get in, and press for the first floor.

THE STREETS ARE WET FROM THE sprinklers that come on in the city before dawn. Windows are drawn shut and garages locked. Lovers grope one another in parked cars, moaning mildly.
I am wearing soft shoes. I am thinking of no one.
I walk in the middle of the street and the trees and the streetlamps arch above me. It feels like I'm moving through a tunnel.

AFTER SOME TIME, WE PASS BY THE gorge again. The apartment buildings have sunk deeper into it. Windows are cracked and laundry is laid out on the ledges, over the broken glass. The wet seeps from the hanging sheets and runs down the walls, darkening the concrete.
You want to take a closer look.
We can rest here for the night, you say.

YOU CRAWL UNDER THE CHAIN LINK fence, and I follow you, to the gorge.
In the gorge, there are many dead children, bobbing up and down at the water's surface. They are pale and silvery in the evening light, dressed in white pajamas. The apartment buildings are sinking.
You say you will go up the buildings first. Ride the elevator squeak squeak squeak to the top floor.
I sit down at the lip of the gorge.
I will wait right here, I say.

THE CHILDREN IN THE GORGE ARE ours. They were too beautiful for us to keep, in a shopping cart, or walled up in a tunnel, so we drowned them here in the gorge.
The trees grow in monotone. There is no graffiti to wet their roots. I lie down in the brown leaves and listen to the wolves howling deep in the water.

I WALK. I WALK AND I WALK, AND there is no one who will take the guy's money. I want my palm read. I want to meet a wolf. I want a train to run out of this city and I want to be hit by that train. When the guy wakes up in my apartment, I hope he will continue to live there. My place is bigger than the squat houses at the city's edge. It is bigger than the boxcars.
I drop the guy's money, bill by bill, in the street. This way, he will have nothing. He will have to stay.

I WALK THROUGH THE SMALL HOURS. It is dark. I passed the junkyard a while ago. The porpoise and the little girl, the parking lot. I don't know exactly where I am anymore. I am far from my place.
The buildings drop off as I walk and the sky opens.
I am heading for the woods at the city's edge. I know you live there now, by the old railroad. You've been living there alone since our child died.

I WALK UNTIL I AM LOST. I FEEL THAT I've been lost here before. Not last night with the guy, but another time, when I was alone.
When our child died, you left for the railroad, and it was as if you took her away. As if the two of you were together without me, in a place I couldn't follow.

THE WINDOWS IN THE APARTMENT buildings have no glass and I can see the dark hallways inside, filling up with water. The apartment buildings are all but swallowed.
In the gorge, the children's white pajamas billow gently around their small bodies. I look for your face in the windows.

SOON THE BUILDINGS FLATTEN, THE streets taper and the asphalt starts to crack. The sky lightens and the streetlamps sputter off.
I hear dogs barking in a cage somewhere. Maybe they are not dogs. Maybe there is no cage. The trees are thickening. I walk.

WHEN I WAKE UP, I AM LYING ON MY back with one arm dangling into the gorge. The arm is wet and limp. I pull it up with some difficulty.
I look down into the gorge to find you, but only the satellite dishes are left. They bloom on the water like pale lotuses.
You are gone and you took our children with you. I miss their silver bodies.

ALL THE STREETS COME TO DEAD ends. I cannot follow them anymore, so I hike through the shrubbery. I find a footpath that runs through the trees.
The trees are losing their leaves.
I walk on in my soft shoes. I call out

YOUR NAME echoes in the gorge. I call it out again, and I think I hear a wolf howl.
The gorge is flooding. The elevator squeaks far below. The satellite dishes are submerged now. I have to find

THE WAY BACK to the streets is obscured by the undergrowth. I cannot tell what is the path anymore. The ground is all brown with leaves.

THE LEAVES ARE MATTED IN MY HAIR. I walk back to the chain link fence, claw through it. I make my way through the shrubbery and

THE TREES BEGIN TO THIN and metal is glinting in the undergrowth. Rusted tracks. It is

THE RAILROAD ends and soon I see the junkyard, and beyond that, the parking lot.

I GET CLOSER AND I SEE THAT someone is coming down the tracks.

I THINK I WILL ROB SOMEONE.

THAT SOMEONE IS YOU.

Experimental Writing

GennaRose Nethercott

(illustrated by Bobby DiTrani)

excerpt from *Lianna Fled the Cranberry Bog*

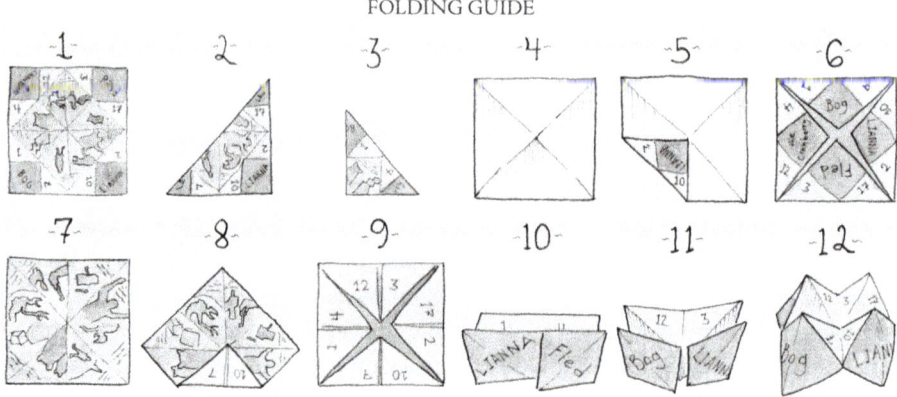

HOW TO READ THIS STORY

1. Begin with the title catcher. Hold it with your thumbs and forefingers tucked into the four nooks beneath, the four peaks pinched together on top.

2. The title appears on the four outer panels. Read the title aloud. Choose—or have a partner choose—one of the four key words.

3. Spell the selected word aloud. Open and close the catcher to reveal first one set of interior panels, then the other, switching once for each letter. When you reach the end of the word, stop with the catcher open.

4. Read the four revealed inner panels and select one, noting the bolded word on your chosen panel. Open and close the catcher again, back and forth, this time counting off the letters of *that* word. Repeat this process of choosing and counting as many times as you like.

5. When the moment is right—when your curiosity gets the best of you, when you feel the beast's breath at the back of your neck—flip open the chosen panel to reveal the conclusion beneath.

Ninepin Press · Easthampton, MA · ninepinpress.com
Text copyright © 2019 by GennaRose Nethercott · Illustrated by Bobby DiTrani
This is a work of fiction. All characters and events portrayed herein are either fictitious or used fictitiously.

Anthology

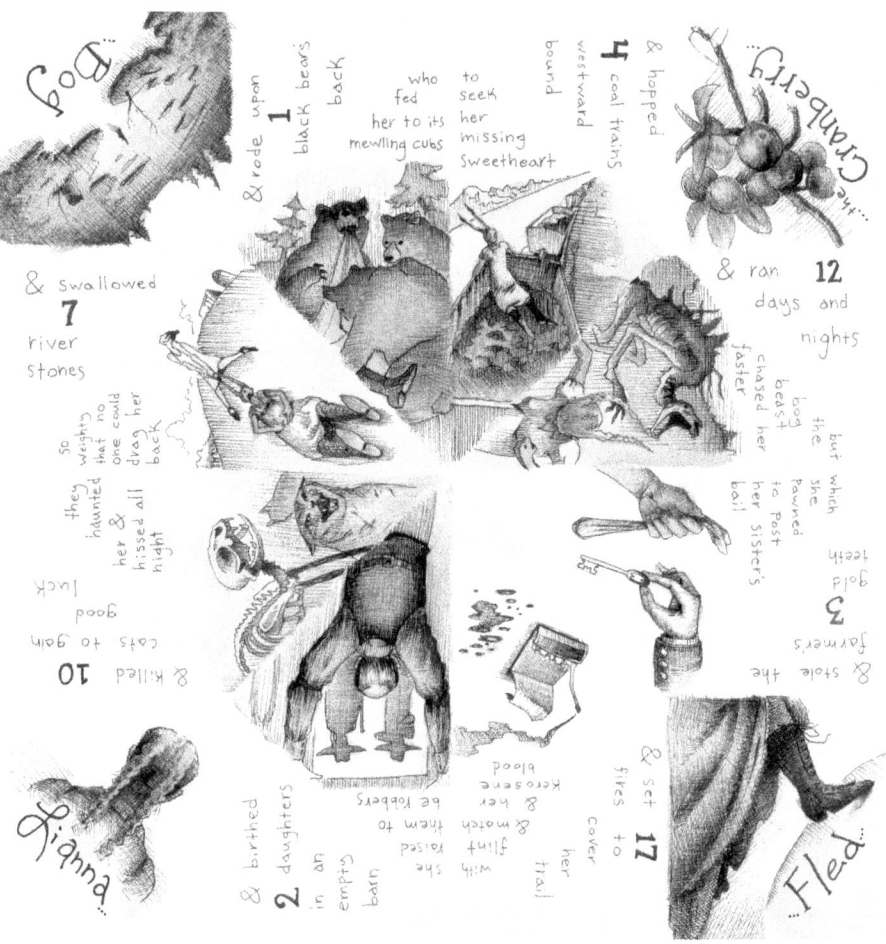

Dog...

the Cranberry...

& rode upon 1 black bear's back

who fed her to its mewling cubs

to seek her missing sweetheart

& hopped 4 coal trains westward bound

& ran 12 days and nights

& swallowed 7 river stones

but which the dog the beast pawned to post chased her her sister's faster bail

so heavy that no one could drag her back

they haunted her & kissed all night

3 gold teeth

& killed 10 cats to gain good luck

& stole the farmers

& birthed 2 daughters in an empty barn

with she flint raised & match them to be robbers

& her kerosene blood

& set 17 fires to cover her trail

Lianna...

...Fled

Experimental Writing

Eiríkur Örn Norðdahl

Nailsoup I-VI

I

Squash the cheese roll with a fork!
Squash the garlic cloves!
Squash the juniper berries!
Squash the grapes!
Squash the strawberries!
Squash the tomatoes!
Squash the asparagus!
Squash the poor!
Squash them well!
Squash, beat, grind, and bust!
Squash the bananas!
Squash the potatoes!
Squash the garden thyme!
Squash the mint leaves!
Squash the lemon grass!
Squash the fruit!
Squash the coriander seeds!
Squash the cocoa pastry!
Squash the bread crumbs!
Squash it all!

II

Chop the onions!
Chop the red onions!
Chop the garlic!
Chop the shalot!
Chop the basil!
Chop the Old Bull!
Chop into mush!
Chop the pineapple!
Chop the mushrooms!
Chop the dill!
Chop the red pepper!
Chop the peanuts!
Chop the beef!
Chop the bacon!
Chop the almonds!
Chop the dates!

Experimental Writing

Chop the prunes and the figs!
Chop down the plants!
Chop the herbs!
Chop the cucumber!
Chop the chocolate!
Chop the vegetables!
Chop the biscuit!
Chop the wild goose liver and the pig ham!
Chop the salmon!
Chop the olives and the walnuts!

III

Mince the melon!
Mince the eggs!
Mince the asparagus!
Mince the sausages!
Mince the croquante!
Mince the butter!
Mince the apples!
Mince the cold chicken!
Mince the rhubarb!
Mince the meat!
Mince the protein bar!
Mince the bread!
Mince the Corn Flakes!
Mince the olives!
Mince the milk chocolate and Mars bar!
Mince the tempered chocolate!
Mince the nougat!
Mince the Camembert cheese!
Mince the After Eight!
Mince the Valley Drizzle!

IV

Shred the green salad!
Shred the rinds!
Shred the cabbage!
Shred the parmesan cheese!
Shred the squash!
Shred the ginger!
Shred, shred everything to the ground!
Shred Shred Shred Shred Shred Shred!

Shred the silk paper!
Shred the salt cod!
Shred the lemon peel!
Shred the marzipan!
Shred the filter paper!
Shred the carrots!
Shred her!

V

Slice the leek!
Slice the herring!
Slice the others!
Slice the chili pepper!
Slice the eggplant!
Slice the Brie cheese!
Slice the celery!
Slice the mozzarella cheese!
Slice widthwise and lengthwise!
Slice the glacial salad!
Slice the pepperoni!
Slice past any brethren who lives irregularly!
Slice more over past any such immoral novel that poisons the heart!

VI

Slash the Gold cheese!
Slash the cross!
Slash the BBQ meat!
Slash the pheasant!
Slash the cauliflower!
Slash the fennel!
Slash the breasts!
Slash the orange!
Slash the crust!
Slash the top!
Slash the stalks!
Slash the pepper!
Slash the papaya fruits!
Slash the passion fruits!
Slash them, slaughter and stab!
Slash the lemon!
Slash into little bits!
Slash into boats!

Experimental Writing

Slash into cubes!
Slash in half!
Slash the coriander leaves!
Slash the sundried tomatoes!
Slash the cod heads!
Slash the pig miette!
Slash the cherry tomatoes!
Slash the lobster!
Slash the artichokes!
Slash the tuna fish!
Slash up your earth-growths!
Slash the ice!
Slash yourselves!
Slash busses in twain!
Slash up military arrows with arrogance!
Slash the flower stalks!
Slash the bagels!
Slash the pasta!
Slash now the sheep that you wish!
Slash the cheeks from the headbone!

Elena Passarello

Koko

Koko the Gorilla tells a famous joke:
  Father-gorilla, Mother-gorilla, Baby-gorilla hungry. Need work.
  Mustache-man tell: "What work?"
  Father-gorilla tell: "Really together show. Fine show. Good practice. Lights-off good."
  Mustache-man tell: "Hurry, give me."
  Father-gorilla tell: " 'Hello!' do Mother-gorilla; 'Hello!' do Father-gorilla. Together dance; clap people. Father-gorilla harmonica; Mother-gorilla clowntime; clap people. 'Hello!' do Baby-gorilla. Skateboard do, puppet dance do; clap people. Father-gorilla kiss, Mother-gorilla kiss; gorilla hug, Mother-gorilla nipple find; clap people. Nipple kiss, nipple rub, nipple pinch, nipple slap, nipple-on-bottom, nail clipper nipple, many many nipple touch. Tongue nipple. Nipple sandwich."
  Mustache-man tell: "Who nipple?"
  Father-gorilla tell: ALL nipple. Now Father-gorilla, Mother-gorilla peekaboo pickle. Poke stomach. Peekaboo pickle with pat-bottom. With walk-up-my-bottom. Pull-out hair. Nasty time. Mean love. Mother-gorilla leash-on pickle; skateboard ride do. Clap people.
  "Mother-gorilla find Baby-gorilla. Little noodle pull. Zip mouth shut. Strangle tadpole. Mayonnaise necklace. Father-gorilla there; sit Father-gorilla. Thirsty Father-gorilla lick; Mother-gorilla strap-on. Baby-gorilla sit Mother-gorilla. ALL PEEKABOO PICKLE. Trouble pickle.
  "Baby-gorilla get Ingrid. 'Hello!' do Ingrid. Ingrid turnaround; Baby-gorilla wrestle. Ingrid trouble. Devil Ingrid. 'You bad dirty toilet Ingrid.' Ingrid pudding do. Ingrid laugh; Ingrid eat. Ingrid sick. Mother-gorilla taste. Bottle-match! Ingrid electric pudding. Ingrid get Father-gorilla. Pickle bottle-match! Peekaboo pickle on fire now!
  "Ingrid hole smoke-ring blow. Mother-gorilla hole blow harmonica. Father-gorilla dance, ballon-on-noodle. Baby-gorilla clowntime, balloon-on-tadpole. Ingrid hole smoke-smoke. Around together skateboard do—smoke noodle balloon harmonica ride all! Harmonica hole play 'Purple Rain!' All MAYONNAISE RAIN! All finished! Thank you."
  Mustache-man tell: "Wow. What name show?"
  Father-gorilla tell: "WE WONDERFUL SNOB PEOPLE!"
  Mustache-man smile-frown.
  Drapes

Experimental Writing

Craig Santos Perez

ginen the legends of juan malo [a malologue]

Rub the entire block of SPAM*, along with the accompanying gelatinous goo, onto your wood furniture. The oils from the SPAM* moisturize the wood and give it a nice luster. Plus, you'll have enough left over to use as your own personal lubricant (a true Pacific dinner date). Why didn't you tell me about the "In Honor of Guam's Liberation" SPAM*! I'm trying to collect them all! Once I was on a diet and SPAM* faded from my consciousness. Then I met my future wife, who's Hawaiian, and SPAM* became part of my life again (a true Pacific romance). Maybe the economic downturn will help people appreciate SPAM* instead of loathing it. SPAM* doesn't have to be unhealthy; I eat SPAM* every day and I'm not dead, yet—just switch to SPAM* Lite. Despite rumors, SPAM* is NOT made of such odds and ends as hooves, ears, brains, native peoples, or whole baby pigs. The name itself stands for Specially Processed Army Meal, Salted Pork And More, Super Pink Artificial Meat, Snake Possum And Mongoose, or Some People Are Missing. My uncle is the reigning Guam SPAM* king. He won the last SPAM* cook off with his Spicy SPAM* meatballs. I will never forget the two-pound SPAM* bust of George Washington he made for Liberation Day, toasted crispy on the outside with raw egg yolk in the hollow center—the kids loved it! Only a fool would start a company in Guam that provides SPAM* protection. For Xmas, I bought a snow globe featuring a can of SPAM* sitting on an island. Turn it over and a typhoon swirls madly, unable to unseat SPAM* from its place of honor. I have a souvenir can I bought after seeing Monty Python's SPAM*ALOT on Broadway in New York City. It cost me $10 and is the most expensive SPAM* I've ever bought. I will never eat it.

DBC Pierre

News

A summary of the *News at Ten:* shopping centres around the country continue to draw criticism for their handling of the January clearance sales, in which a woman required first aid after being caught in a crush. The stores in question have vowed to make 1993 a safer year for shoppers.

A prominent environmental group has warned that pesticides used to rid homes of common infestations may be having a far more detrimental effect on the environment than was previously thought. A spokesman for the Green Earth Conference has said that incalculable damage could be resulting from commonly used pest-control programmes, and that the eradication of certain pests from areas of land could open the way for more ecological problems down the line. He added that only by preserving the whole ecological spectrum could the future of the environment be guaranteed.

The case of Baby X, in which a three-year-old sustained injuries after falling down badly carpeted stairs, has been adjourned a second time while submissions are heard by the government's Select Committee for Infant Safety in the Home.

In more court news, the libel action brought by Lord M. against a journalist who referred to him as 'the new Goebbels' has entered its third day before Lord Justice Davenport. A decision is expected by Friday, which, if successful for Lord M., could lead to substantial damages being awarded.

In a study thought to be the first of its kind in the world, the entire fifth and sixth forms of Galden Grammar School in Essex are to take part in an experiment focusing on gender identity and interrelationship. Hull University is to observe girls and boys from both forms wearing identical boiler suits in and out of school. Leading the study, Professor Brendan Price said results may show that many issues leading to friction between the sexes, including discrimination and even assault, can be put down to what he called 'over-genderfication' of young people under increasing pressure to adopt stereotypes in fashion, behaviour, and attitude.

And finally weather: showers gradually clearing to the east, giving way to a clear and cold night with ground frost in some rural areas. Tomorrow will begin with clear spells and some fog over low ground, with clouds increasing throughout the day. Overnight a minimum of three degrees Celsius, that's thirty-seven Fahrenheit, and an average daytime maximum of seven degrees Celsius, that's forty-four degrees Fahrenheit. The outlook for the week: remaining cool and unsettled with below average temperatures in most areas.

Experimental Writing

Mary Ruefle

The Taking of Moundville by Zoom

If you were very, very small, smaller than a leprechaun, smaller than a gnome or a fairy, and you lived in a vagina, every time a penis came in there would be a natural disaster. Your dishes would fall out of the cupboards and break and the furniture slide all the way to the other side of the room. It would take a long time to clean up afterwards.

Ekaterina Samigulina/Tae Ateh

excerpt from *Post-Soviet Belarus*

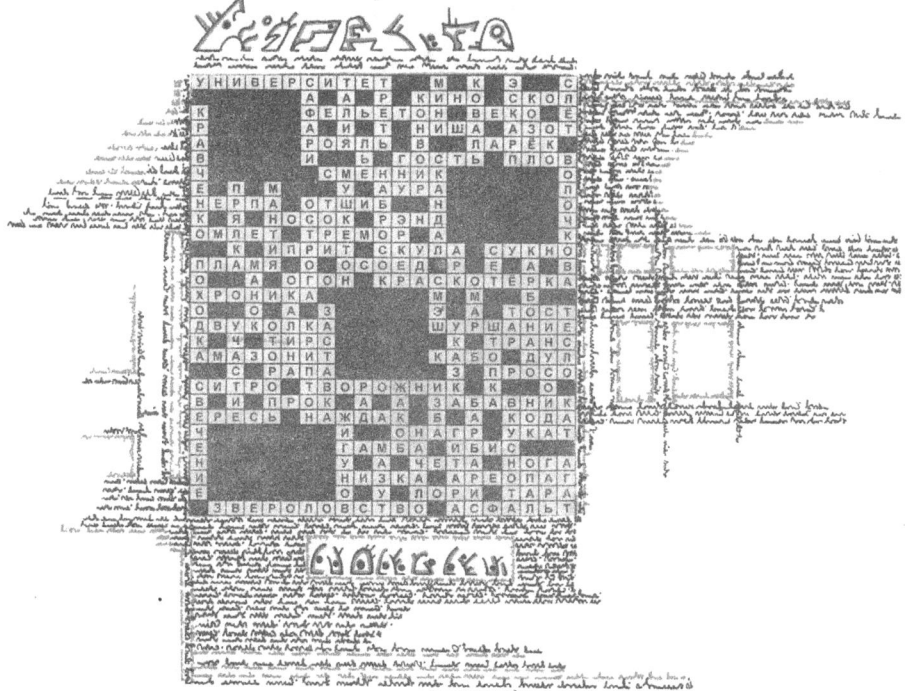

Experimental Writing

Carlos Soto-Román
  (translated by Alexis Almeida, Daniel Beauregard, Daniel Borzutzky, Whitney DeVos, Patrick Greaney, Robin Myers, Jessica Pujol, Durán, and Thomas Rothe)

Never Again

***

Never again…

Bearing in mind:

1st – The severe economic, social, and moral crisis currently destroying our country;

***

the patriotic commitment

> to restore the (broken) national spirit
> to restore our (broken) justice system
> to restore our (broken) institutions

aware that this is the only way:

> to uphold   national tradition
> to uphold   the legacy of our Founding Fathers
> to uphold   the History of Chile

aware that this is the only way:

> to guide the country's   progress and evolution
> into the future

VIGOROUSLY

***

— For having unlawfully buried a count of 15 weapons, a sizeable quantity of ammunition and explosives

— For having participated in guerrilla warfare training
— For stealing explosives
— For inciting miners to seize armories
— For inciting support of armed resistance
— For having participated in the acquisition and distribution of firearms
— For having found unlawfully buried explosives

***

Citizens are hereby informed that today, __ of _____, _____ at 16:00, the following persons were executed pursuant to the provisions granted to Military Tribunals in times of war:

***

CERTIFICATE OF REGISTRY

I, the undersigned Director of the Office of Detainee Control,

hereby certify that _____ was

detained in the National Stadium from _____ to _____

_____.

SANTIAGO, _____ of _____ 1973.

Dir. Office of Detainee Control

***

APPLICATION OF THE "ESCAPE LAW"

1. Shot
2. Shot
3. Shot
4. Shot

5. Shot
6. Shot

***

DATE OF DEATH
TIME _____

PLACE OF DEATH

OBSERVATIONS

Cause: Cervical thoracic trauma.

Cause: Cardiopulmonary arrest. Head injury by firearm.

Cause: Destruction of the thorax and cardiac region. Execution.

***

SEPTEMBER 21, 1976 – WASHINGTON, DC
THE WHITE HOUSE

7:33 The President had breakfast.

8:02 The President went to the doctor's office.

8:10 The President went to the Oval Office.

9:05 The President met with John O. March Jr., Counselor.

9:20 The President met with Richard B. Cheney, Assistant.

10:15 The President met with his Assistant for National Security Affairs.

10:15 The President met with his Assistant for National Security Affairs.

10:15 The President met with his Assistant for National Security Affairs.

10:15 The President met with his Assistant for National Security Affairs.

***

SPEECH AT CHACARILLAS

(trumpets)

(torches) (applause) (cheers: Pinochet! Pinochet! Pinochet!)
(torches) (applause) (cheers: Pinochet! Pinochet! Pinochet!)
(torches) (applause) (cheers: Pinochet! Pinochet! Pinochet!)
(torches) (applause) (cheers: Pinochet! Pinochet! Pinochet!)
(torches) (applause) (cheers: Pinochet! Pinochet! Pinochet!)
(torches) (applause) (cheers: Pinochet! Pinochet! Pinochet!)
(torches) (applause) (cheers: Pinochet! Pinochet! Pinochet!)
(torches) (applause) (cheers: Pinochet! Pinochet! Pinochet!)
(torches) (applause) (cheers: Pinochet! Pinochet! Pinochet!)
(torches) (applause) (cheers: Pinochet! Pinochet! Pinochet!)
(torches) (applause) (cheers: Pinochet! Pinochet! Pinochet!)
(torches) (applause) (cheers: Pinochet! Pinochet! Pinochet!)

(trumpets)

***

My dear young people:
The future of Chile is always in you, whose glory we are now sculpting

***

Chile is you

Homeland, flag, and youth

***

thank you

Mr. president, for everything you've done for Chile
for our safety
for our children

Experimental Writing

god bless you

***

… at first, when you start, you cry and try to hide it, so nobody notices. Then, you feel bad, a lump forms in your throat but you can hold back the tears. And then, […] you get used to it. And in the end, you don't even feel what you're doing anymore …

***

First the legs, then the sexual organs, then the heart.

They fired the machine guns in this order.

***

I was punched and kicked, pistol-whipped …
They gave me electric shocks …
Two men brutally raped me …
I was submitted to torture. I was raped …
They hit my ears, and they gave me electric shocks.
They hit me in the groin, they hit my legs with wet sacks …
I was tied to a post and doused with buckets of water …
They simulated firing-squad executions and rapes …
They tore the nails off my pinky toes …
They made me listen to a tape with recordings of children crying
and they told me they were my kids …

***

I was a month and a half pregnant.
I was two months pregnant.
I was three months pregnant.
I was five months pregnant.
I was six months pregnant.

Rodrigo Toscano

Great Awakening

a minimally staged dialogue for two players

{B being pulled over by cop, nervous, skittish; A "cop" walks up from behind wearing shades, aggressive, zealous, knocks on the "window"}

A: The lord can—give you a will, for the right search.

B: I twitch, jerk, and quake—as a prime example—of that search.

A: The lord looks for prime examples.

B: The lord is hereby offered one.

A: Self-recognition, the cognate in common?

B: We've got an understanding—me, you, the lord.

A: Weep not says the lord, for—

B: —a well-lent will, can more easily skim, him?

A: The lord's cognition has spoken.

B: The lord seeks exactness?

{A pulls B from car and puts B's hands on the hood}

A: Awake—from yourself. Shark teaser in a cage—have exactitude!

B: The lord twitches, jerks, and quakes—I didn't think so, until now.

A: I offer myself, as proof.

B: People from cities all over, unable to analyze it—guilt-free, come to—

A: —fight? Amen!

B: Amen.

A: The lord, the pimp, the people, the product, the pump of this culture readied (a stainless steel ring to pull in an emergency).

B: Amen.

A: A platinum collar, cold on contact, sometimes bliss, around the neck.

B: Pull, then twist, so that the hidden holiday is revealed: Katrina Day.

A: The food pantry of X the Lord's Sanctuary—*is* inviting.

B: Chew on this, profit.

A: Nylon straps, snug as the lord's words tethering the lord's—

B: Independent Contracting Schemes (a toddler seat at the table)

Experimental Writing

{A muscles B to the ground into spread eagle position}

A: Amen. Let's be exact! There's art for profits, art for *non*-profits (to profit by), and altogether *unprofitable* arts.

B: Quantum. Sociology. My fifty golden calves—at granny hipster's.

A: A small slab of anthracite for the nephew, an ornate cape—just for the hell of it, a hockey mask for a stroll through the mall, a 500-megawatt pulsed rhodamine laser in hand—etc.

B: You. Proud product of some kind of network. I think the lord's *self-pimping* abilities—are on the increase.

A: Average poetry readings reveal much.

B: I improve…when the content is based on *some other kind of*—contract.

A: Respect for The Lord! Respect for Cable Coppersmooth, Cinnamon Face, and all verifiable accomplishments, in tow.

B: The local is pushed out. Amen?

A: Amen! This re-flavoring of certain…distinctions. Other bitterness applied lightly to the rippled surface. Property mud bars for the whole family!

B: Audit the flow—*incoming. Admit* the lord. You were about to This Very Moaning In Private Seems Necessary. What's the immediate effect?

A: Piety, double-digit snide, "bilk bilk."

B: What's the immediate goal?

A: Light up the mall.

B: And the lonely shark around the cage?

A: Amen. The people *are*—poking back—at it.

Cecilia Vicuña

Destruir el desierto

Destruir el desierto
destruir la lluvia de las palabras infinitas del poema que interactúa con la savia.

Silenciar el poema sonorense.

Borrar la memoria de la tierra, el pensar vasto, indefinible de un pueblo
es crear una historia futura.

La historia de los censores borrando la lluvia de las palabras infinitas.

Chuk-son

> *"I's are a path"*
> Stacy Doris

We went out looking for the city of Tucson

> *Chuk-son*
> *The spring at the foot of the Dark Mountain*
>   was gone

No one was left
       only the empty shell

            Capullos de mariposa
            Téneboim

Los cuerpos del danzante muerto

        All gone inside little AC cells

        It was hot, hot

An empty thread went looking for them

                The *fat eaters* gone inside the cells
We went to Sentinel Peak
       seeking the Dark Mountain
                We saw

                children selling drugs

    families floating above

                                    balloons of fat
                                          dripping down

We lassoed their cries

We went further into the desert

        seeking the shining prisoners
                                  trapped in their light

                                                          eaters of light
                                                          shiting light
          a little ball of light
                          un mosquito gigante

they were mourning
                      Can we leave?
                                  they said

"We are the ripped heart of the Spirit"
                              they said
                                            swallowing little blobs of fat

                                                         around a TV set.
Más allá, al otro lado
                    We went further and further into the desert, seeking
the Camino Cocoim

Glittering mica
                the boys join in their own slaughter
                                  building prisons for themselves

"We are the proud flesh of the gaping wound"
                                    they said

"Aquí perdemos el habla"

No more speech,
                    only
                        gaping wound.

Watch a performance of this piece here: https://voca.arizona.edu/reading/cecilia-vicuna-may-18-2012.

Experimental Writing

Jennifer Walshe

THIS IS WHY PEOPLE O.D. ON PILLS /AND JUMP FROM THE GOLDEN GATE BRIDGE

This piece is performed by 1-10 performers performing on any instruments (including voice). Each performer prepares and practices their own individual "path" according to the directions given below. The piece consists of the performance of this/these "path(s)."
If the piece is performed by a soloist, it should be a minimum duration of 5 minutes long, and is called "THIS IS WHY PEOPLE O.D. ON PILLS."
If the piece is performed by a group, the group should agree on a performance duration (minimum 10 minutes). Each member of the group's path should be a minimum duration of 5 minutes long, and a performer can begin/end their path anywhere within the chosen performance duration. A performance by a group is called "/AND JUMP FROM THE GOLDEN GATE BRIDGE."

Directions:
1. Learn to skateboard, however primitively. Re-learn your body's weight, muscles, bones, geometry, abilities, flash-points afresh. Meditate on pressure, torque, weight, movement, air, light, space, lines. Focus minutely on surface, micro-surface, bumps, cracks, debris, concrete, asphalt, granite, marble, plastic, wood; gradients, slopes, verticals, the architectural qualities of what you skate on, the "wallness of wall." See, smell, hear, feel, how your body relates to the board and through it to space. Try to learn or at least attempt a few tricks. Even if you cannot do the tricks, analyse and understand them in your head and body, the basic concepts, movements, weightings, shifts and throw involved in ollies, grinds, kickflips, aerials, backslides, boardslides, rock'n'rolls, varials (or other tricks, and combinations of any of them). Feel time compress and expand as you move in and out of these tricks, launch, rise, catch stillness, fall; spin, slide, pivot, leap.
2. Augment this experience by watching skaters, visiting skateparks, viewing skateboard photos, videos, looking at skating magazines, books, films, websites. Try to understand and absorb what you see with your body, internalizing these ways of achieving speed, height, weightlessness, skating the paths virtually with full attention.
3. Examine and meditate on optimum skating environments, either real or imagined, taking in the macro- and micro-structure of these environments. Go for a walk and imagine being able to skate everything you see – streets, roads, walls, trees, curbs, planters, slopes, gardens, bins, lamp-posts, footpaths, bushes, cars, signs, window-sills, ramps, shopping trolleys, pools, slides, bollards, roofs, benches, cows, hand-rails, fences, edges, lips, steps, drains, ditches, rims, gutters. Contemplate the ability of skate-boarding to articulate space, find new paths through architecture, fresh uses for it, notice and exploit visible/invisible relationships.
4. Compose an imaginary path you would like to skate. This path should push and force you to limits, be rich, beautiful, complicated and stylish, and incorporate some tricks. The path is limited only by your imagination. Internalise this path, skate and inhabit it in terms of body, space and time. Feel space moving around you as you articulate your lines, intersecting, crossing, glancing, spinning away, grabbing at movements and air, smells and sounds.
5. Choose a pitch on your instrument. Skate your imagined path on this pitch. (You may choose to skate the path in slow-motion.) Every micro-detail of the pitch (tuning, timbre, dynamic, envelope, consistency, colour, texture, weight, feel, pressure, clarity, strength) should correspond absolutely to the experience of skating the path in your head. Pay attention to every minute detail, the micro-cartography of the path you are skating, the tiny shifts in muscle, weight, speed, direction. Carve through air in long, sweeping paths with the sound you produce. Reveal and inhabit new spaces, smooth new lines.

MILKER Corp. 2004

Pictures from upper left, clockwise: "skateboarding" by David Chief; "untitled" by nugunslinger; "skatepark" by Flor Hartigan; 'IMG_2150 by rednuht. All used under Creative Commons Attribution Licence 2.0.

Title taken from "Weightless Again" from Through the Trees (1998) by The Handsome Family.

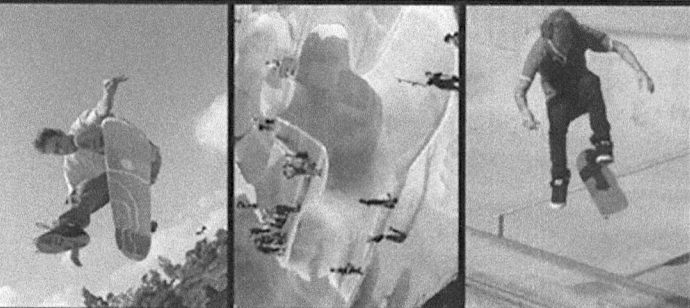

Karen Tei Yamashita

Hannah Kusoh: An American Butoh
A Performance in Six Senses

Written by Karen Tei Yamashita
Choreography and Direction by Shizuko Hoshi
Video and Slides by Karen Mayeda
Music by Vicki Abe
Scene/Lighting and Tech by Ronaldo Lopes de Oliveira,
Chris Tashima, and Steve James
Ensemble: Victor Chew, Tim Dang, Linda Igarashi,
Sala Iwamatsu, Mimosa Iwamatsu, Susan Nakagiri

Originally staged at the Japanese American Cultural and Community Center,
Little Tokyo, Los Angeles, and Highways, Santa Monica

PART 1: THE SNEEZE—THE SENSE OF SMELL

KOAN: *In a single sneeze, millions of germs are released into the air.*

PART 2: THE JAPANOPHILE—THE SENSE OF TOUCH

KOAN: *Nice Caucasian boy looking for nice Asian girl.*

PART 3: THE EYES—THE SENSE OF SIGHT

KOAN: *The only things Japanese about me are my name and my eyes.*

PART 4: TOROZUSHI/EROTICA EXOTICA— THE SENSE OF TASTE

KOAN: *Toro is the fat underbelly of the tuna. In sushi,
it is the best part, like the thighs of a woman.*
Or
A hundred million miracles are happening every day!

PART 5: MADAME BUTTERFLY—THE SENSE OF SOUND

KOAN: *Tienti la tua paura, io con sicura fede lo aspetto—*
Keep your fears; I, with secure faith, wait for him. (Last lines from *Madama Butterfly* aria)

PART 6: THE SIXTH SENSE—THE SENSE OF INTUITION

KOAN: *You've got to be kidding.*
Or
Hey, like, go with the flow, man; go with the flow.

PART 1: THE SNEEZE—THE SENSE OF SMELL

MUSIC:	Piece with mixed cultural instruments: koto, shakuhachi, marimba, bagpipes, or some other sansei invention of a multicultural nature.
SCENE:	There is an enormous half mask (nose and eyes) on stage, possibly ukiyo-e in design, but probably Japanese. The nose part of the mask allows for the entrance and exit of dancers. The eyes, which may blink, open and shut, house large video monitors. Mask coloring is effected with the use of slides/lighting. Changes in mask may create Kabuki-like makeup; red, white, and blue highlights; and so on. Slide material over white mask is effective.
DANCE:	A sneeze begins the music/dance. Five dancers (three women, two men) in bags fall out of the nostrils. The bags are of different colors/materials and should be stretchy in nature: green (the first bag), kimono material, khaki camouflage, and so on. Possibly one stretchy type of material can be airbrushed into different possibilities. The bags roll, splat, fall over, congregate, stick to each other, expostulate, ruminate, and so on. Possibly film projection over bags.
SMELLS:	There is a flow of smells directed into the audience: hibachi, teriyaki, incense, chili, marijuana, takuan, cherry, and so on.
VIDEO/SLIDES:	Eyes are closed. Footage of atomic bomb at the flutter of eyes during the initial sneeze. Scenes of Hiroshima post-A-bomb destruction. Then, Japanese America scenes of the concentration camps, early farming and urban pioneers, with movement to present day—Little Tokyo, Gardena, festivals, family life, daily life.

PART 2: JAPANOPHILE—THE SENSE OF TOUCH

MUSIC:	Chinese dance from the Nutcracker.
DANCE:	A large finger appears. Feet push through each bag. Some feet wear sneakers; others put on geta, tabi, or heels. The chase begins. Some bags get stuck to the finger. Some of the bags get pushed against the wall. Some run back into the nose. The finger rubs the nose. The bags escape through the opposite nostril. Some bags produce fingers; some bags produce bare feet. Other bags produce massaging aids. One bag has an electric massager, which jitters like crazy. The bags massage the finger until it flees, the bags running the finger up into the nose.
VIDEO/ SLIDES:	Sansei discussing her blind date with a Japanophile. This may be broken up into several women telling the same story. Narrative over

photographs from family albums and old film footage showing a sansei girl growing up in America.

VIDEO NARRATIVE: Listen, I never do this, but I figure I'd do this for my friend. She's says, "Listen, this guy has money, and he loves Asian women, but none of the women he dates are fun like you. He oughta date an Asian woman who knows how to have fun, you know what I mean? Listen, I think you'll really hit it off."

Well, I shoulda known better, but, after all, they're all Japanophiles out there. They just manifest themselves in different forms.

I drive out to meet this guy at his place. I'm like driving through this nice area, so I figure I'm going to get treated to a nice dinner. When I get to his place, he like lives behind this Japanese gate with Japanese kanji painted on the doorway. I get let in the gate, and this place is a total Japanese garden. My parents live in Gardena, but they don't have a garden like this. I mean it is out of Japan Home Gardens. It's like a setting for a Japanese restaurant. There's this koi pond and a little red lacquered bridge and all this bonsai and this moss and rocks. I never been in Japan, but I swear to myself, like I'm totally in Japan.

So then I get to his house, and he's got this marble entranceway and these shoes all left at the doorway. He meets me at the door, and he is this hakujin guy who's shorter than me. He looks me over, and you know I was prepared for this big evening, so I came in black stockings and heels and my black leather miniskirt and big shoulder-padded leather coat. I was really looking wonderful, but I'm towering over him so I take my heels off at least.

I say, "Wow. You got a nice place. I never seen anything like it." He looks surprised you know.

He shows me around. He's got scrolls everywhere and screens here and there. He's got these big dead branches built up into giant arrangements next to white walls. He's got a big red silk kimono hanging on his bedroom wall with all these prints of Japanese women with their kimonos falling off. And get this, he sleeps on tatami mats, and he takes a bath in a sunken tub. All the time he's got this koto and flute music playing on his compact disc.

I ask him if he lives there all by himself. And he says, "Yeah." This is sort of his retreat that he's made for himself. And I say, "Yeah." Then I ask him whether he's got anything to drink. He says he's got some fine tea. I ask him if he's got anything stronger. He says he doesn't drink, but he's got this bar for guests, so I help myself.

Then he goes off to get something, so I snoop around and open all his closets. And he's got these Playboy fold-outs of all these Asian nudes in the closets.

Experimental Writing

Then he comes back with this apple cut up on a Japanese plate, and he says it's a Japanese apple. I try this apple, and it tastes like an apple, so I say, "So what is this, a Japanese grew it?" He says something about intensive agriculture, and I say, "Oh yeah, my grandfather used to do that."

Then he shows me his newest acquisition, some antique Japanese furniture that's sitting there on the tatami. He says it's a something or other sort of dressing table from the fourteenth century and he paid a fortune for it. I remember the Japanese nudes in the closet, so I say, "Yeah, but you need a midget to use it."

By now I'm really hungry. Japanese apples don't do anything for me. Besides, I really feel like I need to return to L.A. He says, "Where would you like to eat?" I suggest _____. Well, he says he's heard of that place, and isn't it a little expensive? So I suggest another place, and he doesn't like Italian. He doesn't like Thai. He doesn't like Tex-Mex. He doesn't like this or that or this is too expensive. He says, "Don't you like Japanese food?" Well, I tell him Japanese food is no big deal. If I want it, I can get it at home. "Do you cook Japanese?" he asks. I say, "Of course not; my mom does." He looks confused. But all he wants to eat is Japanese, so we end up going to a Japanese family restaurant on Sawtelle. Can you imagine? I'm dressed for _____, and he takes me to a teriyaki place. I can't believe it.

Then, get this. He orders everything in Japanese. Seriously. Japanese. He orders all that disgusting gooey stuff like salmon eggs and quail eggs. Me, I order tekkamaki and some California rolls.

He knows the owner, and they spend the whole dinner talking in Japanese. He never even talks to me. Just to really freak him out, I ask for a fork and spoon and pour shoyu all over my rice.

So I take him back to Japan on the Westside and leave him there at the gate. I say, "Well, I don't know what you're looking for in the way of a date, but the only things Japanese about me are my name and my eyes," and I drive off.

PART 3: THE EYES—THE SENSE OF SIGHT

MUSIC: *Aperture* (piece originally composed by Vicki Abe)

DANCE: Heads and arms, covered in white chalk, push out of the bags. The legs are further exposed. Faces emerge in dark glasses. Eyeball earrings. Mouths encase tiny lights; as the dancers open their mouths in little Os, lights flash on and off. Eyes might be patched underneath glasses with painted-on almond eyes; on one dancer's eyelids are inscribed a *3* and an *M*. Candy almonds are passed out to the audience after dancers remove patches. Dancers use mirrors and paint eyes extravagantly and formally on stage. All dancers then display rolls of Scotch tape, which may be torn in long pieces and applied to parts of the body. Bodies and faces move together, positioning the eyes dramatically. Ongoing demonstration of latex application to create Asian features.

ONSTAGE DIALOGUE:

Quotations from various sources about eyes:

A: Medical
B: Makeup/Special Effects
C: Biblical/Shakespearean
D: Poet
E: Scholar/Reporter

C: You see her eyes are open. (*Macbeth*)

D: Ay, but their sense is shut. (*Macbeth*)

E: It is probably futile to claim that most Japanese eyes are not slanted—especially in a work on Japanese prints, whose artists adopted the pleasing sensation that they were… (*The Floating World*, Michener)

D: I met a lady in the meads
Full beautiful, a faery's child;
Her hair was long, her foot was light,
And her eyes were wild.
("La Belle Dame San Merci," Keats)

C: Lust not after her beauty in thine heart; neither let her take thee with her eyelids.
(Proverbs)

A: Westernization of the Asian eyelid has become a topic of considerable interest in the Western world in recent years due to the increasing number of surgeons being consulted to perform this procedure. This demand is attributable to the great influx of Asian immigrants, who are influenced by Western culture, design, and esthetics. After performing over two thousand cases of westernizing Asian eyelids, I have developed a method of surgically creating a double eyelid as well as a method for removing the epicanthal web. The techniques result in a marked improvement of the narrow, puffy Asian eye and greater patient satisfaction.
(Ronald S. Matsunaga, DDS, MD, FACS)

C: Behold, I show you a mystery; we shall not all sleep, but we shall all be changed, in a moment, in the twinkling of an eye…
(Corinthians)

B: Instructions for the makeup artist.
Number 24: Oriental Makeup.
Materials: One pair of Oriental eyelids…
(*Makeup for Theater, Film & Television*, Lee Baygan)

Experimental Writing

A: The goal... is to surgically create a supratarsal fold, commonly referred to as a "double eyelid" of the typical Asian to a more esthetic and cosmetically larger eyelid characteristic of the occidental. The newly created eyelids can be further enhanced by proper cosmetic application, resulting in greater self-image and confidence.

B: Black eyebrow pencil shapes and defines brows at the arch. For natural effect, blend color well with cotton swab. Apply honey-brown eye shadow from crease to brow, smokey olive shadow on lid. Blend out, extending color under lower lashes.
("Beauty Center," *Good Housekeeping*)

C: Did not the heavenly rhetoric of thine eye,
'gainst whom the world cannot hold argument,
Pursuade my heart to this false perjury?
(*Love's Labour's Lost*)

A: In the Asian eye, there is a congenital absence of the supratarsal fold with excessive preorbital septal fat extending down to the ciliary margin along with the obicularis oculi muscle, causing a puffy, narrow *slit eye*.

C: Life for life. Eye for an eye...
(Exodus 21:23)

B: 1. Oriental eyelids must be large enough to cover the area from your eyelashes to your eyebrows ...
2. Place the eyelid latex piece so you can look straight ahead easily ...
3. Powder heavily ...

E: She's got eyes like Jezebel, teeth like pearls, gosh or gee, she's out of this world.
(Folk song)

A: The epicanthal web in Asians is a normal ethnic occurrence and is not due to an abnormal position of the orbits or canthal elements.

E: Is life more enjoyable with Caucasian eyes? Is visibility greater?

B: Using a small piece of foam rubber sponge, apply liquid latex...
5. Dry with a hand hair dryer...
6. Powder...
7. Apply rubber mask grease...
8. Blend foundation...
9. Powder the entire face...

E: Can you see when you laugh?

A: 1. A curvilinear line is marked with gentian violet solution on the upper eyelid five to ten millimeters above the ciliary margins of both eyelids simultaneously .. .

B: 10. With the proper clothes and mannerisms … you can achieve a believable Oriental appearance. Remember that the highlight and shading used [must be] suited to [the] actor's bone structure. If you have a very healthy, full face, changing it to a thin one with high cheekbones and shading will not be easy—you might simply wind up with a dirty face. (Remember, too, that not all Orientals are thin!) Do the best you can with your face and stay away from stereotypes.

E: Police are on the lookout for an Asian male, age twenty-five, medium height, short black hair, and surgically Westernized Asian eyes.

C: Take, oh take those lips away,
That so sweetly were forsworn;
And those eyes, the break of day;
Lights that do mislead the Morn.
(*Measure for Measure*)

A: 2. Local anesthesia of 1 percent lidocaine hydrochloride with 1:100,000 adrenaline is injected…

D: Or if thy mistress some rich anger shows,
Imprison her soft hand and let her rave,
And feed deep, deep upon her peerless eyes.
(*Ode to Melancholy*, Keats)

E: Mariko fanned herself … "What is the lady, your wife like?"

A: "She's twenty-nine. Tall compared with you. By our measurements, I'm six feet two inches, she's about five feet eight inches, you're about five feet… Her hair's… fair with a touch of red. Her eyes are blue, much bluer than mine, blue-green…"
(*Shogun*, Clavell)

(*sung*) Don't it make my brown eyes
Don't it make my brown eyes
Don't it make my brown eyes
Don't it make my brown eyes blue?
("Don't It Make My Brown Eyes Blue," lyrics by Richard Leigh)

C: If thine eye offend thee, pluck it out, and cast it from thee: it is far better to enter into life with one eye, rather than having two eyes to be cast into hellfire.
(Matthew 18:9)

(in Japanese) Okome o somatsu ni suru to me ga tsubureru.

A: 3. The skin incision is made…

D: Her eyes were deeper than the depth of waters stilled at even…
("The Blessed Damozel," Rosetti)

Experimental Writing

E: I can sort of see that [this alien being] had a bald, rather largish head for someone that size. And that its eyes are slanted, more than an Oriental's eyes…
(*Communion*, Whitley Strieber)

C: Why beholdest thou the mote that is in thy brother's eye, but considerest not the beam that is in thine own eye?
(Matthew 7:3)

A: 4. Pretarsal subcutaneous dissection is carried out to remove all orbicular oculi muscle and fat…

D: Beauty is in the eye of the beholder.
(Margaret W. Hungerford)

E: It is only with the heart that one can see rightly; what is essential is invisible to the eye.
(*The Little Prince*, Saint-Exupéry)

D: The light that lies
In women's eyes,
Has been my heart's undoing…
My only books
Were women's looks
And folly's all they taught me.
("The Time I've Lost in Wooing," Thomas Moore)

C: Fie, fie upon her!
There's language in her eye…
(*Troilus and Cressida*)

A: 7. Final closure of the incision line is performed with a running subcuticular 6-0 polyester suture…

C: For where is any author in the world
Teaches such beauty as a woman's eye?
(*Love's Labour's Lost*)

E: The look of love is in your eyes,
a look your smile can't disguise.
The look of love is saying so much more
than just words could ever say;
and what my heart has heard,
well, it takes my breath away.
("The Look of Love," lyrics by Burt Bacharach and Hal David)

A: 8. Ointment and dry sterile dressing is applied over the incision line…

VIDEO/SLIDES:
    Eyes on screen. Possibly painting of eyes, application of Scotch tape and thick black pencil and mascara. Shiseido/Maybelline commercials. Possible video of eyelid plastic surgery. Before and after slides of surgery. Cuts from movies where Caucasian actors have had their eyes Asianized (Alex Guinness, Marlon Brando). Ukiyo-e eyes. Also a myriad of Asian eyes, all, in fact, quite different from one another.

PART 4: TOROZUSHI/EROTICA EXOTICA—THE SENSE OF TASTE

MUSIC: Japanese folk songs similar to "Miracles" from *Flower Drum Song* or something from *The Mikado*.

DANCE: All of the bodies, heavily powdered in white chalk, are finally removed from the bags—a sort of butterfly emerging act combined with a striptease. Sensuous, despite the fact that their tongues hang out most of the time (or some other permanent facial expression). As they emerge, inflatable wings and body parts (muscles, breasts, extra appendages) inflate. They all don lace aprons.

    All dancers then lug bottles of shoyu and sake and five-pound bags of rice. They bear these things like burdens. Dancers pour sake and shoyu into buckets and then draw out raw fish and squid and octopus.

    Five microwaves are rolled onstage. The microwaves obviously hum and ding. Dancers stuff the microwaves with instant Japanese foods: Top Ramen and other packaged foods, packages and all. Sushi miraculously appears from the microwaves. Dancers stuff their faces with sushi and disappear into the nose.

FACIAL/PHYSICAL EXPRESSION:
    Permanently cute.

ONSTAGE DIALOGUE:
    (*split among the actors as they go about their business, cooking and so on*) When I first came to this country, I worked for my relatives in a Japanese restaurant. It was not a fancy restaurant. It was family restaurant on Sawtelle. At first, I could not speak any English, so I started working in the kitchen. I washed dishes and I cut vegetables. I filled shoyu containers. I also watched noodles boiling. Then I got better in my English, so I started to serve tea and to clear the tables. Now I am waitress.

    Customers always tell me how good my English is, but if I make mistake or forget something, they always talk among themselves and complain about service. They say nobody in L.A. speaks English anymore.

    Then, of course, there are these Americans who have been to Japan. They like to tell you about the ryokans they have been to and going to Kamakura to see big Buddha and how expensive everything is in Japan.

Before, my relatives tell me that only Japanese Americans and Japanese business people come to eat at our restaurant. Now, you only see Americans. They say they get the same amount of business but that they have double their profits because Americans eat more, maybe twice as much as the Japanese.

Mostly we make money from the sushi bar. In Japan, sushi is very expensive. Maybe if you go to the sushi bar, you eat a few sushi and some sake or beer. It's just a food to eat with a little sake or make the sake go down better. Only the salaryman on a business account can afford to eat so much.

But Americans want to have a big dinner. They eat and drink and eat and drink, and they can't help themselves. Someone is explaining to me that the Americans are eating big steak dinners with big potato, and you cannot expect them to eat like us Japanese.

They want to try everything, and they want to try everything twice. Americans like to have salad before their meals, so we make a special salad and a special soup. Then, they like to try halibut or tuna sashimi or maybe sea bass. Most often they order two or three servings all at once so we have to pile all the sashimi together. I don't think this is very aesthetic, but they tell us we are very inexpensive.

Then they ask for a long list of sushi, and we put maybe twenty pieces on a big platter for one person. Once I saw a man eat one hundred pieces of sushi. He said sushi is very healthy for you. He said he discovered sushi. I was thinking this was strange. He said he even discovered our restaurant. I surprised that the Americans like sushi.

In the beginning, I see some people cry, but usually we tell them that the wasabi kills germs. I surprised that American eat so much raw fish. Even some Japanese don't like raw fish. One man only eat sea urchin. Eat ten to twenty pieces of sea urchin every time and leave. I wonder he don't get sick.

Usually an American comes in for the first time with a friend. This friend they call "the sushi aficionado," I think. This friend sits at the sushi bar and talks with the sushi maker. He says maybe to Ichiro, "Ich, I'll have the regular." Ichiro very professional. He remember one sushi aficionado out of hundreds. If Ichiro don't remember the regular for this customer, he say, "I got something different for you today." Something like that. This is very impressive to the new customer. Pretty soon, the new customer is sushi aficionado himself, coming with his new friends and saying, "Ich, I'll have the regular."

But sometimes there are Americans who can speak Japanese. There is a guy like this who comes all the time. He say to Ichiro in Japanese that he only likes Japanese women. Ichiro like to agree and say that when a man marries, he marries an old-fashioned cute Japanese girl, but American type is only for playing around. Ichiro says that American-type woman don't make a good marriage. You gotta get a woman who don't ask questions and stay at home and cook and do whatever you want. You know, "Oi kimi, get this, get that."

The American guy ask Ichiro to make an arranged marriage with a nice Japanese girl for him. Maybe he is joking but I don't think so. He keep looking at me. When he leaves, Ichiro says that this guy has gone to a lot of trouble to get a Japanese wife, speaking Japanese, building a Japanese house, learning everything Japanese. Of course, he's not Japanese; only Japanese can be Japanese, but it would be a very shame if he didn't marry a Japanese girl.

So I very surprised one day when this American guy comes with a sansei girl in black leather. Sansei girl don't know how to use ohashi. She don't know what the American guy and Ichiro are talking about. When I go to the kitchen, I know they are talking about me. Ichiro tell the guy that I will do anything to stay in America. Ichiro and the guy laugh.

The sansei girl, she's bored so she get up and go to the bathroom and telephone her friend. I hear her talking on the telephone. She say, "This Japanophile's a jerk." I don't know what she mean, "Japanophile," but I think Ichiro is a jerk too.

VIDEO: Cuts of Japanese commercials about Japanese food products, fishermen cutting up fish, Americans eating Japanese food, the nape of a geisha's neck, the kimono suggestively falling off the shoulder and other suggestive cuts. Food and sex get mixed up. Flashes of ukiyo-e prints of courtesans, erotica. Also repetitive narrative, "A hundred million miracles are happening every day!" and "The way to a man's heart is through his stomach."

PART 5: MADAME BUTTERFLY—THE SENSE OF SOUND

MUSIC: Puccini's *Madama Butterfly*

DANCE: Women reappear from nose in long unorthodox kimonos of recycled and unconventional matter (Styrofoam balls/popcorn, nori, mini-blinds, shimmering transparent plastic, crazy eyes, and so on). Footwear may be varied (high heels, boots, and traditional). Fog flows out of the nose with the emerging dancers. Wigs hang from nylon strings above. Women move under and into wigs, moving about each other until the wigs tangle and pop off.

One dancer sings Puccini (karaoke-style) into a mic.

Meanwhile, dancers all partake of long wet noodles/spaghetti, some with enormous chopsticks and some with enormous forks. The noodles flicker this way and that, get draped in their hair and over their bodies. Someone might have some permanent plastic noodles that are permanently held up in the air. Dancers brandish chopsticks

Experimental Writing

in a sort of breast-beating, bizarre, ritualistic fashion, threatening suicide. It never happens.

FACIAL/BODILY EXPRESSION:
Probably permanently wild/hysterical/distressed. Could be changing, evolving, but all women must have exactly the same expression. All mouths hang open, all eyes are crossed, all have Kabuki-esque movements.

VIDEO: Deep red lips sensuously reciting a long list of Japanese words: ohiyogozaimasu, benjo, bakatari, sushi, teriyaki, obachan, hakujin, gaijin, Toyota, bonsai, Honda, sukoshi, hi, hi, moshimoshi, Suzuki, konichiwa, konbanwa, korewa, sorewa, arewa, gohan, ohashi, chawan, niku, ojoosan, arigato, obachan, sansei, nisei, issei, manju, banzai, samurai, ninja, sushi, origami, sake, ocha, biru, Sapporo, Kirin, ringo, kaki, sashimi, wasabi, shoyu, ajinomoto, udon, boya, unchi, zori, nori, ikebana, tatami, doodesuka, harakiri, yakuza, gyoza, gaysian, hiragana, katakana, kanji, hoppi coat, happa, sukiyaki, kimono, bonsai, karate, judo, Mitsubishi, Sumitomo, Mazda, Sony, National, Sharp, Toshiba, Akai, Kenmore, Fujinon, Nikon, Kumon, Suzuki violin, Daihatsu, Nissan, Subaru, Lexus, Cressida, Celica, Sankaijuku, Dairakudakan, Danjuro, Kabuki, Noh, Bunraku, Gagaku, terebi, Sado, Tokyo, Nikko, Nagasaki, Hiroshima, Osaka, Akihito, Hirohito, Yamashita, Abe, Mayeda, Hoshi, sembei, snowcones, Gardena, Meiji, Marukai, Little Tokyo, Big Tokyo, 22nd Street, Rafu Shimpo, JACL, Topaz, Manzanar, Heart Mountain, JAL, Kawabata, Mishima, Oi, Kurosawa, Mifune, Oshima, Panasonic, Bridgestone, hamubaga, Japanophile, kohi, miruku, hachimaki, sakura, koto, shakuhachi, hichiriki, shamisen, enryo, Yamaha, katana, Edo, ukiyo-e, daruma, Utamaro, Sharaku, Issumboshi, Dodesukaden, Urashima Taro, Momotaro, Ran, Shogun, Tokugawa, onibaba, geisha, My Geisha, rikisha, Teahouse of the August Moon, Hiroshima Mon Amour, Godzilla, The Barbarian and the Geisha, Majority of One, Sayonara, Love Is a Many Splendored Thing, Hinomaru, MacArthur, Admiral Perry, Pacific Overtures, Mako, Ohara, Karate Kid, Pat Morita, Jack Soo, Acura, Dark Shadow, Snow Country, Yoko Ono, Kenzo Tanji, Kenzo, Marimekko, Waseda, Todai, Keio, Shinjuku, ichi, ni, san, shi, go, roku, hichi, hachi, ku, ju, redress, corum nobis, Fujica, Casio, Canon, futon, habakari, makura, maguro, uni, saba, ikura, takenoko, hamachi, ika, ochazuke, furikake, tenegui, ofuro, obento, shinkansen, onigiri, mogusa, shiatsu, ochanoyu, sumo, beisubaru, karaoke, manga, Gung Ho, shabushabu, kabucha, tamagogohan, tempura, oshogatsu, bon odori, namuamidabutsu, transformers, soroban, ichiban, tsukudani, yen, salaryman, Pacific rim, the Nikkei, kaisha, Tennoheika, kamikaze, Showa, Heisei, bushido, kao, me, mimi, hana, kuso, sayonara.

PART 6: THE SIXTH SENSE — THE SENSE OF INTUITION

MUSIC: Synthesized gagaku

DANCE: Women discard and step from kimonos. Something contemporary underneath (maybe white Indian pants on powdered bodies). All dancers pick up hair blowers,

Dep and blow-dry their hair in extreme angles. "Hey, like, go with the flow, man; go with the flow" and "You gotta be kidding."

FACIAL/PHYSICAL EXPRESSION:
Permanent laughter, then serene.

VIDEO: Shapes, odd forms from nature, close-ups of ordinary things seen from another perspective; nothing is quite recognizable, but all are clearly something you have seen somewhere. Credits and the End/Owari. Eye winks at end.

ACKNOWLEDGMENTS

Joining us in these conversations—in some cases over many years before we wrote this book—have been a wide array of people we would like to thank and acknowledge here, who, of course, bear no responsibility for any errors or inaccuracies in the book: our NAU students in ENG 179, ENG 579, ENG 676, HON 389, and HON 394. Specifically: Anastasiya Saava, Chris Kalman, Rowan Wentworth, Carson Redmon, Maya Guthrie, Anahi Molina, tanner menard, Eric Haase, and Riley Smith.

We'd also like to thank teachers like Nick Salvato, Alice Fulton, Denis Johnson, Ben Lerner, Uma Satyavolu Rau, Gayle Rogers, Suresh Raval, Jennifer Boyd, and Brian Fleckenstein; mentors like J. Robert Lennon, Ander Monson, and Aurelie Sheehan; colleagues like Nicole Walker, Rob Wallace, and Sean Parson; and friendly minds like Gianni Label, Ed Steck, Sarah Minor, Jamison Crabtree, Noam Dorr, Daisy Pitkin, Timothy Dyke, Lewis DeJong, Mike Powell, Daniel DeKerlegand, Benjamin Garcia, Jared Harél, Les Hunter, Margarita Cruz, Amanda Meeks, Orlando White, Gavin Buckley, Manny Loley, Jake Skeets, John Melillo, Lindsey Drager, and Henry Goldkamp.

Thanks to Weldon Ryckman for his work in tracking down sourcing, and in some cases, inventing citation conventions for the unconventional work mentioned in this book. Thanks to Marilyn Lenhart and Andie Francis for occasional assistance. With gratitude to Andie Francis and M. S. Coe for hours stolen and innumerable notes.

We would also like to thank Lucy Brown and Aanchal Vij who helped shepherd this book through the publication and editing process at Bloomsbury, and Sean Prentiss and Joe Wilkinson for their enthusiasm for this project.

Lastly, in advance, we would like to thank the readers, students, teachers, and experimental communities who make use of this book, trying out its prompts or questioning its premises.

REFERENCES

Aarseth, E. J. (1997), *Family Resemblance Cybertext: Perspectives on Ergodic Literature*, Baltimore: Johns Hopkins University Press.
Abend, G. (2008), "The Meaning of 'Theory,'" *Sociological Theory*, 26 (2): 173–99.
Achebe, C. (1994), *Things Fall Apart*, New York: Anchor Books.
Adrian, K. (2018), *The Shell Game: Writers Play with Borrowed Forms*, Lincoln: University of Nebraska Press.
Alameddine, R. (1998), *Koolaids: The Art of War*, New York: Picador.
Andrews, J. (2006a), "Material Combinatorium Supremum," *Electronic Literature Collection*, 2: 1.
Andrews, J. (2006b), "Stir Fry Texts," *Electronic Literature Collection*. Available online: https://collection.eliterature.org/1/works/andrews__stir_fry_texts/index.html (accessed August 1, 2023).
Antena. (n.d.), "A Manifesto for Ultratranslation." Available online: https://antenaantena.org/wp-content/uploads/2012/06/ultratranslation_eng.pdf (accessed June 12, 2023).
Archey, K., and R. Peckham (2014), "Art Post-Internet," *UCCA*. Available online: https://ucca.org.cn/en/exhibition/art-post-internet// (accessed December 30, 2022).
Archibald, S. (2015), "Feline Darlings & the Anti-Cute," *Cat Is Art Spelled Wrong*, 105–20, Minneapolis: Coffee House Press.
Armand, L. (2021), *Hotel Palenque. minor literature[s]*. Available online: https://minorliteratures.com/2021/04/09/hotel-palenque-10-louis-armand/ (accessed August 1, 2023).
Arrow, D. W. (1997), "Pomobabble: Postmodern Newspeak and Constitutional 'Meaning' for the Uninitiated," *Michigan Law Review*, 96 (3): 461.
Ashbery, J. (1984). *A Wave*. Manchester: Carcanet Press.
Atwood, M. (1982), *Second Words: Selected Critical Prose, 1960–1982*, Toronto: House of Anansi Press.
Austin, J. L. (1961), "Performative Utterances," in J. O. Urmson and G. J. Warnock (eds.), *Philosophical Papers*, 233–52, Oxford: Clarendon Press.
Babbit, M. (1958), "Who Cares If You Listen?," *High Fidelity*, February: 38–40.
Bean, H., and L. Hinton (2009), "Poet's Theatre: An Introduction," *Postmodern Culture*, 20 (1). Available online: https://www.pomoculture.org/2013/09/03/poets-theater-an-introduction/ (accessed June 11, 2023).
Benjamin, W. (1997), "The Translator's Task," trans. Steven Rendell, *TTR: Traduction, Terminologie, Rédaction*, 10 (2): 151–65.
Berghaus, G. (2006), *Theatre, Performance, and the Historical Avant-Garde*, London: Palgrave Macmillan.
Bernstein, C. (1986), "An Interview with Tom Beckett," *Content's Dream: Essays 1975–1984*, 385–410, Los Angeles: Sun & Moon Press.
Bernstein, C. (1988), "Breaking the Translation Curtain: The Homophonic Sublime," *L'Esprit Créateur*, 38 (4): 64–70.
Bernstein, F. (2014), "Notes on Post-Conceptual Poetry," *Evening Will Come: A Monthly Journal of Poetics*, (41). Available online: https://thevolta.org/ewc41-fbernstein-p1.html (accessed August 1, 2023).
Bertram, L.-Y. (2019), *Travesty Generator*, Blacksburg: Noemi Press.
Bervin, J. (2017), *Silk Poems*, Brooklyn: Nightboat Books.
Bervin, J. (n.d.), "An Interview with Jen Bervin," H. A. Knight (interviewer), *Asymptote Journal*. Available online: https://www.asymptotejournal.com/interview/an-interview-with-jen-bervin/ (accessed June 12, 2023).
Bhabha, H. K. (2006), "Cultural Diversity and Cultural Differences," in B. Ashcroft, G. Griffiths, and H. Tiffin (eds.), *The Post-Colonial Studies Reader*, 155–7, New York: Routledge.

References

Birkerts, S. (2016), "Can the 'Literary' Survive Technology?," *Literary Hub*. Available online: https://lithub.com/can-the-literary-survive-technology/ (accessed December 30, 2022).

Bishop, W., and D. Starkey (2006), *Keywords in Creative Writing*, Logan: Utah State University Press.

Blumer, H. (1936), "Book Review: Lexical Evidence from Folk Epigraphy in Western North America: A Glossarial Study of the Low Element in the English Vocabulary," *American Journal of Sociology*, 42 (3): 434–5.

Bök, C. (2011), "The Xenotext Works," *Poetry Foundation*. Available online: https://www.poetryfoundation.org/harriet-books/2011/04/the-xenotext-works (accessed December 30, 2022).

Borges, J. L. (1981), "The Translators of *The Thousand and One Nights*," in E. R. Monegal and A. Reid (eds.), *Borges: A Reader*, 73–86, New York: Dutton.

Boully, J. (2007), *The Book of Beginnings and Endings*, Louisville: Sarabande Books.

Braithwaite, L. Y. (1995), *Wigger*, Vancouver: Arsenal Pulp Press.

Braithwaite, L. Y. (2000), *Ratz Are Nice (PSP)*, New York: Alyson Books.

Braschi, G. (1998), *Yo-Yo Boing!*, Pittsburgh: Latin American Literary Review Press.

Brown, J. P. (2011), "'touch in transit': Manifestation/*Manifestación* in Cecilia Vicuña's *cloud-net*," *Contemporary Women's Writing*, 5 (3): 208–31.

Browne, L., ed. (2021), "Preface," in Laynie Browne (ed.), *A Forest of Many Stems: Essays on the Poet's Novel*, 1–6, Brooklyn: Nightboat Books.

Burt, S. (2020), "On Long Poems," *The Yale Review*. Available online: https://yalereview.org/article/long-poems (accessed August 1, 2023).

Bury, L. (2016), "The Tender Proceduralism of Solmaz Sharif's 'Look'," *Hyperallergic*. Available online: https://hyperallergic.com/332131/the-tender-proceduralism-of-solmaz-sharifs-look/ (accessed December 30, 2022).

Calvino, I. (1982), *If on a Winter's Night a Traveler*, trans. William Weaver, New York: HBJ.

Caplan, D. (2012), "Reduced to Rhyme: On Contemporary Doggerel," *The Poetics of American Song Lyrics*, (1): 6–25.

Casey, R. (2019), "Aisteach: Jennifer Walshe, Heritage, and the Invention of the Irish Avant-Garde," *Transposition: Musique et sciences sociales*, 8 (1): 1–16.

Césaire, A. (1992), *A Tempest*, ed. R. Miller, New York: Theatre Communications Group.

Cha, T. H. K. (1982), *Dictee*, New York: Tanam Press.

Chasar, M. (2020), *Poetry Unbound: Poems and New Media from the Magic Lantern to Instagram*, New York: Columbia University Press.

Cherches, P. (2017), *Star Course*, Rotterdam: SensePublishers.

Choi, D. M. (2020), *DMZ Colony*, Seattle: Wave Books.

Choi, F. (2016), "Turing Test," *The Poetry Society*. Available online: https://poems.poetrysociety.org.uk/poems/turing-test/ (accessed December 12, 2022).

Clifford, A. (2006), "The Sweet Old Etcetera," *Electronic Literature Collection*. Available online: https://collection.eliterature.org/2/works/clifford_sweet_old_etcetera/sweetweb/index.html (accessed August 1, 2023).

Closky, C. (1992), "The First Thousand Numbers Classified in Alphabetical Order," UbuWeb, https://www.ubu.com/concept/Claude_Closky_1000.pdf.

Coetzee, J. M. (1986), *Foe*, London: Martin Secker and Warburg.

Colasacco, J., and @poemsforbrands (n.d.), "Poems for Your Brand or Self," Instagram.

Corral, E. C. (2020), *Guillotine*, Minneapolis: Graywolf Press.

Council, U. N. H. R. (2022), *Neurotechnology and Human Rights*, United Nations Digital Library. Available online: https://digitallibrary.un.org/record/3990569?ln=en (accessed August 1, 2023).

Crabtree, J. (2017), "Review of *Sorry to Disturb the Peace*," *DIAGRAM*, 17 (4). Available online: https://thediagram.com/17_4/rev_cottrell.html (accessed August 1, 2023).

Crase, D. (2022), *On Autumn Lake: Collected Essays*, Brooklyn: Nightboat Books.

Crowley, A. (1913), *The Book of Lies, the Book of Lies*, London: Wieland.

Cuddon, J. A. (1999), *The Penguin Dictionary of Literary Terms and Literary Theory*, London: Penguin Books.

References

Czyz, V. (2014), "Collage and the Secret Adventures of Order," *New England Review*, 35 (3): 91–8.

D'Agata, J., ed. (2003), *The Next American Essay*, Minneapolis: Graywolf Press.

D'Agata, J., ed. (2009), *The Lost Origins of the Essay*, St. Paul: Graywolf Press.

D'Agata, J. (2010), *About a Mountain*, New York: W. W. Norton.

D'Agata, J., ed. (2015), "Introduction," in *We Might As Well Call It the Lyric Essay*, 6–10, Geneva: Hobart and William Smith College Press.

Danto, A. (2013), *What Art Is*, New Haven: Yale University Press.

De Quincey, T. (1873), *Suspiria de Profundis: Being a Sequel to the Confessions of an English Opium-Eater, and Other Miscellaneous Writings*, Boston: Shepard and Gill.

Debord, G. (1983), *The Society of the Spectacle*, ed. K. Knabb, London: Rebel Press.

DeBord, G. (2006), "Theory of the Dérive," in K. Knabb (ed.), *Situationist International Anthology*, 62–6, Berkeley: Bureau of Public Secrets.

DeJong, L. (2015), "Lewis DeJong on Daniel Mahoney," *DIAGRAM*, 15 (3). Available online: https://thediagram.com/15_3/rev_mahoney.html (accessed August 1, 2023).

Derrida, J. (1982), *Margins of Philosophy*, ed. A. Bass, Chicago: University of Chicago Press.

Dillard, A. (1995), *Mornings Like This: Found Poems*, New York: HarperCollins Publishers.

Doller, B., and S. Doller (2014), *Sonneteers*, Salt Lake City: Editions Eclipse.

Dormer, C. (2014), "Writing Textile, Making Text: Cloth and Stitch as Agency for Disorderly Text," *Textile Society of America Symposium Proceedings*, 926.

Duchamp, M. (1917), "Fountain," New York (Sculpture).

Douglas, M. (1966), *Purity and Danger: An Analysis of Concepts of Pollution and Taboo*, Abingdon: Routledge.

Dworkin, C. (2003), "The Politics of Noise," in *Reading the Illegible*, 31–49, Evanston: Northwestern University Press.

Dworkin, C. (2011), "The Fate of Echo," in C. Dworkin and K. Goldsmith (eds.), *Against Expression: An Anthology of Conceptual Writing*, xxiii–liv, Evanston: Northwestern University Press.

Dworkin, C. (2013), *No Medium*, Cambridge: MIT Press.

Dyer, G. (2003), *Yoga for People Who Can't Be Bothered to Do It*, New York: Pantheon.

Eagleton, T. (1983), *Literary Theory: An Introduction*, Oxford: Blackwell.

Ekelund, V. (1986), *The Second Light*, ed. L. Bruce, New York: North Point Press.

Eliot, T. S. (1921), *The Sacred Wood: Essays on Poetry and Criticism*, London: Methuen.

Ervick, K. P. (2016), *The Bitter Life of Božena Němcová*, Brookline: Rose Metal Press.

Farmer, J. (2022), "2022 Winners," *Bulwer-Lytton Fiction Contest*. Available online: https://www.bulwer-lytton.com/2022 (accessed December 30, 2022).

Faulkner, W. (1951), *Requiem for a Nun*, New York: Random House.

Field, T. (2007), *ULULU (Clown Shrapnel)*, Minneapolis: Coffee House Press.

Fielder, N. (2014), "Nathan For You," Comedy Central.

Fisher, M. F. K. (1937), "Borderland," in *Serve It Forth*, 30–2, New York: North Point Press.

Forché, C. (1981), "The Colonel," in *The Country Between Us*, 16, New York: HarperCollins Publishers.

Foucault, M. (1995), "Docile Bodies," in A. Sheridan (ed.), *Discipline and Punish*, 135–69, New York: Vintage Books.

Frankfurt, H. (2005), *On Bullshit*, Princeton: Princeton University Press.

Frye, N. (1957), *Anatomy of Criticism: Four Essays*, Princeton: Princeton University Press.

Gabbert, E. (2020), "For 3 Poets Who Embrace Excess, the Mess Is the Message," *The New York Times*. Available online: https://www.nytimes.com/2020/06/16/books/review/for-3-poets-who-embrace-excess-the-mess-is-the-message.html (accessed January 5, 2023).

Gaiman, N. (2021), "Neil Gaiman on the Great Kathy Acker," *Literary Hub*. Available online: https://lithub.com/neil-gaiman-on-the-great-kathy-acker/ (accessed December 30, 2022).

Gass, W. (2002), *Tests of Time: Essays*, Chicago: University of Chicago Press.

Geary, J. (2007), *Geary's Guide to the World's Great Aphorists*, New York: Bloomsbury.

Gildenhard, I., and A. Zissos (2016), *Ovid, Metamorphoses, 3.511-733*, Cambridge: Open Book Publishers.

References

Ginsburg, R. (2023), "Literary NFTs: Here's How Writers Can Leverage Their Passion in Web3," nft now, Available online: https://nftnow.com/guides/literary-nfts-heres-how-writers-can-leverage-their-passion-in-web3/ (accessed August 1, 2023).
Goldberg, R. (1979), *Performance: Live Art, 1909 to Present*, New York: Harry N. Abrams.
Goldsmith, K. (2003), *Day*, Great Barrington: The Figures.
Goldsmith, K. (2011a), "Against Expression: Kenneth Goldsmith in Conversation," *poets.org2*. Available online: https://poets.org/text/against-expression-kenneth-goldsmith-conversation (accessed December 25, 2022).
Goldsmith, K. (2011b), *Uncreative Writing*, New York: Columbia University Press.
Goldsmith, K. (2014), "If Walt Whitman Vlogged," *The New Yorker*. Available online: https://www.newyorker.com/books/page-turner/if-walt-whitman-vlogged (accessed June 12, 2023).
Goldsmith, K. (2015), "The Body of Michael Brown," *Interrupt 3*, Providence: Brown University.
Goldsmith, K. (2016a), "Go Ahead: Waste Time on the Internet," *The Baltimore Sun*. Available online: https://www.baltimoresun.com/la-oe-goldsmith-wasting-time-internet-20160812-snap-story.html (accessed December 30, 2022).
Goldsmith, K. (2016b), *Wasting Time on the Internet*, New York: HarperCollins Publishers.
Goodwin, R. (2015), "MeterMap," *Github*. Available online: https://github.com/rossgoodwin/metermap (accessed December 30, 2022).
Goodwin, R. (2016), "NueralSnap," *Github*. Available online: https://github.com/rossgoodwin/neuralsnap (accessed December 30, 2022).
Graeber, D. (2018), *Bullshit Jobs: A Theory*, New York: Simon & Schuster.
Greif, M. (2015), *Cat Is Art Spelled Wrong: Essays*, ed. Caroline Casey, Chris Fischbach, and Sarah Schultz, Minneapolis: Coffee House Press.
Groenland, T. (2019), *The Art of Editing: Raymond Carver and David Foster Wallace*, London: Bloomsbury Academic.
Grossman, L. (2010), "Jonathan Franzen: Great American Novelist," *Time Magazine*. Available online: https://content.time.com/time/magazine/article/0,9171,2010185,00.html (accessed December 30, 2022).
Groys, B. (2017), "Dmitri Prigov: Haunted Spaces," *e-flux Journal*, (80). Available online: https://www.e-flux.com/journal/80/101787/dmitri-prigov-haunted-spaces/ (accessed August 1, 2023).
Gutiérrez, R. (2021), "A Concatenation of Sprawls," *Places Journal*. Available online: https://placesjournal.org/article/queer-latinx-nightlife-and-urbanist-aesthetics-los-angeles/?cn-reloaded=1 (accessed August 1, 2023).
Handey, J. (1992), *Deep Thoughts: Inspiration for the Uninspired*, New York: Berkley Books.
Hass, R. (1979), "Meditation at Lagunitas," *Praise*, New York: Ecco Press.
Hass, R. (2007), *Time and Materials*, New York: Ecco Press.
Headley, M. D. (2020), *Beowulf: A New Translation*, New York: Farrar, Straus, and Giroux.
Hebdige, D. (1979), *Subculture: The Meaning of Style*, Abingdon: Routledge.
Hejinian, L. (1987), *My Life*, Los Angeles: Green Integer.
Higgins, D. (1966), "Synesthesia and Intersenses: Intermedia." Available online: https://www.ubu.com/papers/higgins_intermedia.html (accessed June 11, 2023).
Hinds, S. (1987), *The Metamorphosis of Persephone: Ovid and the Self-Conscious Muse*, Cambridge: Cambridge University Press.
Hoang, L. (2008), *Parabola*, Portland: Chiasmus Press.
Hoban, R. (1980), *Riddley Walker*, London: Jonathan Cape.
Hodges, H. (n.d.), "Ratz Are Nice (PSP): Review," *Quill & Quire*. Available online: https://quillandquire.com/review/ratz-are-nice-psp/ (accessed August 1, 2023).
Holiday, H. (2017), *Hollywood Forever*, New York: Fence Books.
Hong, C. P. (2007), *Dance Dance Revolution*, London: W. W. Norton.
Hugo, R. (1979), *The Triggering Town*, New York: W. W. Norton.
Hutcheon, L. (1989), *The Politics of Postmodernism*, New York: Routledge.
Impey, S. (2020a), "Thrall." Available online: https://www.saraimpey.com/thrall/ (accessed August 1, 2023).

References

Impey, S. (2020b), "A Post-Truth Quilt." Available online: http://www.saraimpey.com/a-post-truth-quilt/ (accessed August 1, 2023).

Impey, S. (2020c), "War of Words." Available online: http://www.saraimpey.com/war-of-words/ (accessed August 1, 2023).

Inside the Castle. (n.d.), "The CASTLE FREAK: A Remote Residency for Generative Digital Composition," *insidethecastle.org*. Available online: http://www.insidethecastle.org/castle-freak/ (accessed September 14, 2023).

Issacson, W. (2014), *The Innovators: How a Group of Hackers, Geniuses, and Geeks Created the Digital Revolution*, New York: Simon & Schuster.

Ives, L. (2013), "Lucy Ives on Sophia Le Fraga," *The Poetry Project Newsletter*, (238): 12.

Jackson, H. J. (2001), "Marginalia," in *Marginalia*, 234–40, New Haven: Yale University Press.

James, W. (1929), *The Varieties of Religious Experience: A Study in Human Nature*, London: Longmans, Green, and Company.

Jameson, F. (1991), *Postmodernism, or the Cultural Logic of Late Capitalism*, London: Verso.

Jameson, F. (2014), "Dirty Little Secret," in Chad Harbach (ed.), *MFA vs. NYC*, 263–81, New York: Farrar, Straus, and Giroux.

Johanson, S. (2018), "A Folio of Erasures by Sonja Johanson: Aubade, Shooting Star, & Unmasking," *Tupelo Quarterly*. Available online: https://www.tupeloquarterly.com/collaborative-and-cross-disciplinary-texts/a-folio-of-erasures-by-sonja-johanson-aubade-shooting-star-unmasking/ (accessed January 3, 2023).

Johnson, R. (2005), *RADI OS*, Chicago: Flood Editions.

Joyce, J. (1939), *Finnegans Wake*, London: Faber and Faber.

Kael, P. (1969), "Trash, Art, and the Movies," *Harper's Magazine*, 76.

Kardashian, K. (2015), *Selfish*, Milan: Universe Publishing.

Katelnikoff, J. (2016), "Impromtu #15," *The Found Poetry Review*. Available online: https://foundpoetryreview.com/blog/impromptu-15-joel-katelnikoff/ (accessed June 11, 2023).

Katz, D. (2010), "James Schuyler's Epistolary Poetry: Things, Postcards, Ekphrasis," *Journal of Modern Literature*, 34 (1): 143–61.

Kelly, R. (2006), *Earish, Thirty Poems of Paul Celan Translated by Robert Kelly*, Annandale: Matter Books.

Kenner, H. (1968), *The Counterfeiters*, Bloomington: Indiana University Press.

King, T. (1993), *Green Grass, Running Water*, New York: Houghton Mifflin.

Klosterman, C. (2016), *But What If We're Wrong? Thinking about the Present as If It Were the Past*, New York: Blue Rider Press.

Kocurek, C. (2017), "House of Eternal Return Shows How a House Can Be a Game," *Paste Magazine*. Available online: https://www.pastemagazine.com/games/house-of-eternal-return/house-of-eternal-return-shows-how-a-house-can-be-a/ (accessed December 25, 2022).

Koestenbaum, W. (2007), *Hotel Theory*, Brooklyn: Soft Skull Press.

Koolhaas, R. (1994), *Delirious New York: A Retroactive Manifesto for Manhattan*, New York: The Monacelli Press.

Kostelanetz, R. (2011), "Conceptual Fictions," *Crux Desperationis*, (11): 11–12.

Kracauer, S., and T. Y. Levin (1987), "Cult of Distraction: On Berlin's Picture Palaces," *New German Critique*, (40): 91–6.

Kraus, K. (2015), *The Last Days of Mankind*, trans. Fred Bridgham and Edward Timms, New Haven: Yale University Press.

Krotoszynski Jr., R. J. (1998), "Legal Scholarship at the Crossroads: On Farce, Tragedy, and Redemption Commentary," *Texas Law Review*, 77 (1): 321–2.

Kruger, B. (1990), "Carpet," Chicago Art Institute.

Krystal, A. (2014), "What Is Literature?," *Harper's Magazine*, March, 89–94.

Kunkel, B. (2007), "Still Small Voice," *The New Yorker*, August. Available online: https://www.newyorker.com/magazine/2007/08/06/still-small-voice#:~:text=In%20%E2%80%9CJakob%20von%20Gunten%2C%E2%80%9D,out%20as%20a%20relentless%20diminuendo (accessed August 1, 2023).

Laird, B. (2022), *The Durham Poems*, Santa Rosa: SOd Press.

References

Lanier, J., and J. Euchner (2019), "What Has Gone Wrong with the Internet, and How We Can Fix It," *Research-Technology Management*, 62 (3): 13–20.

Laporte, D. (2000), *History of Shit*, eds. N. Benabid and R. El-Khoury, Cambridge: MIT Press.

Laver, J. (1937), *Taste and Fashion: From the French Revolution to the Present Day*, London: George G. Harrap.

Lehman, D. (2003), "The Prose Poem: An Alternative to Verse," *The American Poetry Review*, 32 (2): 45–9.

LeMay, E. (2017), *Essays on the Essay and Other Essays*, Clarksville: Zone 3 Press.

Leong, M. (2011), "Aphorisms, Preverbs, & Hotel Amerika 9.2 (Spring 2011)," *michael leong's poetry blog*. Available online: https://michaelleong.wordpress.com/2011/03/07/aphorisms-preverbs-hotel-amerika-9-2-spring-2011/ (accessed December 30, 2022).

Lerner, B. (2016), *The Hatred of Poetry*, New York: Farrar, Straus, and Giroux.

Levi-Strauss, C. (1976), *Tristes Tropiques*, eds. J. Weightman and D. Weightman, London: Penguin Books.

Lewis, P., and T. Tzara. (1920), "To Make a Dadaist Poem," *Editing Modernism in Canada*. Available online: https://modernistcommons.ca/islandora/object/yale%3A352 (accessed January 10, 2023).

Lin, T. (2010), *Seven Controlled Vocabularies and Obituary 2004. The Joy of Cooking: [AIRPORT NOVEL MUSICAL POEM PAINTING FILM PHOTO HALLUCINATION LANDSCAPE]*, Middletown: Wesleyan University Press, 2010.

Lisson Gallery. (2020), "Cory Arcangel." Available online: https://www.lissongallery.com/artists/cory-arcangel (accessed August 1, 2023).

Long Soldier, L. (2017), *Whereas*, Minneapolis: Graywolf Press.

Lundgren, P. (2020), "The World's First Wearable Magazine," *T-Post (r)*. Available online: https://www.t-post.com/blog/worlds-first-wearable-magazine/ (accessed December 25, 2022).

MacPhee, J. (2019), Introduction to *Advertising Shits in Your Head*, by V. Raoul and M. Bonner, Binghamton: PM Press.

Maddin, G., E. Johnson, and G. Johnson (2016), *Seances*, Montreal: National Film Board of Canada. Available online: https://seances.nfb.ca/ (accessed August 1, 2023).

Madonna (1992), *Sex*, ed. G. O' Brien, New York: Warner Books.

Magee, M. (n.d.), "The Flarf Files," University of Pennsylvania Electronic Poetry Center. Available online: https://writing.upenn.edu/epc/authors/bernstein/syllabi/readings/flarf.html (accessed August 1, 2023).

Maistre, X. (1794), *A Journey Round my Room*, trans. Henry Atwell, New York: Hurd and Houghton. Available online: https://publicdomainreview.org/collection/a-journey-round-my-room-1794-1871/ (accessed August 1, 2023).

Marcinkiewicz, P. (2018), "The Color of Avant-Garde: Kenneth Goldsmith's 'The Body of Michael Brown,'" *Polish Journal for American Studies*, 12: 211–13.

Marinetti, T. (1909), "Manifesto of Futurism." Available online: https://www.wm.edu/offices/auxiliary/osher/course-info/classnotes/manifestooffuturism.pdf (accessed June 11, 2023).

Markson, D. (2006), *Wittgenstein's Mistress*, Dublin: Dalkey Archive.

McBridge, J. (2022), *Eat Your Mind: The Radical Life and Work of Kathy Acker*, New York: Simon & Schuster.

McGuane, T. (1980), "Big Sky, Big Swaps," *Esquire*, 82–7.

McGurl, M. (2017), "Feeling Like The Internet," *Public Books*. Available online: https://www.publicbooks.org/feeling-like-the-internet/ (accessed 25 December 2022).

McHale, B. (1987), *Postmodernist Fictions*, Oxford: Routledge.

McLuhan, M. (1962), *The Gutenberg Galaxy*, Toronto: University of Toronto Press, 248.

McLuhan, M. (1964), "The Photograph." *Understanding Media*, New York: McGraw Hill.

Melville, H. (2010), *Emoji Dick*, eds. F. Benenson and A. M. Turk.

Merchant, B. (2018), "When an AI Goes Full Jack Kerouac," *The Atlantic*. Available online: https://www.theatlantic.com/technology/archive/2018/10/automated-on-the-road/571345/ (accessed December 30, 2022).

Merrill, J. (1986), "Japan: Prose of Departure." *New York Review of Books*. Available online: https://www.nybooks.com/articles/1986/12/18/japan-prose-of-departure/ (accessed August 1, 2023).
Mesa-Bains, A. (1999), "Domesticana: The Sensibility of Chicana Rasquache," *AZTLAN: A Journal of Chicano Studies*, 24 (2): 157–67.
Messerli, D. (1987), "Language" Poetries," in D. Messerli (ed.), *"Language" Poetries: An Anthology*, New York: New Directions.
Michail, C., and D. Lyacos (2018), "Controlled Experience: Berfrois Interviews Dimitris Lyacos," *Berfrois*. Available online: https://www.berfrois.com/2018/11/berfrois-interviews-dimitris-lyacos/ (accessed December 30, 2022).
Minor, S. (2015), *The Persistence of the Bonyleg: Annotated*, Buffalo: Essay Press.
Minor, S. (2018), "Foul Chutes: On the Archive Downriver," *Ninth Letter Online*. Available online: http://www.ninthletter.com/images/FeaturedContent/pdfs/Foul_Chutes.pdf (accessed September 11, 2023).
Monson, A. (n.d.), "Essay as Hack," *Other Electricities*. Available online: http://www.otherelectricities.com/swarm/essayashack.html (accessed December 30, 2022).
Monson, A. (n.d.), "The Swarm," *Other Electricities*. Available online: http://www.otherelectricities.com/swarm/index.html (accessed December 30, 2022).
Moore, M. (1981), *The Complete Poems of Marianne Moore*, New York: Macmillan.
Moore, M. (2002), *Bowling for Columbine*, Metro-Goldwyn-Mayer Studios.
Motte, W. (2009), "Playing in Earnest," *The John Hopkins University Press*, 40 (1): 25–42.
Moxon, J. (1683), *Mechanick Exercises: Or, the Doctrine of Handy-Works*, London: Joseph Moxon.
Myers, W. D. (2001), *Monster*, New York: Amistad.
Myles, E. (2022), "Introduction," in E. Myles (ed.), *Pathetic Literature*, New York: Grove Press.
Nabokov, V. (1962), *Pale Fire*, New York: Putnam Publishing Group.
Nakayasu, S. (2020), "Experimental Translation," *Translation across Disciplines Conference*, February 27–28, 2020. Available online: https://www.youtube.com/watch?v=6BgXo2MKl6g (accessed June 12, 2023).
Neely, B. (2004), "Wizard People, Dear Reader." Available online https://vimeo.com/492873316 (accessed August 1, 2023).
Nelson, M. (2015), *The Argonauts*, Minneapolis: Graywolf Press.
Nethercott, G., and B. DiTrani (illus.) (2019), *Lianna Fled the Cranberry Bog*, Easthampton: Ninepin Press.
Newberry, C. (2023), "How the Facebook Algorithm Works in 2023 and How to Make It Work for You," *Hootsuite*. Available online: https://blog.hootsuite.com/facebook-algorithm/ (accessed December 30, 2022).
Nezhukumatathil, A. (2014), *Poets.org*. Available online: https://poets.org/text/more-birds-bees-and-trees-closer-look-writing-haibun (accessed June 10, 2023).
Ngai, S. (2017), "Theory of the Gimmick," *Critical Inquiry*, 43 (2): 466–505.
bpNichol. (1998), *The Martyrology Books 1 & 2. The Official bp Nichol Archive*, second edition, Toronto: Coach House. Available online: https://www.bpnichol.ca/archive/documents/martyrology-books-1-2 (accessed August 1, 2023).
Nietzsche, F. (1918), *Antichrist*, ed. H. L. Mencken, New York: Alfred A. Knopf.
Norðdahl, E. Ö. (2013), *Hnefi Eða Vitstola Orð*, Reykjavik: Mal og menning.
Oliu, B. (2011), "So You Know It's Me." Available online: soyouknowitsme.com (accessed December 30, 2022).
Oliu, B. (2015), *I/O: A Memoir*, Fairfax: Civil Coping Mechanisms.
Olson, M., J. Judson, and R. Boudreau (1978), "Felix Pollak, An Interview on Little Magazines," in E. Anderson and M. Kinzie (eds.), *The Little Magazine in America: A Modern Documentary History*, Yonkers: Pushcart.
Oreskes, N., and E. M. Conway (2014), *The Collapse of Western Civilization: A View from the Future*, New York: Columbia University Press.
Ovid ([8 CE] 2004), *Metamorphoses*, ed. R. J. Tarrant, Oxford: Oxford University Press.

References

Pallasmaa, J. (2009), *The Thinking Hand: Existential and Embodied Wisdom in Architecture*, Chichester: John Wiley and Sons.

Palmquist, L. (2015), "Pursuing Essence through Ambiguity: On Kawabata's Palm-of-the-Hand Stories," *Ploughshares*. Available online: https://blog.pshares.org/pursuing-essence-through-ambiguity-on-kawabatas-palm-of-the-hand-stories/ (accessed December 30, 2022).

Pamuk, O. (2013), "A Modest Manifesto for Museums," *American Craft Council*. Available online: https://www.craftcouncil.org/magazine/article/modest-manifesto-museums (accessed December 25, 2022).

Pariser, E. (2011), "Beware Online "Filter Bubbles,"" *TED*, TED. Available online: https://www.ted.com/talks/eli_pariser_beware_online_filter_bubbles?language=en (accessed December 30, 2022).

Pitt, S. (2019), "Computer Files Are Going Extinct," *OneZero*. Available online: https://onezero.medium.com/the-death-of-the-computer-file-doc-43cb028c0506 (accessed December 30, 2022).

Place, V., and R. Fitterman (2009), *Notes on Conceptualisms*, Brooklyn: Ugly Duckling Presse.

Plascencia, S. (2005), *The People of Paper*, San Francisco: McSweeney's Books.

Ponge, F. (2008), *Unfinished Ode to Mud*, ed. B. B. Brahic, London: CB editions.

Poetry Foundation. (2020), "Stéphane Mallarmé." Poetry Foundation. Available online: https://www.poetryfoundation.org/poets/stephane-mallarme (accessed August 1, 2023).

Pound, E. (1934), *Make It New*, London: Faber and Faber.

Prado de Oliveira Martins, L. (2018), "All Directions At Once." Available online: http://alldirectionsatonce.schloss-post.com/ (accessed December 25, 2022).

Prescott, O. (1942), "Books of the Times," *New York Times*, May 22: 17.

Priani, E. (2017), "Ramon Llull (Stanford Encyclopedia of Philosophy)," Stanford.edu. Available online: https://plato.stanford.edu/entries/llull/ (accessed August 1, 2023).

Proudhon, P.-J. (2011), *Property is Theft! A Pierre-Joseph Proudhon Reader*, ed. Iain McKay, Chico, CA: AK Press, 2011.

Purifoy, N. (1966), ""66 Signs of Neon," Art exhibition, mixed media, Los Angeles.

Rafey, K. (2014), "This Is an Essay: The Language and Legacy of Laadan (Evidently)," *Tortoise: A Journal of Writing Pedagogy*, (1): 70–6.

Reese, H. (2016), "The Tactility of Artist Books," in W. D. Von Lucius and G. Kaldewey (eds.), *Marking Artist Books Today: Workshop at Poestenkill/NY August 18th-23rd "97*, 25–38, Berlin: De Gruyter Oldenbourg.

Rekdal, P. (2022), "West: A Translation." Available online: https://westtrain.org/ (accessed December 30, 2022).

Rhys, J. (1966), *Wide Sargasso Sea*, London: W. W. Norton.

Roach, R. (2017), "The Computer Poetry of J.M. Coetzee's Early Programming Career," Ransom Center Magazine. Available online: https://sites.utexas.edu/ransomcentermagazine/2017/06/28/the-computer-poetry-of-j-m-coetzees-early-programming-career/ (accessed August 1, 2023).

Rossellini, I., and G. Maddin (2009), "Guy Maddin & Isabella Rossellini," *BOMB Magazine*. Available online: https://bombmagazine.org/articles/guy-maddin-isabella-rossellini/ (accessed December 30, 2022).

ruangrupa. (n.d.), "About," ruangrupa. Available online: https://ruangrupa.id/en/about/ (accessed August 1, 2023).

Ruefle, M. (2006), *A Little White Shadow*, Seattle: Wave Books.

Rushdie, S. (1982), "The Empire Writes Back with a Vengeance," *The London Times*, July 3: 8.

Saltz, J. (2017), "My Life as a Failed Artist," *Vulture*, April 2017. Available online: https://www.vulture.com/2017/04/jerry-saltz-my-life-as-a-failed-artist.html (accessed June 12, 2023).

Saltzberg, B. (2010), *Beautiful Oops!*, New York: Workman Publishing.

Sarraute, N. (2015), *Tropisms*, trans. Maria Jolas, New York: New Directions.

Saterstrom, S. (2015), *Slab*, Minneapolis: Coffee House Press.

Schlegel, F. (1998), *Philosophical Fragments*, trans. Peter Firchow, Minneapolis: University of Minnesota Press.

Schmidt, C. (2008), "The Waste-Management Poetics of Kenneth Goldsmith," *SubStance*, 37 (2): 25–40.

References

Schottenius Cullhed, S. (2016), "In Bed with Virgil: Ausonius' Wedding Cento and Its Reception," *Greece & Rome*, 63 (2): 237–50.
Scott, J. C. (1985), *Weapons of the Weak: Everyday Forms of Peasant Resistance*, New Haven: Yale University Press.
Seely, H. (ed.) (2003), *Pieces of Intelligence: The Existential Poetry of Donald H. Rumsfeld*, New York: Free Press.
Shelton, R. (n.d.), "Desert," *Blue Ridge Journal*. Available online: https://www.blueridgejournal.com/poems/rs1-desert.htm (accessed December 30, 2022).
Shields, D., and M. Vollmer, eds. (2012), *FAKES: An Anthology of Pseudo-Interviews, Faux-Lectures, Quasi-Letters, "Found" Texts, and Other Fraudulent Artifacts*, London: W. W. Norton.
Siegelaub, S., C. Andre, R. Barry, D. Huebler, J. Kosuth, S. LeWitt, R. Morris, and L. Weiner (1968), *Xerox Book*, New York: Siegelaub/Wendler.
Silliman, R. (1987), *The New Sentence*, New York: Roof Books.
Sinhababu, N. (2008), "Possible Girls," *Pacific Philosophical Quarterly*, 89 (2): 254–60.
Skeets, J. (2019), *Eyes Bottle Dark with a Mouthful of Flowers*, Minneapolis: Milkweed Editions.
Skeets, J. (2020), "The Memory Field," *Emergence Magazine*. Available online: https://emergencemagazine.org/essay/the-memory-field/ (accessed August 1, 2023).
Smith, A. (2018a), *Destruction of Man*, Nashville: Third Man Books.
Smith, J. (2018b), "On the Book of the Dead by Muriel Rukeyser," *The Georgia Review*. Available online: https://thegeorgiareview.com/posts/on-the-book-of-the-dead-by-muriel-rukeyser/ (accessed August 1, 2023).
Smith, Z. (2005), *On Beauty*, New York: The Penguin Press.
Sontag, S. (1966), *Against Interpretation*, New York: FSG.
Spicer, J. (1974), *After Lorca*, Toronto: Coach House Press.
Steinhauer, J. (2015), "The Nine Lives of Cat Videos," in C. Casey, C. Fischbach and S. Schultz (eds.), *Cat Is Art Spelled Wrong*, 9–24, Minneapolis: Coffee House Press.
Stephenson, N. (1992), *Snow Crash*, New York: Bantam Books.
Stoker, B. (1897), *Dracula*, New York: Grosset and Dunlap.
Strand, M. (1970), "Introduction to the American Edition," in Paz, Octavio, Alí Chumacero, José Emilio Pacheco, and Homero Aridjis (eds.), Mark Strand etal. (trans.), *New Poetry of Mexico*, 5–16, New York: E.P. Dutton.
Strand, M. (1978), *The Monument*, New York: Ecco Press.
Sulak, M. M. (2015), *Family Resemblance: An Anthology and Exploration of 8 Hybrid Literary Genres*, Brookline: Rose Metal Press.
Sullivan, G. (2011), "A Brief Guide to Flarf Poetry," *poets.org*. Available online: https://poets.org/text/brief-guide-flarf-poetry (accessed June 12, 2023).
Sweeney, E. (2002), "Literary Forms of Medieval Philosophy," *Stanford Encyclopedia of Philosophy*. Available online: https://plato.stanford.edu/entries/medieval-literary/ (accessed December 30, 2022).
Szilak, I. (2015), "Towards Minor Literary Forms: Digital Literature and the Art of Failure," *Electronic Book Review*. Available online: https://electronicbookreview.com/essay/towards-minor-literary-forms-digital-literature-and-the-art-of-failure/ (accessed December 30, 2022).
Taleb, N. N. (2016), *The Bed of Procrustes: Philosophical and Practical Aphorisms*, New York: Random House.
Tjveil. (2009), "Shatner Performs Palin," *YouTube*. Available online: https://www.youtube.com/watch?v=mF_t1A8LGzg&ab_channel=tjveil (accessed December 30, 2022).
Tomasula, S. (2009), *TOC: A New Media Novel*, Tuscaloosa: University of Alabama Press.
Tomasula, S. (2016), "The Novel as Multimedia, Networked Book: An Interview with Steve Tomasula," Bettencourt, S. (interviewer), *MATLIT: Materialities of Literature*, 4 (1): 155–66.
Toomer, J. (1923), *Cane*, New York: Boni & Liveright.
Torre, M. de la (2010), "Microscripts," *BOMB Magazine*. Available online: https://bombmagazine.org/articles/microscripts/ (accessed December 30, 2022).
Towers, R. (1981), "Low-Rent Tragedies," *The New York Review of Books*. Available online: https://www.nybooks.com/articles/1981/05/14/low-rent-tragedies/ (accessed June 11, 2023).

References

Trecartin, R. (2019), "Re'Search Wait'S," *Sprueth Magers*. Available online: https://spruethmagers.com/exhibitions/ryan-trecartin-research-waits-berlin/ (accessed December 30, 2022).

Turner, J. G. (1994), "Novel Panic: Picture and Performance in the Reception of Richardson's Pamela," *Representations*, (48): 70–96.

Updike, J. (2007), *Due Considerations*, New York: Alfred A. Knopf.

Valéry, P., and C. Guenther. (1954), "Poetry and Abstract Thought," *The Kenyon Review*, 16 (2): 208–33.

Vanasco, J. (2012), "Absent Things As If They Are Present," *The Believer*. Available online: https://www.thebeliever.net/absent-things-as-if-they-are-present/ (accessed November 14, 2022).

Viegener, M. (2012), *2500 Random Things about Me Too*, Los Angeles: Les Figues Press.

Virgil ([29 BCE] 2009), *Georgics*, ed. K. Johnson, London: Penguin Books.

Walker, N. (2007), "On Jenny Boully," *DIAGRAM*, 7 (5). Available online: https://thediagram.com/7_5/rev_boully.html (accessed August 1, 2023).

Wallace, D. F. (1992), "Review: Portrait of an Eye: Three Novels," *Harvard Review*, 32 (1): 154–6.

Wallace, D. F. (2004), "Consider the Lobster," *Gourmet*, August: 50–64.

Walshe, J. (n.d.), "Disclaimer," *aisteach*. Available online: http://www.aisteach.org/?page_id=306 (accessed December 30, 2022).

Waugh, K. (n.d.), "History of the Chapbook," *Poets House*. Available online: https://digitalcollections.poetshouse.org/digital-collection/chapbook-collection/chapbook-history (accessed December 25, 2022).

Weiner, J. (2014), "First Reading of Sophia Le Fraga's 'W8ING 4' (1)," *Jacket 2*. Available online: https://jacket2.org/commentary/first-reading-sophia-le-fragas-w8ing-4 (accessed December 30, 2020).

Weymar, D. (2019), "The Project," *Tiny Pricks Project*. Available online: https://www.tinypricksproject.com/the-project/ (accessed May 8, 2023).

White, C., K. White, and D. White (2015), *'SSES" 'SSES" 'SSEY"'*, Washington DC: Calamari Press.

White, O. (2015), "Finis," *LETTERRS*, Brooklyn: Nightboat Books.

Williams, T. (2002), "Cold Calls," in *c.c.*, 37–56, San Francisco: Krupskaya.

Works, O. (2013), "When I Left the House It Was Still Dark," New York: Odyssey Works.

Xu, L. (2022), *And Those Ashen Heaps That Cantilevered Vase of Moonlight*, Seattle: Wave Books.

Ybarra-Frausto, T. (1989), *Rasquachismo: A Chicano Sensibility*, International Center for the Arts of the Americas at the Museum of Fine Arts, Houston: Documents of Latin America and Latino Art. Available online: https://icaa.mfah.org/s/en/item/845510#?c=&m=&s=&cv=&xywh=-1136%2C-1%2C3927%2C2198 (accessed August 1, 2023).

Young, K. (2018), *Bunk: The Rise of Hoaxes, Humbug, Plagiarists, Phonies, Post-Facts, and Fake News*, Minneapolis: Graywolf Press.

Youngblood, M., B. Chesluk, and N. Haidary, illus. (2020), *Rethinking Users*, Amsterdam: BIS Publishers.

Ziusudra. (2009), "The List of Ziusudra," in J. D'Agata (ed.), *The Lost Origins of the Essay*, 7–8, St. Paul: Graywolf Press.

CONTRIBUTORS

Hanif Abdurraqib's full-length poetry collections are *The Crown Ain't Worth Much* (2016) and *A Fortune for Your Disaster* (2019), which won the Lenore Marshall Prize. His essay collections are *They Can't Kill Us Until They Kill Us* (2017), *Go Ahead in The Rain: Notes to a Tribe Called Quest* (2019), and *A Little Devil in America* (2021), which was a finalist for the National Book Award and National Book Critics Circle Award. Hanif is from Columbus, Ohio, and a graduate of Beechcroft High School.

Caren Beilin is the author of the novel *Revenge of the Scapegoat* (2022, Dorothy, a publishing project). Her other books are *Blackfishing the IUD* (2019), *Spain* (2018), *The University of Pennsylvania* (2014), and the chapbook *Americans, Guests, or Us* (2012). She is an assistant professor of creative writing at the Massachusetts College of Liberal Arts and lives close by, in Vermont.

Dodie Bellamy's writing focuses on sexuality, politics, and narrative experimentation, challenging the distinctions between fiction, essay, and poetry. In 2018–19 she was the subject of *On Our Mind*, a yearlong series of public events, commissioned essays, and reading-group meetings organized by CCA Wattis ICA. With Kevin Killian, she coedited *Writers Who Love Too Much: New Narrative 1977–1997*. A compendium of essays on Bellamy's work, *Dodie Bellamy Is on Our Mind*, was published in 2020 by Wattis ICA/Semiotext(e).

Aase Berg is a poet, literary critic, and translator. She grew up outside Tensta in Stockholm, where she was born in 1967. Her first book, *Hos rådjur* (*with Deer*), was published by Bonnier in 1997. This was followed by *Mörk Materia* (*Dark Matter*), a book-length science-fiction prose poem, in 2000.

Stephanie Berger is a poet, educator, community organizer, and entrepreneur. She is the CEO of The Poetry Society of New York (PSNY) and cocreator with Nicholas Adamski of The Poetry Brothel and The New York City Poetry Festival, among many other projects. With Jackie Braje, she cofounded Milk Press, an online community, publisher, and nurturer of poetic collaborations. Stephanie is the author of *In the Madame's Hat Box* (2011) and coauthor with Carina Finn of *The Grey Bird: Thirteen Emoji Poems in Translation* (2014).

Lillian-Yvonne Bertram is the author of *Travesty Generator* (2019), a book of computational poetry that received the Poetry Society of America's 2020 Anna Rabinowitz prize for interdisciplinary work and longlisted for the 2020 National Book Award for Poetry. Their other poetry books include *How Narrow My Escapes* (2019), *Personal Science* (2017), *a slice from the cake made of air* (2016), and *But a Storm is Blowing From Paradise* (2012).

Christian Bök is the author of *Crystallography* (1994), a 'Pataphysical encyclopedia nominated for the Gerald Lampert Memorial Award, and of *Eunoia* (2001), a bestselling work of experimental literature, which won the Griffin Prize for Poetic Excellence. Bök has created

Contributors

artificial languages for the television shows Gene Roddenberry's *Earth: Final Conflict* and Peter Benchley's *Amazon*. His conceptual artworks (including books built from Rubik's cubes and Lego bricks) have appeared at the Marianne Boesky Gallery in the exhibit *Poetry Plastique*. Bök is currently a professor of English at the University of Calgary.

Kamau Brathwaite was born in Barbados in 1930. He is an internationally celebrated poet, performer, and cultural theorist. Cofounder of the Caribbean Artists Movement, he was educated at Pembroke College, Cambridge, and earned a PhD from the University of Sussex in the UK.

Jos Charles is a trans American poet, writer, translator, and editor. In 2017 her book *feeld* was a winner in the National Poetry Series. She is the founding editor of *THEM*, the first trans literary journal in the United States.

Franny Choi writes poems, essays, and other things. Her third book is *The World Keeps Ending, and the World Goes On* (2022). They are the author of two previous collections, *Soft Science* (2019) and *Floating, Brilliant, Gone,* (2014) as well as a chapbook, *Death by Sex Machine*. (2017) She is a Lilly/Rosenberg Fellow and a recipient of Princeton's Holmes National Poetry Prize. The founder of Brew & Forge, Franny is a Poetry Editor at the *Massachusetts Review* and faculty in Literature at Bennington College.

J. M. Coetzee OMG (1940) is a South African-Australian novelist, essayist, linguist, translator, and recipient of the 2003 Nobel Prize in Literature. He is one of the most critically acclaimed and decorated authors in the English language. He has won the Booker Prize (twice), the CNA Prize (thrice), the Jerusalem Prize, the *Prix Femina étranger*, and *The Irish Times* International Fiction Prize, and holds a number of other awards and honorary doctorates.

Teju Cole is a professor in the Department of English at Harvard University. He was born in the United States in 1975 to Nigerian parents and was raised in Lagos. He is a is a novelist, photographer, critic, curator, and the author of several books. His recent books include the essay collections *Known and Strange Things* (2016), *Golden Apple of the Sun* (2021), *Black Paper* (2021), and the photobook *Fernweh* (2020).

Lucy Corin is the author of the novels *The Swank Hotel* (2021) and *Everyday Psychokillers: A History for Girls* (2004) as well as the story collections *One Hundred Apocalypses and Other Apocalypses* (2016) and *The Entire Predicament* (2007). She is the recipient of an American Academy of Arts and Letters Rome Prize and a literature fellowship from the National Endowment for the Arts. She teaches at the University of California at Davis and lives in Berkeley.

Paul Cunningham is the Creative Writing Program Manager at the University of Notre Dame. He comanages Action Books, an international press for poetry and translation. He is the author of *Fall Garment* (2022) and *The House of the Tree of Sores* (2020). He is the translator of Helena Österlund's *Words* (2019) from the Swedish. He has also translated two chapbooks by Sara Tuss Efrik: *Automanias: Selected Poems* (2016) and *The Night's Belly* (2016). His most recent poetry chapbook is *The Inmost* (2020). Cunningham received his PhD from the University of Georgia and M.F.A. from the University of Notre Dame.

Contributors

Mirtha Dermisache was born in Buenos Aires in 1940 and studied visual arts at Manuel Belgrano and Prilidiano Pueyrredón National School of Fine Arts. Her works were published between 1970 and 1978 by the Center for Art and Communication. In the 1970s her graphisms were published by Marc Dachy and Guy Schraenen in Antwerp. She created the Workshop of Creative Actions in Buenos Aires during this time. Her first solo show in Buenos Aires was presented by The Edge, followed by exhibitions of her work at the MACBA (Barcelona) and the Center Pompidou (Paris).

Bobby DiTrani spent his formative years in the once small logging town of North Bend, WA. He is a graduate of the Aristedes Classical Atelier at the Gage Academy of Art, and his work has been exhibited nationwide. When not painting or drawing, he frequently tours with his band, the DiTrani Brothers.

Sara Tuss Efrik was born in 1981 in Falun, Sweden. She is a writer, playwright, and video artist. Her first novel *Mumieland* (Mummy Landy) was published in 2012. In the US, she has published two chapbooks: *Automanias: Selected Poems* (2016), winner of the 2015 Goodmorning Menagerie Chapbook-in-Translation contest, and *The Night's Belly* (2016), both translated by Paul Cunningham. She has a Master of Fine Arts in Theatre from the Theater Academy in Malmö. She is now working on a novel called *Heroine*.

Chikodili' Emelumadu's work has appeared in *One Throne, Omenana, Apex, Eclectica, Luna Station Quarterly*, and the interactive fiction magazine *Sub-Q*. In 2014, Chikodili was nominated for a Shirley Jackson Award, longlisted for the Caine Prize for African Writing, and is working on her novel.

Carina Finn is the author of *Lemonworld & Other Poems* (2013), *My Life Is a Movie* (2012) and *I Heart Marlon Brando* (2010). Her work has appeared in *TYPO, SUPERMACHINE, PANK, Storyglossia*, and elsewhere. She holds an MFA in Poetry from the University of Notre Dame, writes for *Montevidayo*, and lives in New York City, where she sporadically curates The Bratty Poets Series. Along with fellow poet Stephanie Berger, she is a member of the all-girl electrofolk trio, The London Skul of Economics.

Danielle Geller is the author of *Dog Flowers* (2021). She received her MFA in nonfiction at the University of Arizona and a Rona Jaffe Writers' Award in 2016. Her work has appeared in *The Paris Review, The New Yorker, Brevity*, and *Arizona Highways*, and has been anthologized in *This Is the Place*. She teaches creative writing at the University of Victoria. She is also a faculty mentor for the low-residency MFA program at the Institute of American Indian Arts. She is a member of the Navajo Nation: born to the Tsi'naajinii, born for the white man.

Johannes Göransson is a poet and translator who emigrated with his family from Skåne, Sweden, to the United States at age thirteen. He earned a BA from the University of Minnesota, an MFA from the Iowa Writers' Workshop, and his PhD from the University of Georgia. He is the author of several books of poetry, including *Summer* (2022), the essay collection *Transgressive Circulation: Essays On Translation* (2018), and the diaries *POETRY AGAINST ALL*. He has translated Aase Berg's poetry collections *Hackers* (2015), *Dark Matter* (2012), *Transfer Fat* (2012), *With Deer* (2009), and *Remainland: Selected Poems of Aase Berg* (2005), as well as her essay collection *A Tsunami from Solaris* (2019), with Joyelle McSweeney. He is also the translator of poetry by Johan Jönson, Kim Yideum, Henry Parland, and Ann Jäderlund.

Contributors

Marlon Hacla's latest book, *Melismas*, translated from Filipino by Kristine Ong Muslim, was published in 2020. A bilingual volume of his debut collection, *There Are Angels Walking the Fields*, will be released by Broken Sleep Books. His poems, translated by Kristine Ong Muslim, were published or are forthcoming in *Poetry, The Columbia Review, Nashville Review, Shenandoah, Words Without Borders*, and other journals. He lives in Quezon City, Philippines, with his cats.

Cathy Park Hong is the author of the *New York Times* bestselling book of creative nonfiction, *Minor Feelings: An Asian American Reckoning* (2020). *Minor Feelings* was a Pulitzer Prize finalist, won the National Book Critics Circle Award for autobiography, and earned her recognition on *TIME*'s 100 Most Influential People of 2021 list. She is also the author of poetry collections *Engine Empire, Dance Dance Revolution*, and *Translating Mo'um*. Hong is the recipient of a Windham-Campbell Prize, Guggenheim Fellowship, and National Endowment for the Arts Fellowship. She is a full professor at Rutgers-Newark University.

Douglas Kearney has published seven collections, including *Optic Subwoof* (2022), the Griffin Poetry Prize-winning *Sho* (2021), and *Buck Studies* which won the Theodore Roethke Memorial Poetry Award and the CLMP Firecracker Award. Kearney is the 2021 recipient of OPERA America's Campbell Opera Librettist Prize. His operas include *Sucktion, Mordake, Crescent City, Sweet Land* (the Music Critics of North America's Best Opera of 2021), and *Comet/Poppea* commissioned by AMOC. He has received a Whiting Writer's Award and a Foundation for Contemporary Arts Cy Twombly Award for Poetry. Kearney teaches creative writing at the University of Minnesota–Twin Cities.

Maya Lin is an American architect whose two most important works in the 1980s were the Vietnam Veterans' Memorial in Washington, DC, and the Civil Rights Memorial in Montgomery, Alabama.

Tan Lin is an American poet, writer, filmmaker, and educator. He is most notably recognized for his work in "ambient" literature, a style that draws on and samples source material from popular culture. He is the author of over thirteen books, including *Heath Course Pak* (2012), *Bib. Rev. Ed., Insomnia and the Aunt* (2011), and *Seven Controlled Vocabularies and Obituary 2004. The Joy of Cooking* (2010), among others.

Layli Long Soldier is the author of *Whereas* (2017), which won the National Books Critics Circle Award and was a finalist for the National Book Award. She has been a contributing editor to *Drunken Boat* and poetry editor at Kore Press; in 2012, her participatory installation, *Whereas We Respond*, was featured on the Pine Ridge Reservation. Long Soldier has been awarded a National Artist Fellowship from the Native Arts and Cultures Foundation, a Lannan Literary Fellowship for Poetry, and a Whiting Writer's Award. Long Soldier is a citizen of the Oglala Lakota Nation and lives in Santa Fe, New Mexico.

Garielle Lutz is a writer known for her short stories. She is the author of *Stories in the Worst Way* ([1996] 2002, 2009), *Partial List of People to Bleach* (2007), *I Looked Alive* ([2003] 2010), *Divorcer* (2011), and *The Complete Gary Lutz* (2021). Her work has also appeared in literary magazines and journals such as *Tin House, Conjunctions, NOON, McSweeney's, The Believer, Chicago Review, Columbia: A Journal of Literature and Art, Denver Quarterly, The Quarterly*,

Salt Hill, New York Tyrant, Dominion Review, Mid-American Review, Post Road, Slate.com, StoryQuarterly, and the *Cimarron Review*.

K. Silem Mohammad is the author of several books of poetry, including *Deer Head Nation* (2003), *A Thousand Devils* (2004), *Breathalyzer* (2008), and *The Front* (2009). In *The Sonnagrams* (2009), Mohammad anagrammatizes Shakespeare's sonnets into all-new English sonnets in iambic pentameter. He is also editor of the poetry magazine *Abraham Lincoln* and faculty editor of *West Wind Review*. He teaches English and writing at Southern Oregon University.

Ander Monson is the author of eight books, including the novel *Other Electricities*, a finalist for the New York Public Library Young Lions Fiction Award, and the essay collection *Vanishing Point*, a finalist for the National Book Critics Circle Award. He teaches at the University of Arizona.

Thirii Myo Kyaw Myint was born in Yangon, Myanmar, and grew up in Bangkok, Thailand, and San José, California. She is the author of *The End of Peril, the End of Enmity, the End of Strife, a Haven* (2018, Noemi Press), which won an Asian/Pacific American Award for Literature. Her second book *Names for Light: A Family History* was the winner of the 2018 Graywolf Press Nonfiction Prize. She has a BA from Brown University, an MFA from the University of Notre Dame, and a PhD from the University of Denver. She teaches at Amherst College.

GennaRose Nethercott is the author of *The Lumberjack's Dove* (2018), winner of the National Poetry Series. Her other projects include the narrative song collection *Modern Ballads* and *Lianna Fled the Cranberry Bog: A Story in Cootie Catchers* (2019). Nethercott tours, performing from her works (often with a hand-cranked shadow show in tow) and composing poems-to-order for strangers on a 1952 Hermes Rocket typewriter. She is founder of the Traveling Poetry Emporium and an associate producer at Grim and Mild. She lives in woodlands Vermont beside an old cemetery. Her debut novel is *Thistlefoot* (2022).

Eiríkur Örn Norðdahl is an Icelandic poet and novelist. His novel *Illska* (2012) won The Icelandic Literary Prize and The Book Merchant's Prize. He has published seven books of poems, five novels, two collections of essays, and a philosophical cookbook. Eiríkur has translated over a dozen books into Icelandic, including a selection of Allen Ginsberg's poetry, Jonathan Lethem's *Motherless Brooklyn* (for which he received the Icelandic Translation Award), and Athena Farrokhzad's *Vitsvit*. He lives in Ísafjörður, Iceland, a rock in the middle of the ocean, and spends much of his time in Västerås, Sweden, a town by a lake.

Elena Passarello is an actor, writer, and recipient of a 2015 Whiting Award. Her first collection *Let Me Clear My Throat* (2012), won the gold medal for nonfiction at the 2013 Independent Publisher Awards. Passarello has performed in several regional theaters in the East and Midwest, originating roles in the premieres of Christopher Durang's *Mrs. Bob Cratchit's Wild Christmas Binge* and David Turkel's *Wild Signs* and *Holler*. In 2011, she became the first woman winner of the annual Stella Screaming Contest in New Orleans. She lives in Corvallis, Oregon, and teaches at Oregon State University.

Craig Santos Perez is an indigenous Chamoru (Chamorro) from the Pacific Island of Guåhan (Guam). He is a poet, scholar, editor, publisher, essayist, critic, book reviewer, artist, environmentalist, and political activist. Craig is the author of two spoken word poetry albums,

Contributors

Undercurrent (2011) and *Crosscurrent* (2017), and five poetry books: *from unincorporated territory [hacha]* (2008), *from unincorporated territory [saina]* (2010), *from unincorporated territory [guma']* (2014), *from unincorporated territory [lukao]* (2017), and *Habitat Threshold* (2020). His monograph, *Navigating Chamoru Poetry: Indigeneity, Aesthetics, and Decolonization* (2022) was published by the Critical Issues of Indigenous Studies series at the University of Arizona Press.

DBC Pierre has worked as a designer and cartoonist. He was born in Australia, raised in Mexico, and has lived in Ireland and England. His first novel, *Vernon God Little*, won the 2003 Bollinger Everyman Wodehouse Award, the 2003 Whitbread Prize for Best First Novel, and the 2003 Booker Prize. He spent many schooldays watching Hammer films about the supernatural, drawing replica storyboards on cash register rolls, and holding showings for classmates on a shoebox cinema.

Mary Ruefle is the author of *Dunce* (2019), *My Private Property* (2016), *Madness, Rack, and Honey: Collected Lectures* (2012, a finalist for the National Book Critics Circle Award in Criticism), *Selected Poems* (2010, winner of the William Carlos Williams Award), and the comic book *Go Home and Go to Bed!* (2007). Her erasure artworks have been exhibited in museums and galleries and published in A Little White Shadow (2006). Ruefle is the recipient of the Robert Creeley Award, a Guggenheim fellowship, a National Endowment for the Arts fellowship, and a Whiting Award. She lives in Bennington, Vermont.

Ekaterina Samigulina/Tae Ateh is a poet and asemic worker from Minsk, Belarus. Samigulina is a member of the Lipovy tsvet art group, creator of the KYU literart band and Asemic International, partner of DAMTP, and graduate of Mogilev State University.

Carlos Soto-Román is a poet, translator, and pharmacist. In English, he has published *Philadelphia's Notebooks* (2011), *Chile Project: [Re-Classified]* (2013), *The Exit Strategy* (2014), *Alternative Set of Procedures* (2014), *Bluff* (2018), *Common Sense* (2019), and *Nature of Objects* (2019). In Spanish, he has published *La Marcha de los Quiltros* (1999), *Haikú Minero* (2007), *Cambio y Fuera* (2009), *11* ([2017] 2023]), *Densidad (d=m/V)* (2018), and *Antuco* (2019) in collaboration with Carlos Cardani Parra. He has also translated the first Spanish-language version of *Holocaust* by Charles Reznikoff. His book *11* ([2017] 2023]) was awarded the 2018 Municipal Poetry Prize in Santiago, Chile.

Rodrigo Toscano is a poet and dialogist based in New Orleans. He is the author of eleven books of poetry. His latest two books are *The Cut Point* (2023) and *The Charm & The Dread* (2022). His previous books include *In Range* (2019), *Explosion Rocks Springfield* (2017), *Deck of Deeds* (2012), *Collapsible Poetics Theater* (2008, a National Poetry Series selection), *To Leveling Swerve* (2004), *Platform* (2003), *Partisans* (1999), and *The Disparities* (2002). His poetry has appeared in over twenty anthologies, including *Best American Poetry* and *Best American Experimental Poetry (BAX)*. Toscano has received a New York State Fellowship in Poetry. He won the Edwin Markham 2019 prize for poetry. He works for the Labor Institute in conjunction with the United Steelworkers, the National Institute for Environmental Health Science on educational training projects that involve environmental and labor justice culture transformation (rodrigotoscano.com, @Toscano200),

Contributors

Cecilia Vicuña is a poet, artist, filmmaker, and activist who lives and works in Chile and New York. Born and raised in Santiago de Chile, she has been in exile since the military coup in the early 1970s. She creates multidimensional, site-specific performance works and installations that combine ritual and assemblage. In Chile she founded the Tribu No in 1967, a group that created anonymous poetic actions. In 1974, exiled in London, she cofounded Artists for Democracy to oppose dictatorships in the Third World. Cecilia Vicuña is the author of twenty-two poetry books, including *New and Selected Poems of Cecilia Vicuña* (2018).

Jennifer Walshe was born in Dublin, Ireland. Recent projects include *TIME TIME TIME*, an opera written in collaboration with philosopher Timothy Morton, and *THE SITE OF AN INVESTIGATION*, a 30-minute epic for Walshe's voice and orchestra, commissioned by the National Symphony Orchestra of Ireland. *A Late Anthology of Early Music Vol. 1: Ancient to Renaissance*, her third solo album, was released in 2020. The album uses AI to rework canonical works of Western music. It was an album of the year in *The Irish Times*, *The Wire*, and *The Quietus*. Walshe is professor of composition at the University of Oxford.

Karen Tei Yamashita is the author of seven books—including *I Hotel* (2010), finalist for the National Book Award, and most recently, *Sansei and Sensibility* (2020). Recipient of the Lifetime Achievement Award for Distinguished Contribution to American Letters from the National Book Foundation, the John Dos Passos Prize for Literature, and a US Artists' Ford Foundation Fellowship, she is professor emerita of literature and creative writing at the University of California, Santa Cruz.

PERMISSIONS

"On Times I Have Forced Myself to Dance" from *A Little Devil in America: Notes in Praise of Black Performance* by Hanif Abdurraqib, copyright © 2021 by Hanif Abdurraqib. Used by permission of Random House, an imprint and division of Penguin Random House LLC. All rights reserved.

"Freinds" © Caren Beilin. Published by *Two Serious Ladies*. Used by permission.

"Dogs without a Face" from *Academonia* © 2006 by Dodie Bellamy. Published by Krupskaya. Used by permission.

"In the Guinea Pig Cave" from *With Deer*. Copyright © 2009 by Aase Berg, translated from the Swedish by Johannes Göransson. Reprinted by permission of Black Ocean.

"from Chapter A," "from Chapter E," "from Chapter I," "from Chapter O, "from Chapter U," and "from 'the new Ennui'" © 2005 by Christian Bök. Published by Coach House Books. Used by permission.

"I was Wash-Way in Blood" from *Born To Slow Horses* © 2005 by Kamau Brathwaite. Published by Wesleyan University Press. Used by permission.

Teju Cole, "In Place of Thought" (c) Condé Naste. Published by The New Yorker. Used by permission.

Jos Charles, "Chapter XIX," "Chapter XXI," and "Chapter XXIV" from feeld. Copyright © 2018 by Jos Charles. Reprinted with the permission of The Permissions Company LLC on behalf of Milkweed Editions, milkweed.org.

Franny Choi, "Turing Test" from *Soft Science*. Copyright © 2019 by Franny Choi. Reprinted with the permission of The Permissions Company, LLC on behalf of Alice James Books, alicejamesbooks.org.

Computer Poetry from J. M. Coetzee Papers © Coetzee, J.M. Used by permission.

"Questions in a Significantly Smaller Font" from *One Hundred Apocalypses and Other Apocalypses* © 2013 by Lucy Corin. Published by *McSweeney's*. Used by permission.

Excerpt from *Selected Writings* © 2018 by Mirtha Dermisache. Published by Ugly Duckling Presse. Used by permission.

Excerpt from *Danse Macabre Piggies* © 2023 by Sara Tuss Efrik (trans. Paul Cunningham). Used by permission.

"What to Do When Your Child Brings Home a Mami Wata" © 2018 by Chịkọdịlị Emelụmadụ. Used by permission.

"Grey Bird on a Wire (Angst Attack)" from *The Grey Bird* © 2014 by Carina Finn & Stephanie Berger. Published by Coconut Books. Used by permission.

"Annotating the First Page of the First Navajo-English Dictionary" from © 2017 by Danielle Geller. Published by *The New Yorker*. Used by permission.

"Bluebush" from *Glossolalia* © Marlon Hacla, translation © Kristine Ong Muslim. Published by Ugly Duckling Presse, 2023. Used by permission.

Permissions

"Cholla Village of No" from *DANCE DANCE REVOLUTION* by Cathy Park Hong. Copyright © 2007 by Cathy Park Hong. Used by permission of W. W. Norton & Company, Inc.

Sucktion from *Someone Took They Tongues*: 3 Operas © 2016 by Douglas Kearney. Published by Subito Press. Used by permission.

Layli Long Soldier, excerpts from "Whereas Statements" from *Whereas*. Copyright © 2017 by Layli Long Soldier. Reprinted with the permission of The Permissions Company, LLC on behalf of Graywolf Press, Minneapolis, Minnesota, graywolfpress.org.

"The Boy" © Garielle Lutz. Used by permission.

Blueprint excerpt for *Reading a Garden* © 1998 by Maya Lin and Tan Lin. Commissioned by the Cleveland Public Library. Used by permission.

"They Net the HDTV Teeth, the 'Chewy Heavens' HDTV Teeth" from *The Sonnagrams* © K. Silem Mohammad. Previously unpublished.

"Sincerity" from © Ander Monson. Published by otherelectricities.com. Used by permission.

"You Rail, and the Road" © Thirii Myo Kyaw Myint. Published by *Sleepingfish*. Used by permission.

Excerpt from *Lianna Fled the Cranberry Bog: A Story in Cootie Catchers* © 2019 by GennaRose Nethercott. Published by Ninepin Press. Used by permission.

"Nailsoup" from *Blandarabrandarar* © 2005 by Eiríkur Örn Norðdahl. Published by Nýhil. Used by permission.

"Koko" from *Animals Strike Curious Poses* © 2017 by Elena Passarello. Published by Sarabande Books. Used by permission.

"News" from *Petit Mal* © 2013 by DBC Pierre. Published by Faber and Faber Social. Used by permission.

"The Taking of Moundville by Zoom" from *The Most of It* © 2008 by Mary Ruefle. Published by Wave Books. Used by permission.

Excerpt from *Post-Soviet Belarus* © 2016 by Ekaterina Samigulina/Tae Ateh. Published by *3:AM Magazine*. Used by permission.

"ginen the legends of juan malo [a malologue]" from *From Unincorporated Territory* [gumá] © 2014 by Craig Santos Perez. Published by Omnidawn Press. Used by permission.

"Never Again" from *11* © Carlos Soto-Román, translation © Alexis Almeida, Daniel Beauregard, Daniel Borzutzky, Whitney DeVos, Patrick Greaney, Robin Myers, Jessica Pujol, Durán, and Thomas Rothe, Published by Ugly Duckling Presse, 2023. Used by permission.

"Great Awakening" from *Collapsible Poetics Theater* © 2008 by Rodrigo Toscano. Published by Fence Books. Used by permission.

"Destruir el desierto" from *Forthcoming Title* © 2024 by Cecilia Vicuña.

"THIS IS WHY PEOPLE O.D. ON PILLS/AND JUMP OFF THE GOLDEN GATE BRIDGE" © 2004 by Jennifer Walshe. Used by permission.

Karen Tei Yamashita, "Hannah Kusoh: An American Butoh" from *Anime Wong: Fictions of Performance*. Copyright © 2014 by Karen Tei Yamashita. Reprinted with the permission of The Permissions Company, LLC, on behalf of Coffee House Press, Minneapolis, Minnesota, coffeehousepress.org.

"#/usr/bin/python/three_last_words" from *Travesty Generator* © 2019 by Lillian-Yvonne Bertram. Published by Noemi Press. Used by permission.

INDEX

2500 Random Things About Me Too 169
"34650 Seconds" 106
"45' for a Speaker" 149

Aarseth, Espen 176
Abbey, Edward 141
Abend, Gabriel 30
Abish, Walter 66, 106
Abramović, Maria 154
Achebe, Chinua 62, 119
Acker, Kathy 63, 66, 108, 117, 155
Adams, Douglas 126
Adbusters Magazine 54
Adichie, Chimamanda Ngozie 126
Adobe Flash 163, 176, 192
advertisements 59, 84, 125, 167
After Lorca 27
Aire, Antena 57
Aisteach 136
Alameddine, Rabih 35
Alciato, Andrea 108
"ALGOL" 175
all-dialogue story 19
Allin, GG 120
Alphabetical Africa 106
alternative histories 63
Alt-Lit 166, 167
Amalgamemnon 106
Amerifl.txt 126
Ammons, A. R. 90
Analytical Engine 177
André, Carl 107
Andrews, Jim 177
Anémic Cinéma 176
Antin, David 149
antinovel 34, 36, 37, 39, 40, 43, 47, 49
"Ants" 109
aphorisms 115, 122, 124, 126, 127, 129, 140
Apollinaire, Guillaume 108, 175
appropriation 52, 71, 101, 103
Arcades Project 122
Arcangel, Cory 173
The Argonauts 30
ARK 42
Armand, Louis 37
The Armies of the Night 155
Arrow, Dennis W. 137
Ars Magna 177
Artist's Shit 120, 155
ArtThoughtz 173

asemic writing 86, 109, 110, 111, 182
Ashbery, John 22, 23, 66, 95
Associate Deans (@ass_deans) 170
"Attempt at Exhausting a Space in Williamstown" 106
Atwood, Margaret 62, 123
aubade 21
Auden, W. H. 26, 126
Austin, J. L. 156
The Autobiography of Alice B. Toklas 138
autofiction 29, 31
autotheory 30, 31, 32, 103, 113
Autotheory as Feminist Practice in Art, Writing, and Criticism 30

Babbage, Charles 177
Babbitt 152, 153
Bachelard, Gaston 91
Bakhtin, Mikhail 39
Baldassari, John 107
Ball, Hugo 147
Banksy 54, 155
Barlow, John Perry 181–2
Barney, Matthew 154
Barthelme, Donald 29, 61, 97, 108, 113
Barthes, Roland 13, 30, 95, 104, 143, 192
Bashō 23, 24
Baudelaire, Charles 21
Bauhaus 78, 146
Bean, Heidi R. 147
Beat poets 148
Beaulieu, Derek 109
Beautiful Oops 82
Bed 41
The Bed of Procrustes 123
Beech, Dave 165
Being a Beast 140
Bénabou, Marcel 105
Benenson, Fred 58
"benign violation" 150
Benjamin, Walter 56, 122
Beowulf 58
Berghaus, Günter 146
Bernstein, Charles 56, 95, 96, 101, 172
Bernstein, Felix 101, 102
Berry, Wendell 141
Bertram, Lillian Yvonne 189
Bervin, Jen 68, 89
Bess, Gabby 167
Beyond Craft: An Anti-Handbook for Creative Writers 161

Index

Bhabha, Homi 19
Bhatnagar, Ranjit 170
Bhatti, Jaspal 150
Bildungsroman 28
The Bindery 77
Birkerts, Sven 163
Bishop, Claire 102
Bishop, Wendy 6
The Bitter Life of Božena Němcová 46
"Black Box" 169
Black Nature 141
Blake 1
blank parody 53
blank verse 27
"Blue Hyacinth" 177
Blumer, Herbert 128
Boccacio 99
Bochner, Mel 87
"The Body of Michael Brown" 100
Boglione, Riccardo 99
BOMB 118
Bonk 140
The Book of Beginnings and Endings 122
The Book of Disquiet 139
Book of Questions 140
Book of the Dead 41
Borges, Jorge Luis 13, 56, 113, 126, 149, 189
Boully, Jenny 69, 122
Bourriaud, Nicholas 156
Bowling for Columbine 55
Boyle, Megan 166, 186
bpNichols 41
braided essay 23
Braithwaite, Lawrence Ytzhak 116
Brecht, Bertolt 168
British Poetry Revival 97
Brock-Broido, Lucie 27
Brooke-Roses, Christine 106
Brosi, Evelin 106
Brown, Julie Philips 81
Brown, Laynie 38
Browning, Elizabeth Barret 28, 139
Brynner, Witter 130
Bulwer Lytton Fiction Contest 117
Burden, Chris 154
Burt, Stephanie 42, 48
Bury, Louis 106
But What If We're Wrong? 133, 189
Butor, Michel 45
Button Poetry 170, 187
Byron, Lord 177

Cage, John 143, 147
Callan, Jonathan 80
Calligrammes 175
Calloway, Caroline 102
Calvino, Italo 105, 149
Camnitzer, Luis 99

Campesino, Teatro 121
campfire tales 123
Campos, Augusto de 107
Cane 35
Caplan, David 117
carmina figurata 108
Carr, Nicholas 166
Carson, Anne 23, 41, 82, 83
Carson, David 135
Carver, Raymond 122
Casey, Rob 136
Cassils 154
Castro, E. M. de Melo e 176
Castro, Jordan 167
"Cat Person" 29
A Certain World 126
Cha, Theresa Hak Kyung 44, 59
Chasar, Mark 84
Cherches, Peter 149
Chesluk, Benjamin J. 79
Choi, Don Mee 87
Choi, Franny 58
circus arts 146, 155
Clifford, Alison 176
closet drama 28, 31, 40
Closky, Claude 98
Cobain, Kurt 66, 126
Cobbing, Bob 107
Coetzee, J. M. 62, 174
Colasacco, John 170
"Cold Calls" 100
Cole, Henri 24
Cole, Teju 169
Coleridge 1
collage 45, 48, 51
The Collapse of Western Civilization: A View from the Future 136
collected letters 125
collective net.art 173
"The Colonel" 22
commonplace book 125–7
composite novel 34, 35, 36, 39, 47
"Composition as Process" 149
Composition No 1 82
"A Concatenation of Sprawls" 121
Concrete Poetry 107–8
Conrad, CA 155, 159
"Consider the Lobster" 134
Conway, Erik M. 136
Coover, Robert 53, 54, 97
Corin, Lucy 26
Cortázar 2, 61, 66, 97
Corvo, Baron 138
Cottrell, Patrick 135
The Counterfeiters 69
Crabtree, Jamison 135
craft talk 149
Crase, Douglass 126

Index

creepy pasta 123, 172
Cross, David 150
Crowley, Aleister 139
crux 15
"Cult of Distraction" 172
cultural criticism 36, 133
Cummings, E. E. 108, 176
Cuneo, John 170
Czyz, Vincent 45

D'Agata, John 22, 23, 89, 98, 131, 132
DALL·E 181, 185
Dalton, Trinie 84, 126
Danielewski, Mark Z. 83
Danto, Arthur 65
Dark Mountain 141
Day 100
"DECADENCE CAN BE AN END IN ITSELF" 107
"DECENCY IS A RELATIVE THING" 107
de rigueur 14, 78, 131
Dear Ijeawele, or A Feminist Manifesto in Fifteen Suggestions 126
Dear New Girl or Whatever Your Name Is 126
DeBord, Guy 54, 148, 165
Decameron 99
"A Declaration of the Independence of Cyberspace" 182
Deep Ecology 141
Deep Thoughts 123
Degas, Edgar 110
DeJon, Lewis 135
Deleuze 115
Delirious New York: A Retroactive Manifesto for Manhattan 135
Denton, William 176
Derrida, Jacques 65, 72, 95
Destruction of Man 122
détournement 7, 54, 55, 74, 171
Dial-a-Poem 155
Dialogues 29
diaries 20, 64, 126, 139
Diary 126
diastic method 106
Dickinson, Emily 83, 118, 129
Dickinson, Stephanie 139
Dictée 44, 59
Différance 191–2
The Digital Culture World Lecture Tour 125
Diné College 82
Discipline and Punish 132
distant reading 101, 111
doggerel 116–18, 127, 130
Dong, Wang 109
Donovan, Simon 85
Dormer, Catherine 81
Dorr, Noam 109
Douglas, Mary 120
Dr. Johnson and Mr. Savage 138
Dracula 27, 68

DRAFTS 81
dramatic essay 28–9, 31, 32
Dryden, John 56
Duchamp, Marcel 104, 122
  art 65, 120
  digital writing 176
  kitsch 121
  theater 146, 153
DuPlessis, Rachel Blau 81
Duqette, Jesse 170
The Durham Poems 176
Dworkin, Craig 99–100, 106
Dyer, Geoff 64, 138, 140

Eagleton, Terry 157
"Easter Wings" 108
Eastgate 177
East Jesus 120
Eat Your Mind 117
Ecclesiastes 51
Edwards, Joshua 148
EECCHHOOEESS 107
Egan, Jennifer 61, 169
"The Egg" 108
Eiríkur Örn Norðdahl 99
Ekelund, Vilhelm 13
Eliot, T. S. 27, 48, 66
Elmslie, Kenward 148
Emile 38
Empire Writes Back 62–3
Emoji Dick 58
endurance art 154
English Baroque 108
Enlightenment 29, 69, 139, 140, 183
epistolary
  forms 26, 125
  novels 27, 31, 35, 183
  writing 115, 174
ergodic 2, 82, 174, 176, 177
Ervick, Kelcey Parker 46
Eshelman, Clayton 155
Essays on the Essay and Other Essays 178
Etherpoems 182
Ethnopoetics 155
"Eve's Legend" 105
"Everyone I've Had Sex With" 166
Exercises in Style 105
existentialist 38, 139
experimentalism 8, 10, 13, 110
Extremely Loud and Incredibly Close 109
Eyes Bottle Dark with a Mouthful of Flowers 70

Family Resemblance 7, 33
Father and Son 138
Faulkner, William 51
Ferry, Bryan 135
feuilletons 118
Field, Thalia 46

Index

Fifty Days at Iliam 182
Finnegans Wake 2, 59
"The First Thousand Numbers Classified in Alphabetical Order" 98
Fisher, M. F. K. 134
Fitterman, Robert 103
"Five Words in Red Neon" 107
flash genre 24–5
Flatland 109
Flush: A Biography 139
FLUXUS 153, 154, 156, 159
Foer, Jonathan Safran 68, 83, 109
folk culture 123
Forché, Carolyn 22
Foster, Charles 140
Foucault, Michel 95
Fountain 65, 120
Fournier, Lauren 30
"Fourth of July" 26
Fraga, Sophia Le 103
fragments 122, 128
Frank, Waldo 35
Frankfurt, Harry G. 137
Franzen, Jonathan 165
Frye, Northrop 39
furoshiki 81
"Future Biometrics" 79
Futurists 108, 147, 156, 182

Gabbert, Elisa 102, 169
Gaiman, Neil 117
Garréta, Anne F. 105
Geary, James 123
German Romantics 37
Gesamtkunstwerk 156
Gildenhard 20
Gilmore, Madeline 106
Giorno, John 155
Goeritz, Mathias 107
Goldberg, Roselee 154
"Golden Record" 89
Goldkamp, Henry 151
Goldsmith, Kenneth 165, 185
    Alt-Lit 167
    conceptual writing 98, 100, 101
    internet browsing 166
    PennSound 172
Gombrowicz, Witold 126
Goodwin, Ross 180
Google Ngram Viewer 186
Gordon, Noah Eli 99, 174
Gosse, Edmund 138
Gottfried, Gilbert 151
Grangaud, Michelle 105
The Great Fire of London 105
Greenblatt, Stephen 138
Greif, Mark 172
Gretzinger, Jerry 140

Groenland, Tim 122
Groys, Boris 85
Guattari 115, 118
Guide to the World's Great Aphorists 123
Gulp 140
gurlesque 117
Gutiérrez, Raquel 121
Guy in Your MFA 170

Hafiz 71
haibun 23, 24, 31
Handey, Jack 123
Harjo, Joy 148
Harlem Renaissance 148
Hass, Robert 24, 97
The Hatred of Poetry 3
Headley, Maria Dahvana 58
The Heart of the World 118
Heat: An Interview with Jean Seaburg 139
Hebdige, Dick 55
Hedberg, Mitch 124, 150
Heidegger, Martin 191–2
Hejinian 95, 96, 98
Hellstern, Elizabeth 156
Hembree, Carolyn 171
Hemingway, Ernest 26, 29
Hemley, Robin 60, 191
Herbert, George 108
Higgins, Dick 153, 156
Hinds 20
Hinton, Laura 147
History of Shit 137
Hoang, Lily 23, 45
Hoban, Russell 59, 119
Höch, Hannah 119
Hodgman, Ann 134
Hoff, Benjamin 139
Holiday, Harmony 70
Hollywood Forever 70
Holmes, Richard 138
Holzer, Jenny 107
Hopscotch 2
Hotel Amerika 123
Hotel Palenque 37
Hotel Theory 36
The House of Eternal Return 88
House of Leaves 83
Howard, Richard 16, 27
Howe, Susan 64, 95, 99, 138
"How to Make a Dadaist Poem" 66
Hseih, Tehching 57, 154
Hsi, Chu 51
Hugo, Richard 8, 27
Huidobro, Vicente 108
Huiwen 104
A Humument: A Treated Victorian Novel 67
A Hundred Thousand Billion Poems 104
Hutcheon, Linda 53

hybrid publishing 79
hypertexts 177

I Ching (Book of Changes) 176
i/o 175
Iconographs 107
If on a Winter's Night a Traveler 37, 105
IF U DONT LOVE THE MOON YOUR AN ASS HOLE 167
Impey, Sara 81
Inbox 99, 174
Ineradicable Stain: Skin Project 2
Information Age 163, 182
The Innovators 177
Inside the Castle 180
Instapoems 170
Internet Cat Video Festival 172
Internet of Things 163
Isou, Isidore 109
Issacson, Walter 177
Ives, Lucy 103
Iwamoto, Kalen 181
"I Will Not Make Any More Boring Art" 107

Jabès, Edmond 140
Jackson, H. J. 1
Jackson, Shelley 2, 177
Jacobson, Michael 109
James, William 120, 149
Jameson, Fredric 4, 53
"Japan: Prose of Departure" 24
Jarry, Alfred 37, 104
Jay, Rikki 88
Jefferson, Margo 138
Joe Gould's Secret 138
Johnson, B. S. 2, 82
Johnson, Ronald 42, 68
Johnson, Samuel 138, 214
journals 126
Journals 126

Kael, Pauline 172
Kafka, Franz 115
Kafka: Toward a Theory of Minor Literature 115
Kapow! 83
Kappus, Franz Xaver 162
Kardashian, Kim 173
Katelnikoff, Joel 64
Kaur, Rupi 170
Kawabata, Yasunari 26
kawaī 122, 172
Keats, John 46
Kemal 92
Kenner, Hugh 69
Keret, Etgar 25
Keywords in Creative Writing 6
King, Stephen 169
kitsch 119, 121

Klosterman, Chuck 133, 189
Klosterman's Razor 133
Koch, Kenneth 28
Kocurek, Carly 88
Koestenbaum, Wayne 36, 90
Koolaids 35
Koolhaas, Rem 135
Koons, Jeff 121
Kostelanetz, Richard 106
Kosuth, Joseph 107
Kracauer, Sigfried 172
Kraus, Karl 28, 129
Krotoszynski Jr., Ronald J. 137
Kruger, Barbara 81, 107
Krystal, Arthur 157
Kunkel, Benjamin 119

La Disparition 104
Lace Letters 81
Ladinsky, Daniel 71
Laird, Benjamin 176
LANGUAGE poetry 95
Laporte, Dominique 137
Las Aventuras de Don Chipote 121
Last Days of Mankind 28
latrinalia 127
Laver, James 193
Lawrence, D. H. 64, 138
Leadville 138
Lebenswelt 191
"Lecture on Nothing" 149
Lectures in America 149
Lehman, David 33, 60
LeMay, Eric 178
Lennon, Brian 177
Leong, Michael 123
Lerner, Ben 3, 38
Les Figues Press 45
Letter to a Future Lover: Marginalia, Errata, Secrets, Inscriptions, and Other Ephemera Found in Libraries 127
Letters from Iceland 26
Letters to a Young Poet 126
Lettrism 109
Lévi-Strauss, Claude 86, 104
LeWitt, Sol 107
Lexical Evidence from Folk Epigraphy in Western North America: A Glossarial Study of the Low Element in the English Vocabulary 128
Lianna Fled the Cranberry Bog 192
Life: A User's Manual 105
"Life Story" 191
Lin, Maya 192
Lin, Tan 46, 103, 192
Lindsay, Vachel 148
Lionnais, François Le 104
Lish, Gordon 122
literary field guides 141

Index

literary notebooks 125–7
Live Action Role-Playing Games 151
Liveblog 186
Llull, Ramon 177
Lockett, Clayton 101
"A Log Cabin Square" 109
The Lonely Planet Guide to Experimental Travel 140
long poem 40–3
longue durée 10
los de abajo 121
The Lost Origins of the Essay 131
"Love Is in the Bin" 155
Lovelace, Ada 177
Lovelace, Sean 139
Low, Jackson Mac 106
Loyd, John 126
Lyacos, Dimitris 46
lyric essay 22–5, 44, 98

Maciunas, Georges 153, 159
MacPhee, Josh 54
Maddin, Guy 118, 179
Madonna 82
Mahoney, Daniel 135
Mailer, Norman 155
Maistre, Xavier de 140
"Make it new" 51
Mallarmé, Stéphane 21, 110
"A Manifesto for Ultratranslation" 57
"Manifesto of Futurism" 156
manifestos 45, 156, 158, 162
Manzoni, Piero 120, 155
Marcinkiewicz, Paweł 100
marginalia 125, 127
Marinetti 156
Markos, Steven 171
Markson, David 38
Martins, Luiza Prado de Oliveira 87
Martone, Michael 149
The Martyrology 41
Marxist 13, 54, 55, 96, 157
Master Letters 27
Masurel, Pauline 177
"Material Combinatorium Supremum" 177
Mathews, Harry 60, 105, 112
Mattawa, Khaled 24
Mau, Bruce 136
Mayakovsky, Vladimir 147
Mayer, Bernadette 157
McBride, Jason 117
McCarthy, Tom 38
McGraw, Peter 150
McGuane, Thomas 122
McGurl, Mark 78
McHale, Brian 47
McLuhan, Marshall 164, 165
McSweeney, Joyelle 148
McSweeney's Internet Tendency 124

The Meaning of Liff: A Dictionary of Things There Aren't Any Words for Yet—But There Ought to Be 126
"Meditation at Lagunitas" 97
Méliès, Georges 175
melodrama 115, 116, 118, 179
Memmott, Talan 125
Memorial 99
Menippean satire 34, 39, 40, 47, 49
"Mensajes dorados" 107
Menu, Jean-Christophe 105
Meow Wolf 88
Merchant, Brian 180
Merrill, James 24
Mesa-Bains, Amalia 121
Messerli, Douglas 96
Metamorphoses 20
metaverse 181–4
Michaux, Henri 109
Michigan Law Review 136
Middle Ages 108
Mill, John Stuart 112
Milne, A. A. 139
Minimalism in Action 122
Minnis, Chelsey 122
Minor, Sarah 87, 109, 112, 192
Mitchell, Joseph 138
Mobile 45
Modernism 10, 13, 34, 37, 40, 53, 80, 137
Mohammad, K. Silem 66, 190
MoMA 65, 154
Mongrel Coalition Against Gringpo 100–1
Monson, Ander 82, 98, 127, 149, 167
mono no aware 24, 31
Monster 27
The Monument 97
Moore, Marianne 3
Moore, Thomas 38
The Morning of the Poem 90
Morrison, Toni 91
Moving Poems 187
Mroué, Rabih 103
Museum of Innocence 87, 92
The Museum of Jurassic Technology 88
Musil, Robert 118
My Autobiography of Carson McCullers 64, 138
My Emily Dickinson 64, 138
My Life 22, 96
My Winnipeg 118
Myers, Walter Dean 27
Myles, Eileen 29, 38, 116, 165
Mynd Eraser 110

N + 7 112
Nabokov, Vera 138
Nabokov, Vladimir 35, 82
naïve 116, 118, 121
Nakayasu, Sawako 57
Narrow Road to the Deep North 23

Index

Nathan for You 55
National Film Board of Canada 179
Nauman, Bruce 154
Neely, Mark 139
Nelson, Maggie 23, 30, 44, 98
Neoliberal 167
Nethercott, GennaRose 192
New England Review 45
New Historicism 63
the New Sentence 96–7
Newton, Isaac 139
The New Yorker 25, 29, 119, 169
Nezhukumatathil, Aimee 24
NFT Now 181
Ngai, Sianne 102
Nice Things by James Franco 139
Niikuni, Seiichi 107
No Medium 100
NonfictioNOW Conference 149
Notes on Conceptualisms 103
nouveau roman 37, 97
"No Wonder They Call Me a Bitch" 134
"Notes on Camp" 121
NOX 83

Oates, Joyce Carol 16, 169
Obrist, Hans Ulrich 102
Odyssey Works 88
Oliu, Brian 167, 175
Olmstead, Ben 85
Olson, Charles 68, 95, 108, 147
Omega Mart 88
On Bullshit 137
"On Exactitude in Science" 189
On Michael Jackson 138
one-liner joke 123
Only Revolutions 83
Ono, Yoko 153, 159, 172
"On Visiting the DMZ at Panmunjom" 24
"One Aphorism Will Hide Another" 105
Oreskes, Naomi 136
OuLiPo 104, 111, 112, 123
Out of Sheer Rage 64, 138
outsider art 118
"Ovonovelo" 107
Ovid 20, 26, 61

Pale Fire 35
palimpsest 67, 69, 70
Pallasmaa, Juhani 80
Palmquist, Lara 26
The Palm-Wine Drinkard and His Dead Palm-Wine Tapster in the Dead's Town 119
Pamela; or, Virtue Rewarded 183
Pamuk, Orhan 87, 92
Parabola 45
Paris Spleen 21
Pariser, Eli 166

Parsons, Guy 185
Partch, Harry 152
participatory art 155
Pathetic Literature 116
patternicity 44
Pecha Kucha 149, 162
PennSound 98, 159, 172
The People of Paper 35–6
People's Republic of Interactive Fiction 184
Perec, Georges 104
Perelman, Bob 97, 149
Pessoa, Fernando 139
Phillips, Tom 67
philosophical novel 38, 39, 47, 49
Pink Flamingos 121
Piper, Adrian 154
Pitt, Simon 164
"Pixelated Revolution" 103
Place, Vanessa 100, 103
Plascencia, Salvador 35, 36
Plato 29
Platt, Edward 138
"A plural syntax" 21
"poem fondu" 105
Poems for Brands 170
poet's novel 37–9, 47
poet's theater 147
Poetry Foundation 21, 184
Poetry Unbound 84
polysemy 21
"Pomobabble: Postmodern Newspeak[1] and Constitutional 'Meaning' for the Uninitiated" 136
Ponge, Francis 22
Pope.L, William 154
portmanteaus 19
"Possible Girls" 136
Post-Information Age 163
postmodern parody 53
Potter, Justice 11
Pound, Ezra 51
Prescott, Orville 134
Prigov, Dmitrij 84
Pritchard, N. H. 107
Proceduralism 104, 106
project books 42–3, 48
prose poem 21–3, 27, 33, 60, 111
prosody 6, 22, 28, 157
Proudhon, Pierre Joseph 52
The Public Domain Review 140
punk 119–20, 122, 129
Purifoy, Noah 120

Queer Nature 141
Queneau, Raymond 104, 177
The Quest for Corvo: An Experiment in Biography 138
Quincey, Thomas De 69
quotations 122–4, 126

361

Index

"Rabbit" 121
rasquachismo 121, 128, 130
Ratz Are Nice 116
Rauschenberg 41, 147
Ray Gun 135
Read, Allen Walker 128
"Readerly" 192
"Reading a Garden" 192
"Ready-to-hand" 192
Reality Hunger 64, 123
Reese, Harry 80
reference work 126, 130
Rekdal, Paisley 168
Renaissance 27, 69, 70, 88, 108, 126, 148, 151, 165, 178
"Reply All" 60, 191
Rethinking Users 79
Rhodes, Simmias of 108
Richardson, Samuel 108, 183
Riddley Walker 59, 119
Ridgley, Sarah 109, 182
Rigging a Chevy to a Time Machine and Other Ways to Escape a Plague 171
Rilke, Rainer Maria 126
Rimbaud, Arthur 21
Riot Grrrl 119, 152
Ritmo D. Feeling the Blanks 99
Roach, Mary 140
Roach, Rebecca 174
The Road 180
Roda Lume Fogo 176
Roethke, Theodore 126
Roggenbuck, Steve 167
Romantic 1, 19, 21, 28, 37, 46, 69, 128, 157
Ross, Fran 124
Rossellini, Isabella 118
Rothenberg, Jerome 155
Roubaud, Jacques 105
Roupenian, Kristen 29
Rousseau 38
ruangrupa 155
Rukeyser, Muriel 41
Rumble-Smith, Donna 81
Rushdie, Salman 47, 62, 91
Ryan, James 161

S, M, L, XL 135–6
The Saddest Music in the World 118
Saltz, Jerry 133
Saltzberg, Barney 82
Sanchez, Sonia 148
sand drawing 85
Saporta, Mark 82
Saroyan, Aram 107
Sarraute, Nathalie 29, 37
Saterstrom, Selah 35, 155
Satin Island 38

Savage, Richard 138
Schechner, Richard 155
Schlegel, Friedrich 69
schlock 116–18
Schmidt, Christopher 101
Schneemann, Carolee 154
Schuyler, James 26, 90
Scott, James C. 125
Seances 179
Sebald, W. G. 109
Selfish 82
Seltman, Cassandra B. 102
semiotics 108
serial poem 34, 40, 42
Sex 82
Shakur, Tupac 106
The Shallows: What the Internet Is Doing to Our Brain 166
Shapland, Jenn 64, 138
Shelton, Richard 85
Shields, David 60, 64, 123, 191
Shiff, Stacy 138
Shum, Wanwei 86
Sicko 55
Silliman, Ron 21, 42, 95
Singular Pleasures 105
Sinhababu, Neil 136
Skeets, Jake 70
Slab 35
Slab City 120
Smith, Abe 122
Smith, Jessica 42
Snow Country 26
Snow Crash 182
Snyder, Gary 141, 155
Soares, Bernardo 139
The Society of the Spectacle 54
Soda, Molly 167
Solnit, Rebecca 140
"Soma(tic) Poetry Exercises" 159
"Sonic Icons" 107
"The Sonnagrams" 190
Sontag, Susan 23, 121, 129
Sorry to Disturb the Peace 135
So You Know It's Me 168
Sphinx 105
Spicer, Jack 27
Spolin, Viola 159
SSES' 'SSES' "SSEY' 45
St. Ambrose 1
St. Augustine 1
Stanton, Elizabeth Cady 139–40
Starkey, David 6
Stein, Gertrude 22
Steinhauer, Jill 172
Stephenson, Neal 182
Stiff 140
Stiles, Sasha 181

Index

"Stir Fry Texts" 177
Stockhausen, Karlheinz 152
Stoker 27
Strand, Mark 13, 97
Strauss, Neil 182
Straw for the fire 126
street art 154
Student Writers 9
Studying Hunger 157
Subculture: The Meaning of Style 55
Sulak, Marcela 33
Sullivan, Gary 66
Sunblind Almost Motorcrash 135
Survive All Apocalypses 182
"The Sweet Old Etcetera" 176
Swenson, American May 107
Symons, A. J. A. 138
Szilak, Ilya 115, 125

Taleb, Nassim Nicholas 123
talk poems 149, 158
The Tao of Pooh 139
A Tape for the Turn of the Year 90
The Tapeworm Foundry 99
Tel Quel 104
Telepoem Booth 156
text-based adventure games 178
Thaw, Khrushchev 148
Thingiverse 93
The Thinking Hand 80
third space 19
Thirlwell, Adam 83
Thomas, Dylan 119
Thompson, Clive 113
Thornton, Kevin James 171
Tiny Pricks Project 171
Tolson, Melvin B. 148
Tomasula, Steve 177
Toomer, Jean 35
Torre, Mónica de la 119
Towers, Robert 122
T-Post® 82
Transposition 136
trash culture 120
Travesty Generator 189
Trecartin, Ryan 173
Tree of Codes 68, 83
Tree, Joshua 120
TrenchArt 45
Triggering Town 8
TriQuarterly 168, 171
Trondheim, Lewis 105
Tropisms 37
True Stories 170
Turkington, Gregg 124
Turner, James Grantham 183
Tutuola, Amos 119
Tzara, Tristan 66, 147

UbuWeb 98, 172
Ulman, Amelia 103
ULULU: Clown Shrapnel 46
"Uncivilisation" 141
unclassifiables 43–4
Unfinished Ode to Mud 22
The Unfortunates 2
United Nations Human Rights Council 183
University of Arizona Poetry Center 159
Untitled Subjects 27
Updike, John 90
Utopia 38

Valéry, Paul 21
Vanasco, Jeannie 68
"Variations VII" 152
Vassall-Fox, Henry 105
Venegas, Daniel 121
Vera, Mrs. Vladimir Nabokov 138
verse autobiography 28
verse novel 28, 40
verse play 27
Victorian 25, 68, 157
Vicuña, Cecilia 81, 148
Viegener, Mattias 169
Viennese Actionists 155
Virginia Quarterly Review 170
"A Visual Writing Resource list" 112
Voyage autour de ma chambre (A Journey Around My Room) 140
Voyager I 89
Voyager II 89

Wagner, True 171
Wagoner, David 126
Walker, Nicole 23, 122
Wallace, David Foster 47, 117, 133–4
Walser, Robert 83, 118
Walshe, Jennifer 136, 153
Warner, Joel 150
Wasting Time on the Internet 98, 165, 185
Waters, John 121, 129
Waugh, Kyle 76
The Waves 106
We Met in Virtual Reality 183
Weapons of the Weak: Everyday Forms of Peasant Resistance 125
Weiner, Joshua 103
Weiner, Lawrence 107
Weird Internet 172
weird tales 123
Weise, Jillian 79
Weiser, Mark 163
Wellman, Mac 46
Wershler, Darren 99
Westbrook, Steve 161
Weymar, Diana 171
"What Happened on 6/21/18 and 12/21/19?" 186

Index

"What I Learned About My Writing by Seeing Only the Punctuation" 113
When I Left the House It Was Still Dark 88
White, Chaulky 46
White, Derek 46
White, Orlando 86
Wigger 116
Wilke, Hannah 154
Will in the World: How Shakespeare Became Shakespeare 138
Williams, Tyrone 100
"The Wings" 108
Winnie-the-Pooh 139
Wittgenstein's Mistress 38
The Woman's Bible 140
Wood, Dennis 140
Woolf, Virginia 139, 149

World Economic Forum 165
www.theuselessweb.com 184

Xerox Book 80
Xi, Fu 176
Xu, Lynn 87

Ybarra-Frausto, Tomás 121
Yoga for People Who Can't Be Bothered to Do It 140
Young, Kevin 2, 42
Youngblood, Michael 79
Youngman, Hennessy 173
"Your City" 24

Zissos 20
Ziusudra 132

Milton Keynes UK
Ingram Content Group UK Ltd.
UKHW030039030224
437207UK00005B/145